Philip Dormer Chesterfield

Letters Written by Lord Chesterfield to his Son

Vol. II

Philip Dormer Chesterfield

Letters Written by Lord Chesterfield to his Son
Vol. II

ISBN/EAN: 9783337074081

Printed in Europe, USA, Canada, Australia, Japan

Cover: Foto ©Raphael Reischuk / pixelio.de

More available books at **www.hansebooks.com**

LETTERS

WRITTEN BY

LORD CHESTERFIELD

TO HIS SON.

EDITED, WITH OCCASIONAL ELUCIDATORY NOTES, TRANSLATIONS
OF ALL THE LATIN, FRENCH, AND ITALIAN QUOTATIONS,

AND

A BIOGRAPHICAL NOTICE OF THE AUTHOR,

BY CHARLES STOKES CAREY.

IN TWO VOLUMES.—VOL. II.

LONDON: WILLIAM TEGG.
1872.

LORD CHESTERFIELD'S

LETTERS TO HIS SON.

LETTER CXCIII.

MY DEAR FRIEND,   London, May the 27th, O. S. 1750.

YOUR apprenticeship is near out, and you are soon to set up for yourself; that approaching moment is a critical one for you, and an anxious one for me. A tradesman, who would succeed in his way, must begin by establishing a character of integrity and good manners: without the former, nobody will go to his shop at all; without the latter, nobody will go there twice. This rule does not exclude the fair arts of trade. He may sell his goods at the best price he can, within certain bounds. He may avail himself of the humour, the whims, and the fantastical tastes of his customers; but what he warrants to be good must be really so, what he seriously asserts must be true, or his first fraudulent profits will soon end in a bankruptcy. It is the same in higher life, and in the great business of the world. A man who does not solidly establish, and really deserve, a character of truth, probity, good manners, and good morals, at his first setting out in the world, may impose and shine like a meteor for a very short time, but will very soon vanish, and be extinguished with contempt. People easily pardon, in young men, the common irregularities of the senses; but they do not forgive the least vice of the heart. The heart never grows better by age; I fear rather worse, always harder. A young liar will be an old one; and a young knave will only be a greater knave as he grows older. But should a bad young heart, accompanied with a good head (which, by the way, very seldom is the case), really reform in a more advanced age, from

a consciousness of its folly, as well as of its guilt; such a conversion would only be thought prudential and political, but
never sincere.   I hope in God, and I verily believe, that you
want no moral virtue.   But the possession of all the moral
virtues, *in actu primo*, as the logicians call it, is not sufficient;
you must have them *in actu secundo* too : nay, that is not sufficient neither ; you must have the reputation of them also.
Your character in the world must be built upon that solid foundation, or it will soon fall, and upon your own head.   You cannot therefore be too careful, too nice, too scrupulous, in establishing this character at first, upon which your whole depends.
Let no conversation, no example, no fashion, no *bon mot*, no silly
desire of seeming to be above, what most knaves, and many
fools, call prejudice, ever tempt you to avow, excuse, extenuate,
or laugh at the least breach of morality ; but show upon all
occasions, and take all occasions to show, a detestation and abhorrence of it.   There, though young, you ought to be strict ;
and there only, while young, it becomes you to be strict and
severe.   But there, too, spare the persons, while you lash the
crimes.   All this relates, as you easily judge, to the vices of
the heart, such as lying, fraud, envy, malice, detraction, &c.; and
I do not extend it to the little frailties of youth, flowing from
high spirits and warm blood.   It would ill become you, at your
age, to declaim against them, and sententiously censure a gallantry, an accidental excess of the table, a frolic, an inadvert-
ency ; no, keep as free from them yourself as you can ; but say
nothing against them in others.   They certainly mend by time,
often by reason ; and a man's worldly character is not affected
by them, provided it be pure in all other respects.

   To come now to a point of much less but yet of very great
consequence, at your first setting out.   Be extremely upon your
guard against vanity, the common failing of unexperienced
youth ; but particularly against that kind of vanity that dubs
a man a coxcomb; a character which, once acquired, is more
indelible than that of the priesthood.   It is not to be imagined
by how many different ways vanity defeats its own purposes.
One man decides peremptorily upon every subject, betrays his
ignorance upon many, and shows a disgusting presumption
upon the rest.   Another desires to appear successful among the
women ; he hints at the encouragement he has received from
those of the most distinguished rank and beauty, and intimates
a particular connection with some one ; if it is true, it is ungenerous ; if false, it is infamous : but in either case he destroys
the reputation he wants to get.   Some flatter their vanity by

little extraneous objects, which have not the least relation to themselves; such as being descended from, related to, or acquainted with, people of distinguished merit and eminent characters. They talk perpetually of their grandfather such-a-one, their uncle such-a-one, and their intimate friend, Mr such-a-one, with whom, possibly, they are hardly acquainted. But admitting it all to be as they would have it, what then? Have they the more merit for these accidents? Certainly not. On the contrary, their taking up adventitious, proves their want of intrinsic, merit; a rich man never borrows. Take this rule for granted, as a never-failing one; That you must never seem to affect the character in which you have a mind to shine. Modesty is the only sure bait, when you angle for praise. The affectation of courage will make even a brave man pass only for a bully; as the affectation of wit will make a man of parts pass for a coxcomb. By this modesty, I do not mean timidity, and awkward bashfulness. On the contrary, be inwardly firm and steady, know your own value, whatever it may be, and act upon that principle; but take great care to let nobody discover that you do know your own value. Whatever real merit you have, other people will discover; and people always magnify their own discoveries, as they lessen those of others.

For God's sake revolve all these things seriously in your thoughts before you launch out alone into the ocean of Paris. Recollect the observations that you have yourself made upon mankind, compare and connect them with my instructions, and then act systematically and consequentially from them; not *au jour la journée*. Lay your little plan now, which you will hereafter extend and improve by your own observations, and by the advice of those who can never mean to mislead you; I mean Mr Harte and myself.

———◇———

LETTER CXCIV.

My dear Friend,   London, May the 24th, O. S. 1750.

I received yesterday your letter of the 7th, N. S., from Naples, to which place I find you have travelled classically, critically, and *da virtuoso*. You did right, for whatever is worth seeing at all, is worth seeing well, and better than most people see it. It is a poor and frivolous excuse, when anything curious is talked of, that one has seen, to say, *I saw it, but really I did not much mind it.* Why did they go to see it, if they would not mind it? or why would they not mind it when they saw it?

Now you are at Naples, you pass part of your time there, *en honnête homme, da garbato cavaliere,* in the Court, and the best companies. I am told that strangers are received with the utmost hospitality at Prince —— *que lui il fait bonne chère, et que madame la Princesse donne chère entière; mais que sa chair est plus que hazardée ou mortifiée même;* which in plain English means, that she is not only tender, but rotten. If this be true, as I am pretty sure it is, one may say to her in a literal sense, *juvenumque prodis, publica cura.*[1]

Mr Harte informs me that you are clothed in sumptuous apparel; a young fellow should be so, especially abroad, where fine clothes are so generally the fashion. Next to their being fine, they should be well made, and worn easily; for a man is only the less genteel for a fine coat, if in wearing it he shows a regard for it, and is not as easy in it as if it were a plain one.

I thank you for your drawing, which I am impatient to see, and which I shall hang up in a new gallery that I am building at Blackheath, and very fond of; but I am still more impatient for another copy, which I wonder I have not yet received, I mean the copy of your countenance. I believe, were that a whole length, it would still fall a good deal short of the dimensions of the drawing after Dominichino, which you say is about eight feet high; and I take you, as well as myself, to be one of the family of the *Piccolomini.* Mr Bathurst tells me, that he thinks you rather taller than I am; if so, you may very possibly get up to five feet eight inches, which I would compound for, though I would wish you five feet ten. In truth, what do I not wish you, that has a tendency to perfection? I say a tendency only, for absolute perfection is not in human nature, so that it would be idle to wish it. But I am very willing to compound for your coming nearer to perfection than the generality of your contemporaries: without a compliment to you, I think you bid fair for that. Mr Harte affirms (and, if it were consistent with his character, would, I believe, swear) that you have no vices of the heart; you have undoubtedly a stock both of ancient and modern learning, which, I will venture to say, nobody of your age has, and which must now daily increase, do what you will. What then do you want towards that practicable degree of perfection which I wish you? Nothing, but the knowledge, the turn, and the manners of the world; I mean the *beau monde.* These it is impossible that you can yet have quite right; they are not given, they must be learned. But then, on the other hand, it is impossible not to acquire

[1] Thou comest forth the common pursuit of our young men.

them if one has a mind to them ; for they are acquired insensibly, by keeping good company, if one has but the least
attention to their characters and manners. Every man becomes,
to a certain degree, what the people he generally converses
with are. He catches their air, their manners, and even their
way of thinking. If he observes with attention, he will catch
them soon, but if he does not, he will at long run contract them
insensibly. I know nothing in the world but poetry that is
not to be acquired by application and care. The sum total of
this is a very comfortable one for you, as it plainly amounts to
this, in your favour ; that you now want nothing but what
even your pleasures, if they are liberal ones, will teach you. I
congratulate both you and myself upon your being in such a
situation, that, excepting your exercises, nothing is now wanting but pleasures to complete you. Take them but (as I am sure
you will) with people of the first fashion, wherever you are, and
the business is done ; your exercises at Paris, which I am sure
you will attend to, will supple and fashion your body ; and the
company you will keep there will, with some degree of observation on your part, soon give you their air, address, manners,
in short, *le ton de la bonne compagnie.* Let not those considerations, however, make you vain ; they are only between you
and me : but as they are very comfortable ones, they may
justly give you a manly assurance, a firmness, a steadiness,
without which a man can neither be well bred, or in any light
appear to advantage, or really what he is. They may justly
remove all timidity, awkward bashfulness, low diffidence of
one's self, and mean abject complaisance to every or anybody's
opinion. La Bruyere says, very truly, *on ne vaut dans ce monde,
que ce que l'on veut valoir :* [1] it is a right principle to proceed
upon in the world, taking care only to guard against the appearances and outward symptoms of vanity. Your whole then,
you see, turns upon the company you keep for the future. I
have laid you in a variety of the best at Paris, where, at your
arrival, you will find a cargo of letters, to very different sorts of
people, as *beaux esprits, savants, et belles dames.* These, if you
will frequent them, will form you, not only by their examples,
but by their advice, and admonitions in private, as I have desired them to do ; and consequently add to what you have, the
only one thing now needful.

Pray tell me what Italian books you have read, and whether
that language is now become familiar to you. Read Ariosto
and Tasso through, and then you will have read all the Italian

---

[1] In this world a man is held in no higher estimation than he wishes to be.

poets who, in my opinion, are worth reading. In all events, when you get to Paris, take a good Italian master to read Italian with you three times a week; not only to keep what you have already, which you would otherwise forget, but also to perfect you in the rest. It is a great pleasure, as well as a great advantage, to be able to speak to people of all nations, and well, in their own language. Aim at perfection in everything, though in most things it is unattainable; however, they who aim at it, and persevere, will come much nearer it than those whose laziness and despondency make them give it up as unattainable. *Magnis tamen excidit ausis*[1] is a degree of praise which will always attend a noble and shining temerity, and a much better sign in a young fellow, than *serpere humi, tutus nimium timidusque procellæ.*[2] For men, as well as women,

> ———— born to be controll'd,
> Stoop to the forward and the bold.

A man who sets out in the world with real timidity and diffidence has not an equal chance in it; he will be discouraged, put by, or trampled upon. But, to succeed, a man, especially a young one, should have inward firmness, steadiness, and intrepidity; with exterior modesty, and *seeming* diffidence. He must modestly, but resolutely, assert his own rights and privileges. *Suaviter in modo,* but *fortiter in re.* He should have an apparent frankness and openness, but with inward caution and closeness. All these things will come to you by frequenting and observing good company. And by good company, I mean that sort of company which is called good company by everybody of that place. When all this is over, we shall meet; and then we will talk over, *tête-à-tête,* the various little finishing strokes, which conversation and acquaintance occasionally suggest, and which cannot be methodically written.

Tell Mr Harte that I have received his two letters of the 2nd and 8th, N. S., which, as soon as I have received a third, I will answer. Adieu, my dear! I find you will do.

———◇———

LETTER CXCV.

MY DEAR FRIEND,   London, June the 5th, O. S. 1750.

I HAVE received your picture, which I have long waited for with impatience; I wanted to see your countenance, from

---

[1] Though he failed he had attempted great deeds.
[2] To creep on the ground, in safety, but too fearful of the storm.

whence I am very apt, as I believe most people are, to form some general opinion of the mind. If the painter has taken you as well as he has done Mr Harte (for his picture is by far the most like I ever saw in my life), I draw good conclusions from your countenance, which has both spirit and *finesse* in it. In bulk you are pretty well increased since I saw you; if your height is not increased in proportion, I desire that you will make haste to complete it. Seriously, I believe that your exercises at Paris will make you shoot up to a good size; your legs, by all accounts, seem to promise it. Dancing excepted, the wholesome part is the best part of those academical exercises. *Ils dégraissent leur homme.*[1] *A propos* of exercises; I have prepared everything for your reception at Monsieur de la Guériniere's, and your room, &c., will be ready at your arrival. I am sure you must be sensible how much better it will be for you to be *interne* in the Academy, for the first six or seven months at least, than to be *en hôtel garni*, at some distance from it, and obliged to go to it every morning, let the weather be what it will, not to mention the loss of time too; besides, by living and boarding in the Academy, you will make an acquaintance with half the young fellows of fashion at Paris; and in a very little while be looked upon as one of them in all French companies; an advantage that has never yet happened to any one Englishman that I have known. I am sure you do not suppose that the difference of the expense, which is but a trifle, has any weight with me in this resolution. You have the French language so perfectly, and you will acquire the French *tournure* so soon, that I do not know anybody likely to pass his time so well at Paris as yourself. Our young countrymen have generally too little French, and too bad address, either to present themselves, or be well received in the best French companies; and, as a proof of it, there is no one instance of an Englishman's having ever been suspected of a gallantry with a French woman of condition, though every French woman of condition is more than suspected of having a gallantry. But they take up with the disgraceful and dangerous commerce of prostitutes, actresses, dancing women, and that sort of trash; though, if they had common address, better achievements would be extremely easy. *Un arrangement*, which is in plain English a gallantry, is, at Paris, as necessary a part of a woman of fashion's establishment, as her house, table, coach, &c. A young fellow must therefore be a very awkward one, to be reduced to, or of a very singular taste, to

[1] They prevent corpulency.

prefer drabs and danger to a commerce (in the course of the world not disgraceful) with a woman of health, education, and rank. Nothing sinks a young man into low company, both of men and women, so surely as timidity, and diffidence of himself. If he thinks that he shall not, he may depend upon it he will not, please. But with proper endeavours to please, and a degree of persuasion that he shall, it is almost certain that he will. How many people does one meet with everywhere, who with very moderate parts, and very little knowledge, push themselves pretty far, singly by being sanguine, enterprising, and persevering? They will take no denial from man or woman; difficulties do not discourage them; repulsed twice or thrice, they rally, they charge again, and nine times in ten prevail at last. The same means will much sooner, and more certainly, attain the same ends, with your parts and knowledge. You have a fund to be sanguine upon, and good forces to rally. In business (talents supposed) nothing is more effectual, or successful, than a good, though concealed, opinion of one's self, a firm resolution, and an unwearied perseverance. None but madmen attempt impossibilities; and whatever is possible is one way or another to be brought about. If one method fails, try another, and suit your methods to the characters you have to do with. At the treaty of the Pyrenées, which Cardinal Mazarin and Don Louis de Haro concluded, *dans l'Isle des Faisans;* the latter carried some very important points by his constant and cool perseverance.

The Cardinal had all the Italian vivacity and impatience; Don Louis all the Spanish phlegm and tenaciousness. The point which the Cardinal had most at heart was, to hinder the re-establishment of the Prince of Condé, his implacable enemy; but he was in haste to conclude, and impatient to return to Court, where absence is always dangerous. Don Louis observed this, and never failed at every conference to bring the affair of the Prince of Condé upon the *tapis.* The Cardinal for some time refused even to treat upon it; Don Louis, with the same *sens froid,* as constantly persisted, till he at last prevailed, contrary to the intentions and the interest both of the Cardinal and of his Court. Sense must distinguish between what is impossible and what is only difficult, and spirit and perseverance will get the better of the latter. Every man is to be had one way or another, and every woman almost any way I must not omit one thing, which is previously necessary to this, and indeed to everything else; which is attention, a flexibility of attention; never to be wholly engrossed by any past or future object, but instantly directed to

the present one, be it what it will. An absent man can make
but few observations ; and those will be disjointed and imperfect ones, as half the circumstances must necessarily escape him.
He can pursue nothing steadily, because his absences make him
lose his way. They are very disagreeable, and hardly to be
tolerated in old age ; but in youth they cannot be forgiven.
If you find that you have the least tendency to them, pray
watch yourself very carefully, and you may prevent them now ;
but if you let them grow into a habit, you will find it very
difficult to cure them hereafter ; and a worse distemper I do not
know.

I heard with great satisfaction the other day, from one who
has been lately at Rome, that nobody was better received in the
best companies than yourself. The same thing, I dare say, will
happen to you at Paris ; where they are particularly kind to all
strangers, who will be civil to them, and show a desire of pleasing. But they must be flattered a little, not only by words,
but by a seeming preference given to their country, their manners, and their customs ; which is but a very small price to pay
for a very good reception. Were I in Africa, I would pay it
to a negro for his good-will. Adieu.

LETTER CXCVI.

My dear Friend,   London, June the 11th, O. S. 1750.

The President Montesquieu (whom you will be acquainted
with at Paris), after having laid down, in his book *de l'Esprit
des Loix*, the nature and principles of the three different kinds
of government, *viz.* the democratical, the monarchical, and the
despotic, treats of the education necessary for each respective
form. His chapter upon the education proper for the monarchical, I thought worth transcribing and sending to you. You
will observe that the monarchy which he has in his eye is France.

[1] Ce n'est point dans les maisons publiques où l'on instruit
l'enfance, que l'on reçoit dans les monarchies la principale éducation ; c'est lorsque l'on entre dans le monde que l'éducation
en quelque façon commence. Là est l'école de ce que l'on appelle l'honneur, ce maître universel, qui doit partout nous con-
duire.

[1] In monarchies, the principal branch of education is not taught in colleges or academies. It commences, in some measure, at our setting out in
the world ; for this is the school of what we call honour, that universal pre-
ceptor, which ought everywhere to be our guide.

C'est là que l'on voit et que l'on entend toujours dire trois choses, qu'il faut mettre dans les vertus une certaine noblesse, dans les mœurs une certaine franchise, dans les manières une certaine politesse.

Les vertus qu'on nous y montre sont toujours moins ce que l'on doit aux autres, que ce que l'on se doit à soi-même, elles ne sont pas tant ce qui nous appelle vers nos concitoyens, que ce qui nous en distingue.

On n'y juge pas les actions des hommes commes bonnes, mais comme belles ; comme justes, mais comme grandes ; comme raisonnables, mais comme extraordinaires.

Dès que l'honneur y peut trouver quelque chose de noble, il est ou le juge qui les rend légitimes, ou le sophiste qui les justifie.

Il permet la galanterie lorsqu'elle est unie à l'idée des sentimens du cœur, ou à l'idée de conquête ; et c'est la vraie raison pour laquelle les mœurs ne sont jamais si pures dans les monarchies, que dans les gouvernemens républicains.

Il permet la ruse, lorsqu'elle est jointe à l'idée de la grandeur de l'esprit ou de la grandeur des affaires, comme dans la politique dont les finesses ne l'offensent pas.

Il ne défend l'adulation que lorsqu'elle est séparée de l'idée d'une grande fortune, et n'est jointe qu'au sentiment de sa propre bassesse.

A l'égard des mœurs, j'ai dit que l'éducation des monarchies doit y mettre une certaine franchise. On y veut donc de la vérité dans les discours. Mais est-ce par amour pour elle ? point du tout. On la veut parce qu'un homme qui est accou-

Here it is that we constantly hear three rules or maxims ; viz. that we should have a certain nobleness in our virtues, a kind of frankness in our morals, and a particular politeness in our behaviour.

The virtues we are here taught are less what we owe to others, than to ourselves ; they are not so much what draws us towards society, as what distinguishes us from our fellow-citizens.

Here the actions of men are judged, not as virtuous, but as shining ; not as just, but as great ; not as reasonable, but as extraordinary.

When honour here meets with anything noble in our actions, it is either a judge that approves them, or a sophister by whom they are excused.

It allows of gallantry, when united with the idea of sensible affection, or with that of conquest ; this is the reason why we never meet with so strict a purity of morals in monarchies, as in republican governments.

It allows of cunning and craft, when joined with the notion of greatness of soul or importance of affairs ; as, for instance, in politics, with whose finesses it is far from being offended.

It does not forbid adulation, but when separate from the idea of a large fortune, and connected only with the sense of our mean condition.

With regard to morals, I have observed, that the education of monarchies ought to admit of a certain frankness and open carriage. Truth therefore in conversation is here a necessary point. But is it for the sake of

tumé à la dire paroît être hardi et libre. En effet, un tel
homme semble ne dépendre que des choses, et non pas de la
manière dont un autre les reçoit.

C'est ce qui fait qu'autant qu'on y recommande cette espèce
de franchise, autant on y méprise celle du peuple, qui n'a que
la vérité et la simplicité pour objet.

Enfin l'éducation dans les monarchies éxige dans les manières une certaine politesse. Les hommes nés pour vivre ensemble,
sont nés aussi pour se plaire ; et celui qui n'observeroit pas les
bienséances, choquant tous ceux avec qui il vivroit, se décrédite-
roit au point qu'il deviendroit incapable de faire aucun bien.

Mais ce n'est pas d'une source si pure que la politesse a
coutume de tirer son origine. Elle naît de l'envie de se distinguer. C'est par orgueil que nous sommes polis : nous
nous sentons flattés d'avoir des manières qui prouvent que nous
ne sommes pas dans la bassesse, et que nous n'avons pas vécu
avec cette sorte de gens que l'on a abandonnés dans tous les âges.

Dans les monarchies la politesse est naturalisée à la cour.
Un homme excessivement grand rend tous les autres petits.
De là les égards que l'on doit à tout le monde ; de-là naît la
politesse, qui flatte autant ceux qui sont polis que ceux à l'égard
de qui ils le sont, parce qu'elle fait comprendre qu'on est de la
cour, ou qu'on est digne d'en être.

L'air de la cour consiste à quitter sa grandeur propre pour
une grandeur empruntée. Celle-ci flatte plus un courtisan que

truth ? By no means. Truth is requisite only, because a person habitu-
ated to veracity has an air of boldness and freedom. And indeed a man of
this stamp seems to lay a stress only on the things themselves, not on the
manner in which they are received.

Hence it is, that in proportion as this kind of frankness is commended,
that of the common people is despised, which has nothing but truth and
simplicity for its object.

In fine, the education of monarchies requires a certain politeness of behaviour. Man, a sociable animal, is formed to please in society ; and a person
that would break through the rules of decency, so as to shock those he conversed with, would lose the public esteem, and become incapable of doing
any good.

But politeness, generally speaking, does not derive its original from so
pure a source. It rises from a desire of distinguishing ourselves. It is
pride that renders us polite : we are flattered with being taken notice of for
a behaviour that shows we are not of a mean condition, and that we have
not been bred up with those who in all ages are considered as the scum of
the people.

Politeness in monarchies is naturalized at Court, one man excessively
great renders everybody else little. Hence that regard which is paid to
our fellow-subjects ; hence that politeness, equally pleasing to those by
whom, as to those towards whom, it is practised, because it gives people to
understand, that a person actually belongs, or at least deserves to belong, to
the Court.

A Court air consists in quitting a real for a borrowed greatness. The

la sienne même.   Elle donne une certaine modestie superbe qui
se répand au-loin, mais dont l'orgueil diminue insensiblement,
à proportion de la distance où l'on est de la source de cette
grandeur.

On trouve à la cour une délicatesse de goût en toutes choses,
qui vient d'un usage. continuel des superfluités d'une grande
fortune, de la variété et surtout de la lassitude des plaisirs, de
la multiplicité, de la confusion même des fantaisies, qui lorsqu'-
elles sont agréables y sont toujours reçues.

C'est sur toutes ces choses que l'éducation se porte pour
faire ce qu'on appelle l'honnête homme, qui a toutes les qualités et toutes les vertus que l'on demande dans ce gouverne-
ment.

Là, l'honneur se mêlant par-tout entre dans toutes les façons
de penser et toutes les manières de sentir, et dirige même les
principes.

Cet honneur bisarre fait que les vertus ne sont que ce qu'il
veut et comme il les veut ; il met de son chef des règles à
tout ce qui nous est prescrit ; il étend ou il borne nos devoirs à
sa fantaisie, soit qu'ils aient leur source dans la religion, dans
la politique, ou dans la morale.

Il n'y a rien dans la monarchie que les loix, la religion, et
l'honneur prescrivent tant que l'obéissance aux volontés du
Prince : mais cet honneur nous dicte que le Prince ne doit jamais nous prescrire une action qui nous deshonore, parce
qu'elle nous rendroit incapables de le servir.

Crillon refusa d'assassiner le Duc de Guise, mais il offrit à

latter pleases the Courtier more than the former. It inspires him with a
certain disdainful modesty, which shows itself externally, but whose pride
insensibly diminishes in proportion to its distance from the source of this
greatness.

At Court we find a delicacy of taste in everything, a delicacy arising
from the constant use of the superfluities of life, from the variety, and
especially the satiety, of pleasures, from the multiplicity and even confusion
of fancies, which, if they are but agreeable, are sure of being well received.

These are the things which properly fall within the province of education, in order to form what we call a man of honour, a man possessed of all
the qualities and virtues requisite in this kind of government.

Here it is that honour interferes with everything, mixing even with
people's manner of thinking, and directing their very principles.

To this whimsical honour it is owing that the virtues are only just what
it pleases ; it adds rules of its own invention to everything prescribed to
us ; it extends or limits our duties according to its own fancy, whether they
proceed from religion, politics, or morality.

There is nothing so strongly inculcated in monarchies, by the laws, by
religion, and honour, as submission to the Prince's will ; but this very honour tells us that the Prince never ought to command a dishonourable action,
because this would render us incapable of serving him.

Crillon refused to assassinate the Duke of Guise, but offered to fight him.

Henri Trois de se battre contre lui. Après la Saint Barthé-
lemi, Charles Neuf ayant écrit à tous les gouverneurs de faire
massacrer les Huguenots, le Vicomte Dorte, qui commandoit
dans Bayonne, écrivit au Roi : 'Sire, je n'ai trouvé parmi les
habitans et les gens de guerre, que de bons citoyens, de braves
soldats, et pas un bourreau ; ainsi eux et moi supplions votre
Majesté d'employer nos bras et nos vies à choses faisables.'
Ce grand et généreux courage regardoit une lâcheté comme
une chose impossible.

Il n'y a rien que l'honneur prescrive plus à la Noblesse, que
de servir le Prince à la guerre. En effet, c'est la profession
distinguée, parce que ses hasards, ses succès, et ses malheurs,
même conduisent à la grandeur. Mais en imposant cette loi,
l'honneur veut en être l'arbitre, et s'il se trouve choqué, il exige
ou permet qu'on se retire chez soi.

Il veut qu'on puisse indifféremment aspirer aux emplois ou
les refuser ; il tient cette liberté au dessus de la fortune même.

L'honneur a donc ses règles suprèmes, et l'éducation est
obligée de s'y conformer. Les principales sont, qu'il nous est
bien permis de faire cas de notre fortune, mais qu'il nous est
souverainement défendu d'en faire aucun de notre vie.

La seconde est, que lorsque nous avons été une foi placés
dans un rang, nous ne devons rien faire ni souffrir qui fasse
voir que nous nous tenons inférieurs à ce rang même.

La troisième, que les choses que l'honneur défend, sont
plus rigoureusement défendues, lorsque les Loix ne concourent

After the massacre of St Bartholomew, Charles IX. having sent orders to
the governors in the several provinces for the Hugonots to be murdered,
Viscount Dort, who commanded at Bayonne, wrote thus to the king :
'Sire, among the inhabitants of this town, and your Majesty's troops, I
could not find so much as one executioner ; they are honest citizens and
brave soldiers. We jointly therefore beseech your Majesty to command our
arms and lives in things that are practicable.' This great and generous
soul looked upon a base action as a thing impossible.

There is nothing that honour more strongly recommends to the Nobility,
than to serve their Prince in a military capacity. And, indeed, this is their
favourite profession, because its dangers, its success, and even its miscar-
riages, are the road to grandeur. Yet this very law of its own making,
honour chooses to explain ; and in case of any affront, it requires or permits
us to retire.

It insists also that we should be at liberty either to seek or to reject employments : a liberty which it prefers even to an ample fortune.

Honour therefore has its supreme laws, to which education is obliged
to conform. The chief of these are, that we are permitted to set a value
upon our fortune, but are absolutely forbidden to set any upon our lives.

The second is, that when we are raised to a post or preferment, we should
never do or permit anything which may seem to imply that we look upon
ourselves as inferior to the rank we hold.

The third is, that those things which honour forbids are more rigorously
forbidden when the laws do not concur in the prohibition ; and those it

point à les proscrire, et que celles qu'il exige sont plus forte-
ment exigées, lorsque les Loix ne le demandent pas.

Though our government differs considerably from the
French, inasmuch as we have fixed laws and constitutional
barriers for the security of our liberties and properties, yet
the President's observations hold pretty near as true in England
as in France. Though Monarchies may differ a good deal,
Kings differ very little. Those who are absolute desire to continue so, and those who are not endeavour to become so ; hence,
the same maxims and manners almost in all Courts : voluptu-
ousness and profusion encouraged, the one to sink the people
into indolence, the other into poverty, consequently into de-
pendency. The Court is called the world here, as well as at
Paris ; and nothing more is meant by saying that a man knows
the world, than that he knows Courts. In all Courts you must
expect to meet with connections without friendship, enmities
without hatred, honour without virtue, appearances saved, and
realities sacrificed ; good manners, with bad morals ; and all
vice and virtue so disguised, that whoever has only reasoned
upon both would know neither, when he first met them at
Court. It is well that you should know the map of that country,
that when you come to travel in it you may do it with greater
safety.

From all this you will of yourself draw this obvious conclusion, That you are in truth but now going to the great and
important school, the world ; to which Westminster and Leipsig
were only the little preparatory schools, as Mary-le-bone, Wand-
sor, &c., are to them. What you have already acquired will
only place you in the second form of this new school, instead of
the first. But if you intend, as I suppose you do, to get into
the shell, you have very different things to learn from Latin and
Greek, and which require much more sagacity and attention
than those two dead languages : the language of pure and
simple nature, the language of nature variously modified, and
corrupted by passions, prejudices, and habits : the language of
simulation and dissimulation, very hard but very necessary to
decipher. Homer has not half so many nor so difficult dialects,
as the great book of the school you are now going to. Observe
therefore progressively, and with the greatest attention, what
the best scholars in the form immediately above you do, and so
on, till you get into the shell yourself. Adieu.

---

commands are more strongly insisted upon when they happen not to be
commanded by law.—Mr NUGENT's Translation.

Pray tell Mr Harte that I have received his letter of the 27th May, N. S., and that I advise him never to take the English news-writers literally, who never yet inserted any one thing quite right. I have both his patent and his mandamus, in both which he is Walter, let the newspapers call him what they please.

------o------

LETTER CXCVII.

My dear Friend,   London, July the 9th, O. S. 1750.

I should not deserve that appellation in return from you, if I did not freely and explicitly inform you of every corrigible defect, which I may either hear of, suspect, or at any time discover in you. Those who in the common course of the world will call themselves your friends, or whom, according to the common notions of friendship, you may possibly think such, will never tell you of your faults, still less of your weaknesses. But on the contrary, more desirous to make you their friend than to prove themselves yours, they will flatter both, and, in truth, not be sorry for either. Interiorly, most people enjoy the inferiority of their best friends. The useful and essential part of friendship to you is reserved singly for Mr Harte and myself; our relations to you stand pure, and unsuspected of all private views. In whatever we say to you, we can have no interest but yours. We can have no competition, no jealousy, no secret envy or malignity. We are therefore authorized to represent, advise, and remonstrate; and your reason must tell you that you ought to attend to and believe us.

I am credibly informed that there is still a considerable hitch or hobble in your enunciation; and that when you speak fast, you sometimes speak unintelligibly. I have formerly and frequently laid my thoughts before you so fully upon this subject, that I can say nothing new upon it now. I must therefore only repeat, that your whole depends upon it. Your trade is to speak well, both in public and in private. The manner of your speaking is full as important as the matter, as more people have ears to be tickled than understandings to judge. Be your productions ever so good, they will be of no use, if you stifle and strangle them in their birth. The best compositions of Corelli, if ill executed, and played out of tune, instead of touching, as they do when well performed, would only excite the indignation of the hearers, when murdered by an unskilful performer. But to murder your own productions, and that *coram populo*, is a *Medean cruelty*, which Horace absolutely forbids. Remember of what importance Demosthenes, and one of the Gracchi, thought *enunciation;* read what stress Cicero and Quintilian lay upon it; even the herb-women at Athens were correct judges of it. Oratory with all its graces, that of enunciation in particular, is full as necessary in our government, as it ever was in Greece or Rome. No man can make a fortune or a figure in this country, without speaking, and speaking well, in public. If you will persuade, you must first please; and if you will please, you must tune your voice to harmony; you must articulate every syllable distinctly; your emphasis and cadences must be strongly and properly marked; and the whole together must be graceful and engaging; if you do not speak in that manner, you had much better not speak at all. All the learning you have, or ever can have, is not worth one groat without it. It may be a comfort and an amusement to you in your closet, but can be of no use to you in the world. Let me conjure you therefore to make this your only object, till you have absolutely conquered it, for that is in your power; think of nothing else, read and speak for nothing else. Read aloud, though alone, and read articulately and distinctly, as if you were reading in public, and on the most important occasion. Recite pieces of eloquence, declaim scenes of tragedies, to Mr Harte, as if he were a numerous audience. If there is any particular consonant which you have a difficulty in articulating, as I think you had with the *R*, utter it millions and millions of times, till you have uttered it right. Never speak quick, till you have first learned to speak well. In short, lay aside every book and every thought, that does not directly tend to this great object, absolutely decisive of your future fortune and figure.

The next thing necessary in your destination is, writing correctly, elegantly, and in a good hand too; in which three particulars, I am sorry to tell you that you hitherto fail. Your hand-writing is a very bad one, and would make a scurvy figure in an office-book of letters, or even in a lady's pocket-book. But that fault is easily cured by care, since every man who has the use of his eyes and of his right hand,

As to the correctness and elegancy of your writing, attention to grammar does the one, and to the best authors the other. In your letter to me of the 27th June, N. S., you omitted the date of the place, so that I only conjectured from the contents that you were at Rome.

Thus I have, with the truth and freedom of the tenderest affection, told you all your defects, at least all that I know or have heard of. Thank God they are all very curable, they must be cured, and I am sure you will cure them. That once done, nothing remains for you to acquire, or for me to wish you, but the turn, the manners, the address, and the *graces* of the polite world; which experience, observation, and good company will insensibly give you. Few people at your age have read, seen, and known so much as you have, and consequently few are so near as yourself to what I call perfection, by which I only mean being very near as well as the best. Far, therefore, from being discouraged by what you still want, what you already have should encourage you to attempt, and convince you that by attempting you will inevitably obtain it. The difficulties which you have surmounted were much greater than any you have now to encounter. Till very lately your way has been only through thorns and briars; the few that now remain are mixed with roses. Pleasure is now the principal remaining part of your education. It will soften and polish your manners; it will make you pursue and at last overtake the *graces*. Pleasure is necessarily reciprocal; no one feels who does not at the same time give it. To be pleased, one must please. What pleases you in others, will in general please them in you. Paris is indisputably the seat of the *graces*; they will even court you, if you are not too coy. Frequent and observe the best companies there, and you will soon be naturalized among them; you will soon find how particularly attentive they are to the correctness and elegancy of their language, and to the graces of their enunciation; they would even call the understanding of a man in question, who should neglect or not know the infinite advantages arising from them. *Narrer, réciter, déclamer bien*, are serious studies among them, and well deserve to be so everywhere. The conversations even among the women frequently turn upon the elegancies, and minutest delicacies, of the French language. An *enjouement*, a gallant turn prevails in all their companies, to women, with whom they neither are, nor pretend to be, in love; but should you (as may very possibly happen) fall really in love there with some woman of fashion and sense (for I do not suppose you capable of falling in love with a strumpet), and that your rival, without half your parts or knowledge, should get the better of you, merely by dint of manners, *enjouement, badinage, &c.*, how would you regret not having sufficiently attended to these accomplishments, which you despised as superficial and trifling, but which you would then find of real consequence in the course of the world ! And men, as well as women, are taken by these external graces. Shut up your books, then, now as a business, and open them only as a pleasure: but let the great book of the world be your serious study ; read it over and over, get it by heart, adopt its style, and make it your own.

When I cast up your account as it now stands, I rejoice to see the balance so much in your favour ; and that the items *per contra* are so few, and of such a nature that they may be very easily cancelled. By way of debtor and creditor, it stands thus :

Creditor. By French.	*Debtor.* To English.
German	Enunciation.
Italian.	Manners.
Latin.	
Greek.	
Logic.	
Ethics.	
History.	
Jus { Naturæ. Gentium. Publicum.	

This, my dear friend, is a very true account, and a very encouraging one for you. A man who owes so little, can clear it off in a very little time, and if he is a prudent man, will ; whereas a man who by long negligence owes a great deal, despairs of ever being able to pay ; and therefore never looks into his accounts at all.

When you go to Genoa, pray observe carefully all the *environs* of it, and view them with somebody who can tell you all the situations and operations of the Austrian army during that famous siege, if it deserves to be called one ; for in reality the town never was besieged, nor had the Austrians any one thing necessary for a siege. If Marquis Centurioni, who was last winter in England, should happen to be there, go to him with my compliments, and he will show you all imaginable civilities.

I could have sent you some letters to Florence, but that I knew Mr Mann would be of more use to you than all of them. Pray make him my compliments. Cultivate your Italian while you are at Florence; where it is spoken in its utmost purity, but ill pronounced.

Pray save me the seed of some of the best melons you eat, and put it up dry in paper. You need not send it me; but Mr Harte will bring it in his pocket when he comes over. I should likewise be glad of some cuttings of the best figs, especially *il Fico gentile*, and the Malthese; but as this is not the season for them, Mr Mann will, I dare say, undertake that commission, and send them to me at the proper time by Leghorn. Adieu. Endeavour to please others, and divert yourself as much as ever you can, *en honnête et galant Homme*.

P. S. I send you the enclosed to deliver to Lord Rochford, upon your arrival at Turin.

LETTER CXCVIII.

My dear Friend,　　　　　London, August the 6th, O. S. 1750.

Since your letter from Sienna, which gave me a very imperfect account both of your illness and your recovery, I have not received one word either from you or Mr Harte. I impute this to the carelessness of the post singly; and the great distance between us, at present, exposes our letters to those accidents. But when you come to Paris, from whence the letters arrive here very regularly, I shall insist upon your writing to me constantly once a week, and that upon the same day, for instance, every Thursday, that I may know by what mail to expect your letter. I shall also require you to be more minute in your account of yourself than you have hitherto been, or than I have required, because of the informations which I have received from time to time from Mr Harte. At Paris you will be out of your time, and must set up for yourself: it is then that I shall be very solicitous to know how you carry on your business. While Mr Harte was your partner, the care was his share, and the profit yours. But at Paris, if you will have the latter, you must take the former along with it. It will be quite a new world to you; very different from the little world that you have hitherto seen, and you will have much more to do in it. You must keep your little accounts constantly every morning, if you would not have them run into confusion, and swell to a bulk that would frighten you from ever looking into them at all. You must allow some time for learning what you do not know, and some for keeping what you do know : and you must leave a great deal of time for your pleasures; which (I repeat it again) are now become the most necessary part of your education. It is by conversations, dinners, suppers, entertainments, &c., in the best companies, that you must be formed for the world. *Les manières, les agrémens, les grâces*, cannot be learned by theory; they are only to be got by use among those who have them ; and they are now the main object of your life, as they are the necessary steps to your fortune. A man of the best parts, and the greatest learning, if he does not know the world by his own experience and observation, will be very absurd ; and, consequently, very unwelcome in company. He may say very good things ; but they will probably be so ill-timed, misplaced, or improperly addressed, that he had much better hold his tongue. Full of his own matter, and uninformed of, or inattentive to, the particular circumstances and situations of the company, he vents it indiscriminately : he puts some people out of countenance ; he shocks others ; and frightens all, who dread what may come out next. The most general rule that I can give you for the world, and which your experience will convince you of the truth of, is, Never to give the tone to the company, but to take it from them ; and to labour more to put them in conceit with themselves, than to make them admire you. Those whom you can make like themselves better, will, I promise you, like you very well.

A system-monger, who, without knowing anything of the world by experience, has formed a system of it in his dusty cell, lays it down, for example, that (from the general nature of mankind) flattery is pleasing. He will therefore flatter. But how ? Why, indiscriminately. And instead of repairing and heightening the piece judiciously, with soft colours, and a delicate pencil ; with a coarse brush, and a great deal of whitewash, he daubs and besmears the piece he means to adorn. His flattery offends even his patron ; and is almost too gross for his mistress. A man of the world knows the force of flattery as well as he does; but then he knows how, when, and where to give it ; he proportions his dose to the constitution of the patient. He flatters by application, by inference, by comparison, by hint ; and seldom directly. In the course of the world there is the same difference, in everything, between system and practice.

I long to have you at Paris, which is to be your great school ; you will be then in a manner within reach of me.

Tell me, are you perfectly recovered, or do you still find any remaining complaint upon your lungs? Your diet should

be cooling, and at the same time nourishing. Milks of all kinds
are proper for you; wines of all kinds bad. A great deal of
gentle and no violent exercise is good for you. Adieu. *Gra-
tia, Fama, Valetudo contingat abundè*.[1]

LETTER CXCIX.

My dear Friend,   London, October the 22nd, O. S. 1750.

This letter will, I am persuaded, find you, and I hope safely,
arrived at Montpellier; from whence I trust that Mr Harte's
indisposition will, by being totally removed, allow you to get
to Paris before Christmas. You will there find two people, who,
though both English, I recommend in the strongest manner
possible to your attention; and advise you to form the most
intimate connections with them both, in their different ways.
The one is a man whom you already know something of, but
not near enough: it is the Earl of Huntingdom; who, next to
you, is the truest object of my affection and esteem; and who (I
am proud to say it) calls me and considers me as his adopted
father. His parts are as quick as his knowledge is extensive;
and if quality were worth putting into an account, where every
other item is so much more valuable, his is the first almost in
this country: the figure he will make, soon after he returns to
it, will, if I am not more mistaken than ever I was in my life,
equal his birth and my hopes. Such a connection will be of
infinite advantage to you; and I can assure you that he is extremely disposed to form it upon my account; and will, I hope
and believe, desire to improve and cement it upon your own.

In our parliamentary government, connections are absolutely necessary; and, if prudently formed, and ably maintained,
the success of them is infallible. There are two sorts of connections, which I would always advise you to have in view.
The first I will call equal ones; by which I mean those where
the two connecting parties reciprocally find their account from
pretty near an equal degree of parts and abilities. In those
there must be a freer communication; each must see that the
other is able, and be convinced that he is willing, to be of use
to him. Honour must be the principle of such connections;
and there must be a mutual dependance, that present and
separate interest shall not be able to break them. There must

[1] May favour, reputation, and health be yours in plenty.

be a joint system of action; and in case of different opinions, each must recede a little in order at last to form a unanimous one. Such, I hope, will be your connection with Lord Huntingdon. You will both come into parliament at the same time; and if you have an equal share of abilities and application, you and he, with other young people, whom you will naturally associate, may form a band which will be respected by any Administration, and make a figure in the public. The other sort of connections I call unequal ones; that is, where the parts are all on one side, and the rank and fortune on the other. Here the advantage is all on one side; but that advantage must be ably and artfully concealed. Complaisance, an engaging manner, and a patient toleration of certain airs of superiority, must cement them. The weaker party must be taken by the heart, his head giving no hold; and he must be governed, by being made to believe that he governs. These people, skilfully led, give great weight to their leader. I have formerly pointed out to you a couple that I take to be proper objects for your skill; and you will meet with twenty more, for they are very rife.

The other person whom I recommend to you is a woman; not as a woman, for that is not immediately my business; besides, I fear she is turned of fifty. It is Lady Hervey, whom I directed you to call upon at Dijon; but who, to my great joy, because to your great advantage, passes all this winter at Paris. She has been bred all her life at Courts, of which she has acquired all the easy good breeding and politeness, without the frivolousness. She has all the reading that a woman should have, and more than any woman need have, for she understands Latin perfectly well, though she wisely conceals it. As she will look upon you as her son, I desire that you will look upon her as my delegate: trust, consult, and apply to her without reserve. No woman ever had, more than she has, *le ton de la parfaitement bonne compagnie, les manières engageantes, et le je ne sais quoi qui plaît.* Desire her to reprove and correct any, and every, the least error and inaccuracy in your manners, air, address, &c. No woman in Europe can do it so well; none will do it more willingly, or in a more proper and obliging manner. In such a case she will not put you out of countenance, by telling you of it in company; but either intimate it by some sign, or wait for an opportunity when you are alone together. She is also in the best French company, where she will not only introduce, but *puff* you, if I may use so low a word. And I can assure you that it is no little help, in the *beau monde*, to be puffed there by a fashionable woman. I send you the enclosed billet to carry her, only as a certificate of the identity of your person, which I take it for granted she could not know again.

You would be so much surprised to receive a whole letter from me, without any mention of the exterior ornaments necessary for a gentleman as manners, elocution, air, address, graces, &c., that, to comply with your expectations, I will touch upon them; and tell you, that, when you come to England, I will show you some people, whom I do not now care to name, raised to the highest stations singly by those exterior and adventitious ornaments; whose parts would never have entitled them to the smallest office in the excise. Are they, then, necessary, and worth acquiring, or not? You will see many instances of this kind at Paris, particularly a glaring one, of a person [1] raised to the highest posts and dignities in France, as well as to be absolute sovereign of the *beau monde*, singly by the graces of his person and address; by woman's chit-chat, accompanied with important gestures; by an imposing air, and pleasing *abord*. Nay, by these helps he even passes for a wit, though he hath certainly no uncommon share of it. I will not name him, because it would be very imprudent in you to do it. A young fellow, at his first entrance into the *beau monde*, must not offend the king *de facto* there. It is very often more necessary to conceal contempt than resentment, the former being never forgiven, but the latter sometimes forgot.

There is a small quarto book, entitled *Histoire Chronologique de la France*, lately published by le President Hénault; a man of parts and learning, with whom you will probably get acquainted at Paris. I desire that it may always lie upon your table, for your recourse as often as you read history. The chronology, though chiefly relative to the history of France, is not singly confined to it; but the most interesting events of all the rest of Europe are also inserted, and many of them adorned by short, pretty, and just reflections. The new edition of *les Mémoires de Sully*, in three quarto volumes, is also extremely well worth your reading, as it will give you a clearer and truer notion of one of the most interesting periods of the French history than you can yet have formed from all the other books you may have read upon the subject. That Prince, I mean Henry the Fourth, had all the accomplishments and virtues of a Hero, and of a King; and almost of a man. The last are the most rarely seen; may you possess them all! Adieu.

Pray make my compliments to Mr Harte, and let him know

1 Mr le Maréchal de Richelieu.

that I have this moment received his letter of the 12th, N. S., from Antibes. It requires no immediate answer, I shall therefore delay mine till I have another from him. Give him the enclosed, which I have received from Mr Eliot.

LETTER CC.

My dear Friend,   London, November the 1st, O. S. 1750.

I hope this letter will not find you still at Montpellier, but rather be sent after you from thence to Paris, where I am persuaded that Mr Harte could find as good advice for his leg as at Montpellier, if not better; but if he is of a different opinion, I am sure you ought to stay there as long as he desires.

While you are in France, I could wish that the hours you allot for historical amusement, should be entirely devoted to the history of France. One always reads history to most advantage in that country to which it is relative; not only books, but persons being ever at hand, to solve the doubts and clear up difficulties. I do by no means advise you to throw away your time in ransacking, like a dull antiquarian, the minute and unimportant parts of remote and fabulous times. Let blockheads read what blockheads wrote. A general notion of the history of France, from the conquest of that country by the Franks, to the reign of Lewis the Eleventh, is sufficient for use, consequently sufficient for you. There are, however, in those remote times, some remarkable eras, that deserve more particular attention; I mean those in which some notable alterations happened in the constitution and form of government. As, for example, the settlement of Clovis in Gaul, and the form of government which he then established; for, by the way, that form of government differed in this particular from all the other Gothic governments, that the people, neither collectively nor by representatives, had any share in it. It was a mixture of monarchy and aristocracy: and what were called the States-General of France, consisted only of the Nobility and Clergy, till the time of Philip le Bel, in the very beginning of the fourteenth century, who first called the people to those assemblies, by no means for the good of the people, who were only amused by this pretended honour, but, in truth, to check the Nobility and Clergy, and induce them to grant the money he wanted for his profusion: this was a scheme of Enguerrand de Marigny, his Minister, who governed both him and his kingdom to such a

degree, as to be called the coadjutor and governor of the kingdom. Charles Martel laid aside these assemblies, and governed
by open force. Pepin restored them, and attached them to him,
and with them the nation; by which means he deposed Chil-
deric, and mounted the throne. This is a second period worth
your attention. The third race of Kings, which begins with
Hugues Capet, is a third period. A judicious reader of history
will save himself a great deal of time and trouble by attending
with care only to those interesting periods of history which
furnish remarkable events, and make eras; going slightly over
the common run of events. Some people read history, as others
read the Pilgrim's Progress; giving equal attention to, and indiscriminately loading their memories with, every part alike.
But I would have you read it in a different manner: take the
shortest general history you can find of every country; and
mark down in that history the most important periods, such as
conquests, changes of Kings, and alterations of the form of
government; and then have recourse to more extensive histories, or particular treatises, relative to these great points.
Consider them well, trace up their causes, and follow their consequences. For instance; there is a most excellent though very
short history of France, by Le Gendre. Read that with attention, and you will know enough of the general history; but
when you find there such remarkable periods as are above
mentioned, consult Mezeray, and other the best and minutest
historians, as well as political treatises upon those subjects. In
later times, Memoirs, from those of Philip de Commines, down
to the innumerable ones in the reign of Lewis the Fourteenth,
have been of great use, and thrown great light upon particular
parts of history.

Conversation in France, if you have the address and dexterity to turn it upon useful subjects, will exceedingly improve
your historical knowledge; for people there, however classically
ignorant they may be, think it a shame to be ignorant of the
history of their own country: they read that, if they read nothing else, and having often read nothing else, are proud of
having read that, and talk of it willingly; even the women are
well instructed in that sort of reading. I am far from meaning
by this, that you should always be talking wisely, in company,
of books, history, and matters of knowledge. There are many
companies which you will and ought to keep, where such conversations would be misplaced and ill-timed; your own good
sense must distinguish the company, and the time. You must
trifle with triflers; and be serious only with the serious, but

dance to those who pipe. *Cur in theatrum Cato severe venisti ?*[1] was justly said to an old man : how much more so would it be to one of your age ! From the moment that you are dressed, and go out, pocket all your knowledge with your watch, and never pull it out in company unless desired : the producing of the one unasked implies that you are weary of the company ; and the producing of the other unrequired will make the company weary of you. Company is a republic too jealous of its liberties to suffer a dictator even for a quarter of an hour ; and yet in that, as in all republics, there are some few who really govern ; but then it is by seeming to disclaim, instead of attempting to usurp, the power : that is the occasion in which manners, dexterity, address, and the undefinable *je ne sais quoi* triumph ; if properly exerted, their conquest is sure, and the more lasting for not being perceived. Remember, that this is not only your first and greatest, but ought to be almost your only, object, while you are in France.

I know that many of your countrymen are apt to call the freedom and vivacity of the French, petulancy and ill-breeding ; but should you think so, I desire upon many accounts that you will not say so : I admit that it may be so, in some instances of *petits maîtres étourdis*, and in some young people unbroken to the world ; but I can assure you, that you will find it much otherwise with people of a certain rank and age, upon whose model you will do very well to form yourself. We call their steady assurance impudence : Why ? Only because what we call modesty is awkward bashfulness, and *mauvaise honte*. For my part, I see no impudence, but, on the contrary, infinite utility and advantage, in presenting one's self with the same coolness and unconcern in any and every company : till one can do that, I am very sure that one can never present one's self well. Whatever is done under concern and embarrassment, must be ill-done ; and till a man is absolutely easy and unconcerned in every company, he will never be thought to have kept good, nor be very welcome in it. A steady assurance, with seeming modesty, is possibly the most useful qualification that a man can have in every part of life. A man would certainly make a very inconsiderable fortune and figure in the world, whose modesty and timidity should often, as bashfulness always does, put him in the deplorable and lamentable situation of the pious Æneas, when, *obstupuit steteruntque comæ ; et vox faucibus hæsit.* Fortune (as well as women),

---

[1] Why hast thou, stern Cato, come into the theatre?

—————born to be control'd,
Stoops to the forward and the bold.

Assurance and intrepidity, under the white banner of seeming
modesty, clear the way for merit, that would otherwise be discouraged by difficulties in its journey ; whereas barefaced impudence is the noisy and blustering harbinger of a worthless
and senseless usurper.

You will think that I shall never have done recommending
to you these exterior worldly accomplishments, and you will
think right, for I never shall ; they are of too great consequence
to you, for me to be indifferent or negligent about them : the
shining part of your future figure and fortune depends now
wholly upon them. These are the acquisitions which must
give efficacy and success to those you have already made. To
have it said and believed that you are the most learned man in
England, would be no more than was said and believed of Dr
Bentley : but to have it said, at the same time, that you are
also the best bred, most polite, and agreeable man in the kingdom, would be such a happy composition of a character, as I
never yet knew any one man deserve ; and which I will endeavour, as well as ardently wish, that you may. Absolute
perfection is, I well know, unattainable ; but I know too, that
a man of parts may be unweariedly aiming at and arrive pretty
near it. Try, labour, persevere. Adieu.

LETTER CCI.

MY DEAR FRIEND,   London, November the 8th, O. S. 1750.

BEFORE you get to Paris, where you will soon be left to
your own discretion, if you have any, it is necessary that we
should understand one another thoroughly ; which is the most
probable way of preventing disputes. Money, the cause of
much mischief in the world, is the cause of most quarrels between fathers and sons ; the former commonly thinking, that
they cannot give too little, and the latter, that they cannot have
enough ; both equally in the wrong. You must do me the
justice to acknowledge, that I have hitherto neither stinted nor
grudged any expense that could be of use or real pleasure to
you ; and I can assure you, by the way, that you have travelled
at a much more considerable expense than I did myself : but I
never so much as thought of that, while Mr Harte was at the

head of your finances ; being very sure that the sums granted
were scrupulously applied to the uses for which they were intended. But the case will soon be altered, and you will be
your own receiver and treasurer. However, I promise you
that we will not quarrel singly upon the *quantum*, which shall
be cheerfully and freely granted ; the application and appro-
priation of it will be the material point, which I am now going
to clear up and finally settle with you. I will fix, or even
name, no settled allowance, though I well know in my own
mind, what would be the proper one ; but I will first try your
draughts, by which I can in a good degree judge of your conduct. This only I tell you in general, that, if the channels
through which my money is to go are the proper ones, the
source shall not be scanty ; but should it deviate into dirty,
muddy, and obscure ones (which, by the by, it cannot do for a
week, without my knowing it), I give you fair and timely notice that the source will instantly be dry. Mr Harte, in establishing you at Paris, will point out to you those proper channels ; he will leave you there upon the foot of a man of fashion,
and I will continue you upon the same ; you will have your
coach, your valet de chambre, your own footman, and a valet
de place ; which, by the way, is one servant more than I had.
I would have you very well dressed, by which I mean, dressed
as the generality of people of fashion are ; that is, not to be
taken notice of for being either more or less fine than other
people ; it is by being well dressed, not finely dressed, that a
gentleman should be distinguished. You must frequent *les
spectacles*, which expense I shall willingly supply. You must
play, *à des petits jeux de commerce*, in mixed companies ; that
article is trifling ; I shall pay it cheerfully. All the other
articles of pocket-money are very inconsiderable at Paris in
comparison of what they are here ; the silly custom of giving
money wherever one dines or sups, and the expensive importunity of subscriptions, not being yet introduced there. Having thus reckoned up all the decent expenses of a gentleman,
which I will most readily defray, I come now to those which
I will neither bear nor supply. The first of these is gaming,
which though I have not the least reason to suspect you of, I
think it necessary eventually to assure you that no consideration in the world shall ever make me pay your play debts :
should you ever urge to me that your honour is pawned, I
should most immovably answer you, that it was your honour,
not mine, that was pawned ; and that your creditor might e'en
take the pawn for the debt.

Low company and low pleasures are always much more costly than liberal and elegant ones. The disgraceful riots of a tavern are much more expensive, as well as dishonourable, than the (sometimes pardonable) excesses in good company. I must absolutely hear of no tavern scrapes and squabbles.

I come now to another and very material point; I mean women; and I will not address myself to you upon this subject, either in a religious, a moral, or a parental style. I will even lay aside my age, remember yours, and speak to you, as one man of pleasure, if he had parts too, would speak to another. I will, by no means, pay for whores, and their never-failing consequences, surgeons; nor will I, upon any account, keep singers, dancers, actresses, and *id genus omne;* and, independently of the expense, I must tell you that such connections would give me, and all sensible people, the utmost contempt for your parts and address: a young fellow must have as little sense as address, to venture, or more properly to sacrifice, his health and ruin his fortune with such sort of creatures; in such a place as Paris especially, where gallantry is both the profession and practice of every woman of fashion. To speak plainly; I will not forgive your understanding c—s and p—s; nor will your constitution forgive them you. These distempers, as well as their cures, fall nine times in ten upon the lungs. This argument, I am sure, ought to have weight with you; for I protest to you, that if you meet with any such accident, I would not give one year's purchase for your life. Lastly, there is another sort of expense that I will not allow, only because it is a silly one; I mean the fooling away your money in baubles at toy-shops. Have one handsome snuff-box (if you take snuff) and one handsome sword; but then no more very pretty and very useless things.

By what goes before, you will easily perceive that I mean to allow you whatever is necessary, not only for the figure, but for the pleasures of a Gentleman, and not to supply the profusion of a Rake. This, you must confess, does not savour of either the severity or parsimony of old age. I consider this agreement between us as a subsidiary treaty on my part, for services to be performed on yours. I promise you that I will be as punctual in the payment of the subsidies, as England has been during the last war; but then I give you notice, at the same time, that I require a much more scrupulous execution of the treaty on your part, than we met with on that of our allies; or else that payment will be stopped. I hope that all that I have now said was absolutely unnecessary, and that sentiments more worthy and more noble than pecuniary ones, would of themselves have pointed out to you the conduct I recommend ; but, in all events, I resolved to be once for all explicit with you, that in the worst that can happen, you may not plead ignorance, and complain that I had not sufficiently explained to you my intentions.

Having mentioned the word Rake, I must say a word or two more upon that subject, because young people too frequently, and always fatally, are apt to mistake that character for that of a man of pleasure ; whereas there are not in the world two characters more different. A rake is a composition of all the lowest, most ignoble, degrading, and shameful vices ; they all conspire to disgrace his character, and to ruin his fortune ; while wine and the p—x contend which shall soonest and most effectually destroy his constitution. A dissolute, flagitious footman, or porter, makes full as good a rake as a man of the first quality. By the by, let me tell you, that in the wildest part of my youth, I never was a rake, but, on the contrary, always detested and despised the character.

A man of pleasure, though not always so scrupulous as he should be, and as one day he will wish he had been, refines at least his pleasures by taste, accompanies them with decency, and enjoys them with dignity. Few men can be men of pleasure, every man may be a rake. Remember that I shall know everything you say or do at Paris, as exactly as if, by the force of magic, I could follow you everywhere, like a Sylph or a Gnôme, invisible myself. Seneca says, very prettily, that one should ask nothing of God, but what one should be willing that men should know ; nor of men, but what one should be willing that God should know ; I advise you to say or do nothing at Paris, but what you would be willing that I should know. I hope, nay I believe, that will be the case. Sense, I dare say, you do not want ; instruction, I am sure, you have never wanted ; experience, you are daily gaining ; all which together must inevitably (I should think) make you both *respectable et aimable,* the perfection of a human character. In that case nothing shall be wanting on my part, and you shall solidly experience all the extent and tenderness of my affection for you ; but dread the reverse of both ! Adieu.

P. S. When you get to Paris, after you have been to wait on Lord Albemarle, go to see Mr Yorke, whom I have particular reasons for desiring that you should be well with, as I shall hereafter explain to you. Let him know that my orders,

and your own inclinations, conspired to make you desire his
friendship and protection

LETTER CCII.

My dear Friend,

I HAVE sent you so many preparatory letters for Paris, that
this, which will meet you there, shall only be a summary of
them all.

. You have hitherto had more liberty than anybody of your
age ever had ; and I must do you the justice to own, that you
have made a better use of it than most people of your age would
have done ; but then, though you had not a jailer, you had a
friend with you.   At Paris, you will not only be unconfined,
but unassisted.   Your own good sense must be your only guide ;
I have great confidence in it, and am convinced that I shall receive just such accounts of your conduct at Paris as I could
wish ; for I tell you beforehand that I shall be most minutely
informed of all that you do, and almost of all that you say, there.
Enjoy the pleasures of youth, you cannot do better ; but refine
and dignify them like a man of parts : let them raise and not
sink, let them adorn and not vilify, your character ; let them,
in short, be the pleasures of a gentleman, and taken with your
equals at least, but rather with your superiors, and those chiefly
French.

Inquire into the characters of the several academicians, before you form a connection with any of them ; and be most
upon your guard against those who make the most court to you.

You cannot study much in the academy ; but you may
study usefully there, if you are an economist of your time, and
bestow only upon good books those quarters and halves of
hours, which occur to everybody in the course of almost every
day ; and which, at the year's end, amount to a very considerable sum of time.   Let Greek, without fail, share some part of
every day : I do not mean the Greek poets, the catches of Ana-
creon, or the tender complaints of Theocritus, or even the por-
terlike language of Homer's heroes ; of whom all smatterers in
Greek know a little, quote often, and talk of always ; but I
mean Plato, Aristoteles, Demosthenes, and Thucydides, whom
none but adepts know.   It is Greek that must distinguish you
in the learned world, Latin alone will not.   And Greek must
be sought to be retained, for it never occurs like Latin.   When

you read history, or other books of amusement, let every language you are master of have its turn; so that you may not only retain, but improve in every one. I also desire that you will converse in German and Italian, with all the Germans and the Italians with whom you converse at all. This will be a very agreeable and flattering thing to them, and a very useful one to you.

Pray apply yourself diligently to your exercises; for though the doing them well is not supremely meritorious, the doing them ill is illiberal, vulgar, and ridiculous.

I recommend theatrical representations to you ; which are excellent at Paris. The tragedies of Corneille and Racine, and the comedies of Molière, well attended to, are admirable lessons, both for the heart and the head. There is not, nor ever was, any theatre comparable to the French. If the music of the French operas does not please your Italian ear, the words of them, at least, are sense and poetry, which is much more than I can say of any Italian opera that I ever read or heard in my life.

I send you the enclosed letter of recommendation to Marquis Matignon, which I would have you deliver to him as soon as you can : you will, I am sure, feel the good effects of his warm friendship for me, and Lord Bolingbroke ; who has also wrote to him upon your subject. By that, and by the other letters which I have sent you, you will be at once so thoroughly introduced into the best French company, that you must take some pains if you will keep bad; but that is what I do not suspect you of. You have, I am sure, too much right ambition to prefer low and disgraceful company to that of your superiors, both in rank and age. Your character, and, consequently, your fortune, absolutely depends upon the company you keep, and the turn you take at Paris. I do not in the least mean a grave turn ; on the contrary, a gay, a sprightly, but, at the same time, an elegant and liberal one.

Keep carefully out of all scrapes and quarrels. They lower a character extremely, and are particularly dangerous in France, where a man is dishonoured by not resenting an affront, and utterly ruined by resenting it. The young Frenchmen are hasty, giddy, and petulant; extremely national, and *avantageux.* Forbear from any national jokes or reflections, which are always improper, and commonly unjust. The colder northern nations generally look upon France, as a whistling, singing, dancing, frivolous nation : this notion is very far from being a true one, though many *petits maîtres* by their behaviour seem to justify it ; but those very *petits maîtres*, when mellowed by age and experience, very often turn out very able men. The number of great Generals and Statesmen, as well as excellent Authors, that France has produced, is an undeniable proof, that it is not that frivolous, unthinking, empty nation that northern prejudices suppose it. Seem to like and approve of everything at first, and I promise you that you will like and approve of many things afterwards.

I expect that you will write to me constantly, once every week, which I desire may be every Thursday : and that your letters may inform me of your personal transactions ; not of what you see, but of whom you see, and what you do.

Be your own monitor, now that you will have no other. As to enunciation, I must repeat it to you again and again, that there is no one thing so necessary ; all other talents, without that, are absolutely useless, except in your own closet.

It sounds ridiculously to bid you study with your dancing-master ; and yet I do. The bodily carriage and graces are of infinite consequence to everybody, and more particularly to you.

Adieu for this time, my dear child. Yours tenderly.

———◇———

LETTER CCIII.

My dear Friend,   London, November the 12th, O. S. 1750.

You will possibly think that this letter turns upon strange, little, trifling objects ; and you will think right, if you consider them separately ; but if you take them aggregately you will be convinced that as parts, which conspire to form that whole, called the exterior of a man of fashion, they are of importance. I shall not dwell now upon those personal graces, that liberal air, and that engaging address, which I have so often recommended to you, but descend still lower, to your dress, cleanliness, and care of your person.

When you come to Paris you must take care to be extremely well dressed, that is, as the fashionable people are ; this does by no means consist in the finery, but in the taste, fitness, and manner of wearing your clothes : a fine suit ill made, and slatternly or stiffly worn, far from adorning, only exposes the awkwardness of the wearer. Get the best French tailor to make your clothes, whatever they are, in the fashion, and to fit you : and then wear them, button them, or unbutton

them, as the genteelest people you see do. Let your man learn
of the best *friseur* to do your hair well, for that is a very material part of your dress. Take care to have your stockings well
gartered up, and your shoes well buckled ; for nothing gives a
more slovenly air to a man than ill-dressed legs. In your person
you must be accurately clean ; and your teeth, hands, and nails
should be superlatively so : a dirty mouth has real ill consequences to the owner, for it infallibly causes the decay, as well
as the intolerable pain, of the teeth ; and it is very offensive to
his acquaintance, for it will most inevitably stink. I insist,
therefore, that you wash your teeth the first thing you do every
morning, with a soft sponge and warm water, for four or five
minutes ; and then wash your mouth five or six times. *Mouton*,
whom I desire you will send for upon your arrival at Paris, will
give you an opiate, and a liquor to be used sometimes. Nothing looks more ordinary, vulgar, and illiberal, than dirty hands,
and ugly, uneven, and ragged nails : I do not suspect you of
that shocking, awkward trick, of biting yours ; but that is not
enough ; you must keep the ends of them smooth and clean,
not tipped with black, as the ordinary people's always are.
The ends of your nails should be small segments of circles,
which, by a very little care in the cutting, they are very easily
brought to ; every time that you wipe your hands, rub the skin
round your nails backwards, that it may not grow up, and
shorten your nails too much. The cleanliness of the rest of
your person, which, by the way, will conduce greatly to your
health, I refer from time to time to the bagnio. My mentioning
these particulars arises (I freely own) from some suspicion that
the hints are not unnecessary ; for when you were a schoolboy,
you were slovenly and dirty, above your fellows. I must add
another caution, which is, that upon no account whatever you
put your fingers, as too many people are apt to do, in your nose
or ears. It is the most shocking, nasty, vulgar rudeness, that
can be offered to company ; it disgusts one, it turns one's
stomach ; and, for my own part, I would much rather know
that a man's finger were actually in his breech, than see them
in his nose. Wash your ears well every morning, and blow
your nose in your handkerchief whenever you have occasion :
but, by the way, without looking at it afterwards. There should
be in the least as well as in the greatest parts of a gentleman,
les manières nobles. Sense will teach you some, observation
others : attend carefully to the manners, the diction, the motions, of people of the first fashion, and form your own upon
them. On the other hand, observe a little those of the vulgar,

in order to avoid them : for though the things which they say
or do may be the same, the manner is always totally different :
and in that, and nothing else, consists the characteristic of a
man of fashion.   The lowest peasant speaks, moves, dresses,
eats, and drinks, as much as a man of the first fashion, but
does them all quite differently ; so that by doing and saying
most things in a manner opposite to that of the vulgar, you
have a great chance of doing and saying them right.   There
are gradations in awkwardness and vulgarism, as there are in
everything else.   *Les manières de Robe*, though not quite right,
are still better than *les manières Bourgeoises ;* and these, though
bad, are still better than *les manières de Campagne.*   But the
language, the air, the dress, and the manners, of the Court, are
the only true standard *des manières nobles, et d'un honnête homme.*
Ex pede Herculem [1] is an old and true saying, and very applicable
to our present subject ; for a man of parts, who has been bred
at Courts, and used to keep the best company, will distinguish
himself, and is to be known from the vulgar, by every word, attitude, gesture, and even look.   I cannot leave these seeming
minuties, without repeating to you the necessity of your carving
well ; which is an article, little as it is, that is useful twice
every day of one's life ; and the doing it ill is very troublesome
to one's self, and very disagreeable, often ridiculous, to others.

Having said all this, I cannot help reflecting what a formal
dull fellow, or a cloistered pedant, would say, if they were to
see this letter : they would look upon it with the utmost contempt, and say, that surely a father might find much better
topics for advice to a son.   I would admit it if I had given
you, or that you were capable of receiving, no better ; but if
sufficient pains had been taken to form your heart and improve
your mind, and, as I hope, not without success, I will tell those
solid Gentlemen that all these trifling things, as they think
them, collectively form that pleasing *je ne sais quoi*, that *ensemble*, which they are utter strangers to both in themselves and
others.   The word *aimable* is not known in their language, or
the thing in their manners.   Great usage of the world, great attention, and a great desire of pleasing, can alone give it ; and
it is no trifle.   It is from old people's looking upon these things
as trifles, or not thinking of them at all, that so many young
people are so awkward, and so ill bred.   Their parents, often
careless and unmindful of them, give them only the common run
of education, as school, university, and then travelling ; without
examining, and very often without being able to judge if they

1 You may tell Hercules from his foot.

did examine, what progress they make in any one of these stages. Then they carelessly comfort themselves, and say that their sons will do like other people's sons ; and so they do, that is, commonly very ill. They correct none of the childish, nasty tricks, which they get at school; nor the illiberal manners which they contract at the university; nor the frivolous and superficial pertness which is commonly all that they acquire by their travels. As they do not tell them of these things, nobody else can ; so they go on in the practice of them, without ever hearing or knowing that they are unbecoming, indecent, and shocking. For, as I have often formerly observed to you, nobody but a father can take the liberty to reprove a young fellow grown up for those kind of inaccuracies and improprieties of behaviour. The most intimate friendship, unassisted by the paternal superiority, will not authorize it. I may truly say, therefore, that you are happy in having me for a sincere, friendly, and quick-sighted monitor. Nothing will escape me ; I shall pry for your defects, in order to correct them, as curiously as I shall seek for your perfections, in order to applaud and reward them; with this difference only, that I shall publicly mention the latter, and never hint at the former, but in a letter to, or a *téte-à-téte* with, you. I will never put you out of countenance before company ; and I hope you will never give me reason to be out of countenance for you, as any one of the above-mentioned defects would make me. *Prætor non curat de minimis*,[1] was a maxim in the Roman law; for causes only of a certain value were tried by him ; but there were inferior jurisdictions, that took cognizance of the smallest. Now I shall try you, not only as a Prætor in the greatest, but as Censor in lesser, and as the lowest magistrate in the least, cases.

I have this moment received Mr Harte's letter of the 1st November, new style ; by which I am very glad to find that he thinks of moving towards Paris the end of this month, which looks as if his leg were better ; besides, in my opinion, you both of you only lose time at Montpellier ; he would find better advice, and you better company, at Paris. In the mean time, I hope you go into the best company there is at Montpellier, and there always is some at the Intendant's or the Commandant's. You will have had full time to have learned, *les petites chansons Languedociennes*, which are exceeding pretty ones, both words and tunes. I remember, when I was in those parts, I was surprised at the difference which I found between the people on one side and those on the other side of the Rhône.

---

[1] The Prætor gives no heed to trifles.

The *Provenceaux* were, in general, surly, ill-bred, ugly, and swarthy: the Languedocians the very reverse; a cheerful, well-bred, handsome people. Adieu! Yours most affectionately.

P. S. Upon reflection, I direct this letter to Paris; I think you must have left Montpellier before it could arrive there.

LETTER CCIV.

MY DEAR FRIEND,   London, Nov. the 19th, O. S. 1750.

I WAS very glad to find, by your letter of the 12th, N. S., that you had informed yourself so well of the state of the French marine at Toulon, and of the commerce at Marseilles: they are objects that deserve the inquiry and attention of every man who intends to be concerned in public affairs. The French are now wisely attentive to both; their commerce is incredibly increased within these last thirty years: they have beaten us out of great part of our Levant trade: their East India trade has greatly affected ours: and, in the West Indies, their Martinico establishment supplies, not only France itself, but the greatest part of Europe, with sugars: whereas our islands, as Jamaica, Barbadoes, and the Leeward, have now no other market for theirs but England. New France, or Canada,[1] has also greatly lessened our fur and skin trade. It is true (as you say) that we have no treaty of commerce subsisting (I do not say *with Marseilles*) but with France. There was a treaty of commerce made between England and France immediately after the treaty of Utrecht; but the whole treaty was conditional, and to depend upon the Parliament's enacting certain things, which were stipulated in two of the articles: the Parliament, after a very famous debate, would not do it; so the treaty fell to the ground: however, the outlines of that treaty are, by mutual and tacit consent, the general rules of our present commerce with France. It is true, too, that our commodities, which go to France, must go in our bottoms; the French having imitated, in many respects, our famous Act of Navigation, as it is commonly called. This Act was made in the year 1652, in the Parliament held by Oliver Cromwell. It forbids all foreign ships to bring into England any merchandise or commodities whatsoever, that were not of the growth and produce of that country to which those ships belonged, under penalty of the

[1] It was ceded to England in 1763.

forfeiture of such ships. This Act was particularly levelled at the Dutch, who were at that time the carriers of almost all Europe, and got immensely by freight. Upon this principle of the advantages arising from freight, there is a provision in the same Act, that even the growth and produce of our own colonies in America shall not be carried from thence to any other country in Europe without first touching in England ; but this clause has lately been repealed, in the instances of some perishable commodities, such as rice, &c., which are allowed to be carried directly from our American colonies to other countries. The Act also provides, that two thirds, I think, of those who navi· gate the said ships, shall be British subjects. There is an excellent and little book, written by the famous Monsieur Huet, Evêque d'Avranches, *sur le commerce des anciens*, which is very well worth your reading, and very soon read. It will give you a clear notion of the rise and progress of commerce. There are many other books which take up the history of commerce where Monsieur d'Avranches leaves it, and bring it down to these times : I advise you to read some of them with care : commerce being a very essential part of political knowledge in every country ; but more particularly in this, which owes all its riches and power to it.

I come now to another part of your letter, which is the orthography, if I may call bad spelling *orthography*. You spell induce, *enduce*, and grandeur you' spell grand*ure ;* two faults, of which few of my housemaids would have been guilty. I must tell you that orthography, in the true sense of the word, is so absolutely necessary for a man of. letters, or a gentleman, that one false spelling may fix a ridicule upon him for the rest of his life ; and I know a man of quality who never recovered the ridicule of having spelled *wholesome* without the *w*.

Reading with care will secure everybody from false spelling ; for books are always well spelled, according to the orthography of the times. Some words are indeed doubtful, being spelled differently by different authors of equal authority : but those are few ; and in those cases every man has his option, because he may plead his authority either way ; but where there is but one right way, as in the two words above-mentioned, it is unpardonable, and ridiculous, for a gentleman to miss it : even a woman of a tolerable education would despise and laugh at a lover who should send her an ill-spelled *billetdoux*. I fear, and suspect, that you have taken it into your head, in most cases, that the Matter is all, and the Manner little or nothing. If you have, undeceive yourself, and be convinced that, in everything, the Manner is full as important as the Matter. If you speak the sense of an angel in bad words, and with a disagreeable utterance, nobody will hear you twice who can help it. If you write epistles as well as Cicero, but in a very bad hand, and very ill spelled, whoever receives will laugh at them ; and if you had the figure of Adonis, with an awkward air and motions, it will disgust instead of pleasing. Study Manner, therefore, in everything, if you would be anything. My principal inquiries of my friends at Paris, concerning you, will be relative to your Manner of doing whatever you do. I shall not inquire whether you understand Demosthenes, Tacitus, or the *jus publicum imperii;* but I shall inquire whether your utterance is pleasing, your style not only pure but elegant, your manners noble and easy, your air and address engaging; in short, whether you are a gentleman, a man of fashion, and fit to keep good company, or not ; for till I am satisfied in these particulars you and I must by no means meet ; I could not possibly stand it. It is in your power to become all this at Paris if you please. Consult with Lady Hervey and Madame Monconseil upon all these matters ; and they will speak to you, and advise you freely. Tell them that *bisogna compatire ancora,*[1] that you are utterly new in the world, that you are desirous to form yourself, that you beg they will reprove, advise, and correct you, that you know that none can do it so well ; and that you will implicitly follow their directions. This, together with your careful observation of the manners of the best company, will really form you.

Abbé Guasco, a friend of mine, will come to you as soon as he knows of your arrival at Paris ; he is well received in the best companies there, and will introduce you to them. He will be desirous to do you any service he can ; he is active and curious, and can give you information upon most things. He is a sort of *complaisant* of the President Montesquieu, to whom you have a letter.

I imagine that this letter will not wait for you very long at Paris, where I reckon you will be in about a fortnight. Adieu.

———◇———

LETTER CCV.

Mon Cher Ami,   A Londres, le 24 Dec. V. S. 1750.

Vous voilà à la fin Parisien, et il faut s'adresser à un Pa-

---
[1] They must still have pity upon you.

risien en François. Vous voudrez bien aussi me répondre de même, puisque je serai bien aise de voir à quel point vous possédez l'élégance, la délicatesse, et l'ortographe de cette langue qui est devenue, pour ainsi dire, la langue universelle de l'Europe. On m'assure que vous la parlez fort bien, mais il y a bien et bien. Et tel passera pour la bien parler hors de Paris, qui passeroit lui-même pour Gaulois à Paris. Dans ce Pays des modes, le langage même a la sienne, et qui change presqu' aussi souvent que celle des habits.

L'affecté, le précieux, le néologique, y sont trop à la mode d'aujourd'hui. Connoissez-les, remarquez-les, et parlez-les même, à la bonne heure, mais ne vous en laissez pas infecter : l'esprit aussi a sa mode, et actuellement à Paris, c'est la mode d'en avoir, en dépit même de Minerve ; tout le monde court après l'esprit, qui par parenthèse ne se laisse jamais attraper ; s'il ne se présente pas on a beau courir. Mais malheureusement pour ceux qui courent après, ils attrapent quelque chose qu'ils prennent pour de l'esprit, et qu'ils donnent pour tel. C'est tout au plus la bonne fortune d'Ixion, c'est une vapeur qu'ils embrassent, au lieu de la déesse qu'ils poursuivent. De cette erreur résultent ces beaux sentimens qu'on n'a jamais senti, ces pensées fausses que la nature n'a jamais produites, et ces expressions entortillées et obscures, que non seulement on n'entend point, mais qu'on ne peut pas même déchiffrer ni deviner. C'est de tous ces ingrédiens que sont composés les deux tiers des nouveaux livres François qui paroissent. C'est la nouvelle cuisine du Parnasse, ou l'alambic travaille au lieu du pot et de la broche, et ou les quintessences et les extraits dominent. N. B. Le sel Attique en est banni.

Il vous faudra bien, de tems en tems, manger de cette nouvelle cuisine. Mais ne vous y laissez pas corrompre le goût. Et quand vous voudrez donner à manger à votre tour, étudiez la bonne vieille cuisine du tems de Louis quatorze. Il y avoit alors des chefs admirables, comme Corneille, Boileau, Racine, et la Fontaine. Tout ce qu'ils apprétoient étoit simple, sain, et solide. Sans métaphore, ne vous laissez pas éblouir par le faux brillant, le recherché, les antithèses à la mode ; mais servez vous de votre propre bon sens, et appelez les anciens à votre secours, pour vous en garantir. D'un autre côté, ne vous moquez pas de ceux qui s'y sont laissés séduire ; vous êtes encore trop jeune pour faire le critique, et pour vous ériger en vengeur sévère du bon sens lésé. Seulement ne vous laissez pas pervertir, mais ne songez pas à convertir les autres. Laissez les jouir tranquillement de leurs erreurs dans le goût, comme dans la religion.

Le goût en France a depuis un siècle et demi, eu bien du haut
et du bas, aussi bien que la France même. Le bon goût com-
mença seulement à se faire jour, sous le règne, je ne dis pas de
Louis treize, mais du Cardinal de Richelieu, et fut encore épuré
sous celui de Louis quatorze, grand Roi au moins, s'il n'étoit
pas grand homme. Corneille étoit le restaurateur du vrai, et
le fondateur du théâtre François ; se ressentant toujours un peu
des *Concetti* des Italiens et des *Agudeze* des Espagnols ; témoin
les épigrammes qu'il fait débiter à Chimène dans tout l'excès
de sa douleur.

Mais avant son tems, les Troubadours, et les Romanciers
étoient autant de fous, qui trouvoient des sots pour les admirer.
Vers la fin du règne du Cardinal de Richelieu, et au commence-
ment de celui de Louis quatorze, l'Hôtel de Rambouillet étoit
le Temple du Goût, mais d'un goût pas encore tout à fait épuré.
C'étoit plutôt un laboratoire d'esprit, ou l'on donnoit la torture
au bon sens, pour en tirer une essence subtile. Voiture y tra-
vailloit, et suoit même à grosses gouttes pour faire de l'esprit.
Mais enfin Boileau et Molière fixèrent le goût du vrai ; en dépit
des Scudery et des Calprenèdes, &c. Ils déconfirent et mirent
en fuite les Artamènes, les Jubas, les Oroondates, et tous ces
héros de Romans, qui valoient pourtant chacun seul, une armée.
Ces fous cherchèrent dans les bibliothèques un asile qu'on leur
refusa ; et ils n'en trouvèrent que dans quelques ruelles. Je
vous conseille pourtant de lire un tome de Cléopatre et un de
Clélie, sans quoi il vous sera impossible de vous former une
idée de ces extravagances ; mais Dieu vous garde d'aller jusqu'au douzième.

Le goût resta pur et vrai pendant presque tout le règne de
Louis quatorze, et jusqu'à ce qu'un très-beau génie y donna,
(mais sans le vouloir) quelque atteinte. C'étoit Monsieur de
Fontenelle, qui avec tout l'esprit du monde, et un grand savoir,
sacrifioit peut-être un peu trop aux grâces, dont il étoit le
nourrisson, et l'élève favori. Admiré avec raison, on voulut
l'imiter, mais malheureusement pour le siècle l'auteur des Pas-
torales, de l'Histoire des Oracles, et du théâtre François, trouva
moins d'imitateurs, que le Chevalier d'Her ne trouva de singes.
Contrefait depuis, par mille auteurs, il n'a pas été imité que je
sache par un seul.

A l'heure qu'il est, l'empire du vrai goût ne me paroit pas
trop bien affermi en France ; il subsiste à la vérité, mais il est
déchiré par des partis ; il y a le parti des petits maîtres, celui
des caillettes, celui des fades auteurs dont les ouvrages sont, *verba
et voces et præterea nihil*, et enfin un parti nombreux et fort à

la mode, d'auteurs qui débitent dans un galimatias métaphy-
sique leurs faux raffinemens, sur les mouvemens et les sentimens
de l'âme, du cœur, et de l'esprit.

Ne vous en laissez pas imposer par la mode ; ni par des
cliques que vous pourrez fréquenter ; mais essayez toutes ces
différentes espèces, avant que de les reçevoir en paiement au
coin du bon sens et de la raison ; et soyez bien persuadé que,
rien n'est beau que le vrai. Tout brillant qui ne résulte pas de
la solidité et de la justesse de la pensée n'est qu'un faux brillant.
Le mot Italien sur le diamant est bien vrai à cet égard, *quanto
più sodezza, tanto più splendore.*

Tout ceci n'empêche pas que vous ne deviez vous conformer
extérieurement aux modes et aux tons des différentes compagnies ou vous vous trouverez. Parlez epigrammes avec les
petits maîtres, sentimens faux avec les caillettes, et galimatias
avec les beaux esprits par état. A la bonne heure ; à votre
âge, ce n'est pas à vous à donner le ton à la compagnie, mais
au contraire à le prendre. Examinez bien pourtant, et pesez
tout cela en vous-même ; distinguez bien le faux du vrai, et
ne prenez pas le clinquant du Tasse pour l'or de Virgile.

Vous trouverez en même tems à Paris, des auteurs, et des
compagnies très-solides. Vous n'entendrez point des fadaises,
du précieux, du guindé, chez Madame de Monconseil, ni aux
hôtels de Matignon et de Coigny, ou elle vous présentera ; le
Président Montesquieu ne vous parlera pas *pointes.* Son livre
de l'Esprit des Loix, écrit en langue vulgaire, vous plaira, et
vous instruira également.

Fréquentez le théâtre quand on y jouera les pièces de Corneille, de Racine, et de Molière, ou il n'y a que du naturel et
du vrai. Je ne prétends pas par la donner l'exclusion à plu-
sieurs pièces modernes qui sont admirables, et en dernier lieu,
Cénie, pièce pleine de sentimens, mais de sentimens vrais, naturels, et dans lesquels on se reconnoît. Voulez-vous connoître
les caractères du jour, lisez les ouvrages de Crébillon le fils, et
de Marivaux. Le premier est un peintre excellent ; le second a
beaucoup étudié et connoît bien le cœur, peut-être même un
peu trop. Les égaremens du cœur et de l'esprit par Crébillon
est un livre excellent dans ce genre ; les caractères y sont bien
marquez ; il vous amusera infiniment, et ne vous sera pas inu-
tile. L'Histoire Japonoise de Tanzaï, et de Neadarné, du même
auteur, est une aimable extravagance, et parsemée de réflexions
très-justes ; enfin vous trouverez bien à Paris de quoi vous former un goût sûr et juste, pourvu que vous ne preniez pas le
change.

Comme je vous laisse sur votre bonne foi à Paris sans sur-
veillant, je me flatte que vous n'abuserez pas de ma confiance.
Je ne demande pas que vous soyez Capucin ; bien au contraire,
je vous recommande les plaisirs, mais j'éxige que ce soient les
plaisirs d'un honnête homme. Ces plaisirs la donnent du brillant au caractère d'un jeune homme ; mais la débauche avilit
et dégrade. J'aurai des relations très-vraies et détaillées de
votre conduite, et selon ces relations je serai plus, ou moins, ou
point du tout, à vous. Adieu.

P. S. Ecrivez moi sans faute une fois la semaine, et répondez
à celle-ci en François. Faufilez vous tant que vous le pourrez
chez les ministres étrangers. C'est voyager en différens endroits
sans changer de place. Parlez Italien à tous les Italiens, et
Allemand à tous les Allemands que vous trouverez, pour entretenir ces deux langues.

Je vous souhaite, mon cher, autant de nouvelles années que
vous mériterez, et pas une de plus. Mais puissiez vous en
mériter un grand nombre !

TRANSLATION.

My dear Friend,　　　　　London, December the 24th, 1750.

At length you are become a Parisian, and consequently
must be addressed in French ; you will also answer me in the
same language, that I may be able to judge of the degree in
which you possess the elegancy, the delicacy, and the orthography of that language, which is, in a manner, become the universal one of Europe. I am assured that you speak it well ;
but in that well there are gradations. He who in the provinces might be reckoned to speak correctly, would at Paris be
looked upon as an ancient Gaul. In that country of mode, even
language is subservient to fashion, which varies almost as often
as their clothes.

The *affected*, the *refined*, the *neological, or new and fashionable
style*, are at present too much in vogue at Paris. Know, observe, and occasionally converse (if you please) according to
these different styles ; but do not let your taste be infected by
them. Wit, too, is there subservient to fashion ; and actually,
at Paris, one must have wit, even in despite of Minerva. Everybody runs after it ; although, if it does not come naturally, and
of itself, it never can be overtaken. But, unfortunately for
those who pursue, they seize upon what they take for wit, and

endeavour to pass it for such upon others. This is, at best, the lot of Ixion, who embraced a cloud instead of the Goddess he pursued. Fine sentiments which never existed, false and unnatural thoughts, obscure and far-sought expressions, not only unintelligible, but which it is even impossible to decipher, or to guess at, are all the consequences of this error ; and two thirds of the new French books which now appear, are made up of those ingredients. It is the new cookery of Parnassus, in which the still is employed instead of the pot and the spit, and where quintessences and extracts are chiefly used. N. B. The Attic salt is proscribed.

You will now and then be obliged to eat of this new cookery, but do not suffer your taste to be corrupted by it. And when you, in your turn, are desirous of treating others, take the good old cookery of Lewis the Fourteenth's reign for your rule. There were at that time admirable head cooks, such as Corneille, Boileau, Racine, and la Fontaine. Whatever they prepared was simple, wholesome, and solid. But, laying aside all metaphors, do not suffer yourself to be dazzled by false brilliancy, by unnatural expressions, nor by those Antitheses so much in fashion : as a protection against such innovations, have recourse to your own good sense, and to the ancient authors. On the other hand, do not laugh at those who give in to such errors ; you are as yet too young to act the critic, or to stand forth a severe avenger of the violated rights of good sense. Content yourself with not being perverted, but do not think of converting others ; let them quietly enjoy their errors in taste, as well as in religion. Within the course of the last century and a half, taste in France has (as well as that kingdom itself) undergone many vicissitudes. Under the reign of (I do not say) Lewis the Thirteenth, but of Cardinal de Richelieu, good taste first began to make its way. It was refined under that of Lewis the Fourteenth ; a great king at least, if not a great man. Corneille was the restorer of true taste, and the founder of the French theatre ; although rather inclined to the Italian *Concetti*, and the Spanish *Agudeze*. Witness those epigrams which he makes Chimene utter in the greatest excess of grief.

Before his time that kind of itinerant authors called *Troubadours*, or *Romanciers*, was a species of madmen, who attracted the admiration of fools. Towards the end of Cardinal de Richelieu's reign, and the beginning of Lewis the Fourteenth's, the Temple of Taste was established at the *hôtel* of Rambouillet ; but that taste was not judiciously refined : this Temple of Taste might more properly have been named, a Laboratory of Wit, where good sense was put to the torture, in order to extract from it the most subtil essence. There it was, that Voiture laboured hard and incessantly to create wit. At length Boileau and Molière fixed the standard of true taste. In spite of the Scuderys, the Calprenedes &c., they defeated and put to flight *Artamenes*, *Juba*, *Oroondates*, and all those heroes of romance who were notwithstanding (each of them) as good as a whole army. Those madmen then endeavoured to obtain an asylum in libraries; this they could not accomplish, but were under a necessity of taking shelter in the chambers of some few ladies. I would have you read one volume of Cleopatra, and one of Clelia, it will otherwise be impossible for you to form any idea of the extravagancies they contain; but God keep you from ever persevering to the twelfth.

During almost the whole reign of Lewis the Fourteenth, true taste remained in its purity until it received some hurt, although undesignedly, from a very fine genius, I mean Monsieur de Fontenelle; who, with the greatest sense and most solid learning, sacrificed rather too much to the Graces, whose most favourite child and pupil he was. Admired with reason, others tried to imitate him: but unfortunately for us, the author of the Pastorals, of the History of Oracles, and of the French Theatre, found fewer imitators than the Chevalier d'Her did mimics. He has since been taken off by a thousand authors; but never really imitated by any one that I know of.

At this time, the seat of true taste in France seems to me not well established. It exists, but torn by factions. There is one party of *petits maîtres*, one of half-learned women, another of insipid authors, whose works are *verba et voces et præterea nihil*;[1] and, in short, a numerous and very fashionable party of writers, who, in a metaphysical jumble, introduce their false and subtile reasonings upon the movements and the sentiments of *the soul*, *the heart*, and *the mind*.

Do not let yourself be overpowered by fashion, nor by particular sets of people with whom you may be connected; but try all the different coins before you receive any in payment. Let your own good sense and reason judge of the value of each; and be persuaded that *nothing can be beautiful unless true*. Whatever brilliancy is not the result of the solidity and justness of a thought, is but a false glare. The Italian saying upon a diamond is equally just with regard to thoughts, *Quanto più sodezza, tanto più splendore*.[2]

---

[1] Words and sounds and nothing else.
[2] The more brilliancy the more splendour.

All this ought not to hinder you from conforming externally to the modes and tones of the different companies in which you may chance to be. With the *petits maîtres* speak epigrams, false sentiments with frivolous women ; and a mixture of all these together, with professed *beaux esprits*. I would have you do so ; for, at your age, you ought not to aim at changing the tone of the company, but conform to it. Examine well, however ; weigh all maturely within yourself ; and do not mistake the tinsel of Tasso for the gold of Virgil.

You will find at Paris good authors, and circles distinguished by the solidity of their reasoning. You will never hear *trifling, affected*, and far-sought conversations at Madame de Monconseil's nor at the hôtels of Matignon and Coigni, where she will introduce you. The President Montesquieu will not speak to you in the epigrammatic style. His book, the Spirit of the Laws, written in the vulgar tongue, will equally please and instruct you.

Frequent the theatre, whenever Corneille, Racine, and Molière's pieces are played. They are according to nature, and to truth. I do not mean by this to give an exclusion to several admirable modern plays, particularly Cénie,[1] replete with sentiments that are true, natural, and applicable to one's self. If you choose to know the characters of people now in fashion, read Crébillon the younger, and Marivaux's works. The former is a most excellent painter ; the latter has studied, and knows the human heart, perhaps too well. Crébillon's *Egaremens du Cœur et de l'Esprit* is an excellent work in its kind ; it will be of infinite amusement to you, and not totally useless. The Japanese history of Tanzaï and Neadarné, by the same author, is an amiable extravagancy, interspersed with the most just reflections. In short, provided you do not mistake the objects of your attention, you will find matter at Paris to form a good and true taste.

As I shall let you remain at Paris without any person to direct your conduct, I flatter myself that you will not make a bad use of the confidence I repose in you. I do not require that you should lead the life of a capuchin friar ; quite the contrary : I recommend pleasures to you ; but I expect that they shall be the pleasures of a gentleman. Those add brilliancy to a young man's character ; but debauchery vilifies and degrades it. I shall have very true and exact accounts of your conduct ; and according to the informations I receive shall be more, or less, or not at all yours. Adieu.

[1] Imitated in English by Mr Francis, in a play called Eugenia.

P. S. Do not omit writing to me once a week ; and let your answer to this letter be in French. Connect yourself as much as possible with the foreign Ministers ; which is properly travelling into different countries, without going from one place. Speak Italian to all the Italians, and German to all the Germans, you meet, in order not to forget those two languages.

I wish you, my dear friend, as many happy new years as you deserve, and not one more.—May you deserve a great number!

LETTER CCVI.

MY DEAR FRIEND, London, January the 3rd, O. S. 1751.

BY your letter of the 5th, N. S., I find that your *début* at Paris has been a good one; you are entered into good company, and I dare say you will not sink into bad. Frequent the houses where you have been once invited, and have none of that shyness which makes most of your countrymen strangers, where they might be intimate and domestic if they pleased. Wherever you have a general invitation to sup when you please, profit of it with decency, and go every now and then. Lord Albemarle will, I am sure, be extremely kind to you ; but his house is only a dinner house, and, as I am informed, frequented by no French people. Should he happen to employ you in his bureau, which I much doubt, you must write a better hand than your common one, or you will get no great credit by your manuscripts ; for your hand is at present an illiberal one, it is neither a hand of business, nor of a gentleman ; but the hand of a school-boy writing his exercise, which he hopes will never be read.

Madame de Monconseil gives me a favourable account of you and so do Marquis de Matignon, and Madame du Boccage ; they all say that you desire to please, and consequently promise me that you will : and they judge right ; for whoever really desires to please, and has (as you now have) the means of learning how, certainly will please : and that is the great point of life ; it makes all other things easy. Whenever you are with Madame de Monconseil, Madame du Boccage, or other women of fashion, with whom you are tolerably free, say frankly and naturally, [1] *Je n'ai point d'usage du monde, j'y suis encore bien neuf, je*

------

[1] 'I know little of the world, I am quite a novice in it; and although very desirous of pleasing, I am at a loss for the means. Be so good, Madam, as to let me into your secret of pleasing everybody. I shall owe my success to it, and you will always have more than falls to your share.'

souhaiterois ardemment de plaire, mais je ne sais guères comment m'y prendre ; ayez la bonté, Madame, de me faire part de votre secret de plaire à tout le monde. J'en ferai ma fortune, et il vous en restera pourtant toujours, plus qu'il ne vous en faut. When, in consequence of this request, they shall tell you of any little error, awkwardness, or impropriety, you should not only feel, but express, the warmest acknowledgment. Though nature should suffer, and she will at first hearing them, tell them, [1] *Que la critique la plus sévère est, à votre égard, la preuve la plus marquée de leur amitié.* Madame du Boccage tells me particularly to inform you, [2] *Qu'il me fera toujours plaisir et honneur de me venir voir ; il est vrai qu'a son âge le plaisir de causer est froid, mais je tacherai de lui faire faire connoissance avec des jeunes gens, &c.* Make use of this invitation, and as you live in a manner next door to her, step in and out there frequently. Monsieur Du Boccage will go with you, he tells me, with great pleasure, to the plays, and point out to you whatever deserves your knowing there. This is worth your acceptance too, he has a very good taste. I have not yet heard from Lady Hervey upon your subject, but as you inform me that you have already supped with her once, I look upon you as adopted by her : consult her in all your little matters ; tell her any difficulties that may occur to you ; ask her what you should do or say in such or such cases ; she has *l'usage du monde en perfection*, and will help you to acquire it. Madame de Berkenrode *est paitrie de grâces*, and your quotation is very applicable to her. You may be there, I dare say, as often as you please, and I would advise you to sup there once a week.

You say, very justly, that as Mr Harte is leaving you, you shall want advice more than ever ; you shall never want mine ; and as you have already had so much of it, I must rather repeat, than add to what I have already given you : but that I will do, and add to it occasionally, as circumstances may require.

At present I shall only remind you of your two great objects, which you should always attend to : they are Parliament and Foreign affairs. With regard to the former, you can do nothing, while abroad, but attend carefully to the purity, correctness, and elegancy of your diction, the clearness and gracefulness of your utterance, in whatever language you speak. As for the parliamentary knowledge, I will take care of that, when

[1] 'That you will look upon the most severe criticisms as the greatest proof of their friendship.'

[2] 'I shall always receive the honour of his visits with pleasure : it is true that at his age the pleasures of conversation are cold ; but I will endeavour to bring him acquainted with young people, &c.'

you come home. With regard to foreign affairs, everything you do abroad may and ought to tend that way. Your reading should be chiefly historical ; I do not mean of remote, dark, and fabulous history, still less of jimcrack natural history of fossils, minerals, plants, &c., but I mean the useful, political, and constitutional history of Europe for these last three centuries and a half. The other thing necessary for your foreign object, and not less necessary than either ancient or modern knowledge, is a great knowledge of the world, manners, politeness, address, and *le ton de la bonne compagnie.* In that view, keeping a great deal of good company is the principal point to which you are now to attend. It seems ridiculous to tell you, but it is most certainly true, that your dancing master is at this time the man in all Europe of the greatest importance to you. You must dance well, in order to sit, stand, and walk well ; and you must do all these well, in order to please. What with your exercises, some reading, and a great deal of company, your day is, I confess, extremely taken up ; but the day, if well employed, is long enough for everything ; and I am sure you will not slattern away one moment of it in inaction. At your age people have strong and active spirits, alacrity and vivacity in all they do ; are *impigri*, indefatigable, and quick. The difference is, that a young fellow of parts exerts all those happy dispositions in the pursuit of proper objects ; endeavours to excel in the solid and in the showish parts of life : whereas a silly puppy or a dull rogue throws away all his youth and spirits upon trifles, when he is serious ; or upon disgraceful vices, while he aims at pleasures. This, I am sure, will not be your case ; your good sense and your good conduct hitherto are your guarantees with me for the future. Continue only at Paris as you have begun, and your stay there will make you, what I have always wished you to be, as near perfection as our nature permits.

Adieu, my dear ; remember to write to me once a week, not as to a father, but without reserve as to a friend.

LETTER CCVII.

MY DEAR FRIEND,   London, Jan. the 14th, O. S. 1751.

AMONG the many good things Mr Harte has told me of you, two in particular gave me great pleasure. The first, that you are exceedingly careful and jealous of the dignity of your character : that is the sure and solid foundation upon which you must both stand and rise. A man's moral character is a more delicate thing than a woman's reputation of chastity. A slip or two may possibly be forgiven her, and her character may be clarified by subsequent and continued good conduct : but a man's moral character once tainted is irreparably destroyed. The second was, that you had acquired a most correct and extensive knowledge of foreign affairs, such as the history, the treaties, and the forms of government of the several countries of Europe. This sort of knowledge, little attended to here, will make you not only useful but necessary in your future destination, and carry you very far. He added, that you wanted from hence some books relative to our laws and constitution, our colonies, and our commerce, of which you know less than of those of any other part of Europe. I will send you what short books I can find of that sort, to give you a general notion of those things ; but you cannot have time to go into their depths at present, you cannot now engage with new folios ; you and I will refer the constitutional part of this country to our meeting here, when we will enter seriously into it and read the necessary books together. In the mean time go on in the course you are in, of foreign matters ; converse with Ministers and others of every country, watch the transactions of every Court, and endeavour to trace them up to their source. This, with your physics, your geometry, and your exercises will be all that you can possibly have time for at Paris ; for you must allow a great deal for company and pleasures : it is they that must give you those manners, that address, that *tournure* of the *beau monde*, which will qualify you for your future destination. You must first please, in order to get the confidence, and consequently the secrets, of the Courts and Ministers for whom and with whom you negotiate.

I will send you by the first opportunity a short book written by Lord Bolingbroke, under the name of Sir John Oldcastle, containing remarks upon the History of England, which will give you a clear general notion of our constitution, and which will serve you at the same time (like all Lord Bolingbroke's works) for a model of eloquence and style. I will also send you Sir Josiah Childe's little book upon trade, which may properly be called, the Commercial Grammar. He lays down the true principles of commerce, and his conclusions from them are generally very just.

Since you turn your thoughts a little towards trade and commerce, which I am very glad you do, I will recommend a French book to you, that you will easily get at Paris, and which

I take to be the best book in the world of that kind ; I mean the *Dictionnaire de Commerce de Savary*, in three volumes in folio, where you will find everything that relates to trade, commerce, specie, exchange, &c., most clearly stated ; and not only relative to France, but to the whole world. You will easily suppose that I do not advise you to read such a book *tout de suite ;* but I only mean that you should have it at hand to have recourse to occasionally.

With this great stock of both useful and ornamental knowledge, which you have already acquired, and which, by your application and industry, you are daily increasing, you will lay such a solid foundation of future figure and fortune, that, if you complete it by all the accomplishments of manners, graces, &c., I know nothing which you may not aim at, and, in time, hope for. Your great point at present at Paris, to which all other considerations must give way, is to become entirely a man of fashion ; to be well bred without ceremony, easy without negligence, steady and intrepid with modesty, genteel without affectation, insinuating without meanness, cheerful without being noisy, frank without indiscretion, and secret without mysteriousness ; to know the proper time and place for whatever you say or do, and to do it with an air of condition : all this is not so soon nor so easily learned as people imagine, but requires observation and time. The world is an immense folio, which demands a great deal of time and attention to be read and understood as it ought to be : you have not yet read above four or five pages of it ; and you will have but barely time to dip now and then in other less important books.

Lord Albemarle has (I know) wrote to a friend of his here that you do not frequent him so much as he expected and desired ; that he fears somebody or other has given you wrong impressions of him ; and that I may possibly think, from your being seldom at his house, that he has been wanting in his attentions to you. I told the person who told me this, that, on the contrary, you seemed, by your letters to me, to be extremely pleased with Lord Albemarle's behaviour to you ; but that you were obliged to give up dining abroad, during your course of experimental philosophy. I guessed the true reason, which I believe was, that as no French people frequent his house you rather chose to dine at other places ; where you were likely to meet with better company than your countrymen ; and you were in the right of it. However, I would have you show no shyness to Lord Albemarle, but go to him and dine with him oftener than it may be you would wish, for the sake of having him speak well of you here when he returns. He is a good deal in fashion here, and his *puffing* you (to use an awkward expression) before you return here, will be of great use to you afterwards. People in general take characters, as they do most things, upon trust, rather than be at the trouble of examining them themselves ; and the decisions of four or five fashionable people, in every place, are final, more particularly with regard to characters, which all can hear, and but few judge of. Do not mention the least of this to any mortal, and take care that Lord Albemarle do not suspect that you know anything of the matter.

Lord Huntingdon and Lord Stormont are, I hear, arrived at Paris ; you have, doubtless, seen them. Lord Stormont is well spoken of here ; however, in your connections, if you form any with them, show rather a preference to Lord Huntingdon, for reasons which you will easily guess.

Mr Harte goes this week to Cornwall, to take possession of his living ; he has been installed at Windsor : he will return hither in about a month, when your literary correspondence with him will be regularly carried on. Your mutual concern at parting was a good sign for both.

I have this moment received good accounts of you from Paris. Go on, *vous êtes en bon train.* Adieu.

LETTER CCVIII.

My dear Friend,   London, Jan. the 21st, O. S. 1751.

In all my letters from Paris I have the pleasure of finding, among many other good things, your docility mentioned with emphasis : this is the sure way of improving in those things, which you only want. It is true they are little, but it is as true too that they are necessary, things. As they are mere matters of usage and mode, it is no disgrace for anybody of your age to be ignorant of them ; and the most compendious way of learning them is, fairly to avow your ignorance, and to consult those who, from long usage and experience, know them best. Good sense, and good nature, suggest civility in general ; but in good breeding there are a thousand little delicacies which are established only by custom ; and it is these little elegancies of manners which distinguish a courtier, and a man of fashion, from the vulgar. I am assured by different people that your air is already much improved ; and one of my correspondents makes you the true French compliment of saying, *J'ose vous promettre qu'il sera bientôt comme un de nous autres.*[1] However unbecoming this speech may be in the mouth of a Frenchman, I am very glad that they think it applicable to you ; for I would have you not only adopt, but rival, the best manners and usages of the place you are at, be they what they will ; that is, the versatility of manners, which is so useful in the course of the world. Choose your models well at Paris ; and then rival them in their own way. There are fashionable words, phrases, and even gestures at Paris ; which are called *du bon ton ;* not to mention *certaines petites politesse et attentions, qui ne sont rien en elles-mêmes,*[2] which fashion has rendered necessary. Make yourself master of all these things ; and to such a degree as to make the French say, *qu'on diroit que c'est un François;*[3] and when hereafter you shall be at other Courts, do the same thing there ; and conform to the fashionable manners and usage of the place ; that is what the French themselves are not apt to do : wherever they go, they retain their own manners, as thinking them the best ; but granting them to be so, they are still in the wrong not to conform to those of the place. One would desire to please wherever one is ; and nothing is more innocently flattering than an approbation and an imitation of the people one converses with.

I hope your colleges with Marcel go on prosperously. In those ridiculous, though at the same time really important, lectures pray attend ; and desire your Professor also to attend more particularly to the chapter of the arms. It is they that decide a man's being genteel or otherwise, more than any other part of the body. A twist or stiffness in the wrist, will make any man in Europe look awkward. The next thing to be attended to is, your coming into a room, and presenting yourself to a company. This gives the first impression ; and the first impression is often a lasting one. Therefore, pray desire Professor Marcel to make you come in and go out of his room frequently, and in the supposition of different companies being there, such as ministers, women, mixed companies, &c. Those who present themselves well have a certain dignity in their air: which, without the least seeming mixture of pride, at once engages, and is respected.

I should not so often repeat nor so long dwell upon such trifles with anybody that had less solid and valuable knowledge

---

[1] I can assure you that he will soon be quite one of us.
[2] Certain trifling polite attentions which are nothing in themselves.
[3] One would say he is a Frenchman.

than you have. Frivolous people attend to those things, *par préférence;* they know nothing else; my fear with you is, that from knowing better things you should despise these too much, and think them of much less consequence than they really are, for they are of a great deal, and more especially to you.

Pleasing and governing women may in time be of great service to you. They often please and govern others. *A propos;* are you in love with Madame de Berkenrode still, or has some other taken her place in your affections? I take it for granted, that *quæ te cumque domat Venus, non erubescendis adurit ignibus.*[1] *Un arrangement honnête sied bien à un galant homme.* In that case I recommend to you the utmost discretion, and the profoundest silence. Bragging of, hinting at, intimating, or even affectedly disclaiming and denying such an *arrangement,* will equally discredit you among men and women. An unaffected silence upon that subject is the only true medium.

In your commerce with women, and indeed with men too, *une certaine douceur* is particularly engaging; it is that which constitutes that character, which the French talk of so much, and so justly value; I mean *l'aimable.* This *douceur* is not so easily described as felt. It is the compound result of different things: a complaisance, a flexibility, but not a servility of manners: an air of softness in the countenance, gesture, and expression; equally, whether you concur or differ with the person you converse with. Observe those carefully who have that *douceur* which charms you and others, and your own good sense will soon enable you to discover the different ingredients of which it is composed. You must be more particularly attentive to this *douceur* whenever you are obliged to refuse what is asked of you, or to say what in itself cannot be very agreeable to those to whom you say it. It is then the necessary gilding of a disagreeable pill. *L'aimable* consists in a thousand of these little things aggregately. It is the *suavitèr in modo,* which I have so often recommended to you. The *respectable,* Mr Harte assures me you do not want, and I believe him. Study, then, carefully, and acquire perfectly, the *aimable,* and you will have everything.

Abbé Guasco, who is another of your panegyrists, writes me word that he has taken you to dinner at Marquis de St Germain's, where you will be welcome as often as you please, and the oftener the better. Profit of that, upon the principle of travelling in different countries without changing places. He says, too, that he will take you to the parliament, when any re-

---

[1] Whatever fair one enthralls you, you are not the slave of any disgraceful passion.

markable cause is to be tried. That is very well; go through the several chambers of the parliament, and see and hear what they are doing : join practice and observation to your theoretical knowledge of their rights and privileges. No Englishman has the least notion of them.

I need not recommend you to go to the bottom of the constitutional and political knowledge of countries ; for Mr Harte tells me that you have a peculiar turn that way, and have informed yourself most correctly of them.

I must now put some queries to you, as to a *juris publici peritus*, which I am sure you can answer me, and which I own I cannot answer myself : they are upon a subject now much talked of.

1st, Are there any particular forms requisite for the election of a King of the Romans, different from those which are necessary for the election of an Emperor ?

2ndly, Is not a King of the Romans as legally elected by the votes of a majority of the electors, as by two thirds, or by the unanimity of the electors ?

3rdly, Is there any particular law or constitution of the Empire that distinguishes, either in matter or in form, the election of a King of the Romans from that of an Emperor ? And is not the golden bull of Charles the Fourth equally the rule for both ?

4thly, Were there not at a meeting of a certain number of the electors (I have forgot when) some rules and limitations agreed upon concerning the election of a King of the Romans ? and were those restrictions legal, and did they obtain the force of law ?

How happy am I, my dear child, that I can apply to you for knowledge, and with a certainty of being rightly informed! It is knowledge, more than quick, flashy parts, that makes a man of business. A man who is master of his matter will, with inferior parts, be too hard in parliament, and indeed anywhere else, for a man of better parts, who knows his subject but superficially : and if to his knowledge he joins eloquence and elocution, he must necessarily soon be at the head of that assembly : but without those two, no knowledge is sufficient.

Lord Huntingdon writes me word he has seen you, and that you have renewed your old school-acquaintance. Tell me fairly your opinion of him, and of his friend Lord Stormont ; and also of the other English people of fashion you meet with. I promise you inviolable secrecy on my part. You and I must now write to each other as friends, and without the least reserve ; there will for the future be a thousand things in my letters which I would not have any mortal living but yourself see or know. Those you will easily distinguish, and neither show nor repeat ; and I will do the same by you.

To come to another subject, for I have a pleasure in talking over every subject with you : How deep are you in Italian ? Do you understand Ariosto, Tasso, Boccaccio, and Machiavelli ? If you do, you know enough of it, and may know all the rest by reading when you have time. Little or no business is written in Italian, except in Italy ; and if you know enough of it to understand the few Italian letters that may in time come in your way, and to speak Italian tolerably, to those very few Italians who speak no French, give yourself no farther trouble about that language, till you happen to have full leisure to perfect yourself in it. It is not the same with regard to German ; your speaking and writing that well, will particularly distinguish you from every other man in England ; and is, moreover, of great use to any one who is, as probably you will be, employed in the Empire. Therefore, pray cultivate it sedulously, by writing four or five lines of German every day, and by speaking it to every German you meet with.

You have now got a footing in a great many good houses at Paris, in which I advise you to make yourself domestic. This is to be done by a certain easiness of carriage, and a decent familiarity. Not by way of putting yourself upon the frivolous footing of being *sans conséquence,* but by doing, in some degree, the honours of the house and table, calling yourself *en badinant le galopin d'ici,* saying to the master or mistress, *ceci est de mon département, je m'en charge, avouez que je m'en acquitte à merveille.*[1] This sort of *badinage* has something engaging and *liant* in it, and begets that decent familiarity, which it is both agreeable and useful to establish in good houses, and with people of fashion. Mere formal visits, dinners, and suppers, upon formal invitations, are not the thing ; they add to no connection, nor information : but it is the easy, careless ingress and egress, at all hours, that forms the pleasing and profitable commerce of life.

The post is so negligent, that I lose some letters from Paris entirely, and receive others much later than I should. To this I ascribe my having received no letter from you for above a fortnight, which, to my impatience, seems a long time. I expect to hear from you once a week. Mr Harte is gone to Corn-

---

[1] Jocosely the errand-boy of the house—this is my department, I take this upon myself ; admit that I manage it capitally.

wall, and will be back in about three weeks.   I have a packet
of books to send you by the first opportunity, which I believe
will be Mr Yorke's return to Paris.   The Greek books come
from Mr Harte, and the English ones from your humble servant.

Read Lord Bolingbroke's with great attention, as well to
the style as to the matter.   I wish you could form yourself
such a style in every language.   Style is the dress of thoughts,
and a well-dressed thought, like a well-dressed man, appears to
great advantage.

Yours.   Adieu.

LETTER CCIX.

MY DEAR FRIEND,   London, Jan. the 28th, O. S. 1751.

A BILL for ninety pounds sterling was brought me the other
day, said to be drawn upon me by you ; I scrupled paying it
at first, not upon account of the sum, but because you had sent
me no letter of advice, which is always done in those transactions ; and still more, because I did not perceive that you had
signed it.   The person who presented it desired me to look
again, and that I should discover your name at the bottom ;
accordingly I looked again, and with the help of my magnifying glass did perceive that what I had first taken only for
somebody's mark was, in truth, your name, written in the worst
and smallest hand I ever saw in my life.   I cannot write quite so
ill, but it was something like this, *philip Stanhope*.

However, I paid it at a venture ; though I would almost rather
lose the money, than that such a signature should be yours.
All gentlemen, and all men of business, write their names
always in the same way, that their signature may be so well
known as not to be easily counterfeited ; and they generally
sign in rather a larger character than their common hand ;
whereas your name was in a less, and a worse, than your common writing.   This suggested to me the various accidents
which may very probably happen to you, while you write so
ill.   For instance ; if you were to write in such a character to
the secretary's office, your letter would immediately be sent to
the decipherer, as containing matters of the utmost secrecy, not
fit to be trusted to the common character.   If you were to write
so to an antiquarian, he (knowing you to be a man of learning)
would certainly try it by the Runic, Celtic, or Sclavonian alpha-

bet, never suspecting it to be a modern character. And if you were to send a *poulet* to a fine woman in such a hand, she would think that it really came from the *poulailler*, which, by the by, is the etymology of the word, *poulet;* for Henry the Fourth of France used to send *billets-doux* to his mistresses, by his *poulailler*, under pretence of sending them chickens; which gave the name of *poulets* to those short, but expressive manuscripts. I have often told you that every man who has the use of his eyes and of his hand can write whatever hand he pleases; and it is plain that you can, since you write both the Greek and German characters, which you never learned of a writing-master, extremely well, though your common hand, which you learned of a master, is an exceeding bad and illiberal one, equally unfit for business or common use. I do not desire that you should write the laboured, stiff character of a writing-master: a man of business must write quick and well, and that depends singly upon use. I would therefore advise you to get some very good writing-master at Paris, and apply to it for a month only, which will be sufficient; for, upon my word, the writing of a genteel plain hand of business is of much more importance than you think. You will say, it may be, that when you write so very ill, it is because you are in a hurry: to which I answer, Why are you ever in a hurry? a man of sense may be in haste, but can never be in a hurry, because he knows, that whatever he does in a hurry he must necessarily do very ill. He may be in haste to dispatch an affair, but he will take care not to let that haste hinder his doing it well. Little minds are in a hurry, when the object proves (as it commonly does) too big for them; they run, they hare, they puzzle, confound, and perplex themselves; they want to do everything at once, and never do it at all. But a man of sense takes the time necessary for doing the thing he is about, well; and his haste to dispatch a business, only appears by the continuity of his application to it: he pursues it with a cool steadiness, and finishes it before he begins any other. I own your time is much taken up, and you have a great many different things to do; but remember that you had much better do half of them well, and leave the other half undone, than do them all indifferently. Moreover, the few seconds that are saved in the course of the day, by writing ill instead of well, do not amount to an object of time, by any means equivalent to the disgrace or ridicule of writing the scrawl of a common whore. Consider, that if your very bad writing could furnish me with matter of ridicule, what will it not do to others, who do not view you in that partial light that I do. There was a Pope, I think it was Pope Chigi, who was justly ridiculed for his attention to little things, and his inability in great ones ; and therefore called *maximus in minimis*, and *minimus in maximis*.[1] Why ? Because he attended to little things, when he had great ones to do. At this particular period of your life, and at the place you are now in, you have only little things to do ; and you should make it habitual to you to do them well, that they may require no attention from you when you have, as I hope you will have, greater things to mind. Make a good handwriting familiar to you now, that you may hereafter have nothing but your matter to think of, when you have occasion to write to Kings and Ministers. Dance, dress, present yourself habitually well now, that you may have none of those little things to think of hereafter, and which will be all necessary to be done well occasionally, when you will have greater things to do.

As I am eternally thinking of everything that can be relative to you, one thing has occurred to me, which I think necessary to mention, in order to prevent the difficulties which it might otherwise lay you under : it is this ; as you get more acquaintances at Paris, it will be impossible for you to frequent your first acquaintances so much as you did, while you had no others. As, for example, at your first *début*, I suppose, you were chiefly at Madame Monconseil's, Lady Hervey's, and Madame Du Boccage's. Now that you have got so many other houses, you cannot be at theirs so often as you used ; but pray take care not to give them the least reason to think that you neglect or despise them for the sake of new and more dignified and shining acquaintances ; which would be ungrateful and imprudent on your part, and never forgiven on theirs. Call upon them often, though you do not stay with them so long as formerly ; tell them that you are sorry you are obliged to go away, but that you have such and such engagements, with which good breeding obliges you to comply ; and insinuate that you would rather stay with them. In short, take care to make as many personal friends, and as few personal enemies, as possible. I do not mean, by personal friends, intimate and confidential friends, of which no man can hope to have half-a-dozen in the whole course of his life, but I mean friends in the common acceptation of the word, that is, people who speak well of you, and who would rather do you good than harm, consistently with their own interest, and no farther. Upon the whole, I recommend to you again and again *les grâces*. Adorned by them,

---

[1] Greatest in what is least, least in what is greatest.

you may, in a manner, do what you please ; it will be approved
of: without them, your best qualities will lose half their efficacy.
Endeavour to be fashionable among the French, which will soon
make you fashionable here.   Monsieur de Matignon already
calls you *le petit François*.   If you can get that name generally
at Paris, it will put you *à la mode*.   Adieu, my dear child.

LETTER CCX.

MY DEAR FRIEND,   London, Feb. the 4th, O. S. 1751.

THE accounts which I receive of you from Paris grow every
day more and more satisfactory.   Lord Albemarle has wrote a
sort of panegyric of you, which has been seen by many people
here, and which will be a very useful forerunner for you.   Being
in fashion is an important point for anybody, anywhere ; but
it would be a very great one for you to be established in the
fashion here before you return.   Your business would be half
done by it, as I am sure you would not give people reason to
change their favourable presentiments of you.   The good that
is said of you will not, I am convinced, make you a coxcomb ;
and, on the other hand, the being thought still to want some
little accomplishments, will, I am persuaded, not mortify you,
but only animate you to acquire them : I will, therefore, give
you both fairly in the following extract of a letter which I lately
received from an impartial and discerning friend.

[1] ' J'ose vous assurer que Monsieur Stanhope réussira.   Il
a un grand fond de savoir, et une mémoire prodigieuse, sans
faire parade de l'un ou de l'autre.   Il cherche à plaire, et il
plaira.   Il a de la phisionomie ; sa figure est jolie quoique
petite.   Il n'a rien de gauche, quoi qu'il n'aie pas encore toutes
les grâces requises, que Marcel et les femmes lui donneront
bientôt.   Enfin il ne lui manque que ce qui devoit necessaire-
ment lui manquer à son âge ; je veux dire, les usages, et une

---

[1] 'Permit me to assure you, Sir, that Mr Stanhope will succeed. He
has a great fund of knowledge, and an uncommonly good memory, although
he does not make any parade of either the one or the other. He is desirous
of pleasing, and he will please. He has an expressive countenance ; his
figure is elegant, although little. He has not the least awkwardness, though
he has not as yet acquired all the graces requisite ; which Marcel and the
ladies will soon give him.   In short, he wants nothing but those things
which, at his age, must unavoidably be wanting ; I mean a certain turn
and delicacy of manners, which are to be acquired only by time, and in good
company. Ready as he is, he will soon learn them ; particularly as he fre-
quents such companies as are the most proper to give them.'

certaine délicatesse dans les manières, qui ne s'acquièrent que
par le tems et la bonne compagnie. Avec son esprit, il les
prendra bientôt, il y a déjà fait des progrès, et il fréquente les
compagnies les plus propres à les lui donner.'

By this extract, which I can assure you is a faithful one,
you and I have both of us the satisfaction of knowing how
much you have, and how little you want. Let what you have
give you (if possible) rather more *seeming* modesty, but at the
same time more interior firmness and assurance ; and let what
you want, which you see is very attainable, redouble your attention and endeavours to acquire it. You have, in truth, but
that one thing to apply to ; and a very pleasing application it
is, since it is through pleasures that you must arrive at it. Company, suppers, balls, *spectacles*, which show you the models upon
which you should form yourself, and all the little usages, customs, and delicacies, which you must adopt, and make habitual
to you, are now your only schools and universities ; in which
young fellows and fine women will give you the best lectures.

Monsieur du Boccage is another of your panegyrists ; and
he tells me that Madame du Boccage *a pris avec vous le ton de
mie et de bonne ;* [1] and that you like it very well. You are in
the right of it ; it is the way of improving : endeavour to be
upon that footing with every woman you converse with, excepting where there may be a tender point of connection ; a
point which I have nothing to do with : but if such a one there
is, I hope she has not *de mauvais ni de vilains bras*, which I
agree with you in thinking a very disagreeable thing.

I have sent you, by the opportunity of Pollock the courier,
who was once my servant, two little parcels of Greek and English books ; and shall send you two more by Mr Yorke: but I
accompany them with this caution ; that, as you have not much
time to read, you should employ it in reading what is the most
necessary, and that is, indisputably, modern historical, geogra-
phical, chronological, and political knowledge ; the present constitution, maxims, force, riches, trade, commerce, characters,
parties, and cabals of the several Courts of Europe. Many who
are reckoned good scholars, though they know pretty accurately
the governments of Athens and Rome, are totally ignorant of
the constitution of any one country now in Europe, even of their
own. Read just Latin and Greek enough to keep up your classical learning, which will be an ornament to you while young,
and a comfort to you when old. But the true useful knowledge,
and especially for you, is the modern knowledge above men-

---

[1] Plays the part of friend and preceptress.

tioued. It is that which must qualify you both for domestic and foreign business, and it is to that, therefore, that you should principally direct your attention ; and I know with great pleasure that you do so. I would not thus commend you to yourself if I thought commendations would have upon you those ill effects which they frequently have upon weak minds. I think you are much above being a vain coxcomb, overrating your own merit, and insulting others with the superabundance of it. On the contrary, I am convinced that the consciousness of merit makes a man of sense more modest, though more firm. A man who displays his own merit is a coxcomb, and a man who does not know it is a fool. A man of sense knows it, exerts it, avails himself of it, but never boasts of it ; and always *seems* rather to under than over value it, though, in truth, he sets the right value upon it. It is a very true maxim of la Bruyère's (an author well worth your studying) *qu'on ne vaut dans ce monde que ce que l'on veut valoir*. A man who is really diffident, timid, and bashful, be his merit what it will, never can push himself in the world ; his despondency throws him into inaction ; and the forward, the bustling, and the petulant, will always get the better of him. The Manner makes the whole difference. What would be impudence in one Manner, is only a proper and decent assurance in another. A man of sense, and of knowledge of the world, will assert his own rights and pursue his own objects as steadily and intrepidly as the most impudent man living, and commonly more so ; but then he has art enough to give an outward air of modesty to all he does. This engages and prevails, whilst the very same things shock and fail, from the overbearing or impudent manner only of doing them. I repeat my maxim, *Suavitèr in modo, sed fortitèr in re*. Would you know the characters, modes, and manners of the latter end of the last age, which are very like those of the present, read La Bruyère. But would you know man, independently of modes, read La Rochefoucault, who, I am afraid, paints him very exactly.

Give the enclosed to Abbé Guasco, of whom you make good use to go about with you and see things. Between you and me, he has more knowledge than parts. *Mais un habile homme sait tirer parti de tout ;*[1] and everybody is good for something. President Montesquieu is in every sense a most useful acquaintance. He has parts joined to great reading and knowledge of the world. *Puisez dans cette source tant que vous pourrez.*[2]

---

[1] But a clever man can get profit out of everything.
[2] Get as much as you can from that quarter.

Adieu! May the graces attend you; for without them *ogni fatica è vana.* If they do not come to you willingly, ravish them, and force them to accompany all you think, all you say, and all you do.

LETTER CCXI.

My dear Friend, London, Feb. the 11th, O. S. 1751.

When you go to the play, which I hope you do often, for it is a very instructive amusement, you must certainly have observed the very different effects which the several parts have upon you, according as they are well or ill acted. The very best tragedy of Corneille's, if well spoken and acted, interests, engages, agitates, and affects your passions. Love, terror, and pity alternately possess you. But if ill spoken and acted, it would only excite your indignation or your laughter. Why? It is still Corneille's; it is the same sense, the same matter, whether well or ill acted. It is then merely the manner of speaking and acting that makes this great difference in the effects. Apply this to yourself, and conclude from it that if you would either please in a private company or persuade in a public assembly, air, looks, gestures, graces, enunciation, proper accents, just emphasis, and tuneful cadences, are full as necessary as the matter itself. Let awkward, ungraceful, inelegant, and dull fellows say what they will in behalf of their solid matter and strong reasonings; and let them despise all those graces and ornaments, which engage the senses and captivate the heart; they will find (though they will possibly wonder why) that their rough unpolished matter, and their unadorned, coarse, but strong arguments, will neither please nor persuade; but, on the contrary, will tire out attention, and excite disgust. We are so made, we love to be pleased, better than to be informed; information is, in a certain degree, mortifying, as it implies our previous ignorance; it must be sweetened to be palatable.

To bring this directly to you; know that no man can make a figure in this country, but by parliament. Your fate depends upon your success there as a speaker; and, take my word for it, that success turns much more upon Manner than Matter. Mr Pitt, and Mr Murray the solicitor-general, uncle to Lord Stormont, are, beyond comparison, the best speakers. Why? Only because they are the best orators. They alone can inflame or quiet the House; they alone are so attended to, in that numerous and noisy assembly, that you might hear a pin fall while either of them is speaking. Is it that their matter is better, or their arguments stronger, than other people's ? Does the House expect extraordinary informations from them ? Not in the least ; but the House expects pleasure from them, and therefore attends ; finds it, and therefore approves. Mr Pitt, particularly, has very little parliamentary knowledge ; his matter is generally flimsy, and his arguments often weak : but his eloquence is superior, his action graceful, his enunciation just and harmonious ; his periods are well turned, and every word he makes use of is the very best, and the most expressive, that can be used in that place. This, and not his matter, made him paymaster, in spite of both King and Ministers. From this, draw the obvious conclusion. The same thing holds full as true in conversation ; where even trifles, elegantly expressed, well looked, and accompanied with graceful action, will ever please beyond all the homespun, unadorned sense in the world. Reflect, on one side, how you feel within yourself, while you are forced to suffer the tedious, muddy, and ill-turned narration of some awkward fellow, even though the fact may be interesting ; and on the other hand, with what pleasure you attend to the relation of a much less interesting matter, when elegantly expressed, genteelly turned, and gracefully delivered. By attending carefully to all these *agrémens*, in your daily conversation, they will become habitual to you before you come into parliament ; and you will have nothing then to do, but to raise them a little when you come there. I would wish you to be so attentive to this object, that I would not have you speak to your footman, but in the very best words that the subject admits of, be the language which it will. Think of your words, and of their arrangement, before you speak ; choose the most elegant, and place them in the best order. Consult your own ear, to avoid cacophony ; and what is very near as bad, monotony. Think also of your gesture and looks, when you are speaking even upon the most trifling subjects. The same things differently expressed, looked, and delivered, cease to be the same things. The most passionate lover in the world cannot make a stronger declaration of love, than the *Bourgeois gentilhomme* does in this happy form of words, *Mourir d'amour me font, belle Marquise, vos beaux yeux*.[1] I defy anybody to say more ; and yet I would advise nobody to say that ; and I would recommend to you, rather to smother and conceal your passion entirely, than to reveal it in these words. Seriously, this holds in everything, as well as in that ludicrous instance. The French,

[1] Lovely Marquise, your beauteous eyes make me die of love.

to do them justice, attend very minutely to the purity, the correctness, and the elegancy of their style, in conversation, and in their letters. *Bien narrer* is an object of their study; and though they sometimes carry it to affectation, they never sink into inelegancy, which is much the worst extreme of the two. Observe them, and form your French style upon theirs; for elegancy in one language will reproduce itself in all. I knew a young man, who being just elected a member of parliament, was laughed at for being discovered, through the keyhole of his chamber door, speaking to himself in the glass, and forming his looks and gestures. I could not join in that laugh; but, on the contrary, thought him much wiser than those who laughed at him; for he knew the importance of those little graces in a public assembly, and they did not. Your little person (which I am told by the way is not ill turned), whether in a laced coat, or a blanket, is specifically the same; but yet, I believe, you choose to wear the former; and you are in the right, for the sake of pleasing more. The worst bred man in Europe, if a lady let fall her fan, would certainly take it up and give it her: the best bred man in Europe could do no more. The difference however would be considerable; the latter would please by doing it gracefully; the former would be laughed at for doing it awkwardly. I repeat it, and repeat it again, and shall never cease repeating it to you; air, manners, graces, style, elegancy, and all those ornaments, must now be the only objects of your attention; it is now, or never, that you must acquire them. Postpone, therefore, all other considerations; make them now your serious study: you have not one moment to lose. The solid and the ornamental united, are undoubtedly best; but were I reduced to make an option, I should without hesitation choose the latter.

I hope you assiduously frequent Marcel,[1] and carry graces from him; nobody had more to spare than he had formerly. Have you learned to carve? for it is ridiculous not to carve well. A man who tells you gravely that he cannot carve, may as well tell you that he cannot blow his nose; it is both as necessary and as easy.

Make my compliments to Lord Huntingdon, whom I love and honour extremely, as I dare say you do; I will write to him soon, though I believe he has hardly time to read a letter; and my letters to those I love are, as you know by experience, not very short ones: this is one proof of it, and this would have been longer if the paper had been so.——Good night, then, my dear child.

[1] At that time the most celebrated dancing-master at Paris.

LETTER CCXII.

MY DEAR FRIEND,   London, Feb. the 28th, O. S. 1751.

THIS epigram in Martial,

> Non amo te, Sabidi, nec possum dicere quare,
> Hoc tantum possum dicere, non amo te ; [1]

has puzzled a great many people ; who cannot conceive how it
is possible not to love anybody, and yet not to know the reason
why. I think I conceive Martial's meaning very clearly, though
the nature of epigram, which is to be short, would not allow him
to explain it more fully ; and I take it to be this : *O Sabidis, you
are a very worthy deserving man ; you have a thousand good
qualities, you have a great deal of learning : I esteem, I respect,
but for the soul of me I cannot love, you, though I cannot particularly say why. You are not aimable ; you have not those engaging
manners, those pleasing attentions, those graces, and that address,
which are absolutely necessary to please, though impossible to define.
I cannot say it is this or that particular thing that hinders me from
loving you, it is the whole together ; and upon the whole you are not
agreeable.* How often have I, in the course of my life, found
myself in this situation, with regard to many of my acquaintance, whom I have honoured and respected, without being able
to love ! I did not know why, because, when one is young,
one does not take the trouble, nor allow one's self the time, to
analyze one's sentiments, and to trace them up to their source.
But subsequent observation and reflection have taught me
why.—There is a man, whose moral character, deep learning,
and superior parts, I acknowledge, admire, and respect ; but
whom it is so impossible for me to love, that I am almost in a
fever whenever I am in his company. His figure (without being
deformed) seems made to disgrace or ridicule the common
structure of the human body. His legs and arms are never in
the position which, according to the situation of his body, they
ought to be in ; but constantly employed in committing acts of
hostility upon the graces. He throws anywhere, but down his
throat, whatever he means to drink ; and only mangles what he
means to carve. Inattentive to all the regards of social life, he
mistimes or misplaces everything. He disputes with heat, and

---

[1] I do not love thee, Dr Fell ;
The reason why, I cannot tell ;
But this I'm sure I know full well,
I do not love thee, Dr Fell.—*Anon.*

indiscriminately ; mindless of the rank, character, and situation of those with whom he disputes : absolutely ignorant of the several gradations of familiarity or respect, he is exactly the same to his superiors, his equals, and his inferiors ; and therefore, by a necessary consequence, absurd to two of the three. Is it possible to love such a man ? No. The utmost I can do for him, is to consider him as a respectable Hottentot.

I remember, that when I came from Cambridge, I had acquired, among the pedants of that illiberal seminary, a sauciness of literature, a turn to satire and contempt, and a strong tendency to argumentation and contradiction. But I had been but a very little while in the world, before I found that this would by no means do ; and I immediately adopted the opposite character : I concealed what learning I had ; I applauded often, without approving ; and I yielded commonly, without conviction. *Suaviter in modo* was my Law and my Prophets ; and if I pleased (between you and me) it was much more owing to that than to any superior knowledge or merit of my own. *A propos*, the word *pleasing* puts one always in mind of Lady Hervey : pray tell her that I declare her responsible to me for your pleasing ; that I consider her as a pleasing Falstaff, who not only pleases herself, but is the cause of pleasing in others : that I know she can make anything of anybody ; and that, as your governess, if she does not make you please, it must be only because she will not, and not because she cannot. I hope you are, *du bois dont on en fait ;* [1] and if so, she is so good a sculptor, that I am sure she can give you whatever form she pleases. A versatility of manners is as necessary in social, as a versatility of parts is in political, life. One must often yield in order to prevail ; one must humble one's self to be exalted ; one must, like St Paul, become all things to all men to gain some ; and (by the way) men are taken by the same means, *mutatis mutandis*, that women are gained ; by gentleness, insinuation, and submission : and these lines of Mr Dryden's will hold to a Minister as well as to a Mistress :

> The prostrate lover, when he lowest lies,
> But stoops to conquer, and but kneels to rise.

In the course of the world, the qualifications of the cameleon are often necessary ; nay, they must be carried a little farther, and exerted a little sooner ; for you should, to a certain degree, take the hue of either the man or the woman that you want, and wish to be upon terms with. *A propos*, Have you yet

---

[1] The material out of which [a pleasing man] is made.

found out at Paris any friendly and hospitable Madame de Lursay, *qui veut bien se charger du soin de vous éduquer ?*[1] And have you had any occasion of representing to her, *qu'elle faisoit donc des nœuds ?*[2] But I ask your pardon, Sir, for the abruptness of the question, and acknowledge that I am meddling with matters that are out of my department. However, in matters of less importance I desire to be, *de vos secrets le fidèle dépositaire.*[3] Trust me with the general turn and colour of your amusements at Paris. Is it *le fracas du grand monde,*[4] *comédies, bals, opéras, cour, &c. ?* Or is it *des petites sociétés moins brûlantes mais pas pour cela moins agréables ?*[5] Where are you the most *établi?* Where are you *le petit Stanhope? Voyez-vous encore jour à quelque arrangement honnête?*[6]—Have you made many acquaintances among the young Frenchmen who ride at your Academy ; and who are they ? Send me this sort of chitchat in your letters, which, by the by, I wish you would honour me with somewhat oftener. If you frequent any of the myriads of polite Englishmen who infest Paris, who are they ? Have you finished with Abbé Nolet, and are you *au fait* of all the properties and effects of air ? Were I inclined to quibble, I would say that the effects of *air*, at least, are best to be learned of Marcel. If you have quite done with l'Abbé Nolet, ask my friend l'Abbé Sallier to recommend to you some meagre philomath, to teach you a little geometry and astronomy, not enough to absorb your attention and puzzle your intellects, but only enough not to be grossly ignorant of either. I have of late been a sort of an *astronome malgré moi,* by bringing last Monday, into the House of Lords, a bill for reforming our present Calendar, and taking the New Style. Upon which occasion I was obliged to talk some astronomical jargon, of which I did not understand one word, but got it by heart, and spoke it by rote from a master. I wished that I had known a little more of it myself ; and so much I would have you know. But the great and necessary knowledge of all is, to know yourself and others : this knowledge requires great attention and long experience ; exert the former, and may you have the latter ! Adieu.

P. S. I have this moment received your letters of the 27th

---

[1] Who will charge herself with your education ?
[2] An attachment is formed.
[3] The faithful depositary of your secrets.
[4] The turmoil of the great world, &c.
[5] Little gatherings less brilliant, but not therefore less agreeable.
[6] Do you see your way to an honourable *liaison.*

February, and the 2nd March, N. S. The seal shall be done as soon as possible. I am glad that you are employed in Lord Albemarle's bureau ; it will teach you, at least, the mechanical part of that business, such as folding, entering, and docketing letters ; for you must not imagine that you are let into the *fin fin* of the correspondence, nor indeed is it fit that you should at your age. However, use yourself to secrecy as to the letters you either read or write, that in time you may be trusted with *secret, very secret, separate, apart,* &c. I am sorry that this business interferes with your riding ; I hope it is but seldom ; but I insist upon its not interfering with your dancing-master, who is at this time the most useful and necessary of all the masters you have or can have.

LETTER CCXIII.

My dear Friend,

I mentioned to you, some time ago, a sentence, which I would most earnestly wish you always to retain in your thoughts, and observe in your conduct. It is *suaviter in modo, fortiter in re.* I do not know any one rule so unexceptionably useful and necessary in every part of life. I shall therefore take it for my text to-day ; and as old men love preaching, and I have some right to preach to you, I here present you with my sermon upon these words. To proceed, then, regularly and *pulpitically ;* I will first show you, my beloved, the necessary connection of the two members of my text, *suaviter in modo ; fortiter in re.* In the next place, I shall set forth the advantages and utility resulting from a strict observance of the precept contained in my text; and conclude with an application of the whole. The *suaviter in modo* alone would degenerate and sink into a mean, timid complaisance, and passiveness, if not supported and dignified by the *fortiter in re ;* which would also run into impetuosity and brutality, if not tempered and softened by the *suaviter in modo :* however, they are seldom united. The warm choleric man, with strong animal spirits, despises the *suaviter in modo,* and thinks to carry all before him by the *fortiter in re.* He may possibly, by great accident, now and then succeed, when he has only weak and timid people to deal with ; but his general fate will be, to shock, offend, be hated, and fail. On the other hand, the cunning, crafty man thinks to gain all his ends by the *suaviter in modo* only : *he becomes all things to all men;*

he seems to have no opinion of his own, and servilely adopts the present opinion of the present person; he insinuates himself only into the esteem of fools; but is soon detected, and surely despised by everybody else. The wise man (who differs as much from the cunning as from the choleric man) alone joins the *suaviter in modo* with the *fortiter in re.* Now to the advantages arising from the strict observance of this precept.

If you are in authority, and have a right to command, your commands delivered *suaviter in modo* will be willingly, cheerfully, and consequently well obeyed; whereas, if given only *fortiter*, that is, brutally, they will rather, as Tacitus says, be interpreted than executed. For my own part, if I bid my footman bring me a glass of wine, in a rough, insulting manner, I should expect that, in obeying me, he would contrive to spill some of it upon me; and I am sure I should deserve it. A cool, steady resolution should show, that where you have a right to command you will be obeyed; but, at the same time, a gentleness in the manner of enforcing that obedience should make it a cheerful one, and soften, as much as possible, the mortifying consciousness of inferiority. If you are to ask a favour, or even to solicit your due, you must do it *suaviter in modo*, or you will give those, who have a mind to refuse you either, a pretence to do it, by resenting the manner; but, on the other hand, you must, by a steady perseverance and decent tenaciousness, show the *fortiter in re.* The right motives are seldom the true ones of men's actions, especially of kings, ministers, and people in high stations; who often give to importunity and fear, what they would refuse to justice or to merit. By the *suaviter in modo* engage their hearts, if you can; at least, prevent the pretence of offence: but take care to show enough of the *fortiter in re* to extort from their love of ease, or their fear, what you might in vain hope for from their justice or good nature. People in high life are hardened to the wants and distresses of mankind, as surgeons are to their bodily pains; they see and hear of them all day long, and even of so many simulated ones, that they do not know which are real and which not. Other sentiments are therefore to be applied to than those of mere justice and humanity; their favour must be captivated by the *suaviter in modo:* their love of ease disturbed by unwearied importunity, or their fears wrought upon by a decent intimation of implacable, cool resentment: this is the true *fortiter in re.* This precept is the only way I know in the world of being loved without being despised, and feared without being hated. It

LETTERS TO HIS SON.

constitutes the dignity of character, which every wise man must endeavour to establish.

Now to apply what has been said, and so conclude.

If you find that you have a hastiness in your temper, which unguardedly breaks out into indiscreet sallies, or rough expressions, to either your superiors, your equals, or your inferiors, watch it narrowly, check it carefully, and call the *suaviter in modo* to your assistance : at the first impulse of passion be silent, till you can be soft. Labour even to get the command of your countenance so well, that those emotions may not be read in it : a most unspeakable advantage in business ! On the other hand, let no complaisance, no gentleness of temper, no weak desire of pleasing on your part, no wheedling, coaxing, nor flattery, on other people's, make you recede one jot from any point that reason and prudence have bid you pursue ; but return to the charge, persist, persevere, and you will find most things attainable that are possible. A yielding, timid meekness is always abused and insulted by the unjust and the unfeeling ; but when sustained by the *fortiter in re* is always respected, commonly successful. In your friendships and connections, as well as in your enmities, this rule is particularly useful ; let your firmness and vigour preserve and invite attachments to you ; but, at the same time, let your manner hinder the enemies of your friends and dependants from becoming yours : let your enemies be disarmed by the gentleness of your manner, but let them feel at the same time the steadiness of your just resentment ; for there is great difference between bearing malice, which is always ungenerous, and a resolute self-defence, which is always prudent and justifiable. In negotiations with foreign ministers, remember the *fortiter in re ;* give up no point, accept of no expedient, till the utmost necessity reduces you to it, and even then dispute the ground inch by inch ; but then, while you are contending with the minister *fortiter in re,* remember to gain the man by the *suaviter in modo.* If you engage his heart, you have a fair chance for imposing upon his understanding, and determining his will. Tell him, in a frank gallant manner, that your ministerial wrangles do not lessen your personal regard for his merit ; but that, on the contrary, his zeal and ability, in the service of his master, increase it ; and that, of all things, you desire to make a good friend of so good a servant. By these means you may and will very often be a gainer, you never can be a loser. Some people cannot gain upon themselves to be easy and civil to those who are either their rivals, competitors, or opposers, though, independently of those accidental circumstances, they would like and esteem them. They betray a shyness and an awkwardness in company with them, and catch at any little thing to expose them ; and so, from temporary and only occasional opponents, make them their personal enemies. This is exceedingly weak and detrimental, as, indeed, is all humour in business ; which can only be carried on successfully, by unadulterated good policy and right reasoning. In such situations I would be more particularly and *noblement*, civil, easy, and frank with the man whose designs I traversed ; this is commonly called generosity and magnanimity, but is, in truth, good sense and policy. The manner is often as important as the matter, sometimes more so ; a favour may make an enemy, and an injury may make a friend, according to the different manner in which they are severally done. The countenance, the address, the words, the enunciation, the graces, add great efficacy to the *suaviter in modo*, and great dignity to the *fortiter in re ;* and consequently they deserve the utmost attention.

From what has been said, I conclude with this observation, that gentleness of manners, with firmness of mind, is a short but full description of human perfection, on this side of religious and moral duties : that you may be seriously convinced of this truth, and show it in your life and conversation, is the most sincere and ardent wish of yours.

LETTER CCXIV.

MY DEAR FRIEND, London, March the 11th, O. S. 1751.

I RECEIVED by the last post a letter from Abbé Guasco, in which he joins his representations to those of Lord Albemarle, against your remaining any longer in your very bad lodgings at the Academy ; and as I do not find that any advantage can arise to you from being *interne* in an academy, which is full as far from the riding-house, and from all your other masters, as your lodgings will probably be, I agree to your removing to an *hôtel garni ;* the Abbé will help you to find one, as I desire him by the enclosed, which you will give him. I must, however, annex one condition to your going into private lodgings, which is an absolute exclusion of English breakfasts and suppers at them ; the former consume the whole morning, and the latter employ the evenings very ill, in senseless toasting *à l'Angloise* in their infernal claret. You will be sure to go to the riding-house as often as possible, that is, whenever your new business at Lord Albemarle's does not hinder you. But at all events, I insist upon your never missing Marcel, who is at present of more consequence to you than all the *bureaux* in Europe ; for this is the time for you to acquire *tous ces petits riens*, which, though in an arithmetical account, added to one another *ad infinitum*, they would amount to nothing, in the account of the world amount to a great and important sum. *Les agrémens et les grâces*, without which you will never be anything, are absolutely made up of all those *riens*, which are more easily felt than described. By the way, you may take your lodgings for one whole year certain, by which means you may get them much cheaper ; for though I intend to see you here in less than a year, it will be but for a little time, and you will return to Paris again, where I intend you shall stay till the end of April twelvemonth, 1752 ; at which time, provided you have got all *la politesse, les manières, les attentions, et les grâces du beau monde,* I shall place you in some business suitable to your destination.

I have received, at last, your present of the carton, from Dominichino, by Blanchét. It is very finely done ; it is pity that he did not take in all the figures of the original. I will hang it up where it shall be your own again some time or other.

Mr Harte is returned in perfect health from Cornwall, and has taken possession of his prebendal house at Windsor, which is a very pretty one. As I dare say you will always feel, I hope you will always express, the strongest sentiments of gratitude and friendship for him. Write to him frequently, and attend to the letters you receive from him. He shall be with us at Blackheath, alias *Babiole*, all the time that I propose you shall be there, which, I believe, will be the month of August next.

Having thus mentioned to you the probable time of our meeting, I will prepare you a little for it. Hatred, jealousy, or envy make most people attentive to discover the least defects of those they do not love ; they rejoice at every new discovery they make of that kind, and take care to publish it. I thank God, I do not know what those three ungenerous passions are, having never felt them in my own breast ; but love has just the same effect upon me, except that I conceal, instead of publishing, the defects which my attention makes me discover in those I love. I curiously pry into them ; I analyze them ; and, wishing either to find them perfect, or to make them so, nothing escapes me, and I soon discover every the least gradation towards, or from, that perfection. You must, therefore, expect the most critical *examen* that ever anybody underwent : I shall

discover your least as well as your greatest defects, and I shall
very freely tell you of them, *Non quod odio habeam, sed quod
amem.*[1] But I shall tell them you *tête-à-tête*, and as *Micio*, not
as *Demea ;* and I will tell them to nobody else.   I think it but
fair to inform you beforehand, where I suspect that my criticisms
are likely to fall ; and that is more upon the outward than
upon the inward man : I neither suspect your heart nor your
head ; but, to be plain with you, I have a strange distrust of
your air, your address, your manners, your *tournure*, and particularly of your *énonciation* and elegancy of style.   These will
be all put to the trial ; for while you are with me, you must do
the honours of my house and table ; the least inaccuracy or inelegancy will not escape me ; as you will find by *a look* at the
time, and by a remonstrance afterwards when we are alone.
You will see a great deal of company of all sorts at *Babiole*, and
particularly foreigners.   Make therefore, in the mean time, all
these exterior and ornamental qualifications your peculiar
care, and disappoint all my imaginary schemes of criticism.
Some authors have criticized their own works first, in hopes of
hindering others from doing it afterwards : but then they do it
themselves with so much tenderness and partiality for their own
production, that not only the production itself, but the preventive criticism, is criticized.   I am not one of those authors ;
but, on the contrary, my severity increases with my fondness
for my work ; and if you will but effectually correct all the
faults I shall find, I will insure you from all subsequent criticisms
from other quarters.   •

Are you got a little into the interior, into the constitution
of things at Paris ?   Have you seen what you have seen
thoroughly ?   For, by the way, few people see what they see,
or hear what they hear.   For example ; if you go to *les Inva-
lides*, do you content yourself with seeing the building, the hall
where three or four hundred cripples dine, and the galleries
where they lie ; or do you inform yourself of the numbers, the
conditions of their admission, their allowance, the value and
nature of the fund by which the whole is supported ?   This
latter I call seeing, the former is only staring.   Many people
take the opportunity of *les vacances*, to go and see the empty
rooms, where the several chambers of the parliament did sit ;
which rooms are exceedingly like all other large rooms : when
you go there, let it be when they are full ; see and hear what
is doing in them ; learn their respective constitutions, jurisdictions, objects, and methods of proceeding ; hear some causes

[1] Not because I hate but because I love you.

tried in every one of the different chambers. *Approfondissez les choses.*

I am glad to hear that you are so well at Marquis de St Germain's,[1] of whom I hear a very good character. How are you with the other foreign ministers at Paris? Do you frequent the Dutch Embassador or Embassadress? Have you any footing at the Nuncio's, or at the Imperial and Spanish Embassador's? It is useful. Be more particular in your letters to me as to your manner of passing your time, and the company you keep. Where do you dine and sup oftenest? whose house is most your home? Adieu. *Les grâces, les grâces.*

----◇----

LETTER CCXV.

My dear Friend,　　　　London, March the 18th, O. S. 1751.

I ACQUAINTED you in a former letter, that I had brought a bill into the House of Lords for correcting and reforming our present calendar, which is the Julian; and for adopting the Gregorian. I will now give you a more particular account of that affair; from which reflections will naturally occur to you, that I hope may be useful, and which I fear you have not made. It was notorious that the Julian calendar was erroneous, and had overcharged the solar year with eleven days. Pope Gregory the 13th corrected this error; his reformed calendar was immediately received by all the Catholic Powers of Europe, and afterwards adopted by all the Protestant ones, except Russia, Sweden, and England. It was not, in my opinion, very honourable for England to remain in a gross and avowed error, especially in such company; the inconveniency of it was likewise felt by all those who had foreign correspondences, whether political or mercantile. I determined, therefore, to attempt the reformation; I consulted the best lawyers, and the most skilful astronomers, and we cooked up a bill for that purpose. But then my difficulty began: I was to bring in this bill, which was necessarily composed of law jargon and astronomical calculations, to both which I am an utter stranger. However, it was absolutely necessary to make the House of Lords think that I knew something of the matter; and also to make them believe that they knew something of it themselves, which they do not. For my own part, I could just as soon have talked

----

[1] At that time Embassador from the King of Sardinia at the Court of France.

Celtic or Sclavonian to them, as astronomy, and they would
have understood me full as well: so I resolved to do better than
speak to the purpose, and to please instead of informing them.
I gave them, therefore, only an historical account of calendars,
from the Egyptian down to the Gregorian, amusing them now
and then with little episodes ; but I was particularly attentive
to the choice of my words, to the harmony and roundness of my
periods, to my elocution, to my action.   This succeeded, and
ever will succeed ; they thought I informed, because I pleased
them: and many of them said that I had made the whole very
clear to them ; when, God knows, I had not even attempted it.
Lord Macclesfield, who had the greatest share in forming the
bill, and who is one of the greatest mathematicians and astronomers in Europe, spoke afterwards with infinite knowledge,
and all the clearness that so intricate a matter would admit of;
but as his words, his periods, and his utterance were not near
so good as mine, the preference was most unanimously, though
most unjustly, given to me.   This will ever be the case ; every
numerous assembly is *mob*, let the individuals who compose it
be what they will.   Mere reason and good sense is never to be
talked to a mob : their passions, their sentiments, their senses,
and their seeming interests, are alone to be applied to.   Understanding they have collectively none; but they have ears
and eyes, which must be flattered and seduced ; and this can
only be done by eloquence, tuneful periods, graceful action, and
all the various parts of oratory.

   When you come into the House of Commons, if you imagine
that speaking plain and unadorned sense and reason will do
your business, you will find yourself most grossly mistaken.   As
a speaker, you will be ranked only according to your eloquence,
and by no means according to your matter ; everybody knows
the matter almost alike, but few can adorn it.   I was early
convinced of the importance and powers of eloquence ; and from
that moment I applied myself to it.   I resolved not to utter one
word, even in common conversation, that should not be the most
expressive, and the most elegant, that the language could supply
me with for that purpose ; by which means I have acquired
such a certain degree of habitual eloquence, that I must now
really take some pains, if I would express myself very inelegantly.   I want to inculcate this known truth into you, which
you seem by no means to be convinced of yet, That ornaments
are at present your only objects.   Your sole business now is to
shine, not to weigh.   Weight without lustre is lead.   You had
better talk trifles elegantly, to the most trifling woman, than

coarse inelegant sense to the most solid man; you had better
return a dropped fan genteelly, than give a thousand pounds
awkwardly; and you had better refuse a favour gracefully,
than grant it clumsily. Manner is all, in everything: it is
by Manner only that you can please, and consequently rise.
All your Greek will never advance you from Secretary to
Envoy, or from Envoy to Embassador; but your address, your
manner, your air, if good, very probably may. Marcel can be
of much more use to you than Aristotle. I would, upon my
word, much rather that you had Lord Bolingbroke's style and
eloquence, in speaking and writing, than all the learning of the
Academy of Sciences, the Royal Society, and the two Universities, united.

Having mentioned Lord Bolingbroke's style, which is, undoubtedly, infinitely superior to anybody's, I would have you
read his works, which you have, over and over again, with particular attention to his style. Transcribe, imitate, emulate it,
if possible: that would be of real use to you in the House of
Commons, in negotiations, in conversation; with that, you may
justly hope to please, to persuade, to seduce, to impose; and
you will fail in those articles, in proportion as you fall short of
it. Upon the whole, lay aside, during your year's residence at
Paris, all thoughts of all that dull fellows call solid, and exert
your utmost care to acquire what people of fashion call shining.
Prenez l'éclat et le brillant d'un galant homme.

Among the commonly called little things, to which you do
not attend, your hand-writing is one, which is indeed shame-
fully bad, and illiberal; it is neither the hand of a man of
business, nor of a gentleman, but of a truant school-boy; as
soon, therefore, as you have done with Abbé Nolét, pray get an
excellent writing master, since you think that you cannot teach
yourself to write what hand you please, and let him teach you
to write a genteel, legible, liberal hand, and quick; not the
hand of a *procureur*, or a writing-master, but that sort of hand
in which the first *Commis* in foreign bureaus commonly write:
for I tell you truly, that were I Lord Albemarle, nothing should
remain in my bureau written in your present hand. From
hand to arms the transition is natural; is the carriage and
motion of your arms so too? The motion of the arms is the
most material part of a man's air, especially in dancing; the
feet are not near so material. If a man dances well from the
waist upwards, wears his hat well, and moves his head properly,
he dances well. Do the women say that you dress well? for
that is necessary too for a young fellow. Have you *un goût*

vif, or a passion for anybody ? I do not ask for whom ; an Iphigenia would both give you the desire and teach you the means to please.

In a fortnight or three weeks, you will see Sir Charles Hotham at Paris, in his way to Toulouse, where he is to stay a year or two. Pray be very civil to him, but do not carry him into company, except presenting him to Lord Albemarle ; for as he is not to stay at Paris above a week, we do not desire that he should taste of that dissipation : you may show him a play and au opera. Adieu, my dear child.

LETTER CCXVI.

MY DEAR FRIEND,   London, March the 25th, O. S. 1751.

WHAT a happy period of your life is this! Pleasure is now, and ought to be, your business. While you were younger, dry rules, and unconnected words, were the unpleasant objects of your labours. When you grow older, the anxiety, the vexations, the disappointments, inseparable from public business, will require the greatest share of your time and attention ; your pleasures may, indeed, conduce to your business, and your business will quicken your pleasures; but still your time must, at least, be divided : whereas now it is wholly your own, and cannot be so well employed as in the pleasures of a gentleman. The world is now the only book you want, and almost the only one you ought to read : that necessary book can only be read in company, in public places, at meals, and in *ruelles.* You must be in the pleasures in order to learn the manners of good company. In premeditated or in formal business, people conceal, or at least endeavour to conceal, their characters ; whereas pleasures discover them, and the heart breaks out through the guard of the understanding. Those are often propitious moments for skilful negotiators to improve. In your destination particularly the able conduct of pleasures is of infinite use : to keep a good table, and to do the honours of it gracefully, and *sur le ton de la bonne compagnie,* is absolutely necessary for a foreign minister. There is a certain light table chitchat, useful to keep off improper and too serious subjects, which is only to be learned in the pleasures of good company. In truth, it may be trifling ; but, trifling as it is, a man of parts, and experience of the world, will give an agreeable turn to it. *L'art de badiner ugréablement* is by no means to be despised.

An engaging address, and turn to gallantry, is often of very great service to foreign ministers. Women have, directly or indirectly, a good deal to say in most Courts. The late Lord Strafford governed, for a considerable time, the Court of Berlin, and made his own fortune, by being well with Madame de Wartemberg, the first King of Prussia's mistress. I could name many other instances of that kind. That sort of agreeable *caquet de femmes*, the necessary forerunners of closer conferences, is only to be got by frequenting women of the first fashion, *et qui donnent le ton.* Let every other book, then, give way to this great and necessary book, the World; of which there are so many various readings, that it requires a great deal of time and attention to understand it well : contrary to all other books, you must not stay at home, but go abroad to read it ; and when you seek it abroad, you will not find it in booksellers shops and stalls, but in Courts, in *hôtels*, at entertainments, balls, assemblies, spectacles, &c. Put yourself upon the foot of an easy, domestic, but polite familiarity and intimacy, in the several French houses to which you have been introduced. Cultivate them, frequent them, and show a desire of becoming *enfant de la maison.* Get acquainted as much as you can with *les gens de cour:* and observe, carefully, how politely they can differ, and how civilly they can hate ; how easy and idle they can seem in the multiplicity of their business ; and how they can lay hold of the proper moments to carry it on, in the midst of their pleasures. Courts, alone, teach versatility and politeness ; for there is no living there without them. Lord Albemarle has, I hear, and am very glad of it, put you into the hands of Messieurs de Bissy. Profit by that, and beg of them to let you attend them in all the companies of Versailles and Paris. One of them, at least, will naturally carry you to Madame de la Valières, unless he is discarded by this time, and Gelliot [1] retaken. Tell them frankly, *que vous cherchez à vous former, que vous êtes en mains de maîtres, s'ils veulent bien s'en donner la peine.* [2] Your profession has this agreeable peculiarity in it, which is, that it is connected with, and promoted by, pleasures ; and it is the only one in which a thorough knowledge of the world, polite manners, and an engaging address, are absolutely necessary. If a lawyer knows his law, a parson his divinity, and a *financier* his calculations, each may make a figure and a fortune in his profession, without great knowledge of the world, and without the manners of gen-

---

[1] A famous Opera-singer at Paris.

[2] That you wish to form your manners, that you are in the hands of masters, if they will be good enough to trouble themselves about it.

tlemen. But your profession throws you into all the intrigues and cabals, as well as pleasures, of Courts : in those windings and labyrinths, a knowledge of the world, a discernment of characters, a suppleness and versatility of mind, and an elegancy of manners, must be your clue : you must know how to soothe and lull the monsters that guard, and how to address and gain the fair that keeps, the golden fleece. These are the arts and the accomplishments absolutely necessary for a foreign minister ; in which it must be owned, to our shame, that most other nations outdo the English ; and, *cæteris paribus*, a French minister will get the better of an English one, at any third Court in Europe. The French have something more *liant*, more insinuating and engaging in their manner, than we have. An English minister shall have resided seven years at a Court, without having made any one personal connection there, or without being intimate and domestic in any one house. He is always the English minister, and never naturalized. He receives his orders, demands an audience, writes an account of it to his Court, and his business is done. A French minister, on the contrary, has not been six weeks at a Court, without having, by a thousand little attentions, insinuated himself into some degree of favour with the Prince, his wife, his mistress, his favourite, and his minister. He has established himself upon a familiar and domestic footing in a dozen of the best houses of the place, where he has accustomed the people to be not only easy but unguarded before him ; he makes himself at home there, and they think him so. By these means he knows the interior of those Courts, and can almost write prophecies to his own, from the knowledge he has of the characters, the humours, the abilities, or the weaknesses, of the actors. The Cardinal d'Ossat was looked upon at Rome as an Italian, and not as a French, cardinal ; and Monsieur D'Avaux, wherever he went, was never considered as a foreign minister, but as a native, and a personal friend. Mere plain truth, sense, and knowledge, will by no means do alone in Courts ; art and ornaments must come to their assistance. Humours must be flattered ; the *mollia tempora* must be studied and known : confidence, acquired by seeming frankness, and profited of by silent skill. And, above all, you must gain and engage the heart, to betray the understanding to you. *Hæ tibi erunt artes.*[1]

The death of the Prince of Wales,[2] who was more beloved for his affability and good-nature, than esteemed for his steadiness

---

[1] These must be your arts.
[2] Frederick, the son of George II., and father of George III.

and conduct, has given concern to many, and apprehensions to all. The great difference of the ages of the King and Prince George presents the prospect of a minority ; a disagreeable prospect for any nation ! But it is to be hoped, and is most probable, that the King, who is now perfectly recovered of his late indisposition, may live to see his grandson of age. He is, seriously, a most hopeful boy : gentle and good-natured, with good sound sense. This event has made all sorts of people here historians, as well as politicians. Our histories are rummaged for all the particular circumstances of the six minorities we have had since the Conquest, *viz.* those of Henry III., Edward III., Richard II., Henry VI., Edward V., and Edward VI. ; and the reasonings, the speculations, the conjectures, and the predictions, you will easily imagine, must be innumerable and endless, in this nation, where every porter is a consummate politician. Doctor Swift says, very humorously, ' Every man knows that he understands religion and politics, though he never learned them ; but many people are conscious they do not understand many other sciences, from having never learned them.' Adieu.

LETTER CCXVII.

My dear Friend,   London, April the 7th, O. S. 1751.

Here you have all together, the pocket books, the compasses, and the patterns. When your three Graces have made their option, you need only send me, in a letter, small pieces of the three mohairs they fix upon. If I can find no way of sending them safely, and directly to Paris, I will contrive to have them left with Madame Morel, at Calais ; who, being Madame Monconseil's agent there, may find means of furthering them to your three ladies, who all belong to your friend Madame Monconseil. Two of the three, I am told, are handsome ; Madame Polignac, I can swear, is not so ; but however, as the world goes, two out of three is a very good composition.

You will also find, in the packet, a compass ring set round with little diamonds, which I advise you to make a present of to Abbé Guasco, who has been useful to you, and will continue to be so ; as it is a mere bauble, you must add to the value of it by your manner of giving it him. Show it him first, and, when he commends it, as probably he will, tell him that it is at his service, *et que comme il est toujours par voie et par chemins, il*

est absolument nécessaire qu'il ait une boussole.[1] All those little
gallantries depend entirely upon the manner of doing them ; as,
in truth, what does not ? The greatest favours may be done so
awkwardly and bunglingly as to offend ; and disagreeable
things may be done so agreeably as almost to oblige. Endeavour to acquire this great secret ; it exists, it is to be found,
and is worth a great deal more than the grand secret of the
Alchymists would be if it were, as it is not, to be found. This
is only to be learned in Courts, where clashing views, jarring
opinions, and cordial hatreds, are softened, and kept within
decent bounds, by politeness and manners. Frequent, observe,
and learn Courts. Are you free of that of St Cloud ? Are you
often at Versailles ? Insinuate and wriggle yourself into
favour at those places. L'Abbé de la Ville, my old friend, will
help you at the latter ; your three ladies may establish you in
the former. The good breeding *de la Ville et de la Cour* are
different ; but, without deciding which is intrinsically the best,
that of the Court is, without doubt, the most necessary for you,
who are to live, to grow, and to rise in Courts. In two years'
time, which will be as soon as you are fit for it, I hope to be
able to plant you in the soil of a *young Court* here ; where, if
you have all the address, the suppleness, and versatility of a
good courtier, you will have a great chance of thriving and
flourishing. Young favour is easily acquired, if the proper
means are employed ; and, when acquired, it is warm, if not
durable ; and the warm moments must be snatched and improved. *Quitte pour ce qui en peut arriver après.*[2] Do not mention
this view of mine for you, to any mortal ; but learn to keep
your own secrets, which, by the way, very few people can do.

If your course of experimental philosophy, with Abbé Notél,
is over, I would have you apply to Abbé Sallier, for a master
to give you a general notion of astronomy and geometry ; of
both which you may know as much as I desire you should in
six months' time. I only desire that you should have a clear
notion of the present planetary system, and the history of all
the former systems : Fontenelle's *Pluralité des Mondes* will almost teach you all you need know upon that subject. As for
geometry, the seven first books of Euclid will be a sufficient
portion of it for you. It is right to have a general notion of
those abstruse sciences, so as not to appear quite ignorant of
them, when they happen, as sometimes they do, to be the topics

---

[1] And that as he is always on a journey, it is absolutely necessary that
he should have a compass.

[2] Be ready for the future.

of conversation; but a deep knowledge of them requires too much time, and engrosses the mind too much. I repeat it again and again to you, Let the great book of the world be your principal study. *Nocturnâ versate manu, versate diurnâ;* which may be rendered thus in English : Turn over *men by day, and women by night.* I mean only the best editions.

Whatever may be said at Paris of my speech upon the bill for the reformation of the present calendar, or whatever applause it may have met with here, the whole, I can assure you, is owing to the words and to the delivery, but by no means to the matter ; which, as I told you in a former letter, I was not master of. I mention this again, to show you the importance of well-chosen words, harmonious periods, and good delivery ; for, between you and me, Lord Macclesfield's speech was, in truth, worth a thousand of mine. It will soon be printed, and I will send it you. It is very instructive. You say that you wish to speak but half as well as I did : you may easily speak full as well as ever I did, if you will but give the same attention to the same objects that I did at your age and for many years afterwards ; I mean, correctness, purity, and elegancy of style, harmony of periods, and gracefulness of delivery. Read over and over again the third book of *Cicero de Oratore,* in which he particularly treats of the ornamental parts of oratory : they are indeed properly oratory, for all the rest depends only upon common sense, and some knowledge of the subjects you speak upon. But if you would please, persuade, and prevail in speaking, it must be by the ornamental parts of oratory. Make them, therefore, habitual to you, and resolve never to say the most common things, even to your footman, but in the best words you can find, and with the best utterance. This, with *les manières, la tournure, et les usages du beau monde,* are the only two things you want ; fortunately they are both in your power; may you have them both ! Adieu.

LETTER CCXVIII.

Mon cher Ami,   A Londres, 15 d'Avril, V. S. 1751.

Comment vont les grâces, les manières, les agrémens, et tous ces petits riens si nécessaires pour rendre un homme aimable ? Les prenez-vous ? y faites-vous des progrès ? Le grand secret c'est l'art de plaire, et c'est un art qu'il ne tient qu'à un chacun d'acquérir, supposant un certain fond de sens

commun. Un tel vous plaît par tel endroit ; examinez pourquoi, faites comme lui, et vous plairez par le même endroit aux
autres. Pour plaire aux femmes, il faut être considéré des
hommes. Et pour plaire aux hommes il faut savoir plaire aux
femmes. Les femmes, dont la vanité est sans contredit la passion dominante, la trouvent flattée par les attentions d'un
homme qui est généralement estimé parmi les hommes. Quand
il est marqué à ce coin, elles lui donnent le cours, c'est-à-dire,
la mode. De l'autre côté un homme sera estimable parmi les
hommes, sans pourtant être aimable, si les femmes n'y ont pas
mis la dernière main. Il est aussi nécessaire que les deux
sexes travaillent à sa perfection qu'à son être ; portez aux
femmes le mérite de votre sexe, vous en rapporterez la douceur,
les agrémens et les grâces du leur, et les hommes qui vous
estimoient seulement auparavant, vous aimeront après. Les
femmes sont les véritables raffineuses de l'or masculin ; elles
n'y ajoutent pas du poids, il est vrai, mais elles y donnent
l'éclat et le brillant. A propos, on m'assure que Madame de
Blot, sans avoir des traits, est jolie comme un cœur, et que
nonobstant cela, elle s'en est tenue jusqu'ici scrupuleusement à
son mari, quoiqu'il y ait déjà plus d'un an qu'elle est mariée.
Elle n'y pense pas ; il faut décrotter cette femme-là. Décrottez-
vous donc tous les deux réciproquement. Force, assiduités,
attentions, regards tendres, et déclarations passionées de votre
côté, produiront au moins quelque velléité du sien. Et quand
une fois la velléité y est, les œuvres ne sont pas loin.

Comme je vous tiens pour le premier *juris-peritus* et politique
de tout le corps Germanique, je suppose que vous aurez lu la
lettre du Roi de Prusse à l'Electeur de Mayence, au sujet de
l'élection d'un Roi des Romains. Et de l'autre côté, une pièce,
intitulée, *Représentation impartiale de ce qui est juste à l'égard de
l'élection d'un Roi des Romains, &c.* La première est très-bien
écrite, mais pas fondée sur les loix et les usages de l'Empire ;
la seconde est très-mal écrite, au moins en François, mais
fondée. Je crois qu'elle aura été écrite par quelque Allemand
qui s'étoit mis dans l'esprit qu'il entendoit le François. Je suis
persuadé pourtant que l'élégance et la délicatesse de la lettre du
Roi de Prusse en imposeront aux deux tiers du public en dépit
de la solidité et de la vérité de l'autre pièce. Telle est la force
de l'élégance et de la délicatesse.

Je souhaiterois que vous eussiez la bonté de me détailler un
peu plus particulièrement vos allures à Paris. Où est-ce par
exemple que vous dînez tous les Vendredis, avec cet aimable et
respectable vieillard Fontenelle ? Quelle est la maison qui est

pour ainsi dire votre domicile ? Car on en a toujours une, ou l'on est plus établi, et plus à son aise qu'ailleurs. Qui sont les jeunes François avec lesquels vous êtes le plus lié ? Fréquentez-vous l'hôtel d'Hollande ; et vous êtes vous fourré encore dans celui du Comte de Caunitz ? Monsieur de Pignatelli, a-t-il l'honneur d'être du nombre de vos serviteurs ? Et le Nonce du Pape vous a-t-il compris dans son Jubilé ? Dites-moi aussi naturellement comment vous êtes avec Milord Huntingdon ; le voyez-vous souvent ? Le cultivez-vous ? Répondez spécifiquement à toutes ces questions dans votre première lettre.

On me dit que le livre de du Clos n'est pas à la mode à Paris, et qu'on le critique furieusement, c'est apparemment parce qu'on l'entend, et ce n'est plus la mode d'être intelligible. Je respecte infiniment la mode, mais je respecte bien plus ce livre, que je trouve en même tems vrai, solide, et brillant. Il y a même des epigrammes, que veut-on de plus ?

Mr * * * sera parti (je compte) de Paris pour son séjour de Toulouse. J'espère qu'il y prendra des manières, au moins en a-t-il bien besoin. Il est gauche, il est taciturne, et n'a pas le moindre *entregent :* Qualités pourtant très-nécessaires pour se distinguer ou dans les affaires, ou dans le beau monde. Au vrai, ces deux choses sont si liées, qu'un homme ne figurera jamais dans les affaires qui ne sait pas briller aussi dans le beau monde. Et pour réussir parfaitement bien dans l'un ou dans l'autre, il faut être *in utrumque paratus.* Puissiez vous l'être, mon cher ami, et sur ce, nous vous donnons le bon soir.

P. S. Lord and Lady Blessington, with their son Lord Mount-joy, will be at Paris next week, in their way to the South of France ; I send you a little packet of books by them. Pray go to wait upon them, as soon as you hear of their arrival, and show them all the attentions you çan.

TRANSLATION.

MY DEAR FRIEND,   London, April the 15th, O. S. 1751.

WHAT success with the Graces, and in the accomplishments, elegancies, and all those little nothings so indispensably necessary to constitute an amiable man ? Do you take them, do you make a progress in them ? The great secret is the art of pleasing ; and that art is to be attained by every man who has a good fund of common sense. If you are pleased with any person, examine why ; do as he does, and you will charm others by the same things which please you in him. To be liked by

women, you must be esteemed by men ; and to please men,
you must be agreeable to women. Vanity is unquestionably
the ruling passion in women ; and it is much flattered by the
attentions of a man, who is generally esteemed by men : when
his merit has received the stamp of their approbation, women
make it current, that is to say, put him in fashion. On the
other hand, if a man has not received the last polish from women, he may be estimable among men, but he will never be
amiable. The concurrence of the two sexes is as necessary to
the perfection of our being, as to the formation of it. Go among
women with the good qualities of your sex, and you will acquire from them the softness and the graces of theirs. Men
will then add affection to the esteem which they before had
for you. Women are the only refiners of the merit of men ; it
is true they cannot add weight, but they polish and give lustre
to it. *A propos*, I am assured that Madame de Blot, although
she has no great regularity of features, is, notwithstanding,
excessively pretty ; and that, for all that, she has as yet been
scrupulously constant to her husband, though she has now been
married above a year. Surely she does not reflect, that woman
wants polishing. I would have you polish one another reciprocally. Force, assiduities, attentions, tender looks, and passionate declarations, on your side, will produce some irresolute
wishes, at least, on hers ; and when even the slightest wishes
arise, the rest will soon follow.

As I take you to be the greatest *juris-peritus*, and politician,
of the whole Germanic body, I suppose you will have read the
King of Prussia's letter to the Elector of Maïence, upon the
election of a King of the Romans ; and, on the other side, a
memorial intituled, *Impartial Representation of what is just with
regard to the election of a King of the Romans, &c.* The first is
extremely well written, but not grounded upon the laws and
customs of the Empire. The second is very ill written (at least
in French) but well grounded : I fancy the author is some German, who has taken into his head that he understands French.
I am, however, persuaded, that the elegancy and delicacy of the
King of Prussia's letter will prevail with two thirds of the public,
in spite of the solidity and truths contained in the other piece.
Such is the force of an elegant and delicate style !

I wish you would be so good as to give me a more particular and circumstantial account of the method of passing your
time at Paris. For instance, Where is it that you dine every
Friday, in company with that amiable and respectable old man,
Fontenelle ? Which is the house where you think yourself at

home? for one always has such a one, where one is better established, and more at ease, than anywhere else. Who are the young Frenchmen with whom you are most intimately connected? Do you frequent the Dutch Embassador's? Have you penetrated yet into Count Caunitz's house? Has Monsieur de Pignatelli the honour of being one of your humble servants? And has the Pope's Nuncio included you in the jubilee? Tell me also freely, how you are with Lord Huntingdon: Do you see him often? Do you connect yourself with him? Answer all these questions circumstantially in your first letter.

I am told that du Clos's book is not in vogue at Paris, and that it is violently criticized; I suppose that is because one understands it; and being intelligible is now no longer the fashion. I have a very great respect for fashion, but a much greater for this book; which is, all at once, true, solid, and bright. It contains even epigrams; what can one wish for more?

Mr * * * will, I suppose, have left Paris by this time, for his residence at Toulouse. I hope he will acquire manners there; I am sure he wants them. He is awkward, he is silent, and has nothing agreeable in his address: most necessary qualifications to distinguish one's self in business, as well as in the *polite world!* In truth, these two things are so connected, that a man cannot make a figure in business, who is not qualified to shine in the great world; and to succeed perfectly in either the one or the other, one must be *in utrumque paratus.*[1] May you be that, my dear friend! and so we wish you a good night.

LETTER CCXIX.

MY DEAR FRIEND,   London, April the 22nd, O. S. 1751.

I APPLY to you now, as to the greatest *virtuoso* of this or perhaps any other age; one whose superior judgment and distinguishing eye hindered the King of Poland from buying a bad picture at Venice, and whose decisions in the realms of *virtù* are final, and without appeal. Now to the point. I have had a catalogue sent me, *d'une vente à l'amiable de tableaux des plus grands maîtres appartenans au Sieur Araignon Aperén, valet de chambre de la Reine, sur le quai de la Mégisserie, au coin de l'Arche Marion.*[2] There I observe two large pictures of Titian,

---

[1] Prepared for either.
[2] Of a sale in a friendly way of pictures of the greatest masters, belonging to the Sieur Araignon Aparen, the Queen's valet de chambre, &c.

as described in the enclosed page of the catalogue, No. 18,
which I should be glad to purchase, upon two conditions : the
first is, that they be undoubted originals of Titian, in good preservation ; and the other, that they come cheap. To ascertain
the first (but without disparaging your skill) I wish you would
get some undoubted connoisseurs to examine them carefully ;
and if upon such critical examination they should be unanimously allowed to be undisputed originals of Titian, and well
preserved, then comes the second point, the price : I will not
go above two hundred pounds sterling for the two together;
but as much less as you can get them for. I acknowledge that
two hundred pounds seems to be a very small sum for two undoubted Titians of that size ; but, on the other hand, as large
Italian pictures are now out of fashion at Paris, where fashion
decides of everything, and as these pictures are too large for
common rooms, they may possibly come within the price above
limited. I leave the whole of this transaction (the price excepted, which I will not exceed) to your consummate skill and
prudence, with proper advice joined to them. Should you
happen to buy them for that price, carry them to your own
lodgings, and get a frame made to the second, which I observe
has none, exactly the same with the other frame, and have the
old one new gilt; and then get them carefully packed up, and
sent me by Rouen.

I hear much of your conversing with *les beaux esprits* at
Paris: I am very glad of it; it gives a degree of reputation,
especially at Paris ; and their conversation is generally instructive, though sometimes affected. It must be owned that the polite
conversation of the men and women of fashion at Paris, though
not always very deep, is much less futile and frivolous than ours
here.   It turns at least upon some subject, something of taste,
some point of history, criticism, and even philosophy ; which,
though probably not quite so solid as Mr Locke's, is however
better, and more becoming rational beings, than our frivolous
dissertations upon the weather, or upon whist.   Monsieur du
Clos observes, and I think very justly, *qu'il y a à présent en
France une fermentation universelle de la raison qui tend à se développer.*[1] Whereas, I am sorry to say, that here that fermentation
seem to have been over some years ago, the spirit evaporated,
and only the dregs left. Moreover, *les beaux esprits* at Paris are
commonly well bred, which ours very frequently are not : with
the former your manners will be formed ; with the latter, wit

---

[1] That there is in France at present a universal fermentation of the reason which tends to show itself.

must generally be compounded for at the expense of manners. Are you acquainted with Marivaux, who has certainly studied, and is well acquainted with, the heart; but who refines so much upon its *plis et replis*, and describes them so affectedly, that he often is unintelligible to his readers, and sometimes so, I dare say, to himself? Do you know *Crébillon le fils?* He is a fine painter, and a pleasing writer ; his characters are admirable, and his reflections just. Frequent these people, and be glad, but not proud of frequenting them : never boast of it as a proof of your own merit, nor insult, in a manner, other companies by telling them affectedly what you, Montesquieu, and Fontenelle were talking of the other day ; as I have known many people do here, with regard to Pope and Swift, who had never been twice in company with either : nor carry into other companies the tone of those meetings of *beaux esprits*. Talk literature, taste, philosophy, &c., with them, *à la bonne heure ;* but then with the same ease, and more *enjouement*, talk *pompons, moires*,[1] &c., with Madame de Blot, if she requires it. Almost every subject in the world has its proper time and place ; in which no one is above or below discussion. The point is, to talk well upon the subject you talk upon ; and the most trifling, frivolous subjects will still give a man of parts an opportunity of showing them. *L'usage du grand monde* can alone teach that. This was the distinguishing characteristic of Alcibiades, and a happy one it was ; that he could occasionally, and with so much ease, adopt the most different, and even the most opposite, habits and manners, that each seemed natural to him. Prepare yourself for the great world, as the *athletæ* used to do for their exercises ; oil (if I may use that expression) your mind and your manners, to give them the necessary suppleness and flexibility ; strength alone will not do, as young people are too apt to think.

How do your exercises go on ? Can you manage a pretty vigorous *sauteur* between the pillars ? Are you got into stirrups yet ? *Faites-vous assaut aux armes?* But, above all, what does Marcel say of you ? Is he satisfied ? Pray be more particular in your accounts of yourself ; for though I have frequent accounts of you from others, I desire to have your own too. Adieu.

Yours, truly and tenderly.

---

[1] Trinkets, mohairs, &c.

LETTER CCXX.

My dear Friend,   London, May the 2nd, O. S. 1751.

Two accounts, which I have very lately received of you from two good judges, have put me into great spirits, as they have given me reasonable hopes that you will soon acquire all that I believe you want ; I mean the air, the address, the graces, and the manners of a man of fashion. As these two pictures of you are very unlike that which I received and sent you some months ago, I will name the two painters : the first is an old friend and acquaintance of mine, Monsieur D'Aillon. His picture is, I hope, like you, for it, is a very good one ; Monsieur Tollot's is still a better, and so advantageous a one that I will not send you a copy of it, for fear of making you too vain. So far I will tell you, that there was only one *but* in either of their accounts ; and it was this : I gave D'Aillon the question, ordinary and extraordinary, upon the important article of Manners ; and extorted this from him : [1] *Mais, si vous voulez, il lui manque encore ce dernier beau vernis qui relève les couleurs, et qui donne l'éclat à la pièce. Comptez qu'il l'aura, il a trop d'esprit pour n'en pas connoître tout le prix, et je me trompe bien, ou plus d'une personne travaille à le lui donner.* Monsieur Tollet says, [2]*Il ne lui manque absolument pour être tout ce que vous souhaitez qu'il soit, que ces petits riens, ces grâces de détail, cette aisance aimable, que l'usage du grand monde peut seul lui donner. A cet égard on m'assure qu'il est en de bonnes mains ; je ne sais si on ne veut pas dire par là dans des beaux bras.* Without entering into a nice discussion of the last question, I congratulate you and myself upon your being so near that point which I so anxiously wish you may arrive at. I am sure that all your attention and endeavours will be exerted ; and if exerted they will succeed. Mr Tollot says that you are inclined to be fat ; but I hope you will decline it as much as you can ; not by taking anything corrosive to make you lean, but by taking as little as you can of those things that would make you fat. Drink no chocolate, take your

---

[1] 'But since you will know it, he still wants that last, beautiful varnish, which raises the colours, and gives brilliancy to the piece. Be persuaded that he will acquire it ; he has too much sense not to know its value ; and, if I am not greatly mistaken, more persons than one are now endeavouring to give it him.'

[2] ' In order to be exactly all that you wish him, he only wants those little nothings, those graces in detail, and that amiable ease, which can only be acquired by usage of the great world. I am assured that he is, in that respect, in good hands ; I do not know whether that does not rather imply in fine arms.'

coffee without cream ; you cannot possibly avoid suppers at Paris, unless you avoid company too, which I would by no means have you do ; but eat as little at supper as you can, and make even an allowance for that little at your dinners. Take, occasionally, a double dose of riding and fencing ; and now that the summer is come walk a good deal in the Tuilleries : it is a real inconveniency to anybody to be fat : and, besides, it is ungraceful for a young fellow. *A propos,* I had like to have forgot to tell you that I charged Tollot to attend particularly to your utterance and diction; two points of the utmost importance. To the first he says, [1]*Il ne s'énonce pas mal, mais il seroit à souhaiter qu'il le fît encore mieux ; et il s'exprime avec plus de feu que d'élégance. L'usage de la bonne compagnie mettra aussi ordre à tout cela.* These, I allow, are all little things separately, but, aggregately, they make a most important and great article in the account of a gentleman. In the House of Commons you can never make a figure without elegancy of style, and gracefulness of utterance ; and you can never succeed as a Courtier at your own Court, or as a Minister at any other, without those innumerable *petits riens dans les manières, et dans les attentions.* Mr Yorke is by this time at Paris ; make your court to him, but not so as to disgust, in the least, Lord Albemarle ; who may possibly dislike your considering Mr Yorke as the man of business, and him as only *pour orner la scène.* Whatever your opinion may be upon *that point,* take care not to let it appear : but be well with them both by showing no public preference to either.

Though I must necessarily fall into repetitions, by treating the same subject so often, I cannot help recommending to you again the utmost attention to your air and address. Apply yourself now to Marcel's lectures, as diligently as you did formerly to Professor Mascow's ; desire him to teach you every genteel attitude that the human body can be put into ; let him make you go in and out of his room frequently, and present yourself to him as if he were by turns different persons ; such as a minister, a lady, a superior, an equal, an inferior, &c. Learn to sit genteelly in different companies ; to loll genteelly, and with good manners, in those companies where you are authorized to be free ; and to sit up respectfully where the same freedom is not allowable. Learn even to compose your countenance occasionally to the respectful, the cheerful, and the insinuating. Take particular care that the motions of your hands and arms

---

[1] 'His enunciation is not bad, but it is to be wished that it were still better; and he expresses himself with more fire than elegancy. Usage of good company will instruct him likewise in that.'

be easy and graceful; for the genteelness of a man consists more in them than in anything else, especially in his dancing. Desire some women to tell you of any little awkwardness that they observe in your carriage : they are the best judges of those things ; and if they are satisfied, the men will be so too. Think now only of the decorations.   Are you acquainted with Madame Geoffrain, who has a great deal of wit ; and who, I am informed, receives only the very best company in her house ? Do you know Madame du Pin, who, I remember, had beauty, and I hear has wit and reading?   I could wish you to converse only with those who, either from their rank, their merit, or their beauty, require constant attention ; for a young man can never improve in company where he thinks he may neglect himself. A new bow must be constantly kept bent ; when it grows older and has taken the right turn, it may now and then be relaxed.

I have this moment paid your draught of 89*l.* 15*s.*, it was signed in a very good hand ; which proves that a good hand may be written without the assistance of magic.   Nothing provokes me much more than to hear people indolently say that they cannot do what is in everybody's power to do, if it be but in their will.   Adieu.

LETTER CCXXI.

MY DEAR FRIEND,   London, May the 6th, O. S. 1751.

THE best authors are always the severest critics of their own works ; they revise, correct, file, and polish them, till they think they have brought them to perfection.   Considering you as my work, I do not look upon myself as a bad author, and am there-fore a severe critic.   I examine narrowly into the least inac-curacy or inelegancy, in order to correct, not to expose them, and that the work may be perfect at last.   You are, I know, exceedingly improved in your air, address, and manners, since you have been at Paris ; but still there is, I believe, room for further improvement, before you come to that perfection which I have set my heart upon seeing you arrive at : and till that moment I must continue filing and polishing.   In a letter that I received by last post, from a friend of yours at Paris, there was this paragraph : [1] *Sans flatterie, j'ai l'honneur de vous assurer*

---

[1] 'I have the honour to assure you, without flattery, that Mr Stanhope succeeds beyond what might be expected from a person of his age.   He goes into very good company ; and that kind of manner, which was at first

que Monsieur Stanhope réussit ici au de là de ce qu'on attendroit d'une personne de son âge ; il voit très-bonne compagnie, et ce petit ton qu'on regardoit d'abord comme un peu décidé et un peu brusque, n'est rien moins que cela, parce qu'il est l'effet de la franchise, accompagnée de la politesse et de la déférence. Il s'étudie à plaire, et il y réussit. Madame de Puisieux en parloit l'autre jour avec complaisance et intérêt : vous en serez content à tous égards. This is extremely well, and I rejoice at it : one little circumstance only may, and I hope will, be altered for the better. Take pains to undeceive those who thought that *petit ton un peu décidé et un peu brusque;* as it is not meant so, let it not appear so. Compose your countenance to an air of gentleness and *douceur*, use some expressions of diffidence of your own opinion, and deference to other people's ; such as, [1] *s'il m'est permis de le dire—je croirois—ne seroit-ce pas plutôt comme cela? Au moins j'ai tout lieu de me défier de moi-même :* such mitigating, engaging words do by no means weaken your argument ; but, on the contrary, make it more powerful, by making it more pleasing. If it is a quick and hasty manner of speaking that people mistake, *pour décidé et brusque*, prevent their mistakes for the future, by speaking more deliberately, and taking a softer tone of voice : as in this case you are free from the guilt, be free from the suspicion too. Mankind, as I have often told you, is more governed by appearances than by realities : and, with regard to opinion, one had better be really rough and hard, with the appearance of gentleness and softness, than just the reverse. Few people have penetration enough to discover, attention enough to observe, or even concern enough to examine, beyond the exterior ; they take their notions from the surface, and go no deeper ; they commend, as the gentlest and best natured man in the world, that man who has the most engaging exterior manner, though possibly they have been but once in his company. An air, a tone of voice, a composure of countenance to mildness and softness, which are all easily acquired, do the business ; and without further examination, and possibly with the contrary qualities, that man is reckoned the gentlest, the modestest, and the best natured man alive. Happy the man who, with a certain fund of parts and knowledge, gets acquainted with the

---

thought to be too decisive and peremptory, is now judged otherwise ; because it is acknowledged to be the effect of an ingenuous frankness, accompanied by politeness, and by a proper deference. He studies to please, and succeeds. Madame de Puisieux was the other day speaking of him with complacency and friendship. You will be satisfied with him in all respects.'

[1] If I might be permitted to say—I should think—Is it not rather so ? At least I have the greatest reason to be diffident of myself.

world early enough to make it his bubble, at an age when most people are the bubbles of the world ! for that is the common case of youth. They grow wiser when it is too late : and, ashamed and vexed at having been bubbles so long, too often turn knaves at last. Do not therefore trust to appearances and outside yourself, but pay other people with them ; because you may be sure that nine in ten of mankind do, and ever will, trust to them. This is by no means a criminal or blameable simulation, if not used with an ill intention. I am by no means blameable in desiring to have other people's good word, good will, and affection, if I do not mean to abuse them. Your heart, I know, is good, your sense is sound, and your knowledge extensive. What then remains for you to do ? Nothing, but to adorn those fundamental qualifications with such engaging and captivating manners, softness, and gentleness, as will endear you to those who are able to judge of your real merit, and which always stand in the stead of merit with those who are not. I do not mean ·by this to recommend to you *le fade doucereux*, the insipid softness of a gentle fool : no, assert your own opinion, oppose other people's when wrong ; but let your manner, your air, your terms, and your tone of voice, be soft and gentle, and that easily and naturally, not affectedly. Use palliatives when you contradict ; such as, *I may be mistaken, I am not sure, but I believe, I should rather think,* &c. Finish any argument or dispute with some little good-humoured pleasantry, to show that you are neither hurt yourself, nor meant to hurt your antagonist ; for an argument, kept up a good while, often occasions a temporary alienation on each side. Pray observe particularly, in those French people who are distinguished by that character, *cette douceur de mœurs et de manières,* which they talk of so much, and value so justly ; see in what it consists ; in mere trifles, and most easy to be acquired, where the heart is really good. Imitate, copy it, till it becomes habitual and easy to you. Without a compliment to you, I take it to be the only thing you now want : nothing will sooner give it you than a real passion, or, at least, *un goût vif,* for some woman of fashion ; and as I suppose that you have either the one or the other by this time, you are consequently in the best school. Besides this, if you were to say to Lady Hervey, Madame Monconseil, or such others as you look upon to be your friends, [1] *On dit que j'ai un certain petit ton trop dé-*

---

[1] It is said that I have a kind of manner which is rather too decisive and too peremptory ; it is not however my intention that it should be so : I entreat you to correct, and even publicly to punish me, whenever I am guilty.

*cidé et trop brusque, l'intention pourtant n'y est pas ; corrigez-moi,
je vous en supplie, et châtiez-moi même publiquement quand vous me
trouverez sur le fait. Ne me passez rien, poussez votre critique
jusqu'à l'excès ; un juge aussi éclairé est en droit d'être sévère, et
je vous promets que le coupable tâchera de se corriger.*

Yesterday I had two of your acquaintances to dine with
me, Baron B. and his companion Monsieur S. I cannot say of
the former, *qu'il est paitri de grâces ;* and I would rather advise
him to go and settle quietly at home, than to think of improving himself by further travels, *Ce n'est pas le bois dont on en fait.*
His companion is much better, though he has a strong *tocco di
tedesco.* They both spoke well of you, and so far I liked them
both. [1] *Comment vont nos affaires avec l'aimable petite Blot ? Se
prête-t-elle à vos fleurettes, êtes-vous censé d'être sur les rangs ?
Madame du —— est-elle votre Madame de Lursay, et fait-elle
quelquefois des nœuds ? Seriez vous son Meilcour ? Elle a, dit
on, de la douceur, de l'esprit, des manières ; il y a à apprendre
dans un tel apprentissage.* [2] A woman like her, who has always
pleased, and often been pleased, can best teach the art of
pleasing ; that art, without which *ogni fatica è vana.* Marcel's
lectures are no small part of that art ; they are the engaging
forerunner of all other accomplishments. Dress is also an
article not to be neglected, and I hope you do not neglect it ;
it helps in the *premier abord,* which is often decisive. By dress,
I mean your clothes being well made, fitting you, in the fashion,
and not above it ; your hair well done, and a general cleanliness and spruceness in your person. I hope you take infinite
care of your teeth ; the consequences of neglecting the mouth
are serious, not only to one's self but to others. In short, my
dear child, neglect nothing ; a little more will complete the
whole. Adieu ! I have not heard from you these three weeks,
which I think a great while.

Do not treat me with the least indulgence, but criticize to the utmost. So
clear-sighted a judge as you has a right to be severe ; and I promise you
that the criminal will endeavour to correct himself.

[1] How go you on with the amiable little Blot ? Does she listen to your
flattering tale ? Are you numbered among the list of her admirers ? Is
Madame du —— your Madame de Lursay ? Does she sometimes knot, and
are you her Meilcour ? They say she has softness, sense, and engaging
manners ; in such an apprenticeship much may be learned.

[2] This whole passage, and several others, allude to Crébillon's *Egaremens
du Cœur et de l'Esprit,* a sentimental novel written about that time, and
then much in vogue at Paris.

LETTER CCXXII.

My dear Friend,   London, May the 10th, O. S. 1751.

I received yesterday, at the same time, your letters of the
4th and the 11th, N.S., and being much more careful of my
commissions than you are of yours, I do not delay one moment
sending you my final instructions concerning the pictures. The
Man, you allow to be a Titian, and in good preservation ; the
Woman is an indifferent and a damaged picture ; but as I
want them for furniture for a particular room, companions are
necessary ; and therefore I am willing to take the Woman, for
better for worse, upon account of the Man ; and if she is not too
much damaged, I can have her tolerably repaired, as many a
fine woman is, by a skilful hand here ; but then I expect the
lady should be, in a manner, thrown into the bargain with the
Man : and, in this state of affairs, the Woman being worth
little or nothing, I will not go above fourscore Louis for the two
together. As for the Rembrandt you mention, though it is
very cheap, if good, I do not care for it. I love *la belle nature;*
Rembrandt paints caricaturas. Now for your own commissions,
which you seem to have forgotten. You mention nothing of
the patterns which you received by Monsieur Tollot, though I
told you in a former letter, which you must have had before
the date of your last, that I should stay till I received the
patterns pitched upon by your ladies ; for as to the instructions
which you sent me in Madame Monconseil's hand, I could find
no mohairs[1] in London that exactly answered that description :
I shall, therefore, wait till you send me (which you may easily
do in a letter) the patterns chosen by your three Graces.

I would, by all means, have you go now and then for two
or three days to Maréchal Coigny's, at Orli ; it is but a
proper civility to that family, which has been particularly civil
to you ; and moreover, I would have you familiarize yourself
with and learn the interior and domestic manners of people of
that rank and fashion. I also desire that you will frequent
Versailles and St Cloud, at both which Courts you have been
received with distinction. Profit by that distinction, and
familiarize yourself at both. Great Courts are the seats of true
good breeding ; you are to live at Courts, lose no time in
learning them. Go and stay sometimes at Versailles for three
or four days, where you will be domestic in the best families,

[1] By mohairs we suppose his Lordship means tabbies.

by means of your friend Madame de Puisieux ; and mine,
L'Abbé de la Ville.   Go to the King's and the Dauphin's levees,
and distinguish yourself from the rest of your countrymen, who,
I dare say, never go there when they can help it.   Though the
young Frenchmen of fashion may not be worth forming intimate connections with, they are well worth making acquaintance of; and I do not see how you can avoid it, frequenting so
many good French houses as you do, where, to be sure, many
of them come.   Be cautious how you contract friendships, but
be desirous, and even industrious, to obtain a universal acquaintance.   Be easy, and even forward, in making new acquaintances ; that is the only way of knowing manners and
characters in general, which is at present your great object.
You are *enfant de famille* in three Minister's houses ; but I wish
you had a footing, at least, in thirteen ; and that I should
think you might easily bring about by that common chain,
which, to a certain degree, connects those you do not with
those you do know.   For instance, I suppose that neither Lord
Albemarle, nor Marquis de St Germain, would make the least
difficulty to present you to Comte Caunitz, the Nuncio, &c.   *Il
faut étre rompu au monde,*[1] which can only be done by an extensive, various, and almost universal acquaintance.

When you have got your emaciated Philomath, I desire that
his triangles, rhomboids, &c., may not keep you one moment
out of the good company you would otherwise be in.   Swallow
all your learning in the morning, but digest it in company in
the evenings.   The reading of ten new characters is more your
business now, than the reading of twenty old books ; showish
and shining people always get the better of all others, though
ever so solid.   If you would be a great man in the world when
you are old, shine and be showish in it while you are young ;
know everybody, and endeavour to please everybody, I mean
exteriorly ; for fundamentally it is impossible.   Try to engage
the heart of every woman, and the affections of almost every
man you meet with.   Madame Monconseil assures me that you
are most surprisingly improved in your air, manners, and
address ; go on, my dear child, and never think that you are
come to a sufficient degree of perfection ; *Nil actum reputans si
quid superesset agendum ;* and in those shining parts of the
character of a gentleman, there is always something remaining
to be acquired.   Modes and manners vary in different places,
and at different times ; you must keep pace with them, know
them, and adopt them, wherever you find them.   The great

---

[1] One must be made thoroughly conversant with the world.

usage of the world, the knowledge of characters, the *brillant d'un galant homme,* is all that you now want. Study Marcel and the *beau monde* with great application; but read Homer and Horace only when you have nothing else to do. Pray who is *la belle Madame de Case,* whom I know you frequent? I like the epithet given her very well; if she deserves it, she deserves your attention too. A man of fashion should be gallant to a fine woman, though he does not make love to her, or may be otherwise engaged. *On lui doit des politesses, on fait l'éloge de ses charmes, et il n'en est ni plus ni moins pour cela :*[1] it pleases, it flatters; you get their good word, and you lose nothing by it. These *gentillesses* should be accompanied, as indeed everything else should, with *un air, un ton de douceur et de politesse. Les grâces* must be of the party, or it will never do; and they are so easily had, that it is astonishing to me everybody has them not; they are sooner gained than any woman of common reputation and decency. Pursue them but with care and attention, and you are sure to enjoy them at last: without them, I am sure, you will never enjoy anybody else. You observe, truly, that Mr * * * * is *gauche;* it is to be hoped that he will mend with keeping company; and is yet pardonable in him, as just come from school. But reflect what you would think of a man, who had been any time in the world, and yet should be so awkward. For God's sake, therefore, now think of nothing but shining, and even distinguishing yourself, in the most polite Courts, by your air, your address, your manners, your politeness, your *douceur,* your graces. With those advantages (and not without them) take my word for it, you will get the better of all rivals, in business as well as in *ruelles.* Adieu! Send me your patterns by the next post, and also your instructions to Grevenkop about the seal, which you seem to have forgotten.

LETTER CCXXIII.

MY DEAR FRIEND,   London, May the 16th, O. S. 1751.

IN about three months, from this day, we shall probably meet. I look upon that moment as a young woman does upon her bridal night; I expect the greatest pleasure, and yet cannot help fearing some little mixture of pain. My reason bids me doubt a little of what my imagination makes me expect. In some articles I am very sure that my most sanguine wishes

---

[1] We owe to her politeness, we praise her charms, and it all means nothing.

will not be disappointed ; and those are the most material ones. In others, I fear something or other, which I can better feel than describe. However, I will attempt it. I fear the want of that amiable and engaging *je ne sais quoi*, which, as some philosophers have, unintelligibly enough, said of the soul, is all in all, and all in every part ; it should shed its influence over every word and action. I fear the want of that air, and first *abord*, which suddenly lays hold of the heart, one does not know distinctly how nor why. I fear an inaccuracy, or, at least, inelegancy, of diction, which will wrong, and lower, the best and justest matter. And, lastly, I fear an ungraceful if not an unpleasant utterance, which would disgrace and vilify the whole. Should these fears be at present founded, yet the objects of them are (thank God) of such a nature, that you may, if you please, between this and our meeting, remove every one of them. All these engaging and endearing accomplishments are mechanical, and to be acquired by care and observation, as easily as turning, or any mechanical trade. A common country fellow, taken from the plough, and enlisted in an old corps, soon lays aside his shambling gait, his slouching air, his clumsy and awkward motions ; and acquires the martial air, the regular motions, and the whole exercise of the corps, and, particularly, of his right and left hand man. How so ? Not from his parts ; which were just the same before as after he was enlisted ; but either from a commendable ambition of being like and equal to those he is to live with ; or else from the fear of being punished for not being so. If, then, both or either of these motives change such a fellow, in about six months' time, to such a degree as that he is not to be known again, how much stronger should both these motives be with you, to acquire, in the utmost perfection, the whole exercise of the people of fashion, with whom you are to live all your life ? Ambition should make you resolve to be, at least, their equal in that exercise, as well as the fear of punishment, which most inevitably will attend the want of it. By that exercise, I mean the air, the manners, the graces, and the style of people of fashion. A friend of yours, in a letter I received from him by the last post, after some other commendations of you, says, [1] *Il est étonnant, que pensant avec tant de solidité qu'il fait, et ayant le goût aussi sûr, et aussi délicat qu'il l'a, il s'exprime avec si peu d'élégance et de délicatesse. Il néglige même*

[1] It is surprising, that, thinking with so much solidity as he does, and having so true and refined a taste, he should express himself with so little elegancy and delicacy. He even totally neglects the choice of words and turn of phrases.

totalement le choix des mots et la tournure des phrases. This I should not be so much surprised or concerned at, if it related only to the English language; which, hitherto, you have had no opportunity of studying, and but few of speaking, at least to those who could correct your inaccuracies. But if you do not express yourself elegantly and delicately in French and German (both which languages I know you possess perfectly, and speak eternally), it can be only from an unpardonable inattention, to what you most erroneously think a little object, though, in truth, it is one of the most important of your life. Solidity and delicacy of thought must be given us, it cannot be acquired, though it may be improved; but elegancy and delicacy of expression may be acquired, by whoever will take the necessary care and pains. I am sure you love me so well, that you would be very sorry, when we meet, that I should be either disappointed or mortified; and I love you so well, that, I assure you, I should be both, if I should find you want any of those exterior accomplishments which are the indispensably necessary steps to that figure, and fortune, which I so earnestly wish you may one day make in the world.

I hope you do not neglect your exercises of riding, fencing, and dancing, but particularly the latter; for they all concur to *dégourdir*, and to give a certain air. To ride well is not only a proper and graceful accomplishment for a gentleman, but may also save you many a fall hereafter; to fence well may possibly save your life; and to dance well is absolutely necessary, in order to sit, stand, and walk well. To tell you the truth, my friend, I have some little suspicion, that you now and then neglect or omit your exercises, for more serious studies. But now *non est his locus*, everything has its time; and this is yours for your exercises; for when you return to Paris, I only propose your continuing your dancing; which you shall two years longer, if you happen to be where there is a good dancing-master. Here, I will see you take some lessons with your old master Desnoyers, who is our Marcel.

What says Madame du Pin to you? I am told she is very handsome still; I know she was so some few years ago. She has good parts, reading, manners, and delicacy; such an *arrangement* would be both creditable and advantageous to you. She will expect to meet with all the good breeding and delicacy that she brings; and as she is past the glare and *éclat* of youth, may be the more willing to listen to your story, if you tell it well. For an attachment, I should prefer her to *la petite Blot;* and for a mere gallantry, I should prefer *la petite Blot* to her;

so that they are consistent, *et l'une n'empéche pas l'autre.* Adieu! Remember *la douceur et les grâces.*

———◇———

LETTER CCXXIV.

My dear Friend,   London, May the 23rd, O. S. 1751.

I have this moment received your letter of the 25th, N. S., and being rather somewhat more attentive to my commissions, than you are to yours, return you this immediate answer to the question you ask me about the two pictures : I will not give one livre more than what I told you in my last; having no sort of occasion for them, and not knowing very well where to put them, if I had them.

I wait with impatience for your final orders about the mohairs; the mercer persecuting me every day, for three pieces which I thought pretty, and which I have kept by me eventually to secure them, in case your ladies should pitch upon them.

What do you mean by your [1] Si j'osois? qu'est-ce qui vous empêche d'oser? On ose toujours quand il y a espérance de succès; et on ne perd rien à oser, quand même il n'y en a pas. Un honnête homme sait oser, et quand il faut oser, il ouvre la tranchée par des travaux, des soins, et des attentions; s'il n'en est pas délogé d'abord il avance toujours à l'attaque de la place même. Après de certaines approches le succès est infaillible, et il n'y a que les nigauds qui en doutent, ou qui ne le tentent point. Seroit-ce le caractère respectable de Madame de la Valière, qui vous empêche d'oser, ou seroit-ce la vertu farouche de Madame du Pin qui vous retient! La sagesse invincible de la belle Madame Case vous décourage-t-elle plus que sa beauté ne vous invite? Mais si donc. Soyez convaincu que la femme la plus sage se trouve flattée, bien loin d'être offensée, par une

---

[1] If I durst! What should hinder you from daring? One always dares, if there are hopes of success; and if even there are none, one is no loser by daring. A man of fashion knows how, and when, to dare. He begins his approaches by distant attacks, by assiduities, and by attentions. If he is not immediately and totally repulsed, he continues to advance. After certain steps, success is infallible; and none but very silly fellows can then either doubt or not attempt it. Is it the respectable character of Madame de la Valiere, which prevents your daring; or are you intimidated at the fierce virtue of Madame du Pin? Does the invincible modesty of the handsome Madame Case discourage, more than her beauty invites you? Fie, for shame! Be convinced that the most virtuous woman, far from being offended at a declaration of love, is flattered by it, if it is made in a polite and agreeable *

déclaration d'amour, faite avec politesse, et agrément. Il se peut bien qu'elle ne s'y prétera point, c'est-à-dire, si elle a un goût ou une passion pour quelque autre ; mais en tout cas elle ne vous en saura pas mauvais gré ; de façon qu'il n'est pas question d'oser dès qu'il n'y a pas de danger. Mais si elle s'y prête, si elle écoute, et qu'elle vous permet de redoubler votre déclaration, comptez qu'elle se moquera bien de vous si vous n'osez pas tout le reste. Je vous conseille de débuter plutôt par Madame du Pin, qui a encore de la beauté plus qu'il n'en faut pour un jeune drôle comme vous; elle a aussi du monde, de l'esprit, de la délicatesse ; son âge ne lui laisse pas absolument le choix de ses amans, et je vous réponds qu'elle ne rejetteroit pas les offres de vos très-humbles services. Distinguez-la donc par vos attentions, et des regards tendres ; et prenez les occasions favorables de lui dire à l'oreille que vous voudriez bien que l'amitié et l'estime fussent les seuls motifs de vos égards pour elle, mais que des sentimens bien plus tendres en sont les véritables sources. Que vous souffriez bien en les lui déclarant, mais que vous souffriez encore plus en les lui cachant.

Je sens bien qu'en lui disant cela pour la première fois vous aurez l'air assez sot, et assez penaud, et que vous le direz fort mal. Tant mieux, elle attribuera votre désordre à l'excès de votre amour, au lieu de l'attribuer à la véritable cause, votre peu d'usage du monde, surtout dans ces matières. En pareil cas l'amour propre est le fidèle ami de l'amant. Ne craignez donc rien, soyez galant homme ; parlez bien, et on vous écoutera. Si on ne vous écoute pas la première, parlez une seconde, une

manner. It is possible that she may not be propitious to your vows ; that is to say, if she has a liking or a passion for another person. But, at all events, she will not be displeased with you for it; so that, as there is no danger, this cannot even be called daring. But if she attends, if she listens, and allows you to repeat your declaration, be persuaded that if you do not dare all the rest, she will laugh at you. I advise you to begin rather by Madame du Pin, who has still more than beauty enough for such a youngster as you. She has, besides, knowledge of the world, sense, and delicacy. As she is not so extremely young, the choice of her lovers cannot be entirely at her option. I promise you, she will not refuse the tender of your most humble services. Distinguish her, then, by attentions, and by tender looks. Take favourable opportunities of whispering, that you wish esteem and friendship were the only motives of your regard for her ; but that it derives from sentiments of a much more tender nature : that you made not this declaration without pain ; but that the concealing your passion was a still greater torment.

I am sensible that in saying this for the first time, you will look silly, abashed, and even express yourself very ill. So much the better ; for, instead of attributing your confusion to the little usage you have of the world, particularly in these sort of subjects, she will think that excess of love is the occasion of it. In such a case the lover's best friend is self-love. Do not then be afraid ; behave gallantly ; speak well, and you will be heard. If

troisième, une quatrième fois ; si la place n'est pas déjà prise, soyez sûr qu'à la longue elle est prenable.

I am very glad you are going to Orli, and from thence to St Cloud: go to both, and to Versailles also, often. It is that interior, domestic familiarity with people of fashion, that alone can give you *l'usage du monde, et les manières aisées.* It is only with women one loves, or men one respects, that the desire of pleasing exerts itself ; and without the desire of pleasing, no man living can please. Let that desire be the spring of all your words and actions. That happy talent, the art of pleasing, which so few do, though almost all might, possess, is worth all your learning and knowledge put together. The latter can never raise you high, without the former ; but the former may carry you, as it has carried thousands, a great way, without the latter.

I am glad that you dance so well as to be reckoned by Marcel among his best scholars ; go on, and dance better still. Dancing well is pleasing *pro tanto,* and makes a part of that necessary *whole,* which is composed of a thousand parts, many of them of *les infiniment petits quoiqu' infiniment nécessaires.*

I shall never have done upon this subject, which is indispensably necessary towards your making any figure or fortune in the world ; both which I have set my heart upon, and for both which you now absolutely want no one thing but the art of pleasing ; and I must not conceal from you that you have still a good way to go before you arrive at it. You still want a thousand of those little attentions that imply a desire of pleasing : you want a *douceur* of air and expression that engages : you want an elegancy and delicacy of expression, necessary to adorn the best sense and most solid matter : in short, you still want a great deal of the *brillant* and the *poli.* Get them at any rate ; sacrifice hecatombs of books to them : seek for them in company, and renounce your closet till you have got them. I never received the letter you refer to, if ever you wrote it. Adieu, *et bon soir, Monseigneur.*

LETTER CCXXV.

My dear Friend,   Greenwich, June the 6th, O. S. 1751.

Solicitous and anxious as I have ever been to form your heart, your mind, and your manners ; to bring you as near per-

you are not listened to the first time, try a second, a third, and a fourth. If the place is not already taken, depend upon it, it may be conquered.

fection as the imperfection of our natures will allow ; I have
exhausted, in the course of our correspondence, all that my own
mind could suggest, and have borrowed from others whatever I
thought could be useful to you ; but this has necessarily been
interruptedly and by snatches. It is now time, and you are of
an age, to review and to weigh in your own mind all that you
have heard, and all that you have read, upon these subjects ;
and to form your own character, your conduct, and your manners, for the rest of your life ; allowing for such improvements
as a further knowledge of the world will naturally give you.
In this view, I would recommend to you to read, with the
greatest attention, such books as treat particularly of those subjects ; reflecting seriously upon them, and then comparing the
speculation with the practice. For example ; if you read in the
morning some of La Rochefoucault's maxims, consider them,
examine them well, and compare them with the real characters
you meet with in the evening. Read La Bruyere in the morning, and see in the evening whether his pictures are like.
Study the heart and the mind of man, and begin with your
own. Meditation and reflection must lay the foundation of that
knowledge ; but experience and practice must, and alone can,
complete it. Books, it is true, point out the operations of the
mind, the sentiments of the heart, the influence of the passions ;
and so far they are of previous use : but without subsequent
practice, experience, and observation, they are as ineffectual,
and would even lead you into as many errors in fact, as a map
would do if you were to take your notions of the towns and
provinces from their delineations in it. A man would reap very
little benefit by his travels if he made them only in his closet
upon a map of the whole world. Next to the two books that I
have already mentioned, I do not know a better for you to read,
and seriously reflect upon, than *Avis d'une Mère à un Fils par la
Marquise de Lambert.* She was a woman of a superior understanding and knowledge of the world, had always kept the best
company, was solicitous that her son should make a figure and
a fortune in the world, and knew better than anybody how to
point out the means. It is very short, and will take you much
less time to read, than you ought to employ in reflecting upon
it after you have read it. Her son was in the army, she wished
he might rise there ; but she well knew that, in order to rise,
he must first please : she says to him, therefore, *A l'égard de
ceux dont vous dépendez, le premier mérité est de plaire.*[1] And in

---

[1] With regard to those upon whom you depend, the chief merit is to please.

another place, *Dans les emplois subalternes vous ne vous soutenez que par les agrémens. Les maîtres sont comme les maîtresses ; quelque service que vous leur ayez rendu, ils cessent de vous aimer quand vous cessez de leur plaire.*[1] This, I can assure you, is at least as true in courts as in camps, and possibly more so. If to your merit and knowledge you add the art of pleasing, you may very probably come in time to be Secretary of State ; but, take my word for it, twice your merit and knowledge, without the art of pleasing, would, at most, raise you to the *important post* of Resident at Hamburgh or Ratisbon. I need not tell you now, for I often have, and your own discernment must have told you, of what numberless little ingredients that art of pleasing is compounded, and how the want of the least of them lowers the whole ; but the principal ingredient is, undoubtedly, *la douceur dans les manières:* nothing will give this more than keeping company with your superiors. Madame Lambert tells her son, *que vos liaisons soient avec des personnes au dessus de vous, par la vous vous accoutumez au respect et à la politesse ; avec ses égaux on se néglige, l'esprit s'assoupit.*[2] She advises him, too to frequent those people, and to see their inside ; *il est bon d'approcher les hommes, de les voir à découvert ; et avec leur mérite de tous les jours.*[3] A happy expression ! It was for this reason that I have so often advised you to establish and domesticate yourself, wherever you can, in good houses of people above you, that you may see their *every-day* character, manners, habits, &c. One must see people undressed, to judge truly of their shape ; when they are dressed to go abroad, their clothes are contrived to conceal, or at least palliate, the defects of it : as full-bottomed wigs were contrived for the Duke of Burgundy, to conceal his hump back. Happy those who have no faults to disguise, nor weaknesses to conceal ! there are few, if any such : but unhappy those, who know so little of the world as to judge by outward appearances. Courts are the best keys to characters : there every passion is busy, every art exerted, every character analyzed : jealousy, ever watchful, not only discovers but exposes the mysteries of the trade, so that even bystanders *y apprennent à deviner.* There, too, the great art of pleasing is

---

[1] In subaltern employments, the art of pleasing must be your support. Masters are like mistresses ; whatever services they may be indebted to you for, they cease to love when you cease to be agreeable.

[2] Let your connections be with people above you ; by that means you will acquire a habit of respect and politeness. With one's equals one is apt to become negligent, and the mind grows torpid.

[3] In order to judge of men, one must be intimately connected ; thus you see them without a veil, and with their mere every-day merit.

practised, taught, and learned, with all its graces and delicacies. It is the first thing needful there : it is the absolutely necessary harbinger of merit and talents, let them be ever so great. There is no advancing a step without it. Let misanthropes and would-be philosophers declaim as much as they please against the vices, the simulation, and dissimulation of Courts ; those invectives are always the result of ignorance, ill humour, or envy. Let them show me a cottage, where there are not the same vices of which they accuse Courts ; with this difference only, that in a cottage they appear in their native deformity, and that in Courts, manners and good breeding make them less shocking, and blunt their edge. No, be convinced that the good breeding, the *tournure, la douceur dans les manières*, which alone are to be acquired at Courts, are not the showish trifles only which some people call or think them : they are a solid good ; they prevent a great deal of real mischief ; they create, adorn, and strengthen friendships : they keep hatred within bounds ; they promote good humour and good will in families, where the want of good breeding and gentleness of manners is commonly the original cause of discord. Get, then, before it is too late, a habit of these *mitiores virtutes:* practise them upon every the least occasion, that they may be easy and familiar to you upon the greatest ; for they lose a great degree of their merit if they seem laboured, and only called in upon extraordinary occasions. I tell you truly, this is now the only doubtful part of your character with me ; and it is for that reason that I dwell upon it so much, and inculcate it so often. I shall soon see whether this doubt of mine is founded ; or rather, I hope I shall soon see that it is not.

This moment I receive your letter of the 9th, N. S. I am sorry to find that you have had, though ever so slight, a return of your Carniolan disorder ; and I hope your conclusion will prove a true one, and that this will be the last. I will send the mohairs by the first opportunity. As for the pictures, I am already so full, that I am resolved not to buy one more, unless by great accident I should meet with something surprisingly good, and as surprisingly cheap.

I should have thought that Lord * * * at his age, and with his parts and address, need not have been reduced to keep an opera wh—e, in such a place as Paris, where so many women of fashion generously serve as volunteers. I am still more sorry that he is in love with her ; for that will take him out of good company, and sink him into bad ; such as fiddlers, pipers, and *id genus omne;* most unedifying and unbecoming company for a man of fashion!

Lady Chesterfield makes you a thousand compliments. Adieu, my dear child.

LETTER CCXXVII.

My dear Friend,   London, June the 10th, O. S. 1751.

Your ladies were so slow in giving their specific orders, that the mohairs, of which you at last sent me the patterns, were all sold. However, to prevent further delays (for ladies are apt to be very impatient, when at last they know their own minds), I have taken the quantities desired, of three mohairs. which come nearest to the description you sent me some time ago, in Madame Monconseil's own hand; and I will send them to Calais by the first opportunity. In giving *la petite Blot* her piece, you have a fine occasion of saying fine things, if so inclined.

Lady Hervey, who is your puff and panegyrist, writes me word, that she saw you lately dance at a ball, and that you dance very genteelly. I am extremely glad to hear it; for (by the maxim that *omne majus continet in se minus*[1]) if you dance genteelly, I presume you walk, sit, and stand genteelly too; things which are much more easy, though much more necessary, than dancing well. I have known many very genteel people, who could not dance well; but I never knew anybody dance very well, who was not genteel in other things. You will probably often have occasion to stand in circles, at the levees of princes and ministers, when it is very necessary, *de payer de sa personne, et d'étre bien planté,*[2] with your feet not too near nor too distant from each other. More people stand and walk than sit genteelly. Awkward, ill-bred people, being ashamed, commonly sit up bolt upright, and stiff; others, too negligent and easy, *se vautrent dans leur fauteuil,*[3] which is ungraceful and ill bred, unless where the familiarity is extreme; but a man of fashion makes himself easy, and appears so, by leaning gracefully, instead of lolling supinely; and by varying those easy attitudes, instead of that stiff immobility of a bash-

[1] The greater contains the less.
[2] To show off one's person, and to be properly posed.
[3] Wallow in their easy-chair.

ful booby. You cannot conceive, nor can I express, how advantageous a good air, genteel motions, and engaging address are, not only among women, but among men, and even in the course of business; they fascinate the affections, they steal a preference, they play about the heart till they engage it. I know a man, and so do you, who, without a grain of merit, knowledge, or talents, has raised himself millions of degrees above his level, singly by a good air and engaging manners; insomuch that the very prince who raised him so high, calls him, *mon aimable vaurien:*[1] but of this do not open your lips, *pour cause.* I give you this secret, as the strongest proof imaginable of the efficacy of air, address, *tournure, et tous ces petits riens.*

Your other puff and panegyrist, Mr Harte, is gone to Windsor, in his way to Cornwall, in order to be back soon enough to meet you here; I really believe he is as impatient for that moment as I am, *et c'est tout dire:* but, however, notwithstanding my impatience, if, by chance, you should then be in a situation, that leaving Paris would cost your heart too many pangs, I allow you to put off your journey, and to tell me, as Festus did Paul, *at a more convenient season I will speak to thee.* You see by this, that I eventually sacrifice my sentiments to yours, and this in a very uncommon object of paternal complaisance. Provided always, and be it understood (as they say in Acts of Parliament), that *quæ te cumque domat Venus, non erubescendis adurit ignibus.* If your heart will let you come, bring with you only your valet-de-chambre, Christian, and your own footman; not your valet-de-place, whom you may dismiss for the time, as also your coach; but you had best keep on your lodgings, the intermediate expense of which will be but inconsiderable, and you will want them to leave your books and baggage in. Bring only the clothes you travel in, one suit of black, for the mourning for the Prince will not be quite out by that time, and one suit of your fine clothes, two or three of your laced shirts, and the rest plain ones; of other things, as bags, feathers &c., as you think proper. Bring no books, unless two or three for your amusement on the road; for we must apply singly to English, in which you are certainly no *puriste,* and I will supply you sufficiently with the proper English authors. I shall probably keep you here till about the middle of October, and certainly not longer; it being absolutely necessary for you to pass the next winter at Paris; so that should any fine eyes shed tears for your departure, you may dry them by the promise of your return in two months.

[1] The Maréchal De Richelieu.

Have you got a master for Geometry? If the weather is very hot, you may leave your riding at the *manége* till you return to Paris, unless you think the exercise does you more good than the heat can do you harm; but I desire you will not leave off Marcel for one moment: your fencing likewise, if you have a mind, may subside for the summer; but you will do well to resume it in the winter, and to be *adroit* at it, but by no means for offence, only for defence in case of necessity. Good night.

Yours.

P. S. I forgot to give you one commission, when you come here; which is, not to fail bringing the *grâces* along with you.

----●----

LETTER CCXXVII.

MY DEAR FRIEND,   Greenwich, June the 13th, O. S. 1751.

Les bienséances[1] are a most necessary part of the knowledge of the world. They consist in the relations of persons, things, time, and place; good sense points them out, good company perfects them (supposing always an attention and a desire to please), and good policy recommends them.

Were you to converse with a King, you ought to be as easy and unembarrassed as with your own valet-de-chambre: but yet every look, word, and action should imply the utmost respect. What would be proper and well bred with others, much your superiors, would be absurd and ill bred with one so very much so. You must wait till you are spoken to; you must receive, not give, the subject of conversation; and you must even take care that the given subject of such conversation do not lead you into any impropriety. The art would be to carry it, if possible, to some indirect flattery: such as commending those virtues in some other person, in which that Prince either thinks he does or at least would be thought by others to excel. Almost the same precautions are necessary to be used with Ministers, Generals, &c., who expect to be treated with very near the same respect as their masters, and commonly deserve it better. There is, however, this difference, that one may begin the conversation with them, if on their side it should happen to drop, provided one does not carry it to any subject, upon which it is improper either for them to speak or be spoken to. In these two cases, certain attitudes and actions would be

---

[1] This single word implies decorum, good breeding, and propriety.

extremely absurd, because too easy, and consequently disrespectful. As, for instance, if you were to put your arms across in
your bosom, twirl your snuff-box, trample with your feet, scratch
your head, &c., it would be shockingly ill bred in that company;
and, indeed, not extremely well bred in any other. The great
difficulty in those cases, though a very surmountable one by
attention and custom, is to join perfect inward ease with perfect
outward respect.

In mixed companies with your equals (for in mixed companies all people are to a certain degree equal) greater ease
and liberty are allowed; but they too have their bounds within
bienséance. There is a social respect necessary: you may
start your own subject of conversation with modesty, taking
great care, however, *de ne jamais parler de cordes dans la
maison d'un pendu*.[1] Your words, gestures, and attitudes have a
greater degree of latitude, though by no means an unbounded
one. You may have your hands in your pockets, take snuff, sit,
stand, or occasionally walk, as you like: but I believe you
would not think it very *bienséant* to whistle, put on your hat,
loosen your garters or your buckles, lie down upon a couch, or
go to bed and welter in an easy-chair. These are negligences
and freedoms which one can only take when quite alone: they
are injurious to superiors, shocking and offensive to equals,
brutal and insulting to inferiors. That easiness of carriage and
behaviour, which is exceedingly engaging, widely differs from
negligence and inattention, and by no means implies that one
may do whatever one pleases; it only means that one is
not to be stiff, formal, embarrassed, disconcerted, and ashamed,
like country bumpkins, and people who have never been in
good company; but it requires great attention to, and a scrupulous observation of, *les bienséances:* whatever one ought to do
is to be done with ease and unconcern; whatever is improper
must not be done at all. In mixed companies, also, different
ages and sexes are to be differently addressed. You would not
talk of your pleasures to men of a certain age, gravity, and
dignity; they justly expect, from young people, a degree of
deference and regard. You should be full as easy with them as
with people of your own years: but your manner must be different; more respect must be implied; and it is not amiss to
insinuate, that from them you expect to learn. It flatters and
comforts age, for not being able to take a part in the joy and
titter of youth. To women you should always address yourself
with great outward respect and attention, whatever you feel in-

[1] Never to mention a rope in the family of a man who has been hanged.

wardly ; their sex is by long prescription entitled to it ; and it is among the duties of *bienséance :* at the same time that respect is very properly, and very agreeably, mixed with a degree of *enjouement,* if you have it : but then, that *badinage* must either directly or indirectly tend to their praise, and even not be liable to a malicious construction to their disadvantage. But here, too, great attention must be had to the difference of age, rank, and situation. A *Maréchale* of fifty must not be played with like a young coquette of fifteen : respect and *serious enjouement,* if I may couple those two words, must be used with the former, and mere *badinage, zesté méme d'un peu de polissonnerie,*[1] is pardonable with the latter.

Another important point of *les bienséances,* seldom enough attended to, is, not to run your own present humour and disposition indiscriminately against everybody : but to observe, conform to, and adopt, theirs. For example; if you happened to be in high good humour and a flow of spirits, would you go and sing a *pont neuf,*[2] or cut a caper, to la Maréchale de Coigny, the Pope's Nuncio, or Abbé Sallier, or to any person of natural gravity and melancholy, or who at that time should be in grief? I believe not : as, on the other hand, I suppose that if you you were in low spirits, or real grief, you would not choose to bewail your situation with *la petite Blot.* If you cannot command your present humour and disposition, single out those to converse with, who happen to be in the humour nearest to your own.

Loud laughter is extremely inconsistent with *les bienséances,* as it is only the illiberal and noisy testimony of the joy of the mob, at some very silly thing. A gentleman is often seen, but very seldom heard, to laugh. Nothing is more contrary to *les bienséances* than horse play, or *jeux de main* of any kind whatever, and has often very serious, sometimes very fatal, consequences. Romping, struggling, throwing things at one another's head, are the becoming pleasantries of the mob, but degrade a gentleman ; *giuoco di mano, giuoco di villano,*[3] is a very true saying, among the few true sayings of the Italians.

Peremptoriness and decision in young people is *contraire aux bienséances :* they should seem to assert, and always use some softening mitigating expression ; such as *s'il m'est permis de le dire, je croirois plutôt, si j'ose m'expliquer,*[4] which softens

---

[1] Pleasantry spiced even with a little blackguardism.
[2] Ballad.
[3] Practical jokes are the jokes of a clown.
[4] If I may say so,—I should rather think,—if I may venture to explain myself.

the manner, without giving up, or even weakening, the thing. People of more age and experience expect and are entitled to that degree of deference.

There is a *bienséance* also with regard to people of the lowest degree ; a gentleman observes it with his footman, even with the beggar in the street.   He considers them as objects of compassion, not of insult ; he speaks to neither *d'un ton brusque*, but corrects the one coolly, and refuses the other with humanity.   There is no one occasion in the world, in which *le ton brusque* is becoming a gentleman.   In short, *les bienséances* are another word for *manners*, and extend to every part of life. They are propriety ; the Graces should attend in order to complete them : the Graces enable us to do, genteelly and pleasingly, what *les bienséances* require to be done at all.   The latter are an obligation upon every man ; the former are an infinite advantage and ornament to any man.   May you unite both !

Though you dance well, do not think that you dance well enough, and consequently not endeavour to dance still better. And though you should be told that you are genteel, still aim at being genteeler.   If Marcel should, do not you, be satisfied. Go on, court the Graces all your lifetime ; you will find no better friends at Court : they will speak in your favour, to the hearts of Princes, Ministers, and Mistresses.

Now that all tumultuous passions and quick sensations have subsided with me, and that I have no tormenting cares nor boisterous pleasures to agitate me, my greatest joy is to consider the fair prospect you have before you, and to hope and believe you will enjoy it.   You are already in the world, at an age when others have hardly heard of it.   Your character is hitherto not only unblemished in its moral part, but even unsullied by any low, dirty, and ungentlemanlike vice ; and will, I hope, continue so.   Your knowledge is sound, extensive, and avowed, especially in everything relative to your destination.   With such materials to begin, what then is wanting ? Not fortune, as you have found by experience.   You have had, and shall have, fortune sufficient to assist your merit and your industry ; and, if I can help it, you never shall have enough to make you negligent of either.   You have, too, *mens sana in corpore sano*, the greatest blessing of all.   All therefore that you want is as much in your power to acquire, as to eat your breakfast when set before you : it is only that knowledge of the world, that elegancy of manners, that universal politeness, and those graces, which keeping good company, and seeing variety of places and characters, must inevitably, with the least attention on your part, give you. Your foreign destination leads to the greatest things, and your parliamentary situation will facilitate your progress ; consider, then, this pleasing prospect as attentively for yourself, as I consider it for you. Labour on your part to realize it, as I will on mine to assist and enable you to do it. *Nullum numen abest, si sit prudentia.*

Adieu ! my dear child. I count the days till I have the pleasure of seeing you : I shall soon count the hours, and at last the minutes, with increasing impatience.

P. S. The mohairs are this day gone from hence for Calais ; recommended to the care of Madame Morel, and directed, as desired, to the Comptroller General. The three pieces come to six hundred and eighty French livres.

LETTER CCXXVIII.

My dear Friend,　　　　　London, June the 20th, O. S. 1751.

So very few people, especially young travellers, see what they see, or hear what they hear, that though I really believe it may be unnecessary with you, yet there can be no harm in reminding you, from time to time, to see what you see, and to hear what you hear ; that is, to see and hear as you should do. Frivolous futile people, who make at least three parts in four of mankind, only desire to see and hear what their frivolous and futile precursors have seen and heard ; as St Peter's, the Pope, and High Mass, at Rome ; Notre Dame, Versailles, the French King, and the French Comedy, in France. A man of parts sees and hears very differently from these gentlemen, and a great deal more. He examines and informs himself thoroughly of everything he sees or hears ; and, more particularly, as it is relative to his own profession or destination. Your destination is political ; the object therefore of your inquiries and observations should be the political interior of things : the forms of government, laws, regulations, customs, trade, manufactures, &c., of the several nations of Europe. This knowledge is much better acquired by conversation with sensible and well-informed people, than by books ; the best of which, upon these subjects, are always imperfect. For example ; there are Present States of France, as there are of England ; but they are always defective, being published by people uninformed, who only copy one another : they are, however, worth looking into, because they point out objects of inquiry, which otherwise might possibly never have occurred to one's mind : but an hour's conversation with a sensible *Président*, or *Conseiller*, will let you more into the true state of the parliament of Paris, than all the books in France. In the same manner, the *Almanach Militaire* is worth your having ; but two or three conversations with officers will inform you much better of their military regulations. People have, commonly, a partiality for their own professions, love to talk of them, and are even flattered by being consulted upon the subject ; when, therefore, you are with any of those military gentlemen (and you can hardly be in any company without some), ask them military questions. Inquire into their methods of discipline, quartering, and clothing their men ; inform yourself of their pay, their perquisites, *leurs montres, leurs étapes, &c.* Do the same as to the *marine,* and make yourself particularly master of that *détail ;* which has, and always will have, a geat relation to the affairs of England ; and, in proportion as you get good informations, make minutes of them in writing.

The regulations of trade and commerce in France are excellent, as appears but too plainly for us, by the great increase of both, within these thirty years ; for, not to mention their extensive commerce in both the East and West Indies, they have got the whole trade of the Levant from us; and now supply all the foreign markets with their sugars, to the ruin almost of our sugar colonies, as Jamaica, Barbadoes, and the Leeward Islands. Get, therefore, what informations you can of these matters also.

Inquire, too, into their Church matters ; for which the present disputes between the Court and the Clergy give you fair and frequent opportunities. Know the particular rights of the Gallican Church in opposition to the pretensions of the See of Rome. I need not recommend ecclesiastical history to you, since I hear you study *Du Pin* very assiduously.

You cannot imagine how much this solid and useful knowledge of other countries will distinguish you in your own (where, to say the truth, it is very little known or cultivated), besides the great use it is of in all foreign negotiations ; not to mention that it enables a man to shine in all companies. When Kings and Princes have any knowledge, it is of this sort, and more particularly : therefore it is the usual topic of their levée conversations, in which it will qualify you to bear a considerable part : it brings you more acquainted with them ; and they are pleased to have people talk to them on a subject in which they think to shine.

There is a sort of chit-chat, or *small talk*, which is the general run of conversation at Courts, and in most mixed companies. It is a sort of middling conversation, neither silly nor edifying ; but, however, very necessary for you to be master of. It turns upon the public events of Europe, and then is at its best ; very often upon the number, the goodness, or badness, the discipline, or the clothing of the troops of different Princes ; sometimes upon the families, the marriages, the relations of princes, and considerable people ; and, sometimes, *sur la bonne chere*, the magnificence of public entertainments, balls, masquerades, &c. I would wish you to be able to talk upon all these things better and with more knowledge than other people, insomuch that, upon those occasions, you should be applied to, and that people should say, *I dare say Mr Stanhope can tell us*.

Second-rate knowledge, and middling talents, carry a man further at Courts, and in the busy 'part of the world, than superior knowledge and shining parts. Tacitus very justly accounts for a man's having always kept in favour, and enjoyed the best employments, under the tyrannical reigns of three or four of the very worst Emperors, by saying that it was not *propter aliquam eximiam artem, sed quia par negotiis neque supra erat*.[1] Discretion is the great article ; all those things are to be learned, and only learned by keeping a great deal of the best company. Frequent those good houses where you have already a footing, and wriggle yourself somehow or other into every other. Haunt the Courts particularly, in order to get that *routine*.

This moment I receive yours of the 18th, N. S. You will have had some time ago my final answers concerning the pictures : and, by my last, an account that the mohairs were gone to Madame Morel at Calais, with the proper directions.

I am sorry that your two sons-in-law, the princes B——, are such boobies ; however, as they have the honour of being so nearly related to you, I will show them what civilities I can.

I confess you have not time for long absences from Paris at present, because of your various masters, all which I would have you apply to closely while you are now in that capital ; but when you return thither, after the visit you intend me the honour of, I do not propose your having any master at all, except Marcel once or twice a week. And then the Courts will, I hope, be no longer strange countries to you ; for I would have you run down frequently to Versailles and St Cloud for three or four days at a time. You know the Abbé de la Ville, who will pre-

---

[1] Not on account of any remarkable skill, but because he was equal to business and not above it.

sent you to others, so that you will soon be *faufilé*[1] with the rest of the Court. Court is the soil in which you are to grow and flourish ; you ought to be well acquainted with the nature of it : like all other soil, it is in some places deeper, in others lighter, but always capable of great improvement by cultivation and experience.

You say that you want some hints for a letter to Lady Chesterfield ; more use and knowledge of the world will teach you occasionally to write and talk genteelly, *sur des riens*, which I can tell you is a very useful part of worldly knowledge ; for, in some companies, it would be imprudent to talk upon anything else, and with very many people it is impossible to talk of anything else ; they would not understand you. Adieu !

LETTER CCXXIX.

MY DEAR FRIEND, London, June 24th, O. S. 1751.

AIR, address, manners, and graces are of such infinite advantage to whoever has them, and so peculiarly and essentially necessary for you, that now, as the time of our meeting draws near, I tremble for fear I should not find you possessed of them ; and, to tell you the truth, I doubt you are not yet sufficiently convinced of their importance. There is, for instance, your intimate friend Mr H——, who, with great merit, deep knowledge, and a thousand good qualities, will never make a figure in the world while he lives : Why ? Merely for want of those external and showish accomplishments, which he began the world too late to acquire ; and which, with his studious and philosophical turn, I believe he thinks are not worth his attention. He may, very probably, make a figure in the republic of letters ; but he had ten thousand times better make a figure as a man of the world and of business in the republic of the United Provinces, which, take my word for it, he never will.

As I open myself, without the least reserve, whenever I think that my doing so can be of any use to you, I will give you a short account of myself when I first came into the world, which was at the age you are of now, so that (by the way) you have got the start of me in that important article by two or three years at least. At nineteen, I left the university of Cambridge, where I was an absolute pedant : when I talked my best,

---

[1] Associated.

I quoted Horace; when I aimed at being facetious, I quoted Martial; and when I had a mind to be a fine gentleman, I talked Ovid. I was convinced that none but the ancients had common sense; that the Classics contained everything that was either necessary, useful, or ornamental to men; and I was not without thoughts of wearing the *toga virilis* of the Romans, instead of the vulgar and illiberal dress of the moderns. With these excellent notions, I went first to the Hague, where, by the help of several letters of recommendation, I was soon introduced into all the best company; and where I very soon discovered that I was totally mistaken in almost every one notion I had entertained. Fortunately, I had a strong desire to please (the mixed result of good nature and a vanity by no means blamable), and was sensible that I had nothing but the desire. I therefore resolved, if possible, to acquire the means too. I studied attentively and minutely the dress, the air, the manner, the address, and the turn of conversation of all those whom I found to be the people in fashion, and most generally allowed to please. I imitated them as well as I could; if I heard that one man was reckoned remarkably genteel, I carefully watched his dress, motions, and attitudes, and formed my own upon them. When I heard of another, whose conversation was agreeable and engaging, I listened and attended to the turn of it. I addressed myself, though *de très-mauvaise grâce*, to all the most fashionable fine ladies; confessed, and laughed with them at my own awkwardness and rawness, recommending myself as an object for them to try their skill in forming. By these means, and with a passionate desire of pleasing everybody, I came by degrees to please some; and, I can assure you, that what little figure I have made in the world, has been much more owing to that passionate desire I had of pleasing universally than to any intrinsic merit or sound knowledge I might ever have been master of. My passion for pleasing was so strong (and I am very glad it was so) that I own to you fairly, I wished to make every woman I saw in love with me, and every man I met with admire me. Without this passion for the object, I should never have been so attentive to the means; and I own I cannot conceive how it is possible for any man of good nature and good sense to be without this passion. Does not good nature incline us to please all those we converse with, of whatever rank or station they may be? And does not good sense and common observation show of what infinite use it is to please? Oh! but one may please by the good qualities of the heart, and the knowledge of the head, without that fashionable air, address, and manner, which is mere tinsel. I deny it. A man may be esteemed and respected, but I defy him to please without them. Moreover, at your age, I would not have contented myself with barely pleasing; I wanted to shine, and to distinguish myself in the world as a man of fashion and gallantry, as well as business. And that ambition or vanity, call it what you please, was a right one; it hurt nobody, and made me exert whatever talents I had. It is the spring of a thousand right and good things.

I was talking you over the other day with one very much your friend, and who had often been with you, both at Paris and in Italy. Among the innumerable questions, which you may be sure I asked him concerning you, I happened to mention your dress (for, to say the truth, it was the only thing of which I thought him a competent judge), upon which he said that you dressed tolerably well at Paris; but that in Italy you dressed so ill, that he used to joke with you upon it, and even to tear your clothes. Now, I must tell you, that at your age it is as ridiculous not to be very well dressed, as at my age it would be if I were to wear a white feather and red-heeled shoes. Dress is one of the various ingredients that contribute to the art of pleasing; it pleases the eyes at least, and more especially of women. Address yourself to the senses, if you would please; dazzle the eyes, soothe and flatter the ears, of mankind; engage their heart, and let their reason do its worst against you. *Suaviter in modo* is the great secret. Whenever you find yourself engaged insensibly in favour of anybody, of no superior merit nor distinguished talents, examine, and see what it is that has made those impressions upon you : you will find it to be that *douceur*, that gentleness of manners, that air and address, which I have so often recommended to you; and from thence draw this obvious conclusion, that what pleases you in them will please others in you; for we are all made of the same clay, though some of the lumps are a little finer, and some a little coarser; but, in general, the surest way to judge of others is to examine and analyze one's self thoroughly. When we meet I will assist you in that analysis, in which every man wants some assistance against his own self-love. Adieu.

LETTER CCXXX.

My DEAR FRIEND, Greenwich, June the 30th, O. S. 1751.

PRAY give the enclosed to our friend the Abbé ; it is to congratulate him upon his *canonicat*, which I am really very glad
of, and I hope it will fatten him up to Boileau's *Chanoine ;* at
present he is as meagre as an Apostle or a Prophet. By the
way, has he ever introduced you to la.Duchesse d'Aiguillon ?
If he has not, make him present you ; and if he has, frequent
her, and make her many compliments from me. She has uncommon sense and knowledge for a woman, and her house is the
resort of one set of *les beaux esprits.* It is a satisfaction and a
sort of credit to be acquainted with those gentlemen ; and it
puts a young fellow in fashion. A *propos des beaux esprits ;*
have you *les entrées* at Lady Sandwich's ; who, old as she was,
when I saw her last, had the strongest parts of any woman I
ever knew in my life ? If you are not acquainted with her,
either the Duchess d'Aiguillon or Lady Hervey can, and I dare
say will, introduce you. I can assure you it is very well worth
your while, both upon her own account, and for the sake of the
people of wit and learning who frequent her. In such companies there is always something to be learned, as well as manners :
the conversation turns upon something above trifles : some point
of literature, criticism, history, &c., is discussed with ingenuity
and good manners, for I must do the French people of learning
justice ; they are not bears, as most of ours are ; they are gentlemen.

Our Abbé writes me word that you were gone to Compiegne ; I am very glad of it ; other Courts must form you for
your own. He tells me, too, that you have left off riding at
the *manége ;* I have no objection to that, it takes up a great
deal of the morning, and if you have got a genteel and firm
seat on horseback, it is enough for you, now that tilts and tour-
naments are laid aside. I suppose you have hunted at Compiegne. The king's hunting there, I am told, is a fine sight.
The French manner of hunting is gentlemanlike ; ours is only
for bumpkins and boobies. The poor beasts here are pursued
and run down by much greater beasts than themselves ; and
the true British fox-hunter is most undoubtedly a species appropriated and peculiar to this country, which no other part of the
globe produces.

I hope you apply the time you have saved from the riding-
house to useful, more than to learned, purposes ; for I can assure

you they are very different things. I would have you allow
but one hour a day for Greek ; and that more to keep what you
have than to increase it : by Greek, I mean useful Greek books,
such as Demosthenes, Thucydides, &c., and not the poets, with
whom you are already enough acquainted. Your Latin will
take care of itself. Whatever more time you have for reading,
pray bestow it upon those books which are immediately relative
to your destination, such as modern history, in the modern languages; memoirs, anecdotes, letters, negotiations, &c. Collect
also, if you can, authentically, the present state of all the courts
and countries in Europe, the characters of the Kings and Princes,
their wives, their ministers, and their w—s ; their several
views, connections, and interests ; the state of their *finances*,
their military force, their trade, manufactures, and commerce.
That is the useful, the necessary, knowledge for you, and indeed
for every gentleman. But with all this, remember that living
books are much better than dead ones ; and throw away no
time (for it is thrown away) with the latter, which you can
employ well with the former ; for books must now be only your
amusement, but by no means your business. I had much
rather that you were passionately in love with some determined
coquette of condition (who would lead you a dance, fashion,
supple, and polish you) than that you knew all Plato and
Aristotle by heart : an hour at Versailles, Compiegne, or St
Cloud, is now worth more to you than three hours in your
closet, with the best books that ever were written.

I hear the dispute between the Court and the Clergy is
made up amicably ; both parties have yielded something ; the
King being afraid of losing more of his soul, and the Clergy
more of their revenue. Those gentlemen are very skilful in
making the most of the vices and the weaknesses of the laity.
I hope you have read and informed yourself fully of everything
relative to that affair ; it is a very important question, in which
the priesthood of every country in Europe is highly concerned.
If you would be thoroughly convinced that their tithes are of
divine institution, and their property the property of God himself, not to be touched by any power on earth, read Frà-Paolo
de beneficiis, an excellent and short book ; for which, and some
other treatises against the Court of Rome, he was stilettoed ;
which made him say afterwards, upon seeing an anonymous book
written against him, by order of the Pope, *Conosco bene lo stile
Romano*.

The Parliament of Paris, and the States of Languedoc, will,
I believe, hardly scramble off ; having only reason and justice,

but no terrors, on their side. Those are political and constitutional questions, that well deserve your attention and inquiries, I hope you are thoroughly master of them. It is also worth your while to collect and keep all the pieces written upon those subjects.

I hope you have been thanked by your ladies, at least, if not paid in money, for the mohairs, which I sent by a courier to Paris some time ago, instead of sending them to Madame Morel at Calais, as I told you I should. Do they like them; and do they like you the better for getting them? *La petite Blot devroit au moins payer de sa personne.* As for Madame de Polignac, I believe you will very willingly hold her excused from personal payment.

Before you return to England, pray go again to Orli for two or three days, and also to St Cloud, in order to secure a good reception there at your return. Ask the Marquis de Matignon, too, if he has any orders for you in England, or any letters or packets for Lord Bolingbroke. Adieu! Go on and prosper.

LETTER CCXXXI.

My dear Friend,   Greenwich, July the 8th, O. S. 1751.

The last mail brought me your letter of the 3rd July, N. S. I am glad that you are so well with Colonel Yorke as to be let into secret correspondences. Lord Albemarle's reserve to you is, I believe, more owing to his secretary than to himself, for you seem to be much in favour with him; and possibly, too, *he has no very secret letters* to communicate. However, take care not to discover the least dissatisfaction upon this score : make the proper acknowledgments to Colonel Yorke, for what he does show you; but let neither Lord Albemarle nor his people perceive the least coldness on your part, upon account of what they do not show you. It is very often necessary not to manifest all one feels. Make your court to, and connect yourself as much as possible with, Colonel Yorke, he may be of great use to you hereafter; and when you take leave, not only offer to bring over any letters or packets, by way of security, but even ask, as a favour, to be the carrier of a letter from him to his father the Chancellor. *A propos* of your coming here; I confess that I am weekly impatient for it, and think a few days worth getting; I would therefore, instead of the 25th of next month, N. S., which was the day that some time ago I appointed for your leaving Paris, have you set out on Friday the 20th August, N. S. ; in consequence of which you will be at Calais some time on the Sunday following, and probably at Dover within four-and-twenty hours afterwards.   If you land in the morning, you may in a postchaise get to Sittingborne that day ; if you come on shore in the evening, you can only get to Canterbury, where you will be better lodged than at Dover.   I will not have you travel in the night, nor fatigue and overheat yourself, by running on fourscore miles the moment you land.   You will come straight to Blackheath, where I shall be ready to meet you, and which is directly upon the Dover road to London ; and we will go to town together, after you have rested yourself a day or two here.   All the other directions, which I gave you in my former letter, hold still the same.   But, notwithstanding this regulation, should you have any particular reasons for leaving Paris two or three days sooner, or later, than the above mentioned, *vous êtes le maître*.   Make all your *arrangemens* at Paris for about a six weeks' stay in England, at the furthest.

I had a letter the other day from Lord Huntingdon, of which one half at least was your panegyric : it was extremely welcome to me from so good a hand.   Cultivate that friendship : it will do you honour, and give you strength.   Connections in our mixed parliamentary government are of great use.

I send you here enclosed the particular price of each of the mohairs ; but I do not suppose that you will receive a shilling for any one of them.   However, if any of your ladies should take an odd fancy to pay, the shortest way, in the course of business, is for you to keep the money, and to take so much less from Sir John Lambert, in your next draught upon him.

I am very sorry to hear that Lady Hervey is ill.   Paris does not seem to agree with her ; she used to have great health here.   *A propos* of her ; remember, when you are with me, not to mention her but when you and I are quite alone, for reasons which I will tell you when we meet : but this is only between you and me, and I desire that you will not so much as hint it to her, or anybody else.

If old Kursay goes to the Valley of Jehosaphat, I cannot help it ; it will be an ease to our friend Madame Monconseil, who I believe maintains her, and a little will not satisfy her in any way.

Remember to bring your mother some little presents ; they need not be of value, but only marks of your affection and duty for one who has always been tenderly fond of you.   You may bring Lady Chesterfield a little Martin snuffbox, of about five louis : and you need bring over no other presents ; you and I not wanting *les petits présens pour entretenir l'amitié.*[1]

Since I wrote what goes before, I have talked you over minutely with Lord Albemarle ; who told me that he could very sincerely commend you upon every article but one ; but upon that one you were often joked, both by him and others. I desired to know what that was ; he laughed, and told me it was the article of dress, in which you were exceedingly negligent. Though he laughed, I can assure you that it is no laughing matter for you ; and you will possibly be surprised when I assert (but, upon my word, it is literally true), that to be very well dressed is of much more importance to you than all the Greek you know will be of these thirty years. Remember, the world is now your only business ; and you must adopt its customs and manners, be they silly or be they not. To neglect your dress is an affront to all the women you keep company with ; as it implies, that you do not think them worth that attention which everybody else doth ; they mind dress, and you will never please them if you neglect yours ; and if you do not please the women, you will not please half the men you otherwise might. It is the women who put a young fellow in fashion, even with the men. A young fellow ought to have a certain fund of coquetry, which should make him try all the means of pleasing, as much as any coquette in Europe can do. Old as I am, and little thinking of women, God knows I am very far from being negligent of my dress ; and why ? From conformity to custom ; and out of decency to men, who expect that degree of complaisance. I do not, indeed, wear feathers and red heels, which would ill suit my age ; but I take care to have my clothes well made, my wig well combed and powdered, my linen and person extremely clean. I even allow my footmen forty shillings a year extraordinary, that they may be spruce and neat. Your figure especially, which from its stature cannot be very majestic and interesting, should be the more attended to in point of dress : as it cannot be *imposante*, it should be *gentille, aimable, bien mise.* It will not admit of negligence and carelessness.

I believe Mr Hayes thinks you have slighted him a little of late, since you have got into so much other company. I do not, by any means, blame you for not frequenting his house so much as you did at first, before you had got into so many other houses, more entertaining and more instructing than his : on the contrary, you do very well ; however, as he was ex-

[1] Little presents for keeping up friendship.

tremely civil to you, take care to be so to him, and make up in manner, what you omit in matter. See him, dine with him, before you come away, and ask his commands for England.

Your triangular seal is done, and I have given it to an English gentleman, who sets out in a week for Paris, and who will deliver it to Sir John Lambert for you.

I cannot conclude this letter, without returning again to the showish, the ornamental, the shining parts of your character; which if you neglect, upon my word, you will render the solid ones absolutely useless : nay, such is the present turn of the world, that some valuable qualities are even ridiculous, if not accompanied by the genteeler accomplishments. Plainness, simplicity, and Quakerism, either in dress or manners, will by no means do ; they must both be laced and embroidered : speaking or writing sense, without elegancy and turn, will be very little persuasive ; and the best figure in the world, without air and address, will be very ineffectual. Some pedants may have told you that sound sense, and learning, stand in need of no ornaments ; and to support that assertion, elegantly quote the vulgar proverb, that *good wine needs no bush ;* but surely the little experience you have already had of the world must have convinced you that the contrary of that assertion is true. All those accomplishments are now in your power ; think of them, and of them only. I hope you frequent La Foire St Laurent, which I see is now open : you will improve more by going there with your mistress than by staying at home and reading Euclid with your geometry master. Adieu. *Divertissez vous, il n'y a rien de tel.*[1]

LETTER CCXXXII.

MY DEAR FRIEND,   Greenwich, July the 15th, O. S. 1751.

As this is the last, or the last letter but one, that I think I shall write before I have the pleasure of seeing you here, it may not be amiss to prepare you a little for our interview, and for the time we shall pass together. Before Kings and Princes meet, Ministers on each side adjust the important points of precedence, arm-chairs, right hand and left, &c., so that they know previously what they are to expect, what they have to trust to : and it is right they should ; for they commonly envy or hate, but most certainly distrust, each other. We shall meet upon

---
[1] Amuse yourself, there is nothing like it.

very different terms; we want no such preliminaries: you know my tenderness, I know your affection. My only object, therefore, is to make your short stay with me as useful as I can to you; and yours, I hope, is to coöperate with me. Whether, by making it wholesome, I shall make it pleasant to you, I am not sure. Emetics and cathartics I shall not administer, because I am sure you do not want them; but for alteratives you must expect a great many; and I can tell you that I have a number of *nostrums*, which I shall communicate to nobody but yourself. To speak without a metaphor, I shall endeavour to assist your youth with all the experience that I have purchased, at the price of seven-and-fifty years. In order to this, frequent re-proofs, corrections, and admonitions will be necessary; but then, I promise you, that they shall be in a gentle, friendly, and secret manner; they shall not put you out of countenance in company, nor out of humour when we are alone. I do not expect that, at nineteen, you should have that knowledge of the world, those manners, that dexterity, which few people have at nine-and-twenty. But I will endeavour to give them you; and I am sure you will endeavour to learn them, as far as your youth, my experience, and the time we shall pass together, will allow. You may have many inaccuracies (and to be sure you have, for who has not at your age), which few people will tell you of, and some nobody can tell you of but myself. You may possibly have others, too, which eyes less interested, and less vigilant than mine, do not discover: all those you shall hear of, from one, whose tenderness for you will excite his curiosity, and sharpen his penetration. The smallest in-attention, or error in manners, the minutest inelegance of diction, the least awkwardness in your dress and carriage, will not escape my observation, nor pass without amicable correction. Two the most intimate friends in the world can freely tell each other their faults, and even their crimes; but cannot possibly tell each other of certain little weaknesses, awkwardnesses, and blindnesses of self-love; to authorize that unreserved freedom, the relation between us is absolutely necessary. For example; I had a very worthy friend, with whom I was intimate enough to tell him his faults; he had but few; I told him of them, he took it kindly of me, and corrected them. But, then, he had some weaknesses that I could never tell him of directly, and which he was so little sensible of himself, that hints of them were lost upon him. He had a scrag neck, of about a yard long; notwithstanding which, bags being in fashion, truly he would wear one to his wig, and did so; but never behind him, for, upon every motion of his head, his bag came forwards over one shoulder or the other. He took it into his head, too, that he must occasionally dance minuets, because other people did; and he did so, not only extremely ill, but so awkward, so disjointed, so slim, so meagre, was his figure, that had he danced as well as ever Marcel did it would have been ridiculous in him to have danced at all. I hinted these things to him as plainly as friendship would allow, and to no purpose; but to have told him the whole, so as to cure him, I must have been his father, which, thank God, I am not. As fathers commonly go, it is seldom a misfortune to be fatherless; and, considering the general run of sons, as seldom a misfortune to be childless. You and I form, I believe, an exception to that rule; for I am persuaded that we would neither of us change our relation, were it in our power. You will, I both hope and believe, be not only the comfort, but the pride, of my age; and I am sure I will be the support, the friend, the guide of your youth. Trust me without reserve; I will advise you without private interest, or secret envy. Mr Harte will do so too; but still there may be some little things proper for you to know, and necessary for you to correct, which even his friendship would not let him tell you of so freely as I should; and some of which he may possibly not be so good a judge of as I am, not having lived so much in the great world.

One principal topic of our conversation will be not only the purity but the elegancy of the English language, in both which you are very deficient. Another will be the constitution of this country, which, I believe, you know less of than of most other countries in Europe. Manners, attentions, and address, will also be the frequent subjects of our lectures; and whatever I know of that important and necessary art, the art of pleasing, I will unreservedly communicate to you. Dress, too, (which, as things are, I can logically prove requires some attention,) will not always escape our notice. Thus my lectures will be more various, and in some respects more useful, than Professor Mascow's; and therefore I can tell you that I expect to be paid for them: but, as possibly you would not care to part with your ready money, and as I do not think that it would be quite handsome in me to accept it, I will compound for the payment, and take it in attention and practice. · · : ·

Pray remember to part with all your friends, acquaintances, and mistresses, if you have any at Paris, in such a manner, as may make them not only willing, but impatient, to see you there again. Assure them of your desire of returning to them; and do it in a manner, that they may think you in earnest, that is, *avec onction et une espèce d'attendrissement.* All people say pretty near the same things upon those occasions, it is the manner only that makes the difference ; and that difference is great. Avoid, however, as much as you can, charging yourself with commissions, in your return from hence to Paris : I know, by experience, that they are exceedingly troublesome, commonly expensive, and very seldom satisfactory at last to the persons who give them : some you cannot refuse, to people to whom you are obliged, and would oblige in your turn ; but as to common fiddle-faddle commissions, you may excuse yourself from them with truth, by saying that you are to return to Paris through Flanders, and see all those great towns, which I intend you shall do, and stay a week or ten days at Brussels. Adieu ! A good journey to you, if this is my last ; if not, I can repeat again what I shall wish constantly.

LETTER CCXXXIII.

My dear Friend, London, Dec. the 19th, O. S. 1751.

You are now entered upon a scene of business, where I hope you will one day make a figure. Use does a great deal, but care and attention must be joined to it. The first thing necessary in writing letters of business, is extreme clearness and perspicuity ; every paragraph should be so clear, and unambiguous, that the dullest fellow in the world may not be able to mistake it, nor obliged to read it twice in order to understand it. This necessary clearness implies a correctness, without excluding an elegancy of style. Tropes, figures, antitheses, epigrams, &c., would be as misplaced, and as impertinent, in letters of business, as they are sometimes (if judiciously used) proper and pleasing in familiar letters, upon common and trite subjects. In business, an elegant simplicity, the result of care not of labour, is required. Business must be well, not affectedly, dressed, but by no means negligently. Let your first attention be to clearness, and read every paragraph after you have written it, in the critical view of discovering whether it is possible that any one man can mistake the true sense of it ; and correct it accordingly.

Our pronouns and relatives often create obscurity or ambiguity ; be therefore exceedingly attentive to them, and take care to mark out with precision their particular relations. For example; Mr Johnson acquainted me, that he had seen Mr Smith, who had promised him to speak to Mr Clarke, to return him (Mr Johnson) those papers, which he (Mr Smith) had left some time ago with him (Mr Clarke): it is better to repeat a name, though unnecessarily, ten times, than to have the person mistaken once. *Who*, you know, is singly relative to persons, and cannot be applied to things; *which*, and *that*, are chiefly relative to things, but not absolutely exclusive of persons; for one may say, the man *that* robbed or killed such-a-one; but it is much better to say, the man *who* robbed or killed. One never says, the man or the woman *which*. *Which* and *that*, though chiefly relative to things, cannot be always used indifferently as to things; and the ευφονια must sometimes determine their place. For instance; The letter *which* I received from you, *which* you referred to in your last, *which* came by Lord Albemarle's messenger, and *which* I showed to such-a-one; I would change it thus—The letter *that* I received from you, *which* you referred to in your last, *that* came by Lord Albemarle's messenger, and *which* I showed to such-a-one.

Business does not exclude (as possibly you wish it did) the usual terms of politeness and good breeding; but, on the contrary, strictly requires them: such as, *I have the honour to acquaint your Lordship; Permit me to assure you; If I may be allowed to give my opinion, &c.* For the Minister abroad, who writes to the Minister at home, writes to his superior; possibly to his patron, or at least to one who he desires should be so.

Letters of business will not only admit of, but be the better for, *certain graces :* but then they must be scattered with a sparing and a skilful hand; they must fit their place exactly. They must decently adorn without encumbering, and modestly shine without glaring. But as this is the utmost degree of perfection in letters of business, I would not advise you to attempt those embellishments till you have first laid your foundation well.

Cardinal d'Ossat's letters are the true letters of business; those of Monsieur d'Avaux are excellent; Sir William Temple's are very pleasing, but, I fear, too affected. Carefully avoid all Greek or Latin quotations: and bring no precedents from the *virtuous Spartans, the polite Athenians, and the brave Romans.* Leave all that to futile pedants. No flourishes, no declamation. But (I repeat it again) there is an elegant simplicity and dignity of style absolutely necessary for good letters of business; attend to that carefully. Let your periods be harmonious, without seeming to be laboured; and let them not be too long, for that always occasions a degree of obscurity. I should not mention correct orthography, but that you very often fail in that particular, which will bring ridicule upon you ; for no man is allowed to spell ill. I wish, too, that your handwriting were much better : and I cannot conceive why it is not, since every man may certainly write whatever hand he pleases. Neatness in folding up, sealing, and directing your packets, is by no means to be neglected, though I dare say you think it is. But there is something in the exterior, even of a packet, that may please or displease; and consequently worth some attention.

You say that your time is very well employed, and so it is, though as yet only in the outlines and first *routine* of business. They are previously necessary to be known ; they smooth the way for parts and dexterity. Business requires no conjuration nor supernatural talents, as people unacquainted with it are apt to think. Method, diligence, and discretion will carry a man of good strong common sense much higher than the finest parts without them can do. *Par negotiis, neque supra*, is the true character of a man of business : but then it implies ready attention, and no *absences;* and a flexibility and versatility of attention from one object to another, without being engrossed by any one.

Be upon your guard against the pedantry and affectation of business, which young people are apt to fall into from the pride of being concerned in it young. They look thoughtful, complain of the weight of business, throw out mysterious hints, and seem big with secrets which they do not know. Do you, on the contrary, never talk of business, but to those with whom you are to transact it ; and learn to seem *vacuus,* and idle, when you have the most business. Of all things the *volto sciolto,* and the *pensieri stretti,* are necessary. Adieu.

LETTER CCXXXIV.

MY DEAR FRIEND,   London, Dec. the 30th, O. S. 1751.

THE Parliaments are the courts of justice of France, and are what our courts of justice in Westminster Hall are here. They used anciently to follow the Court, and administer justice in the presence of the King. Philip le Bel first fixed it at Paris, by an edict of 1302. It consisted then of but one *chambre,* which was called *La Chambre des Prélats,* most of the members being ecclesiastics ; but the multiplicity of business made it by degrees necessary to create several other *chambres :* it consists now of seven *chambres.*

La Grand Chambre, which is the highest court of justice, and to which appeals lie from the others.

Les cinq Chambres des Enquétes, which are like our Common Pleas, and Court of Exchequer.

La Tournelle, which is the Court for criminal justice, and answers to our Old Bailey and King's Bench.

There are in all twelve Parliaments in France :—1. Paris. 2. Toulouse. 3. Grenoble. 4. Bourdeaux. 5. Dijon. 6. Rouen. 7. Aix en Provence. 8. Rennes en Bretagne. 9. Pau en Navarre. 10. Metz. 11. Dole en Franche Comté. 12. Douay.

There are three *Conseils souverains*, which may almost be called Parliaments ; they are those of Perpignan, Arras, Alsace.

For further particulars of the French Parliaments, read *Bernard de la Rochefavin des Parlemens de France*, and other authors, who have treated that subject constitutionally. But what will be still better, converse upon it with people of sense and knowledge, who will inform you of the particular objects of the several *chambres*, and the businesses of the respective members, as, *les Présidens, les Présidens à Mortier* (these last so called from their black velvet caps laced with gold), *les Maîtres des Requétes, les Greffiers, le Procureur-Général, les Avocats Généraux, les Conseillers, &c.* The great point in dispute is, concerning the powers of the Parliament of Paris, in matters of state, and relatively to the Crown. They pretend to the powers of the States-General of France, when they used to be assembled (which, I think, they have not been since the reign of Lewis the XIIIth, in the year 1615). The Crown denies those pretensions, and considers them only as courts of justice. Mezeray seems to be on the side of the Parliament in this question, which is very well worth your inquiry. But be that as it will, the Parliament of Paris is certainly a very respectable body, and much regarded by the whole kingdom. The edicts of the Crown, especially those for levying money on the subjects, ought to be registered in Parliament ; I do not say to have their effect, for the Crown would take good care of that ; but to have a decent appearance, and to procure a willing acquiescence in the nation. And the Crown itself, absolute as it is, does not love that strong opposition, and those admirable remonstrances, which it sometimes meets with from the Parliaments. Many of those detached pieces are very well worth your collecting ; and I remember, a year or two ago, a remonstrance of the Parliament of Douay, upon the subject, as I think, of the *vingtième*, which was, in my mind, one of the finest and most moving compositions I ever read. They owned themselves, indeed, to be slaves, and showed their chains ; but humbly begged of his Majesty to make them a little lighter and less galling.

The *States of France* were general assemblies of the three states or orders of the kingdom ; the Clergy, the Nobility, and the *Tiers Etat*, that is, the people. They used to be called together by the King, upon the most important affairs of state, like our Lords and Commons in parliament, and our Clergy in convocation. Our Parliament is our States, and the French Parliaments are only their courts of justice. The nobility consisted of all those of noble extraction, whether belonging to the *sword*, or to the *robe* ; excepting such as were chosen (which sometimes happened) by the *tiers état*, as their deputies to the States-General. The *tiers état* was exactly our House of Commons, that is, the people represented by deputies of their own choosing. Those who had the most considerable places, *dans la robe*, assisted at those assemblies, as commissioners on the part of the Crown. The States met, for the first time that I can find (I mean by the name of *les états*), in the reign of Pharamond, 424, when they confirmed the Salic law. From that time they have been very frequently assembled, sometimes upon important occasions, as making war and peace, reforming abuses, &c. ; at other times, upon seemingly trifling ones, as coronations, marriages, &c. Francis the First assembled them, in 1526, to declare null and void his famous treaty of Madrid, signed and sworn to by him during his captivity there. They grew troublesome to the Kings and to their Ministers, and were but seldom called, after the power of the Crown grew strong ; and they have never been heard of since the year 1615. Richelieu came and shackled the nation, and Mazarin and Lewis the XIVth riveted the shackles.

There still subsist in some provinces in France, which are called *pays d'états*, an humble local imitation, or rather mimicry, of the great *états*, as in *Languedoc, Bretagne, &c.* They meet, they speak, they grumble, and finally submit to whatever the King orders.

Independently of the intrinsic utility of this kind of knowledge to every man of business, it is a shame for any man to be ignorant of it, especially relatively to any country he has been long in. Adieu.

LETTER CCXXXV.

MY DEAR FRIEND,   London, Jan. the 2nd, O. S. 1752.

LAZINESS of mind, or inattention, are as great enemies to knowledge as incapacity ; for, in truth, what difference is there between a man who will not, and a man who cannot, be informed ? This difference only, that the former is justly to be blamed, and the latter to be pitied. And yet how many are there, very capable of receiving knowledge, who from laziness, inattention, and incuriousness, will not so much as ask for it, much less take the least pains to acquire it.

Our young English travellers generally distinguish themselves by a voluntary privation of all that useful knowledge for which they are sent abroad; and yet at that age the most useful knowledge is the most easy to be acquired ; conversation being the book, and the best book, in which it is contained. The drudgery of dry grammatical learning is over, and the fruits of it are mixed with and adorned by the flowers of conversation. How many of our young men have been a year at Rome, and as long at Paris, without knowing the meaning and institution of the Conclave in the former, and of the Parliament in the latter ! and this merely for want of asking the first people they met with in those several places, who could at least have given them some general notions of those matters.

You will, I hope, be wiser, and omit no opportunity (for opportunities present themselves every hour in the day) of acquainting yourself with all those political and constitutional particulars of the kingdom and government of France. For instance ; when you hear people mention *le Chancelier*, or *le Garde des Sceaux*, is it any great trouble for you to ask, or for others to tell you, what is the nature, the powers, the objects, and the profits, of those two employments, either when joined together, as they often are, or when separate, as they are at present ? When you hear of a *Gouverneur*, a *Lieutenant de Roi*, a *Commandant*, and an *Intendant* of the same province, is it not natural, is it not becoming, is it not necessary, for a stranger to inquire into their respective rights and privileges? And yet I dare say there are very few Englishmen, who know the difference between the civil department of the Intendant, and the military powers of the others. When you hear (as I am persuaded you must) every day of the *Vingtième*, which is one in twenty, and consequently five *per cent.*, inquire upon what that tax is laid, whether upon lands, money, merchandise, or upon all three ; how levied ;

and what it is supposed to produce. When you find in books (as you will sometimes) allusion to particular laws and customs, do not rest till you have traced them up to their *source*. To give you two examples ; you will meet in some French comedies, *Cri*, or, *Clameur de Haro ;* ask what it means, and you will be told that it is a term of the law in Normandy, and means citing, arresting, or obliging any person to appear in the courts of justice, either upon a civil or a criminal account ; and that it is derived from *à Raoul*, which Raoul was anciently Duke of Normandy, and a Prince eminent for his justice ; insomuch, that when any injustice was committed, the cry immediately was *venez à Raoul, à Raoul ;* which words are now corrupted and jumbled into *haro*. Another, *Le vol du Chapon*, that is, a certain district of ground immediately contiguous to the mansion seat of a family, and answers to what we call in English *demesnes*. It is in France computed at about sixteen hundred feet round the house, that being supposed to be the extent of the capon's flight from *la basse cour*. This little district must go along with the mansion seat, however the rest of the estate may be divided.

I do not mean that you should be a French lawyer ; but I would not have you be unacquainted with the general principles of their law, in matters that occur every day. Such is the nature of their descents, that is, the inheritance of lands : Do they all go to the eldest son, or are they equally divided among the children of the deceased ? In England, all lands unsettled descend to the eldest son, as heir at law, unless otherwise disposed of by the father's will : except in the county of Kent ; where a particular custom prevails, called Gavel-Kind ; by which, if the father dies intestate, all his children divide his lands equally among them. In Germany, as you know, all lands that are not fiefs are equally divided among all the children, which ruins those families ; but all male fiefs of the empire descend unalienably to the next male heir, which preserves those families. In France, I believe, descents vary in different provinces.

The nature of marriage contracts deserves inquiry. In England the general practice is, the husband takes all the wife's fortune ; and, in consideration of it, settles upon her a proper pin money, as it is called ; that is, an annuity during his life, and a jointure after his death. In France, it is not so, particularly at Paris ; where *la communauté des biens* is established. Any married woman at Paris *(if you are acquainted with one)* can inform you of all these particulars.

These, and other things of the same nature, are the useful

and rational objects of the curiosity of a man of sense and business. Could they only be attained by laborious researches in folio books and worm-eaten manuscripts, I should not wonder at a young fellow's being ignorant of them; but as they are the frequent topics of conversation, and to be known by a very little degree of curiosity, inquiry, and attention, it is unpardonable not to know them.

Thus I have given you some hints only for your inquiries; *l'Etat de la France, L'Almanach Royal*, and twenty other such superficial books, will furnish you with a thousand more. *Approfondissez.*

How often, and how justly, have I since regretted negligences of this kind in my youth! And how often have I since been at great trouble to learn many things, which I could then have learned without any! Save yourself now, then, I beg of you, that regret and trouble hereafter. Ask questions, and many questions; and leave nothing till you are thoroughly informed of it. Such pertinent questions are far from being illbred, or troublesome to those of whom you ask them; on the contrary, they are a tacit compliment to their knowledge; and people have a better opinion of a young man, when they see him desirous to be informed.

I have, by last post, received your two letters of the 1st and 5th January, N. S. I am very glad that you have been at all the shows at Versailles: frequent the Courts. I can conceive the murmurs of the French at the poorness of the fireworks, by which they thought their King or their country degraded; and, in truth, were things always as they should be, when Kings give shows, they ought to be magnificent.

I thank you for the *Thèse de la Sorbonne*, which you intend to send me, and which I am impatient to receive. But pray read it carefully yourself first; and inform yourself what the Sorbonne is, by whom founded, and for what purposes.

Since you have time, you have done very well to take an Italian and a German master; but pray take care to leave yourself time enough for company; for it is in company only that you can learn what will be much more useful to you than either Italian or German; I mean *la politesse, les manières, et les grâces,* without which, as I told you long ago, and I told you true, *ogni fatica è vana.* Adieu.

Pray make my compliments to Lady Brown.

LETTER CCXXXVI.

My dear Friend,   London, Jan. the 6th, O. S. 1752.

I RECOMMENDED to you, in my last, some inquiries into the constitution of that famous society the *Sorbonne ;* but as I cannot wholly trust to the diligence of those inquiries, I will give you here the outlines of that establishment ; which may possibly excite you to inform yourself of particulars, that you are more *à portée* to know than I am.

It was founded by Robert *de Sorbon,* in the year 1256, for sixteen poor scholars in divinity ; four of each nation, of the university of which it made a part ; since that it hath been much extended and enriched, especially by the liberality and pride of Cardinal Richelieu; who made it a magnificent building, for six-and-thirty doctors of that society to live in ; besides which, there are six professors and schools for divinity. This society hath been long famous for theological knowledge and exercitations. There unintelligible points are debated with passion, though they can never be determined by reason. Logical subtleties set common sens? at defiance ; and mystical refinements disfigure and disguise the native beauty and simplicity of true natural religion ; wild imaginations form systems, which weak minds adopt implicitly, and which sense and reason oppose in vain ; their voice is not strong enough to be heard in schools of divinity. Political views are by no means neglected in those sacred places ; and questions are agitated and decided, according to the degree of regard, or rather submission, which the Sovereign is pleased to show the Church. Is the King a slave to the Church, though a tyrant to the laity? the least resistance to his will shall be declared damnable. But if he will not acknowledge the superiority of their spiritual, over his temporal, nor even admit their *imperium in imperio,* which is the least they will compound for, it becomes meritorious, not only to resist, but to depose him. And I suppose, that the bold propositions in the Thesis you mention, are a return for the valuation of *les biens du Clergé.*

I would advise you, by all means, to attend two or three of their public disputations, in order to be informed both of the manner and the substance of those scholastic exercises. Pray remember to go to all such kind of things. Do not put it off, as one is too apt to do things which one knows can be done every day, or any day ; for one afterwards repents extremely, when too late, the not having done them.

But there is another (so called) religious society, of which the minutest circumstance deserves attention, and furnishes great matter for useful reflections. You easily guess that I mean the society of *les R. R. P. P. Jésuites*, established but in the year 1540, by a Bull of Pope Paul III. Its progress, and I may say its victories, were more rapid than those of the Romans; for within the same century it governed all Europe; and in the next it extended its influence over the whole world. Its founder was an abandoned profligate Spanish officer, Ignatius Loyola; who in the year 1521, being wounded in the leg at the siege of Pampelona, went mad from the smart of his wound, the reproaches of his conscience, and his confinement, during which he read the Lives of the Saints. Consciousness of guilt, a fiery temper, and a wild imagination, the common ingredients of enthusiasm, made this madman devote himself to the particular service of the Virgin Mary; whose knight-errant he declared himself, in the very same form in which the old knights-errant in romances used to declare themselves the knights and champions of certain beautiful and incomparable princesses, whom sometimes they had, but oftener had not, seen. For Dulcinea del Toboso was by no means the first Princess, whom her faithful and valorous knight had never seen in his life. The enthusiast went to the Holy Land, from whence he returned to Spain, where he began to learn Latin and Philosophy at three-and-thirty years old, so that no doubt but he made a great progress in both. The better to carry on his mad and wicked designs, he chose four Disciples, or rather Apostles, all Spaniards, *viz.* Laynés, Salmeron, Bobadilla, and Rodriguèz. He then composed the rules and constitutions of his Order; which, in the year 1547, was called the Order of Jesuits, from the church of Jesus in Rome, which was given them. Ignatius died in 1556, aged sixty-five, thirty-five years after his conversion, and sixteen years after the establishment of his society. He was canonized in the year 1609, and is doubtless now a saint in heaven.

If the religious and moral principles of this society are to be detested, as they justly are, the wisdom of their political principles is as justly to be admired. Suspected, collectively as an Order, of the greatest crimes, and convicted of many, they have either escaped punishment, or triumphed after it; as in France, in the reign of Henry IV. They have, directly or indirectly, governed the consciences and the councils of all the Catholic Princes in Europe: they almost governed China, in the reign of Cang-ghi; and they are now actually in possession of the Paraguay in America, pretending, but paying no obedience to the Crown of Spain. As a collective body they are detested even by all the Catholics, not excepting the clergy, both secular and regular ; and yet, as individuals, they are loved, respected ; and they govern wherever they are.

Two things, I believe, chiefly contribute to their success. The first, that passive, implicit, unlimited obedience to their General (who always resides at Rome), and to the Superiors of their several houses, appointed by him. This obedience is observed by them all, to a most astonishing degree ; and, I believe, there is no one society in the world, of which so many individuals sacrifice their private interest to the general one of the society itself. The second is, the education of youth, which they have in a manner engrossed ; there they give the first, and the first are the lasting impressions : those impressions are always calculated to be favourable to the society. I have known many Catholics, educated by the Jesuits, who, though they detested the society, from reason and knowledge, have always remained attached to it, from habit and prejudice. The Jesuits know, better than any set of people in the world, the importance of the art of pleasing, and study it more : they become all things to all men, in order to gain, not a few, but many. In Asia, Africa, and America, they become more than half Pagans, in order to convert the Pagans to be less than half Christians. In private families they begin by insinuating themselves as friends, they grow to be favourites, and they end *directors*. Their manners are not like those of any other Regulars in the world, but gentle, polite, and engaging. They are all carefully bred up to that particular destination, to which they seem to have a natural turn ; for which reason one sees most Jesuits excel in some particular thing. They even breed up some for martyrdom, in case of need ; as the Superior of a Jesuit seminary at Rome told Lord Bolingbroke. *Et abbiamo anche martiri per il martirio, se bisogna.*[1]

Inform yourself minutely of everything concerning this extraordinary establishment : go into their houses, get acquainted with individuals, hear some of them preach. The finest preacher I ever heard in my life is le Père Neufville, who, I believe, preaches still at Paris, and is so much in the best company, that you may easily get personally acquainted with him.

If you would know their *morale*, read Paschal's *Lettres Provinciales*, in which it is very truly displayed from their own writings.

Upon the whole, this is certain, that a society, of which so

[1] We have also martyrs for martyrdom if necessary.

little good is said, and so much ill believed, and that still not only subsists, but flourishes, must be a very able one. It is always mentioned as a proof of the superior abilities of the Cardinal Richelieu, that, though hated by all the nation, and still more by his master, he kept his power in spite of both.

I would earnestly wish you to do everything now, which I wish that I had done at your age, and did not do. Every country has its peculiarities, which one can be much better informed of during one's residence there, than by reading all the books in the world afterwards. While you are in Catholic countries, inform yourself of all the forms and ceremonies of that tawdry church : see their convents both of men and women, know their several rules and orders, attend their most remarkable ceremonies ; have their terms of art explained to you, their *tierce, sexte, nones, matines, vêpres, complies ; their breviaires, rosaires, heures, chapelets, agnus, &c.*, things that many people talk of from habit, though few know the true meaning of any one of them. Converse with and study the characters of some of those incarcerated enthusiasts. Frequent some *parloirs*, and see the air and manners of those Recluse, who are a distinct nation themselves, and like no other.

I dined yesterday with Mrs F———d, her mother, and husband. He is an athletic Hibernian, handsome in his person, but excessively awkward and vulgar in his air and manner. She inquired much after you, and, I thought, with interest. I answered her as a *Mezzano* should do. *Et je prônai votre tendresse, vos soins, et vos soupirs.*[1]

When you meet with any British returning to their own country, pray send me by them any little *brochûres, factums, thèses, &c., qui font du bruit ou du plaisir à Paris* [2] Adieu, child.

LETTER CCXXXVII.

MY DEAR FRIEND,   London, January the 23rd, O. S. 1752.

HAVE you seen the new tragedy of *Varon*, and what do you think of it ? Let me know, for I am determined to form my taste upon yours. I hear that the situations and incidents are well brought on, and the catastrophe unexpected and surprising, but the verses bad. I suppose it is the subject of all the conversations at Paris, where both men and women are judges

---

[1] And I cried up your tenderness, your anxiety, and your sighs.
[2] Which make a stir or give pleasure at Paris.

and critics of all such performances; such conversations, that both form and improve the taste and whet the judgment, are surely preferable to the conversations of our mixed companies here; which, if they happen to rise above bragg and whist, infallibly stop short of everything either pleasing or instructive. I take the reason of this to be, that (as women generally give the tone to the conversation) our English women are not near so well informed and cultivated as the French; besides that they are naturally more serious and silent.

I could wish there were a treaty made between the French and the English theatres, in which both parties should make considerable concessions. The English ought to give up their notorious violations of all the unities; and all their massacres, racks, dead bodies, and mangled carcasses, which they so frequently exhibit upon their stage. The French should engage to have more action, and less declamation; and not to cram and crowd things together, to almost a degree of impossibility, from a too scrupulous adherence to the unities. The English should restrain the licentiousness of their poets, and the French enlarge the liberty of theirs: their poets are the greatest slaves in their country, and that is a bold word; ours are the most tumultuous subjects in England, and that is saying a good deal. Under such regulations, one might hope to see a play, in which one should not be lulled to sleep by the length of a monotonical declamation, nor frightened and shocked by the barbarity of the action. The unity of time extended occasionally to three or four days, and the unity of place broke into, as far as the same street, or sometimes the same town; both which, I will affirm, are as probable, as four-and-twenty hours, and the same room.

More indulgence too, in my mind, should be shown, than the French are willing to allow, to bright thoughts, and to shining images; for though I confess it is not very natural for a Hero or a Princess to say fine things, in all the violence of grief, love, rage, &c., yet I can as well suppose that, as I can that they should talk to themselves for half an hour; which they must necessarily do, or no tragedy could be carried on, unless they had recourse to a much greater absurdity, the choruses of the ancients. Tragedy is of a nature, that one must see it with a degree of self-deception; we must lend ourselves, a little, to the delusion; and I am very willing to carry that complaisance a little farther than the French do.

Tragedy must be something bigger than life, or it would not affect us. In nature the most violent passions are silent;

in Tragedy they must speak, and speak with dignity too. Hence the necessity of their being written in verse, and, unfortunately for the French, from the weakness of their language, in rhymes. And for the same reason, Cato, the Stoic, expiring at Utica, rhymes masculine and feminine, at Paris; and fetches his last breath at London, in most harmonious and correct blank verse.

It is quite otherwise with Comedy, which should be mere common life, and not one jot bigger. Every character should speak upon the stage, not only what it would utter in the situation there represented, but in the same manner in which it would express it. For which reason I cannot allow rhymes in Comedy, unless they were put into the mouth, and came out of the mouth, of a mad poet. But it is impossible to deceive one's self enough (nor is it the least necessary in Comedy) to suppose a dull rogue of a usurer cheating, or *gros Jean* blundering, in the finest rhymes in the world.

As for Operas, they are essentially too absurd and extravagant to mention : I look upon them as a magic scene, contrived to please the eyes and the ears at the expense of the understanding ; and I consider singing, rhyming, and chiming Heroes, and Princesses, and Philosophers, as I do the hills, the trees, the birds, and the beasts, who amicably joined in one common country dance, to the irresistible tune of Orpheus's lyre. Whenever I go to an Opera, I leave my sense and reason at the door with my half guinea, and deliver myself up to my eyes and my ears.

Thus I have made you my poetical confession ; in which I have acknowledged as many sins against the established taste in both countries, as a frank heretic could have owned against the established church in either ; but I am now privileged by my age to taste and think for myself ; and not to care what other people think of me in those respects ; an advantage which youth, among its many advantages, hath not. It must occasionally and outwardly conform, to a certain degree, to established tastes, fashions, and decisions. A young man may, with a becoming modesty, dissent, in private companies, from public opinions and prejudices : but he must not attack them with warmth, nor magisterially set up his own sentiments against them. Endeavour to hear and know all opinions ; receive them with complaisance ; form your own with coolness, and give it with modesty.

I have received a letter from Sir John Lambert, in which he requests me to use my interest to procure him the remittance of Mr Spencer's money when he goes abroad ; and also desires to know to whose account he is to place the postage of my letters. I do not trouble him with a letter in answer, since you can execute the commission. Pray make my compliments to him, and assure him that I will do all I can to procure him Mr Spencer's business ; but that his most effectual way will be by Messrs Hoare, who are Mr Spencer's cashiers, and who will, undoubtedly, have their choice whom they will give him his credit upon. As for the postage of the letters, your purse and mine being pretty near the same, do you pay it, over and above your next draught.

Your relations, the Princes B* * * * *, will soon be with you at Paris ; for they leave London this week : whenever you converse with them, I desire it may be in Italian ; that language not being yet familiar enough to you.

By our printed papers, there seems to be a sort of compromise between the King and the Parliament, with regard to the affairs of the hospitals, by taking them out of the hands of the Archbishop of Paris, and placing them in Monsieur d'Argenson's : if this be true, that compromise, as it is called, is clearly a victory on the side of the Court, and a defeat on the part of the Parliament; for if the Parliament had a right, they had it as much to the exclusion of Monsieur d'Argenson as of the Archbishop. Adieu.

LETTER CCXXXVIII.

MY DEAR FRIEND,   London, February the 6th, O. S. 1752.

YOUR criticism of *Varon* is strictly just; but, in truth, severe. You French critics seek for a fault as eagerly as I do for a beauty : you consider things in the worst light, to show your skill, at the expense of your pleasure ; I view them in the best, that I may have more pleasure, though at the expense of my judgment. *A trompeur trompeur et demi* is prettily said ; and if you please, you may call *Varon, un Normand,* and *Sostrate, un Mançeau, qui vaut un Normand et demi ;* and, considering the *dénouement,* in the light of trick upon trick, it would undoubtedly be below the dignity of the buskin, and fitter for the sock.

But let us see if we cannot bring off the author. The great question, upon which all turns, is to discover and ascertain who *Cleonice* really is. There are doubts concerning her *état;* how shall they be cleared ? Had the truth been extorted from *Varon*

(who alone knew) by the rack, it would have been a true tragi-
cal *dénouement.* But that would probably not have done with
Varon, who is represented as a bold, determined, wicked, and at
that time desperate fellow ; for he was in the hands of an enemy,
who he knew could not forgive him, with common prudence or
safety. The rack would therefore have extorted no truth from
him ; but he would have died enjoying the doubts of his
enemies, and the confusion that must necessarily attend those
doubts. A stratagem is therefore thought of, to discover what
force and terror could not, and the stratagem such as no King
or Minister would disdain to get at an important discovery. If
you call that stratagem *a trick,* you vilify it, and make it comi-
cal ; but call that trick a *stratagem,* or a *measure,* and you dignify it up to tragedy : so frequently do ridicule or dignity turn
upon one single word. It is commonly said, and more particularly by Lord Shaftesbury, that ridicule is the best test of
truth ; for that it will not stick where it is not just. I deny it.
A truth learned in a certain light, and attacked in certain words,
by men of wit and humour, may, and often doth, become ridiculous,
at least so far, that the truth is only remembered and repeated
for the sake of the ridicule. The overturn of Mary of Medicis
into a river, where she was half drowned, would never have
been remembered, if Madame de Vernueil, who saw it, had not
said *la Reine boit.* Pleasure or malignity often gives ridicule a
weight, which it does not deserve. The versification, I must
confess, is too much neglected, and too often bad : but, upon
the whole, I read the play with pleasure.

If there is but a great deal of wit and character in your
new comedy, I will readily compound for its having little or no
plot. I chiefly mind dialogue and character in comedies. Let
dull critics feed upon the carcasses of plays ; give me the taste
and the dressing.

I am very glad you went to Versailles to see the ceremony
of creating the Prince de Condé, *Chevalier de l'Ordre ;* and I do
not doubt but that, upon this occasion, you informed yourself
thoroughly of the institution and rules of that Order. If you
did, you were certainly told it was instituted by Henry III.,
immediately after his return, or rather his flight, from Poland ;
he took the hint of it at Venice ; where he had seen the original
manuscript of an Order of the *St Esprit, ou droit désir,* which
had been instituted in 1352, by Louis d'Anjou, King of Jerusa-
lem and Sicily, and husband to Jane, Queen of Naples, Countess of Provence. This Order was under the protection of St
Nicholas de Bari, whose image hung to the collar. Henry III.

found the Order of St Michael prostituted and degraded, during the civil wars ; he therefore joined it to his new Order of the St Esprit, and gave them both together; for which reason every knight of the St Esprit is now called *Chevalier des Ordres du Roi.* The number of the knights hath been different, but is now fixed to *one hundred*, exclusive of the sovereign. There are many officers who wear the ribbon of this Order, like the other knights ; and what is very singular is, that these officers frequently sell their employments, but obtain leave to wear the blue ribbon still, though the purchasers of those offices wear it also.

As you will have been a great while in France, people will expect that you should be *au fait*, of all these sort of things relative to that country. But the history of all the Orders of all countries is well worth your knowledge ; the subject occurs often, and one should not be ignorant[i] of it, for fear of some such accident as happened to a solid Dane at Paris, who, upon seeing *l'Ordre du St Esprit*, said, *Notre St Esprit chez nous c'est un Eléphant.* Almost all the Princes in Germany have their Orders too, not dated, indeed, from any important events, or directed to any great object, but because they will have Orders, to show that they may ; as some of them, who have the *jus cudendæ monetæ*,[1] borrow ten shillings' worth of gold to coin a ducat. However, wherever you meet with them, inform yourself, and minute down a short account of them : they take in all the colours of Sir Isaac Newton's prisms. N. B. When you inquire about them, do not seem to laugh.

I thank you for *le Mandement de Monseigneur l'Archevéque ;* it is very well drawn, and becoming an Archbishop. But pray do not lose sight of a much more important object, I mean the political disputes between the King and the Parliament and the King and the Clergy ; they seem both to be patching up ; however, get the whole clue to them, as far as they have gone.

I received a letter yesterday from Madame Moncouseil, who assures me you have gained ground *du coté des manières*, and that she looks upon you to be *plus qu'à moitié chemin.* I am very glad to hear this, because if you are got above half way of your journey, surely you will finish it, and not faint in the course. Why do you think I have this affair so extremely at heart, and why do I repeat it so often ? Is it for your sake, or for mine ? You can immediately answer yourself that question ; you certainly have, I cannot possibly have, any interest in it : if, then, you will allow me, as I believe you may, to be a judge

1 Right of coining.

of what is useful and necessary to you, you must, in consequence, be convinced of the infinite importance of a point, which I take so much pains to inculcate.

I hear that the new Duke of Orléans *a remercié Monsieur de Melfort*, and I believe, *pas sans raison*, having had obligations to him ; *mais il ne l'a pas remercié en mari poli*, but rather roughly. *Il faut que ce soit un bourru.* I am told, too, that people get bits of his father's rags, by way of relics ; I wish them joy, they will do them a great deal of good. See from hence what weaknesses human nature is capable of, and make allowances for such in all your plans and reasonings. Study the characters of the people you have to do with, and know what they are, instead of thinking them what they should be ; address yourself generally to the senses, to the heart, and to the weaknesses of mankind, but very rarely to their reason.

Good-night, or good-morrow, to you, according to the time you shall receive this letter. From yours.

LETTER CCXXXIX.

My dear Friend, London, February the 14th, O. S. 1752.

In a month's time, I believe, I shall have the pleasure of sending you, and you will have the pleasure of reading, a work of Lord Bolingbroke's, in two volumes octavo, *upon the use of History ;* in several Letters to Lord Hyde, then Lord Cornbury. It is now put into the press. It is hard to determine whether this work will instruct or please most : the most material historical facts, from the great æra of the treaty of Munster, are touched upon, accompanied by the most solid reflections, and adorned by all that elegancy of style, which was peculiar to himself, and in which, if Cicero equals, he certainly does not exceed him ; but every other writer falls short of him. I would advise you almost to get this book by heart. I think you have a turn to history, you love it, and have a memory to retain it ; this book will teach you the proper use of it. Some people load their memories, indiscriminately, with historical facts, as others do their stomachs with food ; and bring out the one, and bring up the other, entirely crude and undigested. You will find in Lord Bolingbroke's book, an infallible specific against that epidemical complaint.[1]

---

[1] We cannot but observe with pleasure, that at this time Lord Bolingbroke's Philosophical Works had not appeared, which accounts for Lord

I remember a gentleman, who had read History in this thoughtless and undistinguishing manner, and who, having travelled, had gone through the Valteline. He told me that it was a miserable, poor country, and therefore it was, surely, a great error in Cardinal Richelieu, to make such a rout, and put France to so much expense about it. Had my friend read History as he ought to have done, he would have known that the great object of that great Minister was to reduce the power of the house of Austria; and, in order to that, to cut off as much as he could the communication between the several parts of their then extensive dominions; which reflections would have justified the Cardinal to him in the affair of the Valteline. But it was easier to him to remember facts, than to combine and reflect.

One observation I hope you will make in reading History, for it is an obvious and a true one. It is, That more people have made great figures and great fortunes in Courts, by their exterior accomplishments, than by their interior qualifications. Their engaging address, the politeness of their manners, their air, their turn, hath almost alway paved the way for their superior abilities, if they have such to exert themselves. They have been Favourites before they have been Ministers. In courts a universal gentleness and *douceur dans les maniéres* is most absolutely necessary: an offended fool, or a slighted *valet de chambre*, may very possibly do you more hurt at Court, than ten men of merit can do you good. Fools, and low people, are always jealous of their dignity, and never forget nor forgive what they reckon a slight. On the other hand, they take civility, and a little attention, as a favour; remember, and acknowledge it: this, in my mind, is buying them cheap; and, therefore, they are worth buying. The Prince himself, who is rarely the shining genius of his Court, esteems you only by hearsay, but likes you by his senses; that is, from your air, your politeness, and your manner of addressing him; of which alone he is a judge. There is a Court garment, as well as a wedding garment, without which you will not be received. That garment is the *volto sciolto;* an imposing air, an elegant politeness, easy and engaging manners, universal attention, an insinuating gentleness, and all those *je ne sais quoi* that compose the *Grâces*.

I am this moment disagreeably interrupted by a letter; not from you, as I expected, but from a friend of yours at Paris, who informs me that you have a fever, which confines you at home.

Chesterfield's recommending to his Son, in this as well as in some foregoing passages, the study of Lord Bolingbroke's writings.

Since you have a fever, I am glad you have prudence enough with it, to stay at home, and take care of yourself; a little more prudence might probably have prevented it. Your blood is young, and consequently hot; and you naturally make a great deal, by your good stomach and good digestion ; you should therefore necessarily attenuate and cool it, from time to time, by gentle purges or by a very low diet, for two or three days together, if you would avoid fevers.—Lord Bacon, who was a very great physician, in both senses of the word, hath this aphorism in his Essay upon Health, *Nihil magis ad sanitatem tribuit quam crebræ et domesticæ purgationes.* [1] By *domesticæ*, he means those simple uncompounded purgatives, which everybody can administer to themselves ; such as senna-tea, stewed prunes and senna, chewing a little rhubarb or dissolving an ounce and a half of manna in fair water, with the juice of half a lemon to make it palatable. Such gentle and unconfining evacuations would certainly prevent those feverish attacks, to which everybody at your age is subject.

By the way, I do desire and insist, that whenever, from any indisposition, you are not able to write to me upon the fixed days, that Christian shall ; and give me a *true* account how you are. I do not expect from him the Ciceronian epistolary style ; but I will content myself with the Swiss simplicity and truth.

I hope you extend your acquaintance at Paris, and frequent variety of companies ; the only way of knowing the world : every set of company differs in some particulars from another ; and a man of business must, in the course of his life, have to do with all sorts. It is a very great advantage to know the languages of the several countries one travels in ; and different companies may, in some degree, be considered as different countries : each hath its distinctive language, customs, and manners ; know them all, and you will wonder at none.

Adieu, child. Take care of your health: there are no pleasures without it.

LETTER CCXL.

My dear Friend,   London, Feb. the 20th, O. S. 1752.

In all systems whatsoever, whether of religion, government, morals, &c., perfection is the object always proposed, though possibly unattainable ; hitherto, at least, certainly unattained. However, those who aim carefully at the mark itself, will unques-

[1] Nothing conduces more to health than frequent and homely purgatives.

tionably come nearer it, than those who, from despair, negligence, or indolence, leave to chance the work of skill. This maxim holds equally true in common life ; those who aim at perfection will come infinitely nearer it than those desponding or indolent spirits who foolishly say to themselves, nobody is perfect ; perfection is unattainable ; to attempt it is chimerical ; I shall do as well as others ; why, then, should I give myself trouble to be what I never can, and what, according to the common course of things, I need not be, *perfect?*

I am very sure that I need not point out to you the weakness and the folly of this reasoning, if it deserves the name of reasoning. It would discourage and put a stop to the exertion of any one of our faculties. On the contrary, a man of sense and spirit says to himself, Though the point of perfection may (considering the imperfection of our nature) be unattainable, my care, my endeavours, my attention, shall not be wanting to get as near it as I can. I will approach it every day ; possibly I may arrive at it at last, at least (what I am sure is in my own power) I will not be distanced. Many fools (speaking of you) say to me, What, would you have him perfect ? I answer, why not ? what hurt would it do him or me ? Oh, but that is impossible, say they. I reply, I am not sure of that : perfection in the abstract I admit to be unattainable ; but what is commonly called perfection in a character I maintain to be attainable, and not only that, but in every man's power. He hath, continue they, a good head, a good heart, a good fund of knowledge, which will increase daily ; what would you have more ? Why, I would have everything more that can adorn and complete a character. Will it do his head, his heart, or his knowledge, any harm, to have the utmost delicacy of manners, the most shining advantages of air and address, the most endearing attentions, and the most engaging graces ? But as he is, say they, he is loved wherever he is known. I am very glad of it, say I ; but I would have him be liked before he is known, and loved afterwards. I would have him, by his first *abord* and address, make people wish to know him, and inclined to love him : he will save a great deal of time by it. Indeed, reply they, you are too nice, too exact, and lay too much stress upon things that are of very little consequence. Indeed, rejoin I, you know very little of the nature of mankind, if you take those things to be of little consequence : one cannot be too attentive to them ; it is they that always engage the heart, of which the understanding is commonly the bubble. And I would much rather that he erred in a point of grammar, of history, of philosophy, &c., than in a point of manners and address. But consider, he is very young; all this will come in time. I hope so; but that time must be while he is young, or it will never be at all: the right *pli* must be taken young, or it will never be easy, nor seem natural. Come, come, say they (substituting, as is frequently done, assertion instead of argument), depend upon it he will do very well; and you have a great deal of reason to be satisfied with him. I hope and believe he will do well, but I would have him do better than well. I am very well pleased with him, but I would be more, I would be proud of him. I would have him have lustre as well as weight. Did you ever know anybody that reunited all these talents? Yes, I did; Lord Bolingbroke joined all the politeness, the manners, and the graces of a Courtier, to the solidity of a Statesman, and to the learning of a Pedant. He was *omnis homo;* and pray what should hinder my boy from being so too, if he hath, as I think he hath, all the other qualifications that you allow him? Nothing can hinder him, but neglect of, or inattention to, those objects, which his own good sense must tell him are of infinite consequence to him, and which therefore I will not suppose him capable of either neglecting or despising.

This (to tell you the whole truth) is the result of a controversy that passed yesterday, between Lady Hervey and myself, upon your subject, and almost in the very words. I submit the decision of it to yourself; let your own good sense determine it, and make you act in consequence of that determination. The receipt to make this composition is short and infallible; here I give it you.

Take variety of the best company, wherever you are; be minutely attentive to every word and action; imitate respectively those whom you observe to be distinguished and considered for any one accomplishment, then mix all those several accomplishments together, and serve them up yourself to others.

I hope your fair, or rather your brown, *American* is well. I hear that she makes very handsome presents, if she is not so herself. I am told there are people at Paris who expect from this secret connection, to see in time a volume of letters, superior to Madame de Graffigny's Peruvian ones: I lay in my claim to one of the first copies.

Francis's *Cenie*[1] hath been acted twice, with most universal applause; to-night is his third night, and I am going to it. I did not think it would have succeeded so well, considering how long our British audiences have been accustomed to murder,

---

[1] Francis's Eugenia.

racks, and poison in every tragedy; but it affected the heart so much, that it triumphed over habit and prejudice. All the women cried, and all the men were moved. The prologue, which is a very good one, was made entirely by Garrick. The epilogue is old Cibber's; but corrected, though not enough, by Francis. He will get a great deal of money by it; and, consequently, be better able to lend you sixpence upon any emergency.

The Parliament of Paris, I find by the newspapers, has not carried its point concerning the hospitals; and though the King hath given up the Archbishop, yet, as he has put them under the management and direction *du Grand Conseil*, the Parliament is equally out of the question. This will naturally put you upon inquiring into the Constitution of the *Grand Conseil*. You will, doubtless, inform yourself who it is composed of, what things are *de son resort*, whether or not there lies an appeal from thence to any other place, and of all other particulars that may give you a clear notion of this assembly. There are also three or four other *Conseils* in France, of which you ought to know the constitution and the objects: I dare say you do know them already; but if you do not, lose no time in informing yourself. These things, as I have often told you, are best learned in various French companies, but in no English ones, for none of our countrymen trouble their heads about them. To use a very trite image, collect, like the bee, your store from every quarter. In some companies (*parmi les fermiers généraux nommément*) you may, by proper inquiries, get a general knowledge at least of *les affaires des finances*. When you are with *des gens de robe*, suck them with regard to the constitution and civil government, and *sic de cœteris*. This shows you the advantage of keeping a great deal of different French company; an advantage much superior to any that you can possibly receive from loitering and sauntering away evenings in any English company at Paris, not even excepting Lord A* * * *'s. Love of ease, and fear of restraint (to both which I doubt you are, for a young fellow, too much addicted), may invite you among your countrymen; but pray withstand those mean temptations, *et prenez sur vous*, for the sake of being in those assemblies, which alone can inform your mind and improve your manners. You have not now many months to continue at Paris; make the most of them: get into every house there, if you can; extend acquaintance, know everything and everybody there, that when you leave it for other places, you may be *au fait*, and even able to explain whatever you may hear mentioned concerning it. Adieu.

LETTER CCXLI.

MY DEAR FRIEND,   London, March the 2nd, O. S. 1752.

WHEREABOUTS are you in Ariosto? Or have you gone through that most ingenious contexture of truth and lies, of serious and extravagant, of knights-errant, magicians, and all that various matter, which he announces in the beginning of his poem :

> Le Donne, i Cavalier, L'arme, gli amori,
> Le cortesie, L'audaci imprese io canto.

I am by no means sure that Homer had superior invention, or excelled more in description than Ariosto. What can be more seducing and voluptuous than the description of Alcina's person and palace? What more ingeniously extravagant than the search made in the moon for Orlando's lost wits, and the account of other people's that were found there? The whole is worth your attention, not only as an ingenious poem, but as the source of all modern tales, novels, fables, and romances ; as Ovid's Metamorphoses was of the ancient ones : besides, that when you have read this work, nothing will be difficult to you in the Italian language. You will read Tasso's *Gierusalemme*, and the *Decamerone di Boccaccio*, with great facility afterwards ; and when you have read these three authors, you will, in my opinion, have read all the works of invention that are worth reading in that language ; though the Italians would be very angry at me for saying so.

A gentleman should know those which I call classical works, in every language ; such as Boileau, Corneille, Racine, Moliere, &c., in French ; Milton, Dryden, Pope, Swift, &c., in English ; and the three authors above mentioned in Italian : whether you have any such in German I am not quite sure, nor, indeed, am I inquisitive. These sort of books adorn the mind, improve the fancy, are frequently alluded to by, and are often the subjects of conversations of, the best companies. As you have languages to read, and memory to retain them, the knowledge of them is very well worth the little pains it will cost you, and will enable you to shine in company. It is not pedantic to quote and allude to them, which it would be with regard to the ancients.

Among the many advantages which you have had in your education, I do not consider your knowledge of several languages as the least. You need not trust to translations: you can go to the source: you can both converse and negotiate with people of all nations, upon equal terms, which is by no means the case of a man who converses or negotiates in a language which those with whom he hath to do know much better than himself. In business, a great deal may depend upon the force and extent of one word; and in conversation, a moderate thought may gain, or a good one lose, by the propriety or impropriety, the elegancy or inelegancy, of one single word. As therefore you now know four modern languages well, I would have you study (and, by the way, it will be very little trouble to you) to know them correctly, accurately, and delicately. Read some little books that treat of them, and ask questions concerning their delicacies, of those who are able to answer you. As, for instance, should I say in French, *la lettre que je vous ai* écrit, or, *la lettre que je vous ai* écrite? in which, I think the French differ among themselves. There is a short French grammar by the Port Royal, and another by Père Buffier, both which are worth your reading; as is also a little book called *Les Synonymes François.*—There are books of that kind upon the Italian language, into some of which I would advise you to dip: possibly the German language may have something of the same sort; and since you already speak it, the more properly you speak it the better: one would, I think, as far as possible, do all one does correctly and elegantly. It is extremely engaging, to people of every nation, to meet with a foreigner who hath taken pains enough to speak their language correctly: it flatters that local and national pride and prejudice, of which everybody hath some share.

Francis's Eugenia, which I will send you, pleased most people of good taste here: the boxes were crowded till the sixth night; when the pit and gallery were totally deserted, and it was dropped. Distress, without death, was not sufficient to affect a true British audience, so long accustomed to daggers, racks, and bowls of poison; contrary to Horace's rule, they desire to see Medea murder her children upon the stage. The sentiments were too delicate to move them; and their hearts are to be taken by storm, not by parley.

Have you got the things, which were taken from you at Calais, restored? and among them, the little packet, which my sister gave you for Sir Charles Hotham? In this case, have you forwarded it to him? If you have not yet had an opportunity, you will have one soon, which I desire you will not omit: it is by Monsieur D'Aillon, whom you will see in a few days at Paris, in his way to Geneva, where Sir Charles now is, and will remain some time. Adieu.

LETTER CCXLII.

MY DEAR FRIEND,   London, March the 5th, O. S. 1752.

As I have received no letter from you by the usual post, I am uneasy upon account of your health ; for, had you been well, I am sure you would have written, according to your engagement, and my requisition. You have not the least notion of any care of your health : but, though I would not have you be a valetudinarian, I must tell you, that the best and most robust health requires some degree of attention to preserve. Young fellows, thinking they have so much health and time before them, are very apt to neglect or lavish both, and beggar themselves before they are aware : whereas a prudent economy in both, would make them rich indeed ; and so far from breaking in upon their pleasures, would improve and almost perpetuate them. Be you wiser ; and, before it is too late, manage both with care and frugality ; and lay out neither, but upon good interest and security.

I will now confine myself to the employment of your time, which, though I have often touched upon formerly, is a subject that, from its importance, will bear repetition. You have, it is true, a great deal of time before you ; but, in this period of your life, one hour usefully employed may be worth more than four-and-twenty hereafter ; a minute is precious to you now, whole days may possibly not be so forty years hence. Whatever time you allow or can snatch for serious reading (I say snatch, because company, and the knowledge of the world, is now your chief object), employ it in the reading of some one book, and that a good one, till you have finished it : and do not distract your mind with various matters at the same time. In this light I would recommend to you to read *toute de suite* Grotius *de Jure Belli et Pacis*, translated by Barbeyrac, and Puffendorf's *Jus Gentium*, translated by the same hand. For accidental quarters of hours, read works of invention, wit, and humour, of the best, and not of trivial, authors, either ancient or modern.

Whatever business you have, do it the first moment you can ; never by halves, but finish it without interruption, if possible.

Business must not be sauntered and trifled with ; and you must not say to it, as Felix did to Paul, ' at a more convenient season I will speak to thee.'   The most convenient season for business is the first; but study and business, in some measure, point out their own times to a man of sense ; time is much oftener squandered away in the wrong choice and improper methods of amusement and pleasures.

Many people think that they are in pleasures, provided they are neither in study nor in business. Nothing like it ; they are doing nothing, and might just as well be asleep. They contract habitudes from laziness, and they only frequent those places where they are free from all restraints and attentions. Be upon your guard against this idle profusion of time : and let every place you go to be either the scene of quick and lively pleasures, or the school of your improvements : let every company you go into, either gratify your senses, extend your knowledge, or refine your manners. Have some decent object of gallantry in view at some places ; frequent others, where people of wit and taste assemble ; get into others, where people of superior rank and dignity command respect and attention from the rest of the company ; but pray frequent no neutral places, from mere idleness and indolence. Nothing forms a young man so much as being used to keep respectable and superior company, where a constant regard and attention is necessary. It is true, this is at first a disagreeable state of restraint; but it soon grows habitual, and consequently easy ; and you are amply paid for it, by the improvement you make, and the credit it gives you. What you said some time ago was very true, concerning *le Palais Royal ;* to one of your age the situation is disagreeable enough ; you cannot expect to be much taken notice of ; but all that time you can take notice of others ; observe their manners, decipher their characters, and insensibly you will become one of the company.

All this I went through myself, when I was of your age. I have sat hours in company, without being taken the least notice of ; but then I took notice of them, and learned, in their company, how to behave myself better in the next, till by degrees I became part of the best companies myself.   But I took great care not to lavish away my time in those companies, where there were neither quick pleasures nor useful improvements to be expected.

Sloth, indolence, and *mollesse* are pernicious and unbecoming a young fellow ; let them be your *ressource* forty years hence at soonest.   Determine, at all events and however disagreeable it may be to you in some respects, and for some time, to keep the most distinguished and fashionable company of the place you are at, either for their rank, or for their learning, or *le bel esprit et le goût*. This gives you credentials to the best companies, wherever you go afterwards. Pray, therefore, no indolence, no laziness; but employ every minute of your life in active pleasures or useful employments. Address yourself to some woman of fashion and beauty, wherever you are, and try how far that will go. If the place be not secured beforehand, and garrisoned, nine times in ten you will take it. By attentions and respect, you may always get into the highest company; and by some admiration and applause, whether merited or not, you may be sure of being welcome among *les savants et les beaux esprits*. There are but these three sorts of company for a young fellow; there being neither pleasure nor profit in any other.

My uneasiness with regard to your health, is this moment removed by your letter of the 8th, N. S., which, by what accident I do not know, I did not receive before.

I long to read Voltaire's *Rome Sauvée*, which, by the very faults that your *severe* critics find with it, I am sure I shall like; for I will, at any time, give up a good deal of regularity for a great deal of *brillant*; and for the *brillant*, surely nobody is equal to Voltaire. Catiline's conspiracy is an unhappy subject for a tragedy; it is too single, and gives no opportunity to the poet to excite any of the tender passions; the whole is one intended act of horror. Crébillon was sensible of this defect, and to create another interest, most absurdly made Catiline in love with Cicero's daughter, and her with him.

I am very glad you went to Versailles, and dined with Monsieur de St Contest. That is company to learn *les bonnes manières* in; and it seems you had *les bons morceaux* into the bargain. Though you were no part of the King of France's conversation with the foreign ministers, and probably not much entertained with it; do you think that this is not very useful to you to hear it, and to observe the turn and manners of people of that sort? It is extremely useful to know it well. The same in the next rank of people, such as ministers of state, &c., in whose company, though you cannot yet, at your age, bear a part, and consequently be diverted, you will observe and learn, what hereafter it may be necessary for you to act.

Tell Sir John Lambert that I have this day fixed Mr Spencer's having his credit upon him; Mr Hoare had also recommended him. I believe Mr Spencer will set out next month for some place in France, but not Paris. I am sure he wants a great deal of France, for at present he is most entirely English ; and you know very well what I think of that. And so we bid you heartily good night.

——◦——

LETTER CCXLIII.

My dear Friend,   London, March the 16th, O. S. 1752.

How do you go on with the most useful and most necessary of all studies, the study of the world ? Do you find that you gain knowledge ? And does your daily experience at once extend and demonstrate your improvement ? You will possibly ask me how you can judge of that yourself. I will tell you a sure way of knowing. Examine yourself, and see whether your notions of the world are changed, by experience, from what they were two years ago in theory ; for that alone is one favourable symptom of improvement. At that age (I remember it in myself) every notion that one forms is erroneous ; one hath seen few models, and those none of the best, to form one's self upon. One thinks that everything is to be carried by spirit · and vigour ; that art is meanness, and that versatility and complaisance are the refuge of pusillanimity and weakness. This most mistaken opinion gives an indelicacy, a *brusquerie*, and a roughness to the manners. Fools, who can never be undeceived, retain them as long as they live : reflection, with a little experience, makes men of sense shake them off soon. When they come to be a little better acquainted with themselves, and with their own species, they discover that plain right reason is, nine times in ten, the fettered and shackled attendant of the triumph of the heart and the passions ; consequently, they address themselves nine times in ten to the conqueror, not to the conquered : and conquerors, you know, must be applied to in the gentlest, the most engaging, and the most insinuating manner. Have you found out that every woman is infallibly to be gained by every sort of flattery, and every man by one sort or other ? Have you discovered what variety of little things affect the heart, and how surely they collectively gain it ? If you have, you have made some progress. I would try a man's knowledge of the world, as I would a schoolboy's knowledge of Horace ; not by making him construe *Mæcenas atavis edite regibus*, which he could do in the first form, but by examining him as to the delicacy and *curiosa felicitas* [1] of that poet. A man requires very

---

[1] Felicitous elaborateness.

little knowledge and experience of the world, to understand glaring, high coloured, and decided characters ; they are but few, and they strike at first : but to distinguish the almost imperceptible shades, and the nice gradations of virtue and vice, sense and folly, strength and weakness (of which characters are commonly composed), demands some experience, great observation, and minute attention. In the same cases most people do the same things, but with this material difference, upon which the success commonly turns,—A man who hath studied the world knows when to time, and where to place, them : he hath analyzed the characters he applies to, and adapted his address and his arguments to them : but a man of what is called plain good sense, who hath only reasoned by himself, and not acted with mankind, mistimes, misplaces, runs precipitately and bluntly at the mark, and falls upon his nose in the way. In the common manners of social life, every man of common sense hath the rudiments, the A B C of civility ; the means not to offend ; and even wishes to please : and, if he hath any real merit, will be received and tolerated in good company. But that is far from being enough ; for though he may be received, he will never be desired ; though he does not offend, he will never be loved, but, like some little, insignificant, neutral power, surrounded by great ones, he will neither be feared nor courted by any ; but, by turns, invaded by all, whenever it is their interest. A most contemptible situation ! Whereas, a man who hath carefully attended to and experienced the various workings of the heart, and the artifices of the head ; and who, by one shade, can trace the progression of the whole colour ; who can at the proper times employ all the several means of persuading the understanding and engaging the heart ; may and will have enemies ; but will and must have friends ; he may be opposed, but he will be supported too, his talents may excite the jealousy of some, but his engaging arts will make him beloved by many more ; he will be considerable, he will be considered. Many different qualifications must conspire to form such a man, and to make him at once respectable and amiable, and the least must be joined to the greatest ; the latter would be unavailing without the former, and the former would be futile and frivolous without the latter. Learning is acquired by reading books; but the much more necessary learning, the knowledge of the world, is only to be acquired by reading men, and studying all the various editions of them. Many words in every language are generally thought to be synonymous ; but those who study the language attentively will find that there is no such thing ; they will discover some little difference, some distinction, between all those words that are vulgarly called synonymous ; one hath always more energy, extent, or delicacy, than another : it is the same with men ; all are in general, and yet no two in particular, exactly alike. Those who have not accurately studied perpetually mistake them : they do not discern the shades and gradations that distinguish characters seemingly alike. Company, various company, is the only school for this knowledge. You ought to be, by this time, at least in the third form of that school, from whence the rise to the uppermost is easy and quick ; but then you must have application and vivacity, you must not only bear with, but even seek, restraint in most companies, instead of stagnating in one or two only, where indolence and love of ease may be indulged.

In the plan which I gave you in my last,[1] for your future motions, I forgot to tell you, that if a King of the Romans should be chosen this year, you shall certainly be at that election ; and as, upon those occasions, all strangers are excluded from the place of the election, except such as belong to some Ambassador, I have already eventually secured you a place in the *suite* of the King's electoral Ambassador, who will be sent upon that account to Frankfort, or wherever else the election may be. This will not only secure you a sight of the show, but a knowledge of the whole thing, which is likely to be a contested one, from the opposition of some of the Electors, and the protests of some of the Princes of the Empire. That election, if there is one, will, in my opinion, be a memorable era in the history of the Empire ; pens at least, if not swords, will be drawn ; and ink, if not blood, will be plentifully shed, by the contending parties in that dispute. During the fray, you may securely plunder, and add to your present stock of knowledge of the *jus publicum imperii.* The Court of France hath, I am told, appointed le President Ogier, a man of great abilities, to go immediately to Ratisbon, *pour y souffler la discorde.*[2] It must be owned, that France hath always profited skilfully of its having guaranteed the treaty of Munster, which hath given it a constant pretence to thrust itself into the affairs of the Empire. When France got Alsace yielded by treaty, it was very willing to have held it as a fief of the Empire ; but the Empire was then wiser. Every Power should be very careful not to give the least pretence to a neighbouring Power to meddle with the affairs of its interior. Sweden hath already felt the effects of the Czarina's calling herself guarantee of its present form of

---

[1] That letter is missing.   [2] To sow discord there.

government, in consequence of the treaty of Neustadt, confirmed afterwards by that of Abo ; though, in truth, that guarantee was rather a provision against Russia's attempting to alter the then new established form of government in Sweden, than any right given to Russia to hinder the Swedes from establishing what form of government they pleased. Read them both, if you can get them. Adieu.

LETTER CCXLIV.

MY DEAR FRIEND,   London, April the 13th, O. S. 1752.

I RECEIVED this moment your letter of the 19th, N. S., with the enclosed pieces relative to the present dispute between the King and the Parliament. I shall return them by Lord Huntingdon, whom you will soon see at Paris, and who will likewise carry you the piece, which I forgot in making up the packet I sent you by the Spanish Ambassador. The representation of the Parliament is very well drawn, *suaviter in modo, fortiter in re*. They tell the King very respectfully, that in a certain case, *which they should think it criminal to suppose*, they would not obey him. This hath a tendency to what we call here revolution principles. I do not know what the Lord's anointed, his vicegerent upon earth, divinely appointed by him, and accountable to none but him for his actions, will either think or do, upon these symptoms of reason and good sense, which seem to be breaking out all over France ; but this I foresee, that before the end of this century, the trade of both King and Priest will not be half so good a one as it has been. Du Clos, in his reflections, hath observed, and very truly, *qu'il y a un germe de raison qui commence à se développer en France.*[1] A *développement* that must prove fatal to Regal and Papal pretensions. Prudence may, in many cases, recommend an occasional submission to either ; but when that ignorance, upon which an implicit faith in both could only be founded, is once removed, God's Vicegerent, and Christ's Vicar, will only be obeyed and believed, as far as what the one orders, and the other says, is conformable to reason and to truth.

I am very glad (to use a vulgar expression) that *you make as if you* were not well, though you really are ; I am sure it is the likeliest way to keep so. Pray leave off entirely your

---

[1] There is a germ of reason which begins to unfold itself in France.

greasy, heavy pastry, fat creams, and indigestible dumplings; and then you need not confine yourself to white meats, which I do not take to be one jot wholesomer than beef, mutton, and partridge.

Voltaire sent me from Berlin his History *du Siècle de Louis* XIV. It came at a very proper time; Lord Bolingbroke had just taught me how History should be read; Voltaire shows me how it should be written. I am sensible that it will meet with almost as many critics as readers. Voltaire must be criticized: besides, every man's favourite is attacked; for every prejudice is exposed, and our prejudices are our mistresses: reason is at best our wife, very often heard indeed, but seldom minded. It is the history of the human understanding, written by a man of parts, for the use of men of parts. Weak minds will not like it, even though they do not understand it; which is commonly the measure of their admiration. Dull ones will want those minute and uninteresting details, with which most other histories are encumbered. He tells me all I want to know, and nothing more. His reflections are short, just, and produce others in his readers. Free from religious, philosophical, political, and national prejudices, beyond any historian I ever met with, he relates all those matters as truly and as impartially as certain regards, which must always be to some degree observed, will allow him: for one sees plainly, that he often says much less than he would say, if he might. He hath made me much better acquainted with the times of Lewis XIV. than the innumerable volumes which I had read could do; and hath suggested this reflection to me, which I had never made before—His vanity, not his knowledge, made him encourage all, and introduce many arts and sciences in his country. He opened in a manner the human understanding in France, and brought it to its utmost perfection; his age equalled in all, and greatly exceeded in many things (pardon me, pedants!) the Augustan. This was great and rapid; but still it might be done, by the encouragement, the applause, and the rewards of a vain, liberal, and magnificent Prince. What is much more surprising, is, that he stopped the operations of the human mind, just where he pleased; and seemed to say, ' thus far shalt thou go, and no farther.' For, a bigot to his religion, and jealous of his power, free and rational thoughts upon either never entered into a French head during his reign; and the greatest geniuses that ever any age produced never entertained a doubt of the divine right of Kings, or the infallibility of the Church. Poets, Orators, and Philosophers, ignorant of their natural rights, cherished their chains;

and blind active faith triumphed, in those great minds, over silent and passive reason. The reverse of this seems now to be the case in France : reason opens itself; fancy and invention fade and decline.

I will send you a copy of this history by Lord Huntingdon, as I think it very probable that it is not allowed to be published and sold at Paris. Pray read it more than once, and with attention, particularly the second volume ; which contains short but very clear accounts of many very interesting things, which are talked of by everybody, though fairly understood by very few. There are two very puerile affectations, which I wish this book had been free from ; the one is, the total subversion of all the old-established French orthography ; the other is, the not making use of any one capital letter throughout the whole book, except at the beginning of a paragraph. It offends my eyes to see rome, paris, france, cæsar, henry the 4th, &c., begin with small letters ; and I do not conceive that there can be any reason for doing it half so strong as the reason of long usage is to the contrary. This is an affectation below Voltaire ; whom I am not ashamed to say that I admire and delight in, as an author, equally in prose and in verse.

I had a letter, a few days ago, from Monsieur du Boccage ; in which he says, *Monsieur Stanhope s'est jetté dans la politique, et je crois qu'il y réussira :* [1] you do very well, it is your destination ; but remember, that, to succeed in great things, one must first learn to please in little ones. Engaging manners and address must prepare the way for superior knowledge and abilities to act with effect. The late Duke of Marlborough's manners and address prevailed with the first King of Prussia, to let his troops remain in the army of the allies ; when neither their representations, nor his own share in the common cause, could do it. The Duke of Marlborough had no new matter to urge to him ; but had a manner, which he could not, and did not, resist. Voltaire, among a thousand little delicate strokes of that kind, says of the Duke de la Feuillade, *qu'il étoit l'homme le plus brillant et le plus aimable du Royaume, et quoique gendre du Général et Ministre, il avoit pour lui la faveur publique.* [2] Various little circumstances of that sort will often make a man of great real merit be hated, if he hath not address and manners to make him be loved. Consider all your own circum-

---

[1] Mr Stanhope has thrown himself into politics, and I believe he will succeed in them.

[2] That he was the most brilliant and amiable man in the kingdom, and, although the son-in-law of the General and Minister, was in favour with the people.

stances seriously ; and you will find that, of all arts, the art of pleasing is the most necessary for you to study and possess. A silly tyrant said, *oderint modo timeant :* [1] a wise man would have said, *modo ament nihil timendum est mihi.* [2] Judge, from your own daily experience, of the efficacy of that pleasing *je ne sais quoi,* when you feel, as you and everybody certainly do, that in men it is more engaging than knowledge, in women than beauty.

I long to see Lord and Lady * * * (who are not yet arrived), because they have lately seen you ; and I always fancy that I can fish out something new concerning you from those who have seen you last : not that I shall much rely upon their accounts, because I distrust the judgment of Lord and Lady * * *, in those matters about which I am most inquisitive. They have ruined their own son, by what they called and thought loving him. They have made him believe that the world was made for him, not he for the world ; and unless he stays abroad a great while, and falls into very good company, he will expect, what he will never find, the attentions and complaisance from others, which he has hitherto been used to from Papa and Mamma. This, I fear, is too much the case of Mr * * * * ; who, I doubt, will be run through the body, and be near dying, before he knows how to live. However you may turn out, you can never make me any of these reproaches. I indulged no silly womanish fondness for you : instead of inflicting my tenderness upon you, I have taken all possible methods to make you deserve it ; and thank God you do ; at least, I know but one article in which you are different from what I could wish you ; and you very well know what that is. I want that I and all the world should like you, as well as I love you. Adieu.

LETTER CCXLV.

MY DEAR FRIEND, London, April the 30th, O. S. 1752.

A roir du monde is, in my opinion, a very just and happy expression, for having address, manners, and for knowing how to behave properly in all companies ; and it implies, very truly, that a man that hath not these accomplishments is not of the world. Without them, the best parts are inefficient, civility is absurd, and freedom offensive. A learned parson, rusting in his cell at Oxford or Cambridge, will reason admirably well upon

[1] Let them hate me, if only they fear me.
[2] If only they love me, I have nothing to fear.

the nature of man ; will profoundly analyze the head, the heart, the reason, the will, the passions, the senses, the sentiments, and all those subdivisions of we know not what ; and yet, unfortunately, he knows nothing of man : for he hath not lived with him ; and is ignorant of all the various modes, habits, prejudices, and tastes, that always influence, and often determine him. He views man as he does colours in Sir Isaac Newton's prism, where only the capital ones are seen ; but an experienced dyer knows all their various shades and gradations, together with the result of their several mixtures. Few men are of one plain, decided colour ; most are mixed, shaded, and blended ; and vary as much, from different situations, as changeable silks do from different lights. The man *qui a du monde* knows all this from his own experience and observation : the conceited, cloistered philosopher knows nothing of it from his own theory; his practice is absurd and improper ; and he acts as awkwardly as a man would dance, who had never seen others dance, nor learned of a dancing-master; but who had only studied the notes by which dances are now pricked down, as well as tunes. Observe and imitate, then, the address, the arts, and the manners of those *qui ont du monde :* see by what methods they first make, and afterwards improve, impressions in their favour. Those impressions are much oftener owing to little causes, than to intrinsic merit ; which is less volatile, and hath not so sudden an effect. Strong minds have undoubtedly an ascendant over weak ones, as Galigai Maréchale d'Ancre very justly observed, when, to the disgrace and reproach of those times, she was executed for having governed Mary of Medicis by the arts of witchcraft and magic. But the ascendant is to be gained by degrees, and by those arts only which experience and the knowledge of the world teaches : for few are mean enough to be bullied, though most are weak enough to be bubbled. I have often seen people of superior governed by people of much inferior parts, without knowing or even suspecting that they were so governed. This can only happen, when those people of inferior parts have more worldly dexterity and experience than those they govern. They see the weak and unguarded part, and apply to it : they take it, and all the rest follows. Would you gain either men or women, and every man of sense desires to gain both, *il faut du monde.* You have had more opportunities than ever any man had, at your age, of acquiring *ce monde ;* you have been in the best companies of most countries, at an age when others have hardly been in any company at all. You are master of all those languages, which John Trott seldom speaks at all, and never well ; consequently you need be a stranger nowhere. This is the way, and the only way, of having *du monde ;* but if you have it not, and have still any coarse rusticity about you, may one not apply to you the *rusticus expectat* of Horace ?

This knowledge of the world teaches us more particularly two things, both which are of infinite consequence, and to neither of which nature inclines us; I mean, the command of our temper and of our countenance. A man who has no *monde* is inflamed with anger, or annihilated with shame, at every disagreeable incident: the one makes him act and talk like a madman, the other makes him look like a fool. But a man who has *du monde* seems not to understand what he cannot or ought not to resent. If he makes a slip himself, he recovers it by his coolness, instead of plunging deeper by his confusion, like a stumbling horse. He is firm, but gentle ; and practises that most excellent maxim, *suavitèr in modo, fortitèr in re.* The other is the *volto sciolto e pensieri stretti.* People unused to the world have babbling countenances ; and are unskilful enough to show what they have sense enough not to tell. In the course of the world, a man must very often put on an easy, frank countenance upon very disagreeable occasions ; he must seem pleased when he is very much otherwise; he must be able to accost, and receive with smiles, those whom he would much rather meet with swords. In Courts he must not turn himself inside out. All this may, nay must, be done without falsehood and treachery : for it must go no further than politeness and manners, and must stop short of assurances and professions of simulated friendship. Good manners, to those one does not love, are no more a breach of truth than ' your humble servant ' at the bottom of a challenge is ; they are universally agreed upon, and understood, to be things of course. They are necessary guards of the decency and peace of society : they must only act defensively ; and then not with arms poisoned with perfidy. Truth, but not the whole truth, must be the invariable principle of every man, who hath either religion, honour, or prudence. Those who violate it may be cunning, but they are not able. Lies and perfidy are the refuge of fools and cowards. Adieu !

P. S. I must recommend to you again, to take your leave of all your French acquaintance, in such a manner as may make them regret your departure, and wish to see and welcome you at Paris again ; where you may possibly return before it is very long. This must not be done in a cold, civil manner, but with, at least, seeming warmth, sentiment, and concern. Acknowledge the obligations you have to them, for the kindness they have shown you during your stay at Paris; assure them, that, wherever you are, you shall remember them with gratitude; wish for opportunities of giving them proofs of your *plus tendre et respectueux souvenir;* beg of them, in case your good fortune should carry you to any part of the world where you could be of any the least use to them, that they would employ you without reserve. Say all this, and a great deal more, emphatically and pathetically; for you know *si vis me flere.*[1] This can do you no harm, if you never return to Paris; but if you do, as probably you may, it will be of infinite use to you. Remember, too, not to omit going to every house where you have ever been once, to take leave, and recommend yourself to their remembrance. The reputation which you leave at one place, where you have been, will circulate, and you will meet with it at twenty places, where you are to go. That is a labour never quite lost.

This letter will show you, that the accident which happened to me yesterday, and of which Mr Grevenkop gives you an account, hath had no bad consequences. My escape was a great one.

LETTER CCXLVI.

My dear Friend,   London, May the 11th, O. S. 1752.

I break my word by writing this letter; but I break it on the allowable side, by doing more than I promised. I have pleasure in writing to you; and you may possibly have some profit in reading what I write; either of the motives were sufficient for me, both I cannot withstand. By your last, I calculate that you will leave Paris this day se'nnight; upon that supposition, this letter may still find you there.

Colonel Perry arrived here two or three days ago, and sent me a book from you, Cassandra abridged. I am sure it cannot be too much abridged. The spirit of that most voluminous work, fairly extracted, may be contained in the smallest *duodecimo;* and it is most astonishing that there ever could have been people idle enough to write or read such endless heaps of the same stuff. It was, however, the occupation of thousands in the last century; and is still the private, though disavowed,

---

[1] If you would have me weep [you must weep first yourself].

amusement of young girls and sentimental ladies. A lovesick girl finds, in the Captain with whom she is in love, all the courage and all the graces of the tender and accomplished Oroondates ; and many a grown up, sentimental lady, talks delicate Clelia to the hero, whom she would engage to eternal love, or laments with her that love is not eternal.

> Ah ! qu'il est doux d'aimer, si l'on aimoit toujours !
> Mais, hélas ! il n'est point d'éternelles amours.[1]

It is, however, very well to have read one of those extravagant works (of all which La Calprenede's are the best) because it is well to be able to talk, with some degree of knowledge, upon all those subjects that other people talk sometimes upon ; and I would by no means have anything, that is known to others, be totally unknown to you. It is a great advantage for any man to be able to talk or to hear, neither ignorantly nor absurdly, upon any subject ; for I have known people, who have not said one word, hear ignorantly and absurdly ; it has appeared in their inattentive and unmeaning faces.

This, I think, is as little likely to happen to you, as to anybody of your age ; and if you will but add a versatility, and easy conformity of manners, I know no company in which you are likely to be *de trop*.

This versatility is more particularly necessary for you at this time, now that you are going to so many different places ; for though the manners and customs of the several Courts of Germany are in general the same, yet every one has its particular characteristic ; some peculiarity or other which distinguishes it from the next. This you should carefully attend to, and immediately adopt. Nothing flatters people more, nor makes strangers so welcome, as such an occasional conformity. I do not mean by this, that you should mimic the air and stiffness of every awkward German Court ; no, by no means ; but I mean that you should only cheerfully comply and fall in with certain local habits, such as ceremonies, diet, turn of conversation, &c. People who are lately come from Paris, and who have been a good while there, are generally suspected, and especially in Germany, of having a degree of contempt for every other place. Take great care that nothing of this kind appear, at least outwardly, in your behaviour : but commend whatever deserves any degree of commendation, without comparing it with what you may have left, much better, of the same kind at Paris. As,

---

[1] Ah ! how sweet it were to love if one loved always !
But, alas ! there are no everlasting attachments.

for instance, the German kitchen is, without doubt, execrable, and the French delicious; however, never commend the French kitchen at a German table ; but eat of what you can find tolerable there, and commend it, without comparing it to anything better.   I have known many British Yahoos, who, though while they were at Paris conformed to no one French custom, as soon as they got anywhere else, talked of nothing but what they did, saw, and eat at Paris.   The freedom of the French is not to be used indiscriminately at all the Courts in Germany, though their easiness may, and ought; but that, too, at some places more than others.   The Courts of Manheim and Bonn, I take to be a little more unbarbarized than some others ; that of Maïence, an ecclesiastical one,' as well as that of Treves (neither of which is much frequented by foreigners), retains, I conceive, a great deal of the Goth and Vandal still.   There, more reserve and ceremony are necessary ; and not a word of the French. At Berlin, you cannot be too French.   Hanover, Brunswick, Cassel, &c., are of the mixed kind, *un peu décrottés, mais pas assez.*[1]

Another thing, which I most earnestly recommend to you, not only in Germany, but in every part of the world, where you may ever be, is, not only real, but seeming attention, to whomever you speak to, or to whoever speaks to you.   There is nothing so brutally shocking, nor so little forgiven, as a seeming inattention to the person who is speaking to you ; and I have known many a man knocked down, for (in my opinion) a much slighter provocation, than that shocking inattention which I mean.   I have seen many people, who while you are speaking to them, instead of looking at, and attending to, you, fix their eyes upon the ceiling, or some other part of the room, look out of the window, play with a dog, twirl their snuff box, or pick their nose.   Nothing discovers a little, futile, frivolous mind more than this, and nothing is so offensively ill bred : it is an explicit declaration on your part, that every, the most trifling object, deserves your attention more than all that can be said by the person who is speaking to you.   Judge of the sentiments of hatred and resentment, which such treatment must excite, in every breast where any degree of self-love dwells ; and I am sure, I never yet met with that breast where there was not a great deal.   I repeat it again and again (for it is highly necessary for you to remember it), that sort of vanity and self-love is inseparable from human nature, whatever may be its rank or condition ; even your footman will sooner forget and forgive a beating, than any manifest mark of slight and con-

[1] With a little but not enough polish.

tempt. Be therefore, I beg of you, not only really, but seemingly and manifestly, attentive to whoever speaks to you ; nay more, take their tone, and tune yourself to their unison. Be serious with the serious, gay with the gay, and trifle with the triflers. In assuming these various shapes, endeavour to make each of them seem to sit easy upon you, and even to appear to be your own natural one. This is the true and useful versatility of which a thorough knowledge of the world at once teaches the utility, and the means of acquiring.

I am very sure, at least I hope, that you will never make use of a silly expression, which is the favourite expression, and the absurd excuse of all fools and blockheads ; *I cannot do such a thing :* a thing by no means either morally or physically impossible. I *cannot* attend long together to the same thing, says one fool : that is, he is such a fool that he will not. I remember a very awkward fellow, who did not know what to do with his sword, and who always took it off before dinner, saying, that he could not possibly dine with his sword on ; upon which I could not help telling him that I really believed he could, without any probable danger either to himself or others. It is a shame and an absurdity, for any man to say, that he cannot do all those things which are commonly done by all the rest of mankind.

Another thing, that I must earnestly warn you against, is laziness ; by which more people have lost the fruit of their travels, than (perhaps) by any other thing. Pray be always in motion. Early in the morning go and see things ; and the rest of the day go and see people. If you stay but a week at a place, and that an insignificant one, see, however, all that is to be seen there ; know as many people, and get into as many houses, as ever you can.

I recommend to you likewise, though probably you have thought of it yourself, to carry in your pocket a map of Germany, in which the post roads are marked ; and also some short book of travels through Germany. The former will help to imprint in your memory situations and distances ; and the latter will point out many things for you to see, that might otherwise possibly escape you ; and which, though they may in themselves be of little consequence, you would regret not having seen, after having been at the places where they were.

Thus warned and provided for your journey, God speed you ; *Felix faustumque sit !* [1]   Adieu.

[1] May it be fortunate and auspicious!

LETTER CCXLVII.

My dear Friend,   London, May the 27th, O. S. 1752.

I send you the enclosed original, from a friend of ours, with my own commentaries upon the text; a text which I have so often paraphrased and commented upon already, that I believe I can hardly say anything new upon it : but, however, I cannot give it over till I am better convinced, than I yet am, that you feel all the utility, the importance, and the necessity of it ; nay, not only feel, but practise it. Your panegyrist allows you what most fathers would be more than satisfied with in a son, and chides me for not contenting myself with *l'essentiellement bon;* but I, who have been in no one respect like other fathers, cannot neither, like them, content myself with *l'essentiellement bon ;* because I know that it will not do your business in the world, while you want *quelques couches de vernis.*[1] Few fathers care much for their sons, or, at least, most of them care more for their money ; and, consequently, content themselves with giving them, at the cheapest rate, the common run of education ; that is, a school till eighteen ; the university till twenty ; and a couple of years riding post through the several towns of Europe ; impatient till their boobies come home to be married, and, as they call it, settled. Of those who really love their sons, few know how to do it. Some spoil them by fondling them while they are young, and then quarrel with them when they are grown up, for having been spoiled ; some love them like mothers, and attend only to the bodily health and strength of the hopes of their family, solemnize his birthday, and rejoice, like the subjects of the Great Mogul, at the increase of his bulk : while others minding, as they think, only essentials, take pains and pleasure to see in their heir all their favourite weaknesses and imperfections. I hope and believe that I have kept clear of all these errors, in the education which I have given you. No weaknesses of my own have warped it, no parsimony has starved it, no rigour has deformed it. Sound and extensive learning was the foundation which I meaned to lay ; I have laid it ; but that alone, I knew, would by no means be sufficient: the ornamental, the showish, the pleasing superstructure, was to be begun. In that view I threw you into the great world, entirely your own master, at an age when others either guzzle at the university, or are sent abroad in servitude to some awkward, pedantic Scotch Governor. This was to put you in the way, and the

[1] A few layers of varnish.

only way, of acquiring those manners, that address, and those graces, which exclusively distinguish people of fashion; and without which all moral virtues, and all acquired learning, are of no sort of use in Courts and *le beau monde;* on the contrary, I am not sure if they are not a hindrance. They are feared and disliked in those places, as too severe, if not smoothed and introduced by the *graces;* but of these graces, of this necessary *beau vernis,* it seems there are still *quelques couches qui manquent.* Now, pray let me ask you, coolly and seriously, *pourquoi ces couches manquent-elles?* For you may as easily take them, as you may wear more or less powder in your hair, more or less lace upon your coat. I can, therefore, account for your wanting them, no other way in the world, than from your not being yet convinced of their full value. You have heard some English bucks say, 'Damn these finical outlandish airs, give me a manly, resolute manner. They make a rout with their graces, and talk like a parcel of dancing-masters, and dress like a parcel of fops; one good Englishman will beat three of them.' But let your own observation undeceive you of these prejudices. I will give you one instance only, instead of a hundred that I could give you, of a very shining fortune and figure, raised upon no other foundation whatsoever, than that of address, manners, and graces. Between you and me (for this example must go no farther) what do you think made our friend, Lord A ° ° ° ° e, Colonel of a regiment of guards, Governor of Virginia, Groom of the Stole, and Embassador to Paris; amounting in all to sixteen or seventeen thousand pounds a year? Was it his birth? No; a Dutch gentleman only. Was it his estate? No, he had none. Was it his learning, his parts, his political abilities and application? You can answer these questions as easily, and as soon, as I can ask them. What was it then? Many people wondered, but I do not; for I know, and will tell you. It was his air, his address, his manners, and his graces. He pleased, and by pleasing became a favourite; and by becoming a favourite became all that he has been since. Show me any one instance, where intrinsic worth and merit, unassisted by exterior accomplishments, have raised any man so high. You know the Duc de Richelieu, now *Maréchal, Cordon bleu, Gentilhomme de la Chambre,* twice Embassador, &c. By what means? Not by the purity of his character, the depth of his knowledge, or any uncommon penetration and sagacity. Women alone formed and raised him. The Duchess of Burgundy took a fancy to him, and had him before he was sixteen years old; this put him in fashion among the *beau monde:* and the late Regent's eldest daughter, now Madame de Modene, took him next, and was near marrying him. These early connections with women of the first distinction, gave him those manners, graces, and address, which you see he has ; and which, I can assure you, are all that he has ; for strip him of them, and he will be one of the poorest men in Europe. Man or woman cannot resist an engaging exterior ; it will please, it will make its way. You want, it seems, but *quelques couches;* for God's sake lose no time in getting them ; and now you have gone so far, complete the work. Think of nothing else till that work is finished ; unwearied application will bring about anything ; and surely your application can never be so well employed as upon that object, which is absolutely necessary to facilitate all others. With your knowledge and parts, if adorned by manners and graces, what may you not hope one day to be ? But without them, you will be in the situation of a man who should be very fleet of one leg, but very lame of the other. He could not run, the lame leg would check and clog the well one, which would be very near useless.

From my original plan for your education, I meant to make you *un homme universel ;* what depended upon me is executed, the little that remains undone depends singly upon you. Do not, then, disappoint, when you can so easily gratify me. It is your own interest which I am pressing you to pursue, and it is the only return that I desire for all the care and affection of, Yours.

LETTER CCXLVIII.

My dear Friend,   London, May the 31st, O.S., 1752.

The world is the book, and the only one to which, at present, I would have you apply yourself; and the thorough knowledge of it will be of more use to you than all the books that ever were read. Lay aside the best book whenever you can go into the best company ; and depend upon it you change for the better. However, as the most tumultuous life, whether of business or pleasure, leaves some vacant moments every day, in which a book is the refuge of a rational being, I mean now to point out to you the method of employing those moments (which will and ought to be but few) in the most advantageous manner. Throw away none of your time upon those trivial futile books, published by idle or necessitous authors, for the amusement of idle and ignorant readers : such sort of books swarm and buzz about one every day; flap them away, they have no sting. *Certum pete finem,*[1] have some one object for those leisure moments, and pursue that object invariably till you have attained it; and then take some other. For instance; considering your destination, I would advise you to single out the most remarkable and interesting æras of modern history, and confine all your reading to that *Æra.* If you pitch upon the Treaty of Munster (and that is the proper period to begin with, in the course which I am now recommending), do not interrupt it by dipping and deviating into other books, unrelative to it: but consult only the most authentic histories, letters, memoirs, and negotiations relative to that great transaction; reading and comparing them, with all that caution and distrust which Lord Bolingbroke recommends to you, in a better manner and in better words than I can. The next period, worth your particular knowledge, is the Treaty of the Pyrenées; which was calculated to lay, and in effect did lay, the foundation of the succession of the House of Bourbon to the Crown of Spain. Pursue that in the same manner, singling, out of the millions of volumes written upon that occasion, the two or three most authentic ones; and particularly letters, which are the best authorities in matters of negotiation. Next come the Treaties of Nimeguen and Ryswick, postscripts in a manner to those of Munster and the Pyrenées. Those two transactions have had great light thrown upon them by the publication of many authentic and original letters and pieces. The concessions made at the Treaty of Ryswick, by the then triumphant Lewis the Fourteenth, astonished all those who viewed things only superficially; but, I should think, must have been easily accounted for by those who knew the state of the kingdom of Spain, as well as of the health of its King, Charles the Second, at that time. The. interval between the conclusion of the peace of Ryswick, and the breaking out of the great war in 1702, though a short, is a most interesting one. Every week of it almost produced some great event. Two Partition Treaties, the death of the King of Spain, his unexpected Will, and the acceptance of it by Lewis the Fourteenth, in violation of the second treaty of partition, just signed and ratified by him. Philip the Fifth, quietly and cheerfully received in Spain, and acknowledged as King of it, by most of those Powers, who afterwards joined in an alliance to dethrone him. I cannot help making this observation upon that occasion; That character has often more to do in great transactions, than prudence and sound

---

[1] Follow some definite object.

policy : for Lewis the Fourteenth gratified his personal pride, by giving a Bourbon King to Spain, at the expense of the true interest of France; which would have acquired much more solid and permanent strength by the addition of Naples, Sicily, and Lorraine, upon the foot of the second Partition Treaty; and I think it was fortunate for Europe that he preferred the Will. It is true, he might hope to influence his grandson ; but he could never expect that his Bourbon posterity in France should influence his Bourbon posterity in Spain ; he knew too well how weak the ties of blood are among men, and how much weaker still they are among Princes. The Memoirs of Count Harrach, and of Las Torres, give a good deal of light into the transactions of the Court of Spain, previous to the death of that weak King; and the letters of the Maréchal d'Harcourt, then the French Ambassador in Spain, of which I have authentic copies in manuscript, from the year 1698 to 1701, have cleared up that whole affair to me. I keep that book for you. It appears by those letters, that the imprudent conduct of the House of Austria, with regard to the King and Queen of Spain, and Madame Berlips, her favourite, together with the knowledge of the Partition Treaty, which incensed all Spain, were the true and only reasons of the Will in favour of the Duke of Anjou. Cardinal Portocarrero, nor any of the Grandees, were bribed by France, as was generally reported and believed at that time ; which confirms Voltaire's anecdote upon that subject. Then opens a new scene and a new century : Lewis the Fourteenth's good fortune forsakes him, till the Duke of Marlborough and Prince Eugene make him amends for all the mischief they had done him, by making the allies refuse the terms of peace offered by him at Gertruydenberg. How the disadvantageous peace of Utrecht was afterwards brought on, you have lately read ; and you cannot inform yourself too minutely of all those circumstances, that treaty being the freshest source, from whence the late transactions of Europe have flowed. The alterations which have since happened, whether by wars or treaties, are so recent, that all the written accounts are to be helped out, proved, or contradicted, by the oral ones of almost every informed person of a certain age or rank in life. For the facts, dates, and original pieces of this century, you will find them in Lamberti, till the year 1715, and after that time in Rousset's *Recueil.*

I do not mean that you should plod hours together in researches of this kind ; no, you may employ your time more usefully ; but I mean that you should make the most of the moments you do employ, by method, and the pursuit of one single object at a time; nor should I call it a digression from that object, if, when you meet with clashing and jarring pretensions of different Princes to the same thing, you had immediate recourse to other books, in which those several pretensions were clearly stated ; on the contrary, that is the only way of remembering those contested rights and claims : for, were a man to read *tout de suite*, *Schwederus's Theatrum Pretensionum*, he would only be confounded by the variety, and remember none of them ; whereas, by examining them occasionally, as they happen to occur, either in the course of your historical reading, or as they are agitated in your own times, you will retain them, by connecting them with those historical facts which occasioned your inquiry. For example ; had you read, in the course of two or three folios of Pretensions, those, among others, of the two Kings of England and Prussia to Oost Frise, it is impossible that you should have remembered them ; but now that they are become the debated object at the Diet at Ratisbon, and the topic of all political conversations, if you consult both books and persons concerning them, and inform yourself thoroughly, you will never forget them as long as you live. You will hear a great deal of them on one side, at Hanover ; and as much on the other side, afterwards, at Berlin : hear both sides, and form your own opinion ; but dispute with neither.

Letters from foreign Ministers to their Courts, and from their Courts to them, are, if genuine, the best and most authentic records you can read, as far as they go. Cardinal D'Ossat's, President Jeannin's, D'Estrade's, Sir William Temple's, will not only inform your mind, but form your style ; which, in letters of business, should be very plain and simple, but, at the same time, exceedingly clear, correct, and pure.

All that I have said may be reduced to these two or three plain principles : 1st, That you should now read very little, but converse a great deal ; 2ndly, To read no useless, unprofitable books ; and 3rdly, That those which you do read, may all tend to a certain object, and be relative to, and consequential of, each other. In this method, half an hour's reading, every day, will carry you a great way. People seldom know how to employ their time to the best advantage, till they have too little left to employ ; but if, at your age, in the beginning of life, people would but consider the value of it, and put every moment to interest, it is incredible what an additional fund of knowledge and pleasure such an economy would bring in. I look back with regret upon that large sum of time, which, in my youth, I lavished away idly, without either improvement or pleasure. Take warning betimes, and enjoy every moment; pleasures do not commonly last so long as life, and therefore should not be neglected; and the longest life is too short for knowledge, consequently every moment is precious.

I am surprised at having received no letter from you since you left Paris. I still direct this to Strasburgh, as I did my two last. I shall direct my next to the post-house at Maïence, unless I receive, in the mean time, contrary instructions from you. Adieu! Remember *les attentions:* they must be your passports into good company.

LETTER CCXLIX.

MY DEAR FRIEND, London, June the 23rd, O. S. 1752.

I DIRECT this letter to Mayence, where I think it is likely to meet you, supposing, as I do, that you staid three weeks at Manheim after the date of your last from thence; but should you have staid longer at Manheim, to which I have no objection, it will wait for you at Maïence. Maïence will not, I believe, have charms to detain you above a week; so that I reckon you will be at Bonn at the end of July, N. S. There you may stay just as little or as long as you please, and then proceed to Hanover.

I had a letter, by the last post, from a relation of mine at Hanover, Mr Stanhope Aspinwall, who is in the Duke of Newcastle's office, and has lately been appointed the King's Minister to the Dey of Algiers; a post, which, notwithstanding your views of foreign affairs, I believe you do not envy him. He tells me in that letter, there are very good lodgings to be had at one Mrs Meyers', the next door to the Duke of Newcastle's, which he offers to take for you: I have desired him to do it, in case Mrs Meyers will wait for you till the latter end of August, or the beginning of September, N.S., which, I suppose, is about the time when you will be at Hanover. You will find this Mr Aspinwall of great use to you there. He will exert himself to the utmost to serve you: he has been twice or thrice at Hanover, and knows all the *allûres* there: he is very well with the Duke of Newcastle, and will puff you there. Moreover, if you have a mind to work as a volunteer in that *bureau*, he will assist and inform you. In short, he is a very honest, sensible, and informed man; *mais ne paie pas beaucoup de sa figure; il abuse même du privilége qu'ont les hommes d'être laids ; et il ne sera pas en reste, avec les Lions et les Léopards qu'il trouvera à Alger.*[1]

As you are entirely master of the time when you will leave Bonn, and go to Hanover, so are you master to stay at Hanover as long as you please, and to go from thence where you please ; provided that at Christmas you are at Berlin, for the beginning of the Carnival : this I would not have you say at Hanover, considering the mutual disposition of those two Courts ; but, when anybody asks you where you are to go next, say, that you propose rambling in Germany, at Brunswick, Cassel, &c., till the next spring; when you intend to be in Flanders, in your way to England. I take Berlin, at this time, to be the politest, the most shining, and the most useful Court in Europe, for a young fellow to be at : and therefore I would upon no account not have you there, for at least a couple of months of the Carnival. If you are as well received, and pass your time as well, at Bonn, as I believe you will, I would advise you to remain there till about the 20th of August, N. S. ; in four days more you will be at Hanover. As for your stay there, it must be shorter or longer, according to certain circumstances *which you know of ;* supposing them at the best, then stay till within a week or ten days of the King's return to England ; but supposing them at the worst, your stay must not be too short, for reasons which you also know : no resentment must either appear or be suspected ; therefore, at worst, I think you must remain there a month, and at best, as long as ever you please. But I am convinced that all will turn out very well for you there. Everybody is engaged or inclined to help you ; the Ministers, both English and German, the principal Ladies, and most of the foreign Ministers ; so that I may apply to you *nullum numen abest, si sit prudentia.* Du Perron will, I believe, be back there, from Turin, much about the time you get thither : pray be very attentive to him, and connect yourself with him as much as ever you can ; for, besides that he is a very pretty and well-informed man, he is very much in fashion at Hanover, is personally very well with the King, and certain Ladies ; so that a visible intimacy and connection with him will do you credit and service. Pray cultivate Monsieur Hop, the Dutch Minister, who has always been very much my friend, and will, I am sure, be yours : his manners, it is true, are not very engaging ; he is rough, but he is sincere. It is very useful sometimes to see the things which one ought to avoid, as it is right

---

[1] But he is not handsome, he even abuses a man's privilege of being ugly ; and will not lag far behind the lions and leopards of Algiers.

to see very often those which one ought to imitate ; and my friend Hop's manners will frequently point out to you what yours ought to be, by the rule of contraries.

Congreve points out a sort of critics, to whom he says that we are doubly obliged :

> Rules for good writing they with pains indite,
> Then show us what is bad, by what they write.

It is certain that Monsieur Hop, with the best heart in the world, and a thousand good qualities, has a thousand enemies, and hardly a friend : singly from the roughness of his manners.

N.B. I heartily wish you could have stayed long enough at Manheim, to have been seriously and desperately in love with Madame de Taxis ; who I suppose is a proud, insolent fine Lady, and who would consequently have expected attentions little short of adoration : nothing would do you more good than such a passion ; and I live in hopes that somebody or other will be able to excite such a one in you : your hour may not yet be come, but it will come. Love has been not unaptly compared to the smallpox, which most people have sooner or later. Iphigenia had a wonderful effect upon Cimon ; I wish some Hanover Iphigenia may try her skill upon you.

I recommend to you again, though I have already done it twice or thrice, to speak German, even affectedly, while you are at Hanover ; which will show that you prefer that language, and be of more use to you there with *somebody*, than you can imagine. When you carry my letters to Monsieur Munchausen, and Monsieur Schwiegeldt, address yourself to them in German ; the latter speaks French very well, but the former extremely ill. Show great attention to Madame Munchausen's daughter, who is a great favourite : these little trifles please mothers, and sometimes fathers, extremely. Observe and you will find, almost universally, that the least things either please or displease most ; because they necessarily imply, either a very strong desire of obliging, or an unpardonable indifference about it. I will give you a ridiculous instance enough of this truth, from my own experience. When I was Embassador the first time in Holland, Comte de Wassenaer and his wife, people of the first rank and consideration, had a little boy of about three years old, of whom they were exceedingly fond : in order to make my court to them, I was so too, and used to take the child often upon my lap, and play with him. One day his nose was very snotty, upon which I took out my handkerchief and wiped it for him ; this raised a loud laugh, and they called me a very handy nurse ; but the father and mother were so pleased with it, that to this day it is an anecdote in the family ; and I never receive a Letter from Comte Wassenaer, but he makes me the compliments *du morceux que j'ai mouché autrefois :* [1] who, by the way, I am assured, is now the prettiest young fellow in Holland. Where one would gain people, remember that nothing is little. Adieu.

LETTER CCL.

MY DEAR FRIEND,   London, June the 26th, O. S. 1752.

As I have reason to fear, from your last letter of the 18th, N. S., from Manheim, that all, or at least most, of my letters to you, since you left Paris, have miscarried, I think it requisite, at all events, to repeat in this the necessary parts of those several letters, as far as they relate to your future motions.

I suppose that this will either find you, or be but a few days before you, at Bonn, where it is directed ; and I suppose, too, that you have fixed your time for going from thence to Hanover. If things *turn out well at Hanover*, as in my opinion they will, *Chi stà bene non si muova*,[2] stay there till a week or ten days before the King sets out for England; but, should *they turn out ill*, which I cannot imagine, stay however a month, that your departure may not seem a step of discontent or peevishness ; the very suspicion of which is by all means to be avoided. Whenever you leave Hanover, be it sooner or later, where would you go ? *Ella è Padrone*,[3] and I give you your choice : Would you pass the months of November and December at Brunswick, Cassel, &c. ? Would you choose to go for a couple of months to Ratisbon, where you would be very well recommended to, and treated by, the King's Electoral Minister, the Baron de Behr, and where you would improve your *jus publicum?* Or would you rather go directly to Berlin, and stay there till the end of the Carnival ? Two or three months at Berlin are, considering all circumstances, necessary for you ; and the Carnival months are the best ; *pour le reste décidez en dernier ressort, et sans appel comme d'abus.* Let me only know your decree, when you have formed it. Your good or ill success at Hanover will have a very great influence upon your

---

[1] Of the little brat whose nose I once wiped.
[2] He who is well off keeps where he is.
[3] You are master.

subsequent character, figure, and fortune in the world; therefore I confess, that I am more anxious about it, than ever bride
was on her wedding-night, when wishes, hopes, fears, and
doubts, tumultuously agitate, please, and terrify her. It is
your first crisis: the character which you acquire there will,
more or less, be that which will abide by you for the rest of
your life. You will be tried and judged there, not as a boy,
but as a man; and from that moment there is no appeal for
character: it is fixed. To form that character advantageously,
you have three objects particularly to attend to: your character
as a man of morality, truth, and honour; your knowledge in
the objects of your destination, as a man of business; and
your engaging and insinuating address, air, and manners, as a
Courtier; the sure and only steps to favour. Merit at Courts,
without favour, will do little or nothing; favour, without merit,
will do a good deal; but favour and merit together will do
everything. Favour at Courts depends upon so many, such
trifling, such unexpected, and unforeseen events, that a good
courtier must attend to every circumstance, however little, that
either does or can happen; he must have no absences, no *distractions;* he must not say, 'I did not mind it; who would
have thought it?' He ought both to have minded and to
have thought it. A chambermaid has sometimes caused revolutions in Courts, which have produced others in kingdoms.
Were I to make my way to favour in a Court, I would neither
wilfully, nor by negligence, give a dog or a cat there reason to
dislike me. Two *pies grièches*, well instructed, you know, made
the fortune of de Luines with Lewis XIII. Every step a man
makes at Court requires as much attention and circumspection,
as those which were made formerly between hot ploughshares,
in the Ordeal, or fiery trials; which, in those times of ignorance
and superstition, were looked upon as demonstrations of innocence or guilt. Direct your principal battery, at Hanover, at
the D—— of N——'s: there are many very weak places in
that citadel; where, with a very little skill, you cannot fail
making a great impression. Ask for his orders, in everything
you do; talk Austrian and Antigallican to him; and, as soon
as you are upon a foot of talking easily to him, tell him *en
badinant,* that his skill and success, in thirty or forty elections
in England, leave you no reason to doubt of his carrying his
Election for Frankfort; and that you look upon the Archduke
as his Member for the Empire. In his hours of festivity and
compotation, drop, that he puts you in mind of what Sir
William Temple says of the Pensionary de Wit; who at that

time governed half Europe ; that he appeared at balls, assemblies, and public places, as if he had nothing else to do or to think of. When he talks to you upon foreign affairs, which he will often do, say that you really cannot presume to give any opinion of your own upon those matters, looking upon yourself, at present, only as a postscript to the *corps diplomatique;* but that, if his Grace will be pleased to make you an additional volume to it, though but in *duodecimo,* you will do your best, that he shall neither be ashamed nor repent of it. He loves to have a favourite, and to open himself to that favourite : he has now no such person with him ; the place is vacant, and if you have dexterity you may fill it. In one thing alone do not humour him ; I mean drinking; for as I believe you have never yet been drunk, you do not yourself know how you can bear your wine, and what a little too much of it may make you do or say; you might possibly kick down all you had done before.

You do not love gaming, and I thank God for it ; but at Hanover I would have you show, and profess, a particular dislike to play, so as to decline it upon all occasions, unless where one may be wanted to make a fourth at whist or quadrille ; and then take care to declare it the result of your complaisance, not of your inclinations. Without such precaution, you may very possibly be suspected, though unjustly, of loving play, upon account of my former passion for it ; and such a suspicion would do you a great deal of hurt, especially with the King, who detests gaming. I must end this abruptly. God bless you.

LETTER CCLI.

My dear Friend,

VERSATILITY as a Courtier, may be almost decisive to you hereafter ; that is, it may conduce to, or retard, your preferment in your own destination. The first reputation goes a great way ; and if you fix a good one at Hanover, it will operate also to your advantage in England. The trade of a Courtier is as much a trade as that of a shoemaker; and he who applies himself the most will work the best : the only difficulty is to distinguish (what I am sure you have sense enough to distinguish) between the right and proper qualifications and their kindred faults ; for there is but a line between every perfection and its neighbouring imperfection. As, for example, you must be extremely well-bred and polite, but without the troublesome forms and stiffness of ceremony. You must be respectful and assenting, but without being servile and abject. You must be frank, but without indiscretion, and close, without being costive. You must keep up dignity of character, without the least pride of birth or rank. You must be gay, within all the bounds of decency and respect; and grave without the affectation of wisdom, which does not become the age of twenty. You must be essentially secret, without being dark and mysterious. You must be firm, and even bold, but with great seeming modesty.

With these qualifications, which by the way are all in your own power, I will answer for your success, not only at Hanover, but at any Court in Europe. And I am not sorry that you begin your apprenticeship at a little one; because you must be more circumspect, and more upon your guard there, than at a great one, where every little thing is not known, nor reported.

When you write to me, or to anybody else, from thence, take care that your letters contain commendations of all you see and hear there; for they will most of them be opened and read : but, as frequent Couriers will come from Hanover to England, you may sometimes write to me without reserve, and put your letters into a very little box, which you may send safely by some of them.

I must not omit mentioning to you, that at the Duke of Newcastle's table, where you will frequently dine, there is a great deal of drinking; be upon your guard against it, both upon account of your health, which would not bear it, and of the consequences of your being flustered and heated with wine : it might engage you in scrapes and frolics, which the King (who is a very sober man himself) detests. On the other hand, you should not seem too grave and too wise to drink like the rest of the company, therefore use art : mix water with your wine; do not drink all that is in the glass ; and if detected, and pressed to drink more, do not cry out sobriety; but say that you have lately been out of order, that you are subject to inflammatory complaints, and that you must beg to be excused for the present. A young fellow ought to be wiser than he should seem to be ; and an old fellow ought to seem wise, whether he really be so or not.

During your stay at Hanover, I would have you make two or three excursions to parts of that Electorate : the Hartz, where the silver mines are ; Gottingen, for the university ; Stade, for what commerce there is. You should also go to Zell. In short, see everything that is to be seen there, and inform yourself well of all the details of that country. Go to Hamburgh for three or four days, know the constitution of that little Hanseatic Republic, and inform yourself well of the nature of the King of Denmark's pretensions to it.

If all things turn out right for you at Hanover, I would have you make it your head-quarters till about a week or ten days before the King leaves it; and then go to Brunswick, which though a little, is a very polite, pretty Court. You may stay there a fortnight or three weeks, as you like it; and from thence go to Cassel, and there stay till you go to Berlin, where I would have you be by Christmas. At Hanover you will very easily get good letters of recommendation to Brunswick and to Cassel. You do not want any to Berlin; however, I will send you one for Voltaire. *A propos* of Berlin: be very reserved and cautious while at Hanover, as to that King and that country; both which are detested, because feared by everybody there, from his Majesty down to the meanest peasant: but, however, they both extremely deserve your utmost attention; and you will see the arts and wisdom of government better in that country now, than in any other in Europe. You may stay three months at Berlin, if you like it, as I believe you will; and after that I hope we shall meet here again.

Of all the places in the world (I repeat it once more) establish a good reputation at Hanover, *et faites-vous valoir là, autant qu'il est possible; par le brillant, les manières, et les grâces.*[1] Indeed it is of the greatest importance to you, and will make any future application to the King in your behalf very easy. He is more taken by those little things than any man, or even woman, that I ever knew in my life: and I do not wonder at him. In short, exert to the utmost all your means and powers to please; and remember, that he who pleases the most will rise the soonest, and the highest. Try but once the pleasure and advantage of pleasing, and I will answer that you will never more neglect the means.

I send you herewith two letters, the one to Monsieur Munchausen, the other to Monsieur Schwiegeldt, an old friend of mine, and a very sensible knowing man. They will both, I am sure, be extremely civil to you, and carry you into the best company; and then it is your business to please that company. I never was more anxious about any period of your life than I am about this your Hanover expedition, it being of so much more consequence to you than any other. If I hear from thence

---

[1] Make yourself of repute there as much as possible by brilliancy, by good manners, and by the graces.

that you are liked and loved there for your air, your manners, and address, as well as esteemed for your knowledge, I shall be the happiest man in the world ; judge, then, what I must be, if it happens otherwise.   Adieu !

LETTER CCLII.

My dear Friend,   London, July the 21st, O. S. 1752.

By my calculation, this letter may probably arrive at Hanover three or four days before you ; and as I am sure of its arriving there safe, it shall contain the most material points that I have mentioned in my several letters to you since you left Paris, as if you had received but few of them, which may very probably be the case.

As for your stay at Hanover, it must not *in all events* be less than a month ; but if things turn out to *your satisfaction*, it may be just as long as you please.   From thence you may go wherever you like, for I have so good an opinion of your judgment, that I think you will combine and weigh all circumstances, and choose the properest places.—Would you saunter at some of the small Courts, as Brunswick, Cassel, &c., till the Carnival at Berlin ?   You are master.   Would you pass a couple of months at Ratisbon, which might not be ill employed ?   *A la bonne heure.*   Would you go to Brussels, stay a month or two there with Dayrolles, and from thence to Mr Yorke, at the Hague ?   With all my heart.   Or, lastly, would you go to Copenhagen and Stockholm ?   *Ella è anche Padrone :* choose entirely for yourself, without any further instructions from me ; only let me know your determination in time, that I may settle your credit, in case you go to places where at present you have none.   Your object should be to see the *mores multorum hominum et urbes ;* begin and end it where you please.

By what you have already seen of the German Courts, I am sure you must have observed that they are much more nice and scrupulous, in points of ceremony, respect, and attention, than the greater Courts of France and England.   You will therefore, I am persuaded, attend to the minutest circumstances of address and behaviour, particularly during your stay at Hanover, which (I will repeat it, though I have said it often to you already) is the most important preliminary period of your whole life.   Nobody in the world is more exact in all points of good breeding than the King ; and it is the part of every man's character that he informs himself of first. The least negligence, or the slightest inattention, reported to him, may do you infinite prejudices ; as their contraries would service.

If Lord Albemarle (as I believe he did) trusted you with the secret affairs of his department, let the Duke of Newcastle know that he did so, which will be an inducement to him to trust you too, and possibly to employ you in affairs of consequence. Tell him that, though you are young, you know the importancé of secrecy in business, and can keep a secret ; that I have always inculcated this doctrine into you, and have moreover strictly forbidden you ever to communicate, even to me, any matters of a secret nature, which you may happen to be trusted with in the course of business.

As for business, I think I can trust you to yourself ; but I wish I could say as much for you with regard to those exterior accomplishments, which are absolutely necessary to smooth and shorten the way to it. Half the business is done, when one has gained the heart and the affections of those with whom one is to transact it. Air and address must begin, manners and attention must finish, that work. I will let you into one secret concerning myself; which is, that I owe much more of the success which I have had in the world to my manners than to any superior degree of merit or knowledge. I desired to please, and I neglected none of the means. This, I can assure you, without any false modesty, is the truth. You have more knowledge than I had at your age, but then I had much more attention and good breeding than you. Call it vanity, if you please, and possibly it was so ; but my great object was to make every man I met with like me, and every woman love me. I often succeeded ; but why ? By taking great pains, for otherwise I never should ; my figure by no means entitled me to it, and I had certainly an up-hill game : whereas your countenance would help you, if you made the most of it, and proscribed for ever the guilty, gloomy, and funereal part of it. Dress, address, and air would become your best countenance, and make your little figure pass very well.

If you have time to read at Hanover, pray let the books you read be all relative to the history and constitution of that country, which I would have you know as correctly as any Hanoverian in the whole Electorate. Inform yourself of the powers of the States, and of the nature and extent of the several Judicatures ; the particular articles of trade and commerce of Bremen, Harburg, and Stade ; the details and value of the mines of the Hartz. Two or three short books will give you the outlines of all these things ;

and conversation, turned upon those subjects, will do the rest, and better than books can.

Remember of all things to speak nothing but German there ; make it (to express myself pedantically) your vernacular language ; seem to prefer it to any other ; call it your favourite language, and study to speak it with purity and elegancy, if it has any.—This will not only make you perfect in it, but will please, and make your court there better than anything. *A propos* of languages : Did you improve your Italian while you were at Paris, or did you forget it ? Had you a master there ; and what Italian books did you read with him ? If you are master of Italian, 1 would have you afterwards, by the first convenient opportunity, learn Spanish, which you may very easily and in a very little time do ; you will then, in the course of your foreign business, never be obliged to employ, pay, or trust any Translator for any European language.

As I love to provide eventually for everything that can possibly happen, I will suppose the worst that can befall you at Hanover. In that case I would have you go immediately to the Duke of Newcastle, and beg his Grace's advice, or rather orders, what you should do ; adding, that his advice will always be orders to you. You will tell him that, though you are exceedingly mortified, you are much less so than you should otherwise be, from the consideration that, being utterly unknown to his M——, his objection could not be personal to you, and could only arise from circumstances, which it was not in your power either to prevent or remedy : that if his Grace thought that your continuing any longer there would be disagreeable, you entreat him to tell you so ; and that, upon the whole, you referred yourself entirely to him, whose orders you should most scrupulously obey. But this precaution, I dare say, is *ex abundanti*, and will prove unnecessary ; however, it is always right to be prepared for all events, the worst as well as the best ; it prevents hurry and surprise, two dangerous situations in business : for I know no one thing so useful, so necessary in all business as great coolness, steadiness, and *sang froid ;* they give an incredible advantage over whomever one has to do with.

I have received your letter of the 15th, N. S., from Mayence, where I find that you have diverted yourself much better than I expected. I am very well acquainted with Comte Cobentzel's character, both of parts and business. He could have given you letters to Bonn, having formerly resided there himself. You will not be so agreeably *electrified*, where this letter will find you, as you were both at Manheim and Mayence ; but I hope you may meet with a second German Mrs F———d, who may make you forget the two former ones, and practise your German. Such transient passions will do you no harm ; but, on the contrary, a great deal of good : they will refine your manners and quicken your attention ; they give a young fellow *du brillant*, and bring him into fashion, which last is a great article in setting out in the world.

I have wrote, above a month ago, to Lord Albemarle, to thank him for all his kindnesses to you ; but pray have you done as much ? Those are the necessary attentions which should never be omitted, especially in the beginning of life, when a character is to be established.

That ready wit which you so partially allow me, and so justly Sir Charles Williams, may create many admirers; but, take my word for it, it makes few friends. It shines and dazzles like the noonday sun, but, like that too, is very apt to scorch, and therefore is always feared. The milder morning and evening light and heat of that planet, soothe and calm our minds. Good sense, complaisance, gentleness of manners, attentions, and graces, are the only things that truly engage, and durably keep, the heart at long run. Never seek for wit; if it presents itself well and good, but even in that case let your judgment interpose, and take care that it be not at the expense of anybody. Pope says very truly,

> There are whom Heaven has blest with store of wit,
> Yet want as much again to govern it.

And in another place, I doubt with too much truth,

> For wit and judgment ever are at strife,
> Though meant each other's aid, like man and wife.

The Germans are very seldom troubled with any extraordinary ebullitions or effervescences of wit, and it is not prudent to try it upon them ; whoever does, *offendet solido*.[1]

Remember to write me very minute accounts of all your transactions at Hanover, for they excite both my impatience and anxiety. Adieu.

———

LETTER CCLIII.

MY DEAR FRIEND, London, Aug. the 4th, O. S. 1752.

I AM extremely concerned at the return of your old asthmatic

1 Strikes against a solid body.

complaint, which your letter from Cassel of the 28th July, N. S.,
informs me of. I believe it is chiefly owing to your own negligence ; for, notwithstanding the season of the year, and the
heat and agitation of travelling, I dare swear you have not taken
one single dose of gentle, cooling physic, since that which I
made you take at Bath. I hope you are now better, and in
better hands, I mean in Dr Hugo's at Hanover ; he is certainly a
very skilful physician, and therefore I desire that you will inform him most minutely of your own case, from your first attack
in Carniola to this last at Marpurgh ; and not only follow his
prescriptions exactly at present, but take his directions, with
regard to the regimen that he would have you observe to prevent the returns of this complaint ; and in case of any returns,
the immediate applications, whether external or internal, that
he would have you make use of. Consider, it is very well worth
your while to submit at present to any course of medicine or diet,
to any restraint or confinement, for a time, in order to get rid,
once for all, of so troublesome and painful a distemper : the
returns of which would equally break in upon your business or
your pleasures. Notwithstanding all this, which is plain sense
and reason, I much fear that, as soon as ever you are got out of
your present distress, you will take no preventive care, by a
proper course of medicines and regimen ; but, like most people
of your age, think it impossible that you ever should be ill again.
However, if you will not be wise for your own sake, I desire
you will be so for mine, and most scrupulously observe Dr
Hugo's present and future directions.

Hanover, where I take it for granted you are, is at present
the seat and centre of foreign negotiations ; there are Ministers
from almost every Court in Europe ; and you have a fine opportunity of displaying with modesty, in conversation, your
knowledge of the matters now in agitation. The chief I take
to be the Election of the King of the Romans, which, though
I despair of, I heartily wish were brought about, for two reasons.
The first is, that I think it may prevent a war upon the death of
the present Emperor, who, though young and healthy, may possibly die, as young and healthy people often do. The other
is the very reason that makes some Powers oppose it, and
others dislike it who do not openly oppose it ; I mean, that it
may tend to make the Imperial dignity hereditary in the House
of Austria, which I heartily wish, together with a very great
increase of power in the Empire ; till when, Germany will
never be anything near a match for France. Cardinal Richelieu showed his superior abilities in nothing more than in

thinking no pains nor expense too great to break the power of the House of Austria in the Empire. Ferdinand had certainly made himself absolute, and the Empire consequently formidable to France, if that Cardinal had not piously adopted the Protestant cause, and put the Empire, by the treaty of Westphalia, in pretty much the same disjointed situation in which France itself was before Louis the XIth ; when Princes of the blood, at the head of provinces, and Dukes of Brittany, &c., always opposed, and often gave laws to the Crown. Nothing but making the Empire hereditary in the House of Austria, can give it that strength and efficiency which I wish it had, for the sake of the balance of power. For, while the Princes of the Empire are so independent of the Emperor, so divided among themselves, and so open to the corruption of the best bidders, it is ridiculous to expect that Germany ever will or can act as a compact and well-united body against France. But as this notion of mine would as little please *some of our friends*, as many of our enemies, I would not advise you, though you should be of the same opinion, to declare yourself too freely so. Could the Elector Palatine be satisfied, which I confess will be difficult, considering the nature of his pretensions, the tenaciousness and haughtiness of the Court of Vienna, and our inability to do, as we have too often done, their work for them ; I say, if the Elector Palatine could be engaged to give his vote, I should think it would be right to proceed to the election with a clear majority of five votes ; and leave the King of Prussia, and the Elector of Cologne, to protest and remonstrate as much as ever they please. The former is too wise, and the latter too weak in every respect, to act in consequence of those protests. The distracted situation of France, with its ecclesiastical and parliamentary quarrels, not to mention the illness and possibly the death of the Dauphin, will make the King of Prussia, who is certainly no Frenchman in his heart, very cautious how he acts as one. The Elector of Saxony will be influenced by the King of Poland, who must be determined by Russia, considering his views upon Póland, which, by the by, I hope he will never obtain : I mean, as to making that crown hereditary in his family. As for his son's having it by the precarious tenure of election, by which his father now holds it, *à la bonne heure*. But should Poland have a good government under hereditary Kings, there would be a new devil raised in Europe, that I do not know who could lay. I am sure I would not raise him, though on my own side, for the present.

I do not know how I came to trouble my head so much

about politics to-day, which has been so very free from them for some years ; I suppose it was because I knew that I was writing to the most consummate politician of this, and his, age. If I err, you will set me right ; *si quid novisti rectius istis, candidus imperti,*[1] *&c.*

I am excessively impatient for your next letter, which I expect by the first post from Hanover, to remove my anxiety, as I hope it will, not only with regard to your health, but likewise to *other things;* in the mean time, in the language of a pedant, but with the tenderness of a parent, *jubeo te bene valere.*

Lady Chesterfield makes you many compliments, and is much concerned at your indisposition.

LETTER CCLIV.

A Monsieur de Voltaire pour lors à Berlin.

MONSIEUR, A Londres, 27 d'Août, V. S. 1752.

JE m'intéresse infiniment à tout ce qui touche Monsieur Stanhope, qui aura l'honneur de vous rendre cette lettre ; c'est pourquoi je prens la liberté de vous le présenter ; je ne peux pas lui en donner une preuve plus convainquante. Il a beaucoup lu, il a beaucoup vu ; s'il l'a bien digéré, voilà ce que je ne sais pas ; il n'a que vingt ans. Il a déjà été à Berlin il y a quelques années, et c'est pourquoi il y retourne à présent ; car à cette heure on revient au Nord par les mêmes raisons, pour lesquelles on alloit il n'y a pas long tems au Sud.

Permettez, Monsieur, que je vous remercie du plaisir et de l'instruction que m'a donné votre Histoire du Siècle de Louis XIV. Je ne l'ai lu encore que quatre fois, c'est que je voudrois l'oublier un peu avant la cinquième, mais je vois que cela m'est impossible ; j'attendrai donc l'augmentation que vous nous en avez promis, mais je vous supplie de ne me la pas faire attendre long tems. Je croyois savoir passablement l'Histoire du Siècle de Louis XIV. moyennant les milliers d'Histoires, de Mémoires, d'Anecdotes, &c., que j'en avois lu, mais vous m'avez bien montré que je m'étois trompé, et que je n'en avois qu'une idée très-confuse à bien des égards, et très-fausse à bien d'autres. Que je vous sais gré sur tout, Monsieur, du jour dans lequel vous avez mis les folies et les fureurs des sectes. Vous employez

---

[1] If you are better acquainted with any of these matters, communicate it with candour.

contre ces fous ou ces imposteurs les armes convenables ; d'en employer d'autres ce seroit les imiter : c'est par le ridicule qu'il faut les attaquer, c'est par le mépris qu'il faut les punir. A propos de ces fous, je vous envoie ci-jointe une pièce sur leur sujet par le feu Docteur Swift, laquelle je crois ne vous déplaira pas. Elle n'a jamais été imprimée, vous en devinerez bien la raison, mais elle est authentique. J'en ai l'original écrit de sa propre main. Son Jupiter, au jour du jugement, les traite à peu près comme vous les traitéz, et comme ils le méritent.

Au reste, Monsieur, je vous dirai franchement, que je suis embarrassé sur votre sujet, et que je ne peux pas me décider sur ce que je souhaiterois de votre part. Quand je lis votre dernière histoire, je voudrois que vous fussiez toujours historien ; mais quand je lis votre Rome Sauvée (toute mal imprimée et défigurée qu'elle est) je vous voudrois toujours Poëte. J'avoue pourtant qu'il vous reste encore une histoire à écrire digne de votre plume, et dont votre plume est seule digne. Vous nous avez donné il y a long tems l'histoire du plus grand Furieux (je vous demande pardon si je ne peus pas dire du plus grand Héros) de l'Europe. Vous nous avez donné en dernier lieu, l'histoire du plus grand Roi ; donnez-nous, à présent, l'histoire du plus grand et du plus honnête Homme de l'Europe, que je croirois dégrader en appellant Roi. Vous l'avez toujours devant vos yeux, rien ne vous seroit plus facile ; sa gloire n'exigeant pas votre invention poëtique, mais pouvant se reposer en toute sûreté sur votre vérité historique. Il n'a rien à demander à son historien, que son premier devoir comme historien, qui est, *Ne quid falsi dicere audeat, ne quid veri non audeat.* Adieu, Monsieur, je vois bien que je dois vous admirer de plus en plus tous les jours, mais aussi je sais bien que rien ne pourra jamais ajouter à l'estime et à l'attachement avec lesquels je suis actuellement,

Votre très-humble et très-obéissant serviteur,

CHESTERFIELD.

TRANSLATION.

SIR, London, August the 27th, O. S. 1752.

As a most convincing proof how infinitely I am interested in everything which concerns Mr Stanhope, who will have the honour of presenting you this letter, I take the liberty of introducing him to you. He has read a great deal, he has seen a great deal ; whether or not he has made a proper use of that knowledge, is what I do not know : he is only twenty years of age. He was at Berlin some years ago, and therefore he returns thither ; for at present people are attracted towards the north, by the same motives which but lately drew them to the south.

Permit me, Sir, to return you thanks for the pleasure and instruction I have received from your History of Lewis the Fourteenth. I have as yet read it but four times, because I wish to forget it a little before I read it a fifth ; but I find that impossible : I shall therefore only wait till you give us the augmentation which you promised : let me entreat you not to defer it long. I thought myself pretty conversant in the History of the Reign of Lewis the Fourteenth by means of those innumerable histories, memoirs, anecdotes, &c., which I had read relative to that period of time. You have convinced me that I was mistaken, and had upon that subject very confused ideas in many respects, and very false ones in others. Above all, I cannot but acknowledge the obligation we have to you, Sir, for the light which you have thrown upon the follies and outrages of the different sects ; the weapons you employ against those madmen, or those impostors, are the only suitable ones ; to make use of any others would be imitating them : they must be attacked by ridicule, and punished with contempt. *A propos* of those fanatics ; I send you here enclosed, a piece upon that subject, written by the late Dean Swift : I believe you will not dislike it. You will easily guess why it never was printed : it is authentic, and I have the original in his own handwriting. His Jupiter, at the day of judgment, treats them much as you do, and as they deserve to be treated.

Give me leave, Sir, to tell you freely, that I am embarrassed upon your account, as I cannot determine what it is that I wish from you. When I read your last history, I am desirous that you should always write history ; but when I read your *Rome Sauvée* (although ill printed and disfigured), yet I then wish you never to deviate from poetry ; however, I confess that there still remains one history worthy of your pen, and of which your pen alone is worthy. You have long ago given us the history of the greatest and most outrageous Madman (I ask your pardon if I cannot say the greatest Hero) of Europe ; you have given us latterly the history of the greatest King ; give us now the history of the greatest and most virtuous Man in Europe ; I should think it degrading to call him King. To you this cannot be difficult, he is always before your eyes ; your poetical invention is not necessary to his glory, as that may safely rely upon your historical candour. The first duty of an historian is the only one he need require from his, *Ne quid falsi dicere audeat, ne quid veri non audeat.*[1] Adieu, Sir, I find that I must admire you every day more and more; but I also know that nothing ever can add to the esteem and attachment with which I am actually,

Your most humble and most obedient servant,

CHESTERFIELD.

LETTER CCLV.

MY DEAR FRIEND,   London, Sept. the 19th, 1752.

SINCE you have been at Hanover, your correspondence has been both unfrequent and laconic. You made indeed one great effort in folio on the 18th, with a postscript of the 22nd August, N. S., and since that, *vous avez ratté in quarto.* On the 31st August, N. S., you give me no informations of what I want chiefly to know; which is, what Dr Hugo (whom I charged you to consult) said of your asthmatic complaint, and what he prescribed you to prevent the returns of it; and also what is the company that you keep there; who has been kind and civil to you, and who not.

You say that you go constantly to the parade; and you do very well, for though you are not of that trade, yet military matters make so great a part both of conversation and negotiation, that it is very proper not to be ignorant of them. I hope you mind more than the mere exercise of the troops you see; and that you inform yourself at the same time of the more material details; such as their pay, and the difference of it when in and out of quarters, what is furnished them by the country when in quarters, and what is allowed them of ammunition, bread, &c., when in the field; the number of men and officers in the several troops and companies, together with the non-commissioned officers, as *caporals, frey-caporals, anspessades,* serjeants, quarter-masters, &c.; the clothing, how frequent, how good, and how furnished; whether by the Colonel, as here in England, from what we call the *off-reckonings,* that is, deductions from the men's pay, or by Commissaries appointed by the Government for that purpose, as in France and Holland. By these inquiries you will be able to talk military with military men, who, in every country in Europe, except England, make at least half of all the best companies. Your attending the parades has also another good effect, which is, that it brings

[1] To dare to say nothing false, and to leave nothing that is true unsaid. .

you of course acquainted with the officers, who, when of a certain rank and service, are generally very polite, well-bred people, *et du bon ton.*   They have commonly seen a great deal of the World, and of Courts; and nothing else can form a gentleman, let people say what they will of sense and learning : with both which a man may contrive to be a very disagreeable companion.   I dare say there are very few Captains of foot, who are not much better company than ever Descartes or Sir Isaac Newton were.   I honour and respect such superior geniuses ; but I desire to converse with people of this world, who bring into company their share, at least, of cheerfulness, good breeding, and knowledge of mankind.   In common life, one much oftener wants small money, and silver, than gold.   Give me a man who has ready cash about him for present expenses ; sixpences, shillings, half-crowns, and crowns, which circulate easily : but a man who has only an ingot of gold about him is much above common purposes, and his riches are not handy nor convenient.   Have as much gold as you please in one pocket, but take care always to keep change in the other ; for you will much oftener have occasion for a shilling than for a guinea.   In this the French must be allowed to excel all people in the world : they have *un certain entregent, un enjouement, une aimable légéreté dans la conversation, une politesse aisée et naturelle, qui paroit ne leur rien coûter,*[1] which give Society all its charms.   I am sorry to add, but it is too true, that the English and the Dutch are the farthest from this, of all the people in the world ; I do by no means except even the Swiss.

Though you did not think proper to inform me, I know from other hands, that you were to go to the Göhr with a Comte Schullemburgh, for eight or ten days only to see the reviews. I know also, that you had a blister upon your arm, which did you a great deal of good : I know, too, you have contracted a great friendship with Lord Essex ; and that you two were inseparable at Hanover.   All these things I would rather have known from you than from others ; and they are the sort of things that I am the most desirous of knowing, as they are more immediately relative to yourself.

I am very sorry for the Duchess of Newcastle's illness, full as much upon your as upon her account, as it has hindered you from being so much known to the Duke as I could have wished : use and habit going a great way with him, as indeed they do with most people.   I have known many people patronized,

---

[1] A certain acuteness, a gaiety, a charming lightness in conversation, an easy and natural politeness, which appears to cost them nothing.

pushed up, and preferred by those who could have given no other reason for it than that they were used to them. We must never seek for motives by deep reasoning, but we must find them out by careful observation and attention; no matter what they should be; but the point is, what they are. Trace them up, step by step, from the character of the person. I have known *de par le monde*, as Brantôme says, great effects from causes too little ever to have been suspected. Some things must be known, and can never be guessed.

God knows where this letter will find you, or follow you; not at Hanover, I suppose; but wherever it does, may it find you in health and pleasure! Adieu.

———◇———

LETTER CCLVI.

My dear Friend,   London, Sept. the 22d, 1752.

The day after the date of my last, I received your letter of the 8th. I approve extremely of your intended progress, and am very glad that you go to the Göhr with Comte Schullemburg. I would have you see everything with your own eyes, and hear everything with your own ears: for I know, by very long experience, that it is very unsafe to trust to other people's. Vanity and interest cause many misrepresentations, and folly causes many more. Few people have parts enough to relate exactly and judiciously; and those who have, for some reason or other, never fail to sink, or to add some circumstances.

The reception which you have met with at Hanover I look upon as an omen of your being well received everywhere else; for, to tell you the truth, it was the place that I distrusted the most in that particular. But there is a certain conduct, there are *certaines manières* that will, and must, get the better of all difficulties of that kind; it is to acquire them that you still continue abroad, and go from Court to Court: they are personal, local, and temporal; they are modes which vary, and owe their existence to accidents, whim, and humour; all the sense and reason in the world would never point them out; nothing but experience, observation, and what is called knowledge of the world, can possibly teach them. For example; it is respectful to bow to the King of England, it is disrespectful to bow to the King of France; it is the rule to courtesy to the Emperor; and the prostration of the whole body is required by Eastern Monarchs. These are established ceremonies, and must be complied with; but why they were established, I defy sense and reason to tell us. It is the same among all ranks, where certain customs are received, and must necessarily be complied with, though by no means the result of sense and reason. As, for instance, the very absurd, though almost universal, custom of drinking people's healths. Can there be anything in the world less relative to any other man's health, than my drinking a glass of wine? Common sense, certainly, never pointed it out; but yet common sense tells me I must conform to it. Good sense bids one be civil, and endeavour to please; though nothing but experience and observation can teach one the means, properly adapted to time, place, and persons. This knowledge is the true object of a gentleman's travelling, if he travels as he ought to do. By frequenting good company in every country, he himself becomes of every country; he is no longer an Englishman, a Frenchman, or an Italian; but he is an European: he adopts, respectively, the best manners of every country; and is a Frenchman at Paris, an Italian at Rome, an Englishman at London.

This advantage, I must confess, very seldom accrues to my countrymen from their travelling; as they have neither the desire nor the means of getting into good company abroad: for, in the first place, they are confoundedly bashful; and, in the next place, they either speak no foreign language at all, or, if they do, it is barbarously. You possess all the advantages that they want; you know the languages in perfection, and have constantly kept the best company in the places where you have been; so that you ought to be an European. Your canvas is solid and strong, your outlines are good; but remember that you still want the beautiful colouring of Titian, and the delicate graceful touches of Guido. Now is your time to get them. There is, in all good company, a fashionable air, countenance, manner, and phraseology, which can only be acquired by being in good company, and very attentive to all that passes there. When you dine or sup at any well-bred man's house, observe carefully how he does the honours of his table to the different guests. Attend to the compliments of congratulation, or condolence, that you hear a well-bred man make to his superiors, to his equals, and to his inferiors; watch even his countenance and his tone of voice, for they all conspire in the main point of pleasing. There is a certain distinguishing diction of a man of fashion: he will not content himself, like John Trott, to a new married man, Sir, I wish you much joy; or to a man who has lost his son, Sir, I am sorry for your loss; and both with a countenance equally unmoved : but he will say in effect the same thing, in a more elegant and less trivial manner, and with a countenance adapted to the occasion. He will advance with warmth, vivacity, and a cheerful countenance, to the new married man, and embracing him, perhaps say to him, ' If you do justice to my attachment to you, you will judge of the joy that I feel upon this occasion, better than I can express it,' &c. ; to the other in affliction, he will advance slowly, with a grave composure of countenance, in a more deliberate manner, and with a lower voice, perhaps say, ' I hope you do me the justice to be convinced, that I feel whatever you feel, and shall ever be affected where you are concerned.'

Your *abord*, I must tell you, was too cold and uniform; I hope it is now mended. It should be respectfully open and cheerful with your superiors, warm and animated with your equals, hearty and free with your inferiors. There is a fashionable kind of *small talk* that you should get ; which, trifling as it is, is of use in mixed companies, and at table, especially in your foreign department ; where it keeps off certain serious subjects, that might create disputes, or at least coldness for a time. Upon such occasions it is not amiss to know how to *parler cuisine*, and to be able to dissert upon the growth and flavour of wines. These, it is true, are very little things ; but they are little things that occur very often, and therefore should be said *avec gentillesse, et grâce*. I am sure they must fall often in your way, pray take care to catch them. There is a certain language of conversation, a fashionable diction, of which every gentleman ought to be perfectly master, in whatever language he speaks. The French attend to it carefully, and with great reason ; and their language, which is a language of phrases, helps them out exceedingly. That delicacy of diction is characteristical of a man of fashion and good company.

I could write folios upon this subject and not exhaust it, but I think, and hope, that to you I need not. You have heard and seen enough, to be convinced of the truth and importance of what I have been so long inculcating into you upon these points. How happy am I, and how happy are you, my dear child, that these Titian tints, and Guido graces, are all that you want to complete my hopes and your own character! But then, on the other hand, what a drawback would it be to that happiness, if you should never acquire them ? I remember, when I was of your age, though I had not near so good an education as you have, or seen a quarter so much of the world, I observed those masterly touches, and irresistible graces in others, and saw the necessity of acquiring them myself; but then an awkward *mauvaise honte*, of which I had brought a great deal with me from Cambridge, made me ashamed to attempt it, especially if any of my countrymen and particular acquaintance were by. This was extremely absurd in me; for without attempting I could never succeed. But at last, insensibly, by frequenting a great deal of good company, and imitating those whom I saw that everybody liked, I formed myself *tant bien que mal*. For God's sake let this last fine varnish, so necessary to give lustre to the whole piece, be the sole and single object now of your utmost attention: Berlin may contribute a great deal to it, if you please; there are all the ingredients that compose it.

A propos of Berlin; while you are there, take care to seem ignorant of all political matters between the two Courts; such as the affairs of Ostfrise, and Saxe Lawemburg, &c., and enter into no conversations upon those points; however, be as well at Court as you possibly can; live at it, and make one of it. Should General Keith offer you civilities, do not decline them: but return them, however, without being *enfant de la maison chez lui*: say *des choses flatteuses* of the Royal Family, and especially of his Prussian Majesty, to those who are the most like to repeat them. In short, make yourself well there, without making yourself ill *somewhere else*. Make compliments from me to Algarotti, and converse with him in Italian.

I go next week to the Bath, for a deafness, which I have been plagued with these four or five months; and which, I am assured, that pumping on my head will remove. This deafness, I own, has tried my patience; as it has cut me off from society, at an age when I had no pleasures but those left. In the mean time I have, by reading and writing, made my eyes supply the defect of my ears. Madame H——, I suppose, entertained both yours alike; however, I am very glad you were well with her; for she is a good *Prôneuse*, and puffs are very useful to a young fellow at his entrance into the world.

If you should meet with Lord Pembroke again, anywhere, make him many compliments from me; and tell him, I should have written to him, but that I knew how troublesome an old correspondent must be to a young one. He is much commended in the accounts from Hanover.

You will stay at Berlin just as long as you like it, and no longer; and from thence you are absolutely master of your own motions, either to the Hague or to Brussels; but I think you had better go to the Hague first, because that from thence

Brussels will be in your way to Calais, which is a much better passage to England, than from Helvoetsluys. The two Courts of the Hague and Brussels are worth your seeing ; and you will see them both to advantage, by means of Colonel Yorke and Dayrolles. Adieu. Here is enough for this time.

LETTER CCLVII.

MY DEAR FRIEND,. London, September the 26th, 1752.

As you chiefly employ, or rather wholly engross, my thoughts, I see every day, with increasing pleasure, the fair prospect which you have before you. I had two views in your education ; they draw nearer and nearer, and I have now very little reason to distrust your answering them fully. Those two were, Parliamentary and Foreign affairs. In consequence of those views I took care first, to give you a sufficient stock of sound learning, and next, an early knowledge of the world. Without making a figure in Parliament, no man can make any in this country ; and eloquence alone enables a man to make a figure in Parliament, unless it be a very mean and contemptible one, which those make there who silently vote, and who do *pedibus ire in sententiam.*[1], Foreign affairs, when skilfully managed, and supported by a parliamentary reputation, lead to whatever is most considerable in this country. You have the languages necessary for that purpose, with a sufficient fund of historical and treaty knowledge ; that is to say, you have the Matter ready, and only want the Manner. Your objects being thus fixed, I recommended to you to have them constantly in your thoughts, and to direct your reading, your actions, and your words, to those views. Most people think only *ex re natâ*, and few *ex professo :* I would have you do both, but begin with the latter. I explain myself : Lay down certain principles, and reason and act consequentially from them. As, for example : say to yourself, I will make a figure in Parliament, and in order to do that I must not only speak, but speak very well. Speaking mere common sense will by no means do ; and I must speak not only correctly, but elegantly ; and not only elegantly, but eloquently. In order to this, I will first take pains to get an habitual, but unaffected, purity, correctness, and elegancy of style in my common conversation ; I will seek for the best words, and take care to reject improper, inexpressive, and vulgar ones. I will read the great-

[1] Simply fall in with the views of others.

est masters of oratory, both ancient and modern, and I will read
them singly in that view. I will study Demosthenes and Cicero,
not to discover an old Athenian or Roman custom, nor to puzzle
myself with the value of talents, mines, drachms, and sesterces,
like the learned blockheads in *us;* but to observe their choice
of words, their harmony of diction, their method, their distribution, their exordia, to engage the favour and attention of their
audience, and their perorations, to enforce what they have said,
and to leave a strong impression upon the passions. Nor will
I be pedant enough to neglect the moderns; for I will likewise
study Atterbury, Dryden, Pope, and Bolingbroke; nay, I will
read everything that I do read in that intention, and never
cease improving and refining my style upon the best models,
till at last I become a model of eloquence myself, which, by care,
it is in every man's power to be. If you set out upon this principle, and keep it constantly in your mind, every company you
go into, and every book you read, will contribute to your improvement, either by showing you what to imitate, or what to
avoid. Are you to give an account of anything to a mixed
company? or are you to endeavour to persuade either man or
woman? This principle, fixed in your mind, will make you
carefully attend to the choice of your words, and to the clearness
and harmony of your diction.

So much for your parliamentary object; now to the foreign
one.

Lay down first those principles which are absolutely necessary to form a skilful and successful negotiation, and form yourself accordingly. What are they? First, the clear historical
knowledge of past transactions of that kind. That you have
pretty well already, and will have daily more and more; for,
in consequence of that principle, you will read history, memoirs,
anecdotes, &c., in that view chiefly. The other necessary talents
for negotiation are, the great art of pleasing, and engaging the
affection and confidence, not only of those with whom you are
to coöperate, but even of those whom you are to oppose: to
conceal your own thoughts and views, and to discover other
people's: to engage other people's confidence, by a seeming
cheerful frankness and openness, without going a step too far:
to get the personal favour of the King, Prince, Ministers, or
Mistress of the Court to which you are sent: to gain the absolute command over your temper and your countenance, that no
heat may provoke you to say, nor no change of countenance to
betray, what should be a secret. To familiarize and domesticate yourself in the houses of the most considerable people of

the place, so as to be received there rather as a friend to the family, than as a foreigner. Having these principles constantly in your thoughts, everything you do and everything you say, will some way or other tend to your main view: and common conversation will gradually fit you for it. You will get a habit of checking any rising heat; you will be upon your guard against any indiscreet expression ; you will by degrees get the command of your countenance, so as not to change it upon any the most sudden accident; and you will, above all things, labour to acquire the great art of pleasing, without which nothing is to be done. Company is, in truth, a constant state of negotiation ; and if you attend to it in that view, will qualify you for any. By the same means that you make a friend, guard against an enemy, or gain a mistress ; you will make an advantageous treaty, baffle those who counteract you, and gain the Court you are sent to. Make this use of all the Company you keep, and your very pleasures will make you a successful Negotiator. Please all who are worth pleasing ; offend none. Keep your own secret, and get out other people's. Keep your own temper, and artfully warm other people's. Counterwork your rivals with diligence and dexterity, but at the same time with the utmost personal civility to them : and be firm without heat. Messieurs d'Avaux and Servien did no more than this. I must make one observation in confirmation of this assertion, which is, that the most eminent Negotiators have always been the politest and best bred men in company ; even what the women call the *prettiest men.* For God's sake, never lose view of these two your capital objects : bend everything to them, try everything by their rules, and calculate everything for their purposes. What is peculiar to these two objects is, that they require nothing but what one's own vanity, interest, and pleasure would make one do independently of them. If a man were never to be in business, and always to lead a private life, would he not desire to please and to persuade ? So that, in your two destinations, your fortune and figure luckily conspire with your vanity and your pleasures. Nay, more, a foreign minister, I will maintain it, can never be a good man of business, if he is not an agreeable man of pleasure too. Half his business is done by the help of his pleasures : his views are carried on, and perhaps best and most unsuspectedly, at balls, suppers, assembles, and parties of pleasure ; by intrigues with women, and connections insensibly formed with men, at those unguarded hours of amusement.

These objects now draw very near you, and you have no

time to lose in preparing yourself to meet them. You will be in Parliament almost as soon as your age will allow, and I believe you will have a foreign department still sooner, and that will be earlier than ever anybody had one. If you set out well at one-and-twenty, what may you not reasonably hope to be at one-and-forty? All that I could wish you! Adieu.

LETTER CCLVIII.

My dear Friend,   London, September the 29th, 1752.

There is nothing so necessary, but at the same time there is nothing more difficult (I know it by experience), for you young fellows, than to know how to behave yourselves prudently towards those whom you do not like. Your passions are warm, and your heads are light; you hate all those who oppose your views, either of ambition or love; and a rival in either is almost a synonymous term for an enemy. Whenever you meet such a man, you are awkwardly cold to him, at best; but often rude, and always desirous to give him some indirect slap. This is unreasonable; for one man has as good a right to pursue an employment, or a mistress, as another; but it is, into the bargain, extremely imprudent; because you commonly defeat your own purpose by it, and while you are contending with each other a third often prevails. I grant you, that the situation is irksome; a man cannot help thinking as he thinks, nor feeling what he feels; and it is a very tender and sore point to be thwarted and counter-worked in one's pursuits at Court, or with a mistress: but prudence and abilities must check the effects, though they cannot remove the cause. Both the pretenders make themselves disagreeable to their mistress, when they spoil the company by their pouting, or their sparring; whereas, if one of them has command enough over himself (whatever he may feel inwardly) to be cheerful, gay, and easily and unaffectedly civil to the other, as if there were no manner of competition between them, the Lady will certainly like him the best, and his rival will be ten times more humbled and discouraged; for he will look upon such a behaviour as a proof of the triumph and security of his rival; he will grow outrageous with the Lady, and the warmth of his reproaches will probably bring on a quarrel between them. It is the same in business; where he who can command his temper and his countenance the best, will always have an infinite advantage over the other.

This is what the French call *un procédé honnête et galant*, to *pique* yourself upon showing particular civilities to a man, to whom lesser minds would in the same case show dislike, or perhaps rudeness. I will give you an instance of this in my own case; and pray remember it, whenever you come to be, as I hope you will, in a like situation.

When I went to the Hague, in 1744, it was to engage the Dutch to come roundly into the war, and to stipulate their quotas of troops, &c.; your acquaintance, the Abbé de la Ville, was there on the part of France, to endeavour to hinder them from coming into the war at all. I was informed, and very sorry to hear it, that he had abilities, temper, and industry. We could not visit, our two masters being at war; but the first time I met him at a third place, I got somebody to present me to him; and I told him, that though we were to be national enemies, I flattered myself we might be, however, personal friends; with a good deal more of the same kind; which he returned in full as polite a manner. Two days afterwards I went, early in the morning, to solicit the Deputies of Amsterdam, where I found l'Abbé de la Ville, who had been beforehand with me; upon which I addressed myself to the Deputies, and said, smilingly, *Je suis bien fâché, Messieurs, de trouver mon Ennemi avec vous; je le connois déjà assez pour le craindre: la partie n'est pas égale, mais je me fie à vos propres intérêts contre les talens de mon Ennemi; et au moins si je n'ai pas eu le premier mot, j'aurai le dernier aujourd'hui.*[1] They smiled: the Abbé was pleased with the compliment, and the manner of it, stayed about a quarter of an hour, and then left me to my Deputies, with whom I continued upon the same tone, though in a very serious manner, and told them that I was only come to state their own true interests to them, plainly and simply, without any of those arts which it was very necessary for my friend to make use of to deceive them. I carried my point, and continued my *procédé* with the Abbé; and by this easy and polite commerce with him, at third places, I often found means to fish out from him whereabouts he was.

Remember, there are but two *procédés* in the world for a gentleman and a man of parts: either extreme politeness, or knocking down. If a man notoriously and designedly insults and affronts you, knock him down; but if he only injures you,

---

[1] I am very sorry, Gentlemen, to find my enemy with you; my knowledge of his capacity is already sufficient to make me fear him: we are not upon equal terms; but I trust to your own interest, against his talents. If I have not this day had the first word, I shall at least have the last.

your best revenge is to be extremely civil to him in your outward behaviour, though at the same time you counterwork him,
and return him the compliment, perhaps with interest. This
is not perfidy nor dissimulation : it would be so if you were at
the same time to make professions of esteem and friendship to
this man, which I by no means recommend, but, on the contrary,
abhor. All acts of civility are, by common consent, understood
to be no more than a conformity to custom, for the quiet and
conveniency of society, the *agrémens* of which are not to be disturbed by private dislikes and jealousies. Only women and
little minds pout and spar for the entertainment of the company
that always laughs at, and never pities them. For my own part,
though I would by no means give up any point to a competitor,
yet I would pique myself upon showing him rather more civility
than to another man. In the first place, this *procédé* infallibly
makes all *les rieurs* of your side, which is a considerable party ;
and in the next place, it certainly pleases the object of the competition, be it either man or woman ; who never fail to say,
upon such an occasion, that *they must own you have behaved
yourself very handsomely in the whole affair.* The world judges
from the appearances of things, and not from the reality, which
few are able, and still fewer are inclined, to fathom ; and a man,
who will take care always to be in the right in those things,
may afford to be sometimes a little in the wrong in more essential ones : there is a willingness, a desire to excuse him.
With nine people in ten good breeding passes for good nature,
and they take attentions for good offices. At Courts there will
be always coldnesses, dislikes, jealousies, and hatred ; the harvest being but small in proportion to the number of labourers ;
but then, as they arise often, they die soon, unless they are per-
petuated by the manner in which they have been carried on
more than by the matter which occasioned them. The turns
and vicissitudes of Courts frequently make friends of enemies, and
enemies of friends : you must labour, therefore, to acquire that
great and uncommon talent, of hating with good breeding, and
loving with prudence ; to make no quarrel irreconcilable, by
silly and unnecessary indications of anger ; and no friendship
dangerous, in case it breaks, by a wanton, indiscreet, and unreserved confidence.

Few (especially young) people know how to love, or how
to hate ; their love is an unbounded weakness, fatal to the person they love ; their hate is a hot, rash, and imprudent violence,
always fatal to themselves. Nineteen fathers in twenty, and
every mother, who had loved you half as well as I do, would

have ruined you; whereas I always made you feel the weight of my authority, that you might one day know the force of my love. Now, I both hope and believe my advice will have the same weight with you from choice, that my authority had from necessity. My advice is just eight-and-thirty years older than your own, and consequently, I believe you think, rather better. As for your tender and pleasurable passions, manage them yourself; but let me have the direction of all the others. Your ambition, your figure, and your fortune will, for some time at least, be rather safer in my keeping than in your own. Adieu.

LETTER CCLIX.

MY DEAR FRIEND, Bath, October the 4th, 1752.

I CONSIDER you now as at the Court of Augustus,[1] where, if ever the desire of pleasing animated you, it must make you exert all the means of doing it. You will see there, full as well, I dare say, as Horace did at Rome, how States are defended by arms, adorned by manners, and improved by laws. Nay, you have a Horace there, as well as an Augustus; I need not name Voltaire, *qui nil molitur inepte*,[2] as Horace himself said of another poet. I have lately read over all his works that are published, though I had read them more than once before. I was induced to this by his *Siècle de Louis* XIV. which I have yet read but four times. In reading over all his works, with more attention I suppose than before, my former admiration of him is, I own, turned into astonishment. There is no one kind of writing in which he has not excelled. You are so severe a classic, that I question whether you will allow me to call his *Henriade* an Epic poem, for want of the proper number of Gods, Devils, Witches, and other absurdities, requisite for the machinery: which machinery is (it seems) necessary to constitute the Epopèe. But whether you do or not, I will declare (though possibly to my own shame) that I never read any Epic poem with near so much pleasure. I am grown old, and have possibly lost a great deal of that fire which formerly made me love fire in others at any rate, and however attended with smoke: but now I must have all sense, and cannot, for the sake of five righteous lines, forgive a thousand absurd ones.

In this disposition of mind, judge whether I can read all

---

[1] i. e. Frederick the Great of Prussia.
[2] Attempts nothing foolishly.

Homer through *tout de suite*. I admire his beauties ; but, to
tell you the truth, when he slumbers I sleep. Virgil, I confess,
is all sense, and therefore I like him better than his model ; but
he is often languid, especially in his five or six last books, during
which I am obliged to take a good deal of snuff. Besides, I
profess myself an ally of Turnus's, against the pious Æneas,
who, like many *soi-disant* pious people, does the most flagrant
injustice and violence, in order to execute what they imprudently
call the will of Heaven. But what will you say, when I tell
you truly, that I cannot possibly read our countryman Milton
through ? I acknowledge him to have some most sublime passages, some prodigious flashes of light ; but then you must acknowledge, that light is often followed by *darkness visible*, to
use his own expression. Besides, not having the honour to be
acquainted with any of the parties in his Poem, except the Man
and the Woman, the characters and speeches of a dozen or two
of Angels, and of as many Devils, are as much above my reach
as my entertainment. Keep this secret for me : for if it should
be known, I should be abused by every tasteless Pedant, and
every solid Divine, in England.

Whatever I have said to the disadvantage of these three
Poems, holds much stronger against Tasso's Gierusalemme : it
is true he has very fine and glaring rays of poetry ; but then
they are only meteors, they dazzle, then disappear, and are succeeded by false thoughts, poor *concetti*, and absurd impossibilities : witness the Fish and the Parrot ; extravagancies unworthy of an Heroic Poem, and would much better have become
Ariosto, who professes *le coglionerie*.

I have never read the Lusiade of Camoens, except in a prose
translation, consequently I have never read it at all, so shall say
nothing of it ; but the *Henriade* is all sense from the beginning
to the end, often adorned by the justest and liveliest reflections,
the most beautiful descriptions, the noblest images, and the
sublimest sentiments ; not to mention the harmony of the verse,
in which Voltaire undoubtedly exceeds all the French poets :
should you insist upon an exception in favour of Racine, I must
insist, on my part, that he at least equals him. What Hero
ever interested more than Henry the Fourth, who, according to
the rules of Epic poetry, carries on one great and long action,
and succeeds in it at last ? What description ever excited more
horror than those first of the Massacre, and then of the Famine,
at Paris ? Was love ever painted with more truth and *morbidezza*[1]
than in the ninth book ? Not better, in my mind, even in the

---

[1] Delicacy of tint.

fourth of Virgil. Upon the whole, with all your classical rigour, if you will but suppose *St Louis* a God, a Devil, or a Witch, and that he appears in person, and not in a dream, the *Henriade* will be an Epic poem, according to the strictest statute laws of the Epopée ; but in my Court of equity it is one as it is.

I could expatiate as much upon all his different works, but that I should exceed the bounds of a letter, and run into a dissertation. How delightful is his History of that Northern Brute, the King of Sweden ; for I cannot call him a Man ; and I should be sorry to have him pass for a Hero, out of regard to those true Heroes ; such as Julius Cæsar, Titus, Trajan, and the present King of Prussia ; who cultivated and encouraged arts and sciences ; whose animal courage was accompanied by the tender and social sentiments of humanity ; and who had more pleasure in improving, than in destroying, their fellow-creatures. What can be more touching, or more interesting ; what more nobly thought, or more happily expressed, than all his dramatic pieces ? What can be more clear and rational than all his philosophical letters ? and what ever was so graceful, and gentle, as all his little poetical trifles ? You are fortunately *à portée* of verifying, by your knowledge of the man, all that I have said of his works.

Monsieur de Maupertuis (whom I hope you will get acquainted with) is, what one rarely meets with, deep in philosophy and mathematics, and yet *honnête et aimable homme ;* Algarotti is young Fontenelle. Such men must necessarily give you the desire of pleasing them ; and if you can frequent them, their acquaintance will furnish you the means of pleasing everybody else.

A propos of pleasing ; your pleasing Mrs F——d is expected here in two or three days ; I will do all that I can for you with her : I think you carried on the romance to the third or fourth volume ; I will continue it to the eleventh ; but as for the twelfth and last, you must come and conclude it yourself. *Non sum qualis eram.*[1]

Good night to you, child ; for I am going to bed, just at the hour at which I suppose you are beginning to live, at Berlin.

---

[1] I am not such as I was.

LETTER CCLX.

MY DEAR FRIEND,   Bath, November the 16th, 1752.

VANITY, or to call it by a gentler name, the desire of admiration and applause, is perhaps the most universal principle of human actions ; I do not say that it is the best; and I will own that it is sometimes the cause of both foolish and criminal effects. But it is so much oftener the principle of right things, that, though they ought to have a better, yet, considering human nature, that principle is to be encouraged and cherished, in consideration of its effects. Where that desire is wanting, we are apt to be indifferent, listless, indolent, and inert ; we do not exert our powers ; and we appear to be as much below ourselves, as the vainest man living can desire to appear above what he really is.

As I have made you my confessor, and do not scruple to confess even my weaknesses to you, I will fairly own that I had that vanity, that weakness, if it be one, to a prodigious degree ; and, what is more, I confess it without repentance ; nay, I am glad I had it; since, if I have had the good fortune to please in the world, it is to that powerful and active principle that I owe it. I began the world, not with a bare desire, but with an insatiable thirst, a rage of popularity, applause, and admiration. If this made me do some silly things, on one hand, it made me, on the other hand, do almost all the right things that I did : it made me attentive and civil to the women I disliked, and to the men I despised, in hopes of the applause of both : though I neither desired, nor would I have accepted, the favours of the one, nor the friendship of the other. I always dressed, looked, and talked my best; and, I own, was overjoyed whenever I perceived that by all three, or by any one of them, the company was pleased with me. To men, I talked whatever I thought would give them the best opinion of my parts and learning ; and to women, what I was sure would please them ; flattery, gallantry, and love. And moreover I will own to you, under the secrecy of confession, that my vanity has very often made me take great pains to make many a woman in love with me if I could, for whose person I would not have given a pinch of snuff. In company with men I always endeavoured to outshine, or at least, if possible, to equal, the most shining man in it. This desire elicited whatever powers I had to gratify it ; and where I could not perhaps shine in the first, enabled me at least to shine in a second or third, sphere. By these means I soon grew in fashion; and when a man is once in fashion, all he does is right. It was infinite pleasure to me, to find my own fashion and popularity. I was sent for to all parties of pleasure, both of men or women; where, in some measure, I gave the tone. This gave me the reputation of having had some women of condition; and that reputation, whether true or false, really got me others. With the men I was a Proteus, and assumed every shape in order to please them all: among the gay, I was the gayest; among the grave, the gravest; and I never omitted the least attentions of good breeding, or the least offices of friendship, that could either please, or attach them to me: and accordingly I was soon connected with all the men of any fashion or figure in town.

To this principle of vanity, which Philosophers call a mean one, and which I do not, I owe great part of the figure which I have made in life. I wish you had as much, but I fear you have too little of it; and you seem to have a degree of laziness and listlessness about you, that makes you indifferent as to general applause. This is not in character at your age, and would be barely pardonable in an elderly and philosophical man. It is a vulgar, ordinary saying, but it is a very true one, that one should always put the best foot foremost. One should please, shine, and dazzle wherever it is possible. At Paris, I am sure you must observe *que chacun se fait valoir autant qu'il est possible ;* and La Bruyère observes, very justly, *qu'on ne vaut dans ce monde que ce qu'on veut valoir :* wherever applause is in question, you will never see a French man, nor woman, remiss or negligent. Observe the eternal attentions and politeness that all people have there for one another. *Ce n'est pas pour leurs beaux yeux, au moins.* No, but for their own sakes, for commendations and applause. Let me, then, recommend this principle of vanity to you; act upon it *meo periculo;* I promise you it will turn to your account. Practise all the arts that ever Coquette did, to please. Be alert and indefatigable in making every man admire, and every woman in love with you. I can tell you, too, that nothing will carry you higher in the world.

I have had no letter from you since your arrival at Paris, though you must have been long enough there to have written me two or three. In about ten or twelve days I propose leaving this place, and going to London; I have found considerable benefit by my stay here, but not all that I want. Make my compliments to Lord Albemarle.

LETTER CCLXI.

MY DEAR FRIEND,   Bath, November the 28th, 1752.

SINCE my last to you, I have read Madame Maintenon's Letters; I am sure they are genuine, and they both entertained and informed me. They have brought me acquainted with the character of that able and artful Lady; whom I am convinced that I now know, much better than her *directeur* the *Abbé* de Fénélon (afterwards Archbishop of Cambray) did, when he wrote her the one hundred and eighty-fifth letter; and I know him the better too for that letter. The *Abbé*, though brimful of divine love, had a great mind to be first Minister, and Cardinal, in order, *no doubt*, to have an opportunity of doing the more good. His being *directeur* at that time to Madame Maintenon, seemed to be a good step towards those views. She put herself upon him for a saint, and he was weak enough to believe it; he, on the other hand, would have put himself upon her for a saint too, which, I dare say, she did not believe; but both of them knew that it was necessary for them to appear saints to Lewis XIV., who they were very sure was a bigot. It is to be presumed, nay, indeed it is plain by that one hundred and eighty-fifth letter, that Madame Maintenon had hinted to her *directeur* some scruples of conscience, with relation to her commerce with the King; and which I humbly apprehend to have been only some scruples of prudence, at once to flatter the bigot character, and increase the desires of the King. The pious *Abbé*, frightened out of his wits lest the King should impute to the *directeur* any scruples or difficulties which he might meet with on the part of the Lady, writes her the above-mentioned letter; in which he not only bids her not tease the King by advice and exhortations, but to have the utmost submission to his will; and, that she may not mistake the nature of that.submission, he tells her it is the same that Sarah had for Abraham; to which submission Isaac perhaps was owing. No bawd could have written a more seducing letter to an innocent country girl, than the *directeur* did to his *pénitente*; who, I dare say, had no occasion for his good advice. Those who would justify the good *directeur*, alias the pimp, in this affair, must not attempt to do it by saying that the King and Madame Maintenon were at that time privately married; that the *directeur* knew it; and that this was the meaning of his *énigme*. That is absolutely impossible; for that private marriage must have removed all scruples between the parties; nay, could not have been contracted upon any other principle, since it was kept private, and consequently prevented no public scandal. It is therefore extremely evident that Madame Maintenon could not be married to the King at the time when she scrupled granting, and when the *directeur* advised her to grant, those favours which Sarah with so much submission granted to Abraham : and what that *directeur* is pleased to call *le mystère de Dieu*, was most evidently a state of concubinage. The letters are very well worth your reading ; they throw light upon many things of those times.[1]

I have just received a letter from Sir William Stanhope, from Lyons ; in which he tells me that he saw you at Paris, that he thinks you a little grown, but that you do not make the most of it, for that you stoop still; *d'ailleurs* his letter was a panegyric of you.

The young Comte de Schullemburg, the Chambellan whom you knew at Hanover, is come over with the King, *et fait aussi vos éloges.*

Though, as I told you in my last, I have done buying pictures, by way of *virtù*, yet there are some portraits of remarkable people that would tempt me. For instance, if you could by chance pick up at Paris, at a reasonable price, and undoubted originals (whether heads, half-lengths, or whole-lengths, no matter) of Cardinals Richelieu, Mazarin, and Retz; Monsieur de Turenne, le grand Prince de Condé ; Mesdames de Montespan, de Fontanges, de Mombason, de Sévigné, de Maintenon, de Chevreuse, de Longueville, d'Olonne, &c., I should be tempted to purchase them. I am sensible that they can only be met with, by great accident, at family sales and auctions, so I only mention the affair to you eventually.

I do not understand, or else I do not remember, what affair you mean in your last letter ; which you think will come to nothing, and for which, you say, I had once a mind that you should take the road again. Explain it to me.

I shall go to town in four or five days, and carry back with me a little more hearing than I brought : but yet not half enough for common use. One wants ready pocket money much oftener than one wants great sums ; and, to use a very odd expression, I want to hear at sight. I love every-day senses, every-day wit and entertainment ; a man who is only good on holidays is good for very little. Adieu.

[1] There is no doubt Louis XIV. had privately married Madame de Maintenon ; this attack upon Fenelon, therefore, is quite gratuitous.

LETTER CCLXII.

MY DEAR FRIEND,   London, New Year's Day, 1753.

IT is now above a fortnight since I have received a letter from you. I hope, however, that you are well, but engrossed by the business of Lord Albemarle's *bureau* in the mornings, and by business of a genteeler nature in the evenings; for I willingly give up my own satisfaction to your improvement, either in business or manners.

Here have been lately imported from Paris two gentlemen, who, I find, were much acquainted with you there; Comte Sinzendorf, and Monsieur Clairaut, the Academician. The former is a very pretty man, well bred, and with a great deal of useful knowledge; for those two things are very consistent. I examined him about you, thinking him a competent judge. He told me, *que vous parliez l'Allemand comme un Allemand; que vous saviez le droit public de l'Empire parfaitement bien; que vous aviez le goût sûr, et des connoissances fort étendues.*[1] I told him that I knew all this very well; but that I wanted to know whether you had *l'air, les manières, les attentions, enfin le brillant d'un honnête homme:* his answer was, *Mais oui, en vérité, c'est fort bien.* This, you see, is but cold, in comparison of what I do wish, and of what you ought to wish. Your friend Clairaut interposed, and said, *Mais je vous assure qu'il est fort poli;* to which I answered, *Je le crois bien, vis-à-vis des Lapons vos amis; je vous recuse pour Juge, jusqu'à ce que vous ayez été délaponné, au moins dix ans, parmi les honnêtes gens.*[2] These testimonies in your favour are such as perhaps you are satisfied with, and think sufficient: but I am not: they are only the cold depositions of disinterested and unconcerned witnesses, upon a strict examination. When, upon a trial, a man calls witnesses to his character, and those witnesses only say, that they never heard, nor do not know, any ill of him; it intimates at best a neutral and insignificant, though innocent, character. Now I want, and you ought to endeavour, that *les agrémens, les grâces, les attentions,* &c., should be a distinguishing part of your character, and specified of you by people unasked. I wish to hear people say of you, *ah, qu'il est aimable! Quelles manières, quelles grâces,*

---

[1] That you spoke German like a German, that you knew thoroughly the common law of the empire, that you had an exact taste and general knowledge of a very wide compass.

[2] Oh, I assure you he is very polished.—I believe it, as compared with your friends the Laplanders. I will not take you for a judge until for at least ten years you have got rid of the Laplander among decent people.

quel art de plaire! Nature, thank God, has given you all the powers necessary ; and if she has not yet, I hope in God she will give you the will of exerting them.

I have lately read, with great pleasure, Voltaire's two little Histories of *les Croisades*, and *l'Esprit humain;* which I recommend to your perusal, if you have not already read them. They are bound up with a most poor performance, called *Micromégas*, which is said to be Voltaire's too ; but I cannot believe it, it is so very unworthy of him : it consists only of thoughts stolen from Swift, but miserably mangled and disfigured. But his History of the Croisades shows, in a very short and strong light, the most immoral and wicked scheme that was ever contrived by knaves, and executed by madmen and fools, against humanity. There is a strange but never-failing relation between honest madmen and skilful knaves ; and wherever one meets with collected numbers of the former, one may be very sure that they are secretly directed by the latter. The Popes, who have generally been both the ablest and the greatest knaves in Europe, wanted all the power and money of the East : for they had all that was in Europe already. The times and the minds favoured their design, for they were dark and uninformed ; and Peter the Hermit, at once a knave and a madman, was a fine papal tool for so wild and wicked an undertaking. I wish we had good histories of every part of Europe, and indeed of the world, written upon the plan of Voltaire's *de l'Esprit humain;* for, I own, I am provoked at the contempt which most historians show for humanity in general ; one would think by them, that the whole human species consisted but of about a hundred and fifty people, called and dignified (commonly very undeservedly too) by the titles of Emperors, Kings, Popes, Generals, and Ministers.

I have never seen in any of the newspapers any mention of the affairs of the Cevennes, or Grenoble, which you gave me an account of some time ago ; and the Duke de Mirepoix pretends, at least, to know nothing of either. Were they false reports ; or does the French Court choose to stifle them ? I hope that they are both true, because I am very willing that the cares of the French government should be employed and confined to themselves.

Your friend, the Electress Palatine, has sent me six wild boars' heads, and other *pièces de sa chasse*, in return for the fans, which she approved of extremely. This present was signified to me by one Mr Harold, who wrote me a letter in very indifferent English ; I suppose he is a Dane, who has been in England.

Mr Harte came to town yesterday, and dined with me to-day. We talked you over; and I can assure you, that though a Parson, and no member *du beau monde,* he thinks all the most shining accomplishments of it full as necessary for you as I do. His expression was, *that is all that he wants; but if he wants that, considering his situation and destination, he might as well want everything else.*

This is the day when people reciprocally offer, and receive, the kindest and the warmest wishes, though, in general, without meaning them on one side, or believing them on the other. They are formed by the head, in compliance with custom, though disavowed by the heart, in consequence of nature. His wishes, upon this occasion, are the best, that are the best turned; you do not, I am sure, doubt the truth of mine, and therefore I will express them with a Quaker-like simplicity. May this new year be a very new one indeed to you; may you put off the old, and put on the new, man! but I mean the outward, not the inward, man. With this alteration I might justly sum up all my wishes for you in these words:

Dii tibi dent annos, de te nam cætera sumes.

This minute I receive your letter of the 26th past, which gives me a very disagreeable reason for your late silence. By the symptoms which you mention of your illness, I both hope and believe that it was wholly owing to your own want of care. You are rather inclined to be fat, you have naturally a good stomach, and you eat at the best tables; which must of course make you plethoric: and, upon my word, you will be very subject to these accidents, if you will not from time to time, when you find yourself full, heated, or your head aching, take some little easy preventive purge, that would not confine you; such as chewing a little rhubarb, when you go to bed at night, or some senna tea in the morning. You do very well to live extremely low, for some time; and I could wish, though I do not expect it, that you would take one gentle vomit: for those giddinesses, and swimmings in the head, always proceed from some foulness of the stomach. However, upon the whole, I am very glad that your old complaint has not mixed itself with this; which, I am fully convinced, arises singly from your own negligence. Adieu.

I am sorry for Monsieur Kurzé, upon his sister's account.

LETTER CCLXIII.

MY DEAR FRIEND,   London, January the 15th, 1753.

I NEVER think my time so well employed as when I think it employed to your advantage. You have long had the greatest share of it; you now engross it. The moment is now decisive; the piece is going to be exhibited to the public; the mere outlines and the general colouring are not sufficient to attract the eyes, and to secure applause; but the last finishing, artful, and delicate strokes are necessary. Skilful judges will discern and acknowledge their merit; the ignorant will, without knowing why, feel their power. In that view I have thrown together, for your use, the enclosed Maxims;[1] or, to speak more properly, observations on men and things; for I have no merit as to the invention; I am no system-monger; and, instead of giving way to my imagination, I have only consulted my memory; and my conclusions are all drawn from facts, not from fancy. Most maxim-mongers have preferred the prettiness to the justness of a thought, and the turn to the truth; but I have refused myself to everything that my own experience did not justify and confirm. I wish you would consider them seriously, and separately, and recur to them again *pro re natâ* in similar cases. Young men are as apt to think themselves wise enough, as drunken men are to think themselves sober enough. They look upon spirit to be a much better thing than experience; which they call coldness. They are but half mistaken; for though spirit without experience is dangerous, experience without spirit is languid and defective. Their union, which is very rare, is perfection: you may join them if you please; for all my experience is at your service; and I do not desire one grain of your spirit in return. Use them both; and let them reciprocally animate and check each other. I mean here, by the spirit of youth, only the vivacity and presumption of youth; which hinder them from seeing the difficulties or dangers of an undertaking; but I do not mean what the silly vulgar call spirit, by which they are captious, jealous of their rank, suspicious of being undervalued, and tart (as they call it) in their repartees, upon the slightest occasions. This is an evil and a very silly spirit, which should be driven out, and transferred to a herd of swine. This is not the spirit of a man of fashion, who has kept good company. People of an ordinary, low education, when they happen to fall into good company, im-

---

[1] Turn to the end of the volume.

agine themselves the only object of its attention; if the company whispers, it is, to be sure, concerning them; if they laugh, it is at them, and if anything ambiguous, that by the most forced interpretation can be applied to them, happens to be said, they are convinced that it was meant at them; upon which they grow out of countenance first, and then angry. This mistake is very well ridiculed in the Stratagem, where Scrub says, *I am sure they talked of me, for they laughed consumedly.* A well bred man seldom thinks, but never seems to think, himself slighted, undervalued, or laughed at in company, unless where it is so plainly marked out, that his honour obliges him to resent it in a proper manner; *mais les honnêtes gens ne se boudent jamais.*[1] I will admit that it is very difficult to command one's self enough, to behave with ease, frankness, and good-breeding towards those who one knows dislike, slight, and injure one as far as they can without personal consequences; but I assert that it is absolutely necessary to do it: you must embrace the man you hate, if you cannot be justified in knocking him down; for otherwise you avow the injury, which you cannot revenge. A prudent Cuckold (and there are many such at Paris) pockets his horns, when he cannot gore with them; and will not add to the triumph of his maker, by only butting with them ineffectually. A seeming ignorance is very often a most necessary part of worldly knowledge. It is, for instance, commonly advisable to seem ignorant of what people offer to tell you; and when they say, Have not you heard of such a thing? to answer No, and to let them go on, though you know it already. Some have a pleasure in telling it, because they think that they tell it well; others have a pride in it, as being the sagacious discoverers; and many have a vanity in showing that they have been, though very undeservedly, trusted: all these would be disappointed, and consequently displeased, if you said Yes. Seem always ignorant (unless to one most intimate friend) of all matters of private scandal and defamation, though you should hear them a thousand times; for the parties affected always look upon the receiver to be almost as bad as the thief: and whenever they become the topic of conversation, seem to be a sceptic, though you are really a serious believer; and always take the extenuating part. But all this seeming ignorance should be joined to thorough and extensive private informations: and, indeed, it is the best method of procuring them; for most people have such a vanity in showing a superiority over others, though but for a moment, and in the merest trifles, that they

[1] But men of honour never pout.

will tell you what they should not, rather than not show that they
can tell what you did not know : besides that, such seeming
ignorance will make you pass for incurious, and consequently
undesigning. However, fish for facts, and take pains to be
well informed of everything that passes ; but fish judiciously,
and not always, nor indeed often, in the shape of direct questions ; which always put people upon their guard, and often
repeated, grow tiresome. But sometimes take the things that
you would know for granted ; upon which somebody will,
kindly and officiously, set you right : sometimes say that you
have heard so and so ; and at other times seem to know more
than you do, in order to know all that you want : but avoid
direct questioning as much as you can. All these necessary
arts of the world require constant attention, presence of mind,
and coolness. Achilles, though invulnerable, never went to
battle but completely armed. Courts are to be the theatres of
your wars, where you should be always as completely armed,
and even with the addition of a heel-piece. The least inattention, the least *distraction*, may prove fatal. I would fain see
you what pedants call *omnis homo*, and what Pope much better
calls *all accomplished :* you have the means in your power, add
the will, and you may bring it about. The vulgar have a
coarse saying, of *spoiling a hog for a halfpenny-worth of tar :*
prevent the application, by providing the tar; it is very easily
to be had, in comparison with what you have already got.

The fine Mrs Pitt, who, it seems, saw you often at Paris,
speaking of you the other day, said, in French, for she speaks
little English   *   *   *   *   *
*   *   *   *   *   *   *
whether it is that you did not pay the homage due to her beauty,
or that it did not strike you as it does others, I cannot determine ; but I hope she had some other reason than truth, for
saying it. I will suppose that you did not care a pin for her ;
but, however, she surely deserves a degree of propitiatory adoration from you, which I am afraid you neglected. Had I been
in your case I should have endeavoured, at least, to have sup-
planted Mr Mackay in his office of nocturnal reader to her. I
played at cards, two days ago, with your friend Mrs Fitzgerald,
and her most sublime mother, Mrs Seagrave ; they both inquired
after you : and Mrs Fitzgerald said she hoped you went on with
your dancing ; I said Yes, and that you assured me you had
made such considerable improvements in it, that you had now
learned to stand still, and even upright. Your *virtuosa*, la Sig-
nora Vestri, sung here the other day, with great applause : I

presume you are *intimately* acquainted with her merit. Good night to you, whoever you pass it with.

I have this moment received a packet, sealed with your seal, though not directed by your hand, for Lady Hervey. No letter from you! Are you not well?

LETTER CCLXIV.

MY DEAR FRIEND, London, May the 27th, O. S. 1753.

I HAVE this day been tired, jaded, nay, tormented, by the company of a most worthy, sensible, and learned man, a near relation of mine, who dined and passed the evening with me. This seems a paradox, but is a plain truth ; he has no knowledge of the world, no manners, no address ; far from talking without book, as is commonly said of people who talk sillily, he only talks by book ; which, in general conversation, is ten times worse. He has formed in his own closet, from books, certain systems of everything, argues tenaciously upon those principles, and is both surprised and angry at whatever deviates from them. His theories are good, but, unfortunately, are all impracticable. Why? Because he has only read, and not conversed. He is acquainted with books, and an absolute stranger to men. Labouring with his matter, he is delivered of it with pangs ; he hesitates, stops in his utterance, and always expresses himself inelegantly. His actions are all ungraceful ; so that, with all his merit and knowledge, I would rather converse six hours with the most frivolous tittle-tattle woman, who knew something of the world, than with him. The preposterous notions of a systematical man, who does not know the world, tire the patience of a man who does. It would be endless to correct his mistakes, nor would he take it kindly ; for he has considered everything deliberately, and is very sure that he is in the right. Impropriety is a characteristic, and a never-failing one, of these people. Regardless, because ignorant, of custom and manners, they violate them every moment. They often shock, though they never mean to offend ; never attending either to the general character, or the particular distinguishing circumstances of the people to whom, or before whom, they talk: whereas the knowledge of the world teaches one that the very same things which are exceedingly right and proper in one company, time, and place, are exceedingly absurd in others. In short, a man who has great knowledge, from experience and observation of the cha-

racters, customs, and manners of mankind, is a being as different
from, and as superior to, a man of mere book and systematical
knowledge, as a well-managed horse is to an ass. Study therefore, cultivate, and frequent, men and women ; not only in their
outward, and consequently guarded, but in their interior, domestic, and consequently less disguised, characters and manners.
Take your notions of things, as by observation and experience
you find they really are, and not as you read that they are or
should be ; for they never are quite what they should be. For
this purpose do not content yourself with general and common
acquaintance ; but, wherever you can, establish yourself, with
a kind of domestic familiarity, in good houses. For instance ;
go again to Orli for two or three days, and so at two or three *re-
prises.* Go and stay two or three days at a time at Versailles,
and improve and extend the acquaintance you have there. Be
at home at St Cloud ; and whenever any private person of
fashion invites you to pass a few days at his country-house, accept
of the invitation. This will necessarily give you a versatility
of mind, and a facility to adopt various manners and customs ;
for everybody desires to please those in whose house they are ;
and people are only to be pleased in their own way. Nothing
is more engaging than a cheerful and easy conformity to people's
particular manners, habits, and even weaknesses ; nothing (to
use a vulgar expression) should come amiss to a young fellow.
He should be, for good purposes, what Alcibiades was commonly
for bad ones, a Proteus, assuming with ease, and wearing with
cheerfulness, any shape. Heat, cold, luxury, abstinence, gravity,
gaiety, ceremony, easiness, learning, trifling, business, and pleasure, are modes which he should be able to take, lay aside, or
change occasionally, with as much ease as he would take or lay
aside his hat. All this is only to be acquired by use and knowledge of the world, by keeping a great deal of company, analyz-
ing every character, and insinuating yourself into the familiarity
of various acquaintance. A right, a generous ambition to make
a figure in the world, necessarily gives the desire of pleasing ;
the desire of pleasing points out, to a great degree, the means
of doing it ; and the art of pleasing is, in truth, the art of rising,
of distinguishing one's self, of making a figure and a fortune in
the world. But without pleasing, without the Graces, as I have
told you a thousand times, *ogni fatica è vana.* You are now but
nineteen, an age at which most of your countrymen are illiber-
ally getting drunk in Port, at the University. You have greatly
got the start of them in learning ; and if you can equally get
the start of them in the knowledge and manners of the world,

you may be very sure of outrunning them in Court and Parliament, as you set out so much earlier than they. They generally begin but to see the world at one-and-twenty ; you will by that age have seen all Europe. They set out upon their travels unlicked cubs; and in their travels they only lick one another, for they seldom go into any other company. They know nothing but the English world, and the worst part of that too, and generally very little of any but the English language ; and they come home, at three or four-and-twenty, refined and polished (as is said in one of Congreve's plays) like Dutch skippers from a whale-fishing. The care which has been taken of you, and (to do you justice) the care you have taken of yourself, has left you, at the age of nineteen only, nothing to acquire but the knowledge of the world, manners, address, and those exterior accomplishments. But they are great and necessary acquisitions to those who have sense enough to know their true value ; and your getting them before you are one-and-twenty, and before you enter upon the active and shining scene of life, will give you such an advantage over all your contemporaries, that they cannot overtake you ; they must be distanced. You may probably be placed about a young Prince, who will probably be a young King. There all the various arts of pleasing, the engaging address, the versatility of manners, the *brillant*, the Graces, will outweigh and yet outrun all solid knowledge and unpolished merit. Oil yourself therefore, and be both supple and shining for that race, if you would be first, or early, at the goal. Ladies will most probably, too, have something to say there ; and those who are best with them, will probably be best *somewhere else*. Labour this great point, my dear child, indefatigably ; attend to the very smallest parts, the minutest graces, the most trifling circumstances, that can possibly concur in forming the shining character of a complete Gentleman, *un galant homme, un homme de Cour*, a man of business and pleasure ; *estimé des hommes, recherché des femmes, aimé de tout le monde.* In this view observe the shining part of every man of fashion, who is liked and esteemed; attend to, and imitate that particular accomplishment for which you hear him chiefly celebrated and distinguished ; then collect those various parts, and make yourself a Mosaic of the whole. No one body possesses everything, and almost everybody possesses some one thing worthy of imitation : only choose your models well ; and, in order to do so, choose by your, ear more than by your eye. The best model is always that which is most universally allowed to be the best, though in strictness it may possibly not be so. We must take most things as they are, we cannot make them what we would, nor often what they should be; and where moral duties are not concerned it is more prudent to follow, than to attempt to lead.   Adieu. ·

---o---

LETTER CCLXV.

MY DEAR FRIEND,   Bath, October the 3d, 1753.

YOU have set out well at the Hague ; you are in love with Madame Munter, which I am very glad of: you are in the fine company there, and I hope one of it ; for it is not enough, at your age, to be merely in good company ; but you should by your address and attentions make that good company think you one of them.   There is a tribute due to beauty, even independently of further views, which tribute, I hope, you paid with alacrity to Madame Munter and Madame Degenfeldt : depend upon it they expected it, and were offended in proportion as that tribute seemed either unwillingly or scantily paid.   I believe my friend Kreuningen admits nobody now to his table, for fear of their communicating the plague to him, or at least the bite of a mad dog.   Pray profit of the *entrées libres*, that the French Embassador has given you; frequent him, and *speak* to him.   I think you will not do amiss to call upon Mr Burrish, at Aix-la-Chapelle, since it is so little out of your way ; and you will do still better if you would, which I know you will not, drink those waters for five or six days only, to scour your stomach and bowels a little : I am sure it would do you a great deal of good. Mr Burrish can, doubtless, give you the best letters to Munich ; and he will naturally give you some to Comte Preysing, or Comte Sinsheim, and such sort of grave people ; but I could wish that you would ask him for some to young fellows of pleasure or fashionable coquettes, that you may be *dans l'honnête débauche de Munich.   A propos* of your future motions ; I leave you in a great measure the master of them, so shall only suggest my thoughts to you upon that subject.

You have three Electoral Courts in view, Bonn, Munich, and Manheim.   I would advise you to see two of them rather cursorily, and fix your tabernacle at the third, whichever that may be, for a considerable time.   For instance ; should you choose (as I fancy you will) to make Manheim the place of your residence, stay only ten or twelve days at Bonn, and as long at Munich, and then go and fix at Manheim ; and so, *vice versâ*, if you should like Bonn or Munich better than you think you

would Manheim, make that the place of your residence, and
only visit the other two. It is certain that no man can be
much pleased himself, or please others much, in any place where
he is only a bird of passage for eight or ten days; neither party
thinking it worth while to make an acquaintance, still less to
form any connection, for so short a time: but when months are
the case, a man may domesticate himself pretty well; and very
soon not be looked upon as a stranger. This is the real utility
of travelling, when, by contracting a familiarity at any place you
get into the inside of it, and see it in its undress. That is the
only way of knowing the customs, the manners, and all the little
characteristical peculiarities that distinguish one place from
another; but then this familiarity is not to be brought about
by cold, formal visits of half an hour: no, you must show a
willingness, a desire, an impatience, of forming connections, *il
faut s'y prêter, et y mettre du liant, du désir de plaire.*[1] Whatever you do approve, you must be lavish in your praises of;
and you must learn to commend what you do not approve of,
if it is approved of there. You are not much given to praise,
I know; but it is because you do not yet know how extremely
people are engaged by a seeming sanction to their own opinions,
prejudices, and weaknesses, even in the merest trifles. Our self-
love is mortified, when we think our opinions, and even our
tastes, customs, and dresses, either arraigned or condemned; as,
on the contrary, it is tickled and flattered by approbation. I will
give you a remarkable instance of this kind. The famous Earl
of Shaftesbury, in the flagitious reign of Charles the Second, while
he was Chancellor, had a mind to be a Favourite as well as a
Minister of the King: in order therefore to please his Majesty,
whose prevailing passion was women, my Lord kept a w——e,
whom he had no occasion for, and made no manner of use of.
The King soon heard of it, and asked him if it was true; he
owned it was; but that, though he kept that one woman, he had
several others besides, for he loved variety. A few days afterwards, the King, at his public levee saw Lord Shaftesbury at some
distance, and said in the circle, 'One would not think that that
little weak man is the greatest whoremaster in England; but
I can assure you that he is.' Upon Lord Shaftesbury's coming
into the circle there was a general smile; the King said, 'This
is concerning you, my Lord.' 'Me, Sir!' answered the Chancellor, with some surprise. 'Yes, you,' answered the King;
'for I had just said that you were the greatest whoremaster in

---

[1] You must give yourself to it, and seek it by affability and a desire to
please.

England : Is it not true ? ' ' Of a *subject*, Sir,' replied Lord Shaftesbury, ' perhaps I am.' It is the same in everything ; we think a difference of opinion, of conduct, of manners, a tacit reproach, at least, upon our own ; we must therefore use ourselves to a ready conformity to whatever is neither criminal nor dishonourable. Whoever differs from any general custom is supposed both to think and proclaim himself wiser than the rest of the world ; which the rest of the world cannot bear, especially in a young man. A young fellow is always forgiven, and often applauded, when he carries a fashion to an excess ; but never if he stops short of it. The first is ascribed to youth and fire ; but the latter is imputed to an affectation of singularity, or superiority. At your age, one is allowed to *outrer* fashion, dress, vivacity, gallantry, &c., but by no means to be behindhand in any one of them. And one may apply to youth in this case, *Si non errasset, feccrat ille minùs*. Adieu.

LETTER CCLXVI.

MY DEAR FRIEND, Bath, October the 19th, 1753.

OF all the various ingredients that compose the useful and necessary art of pleasing, no one is so effectual and engaging, as that gentleness, that *douceur* of countenance and manners, to which you are no stranger, though (God knows why) a sworn enemy. Other people take great pains to conceal, or disguise, their natural imperfections ; some, by the make of their clothes, and other arts, endeavour to conceal the defects of their shape ; women who unfortunately have natural bad complexions, lay on good ones ; and both men and women, upon whom unkind nature has inflicted a surliness and ferocity of countenance, do at least all they can, though often without success, to soften and mitigate it ; they affect *douceur*, and aim at smiles, though often in the attempt, like the Devil in *Milton*, they *grin horribly a ghastly smile*. But you are the only person I ever knew, in the whole course of my life, who not only disdain, but absolutely reject and disguise, a great advantage, that nature has kindly granted. You easily guess I mean *countenance* ; for she has given you a very pleasing one ; but you beg to be excused, you will not accept it ; on the contrary, take singular pains to put on the most *funeste*, forbidding, and unpleasing one, that can possibly be imagined. This one would think impossible ; but you know it to be true. If you imagine that it gives you a manly, thoughtful, and decisive air, as some, though very few, of your countrymen do, you are most exceedingly mistaken ; for it is at best the air of a German corporal, part of whose exercise is to look fierce, and to *blasemeer-op.* You will say, perhaps, What, am I always to be studying my countenance in order to wear this *douceur ?* I answer No, do it but for a fort-night, and you never will have occasion to think of it more. Take but half the pains to recover the countenance that nature gave you, that you must have taken to disguise and deform it as you have, and the business will be done. Accustom your eyes to a certain softness, of which they are very capable, and your face to smiles, which become it more than most faces I know. Give all your motions, too, an air of *douceur,* which is directly the reverse of their present celerity and rapidity. I wish you would adopt a little of *l'air du Couvent* (you very well know what I mean) to a certain degree ; it has something ex-tremely engaging ; there is a mixture of benevolence, affection, and unction in it : it is frequently really sincere, but is almost always thought so, and consequently pleasing. Will you call this trouble ? It will not be half an hour's trouble to you in a week's time. But suppose it be, pray tell me why did you give yourself the trouble of learning to dance so well as you do ? It is neither a religious, moral, or civil duty. You must own, that you did it then singly to please, and you were in the right on't. Why do you wear fine clothes, and curl your hair ? Both are troublesome ; lank locks, and plain flimsy rags, are much easier. This, then, you also do in order to please, and you do very right. But then, for God's sake, reason and act consequentially ; and endeavour to please in other things too, still more essential ; and without which the trouble you have taken in those is wholly thrown away. You show your dancing, perhaps, six times a year, at most; but you show your counten-ance, and your common motions, every day, and all day. Which, then, I appeal to yourself, ought you to think of the most, and care to render easy, graceful, and engaging? *Douceur* of coun-tenance and gesture can alone make them so. You are by no means ill-natured ; and would you, then, most unjustly be reckoned so ? Yet your common countenance intimates, and would make anybody, who did not know you, believe it. *A propos* of this ; I must tell you what was said the other day to a fine lady whom you know, who is very good-natured, in truth, but whose common countenance implies ill-nature, even to brutality. It was Miss H——n, Lady M——y's niece, whom you have seen, both at Blackheath and at Lady Hervey's.

Lady M——y was saying to me, that you had a very engaging countenance when you had a mind to it, but that you had not always that mind ; upon which Miss H——n said, that she liked your countenance best when it was as glum as her own. Why, then, replied Lady M——y, you two should marry ; for, while you both wear your worst countenances, nobody else will venture upon either of you; and they call her now Mrs Stanhope. To complete this *douceur* of countenance and motions, which I so earnestly recommend to you, you should carry it also to your expressions, and manner of thinking, *mettez y toujours de l'affectueux de l'onction ;* take the gentle, the favourable, the indulgent side of most questions. I own that the manly and sublime John Trott, your countryman, seldom does; but, to show his spirit and decision, takes the rough and harsh side, which he generally adorns with an oath, to seem more formidable. This he only thinks fine ; for, to do John justice, he is commonly as good-natured as anybody. These are among the many little things which you have not, and I have lived long enough in the world to know of what infinite consequence they are in the course of life. Reason then, I repeat it again, within yourself *consequentially ;* and let not the pains you have taken, and still take, to please in some things, be *a pure perte*, by your negligence of, and inattention to, others, of much less trouble, and much more consequence.

I have been of late much engaged, or rather bewildered, in Oriental history, particularly that of the Jews, since the destruction of their temple, and their dispersion by Titus ; but the confusion and uncertainty of the whole, and the monstrous extravagancies and falsehoods of the greatest part of it, disgusted me extremely. Their Thalmud, their Mischna, their Targums, and other traditions and writings of their Rabbins and Doctors, who were most of them Cabalists, are really more extravagant and absurd, if possible, than all that you have read in Comte de Gabalis; and, indeed, most of his stuff is taken from them. Take this sample of their nonsense, which is transmitted in the writings of one of their most considerable Rabbins. ' One Abas Saul, a man ten feet high, was digging a grave, and happened to find the eye of Goliath, in which he thought proper to bury himself, and so he did, all but his head, which the Giant's eye was unfortunately not quite deep enough to receive.' This, I assure you, is the most modest lie of ten thousand. I have also read the Turkish History, which, excepting the religious part, is not fabulous, though very possibly not true. For the Turks, having no notion of letters, and being,

even by their religion, forbid the use of them, except for reading and transcribing the Koran ; they have no historians of their
own, nor any authentic records or memorials for other historians
to work upon : so that what histories we have of that country
are written by foreigners; as Platina, Sir Paul Rycaut, Prince
Cantemir, &c., or else snatches only of particular and short
periods, by some who happened to reside there at those times :
such as Busbequius, whom I have just finished. I like him, as
far as he goes, much the best of any of them : but, then, his
account is, properly, only an account of his own embassy, from
the Emperor Charles the Fifth to Solyman the Magnificent.
However, there he gives, episodically, the best account I know
of the customs and manners of the Turks, and of the nature of
that government, which is a most extraordinary one. For, de- .
spotic as it always seems, and sometimes is, it is in truth a
military republic ; and the real power resides in the Janissaries;
who sometimes order their Sultan to strangle his Vizir, and
sometimes the Vizir to depose or strangle his Sultan, according
as they happen to be angry at the one or the ·other. I own
I am glad that the capital strangler should, in his turn, be
strangle-able, and now and then strangled : for I know of no
brute so fierce, nor criminal so guilty, as the creature called a
Sovereign, whether King, Sultan, or Sophy, who thinks himself,
either by divine or human right, vested with an absolute power
of destroying his fellow-creatures; or who, without inquiring into
his right, lawlessly exerts that power. The most excusable of all
those human monsters are the Turks, whose religion teaches
them inevitable fatalism. *A propos* of the Turks ; my Loyola,
I pretend, is superior to your Sultan. Perhaps you think this
impossible, and wonder who this Loyola is. Know, then, that
I have had a Barbet brought me from France, so exactly like
Sultan, that he has been mistaken for him several times ; only
his snout is shorter, and his ears longer than Sultan's. He has
also the acquired knowledge of Sultan ; and I am apt to think
that he studied under the same master at Paris. His habit,
and his white band, show him to be an Ecclesiastic ; and his
begging, which he does very earnestly, proves him to be of a
Mendicant order ; which, added to his flattery and insinuation,
make him supposed to be a Jesuit, and have acquired him the
name of Loyola. I must not omit too, that, when he breaks
wind, he smells exactly like Sultan.

I do not yet hear one jot the better for all my bathings and
pumpings, though I have been here already full half my time ;
I consequently go very little into company, being very little

fit for any. I hope you keep company enough for us both ; you will get more by that than I shall by all my reading. I read singly to amuse myself, and fill up my time, of which I have too much ; but you have two much better reasons for going into company, Pleasure and Profit. May you find a great deal of both, in a great deal of company ! Adieu.

LETTER CCLXVII.

My dear Friend,   London, November the 20th, 1753.

Two mails are now due from Holland, so that I have no letter from you to acknowledge ; but that, you know by long experience, does not hinder my writing to you : I always receive your letters with pleasure ; but I mean, and endeavour, that you should receive mine with some profit ; preferring always your advantage to my own pleasure.

If you find yourself well settled and naturalized at Manheim, stay there some time, and do not leave a certain for an uncertain good : but if you think you shall be as well, or better established at Munich, go there as soon as you please ; and if disappointed, you can always return to Manheim. I mentioned, in a former letter, your passing the Carnival at Berlin, which, I think, may be both useful and pleasing to you ; however, do as you will ; but let me know what you resolve. That King and that country have, and will have, so great a share in the affairs of Europe, that they are well worth being thoroughly known.

Whether, where you are now, or ever may be hereafter, you speak French, German, or English most, I earnestly recommend to you a particular attention to the propriety and elegancy of your style : employ the best words you can find in the language, avoid *cacophony*, and make your periods as harmonious as you can. I need not, I am sure, tell you what you must often have felt, how much the elegancy of diction adorns the best thoughts, and palliates the worst. In the House of Commons it is almost everything ; and indeed, in every assembly, whether public or private. Words, which are the dress of thoughts, deserve, surely, more care than clothes, which are only the dress of the person, and which, however, ought to have their share of attention. If you attend to your style in any one language, it will give you a habit of attending to it in every other ; and if once you speak either French or German very elegantly,

you will afterwards speak much the better English for it. I
repeat it to you again, for at least the thousandth time ; exert
your whole attention now in acquiring the ornamental parts of
character. People know very little of the world, and talk nonsense, when they talk of plainness and solidity unadorned ; they
will do in nothing : mankind has been long out of a state of
nature, and the golden age of native simplicity will never return. Whether for the better or the worse, no matter ; but we
are refined ; and plain manners, plain dress, and plain diction,
would as little do in life, as acorns, herbage, and the water of
the neighbouring spring, would do at table. Some people are
just come, who interrupt me in the middle of my sermon ; so
good night.

LETTER CCLXVIII.

MY DEAR FRIEND,   London, November the 26th, 1753.

FINE doings at Manheim ! If one may give credit to the
weekly histories of Monsieur Roderigue, the finest writer among
the moderns ; not only *des chasses brillantes et nombreuses, des
opéras ou les acteurs se surpassent, les jours des Saints de L L. A
A. E E. sérénissimes, célébrés en grand gala ;* [1] but, to crown the
whole, Monsieur Zuchmantel is happily arrived, and Monsieur
Wartensleben hourly expected. I hope that you are *pars magna*
of all these delights ; though, as Noll Bluff says, in the Old
Bachelor, *that rascally Gazetteer takes no more notice of you than
if you were not in the land of the living.* I should think that he
might at least have taken notice, that in those rejoicings you
appeared with a rejoicing, and not a gloomy, countenance ; and
you distinguished yourself in that numerous and shining company, by your air, dress, address, and attentions. If this was
the case, as I will both hope and suppose that it was, I will, if
you require it, have him written to, to do you justice in his
next *supplément.* Seriously, I am very glad that you are
whirled in that *tourbillon* of pleasures ; they smooth, polish, and
rub off rough corners : perhaps, too, you have some particular
collision, which is still more effectual.

Schannat's History of the Palatinate was, I find, written originally in German, in which language I suppose it is that you
have read it ; but, as I must humbly content myself with the

---

[1] Brilliant and numerous hunting-parties, operas with first-rate actors.
the saints' days of their Serene Highnesses celebrated with magnificent entertainments.

French translation, Vaillant has sent for it for me, from Holland, so that I have not yet read it. While you are in the Palatinate, you do very well to read everything relative to it; you will do still better if you make that reading the foundation of your inquiries into the more minute circumstances and anecdotes of that country, whenever you are in company with informed and knowing people.

The Ministers here, intimidated by the absurd and groundless clamours of the mob, have, very weakly in my mind, repealed, this session, the bill which they had passed in the last, for rendering Jews capable of being naturalized, by subsequent Acts of Parliament. The clamourers triumph, and will, doubtless, make further demands; which, if not granted, this piece of complaisance will soon be forgotten. Nothing is truer in politics, than this reflection of the Cardinal de Retz, *Que le peuple craint toujours quand on ne le craint pas*,[1] and, consequently, they grow unreasonable and insolent, when they find that they are feared. Wise and honest governors will never, if they can help it, give the people just cause to complain; but then, on the other hand, they will firmly withstand groundless clamour. Besides that this noise against the Jew bill proceeds from that narrow mob spirit of *intoleration* in religious, and inhospitality in civil, matters; both which all wise governments should oppose.

The confusion in France increases daily, as, no doubt, you are informed, where you are. There is an answer of the Clergy's to the remonstrances of the Parliament, lately published; which was sent me by the last post from France, and which I would have sent you, enclosed in this, were it not too bulky. Very probably you may see it at Manheim, from the French Minister: it is very well worth your reading, being most artful and plausibly written, though founded upon false principles; the *jus divinum* of the Clergy, and consequently their supremacy in all matters of faith and doctrine, are asserted; both which I absolutely deny. Were those two points allowed the Clergy of any country whatsoever, they must necessarily govern that country absolutely; everything being, directly or indirectly, relative to faith or doctrine; and whoever is supposed to have the power of saving and damning souls to all eternity (which power the Clergy pretend to), will be much more considered, and better obeyed, than any civil power, that forms no pretensions beyond this world. Whereas, in truth, the Clergy in every country are, like all other subjects, dependent upon the supreme legislative power; and are appointed by that power,

[1] The people always fear when not feared.

under whatever restrictions and limitations it pleases, to keep up decency and decorum in the church, just as constables are to keep peace in the parish. This Fra. Paolo has clearly proved, even upon their own principles of the Old and New Testament, in his book *de Beneficiis*, which I recommend to you to read with attention ; it is short. Adieu !

LETTER CCLXIX.

MY DEAR FRIEND,   London, December the 25th, 1753.

YESTERDAY again I received two letters at once from you, the one of the 7th, the other of the 15th, from Manheim.

You never had in your life so good a reason for not writing, either to me or to anybody else, as your sore finger lately furnished you. I believe it was painful, and I am glad it is cured ; but a sore finger, however painful, is a much lesser evil than laziness of either body or mind, and attended by fewer ill consequences.

I am very glad to hear that you were distinguished at the Court of Manheim, from the rest of your countrymen and fellow-travellers : it is a sign that you had better manners and address than they ; for take it for granted, the best bred people will always be the best received, wherever they go. Good manners are the settled medium of social, as *specie* is of commercial, life ; returns are equally expected for both ; and people will no more advance their civility to a Bear than their money to a Bankrupt. I really both hope, and believe, that the German Courts will do you a great deal of good; their ceremony and restraint being the proper correctives, and antidotes, for your negligence and inattention. I believe they would not greatly relish your weltering in your own laziness, and an easy chair, nor take it very kindly, if when they spoke to you, or you to them, you looked another way, as much as to say, Kiss my b—h. As they give, so they require, attention ; and, by the way, take this maxim for an undoubted truth, That no young man can possibly improve in any company, for which he has not respect enough to be under some degree of restraint.

I dare not trust to Meyssonier's report of his Rhenish, his Burgundy not having answered either his account or my expectations. I doubt, as a wine merchant, he is the *perfidus caupo*,[1] whatever he may be as a banker. I shall therefore venture

---

[1] Faithless inn-keeper.

upon none of his wine ; but delay making my provision of
Old Hock till I go abroad myself next spring; as I told you
in the utmost secrecy, in my last, that I intend to do ; and
then, probably, I may taste some that I like, and go upon
sure ground. There is commonly very good, both at Aix-la-
Chapelle and Liege ; where I formerly got some excellent,
which I carried with me to Spa, where I drank no other
wine.

As my letters to you frequently miscarry, I will repeat in
this, that part of my last which related to your future motions.
Whenever you shall be tired of Berlin, go to Dresden ; where
Sir Charles Williams will be, who will receive you with open
arms. He dined with me to-day ; and sets out for Dresden in
about six weeks. He spoke of you with great kindness, and
impatience to see you again. He will trust and employ
you in business (and he is now in the whole secret of importance) till we fix our place to meet in ; which, probably, will
be Spa. Wherever you are, inform yourself minutely of, and
attend particularly to, the affairs of France ; they grow serious,
and, in my opinion, will grow more and more so every day.
The King is despised, and I do not wonder at it; but he has
brought it about, to be hated at the same time, which seldom
happens to the same man. His Ministers are known to be as
disunited as incapable : he hesitates between the Church and
the Parliaments, like the Ass in the fable, that starved between
two hampers of hay ; too much in love with his mistress to
part with her, and too much afraid for his soul, to enjoy her :
jealous of the Parliaments, who would support his authority ;
and a devoted bigot to the Church, that would destroy it. The
people are poor, consequently discontented : those who have
religion are divided in their notions of it; which is saying,
that they hate one another. The Clergy never do forgive ;
much less will they forgive the Parliament : the Parliament
never will forgive them. The Army must, without doubt,
take, in their own minds at least, different parts in all these
disputes, which, upon occasion, would break out. Armies,
though always the supporters and tools of absolute power for
the time being, are always the destroyers of it too ; by frequently
changing the hands in which they think proper to lodge it.
This was the case of the Prætorian bands, who deposed and
murdered the monsters they had raised to oppress mankind.
The Janissaries in Turkey, and the regiments of guards in
Russia, do the same now. The French nation reasons freely,
which they never did before, upon matters of religion and

government, and begin to be *spregiudicati*,[1] the officers do so too ; in short, all the symptoms, which I have ever met with in history, previous to great changes and revolutions in Government, now exist, and daily increase, in France.[2] I am glad of it ; the rest of Europe will be the quieter, and have time to recover. England, I am sure, wants rest ; for it wants men and money : the Republic of the United Provinces wants both, still more : the other Powers cannot well dance, when neither France, nor the maritime Powers, can, as they used to do, pay the piper. The first squabble in Europe, that I foresee, will be about the Crown of Poland, should the present King die ; and therefore I wish his Majesty a long life, and a merry Christmas.[3] So much for foreign politics ; but, *à propos* of them, pray take care, while you are in those parts of Germany, to inform yourself correctly of all the details, discussions, and agreements, which the several wars, confiscations, bans, and treaties, occasioned between the Bavarian and Palatine Electorates ; they are interesting and curious.

I shall not, upon the occasion of the approaching new year, repeat to you the wishes which I continue to form for you ; you know them already ; and you know that it is absolutely in your own power to satisfy most of them. Among many other wishes, this is my most earnest one, That you would open the new year with a most solemn and devout sacrifice to the Graces ; who never reject those that supplicate them with fervour : without them, let me tell you, that your friend Dame Fortune will stand you in little stead : may they all be your friends ! Adieu.

LETTER CCLXX.

MY DEAR FRIEND,   London, January the 15th, 1754.

I HAVE this moment received your letter of the 26th past, from Munich. Since you are got so well out of the distress and dangers of your journey from Manheim, I am glad that you were in them,

> Condisce i diletti
> Memoria di pene,
> Ne sà che sia bene
> Chi mal non soffrì.[4]

---

[1] Without prejudices.
[2] This was written thirty-six years before the French Revolution.
[3] The then king Augustus III. died in 1763, and the first partition of Poland took place in 1772.
[4] The memory of trouble gives zest to pleasure, and he who has not suffered knows not when he is well off.

They were but little samples of the much greater distress and dangers which you must expect to meet with in your great, and, I hope, long journey through life. In some parts of it flowers are scattered with profusion, the road is smooth, and the prospect pleasant ; but in others (and I fear the greater number) the road is rugged, beset with thorns and briars, and cut by torrents. Gather the flowers in your way ; but at the same time guard against the briars that are either mixed with them, or that most certainly succeed them.

I thank you for your wild boar, who, now he is dead, I assure him *se laissera bien manger malgré qu'il en ait ;* though I am not sure that I should have had that personal valour which so successfully distinguished you in single combat with him, which made him bite the dust like Homer's heroes, and, to conclude my period sublimely, put him into that *pickle* from which I propose eating him. At the same time that I applaud your valour, I must do justice to your modesty ; which candidly admits that you were not overmatched, and that your adversary was of about your own age and size. A *Marcassin*, being under a year old, would have been below your indignation. *Bête de compagnie*, being under two years old, was still, in my opinion, below your glory ; but I guess that your enemy was *un Ragot*, that is, from two to three years old ; an age and size which, between man and boar, answer pretty well to yours.

If accidents of bad roads or waters do not retain you at Munich, I do not fancy that pleasures will ; and I rather believe you will seek for and find them at the Carnival at Berlin ; in which supposition, I eventually direct this letter to your banker there. While you are at Berlin (I earnestly recommend it to you again and again) pray *care* to see, hear, know, and mind everything there. *The ablest Prince in Europe* is surely an object that deserves attention ; and the least thing that he does, like the smallest sketches of the greatest painters, has its value, and a considerable one too.

Read with care the *Code Frederick*, and inform yourself of the good effects of it in those parts of his dominions where it has taken place, and where it has banished the former chicanes, quirks, and quibbles of the old law. Do not think any detail too minute, or trifling, for your inquiry and observation. I wish that you could find one hour's leisure every day to read some good Italian author, and to converse in that language with our worthy friend Signor Angelo Cori : it would both refresh and improve your Italian, which, of the many languages you know, I take to be that in which you are the least perfect ;

but of which too, you already know enough to make yourself master of, with very little trouble, whenever you please.

Live, dwell, and grow, at the several Courts there ; use them so much to your face, that they may not look upon you as a stranger. Observe, and take their tone, even to their affectations and follies ; for such there are, and perhaps should be, at all Courts. Stay, in all events, at Berlin, till I inform you of Sir Charles Williams's arrival at Dresden ; where, I suppose, you would not care.to be before him, and where you may go as soon after him as ever you please. Your time there will neither be unprofitably nor disagreeably spent ; he will introduce you into all the best company, though he can introduce you to none so good as his own. He has of late applied himself very seriously to foreign affairs, especially those of Saxony and Poland ; he knows them perfectly well, and will tell you what he knows. He always expresses, and I have good reason to believe very sincerely, great kindness and affection for you.

The works of the late Lord Bolingbroke are just published, and have plunged me into philosophical studies; which hitherto I have not been much used to, or delighted with : convinced of the futility of those researches : but I have read his Philosophical Essay upon the extent of human knowledge, which, by the way, makes two large quartos and a half. He there shows very clearly, and with most splendid eloquence, what the human mind can and cannot do ; that our understandings are wisely calculated for our place in this planet, and for the link which we form in the universal chain of things ; but that they are by no means capable of that degree of knowledge which our curiosity makes us search after, and which our vanity makes us often believe we arrive at. I shall not recommend to you the reading of that work. But, when you return hither, I shall recommend to your frequent and diligent perusal, all his tracts, that are relative to our history and constitution ; upon which he throws lights, and scatters graces, which no other writer has ever done.

Reading, which was always a pleasure to me, in the time even of my greatest dissipation, is now become my only refuge ; and I fear I indulge it too much, at the expense of my eyes. But what can I do? I must do something ; I cannot bear absolute idleness : my ears grow every day more useless to me, my eyes, consequently, more necessary ; I will not hoard them like a miser, but will rather risk the loss, than not enjoy the use of them.

Pray let me know all the particulars, not only of your reception at Munich, but also at Berlin; at the latter, I believe it will be a good one : for his Prussian Majesty knows that I have long been *an admirer and respecter of his great and various talents.*

Adieu.

LETTER CCLXXI.

MY DEAR FRIEND,   London, February the 1st, 1754.

I RECEIVED, yesterday, yours of the 12th from Munich; in consequence of which I direct this to you there, though I directed my three last to Berlin, where, I suppose, you will find them at your arrival. Since you are not only domesticated, but *niché* at Munich, you are much in the right to stay there. It is not by seeing places that one knows them, but by familiar and daily conversations with the people of fashion. I would not care to be in the place of that prodigy of beauty, whom you are to drive *dans la course de Traineaux;* and I am apt to think you are much more likely to break her bones, than she is, though ever so cruel, to break your heart. Nay, I am not sure but that, according to all the rules of gallantry, you are obliged to overturn her on purpose : in the first place, for the chance of seeing her backside : in the next, for the sake of the contrition and concern which it would give you an opportunity of showing ; and, lastly, upon account of all the *gentillesses et epigrammes,* which it would naturally suggest. Voiture has made several stanzas upon an accident of that kind, which happened to a lady of his acquaintance. There is a great deal of wit in them, rather too much ; for, according to the taste of those times, they are full of what the Italians call *concetti spiritosissimi ;* the Spaniards, *agudeze ;* and we, affectation and quaintness. I hope you have endeavoured to suit your *Traineau* to the character of the fair one whom it is to contain. If she is of an irascible, impetuous disposition (as fine women can sometimes be), you will, doubtless, place her in the body of a lion, a tiger, a dragon, or some tremendous beast of prey and fury ; if she is a sublime and stately beauty, which I think more probable (for unquestionably she is *hogh gebohrne*), you will, I suppose, provide a magnificent swan or proud peacock for her reception ; but if she is all tenderness and softness, you have, to be sure, taken care, amorous doves and wanton sparrows should seem to flutter round her. Proper mottos, I take it for granted, that you have eventually prepared ; but if not, you may find a great many ready made ones in *Les*

Entretiens d'Ariste et d'Eugène, sur les Devises, written by Père Bouhours, and worth your reading at any time. I will not say to you, upon this occasion, like the Father in Ovid,

Parce puer stimulis et fortius utere loris.[1]

On the contrary, drive on briskly ; it is not the chariot of the sun that you drive, but you carry the sun in your chariot; consequently, the faster it goes the less it will be likely either to scorch or consume. This is Spanish enough, I am sure.

If this finds you still at Munich, pray make many compliments from me to Mr Burrish, to whom I am very much obliged for all his kindness to you : it is true, that while I had power, I endeavoured to serve him ; but it is as true too, that I served many others more, who have neither returned nor remembered those services.

I have been very ill this last fortnight, of your old Carniolian complaint, the *arthritis vaga ;* luckily, it did not fall upon my breast, but seized on my right arm ; there it fixed its seat of empire ; but, as in all tyrannical governments, the remotest parts felt their share of its severity. Last post I was not able to hold a pen long enough to write to you, and therefore desired Mr Grevenkop to do it for me ; but that letter was directed to Berlin. My pain is now much abated, though I have still some fine remains of it in my shoulder, where, I fear, it will tease me a great while. I must be careful to take Horace's advice, and consider well, *Quid valeant humeri, quid ferre recusent.*[2]

Lady Chesterfield bids me make you her compliments, and assure you, that the music will be much more welcome to her with you, than without you.

In some of my last letters, which were directed to, and will, I suppose, wait for you at, Berlin, I complimented you, and with justice, upon your great improvement of late in the epistolary way, both with regard to the style and the turn of your letters ; your four or five last to me have been very good ones, and one that you wrote to Mr Harte, upon the New Year, was so pretty a one, and he was so much and so justly pleased with it, that he sent it me from Windsor the instant he had read it. This talent (and a most necessary one it is in the course of life) is to be acquired by resolving, and taking pains to acquire it; and, indeed, so is every talent except poetry, which is, undoubtedly, a gift. Think therefore, night and day, of the turn, the purity, the correctness, the perspicuity, and the elegancy of whatever

---

[1] My boy, be sparing of the goad and thong.
[2] What my shoulders can, and what they cannot, bear.

you speak or write : take my word for it, your labour will not be in vain, but greatly rewarded by the harvest of praise and success which it will bring you.   Delicacy of turn and elegancy of style are ornaments as necessary to common sense, as attentions, address, and fashionable manners are to common civility ; both may subsist without them, but then, without being of the least use to the owner.   The figure of a man is exactly the same in dirty rags, or in the finest and best chosen clothes ; but in which of the two he is the most likely to please, and to be received in good company, I leave to you to determine.

Both my arm and my paper hint to me to bid you good night.

LETTER CCLXXII.

My dear Friend,   London, February the 12th, 1754.

I take my aim, and let off this letter at you, at Berlin ; I should be sorry it missed you, because I believe you will read it with as much pleasure as I write it.   It is to inform you that, after some difficulties and dangers, your seat in the new Parliament is at last absolutely secured, and that without opposition or the least necessity of your personal trouble or appearance.   This success, I must further inform you is, in a great degree, owing to Mr Eliot's friendship to us both ; for he brings you in with himself at his surest borough.   As it was impossible to act with more zeal and friendship than Mr Eliot has acted in this whole affair, I desire that you will, by the very next post, write him a letter of thanks ; warm and young thanks, not old and cold ones.   You may enclose it in yours to me, and I will send it to him, for he is now in Cornwall.

Thus, sure of being a Senator, I dare say you do not propose to be one of the *pedarii senatores et pedibus ire in sententiam ;*[1] for, as the House of Commons is the theatre where you must make your fortune and figure in the world, you must resolve to be an actor, and not a *persona muta,* which is just equivalent to a candle-snuffer upon other theatres.   Whoever does not shine there is obscure, insignificant, and contemptible ; and you cannot conceive how easy it is for a man of half your sense and knowledge to shine there if he pleases.   The receipt to make a speaker, and an applauded one too, is short and easy.   Take of common sense *quantum suﬃcit,* add a little application to the rules and

---

[1] Senators who could not introduce any measure into the Senate, but only vote on what others originated.

orders of the house, throw obvious thoughts in a new light, and make up the whole with a large quantity of purity, correctness, and elegancy of style. Take it for granted, that by far the greatest part of mankind do neither analyze nor search to the bottom ; they are incapable of penetrating deeper than the surface. All have senses to be gratified, very few have reason to be applied to. Graceful utterance and action please their eyes, elegant diction tickles their ears ; but strong reason would be thrown away upon them. I am not only persuaded by theory, but convinced by my experience, that (supposing a certain degree of common sense) what is called a good speaker, is as much a mechanic as a good shoemaker ; and that the two trades are equally to be learned by the same degree of application. Therefore, for God's sake, let this trade be the principal object of your thoughts ; never lose sight of it. Attend minutely to your style, whatever language you speak or write in ; seek for the best words, and think of the best turns. Whenever you doubt of the propriety or elegancy of any word, search the dictionary, or some good author, for it, or inquire of somebody who is master of that language ; and in a little time propriety and elegancy of diction will become so habitual to you, that they will cost you no more trouble. As I have laid this down to be mechanical, and attainable by whoever will take the necessary pains, there will be no great vanity in my saying, that I saw the importance of the object so early, and attended to it so young, that it would now cost me more trouble to speak or write ungrammatically, vulgarly, and inelegantly, than ever it did to avoid doing so. The late Lord Bolingbroke, without the least trouble, talked all day long, full as elegantly as he wrote : Why ? Not by a peculiar gift from heaven ; but, as he has often told me himself, by an early and constant attention to his style. The present Solicitor-general, Murray, has less law than many lawyers, but has more practice than any ; merely upon account of his eloquence, of which he has a never-failing stream. I remember, so long ago as when I was at Cambridge, whenever I read pieces of eloquence (and indeed they were my chief study), whether ancient or modern, I used to write down the shining passages, and then translate them, as well and as elegantly as ever I could ; if Latin or French, into English ; if English, into French. This, which I practised for some years, not only improved and formed my style, but imprinted in my mind and memory the best thoughts of the best authors. The trouble was little, but the advantage, I have experienced, was great. While you are abroad, you can neither have time nor opportunity to read pieces of English, or Parliamentary, eloquence, as I hope you will carefully do when you return ; but, in the mean time, whenever pieces of French eloquence come in your way, such as the speeches of persons received into the Academy, *oraisons funèbres*, representations of the several Parliaments to the King, &c., read them in that view, in that spirit ; observe the harmony, the turn, and elegancy of the style ; examine in what you think it might have been better ; and consider in what, had you written it yourself, you might have done worse. Compare the different manners of expressing the same thoughts, in different authors ; and observe how differently the same things appear in different dresses. Vulgar, coarse, and ill chosen words, will deform and degrade the best thoughts, as much as rags and dirt will the best figure. In short, you now know your object ; pursue it steadily, and have no digressions that are not relative to, and connected with, the main action. Your success in Parliament will effectually remove all *other objections ;* either a foreign or a domestic destination will no longer be refused you, if you make your way to it through Westminster.

I think I may now say that I am quite recovered of my late illness, strength and spirits excepted, which are not yet restored. Aix-la-Chapelle and Spa will, I believe, answer all my purposes.

I long to hear an account of your reception at Berlin, which I fancy will be a most gracious one. Adieu.

LETTER CCLXXIII.

My dear Friend,   London, Feb. the 15th, 1754.

I can now with great truth apply your own motto to you, *Nullum numen abest, si sit prudentia.* You are sure of being, as early as your age will permit, a Member of that House, which is the only road to figure and fortune in this country. Those indeed who are bred up to, and distinguish themselves in, particular professions, as the army, the navy, and the law, may by their own merit raise themselves to a certain degree ; but you may observe, too, that they never get to the top without the assistance of Parliamentary talents and influence. The means of distinguishing yourself in Parliament are, as I told you in my last, much more easily attained than I believe you imagine. Close attendance to the business of the House will soon give you the Parliamentary *routine ;* and strict attention to your style will soon make you not only a speaker, but a good one. The vulgar look upon a man, who is reckoned a fine speaker, as a phenomenon, a supernatural being, and endowed with some peculiar gift of Heaven : they stare at him if he walks in the Park, and cry, *that is he.* You will, I am sure, view him in a juster light, and *nulla formidine.*[1] You will consider him only as a man of good sense, who adorns common thoughts with the graces of elocution, and the elegancy of style. The miracle will then cease ; and you will be convinced, that with the same application and attention to the same objects, you may most certainly equal, and perhaps surpass, this prodigy. Sir W—— Y——, with not a quarter of your parts, and not a thousandth part of your knowledge, has, by a glibness of tongue singly, raised himself successively to the best employments of the kingdom : he has been Lord of the Admiralty, Lord of the Treasury, Secretary at War, and is now Vice-Treasurer of Ireland ; and all this with a most sullied, not to say blasted, character. Represent the thing to yourself as it really is, easily attainable, and you will find it so. Have but ambition enough passionately to desire the object, and spirit enough to use the means, and I will be answerable for your success. When I was younger than you are, I resolved within myself that I would in all events be a speaker in Parliament, and a good one too, if I could. I consequently never lost sight of that object, and never neglected any of the means that I thought led to it. I succeeded to a certain degree ; and, I assure you, with great ease, and without superior talents.—Young people are very apt to overrate both men and things, from not being enough acquainted with them. In proportion as you come to know them better you will value them less. You will find that reason, which always ought to direct mankind, seldom does ; but that passions and weaknesses commonly usurp its seat, and rule in its stead. You will find that the ablest have their weak sides too, and are only comparatively able, with regard to the still weaker herd : having fewer weaknesses themselves, they are able to avail themselves of the innumerable ones of the generality of mankind : being more masters of themselves, they become more easily masters of others. They address themselves to their weaknesses, their senses, their passions ; never to their reason, and consequently seldom fail of success. But then analyze those great, those governing, and, as the vulgar imagine, those perfect Characters, and you will find the great Brutus a thief in Macedonia, the great Cardinal de Richelieu a

---

[1] Without apprehension.

jealous poetaster, and the great Duke of Marlborough a miser. Till you come to know mankind by your own experience, I know no thing, nor no man, that can, in the mean time, bring you so well acquainted with them as le Duc de la Rochefoucault ; his little book of Maxims, which I would advise you to look into, for some moments at least, every day of your life, is, I fear, too like, and too exact, a picture of human nature. I own it seems to degrade it, but yet my experience does not convince me that it degrades it unjustly.

Now, to bring all this home to my first point. All these considerations should not only invite you to attempt to make a figure in Parliament, but encourage you to hope that you shall succeed. To govern mankind, one must not overrate them ; and to please an audience, as a speaker, one must not overvalue it. When I first came into the House of Commons, I respected that assembly as a venerable one, and felt a certain awe upon me ; but, upon better acquaintance, that awe soon vanished, and I discovered that, of the five hundred and sixty, not above thirty could understand reason, and that all the rest were *peuple :* that those thirty only required plain common sense, dressed up in good language ; and that all the others only required flowing and harmonious periods, whether they conveyed any meaning or not, having ears to hear, but not sense enough to judge. These considerations made me speak with little concern the first time, with less the second, and with none at all the third. I gave myself no further trouble about anything, except my elocution and my style ; presuming, without much vanity, that I had common sense sufficient not to talk nonsense. Fix these three truths strongly in your mind : First, that it is absolutely necessary for you to speak in Parliament ; secondly, that it only requires a little human attention, and no supernatural gifts ; and, thirdly, that you have all the reason in the world to think that you shall speak well.—When we meet this shall be the principal subject of our conversations ; and if you will follow my advice I will answer for your success.

Now from great things to little ones ; the transition is to me easy, because nothing seems little to me that can be of any use to you. I hope you take great care of your mouth and teeth, and that you clean them well every morning with a spunge and tepid water, with a few drops of arquebusade water dropped into it : besides washing your mouth carefully after every meal. I do insist upon your never using those sticks, or any hard substance whatsoever, which always rub away the gums, and destroy the varnish of the teeth. I speak this from woful experience ; for my negligence of my teeth, when I was younger than you are, made them bad ; and afterwards, my desire to have them look better made me use sticks, irons, &c., which totally destroyed them, so that I have not now above six or seven left. I lost one this morning, which suggested this advice to you.

I have received the tremendous wild boar, which your still more tremendous arm slew in the immense deserts of the Palatinate ; but have not yet tasted of it, as it is hitherto above my low regimen.   The late King of Prussia, whenever he killed any number of wild boars, used to oblige the Jews to buy them at a high price, though they could eat none of them ; so they defrayed the expense of his hunting.   His son has juster rules of government, as the *Code Frederick* plainly shows.

I hope that by this time you are as well *ancré* at Berlin as you were at Munich ; but if not, you are sure of being so at Dresden.   Adieu.

———◇———

LETTER CCLXXIV.

My dear Friend,   London, February 26th, 1754.

I have received your letters of the 4th from Munich, and of the 11th from Ratisbon ; but I have not received that of the 31st January, to which you refer in the former.   It is to this negligence and uncertainty of the post that you owe your accidents between Munich and Ratisbon ; for had you received my letters regularly, you would have received one from me before you left Munich, in which I advised you to stay, since you were so well there.   But at all events, you were in the wrong to set out from Munich in such weather and such roads ; since you could never imagine that I had set my heart so much upon your going to Berlin as to venture your being buried in the snow for it.   Upon the whole, considering all, you are very well off.   You do very well, in my mind, to return to Munich, or at least to keep within the circle of Munich, Ratisbon, and Manheim, till the weather and the roads are good : stay at each or any of those places as long as ever you please, for I am extremely indifferent about your going to Berlin.

As to our meeting, I will tell you my plan, and you may form your own accordingly.   I propose setting out from hence the last week in April, then drinking the Aix-la-Chapelle waters for a week, and from thence being at Spa about the 15th of May, where I shall stay two months at most, and then returning straight to England. As I both hope and believe that there will be no mortal at Spa during my residence there, the fashionable season not beginning till the middle of July, I would by no means have you come there at first, to be locked up with me and some few *Capucins*, for two months in that miserable hole; but I would advise you to stay where you like best, till about the first week in July, and then to come and pick me up at Spa, or meet me upon the road at Liege or Brussels. As for the intermediate time, should you be weary of Manheim and Munich, you may, if you please, go to Dresden to Sir Charles Williams, who will be there before that time; or you may come for a month or six weeks to the Hague, or, in short, go or stay wherever you like best. So much for your motions.

As you have sent for all the letters directed to you at Berlin, you will receive from thence volumes of mine, among which you will easily perceive that some were calculated for a supposed perusal previous to your opening them. I will not repeat anything contained in them, excepting that I desire you will send me a warm and cordial letter of thanks for Mr Eliot, who has in the most friendly manner imaginable fixed you at his own borough of Liskeard, where you will be elected, jointly with him, without the least opposition or difficulty. I will forward that letter to him into Cornwall, where he now is.

Now, that you are soon to be a man of business, I heartily wish you would immediately begin to be a man of method, nothing contributing more to facilitate and despatch business than method and order. Have order and method in your accounts, in your reading, in the allotment of your time, in short, in everything. You cannot conceive how much time you will save by it, nor how much better everything you do will be done. The Duke of Marlborough did by no means spend, but he slatterned himself into that immense debt, which is not yet near paid off. The hurry and confusion of the Duke of Newcastle do not proceed from his business, but from his want of method in it. Sir Robert Walpole, who had ten times the busiuess to do, was never seen in a hurry, because he always did it with method. The head of a man who has business, and no method nor order, is properly that *rudis indigestaque moles quam dixere chaos.*[1] As you must be conscious that you are extremely negligent and slatternly, I hope you will resolve not to be so for the future. Prevail with yourself only to observe good method and order for one fortnight, and I will venture to assure you that you will never neglect them

[1] Unshaped, unordered mass which men call chaos.

afterwards, you will find such conveniency and advantage arising · from them. Method is the great advantage that lawyers have over other people in speaking in Parliament ; for, as they must necessarily observe it in their pleadings in the Courts of Justice, it becomes habitual to them everywhere else. Without making you a compliment, I can tell you with pleasure, that order, method, and more activity of mind, are all that you want, to make, some day or other, a considerable figure in business. You have more useful knowledge, more discernment of characters, and much more discretion than is common at your age ; much more, I am sure, than I had at that age.— Experience you cannot yet have, and therefore trust in the mean time to mine. I am an old traveller ; am well acquainted with all the by, as well as the great, roads; I cannot misguide you from ignorance, and you are very sure I shall not from design.

I can assure you that you will have no opportunity of subscribing yourself, my Excellency's, &c. Retirement and quiet were my choice some years ago, while I had all my senses, and health and spirits enough to carry on business ; but now I have lost my hearing, and find my constitution declining daily, they are become my necessary and only refuge. I know myself (no common piece of knowledge, let me tell you), I know what I can, what I cannot, and consequently what I ought to do. I ought not, and therefore will not, return to business, when I am much less fit for it than I was when I quitted it. Still less will I go to Ireland, where, from my deafness and infirmities, I must necessarily make a different figure from that which I once made there. My pride would be too much mortified by that difference. The two important senses of seeing and hearing should not only be good, but quick, in business ; and the business of a Lord-Lieutenant of Ireland (if he will do it himself) requires both those senses in the highest perfection. It was the Duke of Dorset's not doing the business himself, but giving it up to favourites, that has occasioned all this confusion in Ireland; and it was my doing the whole myself, without either Favourite, Minister, or Mistress, that made my administration so smooth and quiet. I remember, when I named the late Mr Liddel for my Secretary, everybody was much surprised at it ; and some of my friends represented to me that he was no man of business, but only a very genteel, pretty young fellow ; I assured them, and with truth, that that was the very reason why I chose him : for that I was resolved to do all the business myself, and without even the suspicion of having a Minister ;

which the Lord-Lieutenant's Secretary, if he is a man of business, is always supposed, and commonly with reason, to be. Moreover, I look upon myself now to be *emeritus* in business, in which I have been near forty years together; I give it up to you : apply yourself to it, as I have done, for forty years, and then I consent to your leaving it for a philosophical retirement, among your friends and your books. Statesmen and beauties are very rarely sensible of the gradations of their decay ; and, too sanguinely hoping to shine on in their meridian, often set with contempt and ridicule. I retired in time, *uti conviva satur ;*[1] or, as Pope says, still better, ' Ere tittering youth shall shove you from the stage.' My only remaining ambition is to be the Counsellor and Minister of your rising ambition. Let me see my own youth revived in you ; let me be your Mentor, and, with your parts and knowledge, I promise you, you shall go far. You must bring, on your part, activity and attention, and I will point out to you the proper objects for them. I own I fear but one thing for you, and that is what one has generally the least reason to fear, from one of your age ; I mean your laziness, which, if you indulge, will make you stagnate in a contemptible obscurity all your life. It will hinder you from doing anything that will deserve to be written, or from writing anything that may deserve to be read ; and yet one or other of these two objects should be at least aimed at by every rational being. I look upon indolence as a sort of *suicide ;* for the Man is effectually destroyed, though the appetites of the Brute may survive. Business by no means forbids pleasures ; on the contrary, they reciprocally season each other ; and I will venture to affirm, that no man enjoys either in perfection that does not join both. They whet the desire for each other. Use yourself therefore, in time, to be alert and diligent in your little concerns : never procrastinate, never put off till to-morrow what you can do to-day ; and never do two things at a time : pursue your object, be it what it will, steadily and indefatigably ; and let any difficulties (if surmountable) rather animate. than slacken your endeavours. Perseverance has surprising effects.

I wish you would use yourself to translate, every day, only three or four lines, from any book, in any language, into the correctest and most elegant English that you can think of; you cannot imagine how it will insensibly form your style, and give you an habitual elegancy : it would not take you up a quarter of an hour in a day. This letter is so long, that it will

---

[1] Like a sated diner-out.

hardly leave you that quarter of an hour, the day you receive it. So good night.

LETTER CCLXXV.

MY DEAR FRIEND,   London, March the 8th, 1754.

A GREAT and unexpected event has lately happened in our ministerial world—Mr Pelham died last Monday, of a fever and mortification ; occasioned by a general corruption of his whole mass of blood, which had broke out into sores in his back. I regret him as an old acquaintance, a pretty near relation, and a private man, with whom I have lived many years in a social and friendly way. He meaned well to the public ; and was incorrupt in a post where corruption is commonly contagious. If he was no shining, enterprising Minister, he was a safe one, which I like better. Very shining Ministers, like the Sun, are apt to scorch when they shine the brightest : in our constitution I prefer the milder light of a less glaring Minister. His successor is not yet, at least publicly, *designatus*. You will easily suppose that many are very willing, and very few able, to fill that post. Various persons are talked of, by different people, for it, according as their interest prompts them to wish, or their ignorance to conjecture. Mr Fox is the most talked of, he is strongly supported by the Duke of Cumberland. Mr Legge, the Solicitor-General, and Dr Lee, are likewise all spoken of, upon the foot of the Duke of Newcastle's and the Chancellor's interest. Should it be any one of the three last, I think no great alterations will ensue ; but should Mr Fox prevail, it would, in my opinion, soon produce changes, by no means favourable to the Duke of Newcastle. In the mean time, the wild conjectures of volunteer politicians, and the ridiculous importance which, upon these occasions, blockheads always endeavour to give themselves, by grave looks, significant shrugs, and insignificant whispers, are very entertaining to a bystander, as, thank God, I now am. One *knows something*, but is not yet at liberty to tell it ; another has heard something from a very good hand ; a third congratulates himself upon a certain degree of intimacy, which he has long had with every one of the candidates, though perhaps he has never spoken twice to any one of them. In short, in these sort of intervals, vanity, interest, and absurdity always display themselves in the most ridiculous light. One who has been so long behind the scenes as I have, is much more diverted with the entertainment than those can be who only see it from the pit and boxes. I know the whole machinery of the interior, and can laugh the better at the silly wonder and wild conjectures of the uninformed spectators. This accident, I think, cannot in the least affect your election, which is finally settled with your friend Mr Eliot. For, let who will prevail, I presume, he will consider me enough, not to overturn an arrangement of that sort, in which he cannot possibly be personally interested. So pray go on with your parliamentary preparations. Have that object always in your view, and pursue it with attention.

I take it for granted that your late residence in Germany has made you as perfect and correct in German, as you were before in French, at least it is worth your while to be so ; because it is worth every man's while to be perfectly master of whatever language he may ever have occasion to speak. A man is not himself in a language which he does not thoroughly possess ; his thoughts are degraded, when inelegantly or imperfectly expressed ; he is cramped and confined, and consequently can never appear to advantage. Examine and analyze those thoughts that strike you the most, either in conversation or in books ; and you will find that they owe at least half their merit to the turn and expression of them. There is nothing truer than that old saying, *Nihil dictum quod non prius dictum*.[1] It is only the manner of saying or writing it that makes it appear new. Convince yourself that Manner is almost everything, in everything, and study it accordingly.

I am this moment informed, and I believe truly, that Mr Fox is to succeed Mr Pelham, as first Commissioner of the Treasury and Chancellor of the Exchequer ; and your friend Mr Yorke, of the Hague, to succeed Mr Fox, as Secretary at War. I am not sorry for this promotion of Mr Fox, as I have always been upon civil terms with him, and found him ready to do me any little services. He is frank and gentlemanlike in his manner ; and, to a certain degree, I really believe will be your friend upon my account ; if you can afterwards make him yours upon your own, *tant mieux*. I have nothing more to say now, but Adieu.

---

[1] Nothing is said but has been said before.

LETTER CCLXXVI.

MY DEAR FRIEND,   London, March the 15th, 1754.

WE are here in the midst of a second winter ; the cold is more severe, and the snow deeper, than they were in the first. I presume your weather in Germany is not much more gentle ; and therefore I hope that you are quietly and warmly fixed at some good town ; and will not risk a second burial in the snow, after your late fortunate resurrection out of it. Your letters, I suppose, have not been able to make their way through the ice; for I have received none from you since that of the 12th of February, from Ratisbon. I am the more uneasy at this state of ignorance, because I fear that you may have found some subsequent inconveniencies from your overturn, which you might not be aware of at first.

The curtain of the political theatre was partly drawn up the day before yesterday, and exhibited a scene which the public in general did not expect ; the Duke of Newcastle was declared first Lord Commissioner of the Treasury, Mr Fox Secretary of State in his room, and Mr Henry Legge Chancellor of the Exchequer. The employments of Treasurer of the Navy, and Secretary at War, supposed to be vacant by the promotion of Mr Fox and Mr Legge, were to be kept *in petto* till the dissolution of this Parliament, which will probably be next week, to avoid the expense and trouble of unnecessary reëlections ; but it was generally supposed that Colonel Yorke, of the Hague, was to succeed Mr Fox, and George Grenville Mr Legge. This scheme, had it taken place, you are, I believe, aware, was more a temporary expedient, for securing the elections of the new Parliament, and forming it, at its first meeting, to the interests and the inclinations of the Duke of Newcastle and the Chancellor, than a plan of Administration either intended or wished to be permanent. This scheme was disturbed yesterday : Mr Fox, who had sullenly accepted the seals the day before, more sullenly refused them yesterday. His object was to be first Commissioner of the Treasury and Chancellor of the Exchequer, and consequently to have a share in the election of the new Parliament, and a much greater in the management of it when chosen. This necessary consequence of his view defeated it ; and the Duke of Newcastle, and the Chancellor, chose to kick him up-stairs into the Secretaryship of State, rather than trust him with either the election or the management of the new

Parliament.   In this, considering their respective situations, they certainly acted wisely; but whether Mr Fox has done so or not, in refusing the seals, is a point which I cannot determine. If he is, as I presume he is, animated with revenge, and I believe would not be over-scrupulous in the means of gratifying it, I should have thought he could have done it better as a Secretary of State, with constant admission into the Closet, than as a private man at the head of an opposition.   But I see all these things at too great a distance to be able to judge soundly of them.   The true springs and motives of political measures are confined within a very narrow circle, and known to very few; the good reasons alleged are seldom the true ones.   The Public commonly judges, or rather guesses, wrong, and I am now one of that Public.   I therefore recommend to you a prudent pyrrhonism in all matters of state, until you become one of the wheels of them yourself, and consequently acquainted with the general motion, at least, of the others; for as to all the minute and secret springs, that contribute more or less to the whole machine, no man living ever knows them all, not even he who has the principal direction of it.   As in the human body there are innumerable little vessels and glands that have a good deal to do, and yet escape the knowledge of the most skilful anatomist; he will know more indeed than those who only see the exterior of our bodies; but he will never know all.   This bustle, and these changes at Court, far from having disturbed the quiet and security of your election, have, if possible, rather confirmed them; for the Duke of Newcastle (I must do him justice) has, in the kindest manner imaginable to you, wrote a letter to Mr Eliot, to recommend to him the utmost care of your election.

Though the plan of administration is thus unsettled, mine, for my travels this summer, is finally settled; and I now communicate it to you, that you may form your own upon it.   I propose being at Spa on the 10th or 12th of May, and staying there till the 10th of July.   As there will be no mortal there during my stay, it would be both unpleasant and unprofitable to you to be shut up *téte-à-téte* with me the whole time; I should therefore think it best for you not to come to me there till the last week in June.   In the mean time, I suppose, that by the middle of April you will think you have had enough of Manheim, Munich, or Ratisbon, and that district.   Where would you choose to go then? for I leave you absolutely your choice. Would you go to Dresden for a month or six weeks?   That is a good deal out of your way; and I am not sure that Sir

Charles will be there by that time.   Or would you rather take
Bonn in your way, and pass the time till we meet at the Hague ?
From Manheim you may have a great many good letters of
recommendation to the court of Bonn ; which Court, and its
Elector, in one light or another, are worth your seeing.   From
thence your journey to the Hague will be but a short one ; and
you would arrive there at that season of the year when the
Hague is, in my mind, the most agreeable, smiling scene in
Europe ; and from the Hague you would have but three very
easy days' journeys to me at Spa.   Do as you like ; for, as I told
you before, *Ella èassolutamente padrone.*[1]   But, lest you should
answer, that you desire to be determined by me, I will eventually
tell you my opinion.   I am rather inclined to the latter plan : I
mean, that of your coming to Bonn, staying there according as
you like it, and then passing the remainder of your time, that is,
May and June, at the Hague.   Our connection and transactions
with the Republic of the United Provinces are such, that you
cannot be too well acquainted with that constitution, and with
those people.   You have established good acquaintances there,
and you have been *fêtoyé* round by the foreign Ministers : so that
you will be there *en pays connu.*   Moreover, you have not seen
the Stadthouder, the *Gouvernante*, nor the Court there, which *à
bon compte* should be seen.   Upon the whole, then, you cannot,
in my opinion, pass the months of May and June more agreeably, or more usefully, than at the Hague.   However, if you
have any other plan that you like better, pursue it : only let
me know what you intend to do, and I shall most cheerfully
agree to it.

The Parliament will be dissolved in about ten days, and the
writs for the election of the new one issued out immediately
afterwards ; so that, by the end of next month, you may depend
upon being *Membre de la chambre basse;* a title that sounds
high in foreign countries, and perhaps higher than it deserves.
I hope you will add a better title to it in your own, I mean
that of a good speaker in Parliament : you have, I am sure, all
the materials necessary for it, if you will but put them together
and adorn them.   I spoke in Parliament the first month I was
in it, and a month before I was of age ; and from the day I was
elected, till the day that I spoke, I am sure I thought nor
dreamed of nothing but speaking.   The first time, to say the
truth, I spoke very indifferently as to the matter ; but it passed
tolerably, in favour of the spirit with which I uttered it, and the
words in which I dressed it.   I improved by degrees, till at

[1] You are absolutely your own master.

last it did tolerably well. The House, it must be owned, is always extremely indulgent to the two or three first attempts of a young speaker; and, if they find any degree of common sense in what he says, they make great allowances for his inexperience, and for the concern which they suppose him to be under. I experienced that indulgence; for, had I not been a young Member, I should certainly have been, as I own I deserved, reprimanded by the House for some strong and indiscreet things that I said. Adieu! it is indeed high time.

LETTER CCLXXVII.

My dear Friend, London, March the 26th, 1754.

YESTERDAY I received your letter of the 15th from Manheim, where I find you have been received in the usual gracious manner; which I hope you return in a *graceful* one. As this is a season of great devotion and solemnity in all Catholic countries, pray inform yourself of, and constantly attend to, all their silly and pompous Church ceremonies: one ought to know them. I am very glad that you wrote the letter to Lord ————, which, in every different case that can possibly be supposed, was, I am sure, both a decent and a prudent step. You will find it very difficult, whenever we meet, to convince me that you could have any good reasons for not doing it; for I will, for argument's sake, suppose, what I cannot in reality believe, that he has both said and done the worst he could, of and by you; what then? How will you help yourself? Are you in a situation to hurt him? Certainly not; but he certainly is in a situation to hurt you. Would you show a sullen, pouting, impotent resentment? I hope not: leave that silly, unavailing sort of resentment to women, and men like them, who are always guided by humour, never by reason and prudence. That pettish, pouting conduct is a great deal too young, and implies too little knowledge of the world, for one who has seen so much of it as you have. Let this be one invariable rule of your conduct—Never to show the least symptom of resentment, which you cannot, to a certain degree, gratify; but always to smile, where you cannot strike. There would be no living in Courts, nor indeed in the world, if one could not conceal, and even dissemble, the just causes of resentment, which one meets with every day in active and busy life. Whoever cannot master his humour enough, *pour faire bonne mine à mauvais jeu*, should leave the world, and retire to some hermitage in an unfrequented desert. By showing an unavailing and sullen resentment, you authorize the resentment of those who can hurt you, and whom you cannot hurt; and give them that very pretence, which perhaps they wished for, of breaking with and injuring you; whereas the contrary behaviour would lay them under the restraints of decency at least; and either shackle or expose their malice. Besides, captiousness, sullenness, and pouting, are most exceedingly illiberal and vulgar. *Un honnête homme ne les connoît point.*

I am extremely glad to hear that you are soon to have Voltaire at Manheim : immediately upon his arrival, pray make him a thousand compliments from me. I admire him most exceedingly ; and whether as an Epic, Dramatic, or Lyric Poet, or Prose writer, I think I justly apply to him the *Nil molitur inepte.* I long to read his own correct edition of *Les Annales de l'Empire*, of which the *Abrégé Chronologique de l'Histoire Universelle*, which I have read, is, I suppose, a stolen and imperfect part; however, imperfect as it is, it has explained to me that chaos of history of seven hundred years, more clearly than any other book had done before. You judge very rightly, that I love *le style léger et fleuri*. I do, and so does everybody who has any parts and taste. It should, I confess, be more or less *fleuri*, according to the subject ; but at the same time I assert, that there is no subject that may not properly, and which ought not to be adorned, by a certain elegancy and beauty of style. What can be more adorned than Cicero's Philosophical Works ? What more than Plato's ? It is their eloquence only that has preserved and transmitted them down to us, through so many centuries ; for the philosophy of them is wretched, and the reasoning part miserable. But eloquence will always please, and has always pleased. Study it therefore ; make it the object of your thoughts and attention. Use yourself to relate elegantly ; that is a good step towards speaking well in Parliament. Take some political subject, turn it in your thoughts, consider what may be said, both for and against it, then put those arguments into writing, in the most correct and elegant English you can. For instance, a standing army, a place bill, &c.; as to the former, consider, on one side, the dangers arising to a free country from a great standing military force; on the other side, consider the necessity of a force to repel force with. Examine whether a standing army, though in itself an evil, may not, from circumstances, become a necessary evil, and preventive of greater dangers. As to the latter, consider how far places may bias and warp the conduct of men, from the service of their country, into an unwarrantable complaisance to the Court; and, on the other hand, consider whether they can be supposed to have that effect upon the conduct of people of probity and property, who are more solidly interested in the permanent good of their country, than they can be in an uncertain and precarious employment. Seek for, and answer in your own mind, all the arguments that can be urged on either side, and write them down in an elegant style. This will prepare you for debating, and give you an habitual eloquence; for I would not give a farthing for a mere holiday eloquence, displayed once or twice in a session, in a set declamation; but I want an every-day, ready, and habitual eloquence, to adorn *extempore* and debating speeches; to make business not only clear but agreeable, and to please even those whom you cannot inform, and who do not desire to be informed. All this you may acquire and make habitual to you, with as little trouble as it cost you to dance a minuet as well as you do. You now dance it mechanically and well, without thinking of it.

I am surprised that you found but one letter from me at Manheim, for you ought to have found four or five; there are as many lying for you, at your banker's at Berlin, which I wish you had, because I always endeavoured to put something into them which I hope may be of use to you.

When we meet at Spa next July, we must have a great many serious conversations; in which I will pour out all my experience of the world, and which, I hope, you will trust to, more than to your own young notions of men and things. You will, in time, discover most of them to have been erroneous; and if you follow them long, you will perceive your error too late; but if you will be led by a guide, who, you are sure, does not mean to mislead you, you will unite two things, seldom united in the same person; the vivacity and spirit of youth, with the caution and experience of age.

Last Saturday Sir Thomas Robinson, who had been the King's Minister at Vienna, was declared Secretary of State for the southern department, Lord Holderness having taken the northern. Sir Thomas accepted it unwillingly, and, as I hear, with a promise that he shall not keep it long. Both his health and spirits are bad, two very disqualifying circumstances for that employment; yours, I hope, will enable you some time or other to go through with it. In all events aim at it, and if you fail or

fall, let it at least be said of you, *Magnis tamen excidit ausis.*[1]
Adieu.

LETTER CCLXXVIII.

My dear Friend,   London, April the 5th, 1754.

I received, yesterday, your letter of the 20th March, from
Manheim, with the enclosed for Mr Eliot ; it was a very proper
one, and I have forwarded it to him by Mr Harte, who sets out
for Cornwall to-morrow morning.

I am very glad that you use yourself to translations ; and I
do not care of what, provided you study the correctness and elegancy of your style. The Life of Sextus Quintus is the best
book, of the innumerable books written by Gregorio Leti, whom
the Italians, very justly, call *Leti caca libri.* But I would rather
that you chose some pieces of oratory for your translations ;
whether ancient or modern, Latin or French ; which would give
you a more oratorical train of thoughts, and turn of expression. In
your letter to me you make use of two words, which, though true
and correct English, are, however, from long disuse, become
inelegant, and seem now to be stiff, formal, and in some degree
scriptural : the first is the word *namely,* which you introduce
thus, *You inform me of a very agreeable piece of news,* namely,
that my election is secured. Instead of *namely,* I would always
use *which is,* or *that is,* that my election is secured. The other
word is, *Mine own inclinations :* this is certainly correct, before
a subsequent word that begins with a vowel ; but it is too correct, and is now disused as too formal, notwithstanding the
hiatus occasioned by *my own.* Every language has its peculiarities ; they are established by usage, and, whether right or
wrong, they must be complied with. I could instance many
very absurd ones in different languages ; but so authorized by
the *jus et norma loquendi,*[2] that they must be submitted to. *Namely,*
and *to wit,* are very good words in themselves, and contribute to
clearness, more than the relatives which we now substitute in
their room ; but, however, they cannot be used, except in a
sermon, or some very grave and formal compositions. It is
with language as with manners, they are both established by
the usage of people of fashion ; it must be imitated, it must be
complied with. Singularity is only pardonable in old age and
retirement ; I may now be as singular as I please, but you may

---

[1] He fell, having aimed at noble things.
[2] Law and rule of speaking.

not. We will, when we meet, discuss these and many other points, provided you will give me attention and credit ; without both which it is to no purpose to advise either you or anybody else.

I want to know your determination, where you intend to (if I may use that expression) *while* away your time till the last week in June, when we are to meet at Spa; I continue rather in the opinion which I mentioned to you formerly, in favour of the Hague; but however I have not the least objection to Dresden, or to any other place that you may like better. If you prefer the Dutch scheme, you take Treves and Coblentz in your way, as also Dusseldorp : all which places I think you have not yet seen. At Manheim you may certainly get good letters of recommendation to the Courts of the two Electors of Treves and Cologne, whom you are yet unacquainted with; and I should wish you to know them all. For, as I have often told you, *olim hæc meminisse juvabit.* There is a utility in having seen what other people have seen, and there is a justifiable pride in having seen what others have not seen. In the former case, you are equal to others ; in the latter, superior. As your stay abroad will not now be very long, pray, while it lasts, see everything, and everybody you can ; and see them well, with care and attention. It is not to be conceived of what advantage it is to anybody to have seen more things, people, and countries, than other people in general have : it gives them a credit, makes them referred to, and they become the objects of the attention of the company. They are not out in any part of polite conversation ; they are acquainted with all the places, customs, courts, and families, that are likely to be mentioned ; they are, as Monsieur de Maupertuis justly observes, *de tous les pays, comme les savans sont de tous les tems.* You have, fortunately, both those advantages; the only remaining point is *de savoir les faire valoir;* for, without that, one may as well not have them. Remember that very true maxim of La Bruyère's, *Qu'on ne vaut dans ce monde que ce qu'on veut valoir.* The knowledge of the world will teach you to what degree you ought to show *ce que vous valez.* One must by no means, on one hand, be indifferent about it; as, on the other, one must not display it with affectation, and in an overbearing manner: but, of the two, it is better to show too much than too little. Adieu.

LETTER CCLXXIX.

MY DEAR FRIEND,   Bath, November the 27th, 1754.

I HEARTILY congratulate you upon the loss of your political maidenhead, of which I have received from others a very good account. I hear that you were stopped for some time in your career; but recovered breath, and finished it very well. I am not surprised, nor indeed concerned, at your accident ; for I remember the dreadful feeling of that situation in myself; and as it must require a most uncommon share of impudence to be unconcerned upon such an occasion, I am not sure that I am not rather glad that you stopped. You must therefore now think of hardening yourself by degrees, by using yourself insensibly to the sound of your own voice, and to the act (trifling as it seems) of rising up and sitting down again. Nothing will contribute so much to this as committee work, of elections at night, and of private bills in the morning. There asking short questions, moving for witnesses to be called in, and all that kind of small ware, will soon fit you to set up for yourself. I am told that you are much mortified at your accident ; but without reason ; pray let it rather be a spur than a curb to you. Persevere, and depend upon it, it will do well at last. When I say persevere, I do not mean that you should speak every day, nor in every debate. Moreover, I would not advise you to speak again upon public matters for some time, perhaps a month or two ; but I mean, never lose view of that great object ; pursue it with discretion, but pursue it always. *Pelotez en attendant partie.*[1] You know I have always told you that speaking in public was but a knack, which those who apply to most will succeed in best. Two old Members, very good judges, have sent me compliments upon this occasion ; and have assured me that they plainly find *it will do*, though they perceived, from that natural confusion you were in, that you neither said all, nor perhaps what, you intended. Upon the whole, you have set out very well, and have sufficient encouragement to go on. Attend therefore assiduously, and observe carefully all that passes in the House ; for it is only knowledge and experience that can make a debater. But if you still want comfort, Mrs ———, I hope, will administer it to you ; for in my opinion she may, if she will, be very comfortable ; and with women, as with speaking in Parliament, perseverance will most certainly prevail, sooner or later.

---

[1] Trifle while waiting for your game.

What little I have played for here, I have won ; but that is very far from the considerable sum which you heard of. I play every evening from seven till ten, at a crown whist party, merely to save my eyes from reading or writing for three hours by candlelight. I propose being in town the week after next, and hope to carry back with me much more health than I brought down here. Good night.

Mr Stanhope being returned to England, and seeing his Father almost every day, is the occasion of an interruption of two years in their correspondence.

———◇———

LETTER CCLXXX.

My dear Friend, Bath, November the 15th, 1756.

I received yours yesterday morning, together with the Prussian papers, which I have read with great attention. If Courts could blush, those of Vienna and Dresden ought, to have their falsehoods so publicly and so undeniably exposed. The former will, I presume, next year employ a hundred thousand men, to answer the accusation; and if the Empress of the Two Russias is pleased to argue in the same cogent manner, their logic will be too strong for all the King of Prussia's rhetoric. I well remember the treaty so often referred to in those pieces, between the two Empresses, in 1746. The King was strongly pressed by the Empress Queen to accede to it. Wassenaer communicated it to me for that purpose. I asked him if there were no secret articles; suspecting that there were some, because the ostensible treaty was a mere harmless defensive one. He assured me there were none. Upon which I told him, that as the King had already defensive alliances with those two Empresses, I did not see of what use his accession to this treaty, *if merely a defensive one,* could be either to himself or the other contracting parties ; but that, however, if it was only desired as an indication of the King's good will, I would give him an act, by which his Majesty should accede to that treaty, as far, but no further, as at present he stood engaged to the respective Empresses, by the defensive alliances subsisting with each. This offer by no means satisfied him ; which was a plain proof of the secret articles now brought to light, and into which the Court of Vienna hoped to draw us. I told Wassenaer so, and after that I heard no more of his invitation.

I am still bewildered in the changes at Court, of which I

find that all the particulars are not yet fixed. Who would have thought, a year ago, that Mr Fox, the Chancellor, and the Duke of Newcastle, should all three have quitted together; nor can I yet account for it; explain it to me if you can. I cannot see, neither, what the Duke of Devonshire and Fox, whom I looked upon as intimately united, can have quarrelled about, with relation to the Treasury; inform me, if you know. I never doubted of the prudent versatility of your Vicar of Bray; but I am surprised at Obrien Windham's going out of the Treasury, where I should have thought that the interest of his brother-in-law, George Grenville, would have kept him.

Having found myself rather worse these two or three last days, I was obliged to take some *ipecacuana* last night; and, what you will think odd, for a vomit, I brought it all up again in about an hour, to my great satisfaction and emolument, which is seldom the case in restitutions.

You did well to go to the Duke of Newcastle, who, I suppose, will have no more levees; however, go from time to time, and leave your name at his door, for you have obligations to him. Adieu.

LETTER CCLXXXI.

My dear Friend,   Bath, December the 14th, 1756.

WHAT can I say to you from this place, where *every day is still but as the first*, though by no means so agreeably passed as Anthony describes his to have been? The same nothings succeed one another every day with me, as regularly and uniformly as the hours of the day. You will think this tiresome, and so it is; but how can I help it? Cut off from society by my deafness, and dispirited by my ill health, where could I be better? You will say, perhaps, where could you be worse? Only in prison, or the galleys, I confess. However I see a period to my stay here; and I have fixed, in my own mind, a time for my return to London; not invited there by either politics or pleasures, to both which I am equally a stranger, but merely to be at home; which, after all, according to the vulgar saying, is home, be it never so homely.

The political settlement, as it is called, is, I find, by no means settled: Mr Fox, who took this place in his way to his brother's, where he intended to pass a month, was stopped short by an express, which he received from his connection, to come to town immediately; and accordingly he set out from hence very early, two days ago. I had a very long conversation with him, in which he was, seemingly at least, very frank and communicative : but still I own myself in the dark. In those matters, as in most others, half knowledge (and mine is at most that) is more apt to lead one into error than to carry one to truth ; and our own vanity contributes to the seduction. Our conjectures pass upon us for truths ; we will know what we do not know, and often what we cannot know : so mortifying to our pride is the bare suspicion of ignorance !

It has been reported here that the Empress of Russia is dying ; this would be a fortunate event indeed for the King of Prussia, and necessarily produce the neutrality and inaction, at least, of that great power ; which would be a heavy weight taken out of the opposite scale to the King of Prussia. The *Augustissima* must, in that case, do all herself ; for, though France will no doubt promise largely, it will, I believe, perform but scantily ; as it desires no better, than that the different powers of Germany should tear one another to pieces.

I hope you frequent all the Courts ; a man should make his face familiar there. Long habit produces favour insensibly : and acquaintance often does more than friendship in that climate, where *les beaux sentimens* are not the natural growth.

Adieu ! I am going to the ball, to save my eyes from reading, and my mind from thinking.

LETTER CCLXXXII.

MY DEAR FRIEND, Bath, January the 12th, 1757.

I WAITED quietly, to see when either your leisure, or your inclinations, would allow you to honour me with a letter ; and at last I received one this morning, very near a fortnight after you went from hence. You will say that you had no news to write me ; and that probably may be true ; but, without news, one has always something to say to those with whom one desires to have anything to do.

Your observation is very just with regard to the King of Prussia, whom the most august House of Austria would most unquestionably have poisoned a century or two ago. But now that *Terras Astræa reliquit,* [1] Kings and Princes die of natural deaths ; even war is pusillanimously carried on in this degenerate age ; quarter is given ; towns are taken, and the people

[1] Justice has left the earth.

spared : even in a storm, a woman can hardly hope for the benefit of a rape. Whereas (such was the humanity of former days) prisoners were killed by thousands in cold blood, and the generous victors spared neither man, woman, nor child. Heroic actions of this kind were performed at the taking of Magdebourg. The King of Prussia is certainly now in a situation that must soon decide his fate, and make him Cæsar or nothing. Notwithstanding the march of the Russians, his greatest danger, in my mind, lies westward. I have no great notion of Apraxin's abilities, and I believe many a Prussian Colonel would outgeneral him. But Brown, Piccolomini, Lucchese, and many other veteran officers in the Austrian troops are respectable enemies.

Mr Pitt seems to me to have almost as many enemies to encounter as his Prussian Majesty. The late Ministry, and the Duke's party, will, I presume, unite against him and his Tory friends : and then quarrel among themselves again. His best if not his only chance of supporting himself would be, if he had credit enough in the city, to hinder the advancing of the money to any Administration but his own ; and I have met with some people here who think that he has.

I have put off my journey from hence for a week, but no longer. I find I still gain some strength and some flesh here, and therefore I will not cut, while the run is for me.

By a letter which I received this morning from Lady Allen, I observe that you are extremely well with her ; and it is well for you to be so, for she is an excellent and warm puff.

A propos (an expression which is commonly used to introduce whatever is unrelative to it), you should apply to some of Lord Holderness's people for the perusal of Mr Cope's letters. It will not be refused you ; and the sooner you have them the better. I do not mean them as models for your manner of writing, but as outlines of the matter you are to write upon.

If you have not read Hume's Essays, read them ; they are four very small volumes ; I have just finished, and am extremely pleased with them. He thinks impartially, deep, often new ; and, in my mind, commonly just. Adieu.

LETTER CCLXXXIII.

MY DEAR FRIEND,   Blackheath, September the 17th, 1757.

LORD HOLDERNESS has been so kind as to communicate to

me all the letters which he has received from you hitherto, dated the 15th, 19th, 23rd, and 26th, August ; and also a draught of that which he wrote to you the 9th instant. I am very well pleased with all your letters ; and, what is better, I can tell you that the King is so too ; and he said, but three days ago, to Monsieur Munchausen, *He* (meaning you) *sets out very well, and I like his letters ; provided that, like most of my English Ministers abroad, he does not grow idle hereafter.* So that here is both praise to flatter, and a hint to warn, you. What Lord Holderness recommends to you, being by the King's order, intimates also a degree of approbation ; for the *blacker ink*, *and the larger character*, show that his Majesty, whose eyes are grown weaker, intends to read all your letters himself. Therefore pray do not neglect to get the blackest ink you can ; and to make your Secretary enlarge his hand, though *d'ailleurs* it is a very good one.

Had I been to wish an advantageous situation for you, and a good *début* in it, I could not have wished you either, better than both have hitherto proved. The rest will depend entirely upon yourself ; and I own, I begin to have much better hopes than I had ; for I know, by my own experience, that the more one works, the more willing one is to work. We are all, more or less, *des animaux d'habitude.* I remember very well, that when I was in business, I wrote four or five hours together every day, more willingly than I should now half an hour ; and this is most certain, that when a man has applied himself to business half the day, the other half goes off the more cheerfully and agreeably. This I found so sensibly, when I was at the Hague, that I never tasted company so well, nor was so good company myself, as at the suppers of my post days. I take Hamburgh now, to be *le centre du refuge Allemand.* If you have any Hanover *refugiés* among them, pray take care to be particularly attentive to them. How do you like your house ? Is it a convenient one ? Have the *Casserolles* been employed in it yet ? You will find *les petits soupers fins* less expensive, and turn to better account, than large dinners for great companies.

I hope you have written to the Duke of Newcastle ; I take it for granted that you have to all your brother Ministers of the northern department. For God's sake be diligent, alert, active, and indefatigable in your business. You want nothing but labour and industry, to be, one day, whatever you please, in your own way.

We think and talk of nothing here but Brest, which is universally supposed to be the object of our great expedition. A great and important object it is. I suppose the affair must be

brusqué, or it will not do.   If we succeed, it will make France
put some water to its wine.   As for my own private opinion, I
own I rather wish than hope success.   However, should our
expedition fail, *Magnis tamen excidit ausis*, and that will be
better than our late languid manner of making war.

   To mention a person to you whom I am very indifferent
about, I mean myself, I vegetate still just as I did when we
parted ; but I think I begin to bo sensible of the autumn of the
year, as well as of the autumn of my own life.   I feel an internal
awkwardness, which in about three weeks I shall carry with me
to the Bath, where I hope to get rid of it, as I did last year.
The best cordial I could take would be to hear, from time to
time, of your industry and diligence ; for in that case I should
consequently hear of your success.   Remember your own motto,
Nullum numen abest si sit prudentia.   Nothing is truer.   Yours.

LETTER CCLXXXIV.

My dear Friend,   Blackheath, Sept. the 23rd, 1757.

   I received but the day before yesterday your letter of the 3rd,
from the head-quarters at Selsingen; and, by the way, it is but
the second that I have received from you since your arrival at Hamburgh.   Whatever was the cause of your going to the army, I
approve of the effect ; for I would have you, as much as possible,
see everything that is to be seen.   That is the true useful knowledge, which informs and improves us when we are young, and
amuses us and others when we are old, *Olim hæc meminisse juvabit.*[1]
I could wish that you would (but I know you will not) enter
in a book, a short note only, of whatever you see or hear that
is very remarkable ; I do not mean a German *album*, stuffed
with people's names, and Latin sentences ; but I mean such a
book as, if you do not keep now, thirty years hence you would
give a great deal of money to have kept.   *A propos de bottes*,
for I am told he always wears his ; was his Royal Highness very
gracious to you, or not ?   I have my doubts about it.   The
neutrality, which he has concluded with Maréchal de Richelieu,
will prevent that bloody battle which you expected ; but what
the King of Prussia will say to it is another point.   He was
our only ally ; at present, probably, we have not one in the
world.   If the King of Prussia can get at Monsieur de Soubize's
and the Imperial army, before other troops have joined them, I

---

[1] Later in life it will be pleasant to remember those things.

think he will beat them ; but what then ? He has three hundred thousand men to encounter afterwards. He must submit; but he may say with truth, *Si Pergama dextrâ defendi possent.*[1] The late action between the Prussians and Russians has only thinned the human species, without giving either party a victory; which is plain by each party's claiming it. Upon my word, our species will pay very dear for the quarrels and ambition of a few, and those by no means the most valuable part of it. If the many were wiser than they are, the few must be quieter, and would perhaps be juster and better than they are.

Hamburgh, I find, swarms with *Grafs, Gräffins, Fürsts,* and *Fürstins, Hocheits,* and *Durchlaugticheits.* I am glad of it, for you must necessarily be in the midst of them ; and I am still more glad, that, being in the midst of them, you must necessarily be under some constraint of ceremony ; a thing which you do not love, but which is, however, very useful.

I desired you in my last, and I repeat it again in this, to give me an account of your private and domestic life. How do you pass your evenings ? Have they, at Hamburgh, what are called at Paris *des Maisons,* where one goes without ceremony, sups or not, as one pleases ? Are you adopted in any society ? Have you any rational brother Ministers, and which ? What sort of things are your operas ? In the tender I doubt they do not excel; for *mein lieber schatz,* and the other tendernesses of the Teutonic language, would, in my mind, sound but indifferently, set to soft music ; for the *bravura* parts, I have a very great opinion of them ; and *das, der dönner dich erschlage,*[2] must, no doubt, make a tremendously fine piece of *recitativo,* when uttered by an angry hero, to the rumble of a whole orchestra, including drums, trumpets, and French horns. Tell me your whole allotment of the day, in which I hope four hours, at least, are sacred to writing ; the others cannot be better employed than in *liberal* pleasures. In short, give me a full account of yourself in your unministerial character, your *incognito,* without your *fiocchi.*[3] I love to see those, in whom I interest myself, in their undress, rather than in *gala ;* I know them better so. I recommend to you, *etiam atque etiam,*[4] method and order in everything you undertake. Do you observe it in your accounts ? If you do not you will be a beggar, though

[1] If Troy could be defended it would have been by this right hand. Frederick, however, at the conclusion of the war, retained all his possessions.
[2] This,—'the thunder strikes thee dead.'
[3] Decorations.
[4] Again and again.

you were to receive the appointments of a Spanish Embassador extraordinary, which are a thousand pistoles a month ; and in your ministerial business, if you have not regular and stated hours for such and such parts of it, you will be in the hurry and confusion of the Duke of N——, doing everything by halves, and nothing well nor soon. I suppose you have been feasted through the *Corps diplomatique* at Hamburgh, excepting Monsieur Champeaux ; with whom, however, I hope you live *poliment et galemment*, at all third places.

Lord Loudon is much blamed here for his *retraite des dix milles*, for it is said that he had above that number, and might, consequently, have acted offensively, instead of retreating ; especially, as his retreat was contrary to the unanimous opinion (as it is now said) of the council of war. In our Ministry, I suppose, things go pretty quietly, for the D. N. has not plagued me these two months. When his Royal Highness comes over, which, I take it for granted, he will do very soon, the great push will, I presume, be made at his Grace and Mr Pitt ; but without effect if they agree, as it is visibly their interest to do; and in that case their Parliamentary strength will support them against all attacks. You may remember, I said at first, that the popularity would soon be on the side of those who opposed the popular Militia Bill ; and now it appears so with a vengeance, in almost every county in England, by the tumults and insurrections of the people, who swear that they will not be enlisted. That silly scheme must, therefore, be dropped, as quietly as may be. Now I have told you all that I know, and almost all that I think, I wish you a good supper, and a good night.

LETTER CCLXXXV.

My dear Friend,   Blackheath, Sept. the 30th, 1757.

I have so little to do, that I am surprised how I can find time to write to you so often. Do not stare at the seeming paradox ; for it is an undoubted truth, That the less one has to do, the less time one finds to do it in. One yawns, one procrastinates ; one can do it when one will, and therefore one seldom does it at all : whereas those who have a great deal of business must (to use a vulgar expression) buckle to it ; and then they always find time enough to do it in. I hope your own experience has, by this time, convinced you of this truth.

I received your last, of the 8th. It is now quite over

with a very great man, who will still be a very great man, though a very unfortunate one. He has qualities of the mind that put him above the reach of these misfortunes ; and if reduced, as perhaps he may, to the *marche* of Brandenburgh, he will always find in himself the comfort, and with all the world the credit, of a philosopher, a legislator, a patron, and a professor of arts and sciences. He will only lose the fame of a conqueror : a cruel fame, that arises from the destruction of the human species. Could it be any satisfaction to him to know, I could tell him, that he is at this time the most popular man in this kingdom : the whole nation being enraged at that neutrality which hastens and completes his ruin. Between you and me, the King was not less enraged at it himself, when he saw the terms of it ; and it affected his health more than all that had happened before. Indeed it seems to me a voluntary concession of the very worst that could have happened, in the worst event. We now begin to think that our great and secret expedition is intended for Martinico and St Domingo; if that be true, and we succeed in the attempt, we shall recover, and the French lose, one of the most valuable branches of commerce, I mean sugar. The French now supply all the foreign markets in Europe with that commodity, we only supply ourselves with it. This would make us some amends for our ill luck, or ill conduct, in North America; where Lord Loudon, with twelve thousand men, thought himself no match for the French with but seven ; and Admiral Holbourne, with seventeen ships of the line, declined attacking the French, because they had eighteen, and a greater weight of *metal*, according to the new sea-phrase, which was unknown to Blake. I hear that letters have been sent to both, with very severe reprimands. I am told, and I believe it is true, that we are negotiating with the Corsican, I will not say rebels, but assertors of their natural rights; to receive them, and whatever form of government they think fit to establish, under our protection, upon condition of their delivering up to us Port Ajaccio ; which may be made so strong and so good a one as to be a full equivalent for the loss of Port Mahon. This is, in my mind, a very good scheme ; for though the Corsicans are a parcel of cruel and perfidious rascals, they will in this case be tied down to us by their own interest and their own danger ; a solid security with knaves, though none with fools. His Royal Highness the Duke is hourly expected here : his arrival will make some bustle ; for I believe it is certain that he is resolved to make a push at the Duke of N., Pitt, and Co.; but it will be ineffectual, if they continue to agree, as, to my *certain knowledge*, they do at present. · This Parliament is theirs, *cætera quis nescit.*[1]

Now I have told you all I know, or have heard, of public matters, let us talk of private ones, that more nearly and immediately concern us. Admit me to your fireside, in your little room ; and as you would converse with me there, write to me for the future from thence. Are you completely *nippé*[2] yet ? Have you formed what the world calls connections ; that is, a certain number of acquaintances, whom, from accident or choice, you frequent more than others ? Have you either fine or well-bred women there ? *Y a-t-il quelque bon ton ?* All fat and fair, I presume ; too proud and too cold to make advances, but at the same time too well-bred, and too warm to reject them, when made by *un honnête homme avec des manières.*

Mr * * is to be married in about a month, to Miss * *. I am very glad of it ; for, as he will never be a man of the world, but will always lead a domestic and retired life, she seems to have been made on purpose for him. Her natural turn is as grave and domestic as his ; and she seems to have been kept by her aunts *à la glace*, instead of being raised in a hot-bed, as most young ladies are of late. If, three weeks hence, you write him a short compliment of congratulation upon the occasion, he, his mother, and *tutti quanti*[3] would be extremely pleased with it. Those attentions are always kindly taken, and cost one nothing but pen, ink, and paper. I consider them as draughts upon good breeding, where the exchange is always greatly in favour of the drawer. *A propos* of exchange ; I hope you have, with the help of your Secretary, made yourself correctly master of all that sort of knowledge—Course of Exchange, *Agio, Banco, Reichs-Thalers*, down to *Marien Groschen*. It is very little trouble to learn it : it is often of great use to know it. Good night, and God bless you.

LETTER CCLXXXVI.

MY DEAR FRIEND,   Blackheath, October the 10th, 1757.

IT is not without some difficulty that I snatch this moment of leisure from my extreme idleness, to inform you of the present lamentable and astonishing state of affairs here, which you would know but imperfectly from the public papers, and

[1] What remains, who knows ?
[2] Rigged out.   [3] All the sot.

but partially from your private correspondence. *Or sus* [1] then —Our invincible Armada, which cost at least half-a-million, sailed, as you know, some weeks ago; the object kept an inviolable secret; conjectures various, and expectations great. Brest was perhaps to be taken; but Martinico and St Domingo, at least. When lo! the important island of Aix was taken without the least resistance, seven hundred men made prisoners, and some pieces of cannon carried off. From thence we sailed towards Rochfort, which it seems was our main object; and consequently one should have supposed that we had pilots on board who knew all the soundings and landing-places there and thereabouts; but no; for General M——t asked the Admiral if he could land him and the troops near Rochfort? The Admiral said, With great ease. To which the General replied; But can you take us on board again? To which the Admiral answered, *That*, like all naval operations, will depend upon the wind. If so, said the General, I'll e'en go home again. A Council of War was immediately called, where it was unanimously resolved, that it was *advisable* to return; accordingly they are returned. As the expectations of the whole nation had been raised to the highest pitch, the universal disappointment and indignation have arisen in proportion; and I question whether the ferment of men's minds was ever greater. Suspicions, you may be sure, are various and endless; but the most prevailing one is, that the tail of the Hanover neutrality, like that of a comet, extended itself to Rochfort. What encourages this suspicion is, that a French man-of-war went unmolested through our whole fleet, as it lay near Rochfort. Haddock's whole story is revived; Michel's representations are combined with other circumstances; and the whole together makes up a mass of discontent, resentment, and even fury, greater than perhaps was ever known in this country before. These are the facts, draw your own conclusions from them: for my part, I am lost in astonishment and conjectures, and do not know where to fix. My experience has shown me that many things which seem extremely probable, are not true; and many, which seem highly improbable, are true; so that I will conclude this article, as Josephus does almost every article of his history, with saying, *but of this every man will believe as he thinks proper.* What a disgraceful year will this be in the annals of this country! May its good genius, if ever it appears again, tear out those sheets, thus stained and blotted by our ignominy!

[1] Come on!

Our domestic affairs are, as far as I know anything of them, in the same situation as when I wrote to you last; but they will begin to be in motion upon the approach of the session, and upon the return of the Duke; whose arrival is most impatiently expected by the mob of London; though not to strow flowers in the way.

I leave this place next Saturday, and London the Saturday following, to be the next day at Bath. Adieu.

LETTER CCLXXXVII.

My dear Friend,   London, October the 17th, 1757.

Your last, of the 30th past, was a very good letter: and I will believe half of what you assure me that you returned to the Landgrave's civilities. I cannot possibly go further than half, knowing that you are not lavish of your words, especially in that species of eloquence called the adulatory. Do not use too much discretion, in profiting of the Landgrave's naturalization of you; but go pretty often and feed with him. Choose the company of your superiors, whenever you can have it : that is the right and true pride. The mistaken and silly pride is, to *primer* among inferiors.

Hear, O Israel! and wonder. On Sunday morning last the Duke [1] gave up his commission of Captain-General, and his regiment of Guards. You will ask me why? I cannot tell you; but I will tell you the causes assigned, which, perhaps, are none of them the true ones. It is said that the King reproached him with having exceeded his powers in making the Hanover Convention; which his R. H. absolutely denied, and threw up thereupon. This is certain, that he appeared at the drawing-room, at Kensington, last Sunday, after having quitted, and went straight to Windsor; where, his people say, that he intends to reside quietly, and amuse himself as a private man. But I conjecture that matters will soon be made up again, and that he will resume his employments. You will easily imagine what speculations this event has occasioned in the public; I shall neither trouble you nor myself with relating them; nor would this sheet of paper, or even a quire more, contain them. Some refine enough to suspect that it is a concerted quarrel, to justify *somebody to somebody*, with regard to the Convention; but I do not believe it.

[1] Of Cumberland.

His R. H.'s people load the Hanover Ministers, and more particularly our friend Münchausen here, with the whole blame; but with what degree of truth I know not. This only is certain, that the whole negotiation of that affair was broached, and carried on, by the Hanover Ministers, and Monsieur Stemberg at Vienna, absolutely unknown to the English Ministers till it was executed. This affair, combined (for people will combine it) with the astonishing return of our great armament, not only *re infectâ*, but even *intentatâ*,[1] makes such a jumble of reflections, conjectures, and refinements, that one is weary of hearing them. Our Tacituses and Machiavels go deep, suspect the worst, and perhaps, as they often do, overshoot the mark. For my own part I fairly confess that I am bewildered, and have not certain *postulata* enough not only to found any opinion, but even to form conjectures upon ; and this is the language which I think you should hold to all who speak to you, as to be sure all will, upon that subject. Plead, as you truly may, your own ignorance ; and say that it is impossible to judge of those nice points at such a distance, and without knowing all circumstances, which you cannot be supposed to do. And as to the Duke's resignation ; you should, in my opinion, say, that perhaps there might be a little too much vivacity in the case ; but that, upon the whole, you make no doubt of the things being soon set right again ; as, in truth, I dare say it will. Upon these delicate occasions you must practise the ministerial shrugs and *persiflage ;* for silent gesticulations, which you would be most inclined to, would not be sufficient : something must be said; but that something, when analyzed, must amount to nothing. As, for instance, *Il est vrai qu'on s'y perd, mais que voulez-vous que je vous dise,—il y a bien du pour et du contre, un petit Résident ne voit guères le fond du sac.—Il faut attendre* [2]— Those sort of expletives are of infinite use ; and nine people in ten think they mean something. But, to the Landgrave of Hesse, I think you would do well to say, in seeming confidence, that you have good reason to believe that the principal objection of his Majesty to the Convention was, that his Highness's interests, and the affair of his troops, were not sufficiently considered in it. To the Prussian Minister assert boldly that you know *de science certaine*, that the principal object of his Majesty's, and his British Ministry's attention, is not only to

---

[1] With nothing accomplished, but even with nothing attempted. ·

[2] It is true people lose themselves in conjecture,—but what do you wish me to tell you ? There is much to be said on both sides. An insignificant envoy cannot see the bottom of the sack.—We must wait.

perform all their present engagements with his Master, but to take new and stronger ones for his support ; for this is true— *at least at present.*

You did very well in inviting Comte Bothmar to dine with you. You see how minutely I am informed of your proceedings, though not from yourself. Adieu.

I go to Bath next Saturday ; but direct your letters, as usual, to London.

LETTER CCLXXXVIII.

MY DEAR FRIEND,   Bath, October the 26th, 1757.

I ARRIVED here safe, but far from sound, last Sunday. I have consequently drunk these waters but three days, and yet I find myself something better for them. The night before I left London I was for some hours at Newcastle House ; where the letters, which came in that morning, lay upon the table ; and his Grace singled out yours, with great approbation, and at the same time assured me of his Majesty's approbation too. To these two approbations, I truly add my own, which, *sans vanité*, may perhaps be near as good as the other two. In that letter you venture *vos petits raisonnemens* very properly, and then as properly make an excuse for doing so. Go on so with diligence, and you will be, what I began to despair of your ever being, *somebody.* I am persuaded, if you would own the truth, that you feel yourself now much better satisfied with yourself than you were while you did nothing.

Application to business, attended with approbation and success, flatters and animates the mind ; which, in idleness and inaction, stagnates and putrefies. I would wish that every rational man would, every night when he goes to bed, ask himself this question, *What have I done to-day ?* Have I done anything that can be of use to myself or others ? Have I employed my time, or have I squandered it ? Have I lived out the day, or have I dozed it away in sloth and laziness ? A thinking being must be pleased or confounded, according as he can answer himself these questions. I observe that you are in the secret of what is intended, and what Münchausen is gone to Stade to prepare. A bold and dangerous experiment, in my mind ; and which may probably end in a second volume to the History of the Palatinate, in the last century. His Serene Highness of Brunswick has, in my mind, played a prudent and a saving game; and I am apt to believe that the other Serene Highness, at Hamburgh, is more likely to follow his example, than to embark in the great scheme.

I see no signs of the Duke's resuming his employments; but, on the contrary, I am assured that his Majesty is coolly determined to do as well as he can without him. The Duke of Devonshire, and Fox, have worked hard to make up matters in the closet, but to no purpose. People's self-love is very apt to make them think themselves more necessary than they are; and I shrewdly suspect that his Royal Highness has been the dupe of that sentiment, and was taken at his word when he least expected it: like my predecessor, Lord Harrington; who, when he went into the closet to resign the seals, had them not about him; so sure he thought himself of being pressed to keep them.

The whole talk of London, of this place, and of every place in the whole kingdom, is of our great, expensive, and yet fruitless expedition: I have seen an Officer who was there, a very sensible and observing man; who told me, that, had we attempted Rochfort the day after we took the island of Aix, our success had been infallible; but that after we had sauntered (God knows why) eight or ten days in the island, he thinks the attempt would have been impracticable; because the French had in that time got together all the troops in that neighbourhood to a very considerable number. In short, there must have been some secret in that whole affair which has not yet transpired; and I cannot help suspecting that it came from Stade. *We* had not been successful there; perhaps *we* were not desirous that an expedition in which *we* had neither been concerned nor consulted should prove so: M——t was *our* creature; and a word to the wise will sometimes go a great way. M——t is to have a public trial, from which the public expects great discoveries—Not I.

Do you visit Soltikow, the Russian Minister, whose house, I am told, is the great scene of pleasures at Hamburgh? His, mistress, I take for granted, is by this time dead, and he wears some other body's shackles. Her death comes, with regard to the King of Prussia, *comme la moutarde aprés dîner*. I am curious to see what tyrant will succeed her, not by Divine, but by Military, right; for, barbarous as they are now, and still more barbarous as they have been formerly, they have had very little regard to the more barbarous notion of divine, indefeasible, hereditary right.

The Prætorian bands, that is, the guards, I presume, have been engaged in the interests of the Imperial Prince; but still,

I think, that little John of Archangel will be heard of upon this occasion, unless prevented by a quieting draught of Hemlock or Nightshade ; for I suppose they are not arrived to the politer and genteeler poisons of *Acqua Tufana*,[1] sugar plums, &c.

Lord Halifax has accepted his old employment, with the honorary addition of the Cabinet Council. And so we heartily wish you a good night.

LETTER CCLXXXIX.

MY DEAR FRIEND,   Bath, November the 4th, 1757.

THE sons of Britain, like those of Noah, must cover their parent's shame as well as they can ; for to retrieve its honour is now too late. One would really think that our Ministers and Generals were all as drunk as the Patriarch was. However, in your situation, you must not be Cham ; but spread your cloak over our disgrace, as far as it will go. M——t calls aloud for a public trial ; and in that, and that only, the public agrees with him. There will certainly be one ; but of what kind is not yet fixed. Some are for a Parliamentary inquiry, others for a Martial one : neither will, in my opinion, discover the true secret ; for a secret there most unquestionably is. Why we staid six whole days in the island of Aix mortal cannot imagine ; which time the French employed, as it was obvious they would, in assembling all their troops in the neighbourhood of Rochfort, and making our attempt then really impracticable. The day after we had taken the island of Aix, your friend, Colonel Wolfe, publicly offered to do the business with five hundred men and three ships only. In all these complicated political machines, there are so many wheels within wheels, that it is always difficult, and sometimes impossible, to guess which of them gives direction to the whole. Mr Pitt is convinced that the principal wheel, or, if you will, the *spoke in his wheel*, came from Stade. This is certain, at least, that M——t was the man of confidence with that person. Whatever be the truth of the case, there is, to be sure, hitherto, an *Hiatus valde deflendus*.[2]

The meeting of the Parliament will certainly be very numerous, were it only from curiosity ; but the majority on the side of the Court will, I dare say, be a great one. The people

---

[1] Acqua Tufana, a Neapolitan slow poison, resembling clear water, and invented by a woman at Naples, of the name of Tufana.
[2] Hiatus much to be lamented.

of the late Captain General, however inclined to oppose, will be obliged to concur. Their commissions, which they have no desire to lose, will make them tractable ; for those Gentlemen, though all men of honour, are of Sosia's mind ; *que le vrai Amphitrion est celui où l'on dîne.* The Tories, and the City, have engaged to support Pitt ; the Whigs, the Duke of Newcastle ; the independent, and the impartial, as you well know, are not worth mentioning. It is said that the Duke intends to bring the affair of his Convention into Parliament, for his own justification : I can hardly believe it ; as I cannot conceive that transactions so merely Electoral can be proper objects of inquiry or deliberation for a British Parliament ; and therefore, should such a motion be made, I presume it will be immediately quashed. By the commission lately given to Sir John Ligonier, of General and Commander-in-Chief of all his Majesty's forces in Great Britain, the door seems to be not only shut, but bolted, against his Royal Highness's return ; and I have *good reason* to be convinced that that breach is irreparable. The reports of changes in the Ministry, I am pretty sure, are idle and groundless. The Duke of Newcastle and Mr Pitt really agree very well ; not, I presume, from any sentimental tenderness for each other, but from a sense that it is their mutual interest ; and, as the late Captain General's party is now out of the question, I do not see what should produce the least change.

The visit, lately made to Berlin, was, I dare say, neither a friendly nor an inoffensive one. The Austrians always leave behind them pretty lasting monuments of their visits, or rather visitations ; not so much, I believe, from their thirst of glory, as from their hunger of prey.

This winter, I take for granted, must produce a peace of some kind or another ; a bad one for us, no doubt, and yet perhaps better than we should get the year after. I suppose the King of Prussia is negotiating with France, and endeavouring by those means to get out of the scrape, with the loss only of Silesia, and perhaps Halberstadt, by way of indemnification to Saxony ; and, considering all circumstances, he would be well off upon those terms. But then how is Sweden to be satisfied? Will the Russians restore Memel ? Will France have been at all this expense *gratis?* Must there be no acquisition for them in Flanders ? I dare say they have stipulated something of that sort for themselves by the additional and secret treaty, which I know they made, last May, with the Queen of Hungary. Must we give up whatever the French please to desire in America, besides the cession of Minorca in perpetuity ? I fear we must, or else raise twelve millions more next year, to as little purpose as we did this, and have consequently a worse peace afterwards. I turn my eyes away, as much as I can, from this miserable prospect ; but, as a citizen and member of society, it recurs to my imagination, notwithstanding all my endeavours to banish it from my thoughts. I can do myself or my country no good ; but I feel the wretched situation of both : the state of the latter makes me better bear that of the former; and, when I am called away from my station here, I shall think it rather (as Cicero says of Crassus) *Mors donata quam vita erepta.*[1]

I have often desired, but in vain, the favour of being admitted into your private apartment at Hamburgh, and of being informed of your private life there. Your mornings, I hope and believe, are employed in business ; but give me an account of the remainder of the day, which I suppose is, and ought to be, appropriated to amusements and pleasures. In what houses are you domestic ? Who are so in yours ? In short, let me in, and do not be denied to me.

Here I am, as usual, seeing few people, and hearing fewer ; drinking the waters regularly, to a minute, and am something the better for them. I read a great deal, and vary occasionally my dead company. I converse with grave folios in the morning, while my head is clearest, and my attention strongest; I take up less severe quartos after dinner; and at night I choose the mixed company and amusing chit-chat of octavos and duodecimos. *Je tire parti de tout ce que je puis ;*[2] that is my philosophy ; and I mitigate, as much as I can, my physical ills, by diverting my attention to other objects.

Here is a report that Admiral Holbourne's fleet is destroyed, in a manner, by a storm ; I hope it is not true, in the full extent of the report ; but I believe it has suffered. This would fill up the measure of our misfortunes. Adieu.

LETTER CCXC.

My dear Friend,   Bath, November the 20th, 1757.

I write to you now, because I love to write to you ; and hope that my letters are welcome to you ; for otherwise I have very little to inform you of. The King of Prussia's late victory you are better informed of than we are here. It has given

---

[1] Death bestowed than life taken away.
[2] I reap benefit as far as possible from everything.

infinite joy to the unthinking public, who are not aware that it comes too late in the year, and too late in the war, to be attended with any very great consequences. There are six or seven thousand of the human species less than there were a month ago, and that seems to me to be all. However, I am glad of it, upon account of the pleasure and the glory which it gives the King of Prussia, to whom I wish well as a man, more than as a King. And surely he is so great a man, that had he lived seventeen or eighteen hundred years ago, and his life been transmitted to us in a language that we could not very well understand, I mean either Greek or Latin, we should have talked of him as we do now of your Alexanders, your Cæsars, and others, with whom, I believe, we have but a very slight acquaintance. *Au reste*, I do not see that his affairs are much mended by this victory. The same combination of the great Powers of Europe against him still subsists, and must at last prevail. I believe the French army will melt away, as is usual, in Germany ; but his army is extremely diminished by battles, fatigues, and desertion ; and he will find great difficulties in recruiting it, from his own already exhausted dominions. He must therefore, and to be sure will, negotiate privately with the French, and get better terms that way than he could any other.

The report of the three General Officers, the Duke of Marlborough, Lord George Sackville, and General Waldegrave, was laid before the King last Saturday, after their having sat four days upon M——t's affair : nobody yet knows what it is ; but it is generally believed that M——t will be brought to a Court-martial. That you may not mistake this matter, as *most* people here do, I must explain to you, that this examination before the three above-mentioned General Officers, was by no means a trial, but only a previous inquiry into his conduct, to see whether there was, or was not, cause to bring him to a regular trial before a Court-martial. The case is exactly parallel to that of a grand jury, who, upon a previous and general examination, find, or do not find, a bill, to bring the matter before the petty jury, where the fact is finally tried. For my own part, my opinion is fixed upon that affair : I am convinced that the expedition was to be defeated ; and nothing that can appear before a Court-martial can make me alter that opinion. I have been too long acquainted with human nature to have great regard for human testimony : and a very great degree of probability, supported by various concurrent circumstances, conspiring in one point, will have much greater weight with me than human testimony upon oath, or even upon honour ; both which I have frequently seen considerably warped by private views.

The Parliament, which now stands prorogued to the first of next month, it is thought, will be put off for some time longer, till we know in what light to lay before it the state of our alliance with Prussia, since the conclusion of the Hanover neutrality ; which, if it did not quite break it, made at least a great flaw in it.

The birthday was neither fine nor crowded ; and no wonder, since the King was that day seventy-five. The old Court and the young one are much better together, since the Duke's retirement ; and the King has presented the Prince of Wales with a service of plate.

I am still *unwell*, though I drink these waters very regularly. I will stay here at least six weeks longer, where I am much quieter than I should be allowed to be in town. When things are in such a miserable situation as they are at present, I desire neither to be concerned nor consulted, still less quoted. Adieu !

LETTER CCXCI.

My dear Friend,   Bath, November the 26th, 1757.

I received, by the last mail, your short account of the King of Prussia's victory ; which victory, contrary to custom, turns out more complete than it was at first reported to be. This appears by an intercepted letter from Monsieur de St Germain to Monsieur d'Affry, at the Hague ; in which he tells him, *Cette armée est entièrement fondue*, and lays the blame, very strongly, upon Monsieur de Soubize. But be it greater, or be it less, I am glad of it ; because the King of Prussia (whom I honour and almost adore) I am sure is. Though *d'ailleurs*, between you and me, *où est-ce que cela mène ?* To nothing while that formidable union, of the three great powers of Europe, subsists against him. Could that be any way broken, something might be done ; without which, nothing can. I take it for granted that the King of Prussia will do all he can to detach France. Why should not we, on our part, try to detach Russia ? At least, in our present distress, *omnia tentanda*, and sometimes a lucky and unexpected hit turns up. This thought came into my head this morning ; and I give it to you, not as a very probable scheme, but as a possible one, and consequently worth trying —The year of the Russian subsidies (nominally paid by the court of Vienna, but really by France) is near expired. The former probably cannot, and perhaps the latter will not, renew them. The Court of Petersburgh is beggarly, profuse, greedy, and by no means scrupulous. Why should not we step in there, and outbid them ? If we could, we buy a great army at once ; which would give an entire new turn to the affairs of that part of the world at least. And, if we bid handsomely, I do not believe the *bonne foi* of that court would stand in the way. Both our Court and our Parliament would, I am very sure, give a very great sum, and very cheerfully, for this purpose. In the next place, Why should not you wriggle yourself, if possible, into so great a scheme ? You are, no doubt, much acquainted with the Russian resident Soltikow ; Why should you not sound him, as entirely from yourself, upon this subject ? You may ask him, What, does your Court intend to go on next year in the pay of France, to destroy the liberties of all Europe, and throw universal monarchy into the hands of that already great, and always ambitious, Power ? I know you think, or at least call, yourselves the allies of the Empress Queen ; but is it not plain that she will be, in the first place, and you in the next, the dupes of France ? At this very time you are doing the work of France and Sweden ; and that for some miserable subsidies, much inferior to those which I am sure you might have, in a better cause, and more consistent with the true interest of Russia. Though not empowered, I know the manner of thinking of my own Court so well upon this subject, that I will venture to promise you much better terms than those you have now, without the least apprehensions of being disavowed. Should he listen to this, and what more may occur to you to say upon this subject, and ask you, *En écrirai-je à ma Cour ?* answer him, *Ecrivez, écrivez, Monsieur, hardiment. Je prendrai tout cela sur moi.*[1] Should this happen, as perhaps, and as I heartily wish, it may, then write an exact relation of it to your own Court. Tell them that you thought the measure of such great importance, that you could not help taking this little step towards bringing it about ; but that you mentioned it only as from yourself, and that you have not in the least committed them by it. If Soltikow lends himself in any degree to this, insinuate, that, in the present situation of affairs, and particularly of the King's Electoral dominions, you are very sure that his Majesty would have *une reconnoissance sans bornes* for *all* those, by whose means so desirable a revival of an old and long friendship should be

[1] Shall I write about it to my Court ?—Write, write, Sir, fearlessly. All that I will take upon myself.

brought about. You will, perhaps, tell me, that, without doubt, Mr Keith's instructions are to the same effect : but I will answer you, that you can, *if you please,* do it better than Mr Keith ; and, in the next place, that, be all that as it will, it must be very advantageous to you at home, to show that you have at least a contriving head, and an alertness in business.

I had a letter by the last post from the Duke of Newcastle, in which he congratulates me, in his own name, and in Lord Hardwicke's, upon the approbation which your despatches give, not only to them two, but to *others.* This success, so early, should encourage your diligence, and rouse your ambition, if you have any ; you may go a great way, if you desire it, having so much time before you.

I send you here enclosed the copy of the Report of the three General Officers, appointed to examine previously into the conduct of General M——t ; it is ill written, and ill spelled ; but no matter ; you will decipher it. You will observe, by the tenor of it, that it points strongly to a Court-martial ; which no doubt will soon be held upon him. I presume there will be no shooting, in the final sentence ; but I do suppose there will be breaking, &c.

I have had some severe returns of my old complaints last week, and am still unwell ; I cannot help it.

A friend of yours arrived here three days ago ; she seems to me to be a serviceable strong-bodied bay mare, with black mane and tail ; you easily guess who I mean. She is come with mamma, and without *il caro sposo.*

Adieu ! my head will not let me go on longer.

LETTER CCXCII.

MY DEAR FRIEND,   Bath, December the 31st, 1757.

I HAVE this moment received your letter of the 18th, with the enclosed papers. I cannot help observing that, till then, you never acknowledged the receipt of any one of my letters.

I can easily conceive that party spirit, among your brother Ministers at Hamburgh, runs as high as you represent it, because I can easily believe the errors of the human mind ; but, at the same time, I must observe that such a spirit is the spirit of little minds, and subaltern Ministers, who think to atone by zeal for their want of merit and importance. The political differences of the several Courts should never influence the personal behaviour of their several Ministers towards one another. There is a certain *procédé noble et galant*, which should always be observed among the Ministers, of Powers even at war with each other, which will always turn out to the advantage of the ablest; who will in those conversations find, or make opportunities of throwing out, or of receiving, useful hints. When I was last at the Hague we were at war with both France and Spain ; so that I could neither visit, nor be visited, by the Ministers of those two Crowns : but we met every day, or dined at third places, where we embraced as personal friends, and trifled, at the same time, upon our being political enemies; and by this sort of *badinage* I discovered some things which I wanted to know. There is not a more prudent maxim than to live with one's enemies as if they may one day become one's friends ; as it commonly happens, sooner or later, in the vicissitudes of political affairs.

To your question, which is a rational and prudent one, Whether I was authorized to give you the hints, concerning Russia, by any people in power here ? I will tell you that I was not : but, as I had pressed them to try what might be done with Russia, and got Mr Keith to be dispatched thither some months sooner than otherwise, I dare say, he would, with the proper instructions for that purpose; I wished, that by the hints I gave you, you might have got the start of him, and the merit, at least, of having *entamé* that matter with Soltikow. What you have to do with him now, when you meet with him at any third place, or at his own house (where you are at liberty to go, while Russia has a Minister in London, and we a Minister at Petersburgh) is, in my opinion, to say to him, in an easy cheerful manner, *Hé bien, Monsieur, je me flatte que nous serons bientôt amis publics, aussi bien qu'amis personnels.*[1] To which he will probably ask, Why, or how ? You will reply, Because you know that Mr Keith is gone to his Court with instructions, which you think must necessarily be agreeable there. And throw out to him, that nothing but a change of their present system can save Livonia to Russia ; for, that he cannot suppose that, when the Swedes shall have recovered Pomerania, they will long leave Russia in quiet possession of Livonia. If he is so much a Frenchman as you say, he will make you some weak answers to this; but, as you will have the better of the argument on your side, you may remind him of the old and almost uninterrupted connection between France and Sweden,

---

[1] Well, Sir, I flatter myself we shall soon be public as well as personal friends.

the inveterate enemy of Russia. Many other arguments will naturally occur to you in such a conversation, if you have it. In this case there is a piece of ministerial art, which is sometimes of use ; and that is, to show jealousies among one's enemies, by a seeming preference shown to some one of them. Monsieur Hecht's *rêveries* are *rêveries* indeed.—How should his master have made the *golden arrangements* which he talks of, and which are to be forged into shackles for General Fermor ? The Prussian finances are not in a condition now to make such expensive arrangements. But I think you may tell Monsieur Hecht, in confidence, that you hope the instructions with which you know that Mr Keith is gone to Petersburgh may have some effect upon the measures of that Court.

I would advise you to live with that same Monsieur Hecht in all the confidence, familiarity, and connection, which prudence will allow. I mean it with regard to the King of Prussia himself, by whom I could wish you to be known and esteemed as much as possible. It may be of use to you some day or other. If man, courage, conduct, constancy, can get the better of all the difficulties which the King of Prussia has to struggle with, he will rise superior to them. But still, while this alliance subsists against him, I dread *les gros Escadrons.* His last victory, of the 5th, was certainly the completest that has been heard of these many years. I heartily wish the Prince of Brunswick just such a one over Monsieur de Richelieu's army ; and that he may take my old acquaintance the Maréchal, and send him over here to polish and perfume us.

I heartily wish you, in the plain homespun style, a great number of happy new years, well employed in forming both your mind and your manners, to be useful and agreeable to yourself, your country, and your friends ! That these wishes are sincere your Secretary's brother will, by the time of your receiving this, have remitted you a proof, from   Yours.

LETTER CCXCIII.

MY DEAR FRIEND,   London, February the 8th, 1758.

I RECEIVED by the same post your two letters of the 13th and 17th past ; and yesterday that of the 27th, with the Russian manifesto enclosed ; in which her Imperial Majesty of all the Russias has been pleased to give every reason, except the true one, for the march of her troops against the King of Prussia.

The true one, I take to be, that she has just received a very great sum of money from France, or the Empress Queen, or both, for that purpose. *Point d'argent point de Russe* is now become a maxim. Whatever may be the motive of their march, the effects must be bad; and, according to my speculations, those troops will replace the French in Hanover and Lower Saxony; and the French will go and join the Austrian army. You ask me, If I still despond? Not so much as I did after the battle of Colen: the battles of Rosbach and Lissa were drams to me, and gave me some momentary spirits; but though I do not absolutely despair, I own I greatly distrust. I readily allow the King of Prussia to be *nec pluribus impar ;* [1] but still, when the *plures* amount to a certain degree of plurality, courage and abilities must yield at last. Michel here assures me that he does not mind the Russians; but as I have it from the gentleman's own mouth, I do not believe him. We shall very soon send a squadron to the Baltic, to entertain the Swedes; which, I believe, will put an end to their operations in Pomerania, so that I have no great apprehensions from that quarter; but Russia, I confess, sticks in my stomach.

Everything goes smoothly in Parliament; the King of Prussia has united all our parties in his support; and the Tories have declared that they will give Mr Pitt unlimited credit for this session: there has not been one single division yet upon public points, and I believe will not. Our American expedition is preparing to go soon; the disposition of that affair seems to me a little extraordinary.—Abercrombie is to be the sedentary, and not the acting, Commander; Amherst, Lord Howe, and Wolfe, are to be the acting, and I hope the active, Officers. I wish they may agree. Amherst, who is the oldest Officer, is under the influence of the same great person who influenced Mordaunt, so much to the honour and advantage of this country. This is most certain, that we have force enough in America to eat up the French alive in Canada, Quebec, and Louisbourg, if we have but skill and spirit enough to exert it properly ; but of that I am modest enough to doubt.

When you come to the egotism, which I have long desired you to come to with me, you need make no excuses for it. The egotism is as proper and as satisfactory, to one's friends, as it is impertinent and misplaced with strangers. I desire to see you in your every-day clothes, by your fireside, in your pleasures ; in short, in your private life ; but I have not yet been able to obtain this. Whenever you condescend to do it, as you promise,

---

[1] A host in himself.

stick to truth ; for I am not so uninformed of Hamburgh as perhaps you may think.

As for myself, I am very *unwell*, and very weary of being so ; and with little hopes, at my age, of ever being otherwise. I often wish for the end of the wretched remnant of my life ; and that wish is a rational one ; but then the innate principle of self-preservation, wisely implanted in our natures, for obvious purposes, oppose that wish, and makes us endeavour to spin out our thread as long as we can, however decayed and rotten it may be ; and in defiance of common sense we seek on for that chymic gold, which *beggars us when old.*

Whatever your amusements or pleasures may be at Hamburgh, I dare say you taste them more sensibly than ever you did in your life, now that you have business enough to whet your appetite to them. Business, one half of the day, is the best preparation for the pleasures of the other half. I hope and believe that it will be with you as it was with an apothecary whom I knew at Twickenham. A considerable estate fell to him by an unexpected accident, upon which he thought it decent to leave off his business ; accordingly, he generously gave up his shop and his stock to his head man, set up his coach, and resolved to live like a gentleman ; but in less than a month, the man, used to business, found that living like a gentleman was dying of *ennui* ; upon which he bought his shop and stock, resumed his trade, and lived very happily after he had something to do. Adieu.

LETTER CCXCIV.

My dear Friend, London, February the 24th, 1758.

I received yesterday your letter of the 2nd instant, with the enclosed ; which I return you, that there may be no chasm in your papers. I had heard before of Burrish's death, and had taken some steps thereupon ; but I very soon dropped that affair, for ninety-nine good reasons ; the first of which was, that nobody is to go in his room, and that, had he lived, he was to have been recalled from Munich. But another reason, more flattering for you, was, that you could not be spared from Hamburgh. Upon the whole I am not sorry for it, as the place where you are now is the great *entrepôt* of business ; and when it ceases to be so, you will necessarily go to some of the Courts in the neighbourhood (Berlin, I hope and believe), which will be a much more desirable situation than to rust at Munich, where we can never have any business beyond a subsidy. Do but go on, and exert yourself where you are, and better things will soon follow.

Surely the inaction of our army at Hanover continues too long. We expected wonders from it some time ago, and yet nothing is attempted. The French will soon receive reinforcements, and then be too strong for us; whereas they are now most certainly greatly weakened by desertion, sickness, and deaths. Does the King of Prussia send a body of men to our army or not? or has the march of the Russians cut him out work for all his troops? I am afraid it has. If one body of Russians joins the Austrian army in Moravia, and another body the Swedes in Pomerania, he will have his hands very full, too full, I fear. The French say they will have an army of 180,000 men in Germany this year; the Empress Queen will have 150,000 ; if the Russians have but 40,000, what can resist such a force? The King of Prussia may say, indeed, with more justice than ever any one person could before him, *Moi. Medea superest.*[1]

You promised me some egotism ; but I have received none yet. Do you frequent the Landgrave? *Hantez-vous les grands de la terre?*[2] What are the connections of the evening? All this, and a great deal more of this kind, let me know in your next.

The House of Commons is still very unanimous : there was a little popular squib let off this week, in a motion of Sir John Glyn's, seconded by Sir John Philips, for annual Parliaments. It was a very cold scent, and put an end to by a division of one hundred and ninety to seventy.

Good night. Work hard, that you may divert yourself well.

LETTER CCXCV.

My dear Friend,   London, March the 4th, 1758.

I should have been much more surprised at the contents of your letter of the 17th past, if I had not happened to have seen Sir C. W. about three or four hours before I received it. I thought he talked in an extraordinary manner ; he engaged that the King of Prussia should be master of Vienna in the month of

---

[1] Medea still lives.
[2] Do you often visit the great of the earth ?

May; and he told me that you were very much in love with his daughter. Your letter explained all this to me; and next day, Lord and Lady E—— gave me innumerable instances of his frenzy, with which I shall not trouble you. What inflamed it the more (if it did not entirely occasion it) was a great quantity of cantharides, which, it seems, he had taken at Hamburgh, to recommend himself, I suppose, to Mademoiselle John. He was let blood four times on board the ship, and has been let blood four times more since his arrival here; but still the inflammation continues very high. He is now under the care of his brothers, who do not let him go abroad. They have written to this same Mademoiselle John, to prevent, if they can, her coming to England, and told her the case; which, when she hears, she must be as mad as he is if she takes the journey. By the way, she must be *une Dame aventurière*, to receive a note for ten thousand roubles from a man whom she had known but three days; to take a contract of marriage, knowing he was married already; and to engage herself to follow him to England. I suppose this is not the first adventure of the sort which she has had.

After the news we received yesterday, that the French had evacuated Hanover, all but Hamel, we daily expect much better. We pursue them, we cut them off *en détail*, and at last we destroy their whole army. I wish it may happen, and, moreover, I think it not impossible.

My head is much out of order, and only allows me to wish you good night.

LETTER CCXCVI.

My dear Friend,   London, March the 22nd, 1758.

I have now your letter of the 8th lying before me, with the favourable account of our progress in Lower Saxony, and reasonable prospect of more decisive success. I confess I did not expect this, when my friend Münchausen took his leave of me, to go to Stade, and break the neutrality; I thought it at least a dangerous, but rather a desperate, undertaking; whereas, hitherto, it has proved a very fortunate one. I look upon the French army as *fondue;* and, what with desertion, deaths, and epidemical distempers, I dare say not a third of it will ever return to France. The great object is now what the Russians can or will do; and whether the King of Prussia can hinder their junction with the Austrians, by beating either, before they join : I will trust him for doing all that can be done.

Sir C. W. is still in confinement, and, I fear, will always be so, for he seems *cum ratione insanire ;* the physicians have collected all he has said and done, that indicated an alienation of mind, and have laid it before him in writing ; he has answered it in writing too, and justifies himself by the most plausible arguments that can possibly be urged. He tells his brother, and the few who are allowed to see him, that they are such narrow and contracted minds themselves, that they take those for mad who have a great and generous way of thinking ; as, for instance, when he determined to send his daughter over to you, in a fortnight, to be married, without any previous agreement or settlements, it was because he had long known you, and loved you, as a man of sense and honour; and therefore would not treat with you as with an attorney. That as for Mademoiselle John, he knew her merit and her circumstances ; and asks whether it is a sign of madness, to have a due regard for the one, and a just compassion for the other. I will not tire you with enumerating any more instances of the poor man's frenzy ; but conclude this subject with pitying him, and poor human nature, which holds its reason by so precarious a tenure. The lady, who you tell me is set out, *en sera pour la peine et les fraix du voyage,* for her note is worth no more than her contract. By the way, she must be a kind of *aventurière,* to engage so easily in such an adventure, with a man whom she had not known above a week, and whose *début* of ten thousand roubles showed him not to be in his right senses.

You will probably have seen General Yorke by this time, in his way to Berlin or Breslau, or wherever the King of Prussia may be. As he keeps his commission to the States General, I presume he is not to stay long with his Prussian Majesty : but, however, while he is there, take care to write to him very constantly, and to give all the informations you can. His father, Lord Hardwicke, is your great puff; he commends your office letters exceedingly. I would have the Berlin Commission your object in good time : never lose view of it. Do all you can to recommend yourself to the King of Prussia on your side of the water, and to smooth your way for that commission on this ; by the turn which things have taken of late, it must always be the most important of all foreign commissions from hence.

I have no news to send you, as things here are extremely quiet ; so good night.

LETTER CCXCVII.

MY DEAR FRIEND,   London, April the 25th, 1758.

I AM now two letters in your debt, which I think is the
first time that ever I was so, in the long course of our correspondence. But, besides that my head has been very much out
of order of late, writing is by no means that easy thing that it
was to me formerly. I find by experience that the mind and
the body are more than married, for they are most intimately
united ; and when the one suffers, the other sympathizes. *Non
sum qualis eram :* Neither my memory nor my invention are
now what they formerly were. It is in a great measure my
own fault : I cannot accuse nature, for I abused her ; and it is
reasonable I should suffer for it.

I do not like the return of the oppression upon your lungs ;
but the rigour of the cold may probably have brought it upon
you, and your lungs not in fault. Take care to live very cool,
and let your diet be rather low.

We have had a second winter here, more severe than the
first, at least it seemed so, from a premature summer that we
had for a fortnight, in March ; which brought everything forwards only to be destroyed. I have experienced it at Blackheath ; where the promise of fruit was a most flattering one,
and all nipped in the bud by frost and snow, in April. I shall
not have a single peach or apricot.

I have nothing to tell you from hence concerning public
affairs, but what you read as well in the newspapers. This
only is extraordinary : that last week, in the House of Commons,
above ten millions were granted, and the whole Hanover army
taken into British pay, with but one single negative, which
was Mr Viner's.

Mr Pitt gains ground in the closet, and yet does not lose it
in the public. That is new.

Monsieur Kniphausen has dined with me ; he is one of the
prettiest fellows I have seen ; he has, with a great deal of life
and fire, *les manières d'un honnête homme, et le ton de la parfaitement bonne compagnie.* You like him yourself ; try to be like
him : it is in your power.

I hear that Mr Mitchel is to be recalled, notwithstanding
the King of Prussia's instances to keep him. But why, is a
secret that I cannot penetrate.

You will not fail to offer the Landgrave, and the Princess

of Hesse (who I find are going home) to be their agent and commissioner at Hamburgh.

I cannot comprehend the present state of Russia, nor the motions of their armies. They change their Generals once a week; sometimes they march with rapidity, and now they lie quiet behind the Vistula. We have a thousand stories here of the interior of that government, none of which I believe. Some say that the Great Duke will be set aside. Woronzoff is said to be entirely a Frenchman, and that Monsieur de l'Hôpital governs both him and the Court. Sir C. W. is said, by his indiscretions, to have caused the disgrace of Bestuchef, which seems not impossible. In short, everything of every kind is said, because, I believe, very little is truly known. *A propos* of Sir C. W.; he is out of confinement, and gone to his house in the country for the whole summer. They say he is now very cool and well. I have seen his Circe, at her window in Pallmall; she is painted, powdered, curled, and patched, and looks *l'aventure*. She has been offered, by Sir C. W——'s friends, £500 in full of all demands, but will not accept of it. *La comtesse veut plaider*, and I fancy *faire autre chose si elle peut.*[1] Jubeo te bene valere.

LETTER CCXCVIII.

My dear Friend,   Blackheath, May the 18th, 1758.

I have your letter of the 9th now before me, and condole with you upon the present solitude and inaction of Hamburgh. You are now shrunk from the dignity and importance of a consummate Minister, to be but, as it were, a common man. But this has, at one time or another, been the case of most great men; who have not always had equal opportunities of exerting their talents. The greatest must submit to the capriciousness of fortune; though they can, better than others, improve the favourable moments. For instance, who could have thought, two years ago, that you would have been the Atlas of the Northern Pole? but the good Genius of the North ordered it so; and now that you have set that part of the globe right, you return to *otium cum dignitate.* But, to be serious; now that you cannot have much office business to do, I could tell you what to do, that would employ you, I should think, both usefully and agreeably. I mean, that you should write short memoirs of that busy scene, in which you have been enough

---

[1] Wishes to go to law,—to do something else if she can.

concerned, since your arrival at Hamburgh, to be able to put
together authentic facts and anecdotes. I do not know whether
you will give yourself the trouble to do it or not ; but I do
know, that, if you will *olim hæc meminisse juvabit*. I would
have them short, but correct as to facts and dates.

I have told Alt, in the strongest manner, your lamentations
for the loss of the House of Cassel, *et il en fera rapport à son
Sérénissime Maître.*[1] When you are quite idle (as probably you
may be, some time this summer) why should you not ask leave
to make a tour to Cassel for a week ? which would certainly be
granted you from hence, and which would be looked upon as a
bon procédé, at Cassel.

The King of Prussia is probably, by this time, at the gates
of Vienna, making the Queen of Hungary really do, what Monsieur de Bellisle only threatened, sign a peace upon the ramparts
of her capital. If she is obstinate, and will not, she must fly
either to Presburgh or to Inspruck, and Vienna must fall. But
I think he will offer her reasonable conditions enough for herself ;
and I suppose that, in that case, Caunitz will be reasonable enough
to advise her to accept of them. What turn would the war
take then ? Would the French and Russians carry it on without her ? the King of Prussia, and the Prince of Brunswick,
would soon sweep them out of Germany. By this time too, I
believe, the French are entertained in America, with the loss of
Cape Breton ; and, in consequence of that, Quebec ; for we have
a force there equal to both those undertakings, and officers
there, now, that will execute what Lord L——— never would so
much as attempt. His appointments were too considerable to
let him do anything that might possibly put an end to the war.
Lord Howe, upon seeing plainly that he was resolved to do
nothing, had asked leave to return, as well as Lord Charles Hay.

We have a great expedition preparing, and which will soon
be ready to sail from the Isle of Wight ; fifteen thousand good
troops, eighty battering cannons, besides mortars, and every
other thing in abundance, fit for either battle or siege. Lord
Anson desired, and is appointed, to command the fleet employed
upon this expedition ; a proof that it is not a trifling one. Conjectures concerning its destination are infinite ; and the most
ignorant are, as usual, the boldest conjecturers. If I form any
conjectures, I keep them to myself, not to be disproved by the
event ; but, in truth, I form none ; I might have known, but
would not.

Everything seems to tend to a peace next winter: our suc-

[1] And he will report it to his Most Serene Master.

cess in America, which is hardly doubtful, and the King of Prussia's in Germany, which is as little so, will make France (already sick of the expense of the war) very tractable for a peace. I heartily wish it: for, though people's heads are half turned with the King of Prussia's success, and will be quite turned, if we have any in America, or at sea ; a moderate peace will suit us better than this immoderate war of twelve millions a year.

Domestic affairs go just as they did ; the Duke of Newcastle and Mr Pitt jog on like man and wife ; that is, seldom agreeing, often quarrelling ; but by mutual interest, upon the whole, not parting. The latter, I am told, gains ground in the closet ; though he still keeps his strength in the House, and his popularity in the public : or, perhaps, because of that.

Do you hold your resolution of visiting your dominions of Bremen and Lubeck this summer ? If you do, pray take the trouble of informing yourself correctly of the several constitutions and customs of those places, and of the present state of the federal union of the Hanseatic towns : it will do you no harm, nor cost you much trouble ; and it is so much clear gain on the side of useful knowledge.

I am now settled at Blackheath for the summer ; where unseasonable frost and snow, and hot and parching east winds, have destroyed all my fruit, and almost my fruit trees. I vegetate myself little better than they do ; I crawl about on foot, and on horseback ; read a great deal, and write a little : and am very much yours.

LETTER CCXCIX.

My DEAR FRIEND,   Blackheath, May the 30th, 1758.

I HAVE no letter from you to answer, so this goes to you unprovoked. But à propos of letters ; you have had great honour done you in a letter from a fair and Royal hand, no less than that of her Royal Highness the Princess of Cassel ; she has written your panegyric to her sister, Princess Amelia, who sent me a compliment upon it. This has likewise done you no harm with the King, who said gracious things upon that occasion. I suppose you had, for her Royal Highness, those attentions, which I wish to God you would have in due proportions for everybody. You see, by this instance, the effects of them ; they are always repaid with interest. I am more confirmed by this in thinking, that, if you can conveniently, you should ask leave to go for a week to Cassel, to return your thanks for all favours received.

I cannot expound to myself the conduct of the Russians. There must be a trick in their not marching with more expedition. They have either had a sop from the King of Prussia, or they want an animating dram from France and Austria. The King of Prussia's conduct always explains itself by the events ; and within a very few days we must certainly hear of some very great stroke from that quarter. I think I never, in my life, remember a period of time so big with great events as the present. Within two months the fate of the House of Austria will probably be decided : within the same space of time we shall certainly hear of the taking of Cape Breton, and of our army's proceeding to Quebec : within a few days we shall know the good or ill success of our great expedition, for it is sailed : and it cannot be long before we shall hear something of the Prince of Brunswick's operations, from whom I also expect good things. If all these things turn out, as there is good reason to believe they will, we may once, in our turn, dictate a reasonable peace to France, who now pays seventy *per cent.* insurance upon its trade, and seven *per cent.* for all the money raised for the service of the year.

Comte Bothmar has got the smallpox, and of a bad kind. Kniphausen diverts himself much here ; he sees all places and all people, and is ubiquity itself. Mitchel, who was much threatened, stays at last at Berlin, at the earnest request of the King of Prussia. Lady * * * is safely delivered of a son, to the great joy of that noble family. The expression, of a woman's having brought her husband a son, seems to be a proper and cautious one ; for it is never said from whence.

I was going to ask you how you pass your time now at Hamburgh, since it is no longer the seat of strangers and of business ; but I will not, because I know it is to no purpose. You have sworn not to tell me.

Sir William Stanhope told me that you promised to send him some old Hock from Hamburgh, and so you did—not. If you meet with any superlatively good, and not else, pray send over a *foudre*[1] of it, and write to him. I shall have a share in it. But unless you find some, either at Hamburgh or at Bremen, uncommonly and almost miraculously good, do not send any. *Dixi.*[2] Yours.

---

[1] A large tun used for wine in Germany.
[2] I have said it.

LETTER CCC.

My dear Friend,   Blackheath, June the 13th, 1758.

The secret is out ; St Malo is the devoted place. Our troops began to land at the Bay of Cancale the 5th, without any opposition. We have no further accounts yet, but expect some every moment. By the plan of it, which I have seen, it is by no means a weak place ; and I fear there will be many hats to be disposed of before it is taken.   There are in the port above thirty privateers ; about sixteen of their own, and about as many taken from us.

Now for Africa, where we have had great success.   The French have been driven out of all their forts and settlements upon the gum coast, and upon the river Senegal.   They had been many years in possession of them, and by them annoyed our African trade exceedingly ; which, by the way, *toute proportion gardée*, is the most lucrative trade we have.   The present booty is likewise very considerable, in gold dust, and gum seneca ; which is a very valuable, by being a very necessary, commodity for all our stained and printed linens.

Now for America.   The least sanguine people here expect, the latter end of this month or the beginning of the next, to have the account of the taking of Cape Breton, and of all the forts with hard names in North America.

Captain Clive has long since settled Asia to our satisfaction ; so that three parts of the world look very favourable for us. Europe, I submit to the care of the King of Prussia, and Prince Ferdinand of Brunswick; and I think they will give a good account of it.   France is out of luck, and out of courage ; and will, I hope, be enough out of spirits to submit to a reasonable peace. By reasonable, I mean what all people call reasonable in their own case ; an advantageous one for us.

I have set all right with Münchausen ; who would not own that he was at all offended, and said, as you do, that his daughter did not stay long enough, nor appear enough at Hamburgh, for you possibly to know that she was there. But people are always ashamed to own the little weaknesses of self-love, which, however, all people feel more or less. The excuse, I saw, pleased.

I will send you your quadrille tables by the first opportunity, consigned to the care of Mr Mathias here. *Felices,*

faustæque sint.[1] May you win upon them, when you play with
men ; and when you play with women, either win, or know why
you lose.

Miss — marries Mr —, next week. *Who proffers Love proffers
Death*, says Waller to a dwarf : in my opinion, the conclusion
must instantly choke the little Lady.   Admiral * marries Lady
* * * ; there the danger, if danger is, will be on the other side.
The Lady has wanted a man so long, that she now compounds
for half a one.   Half a loaf——

I have been worse since my last letter ; but am now, I
think, recovering ; *tant va la cruche à l'eau ;* [2]——and I have
been there very often.

Good night.   I am faithfully and truly yours.

———◇———

LETTER CCCI.

MY DEAR FRIEND,   Blackheath, June the 27th, 1758.

You either have received already, or will very soon receive,
a little case from Amsterdam, directed to you at Hamburgh. It
is for Princess Amelia, the King of Prussia's sister, and contains
some books, which she desired Sir Charles Hotham to procure
her from England, so long ago as when he was at Berlin ; he
sent for them immediately ; but, by I do not know what puzzle,
they were recommended to the care of Mr Selwyn, at Paris, who
took such care of them, that he kept them near three years in
his warehouse, and has at last sent them to Amsterdam, from
whence they are sent to you.   If the books are good for anything, they must be considerably improved, by having seen so
much of the world ; but, as I believe they are English books,
perhaps they may, like English travellers, have seen nobody, but
the several bankers to whom they were consigned ; be that as
it will, I think you had best deliver them to Monsieur Hecht,
the Prussian Minister at Hamburgh, to forward to her Royal
Highness, with a respectful compliment from you, which you
will, no doubt, turn in the best manner ; and, *selon le bon ton
de la parfaitement bonne compagnie.*[3]   ·

You have already seen, in the papers, all the particulars of
our St Malo's expedition, so I say no more of that ; only that
Mr Pitt's friends exult in the destruction of three French ships

---

[1] May they be prosperous and lucky.
[2] The pitcher which goes often for water [is broken at last].
[3] In the good style of the best society.

of war, and one hundred and thirty privateers and trading ships; and affirm, that it stopped the march of threescore thousand men, who were going to join the Comte de Clermont's army. On the other hand, Mr Fox and Company call it breaking windows with guineas; and apply the fable of the Mountain and the Mouse. The next object of our fleet was to be the bombarding of Granville, which is the great *entrepôt* of their Newfoundland fishery, and will be a considerable loss to them in that branch of their trade. These, you will perhaps say, are no great matters, and I say so too; but, at least, they are signs of life, which we have not given for many years before; and will show the French, by our invading them, that we do not fear their invading us. Were those invasions, in fishing-boats from Dunkirk, so terrible as they were artfully represented to be, the French would have had an opportunity of executing them, while our fleet, and such a considerable part of our army, were employed upon their coast. *But my Lord Ligonier does not want an army at home.*

The Parliament is prorogued by a most gracious speech neither by nor from his Majesty, who was *too ill* to go to the House; the Lords and Gentlemen are, consequently, most of them, gone to their several counties, to do (to be sure) all the good that is recommended to them in the speech. London, I am told, is now very empty, for I cannot say so from knowledge. I vegetate wholly here. I walk and read a great deal, ride and scribble a little, according as my head allows, or my spirits prompt; to write anything tolerable, the mind must be in a natural, proper disposition; provocatives, in that case, as well as in another, will only produce miserable, abortive performances.

Now you have (as I suppose) full leisure enough, I wish you would give yourself the trouble, or rather the pleasure, to do what I hinted to you some time ago; that is, to write short memoirs of those affairs which have either gone through your hands, or that have come to your certain knowledge, from the inglorious battle of Hastenbeck, to the still more scandalous Treaty of Neutrality. Connect, at least, if it be by ever so short notes, the pieces and letters which you must necessarily have in your hands, and throw in the authentic anecdotes that you have probably heard. You will be glad when you have done it; and the reviving past ideas in some order and method, will be an infinite comfort to you hereafter. I have a thousand times regretted not having done so; it is at present too late for me to begin: this is the right time for you, and your life is likely to be a busy one. Would young men avail themselves of the

advice and experience of their old friends, they would find the
utility in their youth, and the comfort of it in their more advanced age; but they seldom consider that, and you, less than
anybody I ever knew. May you soon grow wiser! Adieu.

<hr>

LETTER CCCII.

MY DEAR FRIEND,   Blackheath, June the 30th, 1758.

THIS letter follows my last very close; but I received yours
of the 15th in the short interval. You did very well not to buy
any Rhenish at the exorbitant price you mention, without
further directions; for both my brother and I think the money
better than the wine, be the wine ever so good. We will
content ourselves with our stock in hand of humble Rhenish, of
about three shillings a bottle. However, *pour la rareté du fait*,
I will lay out twelve ducats, for twelve bottles of the wine of
1665, by way of an eventual cordial, if you can obtain a
senatus consultum for it. I am in no hurry for it, so send it me
only when you can conveniently; well packed up *s'entend*.

You will, I dare say, have leave to go to Cassel; and if you
do go, you will perhaps think it reasonable, that I, who was
the adviser of the journey, should pay the expense of it. I
think so too, and therefore, if you go, I will remit the hundred
pound which you have calculated it at. You will find the House
of Cassel the house of gladness; for Hanau is already, or must
be soon, delivered of its French guests.

The Prince of Brunswick's victory is, by all the skilful,
thought a *chef-d'œuvre*, worthy of Turenne, Condé, or the most
illustrious human butchers. The French behaved better than
at Rosbach, especially the *Carabiniers Royaux*, who could not
be *entamés*.[1] I wish the siege of Olmutz well over, and a
victory after it; and that with good news from America, which,
I think, there is no reason to doubt of, must procure us a good
peace at the end of the year. The Prince of Prussia's death is
no public misfortune; there was a jealousy and alienation
between the King and him, which could never have been made
up between the possessor of the crown and the next heir to it.
He will make something of his nephew, *s'il est du bois dont on
en fait.*[2] He is young enough to forgive, and to be forgiven,
the possession and the expectative, at least for some years.

Adieu! I am *unwell*, but affectionately yours.

[1] Broken up.
[2] If he is of the material out of which anything can be made.

LETTER CCCIII.

My dear Friend,   Blackheath, July the 18th, 1758.

Yesterday I received your letter of the 4th ; and my last will have informed you that I had received your former, concerning the Rhenish, about which I gave you instructions. If *vinum Mosellanum est omni tempore sanum*,[1] as the Chapter of Treves asserts, what must this *vinum Rhenanum* be, from its superior strength and age ? It must be the universal panacea.

Captain Howe is to sail forthwith somewhere or another, with about eight thousand land forces on board him ; and what is much more, Edward the White Prince. It is yet a secret where they are going ; but I think it is no secret, that what sixteen thousand men and a great fleet could not do, will not be done by eight thousand men and a much smaller fleet. About eight thousand five hundred horse, foot, and dragoons, are embarking, as fast as they can, for Embden, to reinforce Prince Ferdinand's army ; late and few, to be sure, but still better than never, and none. The operations in Moravia go on slowly, and Olmutz seems to be a tough piece of work : I own I begin to be in pain for the King of Prussia ; for the Russians now march in earnest, and Marechal Daun's army is certainly superior in number to his. God send him a good delivery.

You have a Danish army now in your neighbourhood, and they say a very fine one ; I presume you will go to see it, and, if you do, I would advise you to go when the Danish Monarch comes to review it himself ; *pour prendre Langue de ce Seigneur*.[2] The Rulers of the earth are all worth knowing ; they suggest moral reflections : and the respect that one [naturally has for God's Vicegerents here on earth, is greatly increased by acquaintance with them.

Your card-tables are gone, and they enclose some suits of clothes, and some of these clothes enclose a letter.

Your friend Lady * * is gone into the country with her Lord, to negotiate, coolly and at leisure, their intended separation. My Lady insists upon my Lord's dismissing the * *, as ruinous to his fortune ; my Lord insists, in his turn, upon my Lady's dismissing Lord * * ; my Lady replies that that is unreasonable, since Lord * * creates no expense to the family, but rather the contrary. My Lord confesses that there is some weight in this argument ; but then pleads sentiment : my Lady

---

[1] Moselle wine is always healthful.
[2] In order to get information about this great man.

says, A fiddlestick for sentiment after having been married so long. How this matter will end is in the womb of time, *nam fuit ante Helenam.*[1]

You did very well to write a congratulatory letter to Prince Ferdinand; such attentions are always right, and always repaid in some way or other.

I am glad you have connected your negotiations and anecdotes; and I hope not with your usual laconism. Adieu! Yours.

LETTER CCCIV.

MY DEAR FRIEND,   Blackheath, August the 1st, 1758.

I THINK the Court of Cassel is more likely to make you a second visit at Hamburgh, than you are to return theirs at Cassel; and therefore, till that matter is clearer, I shall not mention it to Lord Holdernesse.

By the King of Prussia's disappointment in Moravia, by the approach of the Russians, and the intended march of Monsieur de Soubize to Hanover, the waters seem to me to be as much troubled as ever. *Je vois très-noir actuellement;*[2] I see swarms of Austrians, French, Imperialists, Swedes, and Russians, in all near four hundred thousand men, surrounding the King of Prussia and Prince Ferdinand, who have about a third of that number. Hitherto they have only buzzed, but now I fear they will sting.

The immediate danger of this country is being drowned; for it has not ceased raining these three months, and withal is extremely cold. This neither agrees with me in itself, nor in its consequences; for it hinders me from taking my necessary exercise, and makes me very *unwell*. As my head is always the part offending, and is so at present, I will not do, like many writers, write without a head; so adieu.

LETTER CCCV.

MY DEAR FRIEND,   Blackheath, August the 29th, 1758.

YOUR Secretary's last letter brought me the good news, that the fever had left you, and I will believe that it has; but a

---

[1] Horace, Satires, B. I. Sat. iii. 107.
[2] I anticipate the worst.

postscript to it, of only two lines, under your own hand, would have convinced me more effectually of your recovery. An intermitting fever, in the intervals of the paroxysms, would surely have allowed you to have written a very few lines with your own hand, to tell me how you were ; and till I receive a letter (as short as you please) from you yourself, I shall doubt of the exact truth of any other accounts.

I send you no news, because I have none ; Cape Breton, Cherbourg, &c., are now old stories ; we expect a new one soon from Commodore Howe, but from whence we know not. From Germany we hope for good news ; I confess I do not, I only wish it. The King of Prussia is marched to fight the Russians, and I believe will beat them, if they stand ; but what then ? What shall he do next, with the three hundred and fourscore thousand men, now actually at work upon him ? He will do all that man can do, but at last *il faut succomber*.

Remember to think yourself less well than you are, in order to be quite so : be very regular, rather longer than you need ; and then there will be no danger of a relapse. God bless you.

LETTER CCCVI.

My dear Friend,   Blackheath, Sept. the 5th, 1758.

I received, with great pleasure, your letter of the 22nd August ; for, by not having a line from you in your Secretary's two letters, I suspected that you were worse than he cared to tell me ; and so far I was in the right, that your fever was more malignant than intermitting ones generally are ; which seldom confine people to their bed, or at most only the days of the paroxysms. Now, thank God, you are well again, though weak ; do not be in too much haste to be better and stronger : leave that to nature, which, at your age, will restore both your health and strength as soon as she should. Live cool for a time, and rather low, instead of taking what they call heartening things.

Your manner of making presents is noble, *et sent la grandeur d'âme d'un preux Chevalier.* You depreciate their value, to prevent any returns ; for it is impossible that a wine which has counted so many Sindicks, that can only be delivered by a *senatus consultum*, and is the *panacea* of the North, should be sold for a ducat a bottle. The *sylphium* of the Romans, which was stored up in the public magazines, and only distributed by order of the Magistrate, I dare say cost more ; so that, I am convinced, your present is much more valuable than you would make it.

Here I am interrupted, by receiving your letter of the 25th past. I am glad that you are able to undertake your journey to Bremen ; the motion, the air, the new scene, the everything, will do you good, provided you manage yourself discreetly.

Your bill for fifty pounds shall certainly be accepted and paid ; but, as in conscience, I think fifty pounds is too little for seeing a live Landgrave, and especially at Bremen, which this whole nation knows to be a very dear place, I shall, with your leave, add fifty more to it. By the way, when you see the Princess Royal of Cassel, be sure to tell her how sensible you are of the favourable and too partial testimony, which you know she wrote of you to Princess Amelia.

The King of Prussia has had the victory, which you, in some measure, foretold ; and as he has taken *la Caisse Militaire*, I presume *Messieurs les Russes sont hors de combat pour cette campagne ;* for *point d'argent, point de Suisse,* is not truer of the laudable Helvetic body, than *point d'argent, point de Russe,* is of the savages of the Two Russias, not even excepting the Autocratrice of them both. Serbelloni, I believe, stands next in his Prussian Majesty's list to be beaten ; that is, if he will stand ; as the Prince de Soubize does in Prince Ferdinand's, upon the same condition. If both these things happen, which is by no means improbable, we may hope for a tolerable peace this winter ; for, *au bout du compte,* the King of Prussia cannot hold out another year ; and therefore he should make the best of these favourable events, by way of negotiation.

I think I have written a great deal with an actual giddiness of head upon me. So adieu.

I am glad you have received my letter of the Ides of July.

LETTER CCCVII.

MY DEAR FRIEND,   Blackheath, Sept. the 8th, 1758.

THIS letter shall be short, being only an explanatory note upon my last ; for I am not learned enough, nor yet dull enough, to make my comment much longer than my text. I told you then, in my former letter, that, with your leave (which I will suppose granted), I would add fifty pounds to your draught for that sum ; now, lest you should misunderstand this, and wait for the remittance of that additional fifty from hence, know my meaning was, that you should likewise draw upon me for it when you please; which, I presume, will be more convenient to you.

Let the pedants, whose business it is to believe lies, or the poets, whose trade it is to invent them, match the King of Prussia with a hero, in ancient or modern story, if they can. He disgraces history, and makes one give some credit to romances. Calprenede's Juba does not now seem so absurd as formerly.

I have been extremely ill this whole summer; but am now something better: however, I perceive *que l'esprit et le corps baissent;* [1] the former is the last thing that anybody will tell me, or own when I tell it them; but I know it is true. Adieu.

LETTER CCCVIII.

MY DEAR FRIEND,　　　　　　Blackheath, Sept. the 22d, 1758.

I HAVE received no letter from you since you left Hamburgh; I presume that you are perfectly recovered, but it might not have been improper to have told me so. I am very far from being recovered; on the contrary, I am worse and worse, weaker and weaker, every day; for which reason I shall leave this place next Monday, and set out for Bath a few days afterwards. I should not take all this trouble merely to prolong the, fag end of a life, from which I can expect no pleasure, and others no utility; but the cure, or at least the mitigation, of those physical ills which make that life a load, while it does last, is worth any trouble and attention.

We are come off but scurvily from our second attempt upon St Malo: it is our last for this season; and, in my mind, should be our last for ever, unless we were to send so great a sea and land force as to give us a moral certainty of taking some place of great importance, such as Brest, Rochefort, or Toulon.

Monsieur Münchausen embarked yesterday, as he said, for Prince Ferdinand's army; but as it is not generally thought that his military skill can be of any great use to that Prince, people conjecture that his business must be of a very different nature, and suspect separate negotiations, neutralities, and what not? Kniphausen does not relish it in the least, and is by no means satisfied with the reasons that have been given him for it. Before he can arrive there, I reckon that something decisive will have passed in Saxony: if to the disadvantage of the King

---

[1] Body and mind are decaying.

of Prussia, he is crushed; but if, on the contrary, he should get a complete victory (and he does not get half victories) over the Austrians, the winter may probably produce him and us a reasonable peace. I look upon Russia as *hors de combat* for some time; France is certainly sick of the war; under an unambitious King, and an incapable Ministry, if there is one at all: and, unassisted by those two Powers, the Empress Queen had better be quiet. Were any other man in the situation of the King of Prussia, I should not hesitate to pronounce him ruined; but he is such a prodigy of a man, that I will only say, I fear he will be ruined. It is by this time decided.

Your Cassel Court at Bremen is, I doubt, not very splendid : money must be wanting: but, however, I dare say their table is always good, for the Landgrave is a *Gourmand ;* and as you are domestic there, you may be so too, and recruit your loss of flesh from your fever; but do not recruit too fast. Adieu.

LETTER CCCIX.

MY DEAR FRIEND, London, September the 26th, 1758.

I AM sorry to find that you had a return of your fever; but, to say the truth, you in some measure deserved it, for not carrying Dr Middleton's bark and prescription with you. I foresaw that you would think yourself cured too soon, and gave you warning of it; but *by-gones* are *by-gones*, as Chartres, when he was dying, said of his sins: let us look forwards. You did very prudently to return to Hamburgh, to good bark, and, I hope, a good physician. Make all sure there before you stir from thence, notwithstanding the requests or commands of all the Princesses in Europe; I mean a month at least, taking the bark even to supererogation, that is, some time longer than Dr Middleton requires; for, I presume, you are got over your childishness about tastes, and are sensible that your health deserves more attention than your palate. When you shall be thus reëstablished, I approve of your returning to Bremen; and indeed you cannot well avoid it, both with regard to your promise, and to the distinction with which you have been received by the Cassel family.

Now to the other part of your letter. Lord Holdernesse has been extremely civil to you, in sending you, all under his own hand, such obliging offers of his service. The hint is plain, that he will (in case you desire it) procure your leave to come home for some time ; so that the single question is, Whether you should desire it or not, *now*. It will be two months before you can possibly undertake the journey, whether by sea or by land, and either way it would be a troublesome and dangerous one for a *convalescent*, in the rigour of the month of November ; you could drink no mineral waters here in that season, nor are any mineral waters proper in your case, being all of them heating, except Seltzer's ; then, what would do you more harm than all medicines could do you good, would be the pestilential vapours of the House of Commons, in long and crowded days, of which there will probably be many this session ; where your attendance, if here, will necessarily be required. I compare St Stephen's Chapel, upon those days, to *la Grotta del Cane.*

Whatever may be the fate of the war now, negotiations will certainly be stirring all the winter, and of those, the northern ones, you are sensible, are not the least important : in these, if at Hamburgh, you will probably have your share, and perhaps a meritorious one. Upon the whole, therefore, I would advise you to write a very civil letter to Lord Holdernesse; and to tell him, that though you cannot hope to be of any use to his Majesty's affairs anywhere, yet in the present unsettled state of the North, it is possible that unforeseen accidents may throw it in your way to be of some little service, and that you would not willingly be out of the way of those accidents ; but that you shall be most extremely obliged to his Lordship, if he will procure you his Majesty's gracious permission, to return for a few months in the spring, when probably affairs will be more settled one way or another. When things tend nearer to a settlement, and Germany, from the want of money or men, or both, breathes peace more than war, I shall solicit Burrish's commission for you, which is one of the most agreeable ones in his Majesty's gift ; and I shall by no means despair of success. Now I have given you my opinion upon this affair, which does not make a difference of above three months, or four at most, I would not be understood to mean to force your own, if it should happen to be different from mine ; but mine, I think, is more both for your health and your interest. However, do as you please ; may you in this, and everything else, do for the best ! so God bless you.

LETTER CCCX.

MY DEAR FRIEND,   Bath, October the 18th, 1758.

I RECEIVED by the same post your two letters of the 29th past, and of the 3rd instant. The last tells me that you are perfectly recovered ; and your resolution of going to Bremen in three or four days proves it ; for surely you would not undertake that journey a second time, and at this season of the year, without feeling your health solidly restored ; however, in all events, I hope you have taken a provision of good bark with you. I think your attention to her Royal Highness may be of use to you here ; and indeed all attentions, to all sorts of people, are always repaid in some way or other, though real obligations are not. For instance ; Lord Titchfield, who has been with you at Hamburgh, has written an account to the Duke and Duchess of Portland, who are here, of the civilities you showed him ; which he is much pleased, and they delighted, with. At this rate, if you do not take care, you will get the unmanly reputation of a well-bred man ; and your countryman, John Trott, will disown you.

I have received, and tasted of your present ; which is a *très-grand vin*, but more cordial to the stomach than pleasant to the palate. I keep it as physic, only to take occasionally, in little disorders of my stomach ; and in those cases, I believe, it is wholesomer than stronger cordials.

I have been now here a fortnight; and though I am rather better than when I came, I am still far from well. My head is giddier than becomes a head of my age ; and my stomach has not recovered its retentive faculty. Leaning forwards, particularly to write, does not at present agree with, · Yours.

LETTER CCCXI.

MY DEAR FRIEND,   Bath, October the 28th, 1758.

YOUR letter has quieted my alarms ; for I find by it, that you are as well recovered as you could be in so short a time. It is your business now, to keep yourself well, by scrupulously following Dr Middleton's directions. He seems to be a rational and knowing man. Soap and steel are, unquestionably, the proper medicines for your case ; but, as they are alteratives, you must take them for a very long time, six months at least ;

and then drink chalybeate waters. I am fully persuaded that this was your original complaint in Carniola; which those ignorant physicians called, in their jargon, *Arthritis vaga*, and treated as such. But now the true cause of your illness is discovered, I flatter myself that with time and patience on your part, you will be radically cured; but, I repeat it again, it must be by a long and uninterrupted course of those alterative medicines above-mentioned. They have no taste; but if they had a bad one, I will not now suppose you such a child, as to let the frowardness of your palate interfere, in the least, with the recovery or enjoyment of health. The latter deserves the utmost attention of the most rational man; the former is only the proper object of the care of a dainty, frivolous woman.

The run of luck, which some time ago we were in, seems now to be turned against us. Oberg is completely routed; his Prussian Majesty was surprised (which I am surprised at), and had rather the worst of it. I am in some pain for Prince Ferdinand; as I take it for granted, that the detachment from Marechal de Contade's army which enabled Prince Soubize to beat Oberg will immediately return to the grand army, and then it will be infinitely superior. Nor do I see where Prince Ferdinand can take his winter quarters, unless he retires to Hanover; and that I do not take to be at present the land of Canaan. Our second expedition to St Malo I cannot call so much an unlucky, as an ill-conducted, one; as was also Abercrombie's affair in America. *Mais il n'y a pas de petite perte qui revient souvent;* [1] and all these accidents, put together, make a considerable sum total.

I have found so little good by these waters, that I do not intend to stay here above a week longer; and then remove my crazy body to London, which is the most convenient place either to live or die in.

I cannot expect active health anywhere; you may, with common care and prudence, expect it everywhere; and God grant that you may have it! Adieu.

———o———

LETTER CCCXII.

MY DEAR FRIEND,   London, November the 21st, 1758.

You did well to think of Prince Ferdinand's riband, which, I confess, I did not; and I am glad to find you thinking so far

---

[1] But that is no little loss which is repeated so often.

beforehand. It would be a pretty commission, and I will *accingere me* to procure it you. The only competition I fear is that of General Yorke, in case Prince Ferdinand should pass any time with his brother at the Hague, which is not unlikely, since he cannot go to Brunswick to his eldest brother, upon account of their simulated quarrel.

I fear the piece is at an end with the King of Prussia, and he may say *ilicet;* [1] I am sure he may personally say *plaudite*.[2] Warm work is expected this session of Parliament, about continent and no continent : some think Mr Pitt too continent, others too little so ; but a little time, as the newspapers most prudently and truly observe, will clear up these matters.

The King has been ill ; but his illness has terminated in a good fit of the gout, with which he is still confined. It was generally thought that he would have died, and for a very good reason ; for the oldest Lion in the Tower, much about the King's age, died a fortnight ago. This extravagancy, I can assure you, was believed by many above *peuple*. So wild and capricious is the human mind!

Take care of your health, as much as you can ; for, *to be, or not to be*, is a question of much less importance, in my mind, than to be or not to be well. Adieu.

LETTER CCCXIII.

MY DEAR FRIEND,   London, December the 15th, 1758.

IT is a great while since I heard from you, but I hope that good, not ill health, has been the occasion of this silence; I will suppose you have been, or are still, at Bremen, and engrossed by your Hessian friends.

Prince Ferdinand of Brunswick is most certainly to have the Garter, and I think I have secured you the honour of putting it on. When I say *secured*, I mean it in the sense in which that word should always be understood at Courts, and that is, *insecurely ;* I have a promise, but that is not *caution bourgeoise*. In all events, do not mention it to any mortal, because there is always a degree of ridicule that attends a disappointment, though often very unjustly, if the expectation was reasonably grounded ; however, it is certainly most prudent not to communicate, prematurely, one's hopes or one's fears. I cannot tell you when Prince Ferdinand will have it ; though there are

---

[1] It is all over.   [2] Applaud me.

so many candidates for the other two vacant Garters, that I
believe he will have his soon, and by himself, the others must
wait till a third, or rather a fourth, vacancy. Lord Rockingham
and Lord Holdernesse are secure ; Lord Temple pushes strongly,
but, I believe, is not secure. This commission for dubbing a
Knight, and so distinguished a one, will be a very agreeable
and creditable one for you, *et il faut vous en acquitter galamment.*[1]
In the days of ancient chivalry, people were very nice whom
they would be knighted by ; and, if I do not mistake, Francis
the First would only be knighted by the Chevalier Bayard, *qui
étoit preux Chevalier et sans reproche ;* and no doubt but it will
be recorded, *dans les archives de la Maison de Brunswick,* that
Prince Ferdinand received the honour of knighthood from your
hands.

The estimates for the expense of the year 1759 are made up ;
I have seen them; and what do you think they amount to ?
No less than twelve millions three hundred thousand pounds. A
most incredible sum, and yet already all subscribed, and even
more offered ! The unanimity in the House of Commons in
voting such a sum, and such forces, both by sea and land, is not
less astonishing. This is Mr Pitt's doing, *and it is marvellous
in our eyes.*

The King of Prussia has nothing more to do this year ; and,
the next, he must begin where he has left off. I wish he would
employ this winter in concluding a separate peace with the
Elector of Saxony ; which would give him more elbow-room to
act against France and the Queen of Hungary, and put an end
at once to the proceedings of the Diet, and the army of the Empire ; for then no Estate of the Empire would be invaded by
a co-Estate, and France, the faithful and disinterested *guarantee* of the Treaty of Westphalia, would have no pretence to
continue its armies there. I should think that his Polish
Majesty, and his Governor Comte Brühl, must be pretty weary
of being fugitives in Poland, where they are hated, and of being
ravaged in Saxony. This *rêverie* of mine, I hope, will be tried,
and I wish it may succeed. Good night, and God bless you.

[1] You must execute it gracefully.

LETTER CCCXIV.

My dear Friend,   London, New Year's Day, 1759.

Molti e felici,[1] and I have done upon that subject, one truth being fair, upon the most lying day in the whole year.

I have now before me your last letter, of the 21st December, which I am glad to find is a bill of health: but, however, do not presume too much upon it, but obey and honour your physician, 'that thy days may be long in the land.'

Since my last, I have heard nothing more concerning the riband; but I take it for granted it will be disposed of soon. By the way, upon reflection, I am not sure that anybody but a Knight can, according to form, be employed to make a Knight. I remember that Sir Clement Cotterel was sent to Holland, to dubb the late Prince of Orange, only because he was a Knight himself; and I know that the proxies of Knights, who cannot attend their own installations, must always be Knights. This did not occur to me before, and perhaps will not to the person who was to recommend 'you; I am sure I will not stir it; and I only mention it now that you may be in all events prepared for the disappointment, if it should happen.

G * * is exceedingly flattered with your account, that three thousand of his countrymen, all as little as himself, should be thought a sufficient guard upon three-and-twenty thousand of all the nations in Europe; not that he thinks himself by any means a little man, for when he would describe a tall, handsome man, he raises himself up at least half an inch to represent him.

. The private news from Hamburgh is, that his Majesty's Resident there is woundily in love with Madame * * * *; if this be true, God send him, rather than her, a good *delivery*. She must be *étrennée* at this season, and therefore I think you should be so too; so draw upon me, as soon as you please, for one hundred pounds.

Here is nothing new, except the unanimity with which the Parliament gives away a dozen of millions sterling; and the unanimity of the public is as great in approving of it; which has stifled the usual political and polemical argumentations.

Cardinal Bernis's disgrace is as sudden, and hitherto as little understood, as his elevation was. I have seen his Poems, printed at Paris, not by a friend, I dare say; and, to judge by them, I humbly conceive his Eminency is a p—y. I will say

[1] Many and happy [days].

nothing of that excellent headpiece that made him, and unmade him, in the same month, except *O King, live for ever !*

Good night to you, whomever you pass it with.

LETTER CCCXV.

MY DEAR FRIEND, London, February the 2nd, 1759.

I AM now (what I have very seldom been) two letters in your debt: the reason was, that my head, like many other heads, has frequently taken a wrong turn; in which case writing is painful to me, and therefore cannot be very pleasant to my readers.

I wish you would (while you have so good an opportunity as you have at Hamburgh) make yourself perfectly master of that dull, but very useful, knowledge, the Course of Exchange, and the causes of its almost perpetual variations; the value and relation of different Coins, the Specie, the Banco, Usances, Agio, and a thousand other particulars. You may with ease learn, and you will be very glad when you have learned them; ·for, in your business, that sort of knowledge will often prove necessary.

I hear nothing more of Prince Ferdinand's Garter: that he will have one is very certain; but when, I believe, is very uncertain; all the other postulants wanting to be dubbed at the same time, which cannot be, as there is not riband enough for them.

If the Russians move in time, and in earnest, there will be an end of our hopes and of our armies in Germany; three such millstones as Russia, France, and Austria, must, sooner or later, in the course of the year, grind his Prussian Majesty down to a mere *Margrave* of Brandenburgh. But I have always some hopes of a change under a *Gunarchy ;* [1] where whim and humour commonly prevail, reason very seldom, and then only by a lucky mistake.

I except the incomparable fair one of Hamburgh, that prodigy of beauty, and paragon of good sense, who has enslaved your mind, and inflamed your heart. If she is as well *étrennée* as you say she shall, you will be soon out of her chains; for I have, by long experience, found women to be like Telephus's spear, if one end kills, the other cures.

[1] Derived from the Greek word Γυνη, a woman, and means Female Government.

There never was so quiet, or so silent, a session of Parliament as the present : Mr Pitt declares only what he would have them do, and they do it *nemine contradicente*, Mr Viner only excepted.

Duchess Hamilton is to be married, to-morrow, to Colonel Campbell, the son of General Campbell, who will some day or other be Duke of Argyle, and have the estate. She refused the Duke of B——r for him.

Here is a report, but I believe a very groundless one, that your old acquaintance, the fair Madame C——e, is run away from her husband with a Jeweller, that *étrennes* her, and is come over here ; but I dare say it is some mistake, or perhaps a lie. Adieu ! God bless you.

LETTER CCCXVI.

MY DEAR FRIEND,   London, February the 27th, 1759.

IN your last letter, of the 7th, you accuse me, most unjustly, of being in arrears in my correspondence ; whereas, if our epistolary accounts were fairly liquidated, I believe you would be brought in considerably debtor. I do not see how any of my letters to you can miscarry, unless your office packet miscarries too, for I always send them to the office. Moreover, I might have a justifiable excuse for writing to you seldomer than usual, for to be sure there never was a period of time, in the middle of a winter, and the Parliament sitting, that supplied so little matter for a letter. Near twelve millions have been granted this year, not only *nemine contradicente*, but *nemine quicquid dicente.*[1] The proper officers bring in the estimates ; it is taken for granted that they are necessary, and frugal ; the Members go to dinner, and leave Mr West and Mr Martin to do the rest.

I presume you have seen the little poem of the Country Lass, by Soame Jenyns, for it was in the Chronicle ; as was also an answer to it, from the Monitor. They are neither of them bad performances ; the first is the neatest, and the plan of the second has the most invention. I send you none of those *pièces volantes* in my letters, because they are all printed in one or other of the newspapers, particularly the Chronicles ; and I suppose that you and others have all those papers amongst you at Hamburgh ; in which case it would be only putting you to the unnecessary expense of double postage.

[1] No one opposing it—no one saying anything.

I find you are sanguine about the King of Prussia this year ; I allow his army will be what you say ; but will that be *vis-à-vis* French, Austrians, Imperialists, Swedes, and Russians, who must amount to more than double that number ? Were the inequality less, I would allow for the King of Prussia's being so much *ipse agmen*[1] as pretty nearly to balance the account. In war, numbers are generally my omens ; and I confess, that in Germany they seem not happy ones this year. In America, I think, we are sure of success, and great success ; but how we shall be able to strike a balance, as they call it, between good success there, and ill success upon the continent, so as to come at a peace, is more than I can discover.

Lady Chesterfield makes you her compliments, and thanks you for your offer ; but declines troubling you, being discouraged by the ill success of Madame Münchausen's and Miss Chetwynd's commissions, the former for beef, and the latter for gloves ; neither of which have yet been executed, to the dissatisfaction of both. Adieu.

LETTER CCCXVII.

MY DEAR FRIEND, London, March the 16th, 1759.

I HAVE now your letter of the 20th past lying before me, by which you despond, in my opinion too soon, of dubbing your Prince ; for he most certainly will have the Garter ; and he will as probably have it before the campaign opens, as after. His campaign must, I doubt, at best, be a defensive one ; and he will show great skill in making it such ; for, according to my calculation, his enemies will be at least double his number. Their troops, indeed, may perhaps be worse than his ; but then their number will make up that defect, as it will enable them to undertake different operations at the same time. I cannot think that the King of Denmark will take a part in the present war ; which he cannot do without great possible danger : and he is well paid by France for his neutrality ; is safe, let what will turn out ; and, in the mean time, carries on his commerce with great advantage and security : so that that consideration will not retard your visit to your own country, whenever you have leave to return, and your own *arrangemens* will allow you. A short 'absence animates a tender passion, *et l'on ne recule que*

[1] A host in himself.

pour mieux sauter,[1] especially in the summer months ; so that I would advise you to begin your journey in May, and continue your absence from the dear object of your vows till after the dog-days, when love is said to be unwholesome. We have been disappointed at Martinico ; I wish we may not be so at Guada-loupe, though we are landed there ; for many difficulties must be got over before we can be in possession of the whole island. *A propos de bottes ;* you make use of two Spanish words, very properly, in your letter ; were I you, I would learn the Spanish language, if there were a Spaniard at Hamburgh who could teach me ; and then you would be master of all the European languages that are useful ; and, in my mind, it is very convenient, if not necessary, for a public man to understand them all; and not to be obliged to have recourse to an interpreter, for those papers that chance or business may throw in his way. I learned Spanish when I was older than you ; convinced, by experience, that, in everything possible, it was better to trust to one's self than to any other body whatsoever. Interpreters, as well as relators, are often unfaithful, and still oftener incorrect, puzzling, and blundering. In short, let it be your maxim through life, to know all you can know, yourself; and never to trust implicitly to the information of others. This rule has been of infinite service to me, in the course of my life.

I am rather better than I was ; which I owe not to my physicians, but to an ass and a cow, who nourish me, between them, very plentifully and wholesomely ; in the morning the ass is my nurse, at night the cow ; and I have just now bought a milch-goat, which is to graze and nurse me at Black-heath. I do not know what may come of this latter, and I am not without apprehensions that it may make a satyr of me ; but, should I find that obscene disposition growing upon me, I will check it in time, for fear of endangering my life and character by rapes. And so we heartily bid you farewell.

LETTER CCCXVIII.

MY DEAR FRIEND,   London, March the 30th, 1759.

I DO not like these frequent, however short, returns of your illness ; for I doubt they imply either want of skill in your physician, or want of care in his patient. Rhubarb, soap, and chalybeate medicines and waters are almost always specifics for

---

[1] They draw back only to take a better leap.

obstructions of the liver ; but then a very exact regimen is necessary, and that for a long continuance. Acids are good for you, but you do not love them; and sweet things are bad for you, and you do love them. There is another thing very bad for you, and I fear you love it too much. When I was in Holland, I had a slow fever, that hung upon me a great while ; I consulted Boerhaave, who prescribed me what I suppose was proper, for it cured me; but he added, by way of postscript to his prescription, *Venus rariùs colatur;* which I observed, and perhaps that made the medicines more effectual.

I doubt we shall be mutually disappointed in our hopes of seeing one another this spring, as I believe you will find, by a letter which you will receive, at the same time with this, from Lord Holdernesse ; but as Lord Holdernesse will not tell you all, I will, between you and me, supply that defect. I must do him the justice to say, that he has acted in the most kind and friendly manner possible to us both. When the King read your letter, in which you desired leave to return, for the sake of drinking the Tunbridge waters, he said, If he wants steel waters, those of Pyrmont are better than Tunbridge, and he can have them very fresh at Hamburgh. I would rather he had asked to come last autumn, and had passed the winter here ; for, if he returns now, I shall have nobody in those quarters to inform me of what passes ; and yet it will be a very busy and important scene. Lord Holdernesse, who found that it would not be liked, resolved to push it no further ; and replied, he was very sure, that when you knew his Majesty had the least objection to your return at this time, you would think of it no longer ; and he owned that he (Lord Holdernesse) had given you encouragement for this application last year, then thinking and hoping that there would be little occasion for your presence at Hamburgh this year. Lord Holdernesse will only tell you, in his letter, that, as he had some reason to believe, his moving this matter would be disagreeable to the King, he resolved, for your sake, not to mention it. You must answer his letter upon that foot singly, and thank him for this mark of his friendship : for he has really acted as your friend. I make no doubt of your having willing leave to return in autumn, for the whole winter. In the mean time, make the best of your *séjour* where you are ; drink the Pyrmont waters, and no wine but Rhenish, which, in your case, is the only proper one for you.

Next week Mr Harte will send you his Gustavus Adolphus, in two quartos ; it will contain many new particulars of the life of that real hero. as he has had abundant and authentic materials which have never yet appeared. It will, upon the whole, be a very curious and valuable history; though, between you and me, I could have wished that he had been more correct and elegant in his style. You will find it dedicated to one of your acquaintance, who was forced to prune the luxuriant praises bestowed upon him, and yet has left enough of all conscience to satisfy a reasonable man. Harte has been very much out of order these last three or four months, but is not the less intent upon sowing his Lucerne, of which he had six crops last year, to his infinite joy, and, as he says, profit. As a gardener, I shall probably have as much joy, though not quite so much profit, by thirty or forty shillings; for there is the greatest promise of fruit this year, at Blackheath, that ever I saw in my life. Vertumnus and Pomona have been very propitious to me; as for Priapus, that tremendous garden god, as I no longer invoke him, I cannot expect his protection from the birds and the thieves.

Adieu! I will conclude like a pedant, *Leviùs fit patientiâ quicquid corrigere est nefas.*[1]

----◇----

LETTER CCCXIX.

MY DEAR FRIEND,   London, April the 16th, 1759.

WITH humble submission to you, I still say, that if Prince Ferdinand can make a defensive campaign this year, he will have done a great deal, considering the great inequality of numbers. The little advantages of taking a regiment or two prisoners, or cutting another to pieces, are but trifling articles in the great account; they are only the pence, the pounds are yet to come; and I take it for granted, that neither the French, nor the Court of Vienna, will have *le démenti* of their main object, which is unquestionably Hanover; for that is the *summa summarum*; and they will certainly take care to draw a force together for this purpose, too great for any that Prince Ferdinand has, or can have, to oppose them. In short, mark the end on't, *j'en augure mal.* If France, Austria, the Empire, Russia, and Sweden, are not, at long run, too hard for the two Electors of Hanover and Brandenburgh, there must be some invisible power, some tutelar Deities, that miraculously interpose in favour of the latter.

You encourage me to accept all the powers that goats, asses,

[1] Whatever cannot be set right is made easier by patience.

and bulls, can give me, by engaging for my not making an ill use of them; but I own I cannot help distrusting myself a little, or rather human nature; for it is an old and very true observation, that there are misers of money, none of power; and the non-use of the one, and the abuse of the other, increase in proportion to their quantity.

I am very sorry to tell you, that Harte's Gustavus Adolphus does not take at all, and consequently sells very little: it is certainly informing, and full of good matter; but it is as certain too, that the style is execrable: where the devil he picked it up I cannot conceive, for it is a bad style of a new and singular kind; it is full of Latinisms, Gallicisms, German-isms, and all *isms* but Anglicisms; in some places pompous, in others vulgar and low. Surely, before the end of the world, people, and you in particular, will discover, that the *manner*, in everything, is at least as important as the matter; and that the latter never can please, without a good degree of ele-gancy in the former. This holds true in everything in life: in writing, conversing, business, the help of the Graces is ab-solutely necessary; and whoever vainly thinks himself above them, will find he is mistaken, when it will be too late to court them, for they will not come to strangers of an advanced age. There is a History lately come out, of the Reign of Mary Queen of Scots, and her son (no matter by whom) King James, written by one Robertson, a Scotchman, which for clearness, purity, and dignity of style, I will not scruple to compare with the best historians extant, not excepting Davila, Guicciardini, and per-haps Livy. Its success has consequently been great, and a second edition is already published, and bought up. I take it for granted, that it is to be had, or at least borrowed, at Ham-burgh, or I would send it you.

I hope you drink the Pyrmont waters every morning. The health of the mind depends so much upon the health of the body, that the latter deserves the utmost attention, independ-ently of the senses. God send you a very great share of both! Adieu.

LETTER CCCXX.

My DEAR FRIEND,   London, April the 27th, 1759.

I HAVE received your two letters of the 10th and 13th, by the last mail; and I will begin my answer to them, by observing to you, that a wise man, without being a Stoic considers in all misfortunes that befall him, their best as well as their worst side; and everything has a better and a worse side. I have strictly observed that rule for many years, and have found by experience that some comfort is to be extracted, under most moral ills, by considering them in every light, instead of dwelling, as people are too apt to do, upon the gloomy side of the object. Thank God, the disappointment that you so pathetically groan under is not a calamity which admits of no consolation. Let us simplify it, and see what it amounts to. You were pleased with the expectation of coming here next month, to see those who would have been pleased with seeing you. That, from very natural causes, cannot be; and you must pass this summer at Hamburgh, and next winter in England, instead of passing this summer in England, and next winter at Hamburgh. Now, estimating things fairly, is not the change rather to your advantage? Is not the summer more eligible, both for health and pleasure, than the winter, in that northern, frozen Zone? and will not the winter, in England, supply you with more pleasures than the summer, in an empty capital, could have done? So far, then, it appears that you are rather a gainer by your misfortune.

The *tour*, too, which you propose making to Lubeck, Altena, &c., will both amuse and inform you; for at your age one cannot see too many different places and people; since at the age you are now of, I take it for granted that you will not see them superficially, as you did when you first went abroad.

This whole matter, then, summed up, amounts to no more than this—that you will be here next winter, instead of this summer. Do not think that all I have said is the consolation only of an old philosophical fellow, almost insensible of pleasure or pain, offered to a young fellow who has quick sensations of both. No, it is the rational philosophy taught me by experience and knowledge of the world, and which I have practised above thirty years. I always made the best of the best, and never made bad worse, by fretting; this enabled me to go through the various scenes of life, in which I have been an actor, with more pleasure and less pain than most people. You will say, perhaps, One cannot change one's nature: and that, if a person is born of a very sensible gloomy temper, and apt to see things in the worst light, they cannot help it, nor new make themselves. I will admit it, to a certain degree, and but to a certain degree; for though we cannot totally change our nature, we may in a great measure correct it, by reflection and philosophy; and some philosophy is a very necessary companion in this

world, where, even to the most fortunate, the chances are greatly
against happiness.

I am not old enough, nor tenacious enough, to pretend not
to understand the main purport of your last letter ; and to show
you that I do, you may draw upon me for two hundred pounds,
which, I hope, will more than clear you.

Good night, *æquam memento rebus in arduis servare mentem ;*[1]
be neither transported nor depressed by the accidents of life.

LETTER CCCXXI.

MY DEAR FRIEND,   Blackheath, May the 16th, 1759.

YOUR Secretary's last letter, of the 4th, which I received
yesterday, has quieted my fears a good deal, but has not entirely
dissipated them. *Your fever still continues,* he says, *though in a
less degree.* Is it a continued fever, or an intermitting one ? If
the former, no wonder that you are weak, and that your head
aches. If the latter, why has not the bark, in substance and
large doses, been administered ? for, if it had, it must have
stopped it by this time. Next post, I hope, will set me quite
at ease. Surely you have not been so regular as you ought,
either in your medicines, or in your general regimen, otherwise
this fever would not have returned ; for the Doctor calls it *your
fever returned,* as if you had an exclusive patent for it. You
have now had illness enough, to know the value of health, and
to make you implicitly follow the prescriptions of your physician,
in medicines, and the rules of your own common sense in diet;
in which, I can assure you, from my own experience, that
quantity is often worse than quality; and I would rather eat
half a pound of bacon at a meal, than two pounds of any the
most wholesome food.

I have been settled here near a week, to my great satisfaction, *c'est ma place,* and I know it, which is not given to everybody. Cut off from social life by my deafness, as well as other
physical ills, and being at best but the ghost of my former self,
I walk here in silence and solitude, as becomes a ghost; with
this only difference, that I walk by day, whereas, you know, to
be sure, that other ghosts only appear by night. My health,
however, is better than it was last year, thanks to my almost
total milk diet. This enables me to vary my solitary amusements, and alternately to scribble as well as read, which I could

---

[1] Remember in difficulties to keep your mind undisturbed.

not do last year. Thus I saunter away the remainder, be it
more or less, of an agitated and active life, now reduced (and I
am not sure that I am a loser by the change) to so quiet and
serene a one, that it may properly be called still life.

The French whisper in confidence, in order that it may be
the more known and the more credited, that they intend to in-
vade us this year, in no less than three places ; that is, England,
Scotland, and Ireland. Some of our great men, like the Devils,
believe and tremble ; others, and one little one, whom I know,
laugh at it ; and, in general, it seems to be but a poor, instead
of a formidable, scare-crow. While *somebody* was at the head of
a moderate army, and wanted (I know why) to be at the head
of a great one, intended invasions were made an article of
political faith ; and the belief of them was required, as in the
Church the belief of some absurdities, and even impossibilities,
is required upon pain of heresy, excommunication, and consequently damnation, if they tend to the power and interest of the
Heads of the Church. But now there is a general toleration,
and the best Subjects, as well as the best Christians, may believe
what their reason and their consciences suggest : it is generally
and rationally supposed the French will threaten and not strike,
since we are so well prepared, both by armies and fleets, to
receive, and, I may add, to destroy, them. Adieu ! God bless
you.

LETTER CCCXXII.

MY DEAR FRIEND,   Blackheath, June the 15th, 1759.

YOUR letter of the 5th, which I received yesterday, gave me
great satisfaction, being all in your own hand ; though it contains great, and I fear just, complaints of your ill state of health.
You do very well to change the air ; and I hope that change
will do well by you. I would therefore have you write, after
the 20th of August, to Lord Holdernesse, to beg of him to obtain
his Majesty's leave for you to return to England for *two or three
months*, upon account of your health. Two or three months is
an indefinite time, which may afterwards be insensibly stretched
to what length one pleases ; leave that to me. In the mean
time you may be taking your measures with the best economy.

The day before yesterday an express arrived from Guada-
loupe ; which brought an account of our being in possession of
the whole island. And I make no manner of doubt but that,
in about two months, we shall have as good news from Crown-

point, Quebec, &c. Our affairs in Germany, I fear, will not be equally prosperous; for I have very little hopes for the King of Prussia or Prince Ferdinand. God bless you.

***

LETTER CCCXXIII.

My dear Friend,   Blackheath, June the 25th, 1759.

THE two last mails have brought me no letter from you or your Secretray; I will take this silence as a sign that you are better; but however, if you thought that I cared to know, you should have cared to have written. Here the weather has been very fine for a fortnight together: a longer term than in this climate we are used to hold fine weather by. I hope it is so too at Hamburgh, or at least at the *villa* to which you are gone; but pray do not let it be your *villa viciosa*, as those retirements are often called, and too often prove; though (by the way) the original name was villa *vezzoza;* [1] and by wags miscalled *viciosa.*

I have a most gloomy prospect of affairs in Germany; the French are already in possession of Cassel, and of the learned part of Hanover, that is, Göttingen, where I presume they will not stop *pour l'amour des Belles Lettres,* but rather go on to the Capital, and study them upon the coin. My old acquaintance, Monsieur de Richelieu, made a great progress there in metallic learning and inscriptions. If Prince Ferdinand ventures a battle to prevent it, I dread the consequences; the odds are too great against him. The King of Prussia is still in a worse situation; for he has the Hydra to encounter: and though he may cut off a head or two, there will still be enough left to devour him at last. I have, as you know, long foretold the now approaching catastrophe; but I was Cassandra. Our affairs in the new world have a much more pleasing aspect; Guadaloupe is a great acquisition, and Quebec, which I make no doubt of, will still be a greater. But must all these advantages, purchased at the price of so much English blood and treasure, be at last sacrificed as a peace-offering? God knows what consequences such a measure may produce; the germe of discontent is already great, upon the bare supposition of the case; but, should it be realized, it will grow to a harvest of disaffection.

You are now, to be sure, taking the previous necessary measures for your return here in the autumn; and I think you

[1] Charming.

may disband your whole family, excepting your secretary, your
butler, who takes care of your plate, wine, &c., one, or at most
two, maid-servants, and your valet de chambre, and one footman, whom you will bring over with you. But give no mortal,
either there or here, reason to think that you are not to return
to Hamburgh again. If you are asked about it, say, like Lock-
hart, that you are *le serviteur des événemens ;* for your present
appointments will do you no hurt here, till you have some
better destination. At that season of the year, I believe, it
will be better for you to come by sea than by land ; but that
you will be best able to judge of from the then circumstances
of your part of the world.

Your old friend Stevens is dead of the consumption that has
long been undermining him. God bless you, and send you
health !

LETTER CCCXXIV.

MY DEAR FRIEND,   Bath, February the 26th, 1761.

I AM very glad to hear that your election is finally settled,
and, to say the truth, not sorry that Mr * * has been compelled
to do, *de mauvaise grâce,* that which he might have done at first
in a friendly and handsome manner. However, take no notice
of what is past, and live with him as you used to do before ; for
in the intercourse of the world, it is often necessary to seem
ignorant of what one knows, and to have forgotten what one
remembers.

I have just now finished Coleman's play, and like it very
well ; it is well conducted, and the characters are well preserved.
I own I expected from the author more dialogue wit ; but, as
I know that he is a most scrupulous classic, I believe he did not
dare to put in half so much wit as he could have done, because
Terence has not a single grain ; and it would have been *crimen
læsæ antiquitatis.*[1] God bless you !

LETTER CCCXXV.

MY DEAR FRIEND,   Bath, November the 21st, 1761.

I HAVE this moment received your letter of the 19th. If I
find any alterations by drinking these waters, now six days, it

---

[1] High treason against antiquity.

is rather for the better ; but, in six days more, I think I shall find, with more certainty, what humour they are in with me ; if kind, I will profit of, but not abuse, their kindness ; all things have their bounds, *quos ultrà citràve nequit consistere rectum ;* [1] and I will endeavour to nick that point.

The Queen's jointure is larger than, from *some reasons*, I expected it would be, though not greater than the very last precedent authorized. The case of the late Lord Wilmington was, I fancy, remembered.

I have now good reason to believe that Spain will declare war to us ; that is, that it will very soon, if it has not already, avowedly assist France, in case the war continues. This will be a great triumph to Mr Pitt, and fully justify his plan of beginning with Spain first, and having the first blow, which is often half the battle.

Here is a great deal of company, and what is commonly called good company, that is, great quality. I trouble them very little, except at the pump, where my business calls me ; for, what is company to a deaf man, or a deaf man to company ?

Lady Brown, whom I have seen, and who, by the way, has got the gout in her eye, inquired very tenderly after you. And so I elegantly rest,

Yours till death.

LETTER CCCXXVI.

My dear Friend,   Bath, December the 6th, 1761.

I have been in your debt some time, which, you know, I am not very apt to be ; but it was really for want of specie to pay. The present state of my invention does not enable me to coin ; and you would have had as little pleasure in reading, as I should have had in writing, *le coglionerie* of this place ; besides, that I am very little mingled in them. I do not know whether I shall be able to follow your advice, and cut a winner ; for at present I have neither won nor lost a single shilling. I will play on this week only ; and if I have a good run, I will carry it off with me ; if a bad one, the loss can hardly amount to anything considerable in seven days, for I hope to see you in town to-morrow sevennight.

I had a dismal letter from Harte last week ; he tells me that he is at nurse with a sister in Berkshire, that he has got a

------

[1] Outside which everything is wrong.

confirmed jaundice, besides twenty other distempers. The true cause of these complaints I take to be, the same that so greatly disordered, and had nearly destroyed, the most august House of Austria, about one hundred and thirty years ago; I mean Gustavus Adolphus; who neither answered his expectations in point of profit nor reputation, and that merely by his own fault, in not writing it in the vulgar tongue; for as to facts, I will maintain, that it is one of the best histories extant.

Au revoir, as Sir Fopling says, and God bless you.

LETTER CCCXXVII.

MY DEAR FRIEND,   Bath, November the 2nd, 1762.

I ARRIVED here, as I proposed, last Sunday; but as ill as I feared I should be, when I saw you. Head, stomach, and limbs, all out of order.

I have yet seen nobody but Villettes, who is settled here for good, as it is called. What consequences has the Duke of Devonshire's resignation had? He has considerable connections and relations; but whether any of them are resigned enough to resign with him, is another matter. There will be, to be sure, as many and as absurd reports, as there are in the law books; I do not desire to know either; but inform me of what facts come to your knowledge, and of such reports only as you believe are grounded. And so God bless you!

LETTER CCCXXVIII.

MY DEAR FRIEND,   Bath, November the 13th, 1762.

I HAVE received your letter, and believe that your Preliminaries are very near the mark; and, upon that supposition, I think we have made a tolerable good bargain with Spain; at least, full as good as I expected, and almost as good as I wished, though I do not believe that we have got *all* Florida; but if we have St Augustin, as I suppose that, by the figure of *pars pro toto*,[1] will be called all Florida. We have by no means made so good a bargain with France; for, in truth, what do we get by it, except Canada, with a very proper boundary of the river Mississippi, and that is all? As for the restrictions upon the

[1] A part for a whole.

French fishery in Newfoundland, they are very well *per la predica*,[1] and for the Commissary whom we shall employ ; for he will have a good salary from hence, to see that those restrictions are complied with ; and the French will double that salary, that he may allow them all to be broken through. It is plain to me, that the French fishery will be exactly what it was before the war.

The three Leeward islands, which the French yield to us, are not, all together, worth half so much as that of St Lucia, which we give up to them. Senegal is not worth one quarter of Goree. The restrictions of the French, in the East Indies, are as absurd and impracticable as those of Newfoundland ; and you will live to see the French trade to the East Indies just as they did before the war. But, after all I have said, the Articles are as good as I expected with France, when I considered that no one single person, who carried on this negotiation on our parts, was ever concerned or consulted in any negotiation before. Upon the whole, then, the acquisition of Canada has cost us fourscore millions sterling. I am convinced we might have kept Guadaloupe, if our negotiators had known how to have gone about it.

His most Faithful Majesty of Portugal is the best off of anybody in this transaction, for he saves his kingdom by it, and has not laid out one Moidore in defence of it. Spain, thank God, in some measure, *paie les pots cassés ;* for, besides St Augustin, Logwood, &c., it has lost at least four millions sterling, in money, ships, &c.

Harte is here, who tells me he has been at this place these three years, excepting some few excursions to his sister ; he looks ill, and laments that he has frequent fits of the yellow jaundice. He complains of his not having heard from you these four years ; you should write to him. These waters have done me a great deal of good, though I drink but two-thirds of a pint in the whole day, which is less than the soberest of my countrymen drink of claret at every meal.

I should naturally think, as you do, that this session will be a stormy one, that is, if Mr Pitt takes an active part ; but if he is pleased, as the Ministers say, there is no other Æolus to blow a storm. The Dukes of Cumberland, Newcastle, and Devonshire, have no better troops to attack with, than the militia ; but Pitt alone is *ipse agmen.* God bless you !

---

[1] To talk about.

LETTER CCCXXIX.

MY DEAR FRIEND, Bath, November the 27th, 1762.

I RECEIVED your letter this morning, and return you the ball *à la volée.*[1] The King's speech is a very prudent one, and, as I suppose that the Addresses, in answer to it, were, as usual, in almost the same words, my Lord Mayor might very well call them innocent. As his Majesty expatiates so much upon the great *achievements* of the war, I cannot help hoping that, when the Preliminaries shall be laid before Parliament *in due time*, which, I suppose, means after the respective ratifications of all the contracting parties, that some untalked-of and unexpected advantage will break out in our treaty with France ; St Lucia, at least. I see, in the newspapers, an article which I by no means like, in our treaty with Spain ; which is, that we shall be at liberty to cut logwood in the Bay of Campeachy, *but paying for it.* Who does not see that this condition may, and probably will, amount to a prohibition, by the price which the Spaniards may set it at ? It was our undoubted right, and confirmed to us by former treaties, before the war, to cut logwood *gratis ;* but this new stipulation (if true) gives us a privilege, something like a reprieve to a criminal, with a *non obstante* to be hanged.

I now drink so little water, that it can neither do me good nor hurt ; but as I bathe but twice a week, that operation, which does my rheumatic carcass good, will keep me here some time longer than you had allowed.

Harte is going to publish a new edition of his Gustavus in octavo ; which, he tells me, he has altered, and which, I could tell him, he should translate into English, or it will not sell better than the former ; for, while the world endures, style and manner will be regarded, at least as much as matter. And so, *Dieu vous ait dans sa sainte garde.*[2]

LETTER CCCXXX.

MY DEAR FRIEND, Bath, December the 4th, 1762.

I RECEIVED your letter this morning, with the enclosed Preliminaries, which we have had here these three days ; and I

---

[1] In haste.
[2] May God have you in his holy keeping.

return them, since you intend to keep them, which is more than I believe the French will. I am very glad to find that the French are to restore all the conquests they made upon us in the East Indies during this war; and I cannot doubt but they will likewise restore to us all the Cod that they shall take, within less than three leagues of our coast in North America (a distance easily measured, especially at sea), according to the spirit, though not the letter, of the Treaty. I am informed that the strong opposition to the Peace will be in the House of Lords, though I cannot well conceive it; nor can I make out above six or seven who will be against it upon a division, unless (which I cannot suppose) some of the Bishops should vote on the side of their maker. God bless you!

LETTER CCCXXXI.

MY DEAR FRIEND,   Bath, December the 13th, 1762.

YESTERDAY I received your letter, which gave me a very clear account of the debate in your House. It is impossible for a human creature to speak well for three hours and a half; I question even if Belial, who, according to Milton, was the orator of the fallen Angels, ever spoke so long at a time.

There must have been a trick in Charles Townshend's speaking for the Preliminaries; for he is infinitely above having an opinion. Lord Egremont must be ill, or have thoughts of going into some other place: perhaps into Lord Granville's, who they say is dying: when he dies, the ablest head in England dies too, take it for all in all.

I shall be in town, barring accidents, this day sevennight, by dinner time; when I have ordered a *Haricot*, to which you will be very welcome, about four o'clock. *En attendant Dieu vous ait dans sa sainte garde.*

LETTER CCCXXXII.

MY DEAR FRIEND,   Blackheath, June the 14th, 1763.

I RECEIVED, by the last mail, your letter of the 4th, from the Hague; so far so good. You arrived *sonica* at the Hague, for our Embassador's entertainment: I find he has been very civil to you. You are in the right to stop for two or three days, at

Hanau, and make your court to the Lady of that place.[1] Your Excellency makes a figure already in the newspapers ; and let them and others Excellency you as much as they please, but pray suffer not your own servants to do it.

Nothing new of any kind has happened here since you went ; so I will wish you a good night, and hope that God will bless you.

LETTER CCCXXXIII.

MY DEAR FRIEND,   Blackheath, July the 14th, 1763.

YESTERDAY I received your letter from Ratisbon, where I am glad that you are arrived safe. You are, I find, over head and ears engaged in ceremony and *étiquette*. You must not yield in anything essential, where your public character may suffer ; but I advise you, at the same time, to distinguish carefully what may and what may not affect it, and to despise some German *minuties;* such as one step lower or higher upon the stairs, a bow more or less, and such sort of trifles.

By what I see in Cressener's letter to you, the cheapness of wine compensates the quantity, as the cheapness of servants compensates the number, that you must make use of.

Write to your mother often, if it be but three words, to prove your existence ; for when she does not hear from you, she knows, to a demonstration, that you are dead, if not buried.

The enclosed is a letter of the utmost consequence, which I was desired to forward, with care and speed, to the most serene *Louis.*

My head is not well to-day. So God bless you !

LETTER CCCXXXIV.

MY DEAR FRIEND,   Blackheath, August the 1st, 1763.

I HOPE that by this time you are pretty well settled at Ratisbon, at least as to the important points of the ceremonial ; so that you may know to precision to whom you must give, and from whom you must require, the *seine Excellentz*. Those formalities are, no doubt, ridiculous enough in themselves ; but yet they are necessary for manners, and sometimes for business ; and both would suffer by laying them quite aside.

---

[1] Her Royal Highness Princess Mary of England, Landgravine of Hesse.

I have lately had an attack of a new complaint, which I have long suspected that I had in my body, in *actu primo*, as the pedants call it, but I never felt in *actu secundo*, till last week, and that is a fit of the stone or gravel. It was, thank God, but a slight one ; but it was *dans toutes les formes ;* for it was preceded by a pain in my loins, which I at first took for some remains of my rheumatism ; but was soon convinced of my mistake, by making water much blacker than coffee, with a prodigious sediment of gravel.' I am now perfectly easy again, and have no more indications of this dreadful complaint.

God keep you from that and deafness ; other complaints are the common, and almost the inevitable, lot of human nature, but admit of some mitigation. God bless you !

LETTER CCCXXXV.

MY DEAR FRIEND,   Blackheath, August the 22d, 1763.

YOU will, by this post, hear from others that Lord Egremont died two days ago of an apoplexy ; which, from his figure, and the constant plethora he lived in, was reasonably to be expected. You will ask me who is to be Secretary in his room ? to which I answer, that I do not know. I should guess Lord Sandwich, to be succeeded in the Admiralty by Charles Townshend ; unless the Duke of Bedford, who seems to have taken to himself the department of Europe, should have a mind to it. This event may perhaps produce others ; but, till this happened, everything was in a state of inaction, and absolutely nothing was done. Before the next session, this chaos must necessarily take some form, either by a new jumble of its own atoms, or by mixing them with the more efficient ones of the Opposition.

I see by the newspapers, as well as by your letter, that the difficulties still subsist about your ceremonial at Ratisbon ; should they, from pride and folly, prove insuperable, and obstruct your real business, there is one expedient, which may perhaps remove difficulties, and which I have often known practised ; but which I believe our people here know nothing of : it is, to have the character of *Minister*, only, in your ostensible title, and that of Envoy Extraordinary in your pocket, to produce occasionally, especially if you should be sent to any of the Electors in your neighbourhood : or else, in any transactions that you may have, in which your title of Envoy Extraordinary may create great difficulties, to have a reversal given you, declaring, that the temporary suspension of that character, *ne donnera pas la moindre atteinte ni à vos droits ni à vos prétentions.*[1] As for the rest, divert yourself as well as you can, and eat and drink as little as you can ; and so God bless you !

———◇———

LETTER CCCXXXVI.

My dear Friend,   Blackheath, Sept. the 1st, 1763.

GREAT news ! The King sent for Mr Pitt last Saturday, and the conference lasted a full hour ; on the Monday following another conference, which lasted much longer ; and yesterday a third, longer than either. You take for granted that the treaty was concluded and ratified : no such matter, for this last conference broke it entirely off; and Mr Pitt and Lord Temple went yesterday evening to their respective country houses. Would you know what it broke off upon, you must ask the newsmongers, and the coffee-houses, who, I dare say, know it all very minutely ; but I, who am not apt to know anything that I do not know, honestly and humbly confess that I cannot tell you ; probably one party asked too much, and the other would grant too little.—However, the King's dignity was not, in my mind, much consulted, by their making him sole Plenipotentiary of a treaty, which they were not, in all events, determined to conclude. It ought surely to have been begun by some inferior agent, and his Majesty should only have appeared in rejecting or ratifying it. Louis the XIVth never sate down before a town in person, that was not sure to be taken.

However, *ce qui est différé n'est pas perdu ;*[2] for this matter must be taken up again, and concluded before the meeting of the Parliament, and probably upon more disadvantageous terms to the present Ministers, who have tacitly admitted, by this late negotiation, what their enemies have loudly proclaimed, that they are not able to carry on affairs. So much *de re politica.*

I have at last done the best office that can be done, to most married people ; that is, I have fixed the separation between my brother and his wife ; and the definitive treaty of peace will be proclaimed in about a fortnight ; for the only solid and lasting peace between a man and his wife is, doubtless, a separation. God bless you !

---

[1] Will not in the least injure your rights or your claims.
[2] What is put off is not lost.

LETTER CCCXXXVII.

My dear Friend,   Blackheath, Sept. the 30th 1763.

You will have known, long before this, from the office, that the departments are not cast as you wished; for Lord Halifax, as senior, had of course his choice, and chose the Southern, upon account of the colonies. The Ministry, such as it is, is now settled *en attendant mieux;* but, in my opinion, cannot, as they are, meet the Parliament.

The only, and all the efficient people they have, are in the House of Lords; for, since Mr Pitt has firmly engaged Charles Townshend to him, there is not a man of the Court side, in the House of Commons, who has either abilities or words enough to call a coach. Lord B * * * is certainly playing *un dessous de cartes,*[1] and I suspect that it is with Mr Pitt; but what that *dessous* is, I do not know, though all the coffee-houses do most exactly.

The present inaction, I believe, gives you leisure enough for *ennui,* but it gives you time enough, too, for better things; I mean reading useful books; and, what is still more useful, conversing with yourself some part of every day. Lord Shaftesbury recommends self-conversation to all authors; and I would recommend it to all men; they would be the better for it. Some people have not time, and fewer have inclination, to enter into that conversation; nay, very many dread it, and fly to the most trifling dissipations, in order to avoid it; but if a man would allot half an hour every night for this self-conversation, and recapitulate with himself whatever he has done, right or wrong, in the course of the day, he would be both the better and the wiser for it. My deafness gives me more than sufficient time for self-conversation; and I have found great advantages from it. My brother, and Lady Stanhope, are at last finally parted. I was the negotiator between them, and had so much trouble in it, that I would much rather negotiate the most difficult point of the *jus publicum Sacri Romani Imperii,* with the whole Diet of Ratisbon, than negotiate any point with any woman. If my brother had had some of those self-conversations which I recommend, he would not, I believe, at past sixty, with a crazy, battered constitution, and deaf into the bargain, have married a young girl, just turned of twenty, full of health, and consequently of desires. But who takes warning by the fate of others? This, perhaps, proceeds from a negligence of self-conversation. God bless you!

[1] Some secret trick.

LETTER CCCXXXVIII.

MY DEAR FRIEND,   Blackheath, Oct. the 17th, 1763.

THE last mail brought me your letter of the 2nd instant, as the former had brought me that of the 25th past. I did suppose that you would be sent for over, for the first day of the session ; as I never knew a stricter muster, and no furloughs allowed. I am very sorry for it, for the reasons you hint at ; but, however, you did very prudently, in doing *de bonne grâce*, what you could not help doing : and let that be your rule in everything, for the rest of your life. Avoid disagreeable things, as much as, by dexterity, you can ; but when they are unavoidable, do them with seeming willingness and alacrity. Though this journey is ill timed for you in many respects, yet, in point of *finances*, you will be a gainer by it upon the whole ; for depend upon it, they will keep you here till the very last day of the session ; and I suppose you have sold your horses, and dismissed some of your servants. Though they seem to apprehend the first day of the session so much, in my opinion, their danger will be much greater in the course of it.

When you are at Paris, you will of course wait upon Lord Hertford, and desire him to present you to the King ; at the same time make my compliments to him, and thank him for the very obliging message he left at my house in town ; and tell him, that, had I received it in time from thence, I would have come to town on purpose to have returned it in person. If there are any new little books at Paris, pray bring them me. I have already Voltaire's *Zelis dans le Bain*, his *Droit du Seigneur*, and *Olympie*. Do not forget to call once at Madame Monconseil's, and as often as you please at Madame du Pin's. *Au revoir*.

LETTER CCCXXXIX.

MY DEAR FRIEND,   Bath, November the 24th, 1763.

I ARRIVED here, as you suppose in your letter, last Sunday ; but after the worst day's journey I ever had in my life : it snowed and froze that whole morning, and in the evening it rained and thawed, which made the roads so slippery, that I was six hours coming post from the Devizes, which is but eighteen miles from hence ; so that, but for the name of coming post, I might as well have walked on foot. I have not yet quite got over my last violent attack, and am weak and flimsy.

I have now drunk the waters but three days; so that, without a miracle, I cannot yet expect much alteration, and I do not in the least expect a miracle. If they proved *les eaux de Jouvence* to me, that would be a miracle indeed;, but, as the late Pope Lambertini said, *Frà noi, gli miracoli sono passati già un pezzo.*[1]

I have seen Harte, who inquired much after you : he is dejected and dispirited, and thinks himself much worse than he is, though he has really a tendency to the jaundice. I have yet seen ˙nobody else, nor do I know who here is to be seen ; for I have not yet exhibited myself to public view, except at the pump, which, at the time I go to it, is the most private place in Bath.

After all the fears and hopes, occasioned severally by the meeting of the Parliament, in my opinion, it will prove a very easy session. Mr Wilkes is universally given up ; and if the Ministers themselves do not wantonly raise difficulties, I think they will meet with none. A majority of two hundred is a great anodyne. Adieu ! God bless you.

LETTER CCCXL.

MY DEAR FRIEND,   Bath, December the 3rd, 1763.

LAST post brought me your letter of the 29th past. I suppose C—— T—— let off his speech upon the Princess's portion, chiefly to show that he was of the Opposition : for otherwise the point was not debatable, unless as to the *quantum*, against which something might be said ; for the late Princess of Orange (who was the eldest daughter of a King) had no more, and her two sisters but half, if I am not mistaken.

It is a great mercy that Mr Wilkes, the intrepid defender of our rights and liberties, is out of danger, and may live to fight and write again in support of them ; and it is no less a mercy, that God hath raised up the Earl of S—— to vindicate and promote true religion and morality. These two blessings will justly make an epocha in the annals of this country.

I have delivered your message to Harte, who waits with impatience for your letter. He is very happy now in having free access to all Lord Craven's papers, which, he says, give him great

[1] Between ourselves, miracles are somewhat out of date.

lights into the *bellum tricennale ;* the old Lord Craven having been the professed and valorous knight-errant, and perhaps something more, to the Queen of Bohemia; at least, like Sir Peter Pride, he had the honour of spending great part of his estate in her Royal cause.

I am by no means right yet; I am very weak and flimsy still ; but the Doctor assures me that strength and spirits will return : if they do, *lucro apponam,* I will make the best of them ; if they do not, I will not make their want still worse, by grieving and regretting them. I have lived long enough, and observed enough, to estimate most things at their intrinsic, and not their imaginary, value ; and at seventy I find nothing much worth either desiring or fearing. But these reflections, which suit with seventy, would be greatly premature at two-and-thirty. So make the best of your time, enjoy the present hour; but *memor ultimæ.*[1] God bless you !

LETTER CCCXLI.

My dear Friend,   Bath, December the 18th, 1763.

I received your letter this morning, in which you reproach me with not having written to you this week. The reason was that I did not know what to write. There is that sameness in my life here, that *every day is still but as the first.* I see very few people ; and, in the literal sense of the word, I hear nothing.

Mr L—— and Mr C—— I hold to be two very ingenious men ; and your image of the two men ruined, one by losing his lawsuit, and the other by carrying it, is a very just one. To be sure they felt in themselves uncommon talents for business and speaking, which were to reimburse them.

Harte has a great poetical work to publish, before it be long ; he has shown me some parts of it. He had entitled it Emblems; but I persuaded him to alter that name, for two reasons : the first was, because they were not emblems, but fables : the second was, that, if they had been emblems, Quarles had degraded and vilified that name, to such a degree, that it is impossible to make use of it after him : so they are to be called fables, though moral tales would, in my mind, be the properest name. If you ask me what I think of those I have seen, I must say that *sunt plura bona, quædam mediocria, et quædam*——[2]

---

[1] Be mindful of the last.
[2] Many of them are good, some commonplace, and some——

Your report of future changes, I cannot think is wholly groundless : for it still runs strongly in my head that the mine we talked of will be sprung, at, or before, the end of the session.

I have got a little more strength, but not quite the strength of Hercules ; so that I will not undertake, like him, fifty deflorations in one night; for I really believe that I could not compass them. So good night, and God bless you !

LETTER CCCXLII.

MY DEAR FRIEND,   Bath, December the 24th, 1763.

I CONFESS I was a good deal surprised at your pressing me so strongly to influence parson Rosenhagen, when you well know the resolution I had made several years ago, and which I have scrupulously observed ever since, not to concern myself, directly or indirectly, in any party political contest whatsoever. Let Parties go to loggerheads as much and as long as they please, I will neither endeavour to part them, nor take the part of either; for I know them all too well. But you say that Lord Sandwich has been remarkably civil and kind to you. I am very glad of it ; and he can by no means impute to you my obstinacy, folly, or philosophy ; call it what you please : you may with great truth assure him, that you did all you could to obey his commands.

I am sorry to find that you are out of order, but I hope it is only a cold ; should it be anything more, pray consult Dr Maty, who did you so much good in your last illness, when the great medicinal Mattadores did you rather harm. I have found a Monsieur *Diafoirus* here, Dr Moisy, who has really done me a great deal of good ; and I am sure I wanted it a great deal, when I came here first. I have recovered some strength, and a little more will give me as much as I can make use of.

Lady Brown, whom I saw yesterday, makes you many compliments : and I wish you a merry Christmas, and a good night.
            Adieu.

LETTER CCCXLIII.

MY DEAR FRIEND,   Bath, December the 31st, 1763.

GREVENKOP wrote me word, by the last post, that you were laid up with the gout ; but I much question it; that is, whether it is the gout or not. Your last illness, before you went abroad, was pronounced the gout by the skilful ; and proved at last a mere rheumatism. Take care that the same mistake is not made this year ; and that, by giving you strong and hot medicines to throw out the gout, they do not inflame the rheumatism, if it be one.

Mr Wilkes has imitated some of the great men of antiquity, by going into voluntary exile : it was his only way of defeating both his creditors and his prosecutors. Whatever his friends, if he has any, give out of his returning soon, I will answer for it, that it will be a long time before that *soon* comes.

I have been much out of order these four days, of a violent cold ; which I do not know how I got, and which obliged me to suspend drinking the waters : but is now so much better that I propose resuming them for this week, and paying my court to you in town on Monday or Tuesday sevennight ; but this is *sub spe rati* only. God bless you !

LETTER CCCXLIV.

My dear Friend,   Blackheath, July the 20th, 1764.

I have this moment received your letter of the 3rd, from Prague, but I never received that which you mention from Ratisbon ; this made me think you in such rapid motion, that I did not know where to take aim. I now suppose that you are arrived, though not yet settled, at Dresden ; your audiences and formalities are, to be sure, over, and that is great ease of mind to you.

I have no political events to acquaint you with ; the summer is not the season for them, they ripen only in winter ; great ones are expected immediately before the meeting of Parliament, but that, you know, is always the language of fears and hopes. However, I rather believe that there will be something patched up between the *ins* and *outs*.

The whole subject of conversation, at present, is the Death and Will of Lord Bath : he has left above twelve hundred thousand pounds in land and money, four hundred thousand pounds in cash, stocks, and mortgages ; his own estate, in land, was improved to fifteen thousand pounds a year, and the Bradford estate, which he * *, is as much ; both which, at only five-and-twenty years' purchase, amount to eight hundred thousand pounds ; and all this he has left to his brother, General Pulteney, and in his own disposal, though he never loved him. The legacies he has left are trifling, for, in truth, he cared for nobody ; the words *give* and *bequeath* were too shocking to him to repeat, and so he left all, in one word, to his brother. The public, which was long the dupe of his simulation and dissimulation, begins to explain upon him ; and draws such a picture of him as I gave you long ago.

Your late Secretary has been with me three or four times ; he wants something or another, and it seems all one to him what, whether civil or military ; in plain English, he wants bread. He has knocked at the doors of some of the Ministers, but to no purpose. I wish with all my heart that I could help him : I told him fairly that I could not, but advised him to find some channel to Lord B * * *, which, though a Scotchman, he told me he could not. He brought a packet of letters from the office to you, which I made him seal up ; and I keep it for you, as I suppose it makes up the series of your Ratisbon letters.

As for me, I am just what I was when you left me, that is, nobody. Old age steals upon me insensibly. I grow weak and decrepit ; but do not suffer, and so I am content.

Forbes brought me four books of yours, two of which were Bielefeldt's letters ; in which, to my knowledge, there are many notorious lies.

Make my compliments to Comte Einsiedel, whom I love and honour much ; and so good night to *seine Excellentz.*

Now our correspondence may be more regular, and I expect a letter from you every fortnight. I will be regular on my part : but write oftener to your mother, if it be but three lines.

LETTER CCCXLV.

My dear Friend   Blackheath, July the 27th, 1764.

I received, two days ago, your letter of the 11th, from Dresden, where I am very glad that you are safely arrived at last. The prices of the necessaries of life are monstrous there ; and I do not conceive how the poor natives subsist at all, after having been so long and so often plundered by their own as well as by other Sovereigns.

As for procuring you either the title or the appointments of Plenipotentiary, I could as soon procure them from the Turkish as from the English Ministry; and, in truth, I believe they have it not to give.

Now to come to your Civil List, if one may compare small things with great. I think I have found out a better refreshment for it than you propose; for to-morrow I shall send to your cashier, Mr Larpent, five hundred pounds at once, for your use, which, I presume, is better than by quarterly payments; and I am very apt to think, that, next Midsummer-day, he will have the same sum, and for the same use, consigned to him.

It is reported here, and I believe not without some foundation, that the Queen of Hungary has acceded to the Family Compact between France and Spain; if so, I am sure it behoves us to form in time a counter alliance, of at least equal strength; which I could easily point out, but which, I fear, is not thought of here.

The rage of marrying is very prevalent; so that there will be probably a great crop of cuckolds next winter, who are at present only *cocus en herbe.* It will contribute to population, and so far must be allowed to be a public benefit. Lord G—, Mr B—, and Mr D——, are, in this respect, very meritorious; for they have all married handsome women, without one shilling fortune. Lord —— must indeed take some pains to arrive at that dignity; but I dare say he will bring it about, by the help of some young Scotch or Irish officer. Good night, and God bless you!

———◇———

LETTER CCCXLVI.

MY DEAR FRIEND,   Blackheath, Sept. the 3rd, 1764.

I HAVE received your letter of the 13th past. I see that your complete arrangement approaches, and you need not be in a hurry to give entertainments, since so few others do.

Comte Flemming is the man in the world the best calculated to retrieve the Saxon finances, which have been all this century squandered and lavished with the most absurd profusion: he has certainly abilities, and I believe integrity; I dare answer for him, that the gentleness and flexibility of his temper will not prevail with him to yield to the importunities of craving and petulant applications. I see in him another Sully; and therefore I wish he were at the head of our finances.

France and Spain both insult us, and we take it too tamely: for this is, in my opinion, the time for us to talk high to them. France, I am persuaded, will not quarrel with us till it has got a Navy at least equal to ours, which cannot be these three or four years, at soonest; and then, indeed, I believe, we shall hear of something or other; therefore this is the moment for us to speak loud, and we shall be feared, if we do not show that we fear.

Here is no domestic news of changes and chances in the political world; which, like oysters, are only in season in the R months, when Parliament sits. I think there will be some then, but of what kind, God knows.

I have received a book for you, and one for myself, from Harte. It is upon agriculture, and will surprise you, as, I confess, it did me. This work is not only in English, but good and elegant English; he has even scattered graces upon his subject, and, in prose, has come very near Virgil's Georgics in verse. I have written to him, to congratulate his happy transformation. As soon as I can find an opportunity I will send you your copy. You (though no Agricola) will read it with pleasure.

I know Mackenzie, whom you mention. *C'est un délié, sed cave.*[1]

Make mine and Lady Chesterfield's compliments to Comte et Comtesse Flemming: and so, *Dieu vous ait en sa sainte garde.*

LETTER CCCXLVII.

My dear Friend,   Blackheath, Sept. the 14th, 1764.

YESTERDAY I received your letter of the 30th past, by which I find that you had not then got mine, which I sent you the day after I had received your former; you have had no great loss of it; for, as I told you in my last, this inactive season of the year supplies no materials for a letter; the winter may, and probably will, produce an abundant crop, but of what grain, I neither know, guess, nor care. I take it for granted that Lord B * * * *surnagera encore*,[2] but by the assistance of what bladders or cork-waistcoats, God only knows. The death of poor Mr Legge, the epileptic fits of the Duke of Devonshire, for which he is gone to Aix-la-Chapelle, and the advanced age of the Duke of Newcastle, seem to facilitate an accommodation, if Mr Pitt and Lord Bute are inclined to it.

You ask me what I think of the death of poor Iwan, and

---

[1] He is a sharp fellow, but beware.
[2] Float again yet.

of the person [1] who ordered it. You may remember that I
often said she would murder or marry him, or probably both ;
she has chosen the safest alternative ; and has now completed
her character of *femme forte*, above scruples and hesitation.
If Machiavel were alive, she would probably be his Heroine, as
Cæsar Borgia was his Hero. Women are all so far Machiave-
lians, that they are never either good or bad by halves ; their
passions are too strong, and their reason too weak, to do anything with moderation. She will perhaps meet, before it is
long, with some Scythian as free from prejudices as herself. If
there is one Oliver Cromwell in the three regiments of guards,
he will probably, for the sake of his dear country, depose and
murder her : for that is one and the same thing in Russia.

You seem now to be settled, and *bien nippé* [2] at Dresden.
Four sedentary footmen, and one running one, *font Equipage
leste*.[3] The German ones will give you, *seine Excellentz ;* and
the French ones, if you have any, *Monseigneur*.

My own health varies, as usual, but never deviates into
good. God bless you, and send you better !

LETTER CCCXLVIII.

MY DEAR FRIEND,   Blackheath, Oct. the 4th, 1764.

I HAVE now your last letter of the 16th past lying before
me ; and I gave your enclosed to Grevenkop, which has put
him into a violent bustle to execute your commissions, as well
and as cheap as possible. I refer him to his own letter. He
tells you true, as to Comtesse Cosel's diamonds, which certainly
nobody will buy here, unsight unseen, as they call it : so many
minuties concurring to increase or lessen the value of a diamond. Your Cheshire cheese, your Burton ale and beer, I
charge myself with, and they shall be sent you as soon as possible. Upon this occasion I will give you a piece of advice,
which, by experience, I know to be useful. In all commissions,
whether from men or women, *point de galanterie*, bring them in
your account, and be paid to the uttermost farthing ; but if you
would show them *une galanterie*, let your present be of something that is not in your commission, otherwise you will be the
Commissionaire banal of all the women of Saxony. *A propos ;*
Who is your Comtesse de Cosel ? Is she daughter, or grand-

---

[1] Catherine II. of Russia.
[2] Well rigged out.   [3] Make a smart turn out.

daughter, of the famous Madame de Cosel, in King Augustus's time? Is she young or old, ugly or handsome?

I do not wonder that people are wonderfully surprised at our tameness and forbearance, with regard to France and Spain. Spain, indeed, has lately agreed to our cutting logwood, according to the treaty, and sent strict orders to their Governor to allow it; but you will observe, too, that there is not one word of reparation for the losses we lately sustained there. But France is not even so tractable; it will pay but half the money due, upon a liquidated account, for the maintenance of their prisoners. Our request, to have Comte d'Estaing recalled and censured, they have absolutely rejected, though by the laws of war he might be hanged for having twice broke his parole. This does not do France honour; however, I think we shall be quiet, and that at the only time, perhaps this century, when we might with safety be otherwise; but this is nothing new, nor the first time, by many, when national honour and interest have been sacrificed to private. It has always been so: and one may say, upon this occasion, what Horace says upon another, *Nam fuit ante Helenam.*

I have seen *les Contes de Guillaume Vadé*, and like most of them, so little, that I can hardly think them Voltaire's, but rather the scraps that have fallen from his table, and been worked up by inferior workmen under his name. I have not seen the other book you mention, the *Dictionnaire Portatif.* It is not yet come over.

I shall next week go to take my winter-quarters in London, the weather here being very cold and damp, and not proper for an old, shattered, and cold carcass, like mine. In November I will go to the Bath, to careen myself for the winter, and to shift the scene. Good night.

LETTER CCCXLIX.

My dear Friend,   London, October the 19th, 1764.

Yesterday morning Mr * * came to me, from Lord Halifax, to ask me whether I thought you would approve of vacating your seat in Parliament, during the remainder of it, upon a valuable consideration, meaning *money.* My answer was, that I really did not know your disposition upon that subject; but that I knew you would be very willing, in general, to accommodate them, as far as lay in your power. That your Election, to my knowledge, had cost you two thousand pounds ; that this Parliament had not sat above half its time ; and that, for my part, I approved of the measure well enough, provided you had an equitable equivalent. I·take it for granted that you will have a letter from ——, by this post, to that effect, so that you must consider what you will do. What I advise, is this ; give them a good deal of *Galbanum* [1] in the first part of your letter. *Le Galbanum ne coute rien ;* and then say, that you are willing to do as they please ; but that you hope an equitable consideration will be had to the two thousand pounds, which your seat cost you in the present Parliament, of which not above half the term is expired. Moreover, that you take the liberty to remind them, that your being sent for from Ratisbon, last session, when you were just settled there, put you to the expense of three or four hundred pounds, for which you were allowed nothing ; and that, therefore, you hope they will not think one thousand pounds too much, considering all these circumstances ; but that, in all events, you will do whatever they desire. Upon the whole, I think this proposal advantageous to you, as you probably will not make use of your seat this Parliament ; and further, as it will secure you from another unpaid journey from Dresden, in case they meet or fear to meet with difficulties in any ensuing session of the present Parliament. Whatever one must do, one should do *de bonne grâce*. *Dixi.* God bless you !

LETTER CCCL.

MY DEAR FRIEND, Bath, November the 10th, 1764.

I AM much concerned at the account you gave me of yourself in your last letter. There is, to be sure, at such a town as Dresden, at least some one very skilful physician ; whom I hope you have consulted ; and I would have you acquaint him with all your several attacks of this nature, from your great one at Laubach, to your late one at Dresden : tell him too, that, in your last illness in England, the physicians mistook your case, and treated it as the gout, till Maty came, who treated it as a rheumatism, and cured you. In my own opinion you have never had the gout, but always the rheumatism ; which, to my knowledge, is as painful as the gout can possibly be, and should be treated in a quite different way ; that is, by cooling medicines

[1]·Soft sawder.

and regimen, instead of those inflammatory cordials which they always administer, where they suppose the gout, to keep it, as they say, out of the stomach.

I have been here now just a week ; but have hitherto drank so little of the water that I can neither speak well nor ill of it. The number of people in this place is infinite ; but very few whom I know. Harte seems settled here for life. He is not well, that is certain ; but not so ill neither as he thinks himself, or at least would be thought.

I long for your answer to my last letter, containing a certain proposal, which by this time, I suppose, has been made you, and which, in the main, I approve of your accepting.

God bless you, my dear friend, and send you better health ! Adieu.

LETTER CCCLI.

My dear Friend,   London, Feb. the 26th, 1765.

Your last letter of the 5th, gave me as much pleasure as your former had given me uneasiness; and Larpent's acknowledgment of his negligence frees you from those suspicions, which I own I did entertain, and which I believe every one would, in the same concurrence of circumstances, have entertained. So much for that.

You may depend upon what I promised you, before Mid-summer next, at furthest, and *at least.*

All I can say of the affair between you of the *Corps Diplomatique,* and the Saxon Ministers, is *que violà bien du bruit pour une omelette au lard.*[1] It will most certainly be soon made up ; and in that negotiation show yourself as moderate and healing as your instructions from hence will allow, especially to Comte Flemming. The King of Prussia, I believe, has a mind to insult him personally, as an old enemy, or else to quarrel with Saxony, that does not quarrel with him ; but some of the *Corps Diplomatique* here assure me, it is only a pretence to recall his Envoy, and to send, when matters shall be made up, a little Secretary there, *à moins de fraix,* as he does now to Paris and London.

Comte Brühl is much in fashion here ; I like him mightily; he has very much *le ton de la bonne compagnie.* Poor Schrader died last Saturday, without the least pain or sickness. God bless you !

[1] A great noise about an omelette of bacon, i.e. much ado about nothing.

LETTER CCCLII.

MY DEAR FRIEND,   London, April the 22nd, 1765.

THE day before yesterday I received your letter of the 3rd instant. I find that your important affair of the Ceremonial is adjusted at last, as I foresaw it would be. Such *minuties* are often laid hold on as a pretence, for Powers who have a mind to quarrel ; but are never tenaciously insisted upon, where there is neither interest nor inclination to break. Comte Flemming, though a hot, is a wise man ; and I was sure would not break both with England and Hanover, upon so trifling a point, especially during a minority. *A propos* of a minority ; the King is to come to the House to-morrow, to recommend a bill to settle a Regency, in case of his demise while his successor is a minor. Upon the King's late illness, which was no trifling one, the whole nation cried out aloud for such a bill, for reasons which will readily occur to you, who know situations, persons, and characters here. I do not know the particulars of this intended bill ; but I wish it may be copied exactly from that which was passed in the late King's time, when the present King was a minor. I am sure there cannot be a better.

You inquire about Monsieur de Guerchy's affair, and I will give you as succinct an account as I can of so extraordinary and perplexed a transaction ; but without giving you my own opinion of it, by the common post. You know what passed at first between Mr de Guerchy and Monsieur D'Eon, in which both our Ministers and Monsieur de Guerchy, from utter inexperience in business, puzzled themselves into disagreeable difficulties. About three or four months ago Monsieur du Vergy published, in a *brochure,* a parcel of letters, from himself to the Duc de Choiseul ; in which he positively asserts that Monsieur de Guerchy prevailed with him (Vergy) to come over into England to assassinate D'Eon ; the words are, as well as I remember, *que ce n'étoit pas pour se servir de sa plume, mais de son Epée, qu'on le demandoit en Angleterre.*[1] This accusation of assassination, you may imagine, shocked Monsieur de Guerchy, who complained bitterly to our Ministers ; and they both puzzled on for some time, without doing anything, because they did not know what to do. At last du Vergy, about two months ago, applied himself to the Grand Jury of Middlesex, and made oath, that Mr de Guerchy had hired him (du Vergy) to assassinate

[1] That it was not to use his pen, but his sword, that they required him in England.

D'Eon. Upon this deposition, the Grand Jury found a bill of intended murder against Monsieur de Guerchy ; which bill, however, never came to the Petty Jury. The King granted a *noli prosequi* in favour of Monsieur de Guerchy ; and the Attorney General is actually prosecuting du Vergy. Whether the King can grant a *noli prosequi* in a criminal case, and whether *le Droit des gens* extends to criminal cases, are two points which employ our domestic politicians, and the whole *Corps Diplomatique*. *Enfin*, to use a very coarse and vulgar saying, *il y a de la merde au bout du bâton, quelque part*.[1]

I see and hear these storms from shore, *suave mari magno, &c.* I enjoy my own security and tranquillity, together with better health than I had reason to expect, at my age, and with my constitution : however, I feel a gradual decay, though a gentle one ; and I think I shall not tumble, but slide gently to the bottom of the hill of life. When that will be I neither know nor care, for I am very weary. . God bless you !

Mallet died, two days ago, of a diarrhœa, which he had carried with him to France, and brought back again hither.

LETTER CCCLIII.

My dear Friend,   Blackheath, July the 2nd, 1765.

I have this moment received your letter of the 22nd past ; and I delayed answering your former, in daily, or rather hourly, expectation of informing you of the birth of a new Ministry ; but in vain ; for, after a thousand conferences, all things remain still in the state which I described to you in my last. Lord S. has, I believe, given you a pretty true account of the present state of things ; but my Lord is much mistaken, I am persuaded, when he says that *the King has thought proper to re-establish his old servants in the management of his affairs ;* for he shows them all the public dislike possible ; and, at his levee, hardly speaks to any of them ; but speaks by the hour to anybody else. Conferences, in the mean time, go on, of which it is easy to guess the main subject, but impossible, for me at least, to know the particulars ; but this I will venture to prophesy, that the whole will soon centre in Mr Pitt.

You seem not to know the character of the Queen : here it is—She is a good woman, a good wife, a tender mother, and an unmeddling Queen. The King loves her as a woman ; but,

[1] There is dirt somewhere at the end of the stick.

I verily believe, has never yet spoken one word to her about business. I have now told you all that I know of these affairs; which, I believe, is as much as anybody else knows, who is not in the secret. In the mean time, you easily guess, that surmises, conjectures, and reports, are infinite; and if, as they say, truth is but one, one million at least of these reports must be false; for they differ exceedingly.

You have lost an honest servant, by the death of poor *Louis*; I would advise you to take a clever young Saxon in his room, of whose character you may get authentic testimonies; instead of sending for one to France, whose character you can only know from far.

When I hear more, I will write more; till when, God bless you!

———

LETTER CCCLIV.

My dear Friend,   Blackheath, July the 15th, 1765.

I TOLD you in my last that you should hear from me again, as soon as I had anything more to write; and now I have too much to write, therefore will refer you to the Gazette, and the office letters, for all that has been done; and advise you to suspend your opinion, as I do, about all that is to be done. Many more changes are talked of; but so idly, and variously, that I give credit to none of them. There has been pretty clean sweeping already; and I do not remember, in my time, to have seen so much at once, as an entire new Board of Treasury, and two new Secretaries of State, *cum multis aliis, &c.*

Here is a new political arch almost built, but of materials of so different a nature, and without a key-stone, that it does not, in my opinion, indicate either strength or duration. It will certainly require repairs, and a key-stone, next winter; and that key-stone will and must necessarily be Mr Pitt. It is true, he might have been that key-stone now; and would have accepted it, but not without Lord Temple's consent; and Lord Temple positively refused. There was evidently some trick in this, but what, is past my conjecturing. *Davus sum non Œdipus.*[1]

There is a manifest interregnum in the Treasury; for I do suppose that Lord Rockingham and Mr Dowdeswell will not think proper to be very active. General Conway, who is your Secretary, has certainly parts at least equal to his business, to which I dare say he will apply. The same may be said, I

[1] I am Davus not Œdipus.

believe, of the Duke of Grafton ; and indeed there is no magic requisite for the executive part of those employments. The ministerial part is another thing ; they must scramble with their fellow-
servants, for power and favour, as well as they can. Foreign
affairs are not so much as mentioned, and, I verily believe,
not thought of. But surely some counterbalance would be necessary to the Family Compact ; and, if not soon contracted, will be
too late. God bless you !

LETTER CCCLV.

MY DEAR FRIEND,   Blackheath, Aug. the 17th, 1765.

YOU are now two letters in my debt ; and I fear the gout
has been the cause of your contracting that debt. When you
are not able to write yourself, let your Secretary send me two
or three lines to acquaint me how you are.

You have now seen, by the London Gazette, what changes
have really been made at Court; but, at the same time, I believe
you have seen that there must be more, before a Ministry can
be settled ; what those will be, God knows. Were I to conjecture, I should say that the whole will centre, before it is long,
in Mr Pitt and Co., the present being an heterogeneous jumble
of youth and caducity, which cannot be efficient.

Charles Townshend calls the present a Lutestring Ministry;
fit only for the summer. The next session will be not only a
warm but a violent one, as you will easily judge, if you look
over the names of the *ins* and of the *outs*.

I feel this beginning of the autumn, which is already
very cold : the leaves are withered, fall apace, and seem to
intimate that I must follow them ; which I shall do without
reluctance, being extremely weary of this silly world. God
bless you, both in it and after it !

LETTER CCCLVI.

MY DEAR FRIEND,   Blackheath, Aug. the 25th, 1765.

I RECEIVED but four days ago your letter of the 2nd instant.
I find by it that you are well, for you are in good spirits.
Your notion of the new birth or regeneration of the Ministry,
is a very just one ; and that they have not yet the true seal of

the covenant is, I dare say, very true ; at least, it is not in the possession of either of the Secretaries of State, who have only the King's seal ; nor do I believe (whatever his Grace may imagine) that it is even in the possession of the Lord Privy Seal. I own I am lost, in considering the present situation of affairs ; different conjectures present themselves to my mind, but none that it can rest upon. The next session must necessarily clear up matters a good deal ; for I believe it will be the warmest and most acrimonious one that has been known, since that of the Excise. The late Ministry, *the present Opposition*, are determined to attack Lord B—— publicly in Parliament, and reduce the late Opposition, *the present Ministry*, to protect him publicly, in consequence of their supposed treaty with him. *En attendant mieux*, the paper war is carried on with much fury and scurrility on all sides, to the great entertainment of such lazy and impartial people as myself. I do not know whether you have the Daily Advertiser and the Public Advertiser ; in which all the political letters are inserted, and some very well written ones on both sides ; but I know that they amuse me, *tant bien que mal*, for an hour or two every morning. Lord T—— is the supposed author of the pamphlet you mention ; but I think it is above him. Perhaps his brother C—— T——, who is by no means satisfied with the present arrangement, may have assisted him privately. As to this latter, there was a good ridiculous paragraph in the newspapers two or three days ago : *We hear that the Right Honourable Mr C—— T—— is indisposed at his house in Oxfordshire, of a pain in his side ; but it is not said in which side.*

I do not find that the Duke of York has yet visited you ; if he should, it may be expensive, *mais on trouvera moyen*. As for the Lady, if you should be very sharp set for some English flesh, she has it amply in her power to supply you, if she pleases. Pray tell me, in your next, what you think of, and how you like, Prince Henry of Prussia. God bless you !

———⋄———

LETTER CCCLVII.

My dear Friend,   .

Your great character of Prince Henry, which I take to be a very just one, lowers the King of Prussia's a great deal ; and probably that is the cause of their being so ill together. But the King of Prussia, with his good parts, should reflect upon that trite and true maxim, *Qui invidet minor*,[1] or Mr de la Rochefoucault's *Que l'envie est la plus basse de toutes les passions, puisqu'on avoue bien des crimes, mais que personne n'avoue l'envie.*[2] I thank God, I never was sensible of that dark and vile passion, except, that formerly I have sometimes envied a successful rival with a fine woman. But now that cause is ceased, and consequently the effects.

What shall I, or rather what can I, tell you of the political world here? The late Ministers accuse the present with having done nothing; the present accuse the late ones with having done much worse than nothing. Their writers abuse one another most scurrilously, but sometimes with wit. I look upon this to be *peloter en attendant partie*, till battle begins in St Stephen's Chapel. How that will end I protest I cannot conjecture; any further than this, that, if Mr Pitt does not come in to the assistance of the present Ministers, they will have mnch to do to stand their ground. C—— T—— will play booty; and whom else have they? Nobody but C——; who has only good sense, but not the necessary talents nor experience, *Ære ciere viros martemque accendere cantu.*[3] I never remember, in all my time, to have seen so problematical a state of affairs; and a man would be much puzzled which side to bet on.

Your guest, Miss C——, is another problem which I cannot solve. She no more wanted the waters of Carlsbadt than you did. Is it to show the Duke of K—— that he cannot live without her? A dangerous experiment! which may possibly convince him that he can. There is a trick, no doubt, in it; but what, I neither know nor care; you did very well to show her civilities, *cela ne gâte jamais rien.* I will go to my waters, that is, the Bath waters, in three weeks or a month, more for the sake of bathing than of drinking. The hot bath always promotes my perspiration, which is sluggish, and supples my stiff rheumatic limbs. *D'ailleurs*, I am at present as well, and better, than I could reasonably expect to be, *anno septuagesimo primo.* May you be so as long, *y mas.*[4] God bless you!

[1] It is the inferior who envies.
[2] Envy is the basest of all passions, since men confess to many crimes, but no one confesses to envy.
[3] To rouse men by the sword, and incite war by a song.
[4] And more.

LETTER CCCLVIII.

MY DEAR FRIEND,   London, October the 25th, 1765.

I RECEIVED your letter of the 10th *sonica ;* for I set out for
Bath to-morrow morning. If the use of those waters does me
no good, the shifting the scene for some time will at least amuse
me a little ; and at my age, and with my infirmities, *il faut
faire de tout bois fléche.*[1]   Some variety is as necessary for the
mind as some medicines are for the body.

Here is a total stagnation of politics, which, I suppose, will
continue till the Parliament sits to do business, and that will not
be till about the middle of January ; for the meeting on the
17th December is only for the sake of some new writs.   The
late Ministers threaten the present ones ; but the latter do not
seem in the least afraid of the former, and for a very good
reason, which is, that they have the distribution of the loaves
and fishes.   I believe it is very certain that Mr Pitt will never
come into this or any other Administration ; he is absolutely a
cripple all the year, and in violent pain at least half of it.
Such physical ills are great checks to two of the strongest passions to which human nature is liable, love and ambition.
Though I cannot persuade myself that the present Ministry can
be long-lived, I can as little imagine who or what can succeed
them, *telle est la disette de sujets Papables.*[2]   The Duke of ——
swears that he will have Lord —— personally attacked in both
Houses ; but I do not see how, without endangering himself at
the same time.

Miss C—— is safely arrived here, and her Duke is fonder of
her than ever.   It was a dangerous experiment that she tried,
in leaving him so long ; but it seems she knew her man.

I pity you, for the inundation of your good countrymen,
which overwhelms you ; *je sais ce qu'en vaut l'aune.*[3]   It is, besides, expensive ; but, as I look upon the expense to be the
least evil of the two, I will see if a New-year's gift will not
make it up.

As I am now upon the wing, I will only add, God bless
you !

[1] To make any shift.   [2] Such is the scarcity of great men.
[3] I know what a yard is worth.

LETTER CCCLIX.

MY DEAR FRIEND,   Bath, November the 28th, 1765.

I HAVE this moment received your letter of the 10th. I have now been here near a month, bathing and drinking the waters, for complaints much of the same kind as yours ; I mean pains in my legs, hips, and arms ; whether gouty or rheumatic, God knows ; but, I believe, both, that fight without a decision in favour of either, and have absolutely reduced me to the miserable situation of the Sphynx's riddle, to walk upon three legs ; that is, with the assistance of my stick, to walk, or rather hobble, very indifferently. I wish it were a declared gout, which is the distemper of a gentleman ; whereas the rheumatism is the distemper of a hackney-coachman or chairman, who are obliged to be out in all weathers and at all hours.

I think you will do very right to ask leave, and I dare say you will easily get it, to go to the baths in Suabia ; that is, supposing you have consulted some skilful physician, if such a one there be, either at Dresden or at Leipsic, about the nature of your distemper, and the nature of those baths ; but, *suos quisque patimur manes.*[1] We have but a bad bargain, God knows, of this life, and patience is the only way not to make bad worse. Mr Pitt keeps his bed here, with a very real gout, and not a political one, as is often suspected.

Here has been a congress of most of the *ex Ministres.* If they have raised a battery, as I suppose they have, it is a masked one, for nothing has transpired ; only they confess, that they intend a most vigorous attack. *D'ailleurs*, there seems to be a total suspension of all business, till the meeting of the Parliament, and then *Signa canant.*[2] I am very glad that, at this time, you are out of it ; and for reasons that I need not mention : you would certainly have been sent for over, and, as before, not paid for your journey.

Poor Harte is very ill, and condemned to the Hot-well at Bristol. He is a better poet than philosopher ; for all this illness and melancholy proceeds originally from the ill success of his Gustavus Adolphus. He is grown extremely devout, which I am very glad of, because that is always a comfort to the afflicted.

I cannot present Mr Larpent with my New-year's gift, till I

---

[1] We all suffer our own punishments.
[2] They will give the watch-word.

come to town, which will be before Christmas, at furthest; till when, God bless you! Adieu.

LETTER CCCLX.

MY DEAR FRIEND,   London, December the 27th, 1765.

I ARRIVED here from Bath last Monday, rather, but not much, better than when I went thither. My rheumatic pains, in my legs and hips, plague me still; and I must never expect to be quite free from them.

You have, to be sure, had from the office an account of what the Parliament did, or rather did not do, the day of their meeting: and the same point will be the great object at their next meeting; I mean the affair of our American Colonies, relatively to the late imposed Stamp duty; which our Colonists absolutely refuse to pay. The Administration are for some indulgence and forbearance to those froward children of their mother country: the Opposition are for taking vigorous, as they call them, but I call them violent, measures; not less than *les dragonades;* and to have the tax collected by the troops we have there. For my part, I never saw a froward child mended by whipping: and I would not have the mother country become a stepmother. Our trade to America brings in, *communibus annis,* two millions a year; and the Stamp-duty is estimated at but one hundred thousand pounds a year; which I would by no means bring into the stock of the Exchequer, at the loss, or even the risk, of a million a year to the national stock.

I do not tell you of the Garter, given away yesterday, because the newspapers will; but I must observe, that the Prince of Brunswick's riband is a mark of great distinction to that family; which, I believe, is the first (except our own Royal family) that has ever had two blue ribands at a time; but it must be owned they deserved them.

One hears of nothing now, in town, but the separation of men and their wives. Will Finch the ex-vice-Chamberlain, Lord Warwick, and your friend Lord Bolingbroke. I wonder at none of them for parting; but I wonder at many for still living together; for in this country it is certain that marriage is not well understood.

I have this day sent Mr Larpent two hundred pounds for your Christmas-box, which I suppose he will inform you of by this post. Make this Christmas as merry a one as you can;

for *pour le peu de bon tems qui nous reste, rien n'est si funeste qu'un noir chagrin.*[1] For the new years, God send you many, and happy ones! Adieu.

LETTER CCCLXI.

MY DEAR FRIEND,   London, February the 11th, 1766.

I RECEIVED, two days ago, your letter of the 25th past; and your former, which you mention in it, but ten days ago; this may easily be accounted for from the badness of the weather, and consequently of the roads. I hardly remember so severe a winter; it has occasioned many illnesses here. I am sure it pinched my crazy carcass so much, that, about three weeks ago, I was obliged to be let blood twice in four days; which I found afterwards was very necessary, by the relief it gave to my head, and to the rheumatic pains in my limbs; and from the execrable kind of blood which I lost.

Perhaps you expect from me a particular account of the present state of affairs here; but, if you do, you will be disappointed; for no man living (and I still less than any one) knows what it is; it varies, not only daily, but hourly. Most people think, and I among the rest, that the date of the present Ministers is pretty near out; but how soon we are to have a new style, God knows. This, however, is certain, that the Ministers had a contested election in the House of Commons, and got it by eleven votes; too small a majority to carry anything: the next day they lost a question in the House of Lords, by three. The question in the House of Lords was, to enforce the execution of the Stamp Act in the Colonies *vi et armis*. What conclusions you will draw from these premises, I do not know: I protest I draw none; but only stare at the present undecipherable state of affairs, which, in fifty years' experience, I have never seen anything like. The Stamp Act has proved a most pernicious measure; for, whether it is repealed or not, which is still very doubtful, it has given such terror to the Americans, that our trade with them will not be, for some years, what it used to be. Great numbers of our manufacturers at home will be turned a starving, for want of that employment, which our very profitable trade to America found them: and hunger is always the cause of tumults and sedition.

[1] For the few happy seasons which are left us, nothing is so fatal as peevish vexation.

As you have escaped a fit of the gout in this severe cold weather, it is to be hoped you may be entirely free from it, till next winter at least.

P. S. Lord ——, having parted with his wife, now keeps another w——e, at a great expense. I fear he is totally undone.

LETTER CCCLXII.

MY DEAR FRIEND,   London, March the 17th, 1766.

You wrong me, in thinking me in your debt ; for I never receive a letter of yours, but I answer it by the next post, or the next but one, at furthest: but I can easily conceive that my two last letters to you may have been drowned or frozen in their way ; for portents, and prodigies of frost, snow, and inundations, have been so frequent this winter, that they have almost lost their names.

You tell me that you are going to the baths of *Baden ;* but that puzzles me a little, so I recommend this letter to the care of Mr Larpent, to forward to you ; for Baden I take to be the general German word for baths, and the particular ones are distinguished by some epithet, as Weissbaden, Carlsbaden, &c. I hope they are not cold baths, which I have a very ill opinion of, in all arthritic or rheumatic cases ; and your case I take to be a compound of both, but rather more of the latter.

You will probably wonder that I tell you nothing of public matters ; upon which I shall be as secret as Hotspur's gentle Kate, who would not tell what she did not know ; but, what is singular, nobody seems to know any more of them than I do. People gape, stare, conjecture, and refine. Changes of the Ministry, or in the Ministry, at least are daily reported and foretold ; but of what kind God only knows. It is also very doubtful whether Mr Pitt will come into the Administration or not ; the two present Secretaries are extremely desirous that he should ; but the others think of the horse that called the man to its assistance. I will say nothing to you about American affairs, because I have not pens, ink, or paper enough to give you an intelligible account of them. They have been the subjects of warm and acrimonious debates, both in the Lords and Commons, and in all companies.

The repeal of the Stamp Act is at last carried through. I am glad of it, and gave my proxy for it ; because I saw many more inconveniences from the enforcing than from the repealing it.

Colonel Browne was with me the other day, and assured me that he left you very well. He said that he saw me at Spa; but I did not remember him; though I remember his two brothers, the Colonel and the ravisher, very well. Your Saxon Colonel has the brogue exceedingly. Present my respects to Count Flemming; I am very sorry for the Countess's illness; she was a most well-bred woman.

You would hardly think that I gave a dinner to the Prince of Brunswick, your old acquaintance. I am glad it is over; but I could not avoid it. *Il m'a-voit accablé de politesses.*[1] God bless you!

LETTER CCCLXIII.

My DEAR FRIEND, Blackheath, June the 13th, 1766.

I RECEIVED, yesterday, your letter of the 30th past. I waited with impatience for it, not having received one from you of six weeks; nor your mother neither, who began to be very sure that you were dead, if not buried. You should write to her once a week, or at least once a fortnight; for women make no allowance for either business or laziness; whereas I can, by experience, make allowances for both: however, I wish you would generally write to me once a fortnight.

Last week I paid my Midsummer offering of five hundred pounds to Mr Larpent, for your use, as I suppose he has informed you. I am punctual, you must allow.

What account shall I give you of Ministerial affairs here? I protest I do not know: your own description of them is as exact a one as any I, who am upon the place, can give you. It is a total dislocation and *dérangement;* consequently, a total inefficiency. When the Duke of Grafton quitted the seals, he gave that very reason for it, in a speech in the House of Lords; he declared *that he had no objection to the persons or to the measures of the present Ministers; but that he thought they wanted strength and efficiency to carry on proper measures with success; and that he knew but one man* (meaning, as you will easily suppose, Mr Pitt) *who could give them that strength and solidity; that, under this person, he should be willing to serve in any capacity, not only as a General Officer, but as a pioneer; and would take up a spade and*

[1] He had overwhelmed me with polite attentions.

a mattock. When he quitted the seals, they were offered first to Lord Egmont, then to Lord Hardwicke ; who both declined them, probably for the same reasons that made the Duke of Grafton resign them : but, after their going a begging for some time, the Duke of —— begged them, and has them *faute de mieux.* Lord Mountstuart was never thought of for Vienna, where Lord Stormont returns in three months ; the former is going to be married to one of the Miss Windsors, a great fortune. To tell you the speculations, the reasonings, and the conjectures, either of the uninformed, or even of the best informed, public, upon the present wonderful situation of affairs, would take up much more time and paper than either you or I can afford, though we have neither of us a great deal of business at present.

I am in as good health as I could reasonably expect, at my age, and with my shattered carcass ; that is, from the waist up-wards : but downwards it is not the same ; for my limbs retain that stiffness and debility of my long rheumatism, I cannot walk half-an-hour at a time. As the autumn, and still more as the winter, approaches, take care to keep yourself very warm especially your legs and feet.

Lady Chesterfield sends you her compliments, and triumphs in the success of her plaster. God bless you !

———◇———

LETTER CCCLXIV.

My dear Friend,   Blackheath, July the 11th, 1766.

You are a happy mortal, to have your time thus employed between the Great and the Fair ; I hope you do the honours of your country to the latter. The Emperor by your account, seems to be very well for an Emperor ; who, by being above the other Monarchs in Europe, may justly be supposed to have had a proportionably worse education. I find, by your account of him, that he has been trained up to homicide, the only science in which Princes are ever instructed ; and with good reason, as their greatness and glory singly depend upon the numbers of their fellow-creatures, which their ambition exterminates. If a Sovereign should, by great accident, deviate into modera-tion, justice, and clemency, what a contemptible figure would he make in the catalogue of Princes ! I have always owned a great regard for King Log. From the interview at Torgaw, between the two Monarchs, they will be either a great deal better or worse together ; but I think rather the latter ; for our namesake, Philip de Comines, observes, that he never knew any good come from *l'abouchement des Rois*.[1] The King of Prussia will exert all his perspicacity to analyze his Imperial Majesty; and I would bet upon the one head of his Black Eagle, against the two heads of the Austrian Eagle; though two heads are said, proverbially, to be better than one. I wish I had the direction of both the Monarchs, and they should, together with some of their Allies, take Lorraine and Alsace from France. You will call me l'Abbé de St Pierre; but I only say what I wish; whereas he thought everything that he wished practicable.

Now to come home. Here are great bustles at Court, and a great change of persons is certainly very near. You will ask me, perhaps, who is to be out, and who is to be in? To which I answer, I do not know. My conjecture is, that, be the new settlement what it will, Mr Pitt will be at the head of it. If he is, I presume *qu'il aura mis de l'Eau dans son Vin par rapport à Mylord B——* ;[2] when that shall come to be known, as known it certainly will soon be, he may bid adieu to his popularity. A Minister, as Minister, is very apt to be the object of public dislike; and a Favourite, as Favourite, still more so. If any event of this kind happens, which (if it happens at all) I conjecture will be some time next week, you shall hear further from me.

I will follow your advice, and be as well as I can next winter, though I know I shall never be free from my flying rheumatic pains as long as I live; but whether that will be many years or few is extremely indifferent to me: in either case, God bless you!

LETTER CCCLXV.

My dear Friend,   Blackheath, August the 1st, 1766.

THE curtain was at last drawn up, the day before yesterday, and discovered the new actors, together with some of the old ones. I do not name them to you, because to-morrow's Gazette will do it full as well as I could. Mr Pitt, who had *carte blanche* given him, named every one of them: but what would you think he named himself for? Lord Privy Seal; and (what will astonish you, as it does every mortal here) Earl of Chatham. The joke here is, that he has had *a fall up-stairs*, and has done

---

[1] Conference between kings.
[2] Will have put water into his wine, i. e. be more prudent in respect to.

himself so much hurt, that he will never be able to stand upon his legs again. Everybody is puzzled how to account for this step; though it would not be the first time that great abilities have been duped by low cunning. But, be it what it will, he is now, certainly, only Earl of Chatham; and no longer Mr Pitt, in any respect whatever. Such an event, I believe, was never read nor heard of. To withdraw, in the fulness of his power, and in the utmost gratification of his ambition, from the House of Commons (which procured him his power, and which could alone insure it to him), and to go into that Hospital of Incurables, the House of Lords, is a measure so unaccountable, that nothing but proof positive could have made me believe it: but true it is. Hans Stanley is to go Embassador to Russia; and my Nephew, Ellis, to Spain, decorated with the red riband. Lord Shelburne is your Secretary of State, which I suppose he has notified to you this post, by a circular letter. Charles Townshend has now the sole management of the House of Commons; but how long he will be content to be only Lord Chatham's vicegerent there, is a question which I will not pretend to decide. There is one very bad sign for Lord Chatham, in his new dignity; which is, that all his enemies, without exception, rejoice at it; and all his friends are stupified and dumbfounded. If I mistake not much, he will, in the course of a year, enjoy perfect *otium cum dignitate*. Enough of politics.

Is the fair, or at least the fat, Miss C—— with you still? It must be confessed that she knows the arts of Courts; to be so received at Dresden, and so connived at in Leicester-fields.

There never was so wet a summer as this has been, in the memory of man; we have not had one single day, since March, without some rain; but most days a great deal. I hope that does not affect your health, as great cold does; for, with all these inundations, it has not been cold. God bless you!

LETTER CCCLXVI.

My dear Friend,   Blackheath, Aug. the 14th, 1766.

I received yesterday your letter of the 30th past; and I find by it that it crossed mine upon the road, where they had no time to take notice of one another.

The newspapers have informed you, before now, of the changes actually made; more will probably follow, but what,

I am sure I cannot tell you; and I believe nobody can, not even those who are to make them: they will, I suppose, be occasional, as people behave themselves. The causes and consequences of Mr Pitt's quarrel now appear in print, in a pamphlet published by Lord T——; and in a refutation of it, not by Mr Pitt himself, I believe, but by some friend of his, and under his sanction. The former is very scurrilous and scandalous, and betrays private conversation. My Lord says, that in his last conference, he thought he had as good a right to nominate the new Ministry as Mr Pitt, and consequently named Lord G——, Lord L——, &c., for Cabinet Council employments; which Mr Pitt not consenting to, Lord T—— broke up the conference, and in his wrath went to Stowe; where, I presume, he may remain undisturbed a great while, since Mr Pitt will neither be willing nor able to send for him again. The pamphlet, on the part of Mr Pitt, gives an account of his whole political life; and, in that respect, is tedious to those who were acquainted with it before; but, at the latter end, there is an article that expresses such supreme contempt of Lord T——, and in so pretty a manner, that I suspect it to be Mr Pitt's own: you shall judge yourself, for I here transcribe the article.—' But this I will be bold to say, that had he (Lord T——) not fastened himself into Mr Pitt's train, and acquired thereby such an interest in that great man, he might have crept out of life with as little notice as he crept in; and gone off with no other degree of credit than that of adding a single unit to the bills of mortality.'—I wish I could send you all the pamphlets and half-sheets that swarm here upon this occasion; but that is impossible; for every week would make a ship's cargo. It is certain that Mr Pitt has, by his dignity of Earl, lost the greatest part of his popularity, especially in the City; and I believe the Opposition will be very strong, and perhaps prevail, next session, in the House of Commons; there being now nobody there who can have the authority and ascendant over them that Pitt had.

People tell me here, as young Harvey told you at Dresden, that I look very well; but these are words of course, which every one says to everybody. So far is true, that I am better than, at my age, and with my broken constitution, I could have expected to be. God bless you!

LETTER CCCLXVII.

MY DEAR FRIEND,   Blackheath, Sept. the 12th, 1766.

I HAVE this moment received your letter of the 27th past. I was in hopes that your course of waters this year, at Baden, would have given you a longer reprieve from your painful complaint. If I do not mistake, you carried over with you some of Dr Monsey's powders ; Have you taken any of them, and have they done you any good ? I know they did me a great deal. I, who pretend to some skill in physic, advise a cool regimen, and cooling medicines.

I do not wonder that you do wonder at Lord C——'s conduct. If he was not outwitted into his Peerage by Lord B——, his accepting it is utterly inexplicable. The instruments he has chosen for the great Offices, I believe, will never fit the same case. It was cruel to put such a boy as Lord G—— over the head of old Ligonier ; and if I had been the former, I would have refused that commission during the life of that honest and brave old General. All this to quiet the Duke of R—— to a resignation, and to make Lord B—— Lieutenant of Ireland, where, I will venture to prophesy, that he will not do. Ligonier was much pressed to give up his regiment of guards, but would by no means do it ; and declared that the King might break him, if he pleased, but that he would certainly not break himself.

I have no political events to inform you of ; they will not be ripe till the meeting of the Parliament. Immediately upon the receipt of this letter, write me one to acquaint me how you are.

God bless you ; and, particularly, may he send you health, for that is the greatest blessing !

LETTER CCCLXVIII.

MY DEAR FRIEND,   Blackheath, Sept. the 30th, 1766.

I RECEIVED yesterday, with great pleasure, your letter of the 18th, by which I consider this last ugly bout as over ; and, to prevent its return, I greatly approve of your plan for the South of France, where I recommend for your principal residence, Pezenas, Toulouse, or Bordeaux ; but do not be persuaded to go to Aix en Provence, which by experience I know to be at once the hottest and the coldest place in the world, from the ardour of the Provençal Sun, and the sharpness of the Alpine winds. I also earnestly recommend to you, for your complaint upon your breast, to take, twice a day, asses' or (what is better) mares' milk, and that for these six months at least. Mingle turnips, as much as you can, with your diet.

I have written, as you desired, to Mr Secretary Conway ; but I will answer for it, there will be no difficulty to obtain the leave you ask.

There is no new event in the political world since my last ; so God bless you !

LETTER CCCLXIX.

My dear Friend, London, October the 29th, 1766.

The last mail brought me your letter of the 17th. I am glad to hear that your breast is so much better. You will find both asses' and mares' milk enough in the South of France, where it was much drunk when I was there. Guy Patin recommends to a patient to have no Doctor but a Horse, and no Apothecary but an Ass. As for your pains and weakness in your limbs, *je vous en offre autant;* [1] I have never been free from them since my last rheumatism. I use my legs as much as I can, and you should do so too, for disuse makes them worse. I cannot now use them long at a time, because of the weakness of old age ; but I contrive to get, by different snatches, at least two hours' walking every day, either in my garden or within doors, as the weather permits. I set out to-morrow for Bath, in hopes of half repairs, for Medea's kettle could not give me whole ones ; the timbers of my wretched vessel are too much decayed to be fitted out again for use. I shall see poor Harte there, who, I am told, is in a miserable way, between some real and some imaginary distempers.

I send you no political news, for one reason, among others, which is, that I know none. Great expectations are raised of this session, which meets the 11th of next month : but of what kind nobody knows, and consequently everybody conjectures variously. Lord Chatham comes to town to-morrow, from Bath, where he has been to refit himself for the winter campaign : he has hitherto but an indifferent set of *Aides de Camp;* and where he will find better I do not know. Charles Towns-

[1] I offer you as much in return.

hend and he are already upon ill terms. *Enfin je n'y vois goutte;*[1] and so God bless you !

----o----

LETTER CCCLXX.

MY DEAR FRIEND,   Bath, November the 15th, 1766.

I HAVE this moment received your letter of the 5th instant, from Basle.   I am very glad to find that your breast is relieved, though perhaps at the expense of your legs : for if the humour be either gouty or rheumatic, it had better be in your legs than anywhere else.   I have consulted Moisy, the great physician of this place, upon it ; who says, that at this distance he dares not prescribe anything, as there may be such different causes for your complaint, which must be well weighed by a physician upon the spot : that is, in short, that he knows nothing of the matter.   I will therefore tell you my own case, in 1732, which may be something parallel to yours.   I had that year been dangerously ill of a fever, in Holland; and when I was recovered of it, the febrific humour fell into my legs, and swelled them to that degree, and chiefly in the evening, that it was as painful to me as it was shocking to others.   I came to England with them in this condition, and consulted Mead, Broxholme, and Arbuthnot, who none of them did me the least good ; but on the contrary, increased the swelling, by applying poultices and emollients.   In this condition I remained near six months, till, finding that the doctors could do me no good, I resolved to consult Palmer, the most eminent surgeon of St Thomas's Hospital.   He immediately told me that the physicians had pursued a very wrong method, as the swelling of my legs proceeded only from a relaxation and weakness of the cutaneous vessels ; and he must apply strengtheners instead of emollients. Accordingly he ordered me to put my legs, up to the knees, every morning, in brine from the salters, as hot as I could bear it : the brine must have had meat salted in it.   I did so ; and after having thus pickled my legs for about three weeks, the complaint absolutely ceased, and I have never had the least swelling in them since.   After what I have said, I must caution you not to use the same remedy rashly, and without the most skilful advice you can find, where you are ; for if your swelling proceeds from a gouty, or rheumatic humour, there may be great danger in applying so powerful an astringent, and per-

[1] In a word, I do not see into it at all.

haps *repellent*, as brine. So go *piano*,[1] and not without the best advice, upon a view of the parts.

I shall direct all my letters to you *Chez Monsieur Sarrazin*, who by his trade is, I suppose, *sédentaire* at Basle, which it is not sure that you will be at any one place, in the South of France. Do you know that he is a descendant of the French Poet Sarrazin ?

Poor Harte, whom I frequently go to see here, out of compassion, is in a most miserable way ; he has had a stroke of the palsy, which has deprived him of the use of his right leg, affected his speech a good deal, and perhaps his head a little. Such are the intermediate tributes that we are forced to pay, in some shape or other, to our wretched nature, till we pay the last great one of all. May you pay this very late, and as few intermediate tributes as possible ; and so *jubeo te bene valere.* God bless you.

LETTER CCCLXXI.

My dear Friend,   Bath, December the 9th, 1766.

I received, two days ago, your letter of the 26th past. I am very glad that you begin to feel the good effects of the climate where you are ; I know it saved my life, in 1741, when both the skilful and the unskilful gave me over. In that ramble I stayed three or four days at Nîmes, where there are more remains of antiquity, I believe, than in any town in Europe, Italy excepted. What is falsely called *la maison quarrée*, is, in my mind, the finest piece of architecture that I ever saw ; and the Amphitheatre the clumsiest and the ugliest ; if it were in England everybody would swear it had been built by Sir John Vanbrugh.

This place is, now, just what you have seen it formerly ; here is a great crowd of trifling and unknown people, whom I seldom frequent, in the public rooms ; so that I pass my time *très-uniment*, in taking the air in my post-chaise every morning, and reading in the evenings. And *à propos* of the latter, I shall point out a book, which, I believe, will give you some pleasure ; at least it gave me a great deal : I never read it before. It is *Réflexions sur la Poësie et la Peinture, par l'Abbé de Bos*, in two octavo volumes ; and is, I suppose, to be had at every great town in France. The criticisms and the reflections are just and lively.

[1] Gently.

It may be you expect some political news from me; but I can tell you that you will have none; for no mortal can comprehend the present state of affairs. Eight or nine people, of some consequence, have resigned their employments; upon which Lord C—— made overtures to the Duke of B—— and his people; but they could by no means agree, and his Grace went, the next day, full of wrath, to Woburn; so that negotiation is entirely at an end. People wait to see who Lord C—— will take in, for some he must have; even *he* cannot be alone, *contra Mundum.* Such a state of affairs, to be sure, was never seen before, in this or in any other country. When this Ministry shall be settled, it will be the sixth Ministry in six years' time.

Poor Harte is here, and in a most miserable condition; those who wish him the best, as I do, must wish him dead. God bless you!

LETTER CCCLXXII.

My dear Friend,   London, February the 13th, 1767.

It is so long since I have had a letter from you, that I am alarmed about your health: and fear that the southern parts of France have not done so well by you as they did by me in the year 1741, when they snatched me from the jaws of death. Let me know, upon the receipt of this letter, how you are, and where you are.

I have no news to send you from hence; for everything seems suspended both in the Court and in the Parliament, till Lord Chatham's return from the Bath, where he has been laid up this month, by a severe fit of the gout; and, at present, he has the sole apparent power. In what little business has hitherto been done in the House of Commons, Charles Townshend has given himself more Ministerial airs than Lord Chatham will, I believe, approve of. However, since Lord Chatham has thought fit to withdraw himself from that House, he cannot well do without Charles's abilities to manage it as his Deputy.

I do not send you an account of weddings, births, and burials, as I take it for granted that you know them all from the English printed papers; some of which, I presume, are sent after you. Your old acquaintance, Lord Essex, is to be married this week to Harriet Bladen, who has £20,000 down, besides the reasonable expectation of as much at the death of her father. My kinsman, Lord Strathmore, is to be married, in a fortnight, to Miss Bowes, the greatest heiress, perhaps, in Europe. In short, the matrimonial frenzy seems to rage at present, and is epidemical. The men marry for money, and I believe you guess what the women marry for. God bless you, and send you health!

—◦—

LETTER CCCLXXIII.

My dear Friend,   London, March the 3rd, 1767.

YESTERDAY I received two letters at once from you, both dated Montpellier ; one of the 29th of last December, and the other the 12th of February : but I cannot conceive what became of my letters to you ; for I assure you that I answered all yours the next post after I received them ; and, about ten days ago, I wrote you a volunteer, because you had been so long silent; and I was afraid that you were not well ; but your letter of the 12th February has removed all my fears upon that score. The same climate that has restored your health so far, will, probably, in a little more time, restore your strength too ; though you must not expect it to be quite what it was before your late painful complaints. At least I find, that, since my late great rheumatism, I cannot walk above half-an-hour at a time, which I do not place singly to the account of my years, but chiefly to the great shock given then to my limbs. *D'ailleurs* I am pretty well for my age and shattered constitution.

As I told you in my last, I must tell you again in this, that I have no news to send. Lord Chatham, at last, came to town yesterday, full of gout, and is not able to stir hand or foot. During his absence Charles Townshend has talked of him and at him, in such a manner, that henceforwards they must be either much worse or much better together than ever they were in their lives. On Friday last Mr Dowdeswell and Mr Grenville moved to have one shilling in the pound of the land tax taken off; which was opposed by the Court ; but the Court lost it by eighteen. The Opposition triumph much upon this victory ; though, I think, without reason ; for it is plain that all the landed gentlemen bribed themselves with this shilling in the pound.

The Duke of Buccleugh is very soon to be married to Lady Betty Montague. Lord Essex was married, yesterday, to Harriet Bladen ; and Lord Strathmore, last week, to Miss Bowes ; both couples went directly from the church to consummation in the country, from an unnecessary fear that they should not be tired of each other if they stayed in town. And now *dixi ;* God bless you !

You are in the right to go to see the Assembly of the States of Languedoc, though they are but the shadow of the original *Etats,* while there was some liberty subsisting in France.

LETTER CCCLXXIV.

MY DEAR FRIEND,   London, April the 6th, 1767.

YESTERDAY I received your letter from Nîmes, by which I find that several of our letters have reciprocally miscarried. This may probably have the same fate ; however, if it reaches Monsieur Sarrazin, I presume he will know where to take his aim at you : for I find you are in motion, and with a Polarity to Dresden. I am very glad to find by it, that your Meridional journey has perfectly recovered you, as to your general state of health ; for as to your legs and thighs, you must never expect that they will be restored to their original strength and activity, after so many rheumatic attacks as you have had. I know that my limbs, besides the natural debility of old age, have never recovered the severe attack of rheumatism that plagued me five or six years ago. I cannot now walk above half-an-hour at a time, and even that in a hobbling kind of way.

I can give you no account of our political world, which is in a situation that I never saw in my whole life. Lord Chatham has been so ill these last two months, that he has not been able (some say not willing) to do or hear of any business : and for his *sous Ministres,* they either cannot, or dare not, do any without his directions ; so that everything is now at a stand. This situation, I think, cannot last much longer ; and if Lord Chatham should either quit his post, or the world, neither of which is very improbable, I conjecture that what is called the Rockingham Connection stands the fairest for the Ministry. But this is merely my conjecture ; for I have neither *data* nor *postulata* enough to reason upon.

When you get to Dresden, which I hope you will not do till next month, our correspondence will be more regular. God bless you !

LETTER CCCLXXV.

MY DEAR FRIEND,   London, May the 5th, 1767.

BY your letter of the 25th past, from Basle, I presume this will find you at Dresden, and accordingly I direct to you there. When you write me word that you are at Dresden, I will return you an answer, with something better than the answer itself. If you complain of the weather, north of Besançon, what would you say to the weather that we have had here, for these last two months, uninterruptedly? Snow often, northeast wind constantly, and extreme cold. I write this by the side of a good fire; and at this moment it snows very hard. All my promised fruit at Blackheath is quite destroyed; and, what is worse, many of my trees.

I cannot help thinking, that the King of Poland, the Empress of Russia, and the King of Prussia, *s'entendent comme Larrons en foire*,[1] though the former must not appear in it, upon account of the stupidity, ignorance, and bigotry of his Poles. I have a great opinion of the cogency of the controversial arguments of the Russian troops, in favour of the Dissidents: I am sure, I wish them success; for I would have all intoleration intolerated in its turn. We shall soon see more clearly into this matter; for I do not think that the Autocratrice of all the Russias will be trifled with by the Sarmatians.

What do you think of the late extraordinary event in Spain? Could you ever have imagined that those ignorant Goths would have dared to banish the Jesuits? There must have been some very grave and important reasons for so extraordinary a measure: but what they were, I do not pretend to guess; and perhaps I shall never know, though all the coffee-houses here do

Things are here in exactly the same situation in which they were when I wrote to you last. Lord Chatham is still ill, and only goes abroad for an hour in a day, to take the air, in his coach. The King has, to my certain knowledge, sent him repeated messages, desiring him not to be concerned at his confinement, for that he is resolved to support him *pour et contre tous*. God bless you!

---

[1] Are in secret agreement like rogues in a fair.

LETTER CCCLXXVI.

My dear Friend,   London, June the 1st, 1767.

I received yesterday your letter of the 20th past, from Dresden, where I am glad to find that you are arrived safe and sound. This has been everywhere an *annus mirabilis* for bad weather ; it continues here still. Everybody has fires, and their winter clothes, as at Christmas. The town is extremely sickly; and sudden deaths have been very frequent.

I do not know what to say to you upon public matters ; things remain *in statu quo*, and nothing is done. Great changes are talked of, and I believe will happen soon, perhaps next week ; but who is to be changed, for whom, I do not know, though everybody else does. I am apt to think that it will be a Mosaic Ministry, made up *de pièces rapportées* from different connections.

Last Friday I sent your subsidy to Mr Larpent, who, I suppose, has given you notice of it. I believe it will come very seasonably, as all places, both foreign and domestic, are so far in arrears. They talk of paying you all up to Christmas. The King's inferior servants are almost starving.

I suppose you have already heard, at Dresden, that Count Brühl is either actually married, or very soon to be so, to Lady Egremont. She has, together with her salary as Lady of the Bedchamber, 2,500*l.* a year ; besides ten thousand pounds in money left her, at her own disposal, by Lord Egremont. All this will sound great *en écus d'Allemagne.*[1] I am glad of it ; for he is a very pretty man. God bless you !

I easily conceive why Orloff influences the Empress of all the Russias ; but I cannot see why the King of Prussia should be influenced by that motive.

LETTER CCCLXXVII.

My dear Friend,   Blackheath, July the 2nd, 1767.

Though I have had no letter from you since my last, and though I have no political news to inform you of, I write this to acquaint you with a piece of Greenwich news, which I believe you will be very glad of; I am sure I am. Know, then, that your friend Miss * * was happily married, three days ago, to Mr * * *, an Irish gentleman, and a Member of that Parliament,

[1] In German crowns.

with an estate of above two thousand pounds a year. He settles upon her 600*l.* jointure, and, in case they have no children, 1500*l.* He happened to be by chance in her company one day here, and was at once shot dead by her charms ; but, as dead men sometimes walk, he walked to her the next morning, and tendered her his person and his fortune ; both which, taking the one with the other, she very prudently accepted ; for his person is sixty years old.

Ministerial affairs are still in the same ridiculous and doubtful situation as when I wrote to you last. Lord Chatham will neither hear of nor do any business, but lives at Hampstead, and rides about the heath ; his gout is said to be fallen upon his nerves. Your Provincial Secretary, Conway, quits this week, and returns to the army, for which he languished. Two Lords are talked of to succeed him ; Lord Egmont, and Lord Hillsborough : I rather hope, the latter. Lord Northington certainly quits this week ; but nobody guesses who is to succeed him, as President. A thousand other changes are talked of, which I neither believe nor reject.

Poor Harte is in a most miserable condition : he has lost one side of himself, and in a great measure his speech ; notwithstanding which, he is going to publish his *divine poems* as he calls them. I am sorry for it, as he had not time to correct them before this stroke, nor abilities to do it since. God bless you !

———◇———

LETTER CCCLXXVIII.

MY DEAR FRIEND,   Blackheath, July the 9th, 1767.

I HAVE received yours of the 21st past, with the enclosed proposal from the French *refugiés*, for a subscription towards building them *un Temple.* I have shown it to the very few people I see, but without the least success. They told me (and with too much truth) that while such numbers of poor were literally starving here, from the dearness of all provisions, they could not think of sending their money into another country, for a building which they reckoned useless. In truth, I never knew such misery as is here now ; and it affects both the hearts and the purses of those who have either : for my own part, I never gave to a building in my life ; which I reckon is only giving to masons and carpenters, and the treasurer of the undertaking.

Contrary to the expectations of all mankind here, everything still continues *in statu quo.* General Conway has been desired by the King to keep the seals till he has found a successor for him, and the Lord President the same. Lord Chatham is relapsed, and worse than ever; he sees nobody, and nobody sees him : it is said, that a bungling Physician has checked his gout, and thrown it upon his nerves ; which is the worst distemper that a Minister or a Lover can have, as it debilitates the mind of the former, and the body of the latter. Here is at present an interregnum. We must soon see what order will be produced from this chaos.

The Electorate, I believe, will find the want of Comte Flemming ; for he certainly had abilities ; and was as sturdy and inexorable as a Minister at the head of the finances ought always to be. When you see Comtesse Flemming, which I suppose cannot be of some time, pray make her Lady Chesterfield's and my compliments of condolence.

You say that Dresden is very sickly ; I am sure London is at least as sickly now, for there reigns an epidemical distemper, called by the genteel name of *l'influenza*. It is a little fever, which scarcely anybody dies of : and it generally goes off with a little looseness. I have escaped it, I believe, by being here. God keep you from all distempers, and bless you !

LETTER CCCLXXIX.

My dear Friend, London, October the 30th, 1767.

I have now left Blackheath, till the next summer, if I live till then ; and am just able to write, which is all I can say, for I am extremely weak, and have, in a great measure, lost the use of my legs ; I hope they will recover both flesh and strength, for at present they have neither. I go to the Bath next week, in hopes of half repairs at most, for those waters, I am sure, will not prove Medea's kettle, nor *les eaux de Jouvence* to me ; however, I shall do as good Courtiers do, and get what I can, if I cannot get what I will. I send you no politics, for here are neither politics nor Ministers ; Lord Chatham is quiet at Pynsent, in Somersetshire, and his former subalterns do nothing, so that nothing is done. Whatever places or preferments are disposed of, come evidently from Lord ——, who affects to be invisible ; and who, like a woodcock, thinks, that if his head is but hid, he is not seen at all.

General Pulteney is at last dead, last week, worth above thirteen hundred thousand pounds. He has left all his landed estate, which is eight-and-twenty thousand pounds a year, including the Bradford estate, which his brother had * * * * from that ancient family, to a cousin-german. He has left two hundred thousand pounds, in the funds, to Lord Darlington, who was his next nearest relation; and at least twenty thousand pounds in various legacies. If riches alone could make people happy, the last two proprietors of this immense wealth ought to have been so, but they never were.

God bless you, and send you good health, which is better than all the riches of the world!

LETTER CCCLXXX.

My dear Friend,   London, November the 3rd, 1767.

Your last letter brought me but a scurvy account of your health. For the headaches you complain of, I will venture to prescribe a remedy, which, by experience, I found a specific, when I was extremely plagued with them. It is, either to chew ten grains of rhubarb every night going to bed; or, what I think rather better, to take, immediately before dinner, a couple of rhubarb pills, of five grains each; by which means it mixes with the aliments, and will, by degrees, keep your body gently open. I do it to this day, and find great good by it. As you seem to dread the approach of a German winter, I would advise you to write to General Conway, for leave of absence for the three rigorous winter months, which I dare say will not be refused. If you choose a worse climate, you may come to London; but if you choose a better and a warmer, you may go to Nice en Provence, where Sir William Stanhope is gone to pass his winter, who, I am sure, will be extremely glad of your company there.

I go to the Bath next Saturday. *Utinam ne frustra.* God bless you!

LETTER CCCLXXXI.

My dear Friend,   Bath, December the 19th, 1767.

Yesterday I received your letter of the 29th past, and am very glad to find that you are well enough to think, that you may perhaps stand the winter at Dresden; but if you do, pray take care to keep both your body and your limbs exceedingly warm.

As to my own health, it is, in general, as good as I could expect it, at my age; I have a good stomach, a good digestion, and sleep well; but find that I shall never recover the free use of my legs, which are now full as weak as when I first came hither.

You ask me questions, concerning Lord C——, which neither I, nor, I believe, anybody but himself can answer; however, I will tell you all that I do know, and all that I guess concerning him.—This time twelvemonth he was here, and in good health and spirits, except now and then some little twinges of the gout. We saw one another four or five times, at our respective houses; but for these last eight months he has been absolutely invisible to his most intimate friends, *les sous Ministres:* he would receive no letters, nor so much as open any packet about business.

IIis physician, Dr ——, as I am told, had very ignorantly checked a coming fit of the gout, and scattered it about his body; and it fell particularly upon his nerves, so that he continues exceedingly vapourish; and would neither see nor speak to anybody, while he was here. I sent him my compliments, and asked leave to wait upon him; but he sent me word that he was too ill to see anybody whatsoever. I met him frequently taking the air in his postchaise, and he looked very well. He set out from hence, for London, last Tuesday; but what to do, whether to resume, or finally to resign, the Administration, God knows; conjectures are various. In one of our conversations here, this time twelvemonth, I desired him to secure you a seat in the new Parliament; he assured me he would; and, I am convinced, very sincerely; he said even that he would make it his own affair; and desired I would give myself no more trouble about it. Since that, I have heard no more of it; which made me look out for some venal borough: and I spoke to a borough-jobber, and offered five-and-twenty hundred pounds for a secure seat in Parliament; but he laughed at my offer, and said, That there was no such thing as a borough to be had now; for that the rich East and West Indians had secured them all, at the rate of three thousand pounds at least; but many at four thousand; and two or three, that he knew, at five thousand. This, I confess, has vexed me a good deal; and made me the more impatient to know whether Lord C—— had done anything in it; which I shall know when I go to town, as I propose to do in about a fortnight; and as soon as I know it, you shall. To tell you truly what I think—I doubt, from all these *nervous disorders*, that Lord C—— is *hors de combat*, as a Minister ; but do not even hint this to anybody. God bless you !

LETTER CCCLXXXII.

My dear Friend,　　　　　　Bath, December the 27th, 1767.

En nova progenies ! [1]

THE outlines of a new Ministry are now declared ; but they are not yet quite filled up : it was formed by the Duke of Bedford. Lord Gower is made President of the Council, Lord Sandwich Postmaster, Lord Hillsborough Secretary of State, for America only, Mr Rigby Vice-treasurer of Ireland. General Conway is to keep the seals a fortnight longer, and then to surrender them to Lord Weymouth. It is very uncertain whether the Duke of Grafton is to continue at the head of the Treasury or not ; but, in my private opinion, George Grenville will very soon be there. Lord Chatham seems to be out of the question, and is at his repurchased house at Hayes, where he will not see a mortal. It is yet uncertain whether Lord Shelburne is to keep his place ; if not, Lord Sandwich, they say, is to succeed him. All the Rockingham people are absolutely excluded. Many more changes must necessarily be ; but no more are yet declared. It seems to be a resolution taken by somebody, that Ministries are to be annual.

Sir George Macartney is, next week, to be married to Lady Jane Stuart, Lord Bute's second daughter.

I never knew it so cold in my life as it is now, and with a very deep snow ; by which, if it continues, I may be snow-bound here for God knows how long, though I proposed leaving this place the latter end of the week.

Poor Harte is very ill here ; he mentions you often, and with great affection. God bless you !

When I know more, you shall.

---

[1] Lo! a new race!

LETTER CCCLXXXIII.

MY DEAR FRIEND   London, March the 12th, 1768.

THE day after I received your letter of the 21st past, I wrote
to Lord Weymouth, as you desired ; and I send you his answer
enclosed : from which (though I have not heard from him since)
I take it for granted, and so may you, that his silence signifies
his Majesty's consent to your request. Your complicated complaints give me great uneasiness, and the more, as I am convinced that the Montpellier physicians have mistaken a material
part of your case ; as indeed all the physicians here did, except
Dr Maty. In my opinion, you have no gout, but a very scor-
butic and rheumatic habit of body, which should be treated in
a very different manner from the gout ; and, as I pretend to be
a very good quack, at least, I would prescribe to you a strict
milk diet, with the seeds, such as rice, sago, barley, millet, &c.,
for the three summer months at least, and without ever tasting
wine. If climate signifies anything (in which, by the way, I
have very little faith) you are, in my mind, in the finest climate
in the world ; neither too hot nor too cold, and always clear :
you are with the gayest people living ; be gay with them, and
do not wear out your eyes with reading at home. *L'ennui* is
the English distemper ; and a very bad one it is, as I find by
every day's experience ; for my deafness deprives me of the only
rational pleasure that I can have at my age, which is society ;
so that I read my eyes out every day, that I may not hang
myself.

You will not be in this Parliament, at least not at the beginning of it. I relied too much upon Lord C——'s promise,
above a year ago, at Bath. He desired that I would leave it to
him ; that he would make it his own affair, and give it in charge
to the Duke of G——, whose province it was to make the parliamentary arrangement. This I depended upon, and I think
with reason ; but, since that, Lord C—— has neither seen or
spoken to anybody, and has been in the oddest way in the world.
I sent to the D— of G——, to know if L— C—— had either
spoken or sent to him about it ; but he assured me that he had
done neither : that all was full, or rather running over, at present ; but that if he could crowd you in upon a vacancy, he
would do it with great pleasure. I am extremely sorry for this
accident ; for I am of a very different opinion from you, about
being in Parliament, as no man can be of consequence, in this
country, who is not in it ; and, though one may not speak like

a Lord Mansfield, or a Lord Chatham, one may make a very good figure in a second rank. *Locus est et pluribus umbris.*[1] I do not pretend to give you any account of the present state of this country, or Ministry, not knowing nor guessing it myself.

God bless you, and send you health, which is the first and greatest of all blessings !

LETTER CCCLXXXIV.

MY DEAR FRIEND,   London, April the 12th, 1768.

I RECEIVED, yesterday, your letter of the 1st ; in which you do not mention the state of your health, which I desire you will do for the future.

I believe you have guessed the true reason of Mr Keith's mission ; but, by a whisper that I have since heard, Keith is rather inclined to go to Turin, as *Chargé d'Affaires.* I forgot to tell you, in my last, that I was most positively assured, that the instant you return to Dresden, Keith should decamp. I am persuaded they will keep their words with me, as there is no one reason in the world why they should not. I will send your annual to Mr Larpent, in a fortnight, and pay the forty shillings a day quarterly, if there should be occasion; for, in my own private opinion, there will be no *Chargé d'Affaires* sent. I agree with you, that *point d'Argent plint d'Aloemand,*[2] as was used to be said, and not without more reason, of the Swiss ; but, as we have neither the inclination, nor (I fear) the power, to give subsidies, the Court of Vienna can give good things that cost them nothing, as Archbishoprics, Bishoprics, besides corrupting their Ministers and Favourites with places.

Elections, here, have been carried to a degree of frenzy hitherto unheard of; that for the town of Northampton has cost the contending parties at least thirty thousand pounds a side, and ———— ———— has sold his borough of ————, to two Members, for nine thousand pounds. As soon as Wilkes had lost his election for the City, he set up for the County of Middlesex, and carried it hollow, as the jockeys say. Here were great mobs and riots upon that occasion, and most of the windows in town broke, that had no lights *for Wilkes and Liberty*, who were thought to be inseparable. He will appear, the 20th of this month, in the Court of King's Bench, to receive

---

[1] There is room for many chance guests.
[2] No pay, no German.

his sentence ; and then great riots are again expected, and probably will happen.   God bless you !

————◇————

LETTER CCCLXXXV.

MY DEAR FRIEND,   Bath, October the 17th, 1768.

YOUR two last letters, to myself and Grevenkop, have alarmed me extremely ; but I comfort myself a little, by hoping that you, like all people who suffer, think yourself worse than you are.   A dropsy never comes so suddenly ; and I flatter myself that it is only that gouty or rheumatic humour, which has plagued you so long, that has occasioned a temporary swelling of your legs.   Above forty years ago, after a violent fever, my legs were swelled as much as you describe yours to be ;   I immediately thought that I had a dropsy ; but the Faculty assured me that my complaint was only the effect of my fever, and would soon be cured ; and they said true.   Pray let your amanuensis, whoever he may be, write an account regularly, once a week, either to Grevenkop or myself, for that is the same thing, of the state of your health.

I sent you, in four successive letters, as much of the Duchess of Somerset's snuff as a letter could well convey to you.   Have you received all or any of them ?   and have they done you any good ?   Though, in your present condition, you cannot go into company, I hope you have some acquaintances that come and sit with you ; for if originally it was not good for man to be alone, it is much worse for a sick man to be so ; he thinks too much of his distemper, and magnifies it.   Some men of learning amongst the Ecclesiastics, I dare say, would be glad to sit with you ; and you could give them as good as they brought.

Poor Harte, who is here still, is in a most miserable condition ; he has entirely lost the use of his left side, and can hardly speak intelligibly.   I was with him yesterday.   He inquired after you with great affection, and was in the utmost concern when I showed him your letter.

My own health is as it has been ever since I was here last year.   I am neither well nor ill, but *unwell*.   I have, in a manner, lost the use of my legs ; for though I can make a shift to crawl upon even ground for a quarter of an hour, I cannot go up or down stairs, unless supported by a servant.

God bless, and grant you a speedy recovery !

Here end the letters to Mr Stanhope, as he died the 16th of
November following.

LETTER CCCLXXXVI.

To Mrs Stanhope, then at Paris.

MADAM,   London, March the 16th, 1769.

A TROUBLESOME and painful inflammation in my eyes obliges me to use another hand than my own, to acknowledge the receipt of your letter from Avignon, of the 27th past.

I am extremely surprised that Mrs du-Bouchet should have any objection to the manner in which your late husband desired to be buried, and which you, very properly, complied with. All I desire, for my own burial, is not to be buried alive; but how or where, I think, must be entirely indifferent to every rational creature.

I have no commission to trouble you with, during your stay at Paris; from whence, I wish you and the boys a good journey home; where I shall be very glad to see you all: and assure you of my being, with great truth,

Your faithful, humble servant,

CHESTERFIELD.

LETTER CCCLXXXVII.

To the same, at London.

MADAM,

THE last time I had the pleasure of seeing you, I was so taken up in playing with the boys, that I forgot their more important affairs. How soon would you have them placed at school? When I know your pleasure as to that, I will send to Monsieur Perny, to prepare everything for their reception. In the mean time, I beg that you will equip them thoroughly with clothes, linen, &c., all good, but plain; and give me the account, which I will pay; for I do not intend, that, from this time forwards, the two boys should cost you one shilling.

I am, with great truth, Madam,

Your faithful, humble servant,

Wednesday.   CHESTERFIELD.

LETTER CCCLXXXVIII.

MADAM,

As some day must be fixed for sending the boys to school, do you approve of the 8th of next month? by which time the weather will probably be warm and settled, and you will be able to equip them completely.

I will, upon that day, send my coach to you, to carry you and the boys to Loughborough House, with all their immense baggage. I must recommend to you, when you leave them there, to suppress, as well as you can, the overflowings of maternal tenderness; which would grieve the poor boys the more, and give them a terror of their new establishment.

I am, with great truth, Madam,
Your faithful, humble servant,

Thursday Morning.
CHESTERFIELD.

LETTER CCCLXXXIX.

MADAM,
Bath, October the 11th, 1769.

NOBODY can be more willing or ready to obey orders than I am; but then I must like the orders and the orderer. Your orders and yourself come under this description; and therefore I must give you an account of my arrival and existence, such as it is, here. I got hither last Sunday, the day after I left London, less fatigued than I expected to have been; and now crawl about this place upon my three legs, but am kept in countenance by many of my fellow-crawlers: the last part of the Sphynx's riddle approaches, and I shall soon end, as I began, upon all fours.

When you happen to see either Monsieur or Madame Perny, I beg you will give them this *melancholic* proof of my caducity, and tell them, that the last time I went to see the boys, I carried the Michaelmas quarteridge in my pocket, and when I was there I totally forgot it; but assure them that I have not the least intention to bilk them, and will pay them faithfully, the two quarters together, at Christmas.

I hope our two boys are well; for then I am sure you are so.

I am, with great truth and esteem,
Your most faithful, humble servant,

CHESTERFIELD.

LETTER CCCXC.

MADAM, Bath, October the 28th, 1769.

YOUR kind anxiety for my health and life is more than, in my opinion, they are both worth : without the former, the latter is a burthen ; and, indeed, I am very weary of it. I think I have got some benefit by drinking these waters, and by bathing, for my old, stiff, rheumatic limbs ; for I believe I could now outcrawl a snail, or perhaps even a tortoise.

I hope the boys are well. Phil, I dare say, has been in some scrapes ; but he will get triumphantly out of them, by dint of strength and resolution.

I am, with great truth and esteem,
Your most faithful, humble servant,

CHESTERFIELD.

———◇———

LETTER CCCXCI.

MADAM, Bath, November the 5th, 1769.

I REMEMBER very well the paragraph which you quote from a letter of mine to Mrs du-Bouchet, and see no reason yet to retract that opinion, *in general*, which at least nineteen widows in twenty had authorized. I had not then the pleasure of your acquaintance ; I had seen you but twice or thrice ; and I had no reason to think that you would deviate, as you have done, from other widows, so much, as to put perpetual shackles upon yourself, for the sake of your children : but (if I may use a vulgarism) one swallow makes no summer : five righteous were formerly necessary to save a city, and they could not be found ; so, till I find four more such righteous widows as yourself, I shall entertain my former notions of widowhood in general.

I can assure you that I drink here very soberly and cautiously, and at the same time keep so cool a diet, that I do not find the least symptom of heat, much less of inflammation. By the way, I never had that complaint, in consequence of having drunk these waters ; for I have had it but four times, and always in the middle of summer. Mr Hawkins is timorous, even to *minuties*, and my sister delights in them.

Charles will be a scholar, if you please ; but our little Philip, without being one, will be something or other as good, though I do not yet guess what. I am not of the opinion generally entertained in this country, that man lives by Greek and Latin alone; that is, by knowing a great many words of two dead languages, which nobody living knows perfectly, and which are of no use in the common intercourse of life. Useful knowledge, in my opinion, consists of modern languages, history, and geography; some Latin may be thrown into the bargain, in compliance with custom, and for closet amusement.

You are, by this time, certainly tired with this long letter, which I could prove to you from Horace's own words (for I am a *scholar*) to be a bad one; he says, that water drinkers can write nothing good; so I am, with real truth and esteem,

Your most faithful, humble servant,

CHESTERFIELD.

LETTER CCCXCII.

MADAM,   Bath, October the 9th, 1770.

I AM extremely obliged to you for the kind part which you take in my health and life: as to the latter, I am as indifferent myself, as any other body can be; but as to the former, I confess care and anxiety; for, while I am to crawl upon this Planet, I would willingly enjoy the health at least of an insect. How far these waters will restore me to that moderate degree of health, which alone I aspire at, I have not yet given them a fair trial, having drunk them but one week; the only difference I hitherto find is, that I sleep better than I did.

I beg that you will neither give yourself, nor Mr Fitzhugh, much trouble about the Pine plants; for, as it is three years before they fruit, I might as well, at my age, plant Oaks, and hope to have the advantage of their timber; however, somebody or other, God knows who, will eat them, as somebody or other will fell and sell the Oaks I planted five-and-forty years ago.

I hope our boys are well; *my respects* to them both.

I am, with the greatest truth,

Your faithful, humble servant,

CHESTERFIELD.

LETTER CCCXCIII.

MADAM, Bath, November the 4th, 1770.

THE post has been more favourable to you than I intended it should, for, upon my word, I answered your former letter the post after I had received it. However you have *got a loss*, as we say, sometimes, in Ireland.

My friends, from time to time, require bills of health from me, in these suspicious times, when the Plague is busy in some parts of Europe. All I can say, in answer to their kind inquiries, is, that I have not the distemper properly called the Plague; but that I have all the plagues of old age, and of a shattered carcass. These waters have done me what little good I expected from them; though by no means what I could have wished, for I wished them to be *les eaux de Jouvence*.

I had a letter, the other day, from our two boys; Charles's was very finely written, and Philip's very prettily: they are perfectly well, and say that they want nothing. What grown-up people will or can say as much?

I am, with the truest esteem,
MADAM,
Your most faithful servant,
CHESTERFIELD.

LETTER CCCXCIV.

MADAM, Bath, October the 27th, 1771.

UPON my word, you interest yourself in the state of my existence more than I do myself; for it is worth the care of neither of us. I ordered my *valet de chambre*, according to your orders, to inform you of my safe arrival here; to which I can add nothing, being neither better nor worse than I was then.

I am very glad that our boys are well. Pray give them the enclosed.

I am not at all surprised at Mr ——'s conversion; for he was, at seventeen, the idol of old women, for his gravity, devotion, and dulness.

I am, MADAM,
Your most faithful, humble servant,
CHESTERFIELD.

LETTER CCCXCV.

To Charles and Philip Stanhope.

Bath, October the 27th, 1771.

I RECEIVED, a few days ago, two the best written letters that ever I saw in my life ; the one signed Charles Stanhope, the other Philip Stanhope. As for you, Charles, I did not wonder at it ; for you will take pains, and are a lover of letters : but you idle rogue, you Phil, how came you to write so well, that one can almost say of you two, *et cantare pares et respondere parati?* Charles will explain this Latin to you.

I am told, Phil, that you have got a nickname at school, from your intimacy with Master Strangeways ; and that they call you Master *Strangeways;* for, to be sure, you are a strange boy. Is this true?

Tell me what you would have me bring you both from hence, and I will bring it you, when I come to town. In the mean time, God bless you both!

CHESTERFIELD.

THE END OF THE LETTERS.

MISCELLANEOUS PIECES.

SOME ACCOUNTS OF THE GOVERNMENT OF THE REPUBLIC
OF THE SEVEN UNITED PROVINCES.

THE Government of the Republic of the Seven United Provinces is thought by many to be Democratical; but it is merely Aristocratical;[1] the people not having the least share in it, either themselves, or by representatives of their own choosing : they have nothing to do but to pay and grumble.

The Sovereign Power is commonly thought to be in the States General, *as they are called*, residing at the Hague. It is no such thing ; they are only limited Deputies, obliged to consult their Constituents upon every point of any importance that occurs. It is very true, that the Sovereign Power is lodged in the States General ; but who are those States General ? Not those who are commonly called so ; but the Senate Council, or *Vrootschaps*, call it what you will, of every town, in every Province, that sends Deputies to the Provincial States of the said Province. These *Vrootschaps* are in truth the States General ; but were they to assemble, they would amount, for aught I know, to two or three thousand : it is, therefore, for conveniency and dispatch of business, that every Province sends Deputies to the Hague, who are constantly assembled there ; who are commonly called the States-General, and in whom many people falsely imagine that the Sovereign Power is lodged. These Deputies are chosen by the *Vrootschaps ;* but their powers are extremely circumscribed ; and they can consent to nothing,[2] without writing,

---

[1] The Members of the Senate, or *Vrootschaps*, were originally elected by the Burghers, in a general, and often a tumultuous, assembly : but now, for near two hundred years, the *Vrootschaps* found means to persuade the people, that these elections were troublesome and dangerous ; and kindly took upon themselves to elect their own Members, upon vacancies ; and to keep their own body full, without troubling the people with an election : it was then that the Aristocracy was established.

[2] When the Deputies of the States signed the Triple Alliance with Sir William Temple, in two or three days' time, and without consulting their Principals (however Sir William Temple values himself upon it) in reality, they only signified *Sub Spe Rati*. The act was not valid ; and had it not been ratified by the several Constituents of the several Provinces, it had been

or returning themselves, to their several constituent towns, for in- structions in that particular case.   They are authorized to con- cur in matters of order ; that is, to continue things in the common, current, ordinary train ; but for the least innovation, the least step out of the ordinary course, new instructions must be given, either to deliberate or to conclude.

Many people are ignorant enough to take the Province of Holland, singly, for the Republic of the Seven United Provinces ; and when they mean to speak of the Republic, they say, *Holland* [1] will, or will not, do such a thing : but most people are ignorant enough to imagine, that the Province of Holland has a legal, a consti- tutional, power over the other six ; whereas, by the Act of Union, the little Province of *Groningen* is as much Sovereign as the Province of Holland.   The Seven Provinces are Seven distinct Sovereignties, confederated together in one Republic ; no one having any superiority over, or dependence upon, any other : nay, in point of precedence, Holland is but the second, *Gueldres* being the first.   It is very natural to suppose, and it is very true in fact, that Holland, from its superiority of strength and

as *non avenu*. The Deputies who signed that treaty, *Sub Spe Rati*, knew well enough that, considering the nature of the treaty, and the then situation of affairs, they should not only be avowed, but approved of, by their Masters the States.

[1] When the Province of Holland has once taken an important resolution of Peace, or War, or Accession to any treaty, it is very probable that the other Provinces will come into that measure, but by no means certain : it is often a great while first ; and when the little Provinces know that the Pro- vince of Holland has their concurrence much at heart, they will often annex conditions to it ; as the little towns in Holland frequently do, when the great ones want their concurrence.   As, for instance, when I was soliciting the accession of the Republic to the treaty of Vienna, in 1731 ; which the Pensionary, Comte Sinzendorf, and I, had made secretly at the Hague ; all the towns in Holland came pretty readily into it, except the little town of Briel ; whose Deputies frankly declared, that they would not give their con- sent till *Major such a one*, a very honest gentleman of their town, was pro- moted to the rank of Lieutenant-colonel ; and that, as soon as that was done, they would agree, for they approved of the treaty.   This was accordingly done in two or three days, and then they agreed.   This is a strong instance of the absurdity of the unanimity required, and of the use that is often made of it.

However, should one, or even two, of the lesser Provinces, who contri- bute little, and often pay less, to the public charge, obstinately and frivolously, or perhaps corruptly, persist in opposing a measure which Holland and the other more considerable Provinces thought necessary, and had agreed to, they would send a Deputation to those opposing Provinces, to reason with, and persuade them to concur ; but if this would not do, they would, as they have done in many instances, conclude without them.   The same thing is done in the Provincial States of the respective Provinces ; where, if one or two of the least considerable towns pertinaciously oppose a necessary measure, they conclude without them.   But as this is absolutely unconstitutional, it is avoided as much as possible, and a complete unanimity procured, if it can be, by such little concessions as that which I have mentioned to the Briel Major.

riches, and paying 58 *per cent.*, should have great weight and influence in the other six Provinces ; but power it has none.

The unanimity, which is constitutionally requisite for every act of each Town, and each Province, separately ; and then for every act of the Seven collectively ; is something so absurd, and so impracticable in government, that one is astonished that even the form of it has been tolerated so long ; for the substance is not strictly observed. And five Provinces will often conclude, though two dissent, provided that Holland and Zealand are two of the five. As fourteen or fifteen of the principal towns of Holland will conclude an affair, notwithstanding the opposition of four or five of the lesser. I cannot help conjecturing, that William, the first Prince of Orange, called the *Taciturne*, the ablest man, without dispute, of the age he lived in, not excepting even the Admiral Coligny,[1] and who had the modelling of the Republic as he pleased ; I conjecture, I say, that the Prince of Orange would never have suffered such an absurdity to have crippled that government, which he was at the head of, if he had not thought it useful to himself and his family. He covered the greatest ambition with the greatest modesty, and declined the insignificant, outward signs, as much' as he desired the solid substance of power : Might he not therefore think, that this absurd, though requisite unanimity, made a Stadthouder absolutely necessary, to render the government practicable ? In which case he was very sure the Stadthouder would always be taken out of his family ; and he minded things, not names. The Pensionary[2] thinks this conjecture probable ; and as we were talking the other day, confidentially, upon this subject, we both agreed that this monstrous and impracticable unanimity, required by the constitution, was alone sufficient to bring about a Stadthouder, in spite of all the measures of the Republican party to prevent it. He confessed to me, that upon his being made Pensionary, he entered into solemn engagements, not to contribute, directly nor indirectly, to any change of the present form of government, and that he would scrupulously observe those engagements ; but that he foresaw the defects in their form of government, and

---

[1] I am persuaded, that had the *Taciturne* been in the place of the Admiral Coligny, he would never have been prevailed upon to have come to Paris, and to have put himself into the power of those two monsters of perfidy and cruelty, Catharine of Medicis and Charles the Ninth. His prudent escape from Flanders is a proof of it ; when he rather chose to be *Prince sans terre* than *Prince sans tête.*

[2] Monsieur Slingelandt, the ablest Minister, and the honestest man I ever knew. I may justly call him my Friend, my Master, and my Guide. For I was then quite new in business ; he instructed me, he loved, he trusted me.

the abuses crept into every part of it, would infallibly produce a
Stadthouder,[1] tumultuously imposed upon the Republic, by an in-
surrection of the populace, as in the case of King William. I told
him that, in my opinion, if that were to happen a second time, the
Stadthouder so made would be their King.[2] He said, he believed
so too ; and that he had urged all this to the most considerable
Members of the Government, and the most jealous Republicans.
That he had even formed a plan which he had laid before them,
as the only possible one to prevent this impending danger.
That a Stadthouder was originally the chief spring upon which
their government turned ; and that, if they would have no Stadthouder, they must substitute a *succedaneum.* That one part of
that *succedaneum* must be to abolish the unanimity required by the
present form of government, and which only a Stadthouder could
render practicable by his influence. That the abuses which
were crept into the military part of the government, must be
corrected, or that they alone, if they were suffered to go on, would
make a Stadthouder, in order that the army and the navy, which
the public paid for, might be of some use, which at present they
were not. That he had laid these and many other considerations
of the like nature before them, in the hopes of one of these
two things ; either to prevail with them to make a Stadthouder
unnecessary, by a just reformation of the abuses of the government, and substituting a majority, or, at most, two-thirds, to the
absurd and impracticable unanimity now requisite. Or, if they
would not come into these preventive regulations, that they
would treat amicably with the Prince of Orange, and give him
the *Stadthouderat,* under strict limitations, and with effectual provisions for their liberty. But they would listen to neither of
these expedients ; the first affected the private interests of most

---

[1] It has since appeared that he judged very rightly.
[2] And so he ought to be now, even for the sake and preservation of the
Seven Provinces. The necessary principle of a Republic, *Virtue,* subsists
no longer there. The great riches of private people (though the public is
poor) have long ago extinguished that principle, and destroyed the equality
necessary to a Commonwealth. A Commonwealth is unquestionably, upon
paper, the most rational and equitable form of government; but it is as unquestionably impracticable, in all countries where riches have introduced
luxury, and a great inequality of conditions. It will only do in those
Countries that poverty keeps virtuous. In England, it would very soon
grow tyrannical Aristocracy; soon afterwards, an Oligarchy; and soon after
that, an absolute Monarchy: from the same causes that Denmark, in the
last century, became so; the intolerable oppression of the bulk of the people,
from those whom they looked upon as their equals. If the young Stadthouder has abilities, he will, when he grows up, get all the powers of a
limited Monarchy, such as England, no matter under what name; and if
he is really wise, he will desire no more: if the people are wise, they will
give it him.

of the considerable people of the Republic, whose power and profit arose from those abuses. And the second was too contrary to the violent passions and prejudices of Messrs d'Obdam, Booteslaer, Hallewyn, and other Heads of the high Republican party. Upon this, I said to the Pensionary, that he had fully proved to me, not only that there would, but that there ought to be a Stadthouder. He replied, ' There will most certainly be one, and you are young enough to live to see it. I hope I shall be out of the way first; but, if I am not out of the world at that time, I will be out of my place, and pass the poor remainder of my life in quiet. I only pray that our new Master, whenever we have him, may be gently given us. My friend, the Greffier,[2] thinks a Stadthouder absolutely necessary to save the Republic, and so do I, as much as he, if they will not accept of the other expedient; but we are in very different situations; he is under no engagements to the contrary, and I am.' He then asked me, in confidence, whether I had any instructions to promote the Prince of Orange's views and interest. I told him truly, I had not; but that, however, I would do it, as far as ever I could, quietly and privately. That he himself had convinced me, that it was for the interest of the Republic, which I honoured and wished well to ; and also that it would be a much more efficient Ally to England, under that form of government. ' I must own,' replied he,' that at present we have neither strength, secrecy, nor despatch.' I said, that I knew that but too well, by my own experience ; and I added (laughing) that I looked upon him as the Prince of Orange's greatest enemy ; and upon that Prince's violent and impetuous enemies[2] to be his best

---

[1] The Greffier Fagel, who had been *Greffier*, that is, Secretary of State, above fifty years. He had the deepest knowledge of business, and the soundest judgment of any man I ever knew in my life: but he had not that quick, that intuitive sagacity, which the Pensionary Slingelandt had. He has often owned to me, that he thought things were gone too far, for any other remedy but a Stadthouder.

[2] These hot-headed Republicans pushed things with the unjustest acrimony against the Prince of Orange. They denied him his rank in the army ; and they kept him out of the possession of the Marquisat of Tervere and Flessingen, which were his own patrimony ; and by these means gave him the merit with the people, of being unjustly oppressed.

Had he been an abler man himself, or better advised by others, he might have availed himself much more solidly than he did, of the affection, or rather the fury, of the people, in his favour, when they tumultuously made him Stadthouder; but he did not know the value and importance of those warm moments, in which he might have fixed and clinched his power. Dazzled with the show and trappings of power, he did not enough attend to the substance. He attempted a thing impossible, which was, to please everybody : he heard everybody, begun everything, and finished nothing. When the people, in their fury, made him Stadthouder, they desired nothing better than totally to dissolve the Republican form of government. He should

friends; for that, if his (the Pensionary's) plan were to take place, the Prince would have very little hopes. He interrupted me here, with saying, *Ne craignez rien, Milord, de ce côté la ; mon plan blesse trop l'intérêt particulier, pour être reçu à présent que l'amour du public n'existe plus.*[1] I thought this conversation too remarkable not to write down the heads of it when I came home.

The Republic has hardly any Navy at all ; the single fund for the Marine being the small duties upon exports and imports ; which duties are not half collected, by the connivance of the Magistrates themselves, who are interested in smuggling : so that the Republic has now no other title, but courtesy, to the name of a Maritime Power. Their trade decreases daily, and their national debt increases. I have good reason to believe that it amounts to at least fifty millions sterling.

The decrease of their Herring-fishery, from what it appears by Monsieur de Wit's Memoirs of Holland, in his time, is incredible ; and will be much greater, now we are, at last, wise enough to take our own Herrings upon our own coasts.

They do not, now, get by freight one quarter of what they used to get : they were the general sea-carriers of all Europe. The Act of Navigation, passed in Cromwell's time, and afterwards confirmed in Charles the Second's, gave the first blow to that branch of their profit ; and now we carry more than they do. Their only profitable remaining branches of commerce are, their trade to the East Indies, where they have engrossed the spices ; and their illicit trade in America from Surinam, St Eustatia, Curaçoa, &c.

Their woollen and silk manufactures bear not the least comparison with ours, neither in quantity, quality, nor exportation.

Their *police* is still excellent, and is now the only remains

have let them. The tumultuous love of the populace must be seized and enjoyed in its first transports ; there is no hoarding of it to use upon occasions ; it will not keep. The most considerable people of the former government would gladly have compounded for their lives, and would have thought themselves very well off in the castle of Louvestein ; where one of the Prince of Orange's predecessors sent some of their ancestors, in times much less favourable. An affected moderation made him lose that moment. The government is now in a disjointed, loose state. Her R. H. the Gouvernante has not power enough to do much good ; and yet she has more power than authority. Peace and economy, both public and domestic, should, therefore, be the sole objects of her politics, during the minority of her son. The Public is almost a bankrupt ; and her son's private fortune extremely incumbered. She has sense and ambition ; but it is, still, the sense and ambition of a woman ; that is, *inconsequential*. What remains to be done requires a firm, manly, and vigorous mind.

[1] *Never fear, my Lord ; a plan so prejudicial to private interest will not be adopted, where Patriotism no longer subsists.*

of that prudence, vigilance, and good discipline, which formerly made them esteemed, respected and courted.

MAXIMS.

BY THE EARL OF CHESTERFIELD.[1]

A PROPER secrecy is the only mystery of able men; mystery is the only secrecy of weak and cunning ones.

A man who tells nothing, or who tells all, will equally have nothing told him

If a fool knows a secret, he tells it because he is a fool; if a knave knows one, he tells it wherever it is his interest to tell it. But women, and young men, are very apt to tell what secrets they know, from the vanity of having been trusted. Trust none of these, whenever you can help it.

Inattention to the present business, be it what it will; the doing one thing, and thinking at the same time of another, or the attempting to do two things at once; are the never-failing signs of a little, frivolous mind.

A man who cannot command his temper, his attention, and his countenance, should not think of being a man of business. The weakest man in the world can avail himself of the passion of the wisest. The inattentive man cannot know the business, and consequently cannot do it. And he who cannot command his countenance, may e'en as well tell his thoughts as show them.

Distrust all those who love you extremely upon a very slight acquaintance, and without any visible reason. Be upon your guard, too, against those who confess, as their weaknesses, all the Cardinal virtues.

In your friendships, and in your enmities, let your confidence and your hostilities have certain bounds: make not the former dangerous, nor the latter irreconcilable. There are strange vicissitudes in business!

Smooth your way to the head, through the heart. The way of reason is a good one; but it is commonly something longer, and perhaps not so sure.

Spirit is now a very fashionable word: to act with Spirit, to speak with Spirit, means only, to act rashly, and to talk indiscreetly. An able man shows his Spirit by gentle words and resolute actions: he is neither hot nor timid.

[1] These Maxims are referred to in Letter CCLXIII., p. 213., of this Volume.

When a man of sense happens to be in that disagreeable situation, in which he is obliged to ask himself more than once, *What shall I do?* he will answer himself, Nothing. When his reason points out to him no good way, or at least no one way less bad than another, he will stop short, and wait for light. A little busy mind runs on at all events, must be doing ; and, like a blind horse, fears no dangers, because he sees none, *Il faut savoir s'ennuyer.*

Patience is a most necessary qualification for business ; many a man would rather you heard his story, than granted his request. One must seem to hear the unreasonable demands of the petulant, unmoved, and the tedious details of the dull, untired. That is the least price that a man must pay for a high station.

It is always right to detect a fraud, and to perceive a folly ; but it is often very wrong to expose either. A man of business should always have his eyes open ; but must often seem to have them shut.

In Courts, nobody should be below your management and attention : the links that form the Court-chain are innumerable and inconceivable. You must hear with patience the dull grievances of a Gentleman Usher, or a Page of the Back-stairs ; who, very probably, lies with some near relation of the favourite maid, of the favourite Mistress, of the favourite Minister, or perhaps of the King himself ; and who, consequently, may do you more dark and indirect good, or harm, than the first man of quality.

One good patron at Court may be sufficient, provided you have no personal enemies ; and, in order to have none, you must sacrifice (as the Indians do to the Devil) most of your passions, and much of your time, to the numberless evil Beings that infest it : in order to prevent and avert the mischiefs they can do you.

A young man, be his merit what it will, can never raise himself ; but must, like the ivy round the oak, twine himself round some man of great power and interest. You must belong to a Minister some time, before anybody will belong to you. And an inviolable fidelity to that Minister, even in his disgrace, will be meritorious, and recommend you to the next. Ministers love a personal much more than a party attachment.

As Kings are begotten and born like other men, it is to be presumed that they are of the human species ; and perhaps, had they the same education, they might prove like other men. But, flattered from their cradles, their hearts are corrupted, and their heads are turned, so that they seem to be a species by themselves. No King ever said to himself, *Homo sum, nihil humani a me alienum puto.*

Flattery cannot be too strong for them; drunk with it from their infancy, like old drinkers, they require drams.

They prefer a personal attachment to a public service, and reward it better. They are vain and weak enough to look upon it as a free-will offering to their merit, and not as a burnt sacrifice to their power.

If you would be a favourite of your King, address yourself to his weaknesses. An application to his reason will seldom prove very successful.

In Courts, bashfulness and timidity are as prejudicial on one hand, as impudence and rashness are on the other. A steady assurance, and a cool intrepidity, with an exterior modesty, are the true and necessary medium.

Never apply for what you see very little probability of obtaining; for you will, by asking improper and unattainable things, accustom the Ministers to refuse you so often, that they will find it easy to refuse you the properest and most reasonable ones. It is a common, but a most mistaken rule at Court, to ask for everything, in order to get something: you do get something by it, it is true; but that something is refusals and ridicule.

There is a Court jargon, a chit-chat, a small talk, which turns singly upon trifles; and which, in a great many words, says little or nothing. It stands fools instead of what they cannot say, and men of sense instead of what they should not say. It is the proper language of Levees, Drawing-rooms, and Antichambers: it is necessary to know it.

Whatever a man is at Court, he must be genteel and well bred; that cloak covers as many follies, as that of charity does sins. I knew a man of great quality, and in a great station at Court, considered and respected, whose highest character was, that he was humbly proud, and genteelly dull.

It is hard to say which is the greatest fool; he who tells the whole truth, or he who tells no truth at all. Character is as necessary in business as in trade. No man can deceive often in either.

At Court, people embrace without acquaintance, serve one another without friendship, and injure one another without hatred. Interest, not sentiment, is the growth of that soil.

A difference of opinion, though in the merest trifles, alienates little minds, especially of high rank. It is full as easy to commend as to blame a great man's cook, or his tailor : it is shorter too ; and the objects are no more worth disputing about, than the people are worth disputing with. It is impossible to inform, but very easy to displease, them.

A cheerful, easy countenance and behaviour are very useful at Court ; they make fools think you a good-natured man ; and they make designing men think you an undesigning one.

There are some occasions in which a man must tell half his secret, in order to conceal the rest : but there is seldom one in which a man should tell it all. Great skill is necessary to know how far to go, and where to stop.

Ceremony is necessary in Courts, as the outwork and defence of manners.

Flattery, though a base coin, is the necessary pocket-money at Court ; where, by custom and consent, it has obtained such a currency, that it is no longer a fraudulent, but a legal, payment.

If a Minister refuses you a reasonable request, and either slights or injures you ; if you have not the power to gratify your resentment, have the wisdom to conceal and dissemble it. Seeming good humour on your part may prevent rancour on his, and perhaps bring things right again : but if you have the power to hurt, hint modestly, that if provoked, you may possibly have the will too. Fear, when real, and well founded, is perhaps a more prevailing motive at Courts than love.

At Court, many more people can hurt than can help you ; please the former, but engage the latter.

Awkwardness is a more real disadvantage than it is generally thought to be ; it often occasions ridicule, it always lessens dignity.

A man's own good breeding is his best security against other people's ill manners.

Good breeding carries along with it a dignity, that is respected by the most petulant. Ill breeding invites and authorizes the familiarity of the most timid. No man ever said a pert thing to the Duke of Marlborough. No man ever said a civil one (though many a flattering one) to Sir Robert Walpole.

When the old clipped money was called in for a new coinage in King William's time ; to prevent the like for the future, they stamped on the edges of the crown pieces these words, et Decus et Tutamen. That is exactly the case of good breeding.

Knowledge may give weight, but accomplishments only give lustre ; and many more people see than weigh.

Most arts require long study and application ; but the most useful art of all, that of pleasing, requires only the desire.

'It is to be presumed, that a man of common sense, who does not desire to please, desires nothing at all ; since he must know that he cannot obtain anything without it.

A skilful Negotiator will most carefully distinguish between the little and the great objects of his business, and will be as frank and open in the former, as he will be secret and pertinacious in the latter.

He will, by his manners and address, endeavour, at least, to make his public adversaries his personal friends. He will flatter and engage the Man, while he counterworks the Minister ; and he will never alienate people's minds from him, by wrangling for points, either absolutely unattainable, or not worth attaining. He will make even a merit of giving up what he could not, or would not, carry, and sell a trifle for a thousand times its value.

A foreign Minister, who is concerned in great affairs, must necessarily have spies in his pay ; but he must not too easily credit their informations, which are never exactly true, often very false. His best spies will always be those whom he does not pay, but whom he has engaged in his service by his dexterity and address, and who think themselves nothing less than spies.

There is a certain jargon, which, in French, I should call *un Persiflage d'Affaires*, that a foreign Minister ought to be perfectly master of, and may use very advantageously at great entertainments in mixed companies, and in all occasions where he must speak, and should say nothing. Well turned and well spoken, it seems to mean something, though in truth it means nothing. It is a kind of political *badinage*, which prevents or removes a thousand difficulties, to which a foreign Minister is exposed in mixed conversations.

If ever the *Volto sciolto* and the *Pensieri stretti* are necessary, they are so in these affairs. A grave, dark, reserved, and mysterious air has *fœnum in cornu*. An even, easy, unembarrassed one invites confidence, and leaves no room for guesses and conjectures.

Both simulation and dissimulation are absolutely necessary for a foreign Minister ; and yet they must stop short of falsehood and perfidy : that middle point is the difficult one: there ability consists. He must often seem pleased, when he is vexed ; and grave, when he is pleased; but he must never say either : that would be falsehood, an indelible stain to character.

A foreign Minister should be a most exact economist ; an expense proportioned to his appointments and fortune is necessary : but, on the other hand, debt is inevitable ruin to him. It sinks him into disgrace at the Court where he resides, and into

the most servile and abject dependance on the Court that sent
him.   As he cannot resent ill usage, he is sure to have enough
of it.

The Duc de Sully observes very justly, in his Memoirs, that
nothing contributed more to his rise, than that prudent economy
which he had observed from his youth ; and by which he had
always a sum of money beforehand, in case of emergencies.

It is very difficult to fix the particular point of economy ;
the best error of the two is on the parsimonious side.   That may
be corrected, the other cannot.

The reputation of generosity is to be purchased pretty cheap :
it does not depend so much upon a man's general expense, as it
does upon his giving handsomely where it is proper to give at
all.   A man, for instance, who should give a servant four shillings
would pass for covetous, while he who gave him a crown, would
be reckoned generous : so that the difference of those two
opposite characters turns upon one shilling.   A man's character,
in that particular, depends a great deal upon the report of his
own servants ; a mere trifle above common wages makes their
report favourable.

Take care always to form your establishment so much within
your income, as to leave a sufficient fund for unexpected contin-
gencies, and a prudent liberality.   There is hardly a year, in any
man's life, in which a small sum of ready money may not be
employed to great advantage.[1]

POLITICAL MAXIMS

OF THE CARDINAL DE RETZ, IN HIS MEMOIRS ; AND THE
LATE EARL OF CHESTERFIELD'S REMARKS.

1. IL y a souvent de la folie à conjurer ; mais il n'y a rien
de pareil pour faire les gens sages dans la suite : au moins pour
quelque tems.   Comme le péril dans ces sortes d'affaires dure
même après les occasions, l'on est prudent et circonspect dans les
momens qui les suivent.

2. Un esprit médiocre, et susceptible par conséquent d'in-
justes défiances, est de tous les charactères celui qui est le plus
opposé à un bon chef de Parti ; dont la qualité la plus souvent

---

[1] Upon the back of the original is written, in Mr Stanhope's hand,
' Excellent Maxims, but more calculated for the Meridian of France or Spain,
than of England.'

et la plus indispensablement nécessaire, est de supprimer en beaucoup d'occasions, et de cacher en toutes, les soupçons même les plus légitimes.

3. Rien n'anime et n'appuie plus un mouvement, que le ridicule de celui contre lequel on le fait.

4. Le secret n'est pas si rare qu'on le croit, entre des gens qui sont accoutumés à se mêler des grandes affaires.

5. Descendre jusqu'aux petits est le plus sûr moyen de s'égaler aux grands.

6. La mode qui a du pouvoir en toutes choses ne l'a si sensiblement en aucune, qu'à être bien ou mal à la Cour : il y a des tems ou la disgrâce est une manière de feu qui purifie toutes les mauvaises qualités, et qui illumine toutes les bonnes ; il y a des tems ou il ne sied pas bien à un honnête homme d'être disgracié.

7. La souffrance aux personnes d'un grand rang tient lieu d'une grande vertu.

8. Il y a une espèce de galimatias que la pratique fait connoître quelquefois, mais que la spéculation ne fait jamais entendre.

9. Toutes les Puissances ne peuvent rien contre la réputation d'un homme qui se la conserve dans son Corps.

10. On est aussi souvent dupe par la défiance que par la confiance.

11. L'extrêmité du mal n'est jamais à son période, que quand ceux qui commandent ont perdu la honte ; parce que c'est justement le moment dans lequel ceux qui obéissent perdent le respect ; et c'est dans ce même moment que l'on revient de la léthargie : mais par des convulsions.

12. Il y a un voile qui doit toujours couvrir tout ce que l'on peut dire, et tout ce que l'on peut croire du Droit des Peuples et de celui des Rois, qui ne s'accordent jamais si bien ensemble que dans le silence.

13. Il y a des conjonctures dans lesquelles on ne peut plus faire que des fautes ; mais la fortune ne met jamais les hommes dans cet état, qui est de tous le plus malheureux, et personne n'y tombe que ceux qui s'y précipitent par leur faute.

14. Il sied plus mal à un Ministre de dire des sottises, que d'en faire.

15. Les avis que l'on donne à un Ministre passent pour des crimes, toutes les fois qu'on ne lui est point agréable.

16. Auprès des Princes, il est aussi dangereux, et presqu' aussi criminel, de pouvoir le bien que de vouloir le mal.

17. Il est bien plus naturel à la peur de consulter que de décider.

18. Cette circonstance paroît ridicule ; mais elle est fondée. A Paris, dans les émotions populaires, les plus échauffés ne veulent pas, ce qu'ils appellent, *se désheurer.*

19. La flexibilité est de toutes les qualités la plus nécessaire pour le maniement des grandes affaires.

20. On a plus de peine dans les Partis, de vivre avec ceux qui en sont, que d'agir contre ceux qui y sont opposés.

21. Les plus grands dangers ont leurs charmes, pour peu que l'on apperçoive de gloire dans la perspective des mauvais succès ; les médiocres dangers n'ont que des horreurs, quand la perte de la réputation est attachée à la mauvaise fortune.

22. Les extrêmes sont toujours fâcheux. Mais ce sont des moyens sages quand ils sont nécessaires : ce qu'ils ont de consolant c'est qu'ils ne sont jamais médiocres, et qu'ils sont décisifs quand ils sont bons.

23. Il y a des conjonctures où la prudence même ordonne de ne consulter que le chapître des accidens.

24. Il n'y a rien dans le monde qui n'ait son moment décisif ; et le chef d'œuvre de la bonne conduite est de connoître et de prendre ce moment.

25. L'abomination joint au ridicule fait le plus dangereux et le plus irrémédiable de tous les composés.

26. Les gens foibles ne plient jamais quand ils le doivent.

27. Rien ne touche et n'émeut tant les peuples, et même les Compagnies qui tiennent beaucoup du peuple, que la variété des spectacles.

28. Les exemples du passé touchent sans comparaison plus les hommes, que ceux de leur siècle : nous nous accoutumons à tout ce que nous voyons ; et peut-être que le Consulat du Cheval de Caligula, ne nous auroit pas tant surpris, que nous nous l'imaginons.

29. Les hommes foibles se laissent aller ordinairement au plus grand bruit.

30. Il ne faut jamais contester ce qu'on ne croit pas pouvoir obtenir.

31. Le moment où l'on reçoit les plus heureuses nouvelles est justement celui où il faut redoubler son attention pour les petites.

32. Le pouvoir dans les peuples est fâcheux, en ce qu'il nous rend responsables de ce qu'ils font malgré nous.

33. L'une des plus grandes incommodités des guerres civiles est qu'il faut encore plus d'application à ce que l'on ne doit pas dire à ses amis, qu'à ce que l'on doit faire contre ses ennemis.

34. Il n'y a point de qualité qui dépare tant un grand homme,

que de n'être pas juste à prendre le moment décisif de la réputation. L'on ne le manque presque jamais que pour mieux prendre celui de la fortune ; c'est en quoi l'on se trompe, pour l'ordinaire, doublement.

35. La vue la plus commune dans les imprudences, c'est celle, que l'on a, de la possibilité des ressources.

36. Toute Compagnie est peuple ; ainsi tout y dépend des instans.

37. Tout ce qui paroit hazardeux, et qui pourtant ne l'est pas, est presque toujours sage.

38. Les gens irrésolus prennent toujours, avec facilité, les ouvertures qui les mènent à deux chemins, et qui par conséquent ne les pressent pas d'opter.

39. Il n'y a point de petits pas dans les grandes affaires.

40. Il y a des tems où certaines gens ont toujours raison.

41. Rien ne persuade tant les gens qui ont peu de sens que ce qu'ils n'entendent pas.

42. Il n'est pas sage de faire, dans les factions, où l'on n'est que sur la défensive, ce qui n'est pas pressé. Mais l'inquiétude des subalternes est la chose la plus incommode dans ces rencontres ; ils croient que, des qu'on n'agit pas, on est perdu.

43. Les chefs dans les factions n'en sont les maîtres, qu'autant qu'ils savent prévenir ou appaiser les murmures.

44. Quand la frayeur est venue à un certain point, elle produit les mêmes effets que la témérité.

45. Il est aussi nécessaire de choisir les mots dans les grandes affaires, qu'il est superflu de les choisir dans les petites.

46. Rien n'est plus rare ni plus difficile aux Ministres qu'un certain ménagement dans le calme qui suit immédiatement les grandes tempêtes, parce que la flatterie y redouble, et que la défiance n'y est pas éteinte.

47. Il ne faut pas nous choquer si fort des fautes de ceux qui sont nos amis, que nous en donnions de l'avantage à ceux contre lesquels nous agissons.

48. Le talent d'insinuer est plus utile que celui de persuader, parce que l'on peut insinuer à tout le monde, et que l'on ne persuade presque jamais personne.

49. Dans les matières qui ne sont pas favorables par elles-mêmes, tout changement qui n'est pas nécessaire est pernicieux, parce qu'il est odieux.

50. Il faut faire voir à ceux qui sont naturellement foibles toutes sortes d'abîmes : parce que c'est le vrai moyen de les obliger de se jetter dans le premier chemin qu'on leur ouvre.

51. L'on doit hazarder le possible toutes les fois que l'on se

sent en état de profiter même du manquement de succès.

52. Les hommes irrésolus se déterminent difficilement pour les moyens, quoique même ils soient déterminés pour la fin.

53. C'est presque jeu sûr avec les hommes fourbes, de leur faire croire que l'on veut tromper ceux que l'on veut servir.

54. L'un des plus grands embarras que l'on ait avec les Princes, c'est que l'on est souvent obligé, par la considération de leur propre service, de leur donner des conseils dont on ne peut pas leur dire les véritables raisons.

55. Quand on se trouve obligé de faire un discours que l'on prévoit ne devoir pas agréer, l'on ne peut lui donner trop d'apparence de sincérité : parce que c'est l'unique moyen de l'adoucir.

56. On ne doit jamais se jouer avec la faveur, on ne la peut trop embrasser quand elle est véritable ; on ne la peut trop éloigner quand elle est fausse.

57. Il y a de l'inconvénient à s'engager sur des suppositions de ce que l'on croit impossible ; et pourtant il n'y a rien de si commun.

58. La plûpart des hommes examinent moins les raisons de ce qu'on leur propose contre leur sentiment, que celles qui peuvent obliger, celui qui les propose, de s'en servir.

59. Tout ce qui est vide dans les tems de faction et d'intrigue, passe pour mystérieux dans les esprits de ceux qui ne sont pas accoutumés aux grandes affaires.

60. Il n'est jamais permis à un inférieur de s'égaler en paroles à celui à qui il doit du respect, quoi qu'il s'y égale dans l'action.

61. Tout homme que la fortune seule, par quelque accident, a fait homme public, devient presque toujours avec un peu de tems un particulier ridicule.

62. La plus grande imperfection des hommes est la complaisance, qu'ils trouvent, à se persuader que les autres ne sont point exempts des défauts qu'ils se reconnoissent à eux-mêmes.

63. Il n'y a que l'expérience qui puisse apprendre aux hommes à ne pas préférer ce qui les pique dans le présent, à ce qui les doit toucher bien plus essentiellement dans l'avenir.

64. Il faut s'appliquer, avec soin, dans les grandes affaires encore plus que dans les autres, à se défendre du goût qu'on trouve pour la plaisanterie

65. On ne peut assez peser les moindres mots, dans les grandes affaires.

66. Il n'y a que la continuation du bonheur qui fixe la plupart des amitiés.

67. Quiconque assemble le peuple, l'émeut.

TRANSLATION.

1. IT is often madness to engage in a conspiracy ; but nothing is so effectual to bring people afterwards to their senses, at least for a time. As in such undertakings, the danger subsists, even after the business is over ; this obliges to be prudent and circumspect in the succeeding moments.

2. A middling understanding, being susceptible of unjust suspicions, is, consequently, of all characters, the least fit to head a faction. As the most indispensable qualification in such a Chief is to suppress, in many occasions, and to conceal in all, even the best grounded suspicions.

3. Nothing animates and gives strength to a commotion, so much as the ridicule of him against whom it is raised.

4. Among people used to affairs of moment, secrecy is much less uncommon than is generally believed.

5. Descending to the Little is the surest way of attaining to an equality with the Great.

6. Fashion, though powerful in all things, is not more so in any, than in being well or ill at Court. There are times when disgrace is a kind of fire, that purifies all bad qualities, and illuminates every good one. There are others, in which the being out of favour is unbecoming a man of character.

7. Sufferings, in people of the first rank, supply the want of virtue.

8. There is a confused kind of jumble, which practice sometimes teaches ; but is never to be understood by speculation.

9. The greatest Powers cannot injure a man's character, whose reputation is unblemished among his party.

10. We are as often duped by diffidence, as by confidence.

11. The greatest evils are not arrived at their utmost period, until those who are in power have lost all sense of shame. At such a time, those who should obey shake off all respect and subordination. Then is lethargic indolence roused ; but roused by convulsions.

12. A veil ought always to be drawn over whatever may be said or thought concerning the rights of the People, or of Kings ; which agree best when least mentioned.[1]

· 13. There are, at times, situations so very unfortunate, that whatever is undertaken must be wrong. Chance, alone, never

---

[1] This Maxim, as well as several others, evidently prove they were written by a man subject to despotic government.

throws people into such dilemmas; and they happen only to those who bring them upon themselves.

14. It is more unbecoming a Minister to say, than to do, silly things.

15. The advice given to a Minister, by an obnoxious person, is always thought bad.

16. It is as dangerous, and almost as criminal, with Princes, to have the power of doing good, as the will of doing evil.

17. Timorous minds are much more inclined to deliberate than to resolve.

18. It appears ridiculous to assert, but it is not the less true, that at Paris, during popular commotions, the most violent will not quit their homes past a stated hour.

19. Flexibility is the most requisite qualification for the management of great affairs.

20. It is more difficult for the member of a faction to live with those of his own party, than to act against those who oppose it.

21. The greatest dangers have their allurements, if the want of success is likely to be attended with a degree of glory. Middling dangers are horrid, when the loss of reputation is the inevitable consequence of ill success.

22. Violent measures are always dangerous, but when necessary, may then be looked upon as wise. They have, however, the advantage of never being matter of indifference ; and, when well concerted, must be decisive.

23. There may be circumstances, in which even prudence directs us to trust entirely to chance.

24. Everything in this world has its critical moment ; and the height of good conduct consists in knowing and seizing it.

25. Profligacy, joined to ridicule, form the most abominable and most dangerous of all characters.

26. Weak minds never yield when they ought.

27. Variety of sights have the greatest effect upon the mob, and also upon numerous assemblies, who, in many respects, resemble mob.

28. Examples taken from past times have infinitely more power over the minds of men, than any of the age in which they live. Whatever we see, grows familiar ; and perhaps the Consulship of Caligula's Horse might not have astonished us so much as we are apt to imagine.

29. Weak minds are commonly overpowered by clamour.

30. We ought never to contend for what we are not likely to obtain.

31. The instant in which we receive the most favourable accounts, is just that wherein we ought to redouble our vigilance, even in regard to the most trifling circumstances.

32. It is dangerous to have a known influence over the people ; as thereby we become responsible even for what is done against our will.

33. One of the greatest difficulties in civil war is, that more art is required to know what should be concealed from our friends, than what ought to be done against our enemies.

34. Nothing lowers a great man so much, as not seizing the decisive moment of raising his reputation. This is seldom neglected, but with a view to fortune : by which mistake, it is not unusual to miss both.

35. The possibility of remedying imprudent actions is commonly an inducement to commit them.

36. Every numerous assembly is mob ; consequently everything there depends upon instantaneous turns.

37. Whatever measure seems hazardous, and is in reality not so, is generally a wise one.

38. Irresolute minds always adopt with facility whatever measures can admit of different issues, and consequently do not require an absolute decision.

39. In momentous affairs, no step is indifferent.

40. There are times in which certain people are always in the right.

41. Nothing convinces persons of a weak understanding so effectually as what they do not comprehend.

42. When Factions are only upon the defensive, they ought never to do that which may be delayed. Upon such occasions, nothing is so troublesome as the restlessness of subalterns ; who think a state of inaction total destruction.

43. Those who head Factions have no way of maintaining their authority, but by preventing, or quieting, discontent.

44. A certain degree of fear produces the same effects as rashness.

45. In affairs of importance, the choice of words is of as much consequence, as it would be superfluous in those of little moment.

46. During those calms which immediately succeed violent storms, nothing is more difficult for Ministers than to act properly ; because, while flattery increases, suspicions are not yet subsided.

47. The faults of our friends ought never to anger us so far as to give an advantage to our enemies.

48. The talent of insinuation is more useful than that of persuasion ; as everybody is open to insinuation, but scarce any to persuasion.

49. In matters of a delicate nature, all unnecessary alterations are dangerous ; because odious.

50. The best way to compel weakminded people to adopt our opinion is to frighten them from all others, by magnifying their danger.

51. We must run all hazards, where we think ourselves in a situation to reap some advantage, even from the want of success.

52. Irresolute men are diffident in resolving upon the means, even when they are determined upon the End.

53. It is almost a sure game, with crafty men, to make them believe we intend to deceive those whom we mean to serve.

54. One of the greatest difficulties with Princes is the being often obliged, in order to serve them, to give advice the true reasons of which we dare not mention.

55. The saying things which we foresee will not be pleasing, can only be softened by the greatest appearance of sincerity.

56. We ought never to trifle with favour. If real, we should hastily seize the advantage ; if pretended, avoid the allurement.

57. It is very inconsequent to enter into engagements upon suppositions we think impossible, and yet it is very usual.

58. The generality of mankind pay less attention to arguments urged against their opinion, than to such as may engage the disputant to adopt their own.

59. In times of faction and intrigue, whatever appears inert is reckoned mysterious by those who are not accustomed to affairs of moment.

60. It is never allowable in an inferior to equal himself in words to a superior, although he may rival him in actions.

61. Every man whom chance alone has, by some accident, made a public character, hardly ever fails of becoming, in a short time, a ridiculous private one.

62. The greatest imperfection of men is, the complacency with which they are willing to think others not free from faults, of which they are themselves conscious.

63. Experience only can teach men not to prefer what strikes them for the present moment, to what will have much greater weight with them hereafter.

64. In the management of important business, all turn to raillery must be more carefully avoided than in any other.

65. In momentous transactions, words cannot be sufficiently weighed.

66. The permanency of most friendships depends upon the continuity of good fortune.

67. Whoever assembles the multitude will raise commotions.

----◇----

LORD CHESTERFIELD'S REMARKS UPON THE FOREGOING MAXIMS.

I HAVE taken the trouble of extracting and collecting, for your use, the foregoing Political Maxims of the Cardinal de Retz, in his Memoirs. They are not aphorisms of his invention, but the true and just observations of his own experience, in the course of great business. My own experience attests the truth of them all. Read them over with attention as here above, and then read with the same attention, and *tout de suite*, the Memoirs; where you will find the facts and characters from whence those observations are drawn, or to which they are applied ; and they will reciprocally help to fix each other in your mind. I hardly know any book so necessary for a young man to read and re-member. You will there find how great business is really carried on ; very differently from what people, who have never been concerned in it, imagine. You will there see what Courts and Courtiers really are, and observe that they are neither so good as they should be, nor so bad as they are thought by most people. The Court Poet, and the sullen, cloistered Pedant, are equally mistaken in their notions, or at least in the accounts they give us of them. You will observe the coolness in general, the per-fidy in some cases, and the truth in a very few, of Court friend-ships. This will teach you the prudence of a general distrust : and the imprudence of making no exception to that rule, upon good and tried grounds. You will see the utility of good breeding towards one's greatest enemies; and the high impru-dence and folly of either insulting or injurious expressions. You will find, in the Cardinal's own character, a strange, but by no means an uncommon, mixture of high and low, good and bad, parts and indiscretion. In the character of Monsieur le Duc d'Orleans, you may observe the model of weakness, irresolution, and fear, though with very good parts. In short, you will, in every page of that book, see that strange, inconsistent creature, Man, just as he is. If you would know that period of history (and it is well worth knowing) correctly, after you have read the Cardinal's Memoirs, you should read those of Joly, and of Madame de Motteville; both which throw great light upon the first. By all those accounts put together, it appears that Anne of Austria (with great submission to a Crowned Head do I say it) was a B——. She had spirit and courage without parts, devotion without common morality, and lewdness without tenderness either to justify or to dignify it. Her two sons were no more Lewis the Thirteenth's than they were mine ; and if Buckingham had staid a little longer, she would probably have had another by him.

Cardinal Mazarin was a great knave, but no great man ; much more cunning than able ; scandalously false, and dirtily greedy. As for his enemy, Cardinal de Retz, I can truly call him a man of great parts, but I cannot call him a great man. He never was so much so as in his retirement. The Ladies had then a great, and have always had some, share in State affairs in France ; the spring and the streams of their politics have always been, and always will be, the interest of their present Lover, or their resentment against a discarded and perfidious one. Money is their great object ; of which they are extremely greedy, if it coincides with their arrangement with the Lover for the time being : but true glory, and public good, never enter into their heads. They are always governed by the man they love, and they always govern the man who loves them. He or she, who loves the most, is always governed by him or her who loves the least. Madame de Montbazon governed Monsieur de Beaufort, who was fond of her ; whereas she was only proud of his rank and popularity. The *Drudi* for the time being always governed Madame and Mademoiselle de Chevreuse, and steered their politics. Madame de Longueville governed her brother the Prince de Conti, who was in love with her ; but Marsillac, with whom she was in love, governed her. In all female politics, the head is certainly not the part that takes the lead : the true and secret spring lies lower and deeper. La Palatine, whom the Cardinal celebrates as the ablest and most sensible woman he ever met with, and who seems to have acted more systematically and consequentially than any of them, starts aside however, and deviates from her plan, whenever the interests or the inclinations of La Vieuville, her Lover, require it. I will add (though with great submission to a late friend of yours at Paris) that no woman ever yet either reasoned or acted long together consequentially ; but some little thing, some love, some resentment, some present momentary interest, some sup-

posed slight, or some humour, always breaks in upon, and over-
sets, their most prudent resolutions and schemes.

CONSIDERATIONS

UPON THE REPEAL OF THE LIMITATION, RELATIVE TO FOREIGNERS, IN THE ACT OF SETTLEMENT.

THE particular Limitation relative to Foreigners, in the Act
of Settlement, and now to be repealed, was marked out as
peculiarly sacred, by the first Parliament, and that no uncom-
plaisant one, of the late King, by enacting, that that Limitation
should be inserted in all future acts of Naturalization; and it
was so, even in the act for naturalizing the Prince of Orange,
the King's son-in-law.

But, it seems, Messieurs Prevot, Boquet, and others, are now
to receive a mark of distinction, which the King's son-in-law
could not then obtain : But, can the same indulgence, hereafter,
ever be refused to foreign Protestant Princes of the highest birth,
and greatest merit, and, many of them, nearly related to his
Majesty and the Royal Family; who may, very probably, prefer
the British service to any other ?

The poor military arguments, urged in justification of the
Repeal of this most sacred Law, are too trifling to be the true
ones, and too wretched to be seriously answered, unless by the
unfortunate British Officers ; who are hereby, in a manner,
declared and enacted to be incapable of doing the duty of Captains, Majors, &c.

Some other reason, therefore, must be sought for ; and, perhaps, it is but too easily found.

May it not be *periculum faciamus in anima vili?*[1] If this
goes down, it shall be followed ; some foreign Prince, of allowed
merit, shall make the first application to the Crown, and to the
Parliament, for the same favour which was shown to Messieurs
Prevot, Bouquet, and Company. Can either of them, in common
decency, refuse it ? Besides that, perhaps a time may come when
Generals, and superior Officers, may be as much wanted in England, as great Captains and Majors are now wanted in America.

Great evils have always such trifling beginnings, to smooth
the way for them insensibly ; as Cardinal de Retz most justly
observes, when he says, that he is persuaded, that the Romans

---

[1] Let us make an experiment upon a worthless life.

were carried on by such shades and gradations of mischief and extravagancy, as not to have been much surprised or alarmed when Caligula declared his intention of making his horse Consul. So that, by the natural progression of precedents, the next generation may probably see, and even without surprise or abhorrence, Foreigners commanding your troops, and voting the supplies for them in both Houses of Parliament.

As to the pretended utility of these foreign Heroes, it is impossible to answer such arguments seriously. What experience evinces the necessity? Cape Breton, the strongest place in America, was very irregularly taken in the last war, by our irregular American troops. Sir William Johnson lately beat, and took most irregularly, the regular General Dieskau, at the head of his regular forces: and General Braddock, who was most judiciously selected out of the whole British army, to be our *Scipio Americanus*, was very irregularly destroyed, by unseen, and to this day unknown, enemies.

How will these foreign Heroes agree with the English Officers of the same corps, who are, in a manner, by Act of Parliament, declared unfit for their business, till instructed in it by the great foreign masters of Homicide. Will they not even be more inclined to advise than to obey their Colonel: to interpret than to execute his orders? Will they co-operate properly with our American troops and Officers, whom they will certainly look upon, and treat, as an inexperienced and undisciplined rabble? Can it possibly be otherwise? or, can it be wondered at, when those Gentlemen know that they are appointed Officers by one Act of Parliament, and at the expense of another, the most sacred of the statute book.

O! but there is to be but one half of the Officers, of this thundering Legion, who are to be Foreigners: so much the worse: for then, according to the principle laid down, it can be but half disciplined. Besides, the less the object, to which a very great object is sacrificed, the more absurd and the more suspicious such a sacrifice becomes. At first, this whole legion was to consist of all Foreigners, Field officers and all; which, upon the principle of the absolute utility and necessity of foreign Officers, was much more rational; but, thus mitigated, as it is called, is a thousand times more absurd. And how does it stand now? Why truly, the sacred Act of Settlement is to be repealed, and in the tenderest part, for the sake of some foreign Captains and Majors, who are to be commanded by British superior Officers, who, by this Act of Parliament, are supposed not to know their trade.

One has heard (but one hears a thousand false reports) that this absurd scheme was, some time ago, quashed by his Majesty's own prudence and goodness; and, from the rightness of the thing, I am inclined to believe that it is true : and I am sure I will not suppose that ever that might be among the reasons for resuming it in this shape, and forcing it down the throats of the reluctant Nation : but this is certain, that it was once dropped, and at some expense too. The foreign Heroes were contented with Money instead of Laurels, and were going away about their own business ; but, perhaps, a condescension to the unanimous wishes of the whole *people of England, at least,* was looked upon as a dangerous precedent, and the repeal of the Act of Settlement as a useful one. But however I will have candour enough to believe, that this was merely an absurd, wrong-headed measure ; for, if I did not, I must think it the wickedest that ever was pushed.

AXIOMS IN TRADE.

To sell, upon the whole, more than you buy.

To buy your materials as cheap, and to sell your manufactures as dear, as you can.

To ease the manufacturers, as much as possible, of all taxes and burthens.

To lay small or no duties upon your own manufactures exported, and to lay high duties upon all foreign manufactures imported.

To lay small or no duties upon foreign materials, that are necessary for your own manufactures ; but to lay very high duties upon, or rather totally prohibit, the exportation of such of your own materials as are necessary for the manufactures of other countries; as Wool, Fuller's earth, &c.

To keep the interest of money low, that people may place their money in trade.

Not to imagine (as people commonly do) that it is either prudent or possible to prohibit the exportation of your gold and silver, whether coined or uncoined. For, if the balance of trade be against you, that is, if you buy more than you sell, you must necessarily make up that difference in money ; and your Bullion or your Coin, which are in effect the same thing, must and will be exported, in spite of all laws. But if you sell more than you buy, then foreigners must do the same by you, and make up their deficiency in Bullion or Coin. Gold and silver are but merchandise, as well as Cloth or Linen : and that nation that buys the least, and sells the most, must always have the most money.

A free trade is always carried on with more advantage to the public, than an exclusive one by a company. But the particular circumstances of some trades may sometimes require a joint stock and exclusive privileges.

All monopolies are destructive to trade.

To get, as much as possible, the advantages of manufacturing and freight.

To contrive to undersell other nations, in foreign markets.

TO THE KING'S MOST EXCELLENT MAJESTY.

The humble PETITION *of Philip Earl of Chesterfield Knight of the most noble Order of the Garter,*

SHOWETH,

THAT your Petitioner, being rendered, by deafness, as useless and insignificant as most of his equals and contemporaries are by nature, hopes, in common with them, to share your Majesty's Royal favour and bounty ; whereby he may be enabled either to save or spend, as he shall think proper, more than he can do at present.

That your Petitioner, having had the honour of serving your Majesty in several very lucrative employments, seems thereby entitled to a lucrative retreat from business, and to enjoy *otium cum dignitate;* that is, leisure and a large pension.

Your Petitioner humbly presumes, that he has, at least, a common claim to such a pension : he has a vote in the most august assembly in the world ; he has an estate that puts him above wanting it; but he has, at the same time (though he says it), an elevation of sentiment, that makes him not only desire, but (pardon, dread Sir, an expression you are used to) *insist* upon it.

That your Petitioner is little apt, and always unwilling, to speak advantageously of himself; but as, after all, some justice is due to one's self, as well as to others, he begs leave to represent, That his loyalty to your Majesty has always been unshaken, even in the worst of times ; That, particularly, in the late unnatural rebellion, when the Pretender advanced as far as Derby, at the head of, at least, three thousand undisciplined men, the flower of the Scottish Nobility and Gentry, your Petitioner did not join him, as, unquestionably, he might have done, had he been so inclined; but, on the contrary, raised sixteen companies, of one hundred men each, at the public expense, in support of your Majesty's undoubted right to the Imperial Crown of these Realms; which distinguished proof of his loyalty is, to this hour, unrewarded.

Your Majesty's Petitioner is well aware, that your Civil List must necessarily be in a low and languid state, after the various, frequent, and profuse evacuations, which it has of late years undergone; but, at the same time, he presumes to hope, that this argument, which seems not to have been made use of against any other person whatsoever, shall not, in this single case, be urged against him; and the less so, as he has good reasons to believe that the deficiencies of the Pension fund are, by no means, the last that will be made good by Parliament.

Your Petitioner begs leave to observe, That a small pension is disgraceful and opprobrious, as it intimates a shameful necessity on one part, and a degrading sort of charity on the other: but that a great one implies dignity and affluence on one side; on the other, regard and esteem; which, doubtless, your Majesty must entertain in the highest degree, for those great personages whose respectable names stand upon your Eleemosynary list. Your Petitioner, therefore, humbly persuades himself, upon this principle, that less than three thousand pounds a year will not be proposed to him: if made up gold the more agreeable; if for life, the more marketable.

Your Petitioner persuades himself, that your Majesty will not suspect this his humble application to proceed from any mean, interested motive, of which he has always had the utmost abhorrence. No, Sir, he confesses his own weakness; Honour alone is his object; Honour is his passion; Honour is dearer to him than life. To Honour he has always sacrificed all other considerations; and upon this generous principle, singly, he now solicits that honour, which, in the most shining times, distinguished the greatest men of Greece; who were fed at the expense of the public.

Upon this Honour, so sacred to him as a Peer, so tender to him as a Man, he most solemnly assures your Majesty, that, in case you shall be pleased to grant him this his humble request, he will gratefully and honourably support, and promote with zeal and vigour, the worst measure that the worst Minister can ever suggest to your Majesty: but, on the other hand, should he be singled out, marked, and branded by a refusal, he thinks

himself obliged in Honour to declare, that he will, to the utmost
of his power, oppose the best and wisest measures, that your
Majesty yourself can ever dictate.

And your Majesty's Petitioner shall ever pray.

———◇———

A FRAGMENT.

A CHAPTER of the Garter is to be held at St James's next
Friday ; in which Prince Edward, the Prince of Orange, the
Earls of Lincoln, Winchelsea, and Cardigan, are to be
elected Knights Companions of the Order of the Garter.
Though solely nominated by the Crown, they are said to be
elected ; because there is a pretended election. All the
Knights are summoned to attend the Sovereign at a Chapter,
to be held on such a day, in order to elect so many new
Knights into the vacant Stalls of the deceased ones ; accordingly they meet in the Council Chamber, where they all sit
down according to their seniority, at a long table, where the
Sovereign presides. There every Knight pretends to write a
list of those for whom he intends to vote ; and, in effect, writes
down nine names, such as he thinks proper, taking care, however, to insert the names of those who are really to be elected ;
then the Bishop of Salisbury, who is always the Chancellor of
the Order, goes round the table, and takes the paper of each
Knight, pretends to look into them, and then declares the
majority of votes to be for those persons who were nominated
by the Crown. Upon this declaration, two of the old Knights
go into the outward room, where the new ones are attending,
and introduce them, one after another, according to their
ranks. The new Knight kneels down before the King, who
puts the riband about his neck ; then he turns to the Prince of
Wales, or, in his absence, to the oldest Knight, who puts the
Garter about his leg. This is the ceremony of the Chapter :
that of the Installation, which is always performed in St
George's Chapel at Windsor, completes the whole thing ; for
till then the new Knights cannot wear the Star, unless by particular dispensation from the Sovereign, which is very seldom
granted. All ceremonies are in themselves very silly things ;
but yet, a man of the world should know them. They are the
outworks of Manners and Decency, which would be too often
broken in upon, if it were not for that defence, which keeps the
enemy at a proper distance. It is for that reason that I always

treat fools and coxcombs with great ceremony ; true good
breeding not being a sufficient barrier against them. The
knowledge of the world teaches one to deal with different people
differently, and according as characters and situations require.
The *versatile ingenium* is a most essential point; and a man
must be broke to it while he is young. Have it always in
your thoughts, as I have you in mine. Adieu.

P. S. This moment I receive your letter of the 15th, N. S.,
with which I am very well pleased : it informs me, and what I
like still better, it shows me that you are informed.

A FRAGMENT.

YOUR riding, fencing, and dancing, constantly, at the Academy, will, I hope, lengthen you out a little ; therefore pray
take a great deal of those exercises : for I would very fain have
you be, at least, five feet eight inches high, as Mr Harte once
wrote me word that he hoped you would. Mr Pelham likewise
told me, that you speak German and French as fluently and
correctly as a Saxon or a Parisian. I am very glad of both :
take care not to forget the former ; there is no danger of your
forgetting the latter. As I both thank and applaud you for
having, hitherto, employed yourself so well abroad, I must again
repeat to you, that the manner in which you shall now employ
it, at Paris, will be finally decisive of your fortune, figure, and
character in the world, and consequently of my esteem and
kindness. Eight or nine months determine the whole ; which
whole is very near complete. It consists in this only : to retain
and increase the learning you have already acquired ; to add to
it the still more useful knowledge of the world ; and to adorn
both, with the Manners, the Address, the Air, and the Graces
of a Man of Fashion. Without the last, I will say of your youth
and your knowledge, what Horace says to Venus ;

> Parum comis sine te Juventas,
> Mercuriusque.[1]

The two great subjects of conversation now at Paris are,
the dispute between the Crown and the Clergy, and between the
Crown and the States of Brittany : inform yourself thoroughly of
both ; which will let you into the most material parts of the
French history and constitution. There are four letters printed,

> Without thee Youth itself can charm but little,
> And Mercury.

and very well written, against the pretended rights and *immunities* of the Clergy ; to which there is an Answer, very well written too, in defence of those *immunities*. Read them both with attention ; and also all representations, memorials, and whatever shall appear, for or against the claims of the States of Brittany. I dare say, that ninety-nine in a hundred, of the English at Paris, do not give themselves the trouble of inquiring into those disputes ; but content themselves with saying, that there is a confounded bustle and rout between the King and the Priests, and between the King and the States of Brittany ; but that, for their parts, they do not trouble their heads about them ; fight Dog, fight Bear : but, with submission to them, these are objects worthy the attention and inquiries of a man of sense and business.

Adieu, my dear child !   Yours tenderly.

———◇———

We have been favoured with the following letters, written by the late EARL of CHESTERFIELD to different persons.

LETTRE DE RECOMMANDATION,

EN FAVEUR DE MADAME CLELAND, ADRESSÉE A MADAME DE TENCIN.

Londres, ce 20 Août, V. S.

COMBATTU par des mouvemens bien différents, j'ai long tems ballancé, avant que d'oser me déterminer, à vous envoyer cette lettre. Je sentois toute l'indiscrétion d'une telle démarche, et à quel point c'étoit abuser de la bonté que vous avez eu pour moi, pendant mon séjour à Paris, que de vous la redemander pour un autre : mais sollicité vivement par une Dame que son mérite met à l'abri des refus, et porté, d'ailleurs, à profiter du moindre prétexte pour rappeler un souvenir qui m'est si précieux que le vôtre ; le penchant (comme il arrive presque toujours) a triomphé de la discrétion ; et je satisfais en même tems à mes propres inclinations et aux instances de Madame Cleland, qui aura l'honneur de vous rendre cette lettre.

Je sais par expérience, Madame (car j'en suis moi-même un exemple), que ce n'est pas la première affaire de la sorte, à laquelle votre réputation, qui ne se renferme point dans les bornes de la France, vous a exposée : mais je me flatte, aussi, que vous ne la trouverez pas la plus désagréable. Un mérite supérieur, un esprit juste, délicat, orné par la lecture de tout ce qu'il y a de bon dans toutes les langues, et un grand usage

du monde, qui ont acquis à Madame Cleland l'estime et la
considération de tout ce qu'il y a d'honnêtes gens ici, me
rassurent sur la liberté, que je prends, de vous la recom-
mander ; et me persuadent même que vous ne m'en saurez pas
mauvais gré.

Si vous me demandez, par hasard, pourquoi elle m'a choisi
pour son introducteur chez vous, et pourquoi elle a crû, que je
m'étois acquis ce droit-là, je vous dirai naturellement, que c'est
moi, qui en suis cause. En cela j'ai suivi l'exemple de la plupart des voyageurs, qui, à leur retour, se font valoir chez eux,
par leurs prétendues liaisons avec ce qu'il y a de plus distingué,
chez les autres. Les Rois, les Princes et les Ministres les ont
toujours comblé de leurs grâces. Et moyennant ce faux étalage
d'honneurs qu'ils n'ont point reçu, ils acquièrent une considération
qu'ils ne méritent point.

J'ai vanté vos bontés pour moi ; je les ai exagérées même,
s'il étoit possible ; et enfin, pour ne vous rien cacher, ma vanité
a poussé l'effronterie au point même de me donner pour votre
ami favori, et enfant de la maison. Quand Madame Cleland m'a
pris au mot, et m'a dit ; ' Je vais bientôt en France ; je n'y am-
bitionne rien tant, que l'honneur de connoître Madame de Tencin ;
vous qui êtes si bien-là, il ne vous coutera rien de me donner
une lettre pour elle.'

Le cas étoit embarrassant : car, après ce que j'avois dit, un
refus auroit été trop choquant à Madame Cleland, et l'aveu, que
je n'étois pas en droit de le faire, trop humiliant pour mon amour
propre. Si bien que je me suis trouvé réduit à risquer le pacquet,
et je crois même que je l'aurois fait, si je n'avois pas eu l'honneur
de vous connoître du tout, plûtot que de me donner le démenti
sur un article si sensible.

Ayant donc franchi le pas ; je voudrois bien en profiter, pour
vous exprimer les sentimens de reconnoissance que j'ai, et que
j'aurai toujours des bontés que vous m'avez temoigné à Paris ;
je voudrois aussi vous exprimer tout ce que je pense des qualités
qui distinguent votre cœur et votre esprit, de tous les autres :
mais cela me méneroit également au delà des bornes d'une lettre,
et au-dessus de mes forces.

Je souhaiterois que Monsieur de Fontenelle voulut bien s'en
charger pour moi. Sur cet article, je puis dire, sans vanité, que
nous pensons de même ; avec cette différence, qu'il vous le
diroit avec cet esprit, cette délicatesse, et cette élégance, qui lui
sont propres et seules convenables au sujet.

Permettez donc, Madame, que, destitué de tous ces avantages
de l'esprit, je vous assure simplement des sentimens de mon cœur,

de l'estime, de la vénération, et de l'attachement respectueux, avec lequel je serai toute ma vie, Madame,

Votre, &c.

Je crois que vous me pardonnerez bien, si je vous supplie de faire mes complimens à Monsieur de Fontenelle.

TRANSLATION.

LETTER OF RECOMMENDATION, IN FAVOUR OF MRS CLELAND, TO MADAME DE TENCIN.

London, August the 20th, O. S.

AGITATED by various thoughts, I have long been in suspense, before I durst resolve to send this letter. I felt all the indiscretion of such a step, and how much it would be trespassing upon the goodness I had experienced from you during my stay at Paris, to require the same for another. A Lady, whose merit secures her from a refusal, has entreated me in the most pressing manner, and my own inclinations have concurred, to make use of the first opportunity, to recall a remembrance which will always give me pleasure; so that, inclination having (as it generally happens) overpowered discretion, my own wishes, and Mrs Cleland's desires, will both be gratified, by her having the honour of presenting this letter to you.

I know, Madam, by experience, and am myself a proof, that this is not the first affair of that kind, which your reputation, not confined within the limits of France, has brought upon you; but I flatter myself that you will not look upon this as the most disagreeable. Superior merit, exquisite and refined sense, adorned by the knowledge of the best authors in every language, and a thorough usage of the world, have acquired Mrs Cleland the esteem and consideration of all people of most merit here. These motives encourage me to take the liberty of recommending her to you, and even persuade me that you will not be offended at it.

If, by chance, you should ask why this Lady has made choice of me to be her introductor towards you, and how she came to believe that I had any such right; I will candidly own, that I myself have been the cause of it; and, in this respect, I have followed the example of most travellers; who, at their return to their own country, endeavour to raise their reputation, by boasting of imaginary connections with the most distinguished people abroad. Kings, Princes, and Ministers, have always loaded them with favours: in consequence of those boasted honours, which they never received, they often acquire a degree of consideration which they do not deserve.

I have boasted of your goodness to me; I have even, if possible, exaggerated it; and, in short (not to conceal anything from you), Vanity has even drove me to declare that I was your favourite friend, and domesticated in your house. Mrs Cleland immediately seized this opportunity, to say; 'I am going to France soon; I wish for nothing so much, as to have the honour of knowing Madame de Tencin : since you are so much connected, you can easily give me a letter for her.'

This was an intricate affair; for after what I had said, Mrs Cleland might have been shocked by a refusal, and my self-love would have been too cruelly hurt, if I had owned that I had no right to do any such thing. So that I find myself under a necessity of running all hazards; and I really believe, that even if I had not been known to you at all, I should still have done it, rather than have confessed so mortifying a thing.

As the first step is now taken; I wish to make the best use of it, by expressing to you the sentiments of gratitude which I have, and ever shall retain, for your goodness to me during my stay at Paris. I wish it were in my power to tell you also, what I think of those perfections, which distinguish your heart and your mind so eminently from all others; but this would carry me beyond the bounds of a letter, and is, indeed, more than I know how to express. Mr de Fontenelle might undertake this for me; for, to say the truth, I know that our opinions upon that subject coincide; with this difference only, that he would express those sentiments with all that energy, delicacy, and elegancy, so peculiar to him, and so very proper for the subject.

Permit me then, Madam, though destitute of all those advantages of mind, to assure you simply of the sentiments of my heart; and of the esteem, veneration, and respectful attachment with which I shall always remain Yours, &c.

P. S. I am persuaded that you will forgive my troubling you to make my compliments to Mr de Fontenelle.

LETTER.

MADAME,　　　　　　　　　　　　Londres, ce 1 Janvier, V. S.

JE ne suis pas diseur de bonne aventure, mais au contraire ;

car je vous annonce que ces quatre billets, que j'ai choisi avec
tant d'attention, et que j'estimois, l'un portant l'autre, à vingt
mille pièces au moins, se sont avisés d'être tous blancs.

Je ne me console de votre malheur que par les belles réflexions qu'il me fait faire, et par la morale utile que j'en tire,
pour le reste de mes jours.—Oui ! Je vois bien, à présent,
que toute la prudence humaine, les mesures les plus sages, et les
projets les mieux concertés sont frivoles, si la fortune, cette
Divinité inconstante, bizarre et *féminine*, n'est pas d'humeur à
les favoriser.   Car que pouvoit-on faire de plus que je n'ai fait,
et qu'en pouvoit-il arriver de moins ?

Se donnera-t'on, après cela, du mouvement, formera-t'on des
plans, et s'inquiétera-t'on, pour les choses de ce monde ? J'ose
dire, que si ces réflexions, aussi judicieuses que nouvelles, font
la même impression sur votre esprit qu'elles ont fait sur le mien,
elles vous vaudront plus, que tout ce que vous auriez pû gagner
dans la lotterie.

Vous êtes bien querelleuse, Madame ; jusqu'à m'accorder un
talent, que je n'ai pas, pour pouvoir, après, me reprocher de ne
le pas employer avec vous ; et je m'épuise, dites vous, en *bon
ton*, avec Madame de Monconseil.   Quelle accusation injuste, et
denuée de toute vraisemblance !   Un Milord Anglois avec le
bon ton !   Ce sont deux choses absolument contradictoires ; ou,
pour m'expliquer plus clairement, et simplifier mon idée, ce
sont deux Etres hétérogènes, dont l'existence de l'un implique
nécessairement la privation de l'autre.

Me voici donc justifié dans toutes les formes de la logique ;
et si vous n'en êtes pas contente, Madame de Monconseil, qui a
en main mes pièces justificatives, pourra vous en convaincre.
Au reste ; si j'en possédois tant soit peu, ce nouvel an me
fourniroit une belle occasion de l'étaler.   Et quoique depuis plus
de cinq mille ans, toute la terre ait traité ce sujet, je vous
dirois quelque chose de nouveau, de galant, et d'obscur, dont
on ne s'est jamais avisé auparavant : votre mérite, et les sentimens de mon cœur, y seroient alembiquées, jusqu'à la plus fine
quintessence.

TRANSLATION.

MADAM,   London, January the 1st, O. S.

I HAVE no skill in fortune-telling : for I must acquaint you,
that the four lottery tickets I had chosen with so much care,
and valued one with another at the rate of (at least) twenty
thousand pounds, are all come out blanks.

My only consolation in this misfortune is, the fine reflections which it occasions, and the most useful Moral drawn from it, for the rest of my days. Now, I plainly see that all human prudence, the wisest projects, and the best concerted schemes, are vain and frivolous ; if Fortune, that capricious, inconstant, and *feminine* Deity, is not disposed to favour them : for what more could have been done than I did, and what less could have happened ?

After such a reverse, shall we ever take pains, form projects, or be uneasy concerning worldly events ? I will venture to say, that if such reflections, equally judicious as new, make the same impression upon your mind, that they do upon mine, they will be more valuable than all you could have won in the Lottery.

Surely, Madam, you must have a great inclination to quarrel, since you allow me to be in possession of a talent which I really have not ; in order to reproach me with not availing myself of it towards you, while, say you, ' I exhaust that talent of saying agreeable things in favour of Madame de Monconseil.' What an unjust accusation, and how void of all probability ! An English Lord, and say things in fashionable French phrases ! This is quite contradictory ; or to explain myself more clearly, and to simplify my idea, I must answer, that they are two heterogeneous Beings ; the existence of the one necessarily implying the non-existence of the other.

Now I think my justification complete, according to all the rules of logic ; but if that does not suffice, Madame de Monconseil has it in her power to convince you, by producing my letters.

Was I possessed of the talent you suppose, the New Year would be a proper occasion to display it on ; and, although that subject has been treated by the whole world for above five thousand years, yet I should then say something new, gallant, and unintelligible, which never before was thought of. Your merit, and the sentiments of my heart, would then be distilled to the most refined quintessence.

LETTER.

A Londres, ce 9me Fevrier, V. S.

ADIEU donc toute coquetterie, de part et d'autre, et vive la vraie et solide amitié ! Heureux ceux qui peuvent s'y atteindre : c'est le gros lot, dans la lotterie du monde, contre lequel il y a des millions de billets blancs.

S'il pouvoit y avoir quelque chose de flatteur dans mon amitié, je dirois, que nous pourrions nous flatter que la nôtre seroit également vraie et durable ; puisqu'elle est à l'abri de tous ces petits incidens, qui brouillent la plûpart des autres. D'abord, nous sommes de différent sexe, article assez important ; et qui nous garantit de ces défiances et de ces rivalités, sur les objets les plus sensibles, et contre lesquels la plus belle amitié du monde ne tient point. En second lieu ; il n'entre point d'amour dans notre fait ; qui, quoique, à la vérité, il donne un grand feu à l'amitié, pendant un certain tems, la flamme de l'un venant à s'éteindre, on voit bientôt les cendres de l'autre. Et enfin (ce qui me regarde uniquement) nous ne nous voyons pas trop. Vous ne me connoissez que par mon bon côté ; et vous ne voyez pas ces moments de langueur, d'humeur, et de chagrin, qui causent, si souvent, le dégoût ou le repentir des liaisons, qu'on a formé, et qui font, qu'on se dit à soi-même, L'auroit-on crû ? Qui l'auroit dit ? Comme on peut se tromper aux dehors ? Et la perspective, dans laquelle vous me voyez, m'est si favorable, qu'elle me console un peu *della lontananza*, où je suis obligé de vous chercher.

Une caillette, à beaux sentiments, critiqueroit impitoyable-ment ceux-ci comme très-*indélicats ;* mais en sont-ils moins naturels pour cela ? Et ne sommes nous pas, pour la plûpart, redevables de nos vertus à des situations et des circonstances un peu fortuites ? Au moins j'ai assez d'humilité pour le croire ; et (si je voulois dire toute la vérité) assez d'expérience, de moi-même, pour le savoir. En tous cas ; tel que je suis, je vous suis acquis, et vous voyez que je suis de trop bonne foi pour vous surfaire dans le prix de l'acquisition, que vous avez faite.

Vous avez beau faire les honneurs de votre pays, et désavouer votre propriété exclusive des Grâces ; il faut con-venir, pourtant, que la France est leur séjour, ou plûtot leur pays natal. Si elles pouvoient se fâcher contre vous, dont il y a peu d'apparence, elles seroient piquées, au point de vous quitter, de ce que vous les envoyez promener dans un pays, ou elles ne connoissent, ni ne sont connues de personne : et si par hasard je les connoissois, ce ne seroit que pour les avoir vues si souvent, chez vous.

Il est bien sûr que les Grâces sont un don de la nature, qu'on ne peut pas acquérir ; l'art en peut relever l'éclat, mais il faut que la nature ait donné le fond. On voit cela en tout.

Combien de gens ne dansent-ils pas parfaitement bien, mais saus grâce ; comme il y en a qui dausent très-mal avec beaucoup : combien trouve-t'on d'esprits vigoureux et délicats, qui instruits et ornés par tout ce que l'art et l'étude peuvent faire, ne plaisent pourtant guère, faute de ces grâces naturelles, qui ne s'acquièrent point : chaque pays a ses talens, aussi bien que ses fruits et ses denrées particulières. Nous pensons *creux*, et nous approfondissons ; les Italiens pensent *haut*, et se perdent dans les nues : vous tenez le milieu ; on vous voit, on vous suit, on vous aime.

Servez vous, Madame, de tout ce que cet esprit et ces grâces, que je vous connois, peuvent faire en ma faveur, et dites, je vous en supplie, tout ce qu'elles vous suggéreront, à Monsieur de Matignon, de ma part. Mon cœur ne vous désavouera pas sur tout ce que vous pourrez lui dire de plus fort, à propos du mariage de Mademoiselle sa fille : mais ne vous bornez pas à ce seul article, car il n'y en a pas un, au monde, qui peut le regarder, auquel je ne prendrois pas également part. Ce seroit abuser de sa bonté que de lui écrire moi-même : une messagère comme vous me fera bien plus d'honneur, et à lui plus de plaisir.

Adieu, Madame. Je rougis de la longueur de ma lettre.

TRANSLATION.

London, February the 9th, O. S.

ADIEU, then, to all coquetry, on both sides, and prosperity to real and solid friendship ! In this lottery of the world, happy are those who can obtain that greatest prize, to which there are millions of blanks. If anything could be pleasing in my friendship, I would urge that we have reason to flatter ourselves, that with us, friendship may be equally true and permanent, since ours will be unattended by all those little incidents, which are the bane of others. We are of different sexes ; an important article, and such a one as prevents those suspicions, and sentiments of rivalship, which the finest friendships that ever were formed cannot withstand. Secondly, we are free from love, which though it may, during a time, add warmth to friendship ; yet, when the flames of the one begin to extinguish, you soon perceive the ashes of the other. And lastly (but this relates only to myself), we do not see one another too frequently. You view me in the best light, and do not perceive those moments of languor, caprice, or ill humour, which are so generally the occasion of dislike, cause us to repent of the connections we have formed, and are the motives that occasion our saying, Who would have thought it ? Who could have imagined it ?—How one may be deceived by outward appearances! The distant point from which you view. me is so very favourable, that it affords me some consolation for being under the necessity of remaining so far from you.

A trifling woman, with pretensions to refined sentiments, would criticize these unmercifully, as very indelicate ; but are they the less natural ? And are not most of us beholden for our virtue to particular circumstances, or to accidental causes ? As for me, I have humility to own, and (were I to tell the whole truth) self-experience to confirm it. At all events, such as I am, you may dispose of me ; and you see I am too ingenuous to deceive you, by enhancing the merits of the person who is entirely yours.

It is in vain you strive to do the honours of your country, by disavowing your exclusive right to the Graces ; for it must be confessed that France is their abode, or rather their native country. It is highly improbable that they can be angry with you ; but were that possible, they would be provoked to leave you, as a punishment for sending them a rambling into a country where they neither know nor are known by any mortal. If, by chance, I had any knowledge of those Goddesses, it could only be from having seen them so frequently with you. It is true that the Graces cannot be acquired ; art may add to their lustre, but nature must have given them. It is the same in everything. How many people are there who dance exceedingly well, but ungracefully ; and what numbers who dance very ill, and yet gracefully! Do we not see frequently, people with great and good sense ; who, though instructed and adorned by knowledge and study, yet never can please, for want of those natural Graces, not to be acquired ?

Every country has talents peculiar to it, as well as fruits, or other natural productions. We here think deeply, and fathom to the very bottom. Italian thoughts are sublime, to a degree beyond all comprehension. You keep the middle path, and are consequently seen, followed, and beloved.

I beg of you, Madam, make use of all that sense, and those Graces, which I know you to be possessed of, in my favour, by telling Mr de Matignon, whatever they may inspire you, from me. The most friendly things you can say to him, upon the marriage of his daughter, will best explain the sentiments of my heart. But do not confine yourself to that circumstance alone, for there is no event whatever that concerns him, in which I should not take an equal share. To write myself to Mr de Matignon would be encroaching upon his goodness ; such a messenger as you must be more honourable to me, and more pleasing to him.

Adieu, Madam : I am ashamed of the length of this letter.

These Lines are inserted, in order to introduce the following Letter with greater propriety.

TO THE EARL OF CHESTERFIELD.

AUGUST THE 7TH, 1763.

Reclined beneath thy shade, Blackheath,
    From politics and strife apart,
His temples twined with laurel-wreath,
    And virtues smiling at his heart :

Will Chesterfield the Muse allow
    To break upon his still retreat ?
To view, if health still smooths his brow,
    And prints his grove with willing feet ?

'Twas this awaked the present theme,
    And bade it reach thy distant ear,
Where, if no rays of genius beam,
    Sincerity at least is there.

May pale disease fly far aloof,
    O'er venal domes its flag display,
And health beneath thy peaceful roof
    Add lustre to thine evening ray.

If this my fervent wish be crown'd,
    I'll dress with flowers Hygeia's shrine ;
Nor thou, with wisdom's chaplet bound,
    At any absent gift repine.

What though thou dost not grace a throne,
    While subjects bend the supple knee ;
No other King the Muses own,
    And Science lifts her eye to thee.

Though deafness, by a doom severe,
  Steals from thy ear the murmuring rill,
And Philomel's delightful air ;
  Even deem not this a partial ill.

Ah ! if anew thine ear was strung,
  Awake to every voice around,
Thy praises by the many sung,
  Would stun thee with the choral sound.

EDWARD JERNINGHAM.

LETTER TO EDWARD JERNINGHAM, Esq.

SIR,   Blackheath, August the 12th, 1763.

  I DO not know whether I can, with decency, acknowledge
the favour of your poetical letter of the 7th.   But Men, as well
as Women, are very apt to break through decency, when desire
is very strong, as mine I assure you is, to thank you for it.   Could
I give you as good as you bring, my thanks should be conveyed
to you in rhyme and metre : but the Muses, who never were
very propitious to me when I was young, would now laugh at,
and be as deaf as I am to, the invocation of a *septuagenary*
invalid.   Accept, then, my humblest thanks, in humble prose,
for your very good verses, upon a very indifferent subject ;
which, should you be reproached with, you may very justly
make the same answer that your predecessor, Waller, did to
King Charles, after the Restoration : the King accused him of
having made finer verses in praise of Oliver Cromwell than of
himself ; to which he agreed, saying, that Fiction was the soul
of Poetry.   Am I not generous to help you out of this scrape
at my own expense ?   I am sensible, that before I end this
letter, I ought to show some commonplace modesty at least ;
and protest to you that I am ashamed, confounded, and in a
manner annihilated, by the praises you most undeservedly bestow upon me ; but I will not, because if I did I should lie
confoundedly ; for every human creature has vanity, and perhaps I have full as much as another.   The only difference is,
that some people disown any, and others avow it ; whereas I
have truth and impudence enough to say, *tu m'aduli ma tu mi
piaci.*
  What am I to suppose that you are now doing in Norfolk ?

Scribere quod Cassī Parmensis opuscula vincat,
An tacitum sylvas inter reptare salubres ?[1]

If you stray among the hills, vales, and purling streams, it is
to make your court to the Muses, who have long had such an
affection for you, that (I will answer for it) they will meet you
wherever you please to appoint them.   If to those nine ideal
Ladies you add a tenth of real good country flesh and blood,
I cannot help it : but God forbid that I should advise it.   In
all events, I believe you would be equal to the ten.

I am, with equal truth and esteem,
                    Sir,
          Your most faithful, humble servant,
                                    CHESTERFIELD.

P. S.—I desire my respects to Lady Jerningham. But not
one word of the tenth Muse.

LETTER TO DOCTOR MONSEY.

DEAR DOCTOR,   Bath, December the 23d, 1767.

YOUR friend and my Governor, Mr W——, told me that he
had received a letter from you with your kind inquiries after
my health ; but at the same time said, that I might even
answer it myself; for how the devil should he know how I did,
so well as I myself did ? I thought there was reason in what he
said ; so take the account of myself from myself, as follows.
When I first came here, which was just six weeks ago, I was
very weak of my legs, and am so still. A fortnight ago I had
a little return of my fever, which Doctor Moisy called only a
Febricula ; for which he prescribed phlebotomy, and, of course,
the saline draughts.   The phlebotomy did me good, and the
saline draughts did me no harm ; which is all I ask of any
medicine, or any *medicus.* My general state of health has, ever
since that, been as good as, at my age, I can hope for ; that is,
I have a good appetite, a good digestion, and good sleep. You
will, perhaps, ask me what more I would have ?   I answer,
that I would have a great deal more, if I could ; I would have
the free use of my legs, and of all my *members.* But that, I
know, is past praying for. Perhaps you may be in the same
case.   Whom have you quarrelled with, or whom have you
been reconciled to, lately ?   The house of G——, or the

[1] Writing what will excel the smaller works of Cassius Parmensis, or
sauntering in silence along the healthful groves ?

house of M——?. And where are you now; in Norfolk or
Monmouthshire? Wherever you are, I hope you are *vastly*
well; for I am, very sincerely,

Your most faithful friend and servant,

CHESTERFIELD.

LETTER TO DOCTOR MONSEY.

PRAY, dear Doctor, why must I not write to you? Do you
gentlemen of the faculty pretend to monopolize writing in your
prescriptions or proscriptions? I will write, and thank you for
your kind letters; and my writing shall do no hurt to any person living or dying: let the Faculty say as much of theirs, if
they can. I am very sorry to find that you have not been *vastly*
well of late; but it is *vastly* to the honour of your skill to have
encountered and subdued almost all the ills of Pandora's Box.
As you are now got to the bottom of it, I trust that you have
found Hope; which is what we all live upon, much more than
upon Enjoyment; and without which we should be, from our
boasted Reason, the most miserable animals of the Creation. I
do not think that a Physician should be admitted into the Col-
lege till he could bring proofs of his having cured in his own
person, at least four *incurable* distempers. In the old days of
laudable and rational Chivalry, a Knight could not even present
himself to the adorable object of his affections, till he had been
unhorsed, knocked down, and had two or three spears or lances
in his body; but, indeed, he must be conqueror at last, as you
have been. I do not know your Goddess Venus or *Vana*, nor
ever heard of her; but if she is really a Goddess, I must know
her as soon as ever I see her walk into the rooms; for *vera in-
cessu patuit Dea.*[1] It is for her sake, I presume, that you now
make yourself a year younger than you are; for last year you
and I were exactly of an age, and now I am turned of seventy-
three. As to my body natural, it is as you saw it last; it
labours under no particular distemper but one, which may very
properly be called Chronical, for it is Χρονος itself, that daily
steals away some part of me. But I bear with philosophy these
gradual depredations upon myself; and well know, that *levius
fit patientiâ quicquid corrigere est nefas.* And so good night, dear
Doctor.

Bath, November 26th, 1766.

[1] The true goddess was manifest by her gait.
[2] What cannot be remedied patience enables one to bear more easily.

LETTER

FROM THE EARL OF CHESTERFIELD TO SIR THOMAS ROBINSON,
OF CHELSEA.

SIR,   Bath, November 17th, 1757.

YOUR letters always give me pleasure and information ; but your last gave me something more, for it showed me that you were recovered from that illness, which the fears of Mr Walsh, junior, had magnified into a dangerous one. I did not like your being sent to Hampstead for the air ; that sounded very like Kensington Gravelpits. I am sure I need not tell you the part I take in your recovery.

As to General ——'s affairs, my opinion is fixed ; and I am very sure that nothing will appear upon this examination to make me alter it. There is a mystery in it : and wherever there is a mystery, I have done ; I respect, but never reason. The Ode upon that expedition is written by a master, whoever it is : the author of the verses upon the skull is certainly a Poet, though he has spun out his matter too fine ; half the length would have been much better. I cannot imagine why the Grub upon the Comet was laid at my door : but people have long thrown out their wit and humour under my name, by way of trial ; if it takes, the true father owns his child ; if it does not, the foundling is mine.

I take it for granted, that the King of Prussia's victory engrosses the thoughts of all your great politicians in town, and gives you what you call great spirits : he has shown his abilities in it ; which I never doubted of ; but then—nothing, only that there are now seven or eight thousand of the human species less than there were a month ago. France will send double that number immediately, and the match will be as unequal as it was before ; since all Europe is still combined against him ; I will not say, *and us*, because I think it would be impudent *for us*, now, to reckon ourselves among the Powers of Europe ; I might as well reckon myself among the living, who only crawl upon the earth from day to day, exhibiting a shattered carcass, and a weakened mind.

Though these waters always do me some good, it is merely temporary ; but they do by no means regenerate me. I grow deafer and deafer, consequently duller and duller ; and therefore, for your sake, I will put an end to this dull letter ; and assure you, with all the truth of a man who has no invention, that I am,

Your most faithful, humble servant,
CHESTERFIELD.

LETTER

FROM LORD CHESTERFIELD TO SIR T. ROBINSON.

SIR,   Bath, December 3rd, 1765.

I ALWAYS thought myself much obliged to you for your letters from Yorkshire, while you were in the hurry both of business and pleasure ; your land-steward, your tenants, and your agreeable country neighbours, employing your whole day in pleasure and profit : but I think myself still more obliged to you for your last letter, from your Monastic retreat in the midst of Ranelagh Garden ; the place in the world the best calculated for serious reflections upon the vanities of this world, and the hopes of a better. There you may enjoy a philosophical and religious solitude, uninterrupted ; except, now and then, by the rolling of coaches, the sound of forty instruments of music, and the much shriller sound of the tongues of about two thousand women. This is being a *Chartreux* indeed ; and, in addressing myself to you, I will take care to mix no levity in my letter ; but confine myself to grave and moral reflections. For instance ; see the dire effects of passion, or brandy, or both, in the case of Mr ——, whose usual tranquillity and immobility have been transported to the most violent excesses, of assault and battery, even upon the wife of his body ; whom, I really believe, he never assaulted with so much spirit before ; and if he gets the reputation of madness, he will rather be a gainer by it ; for nobody ever thought it could have happened to him. We have here a great many great folks, and a great many fine folks : the former met in council, to consider how they should best serve their country in the approaching session, that being their only view ; and the latter, I mean the Ladies, in the intention of serving themselves, or of being served right enough by others. But all these are dispersed, or dispersing, now ; and, I believe, I shall follow their example soon, and take myself away from hence to London ; where I am too material a part of the busy as well as of the gallant world, to be longer absent. But, whatever I am, and wherever I am, I am, very truly,

Sir,

Your very faithful, humble servant,

CHESTERFIELD.

THE END.

INDEX.

28

JOHN CHILDS AND SON, PRINTERS.

www.ingramcontent.com/pod-product-compliance
Lightning Source LLC
Chambersburg PA
CBHW021327110726
47900CB00005B/1377